CW00419520

**Acknowled**

**Extra special**

**Ale**

**A gifted young graphic designer who p**

(Alex is willing to undertake commissions and can be contacted on Instagram)

**Since I would not have managed to do this without them**

**Special thanks goes to my Personal Production Team**

**Hazel and Mehmet**

For making me one of the family

**Jamie**

For accepting me as one of the family

**Sandra and Derek**

For allowing me to borrow their son

**Sue and Father Martin**

For helping me to believe in myself and my capabilities

**Alex**

Who for the last five years has been a marvellous

Personal Assistant/graphic designer/computer expert and listener!

and

**Charlie and Hannah**

Who also accepted me as one of the family

# The Deadly Sound of Silence

Jan Attwater © 2015

**For**

**David and Aunt Nancy (Margaret Nancy Chapman)**

Who have been watching me/watching over me

**Uncle Fred**

Who identified and then encouraged the God given gift when I was a child

**Dad and Mum**

Who bought me a Brother Deluxe typewriter at the age of 11

**Janet**

Who turned out to be the original Ab Fab daughter

# CONTENTS

# PROLOGUE

*Perhaps this is how my sanctimonious silence was destined to end, trapped in a room like this---talking---to comparative strangers like John Bland and Bill Powell and yet, standing by the window with my arms loosely folded, I am reminded of a day when I sat on the beach, watching the dawn break.*

*Deafened rather than defended by the sound of my silence, I was sheltering in the sand dunes from a brisk sea breeze, and with my arms hugging my knees to my chest like a disturbed child, I was rocking back and forth. Frustrated and angry, the crying had given way to sobbing and when the pain refused to be diminished that same disturbed child had become inconsolable, and as if it were yesterday, instead of almost four years ago, I can still hear this woman screaming, screaming for no other reason than nobody could hear me.*

*One--possibly two--hours later, when my resolve had been restored, I was prepared to accept that there was no other way, somehow I had to learn to live within the confines of my captivity. But as I paddled through a pool of salt water left behind by the ebbing tide, I caught sight of my reflection, and this woman had vowed that regardless of how long it might take, I would never stop searching, until I found a way to regain my freedom. After that, I would make sure that nobody except my God would be able to take me alive again.*

*Of course, for someone well accustomed to neither winning nor losing, it had been a dangerous delusion, because finding myself---for want of a better description---under house arrest in this magnificent Victorian country retreat, not only have the events of June 22 necessitated that this woman be taken alive, as a result of subsequent occurrences the odds have become more unevenly stacked than at any time in my life.*

*Yes, in this ground floor room, with its splendid view across the lake to the woodland beyond, this woman understands that despite the polite reference to---talking---these two trained inquisitors intend to meticulously manipulate my memories, until each and every grey area has been hideously coloured by the truth.*

*Oh dear, the truth! Taking into account that throughout the last seventeen years, I have never been paid a salary by any of Her Majesty's Governments and yet, for various reasons I have been subjected to security screening on a regular basis. So surely I cannot be held responsible if the truth has been hiding in plain sight, but nobody has been clever enough to uncover its harsh reality?*

*However, since two of my Godfather's Operatives have managed to take me alive, without me needing to put in an appearance at a High Court hearing at the insistence of Philip Maddox, who is Commander-in-Chief of Special Operations a Judge has deprived me of my freedom by making me the subject of a Protective Custody Order.*

*Aware that my inquisitors will soon finish setting the scene so that we can begin, I am grateful that these few moments spent reflecting on the past have reminded me that once I start hauling the family skeletons from their hiding places, and the suspects start jostling for pole position in the disorderly queue, finding yourselves cast into the role of my personal invisible audience, you are destined to discover that despite having some kind of defence to offer, the question needing to be answered by anyone--who is assigned to protect me--is from whom will I need to be protected?*

*Charlie Anne Daltry, nee Charlotte Anne Forsyth    June 29th*

# PART ONE

## JUNE 22 --- JUNE 28

# Coincidences

**JUNE 22    181 CHELTENHAM WAY**
**3:17    INCIDENT 3956---report of suspicious vehicle---Officers responding**
**JUNE 22    187 CHELTENHAM WAY**
**3:36    INCIDENT 3957---occupier I.D. Mrs Charlie Daltry---vehicle unattended**
    **checking property status and D.V.L.A. registration.**
    "Mrs Daltry?"

In the master bedroom silence descended, prompting the stranger's voice to elaborate. "I'm an Officer with Thames Valley Police Mrs Daltry. The back door was unlocked and the alarm has been deactivated. Is everything all right?"

Despite the hand Tony Shaw had clamped over Charlie's nose and mouth, out of the corner of her eye, she caught sight of someone taking a step towards the door, and because she wanted to warn the Police Officer, she dared to resist Shaw's hold and yet, one step ahead of her with Peterson's help, they managed to render her not only motionless, but also silent which left Blake free to deal with the interloper.

**3:44    INCIDENT 3957---vehicle reported stolen---original paintwork sky blue**
    **June 02 Special Operations downgraded property from red to amber security**
    **alert---Operatives deployed---proceed with caution**

Sadly, the warning to---*proceed with caution*---had arrived too late, and because their position had been compromised even before Blake returned with the gun in his hand, Charlie was experienced enough to appreciate that they would start working, as if they were moving parts, in the same piece of well-oiled machinery.

"One uniformed and he's dead," Blake announced. "But it changes everything…"

Then, while monitoring the relay of messages from the Police Officer's R.T., Blake moved to the window, in order to watch the rear of the house, while Peterson went onto the landing so that he could deal with, any further activity on the ground floor, and for his part Tony Shaw who had been the principal player, throughout their visit, placed a precautionary finger to his lips, before easing his hand away from Charlie's mouth. But even though she was free to warn anyone who might be foolish enough to attempt the same thing, all courageous gestures were discounted, when Shaw began fishing inside one of the pockets of his jacket, and he produced what she suspected was some kind of knife.

Having defied him, Charlie watched in obedient silence as his finger moved down the object's smooth surface, until a blade sprang free, before he lowered his arm, so that the razor sharp edge slid underneath the plastic ties which Blake had used to secure her hands. Then, when Shaw raised his arm, drawing her wrists closer together to achieve the tautness he required, Charlie tried to close her mind to the possible consequences of his carelessness.

Nevertheless, with one quick upward jerk of his arm, her hands were free and yet, there was no time to restore an adequate blood supply to her wrists.

"Get up, Mrs Daltry," Shaw growled at her. "We're leaving…"

Although the words---*hell and freeze over*---sprang to mind, as a sign of her willingness to cooperate, Charlie rolled onto her side, but then along with everyone else via the R.T. came the relay she had dreaded hearing.

**3:48 INCIDENT LOG 3957----firearm discharged--STAND DOWN---repeat---DO NOT PROCEED—wait for the arrival of Special Operatives**

Those words---*stand down, do not proceed, wait for Special Operatives*---changed everything, especially when the frequency must have been closed leaving nothing in its wake except for the return of the deadly sound of silence, and after her spirits had been lifted by the glimmer of hope that her nightmare might be about to end, Charlie was left with an overpowering awareness of her aloneness.

Turning away from the window, Blake began to approach the bed. "There's no sign of any activity at the rear of the house, but if you want to take her with us, then I reckon that you have less than ten minutes to persuade her to put on some clothes…"

Yet again the words---*hell and freeze over*---sprang to the forefront of her mind, and aware that like any hired assassin, Shaw would not risk being trapped in the house and knowing that Special Operatives were on their way, Charlie was prepared to make this part as difficult as possible, by robbing him of every available second until--dead or alive--they would have to leave her behind.

It was a dangerous game to play, but the alternative was no less appealing, and wanting to avoid being---*persuaded*---Charlie was responding to Shaw's original request and she had begun to ease herself from her side into an upright position. However, her deliberate slowness proved to be a mistake, because when Shaw attempted to hasten her progress by forcing her onto her feet, she could do nothing to stop herself from falling off the edge of the bed, and as she hit the floor with an agonising thud, there was no pretence about the pained gasp which she emitted through her clenched teeth.

After demonstrating their ability to inflict a variety of physical, mental, or emotional pain, amid the urgency, there was an even greater risk of indiscriminate acts of violence, and because Charlie wanted to avoid the physical impact of his impatience, yet again she began to haul herself upright and in all fairness, despite the added hindrance of Shaw's hand twisting her arm in its shoulder socket, she had managed to rise to her knees.

"Do you think I'm stupid?" snarled Shaw. "There's no point trying to play for time, because we'll be gone before the cavalry arrives. Now, I told you to get on your feet, and I suggest you do it, or I'm sure one of my colleagues will be only too pleased to assist you…"

In keeping with his disregard for any other human being, Shaw had not taken into account that after the abuse he had encouraged his two associates to inflict upon her, she might not be capable of obeying any further orders, and responding to his unreasonableness, she lifted her head until she could see his face, before she gasped, "I'm trying…"

Then, having recalled the triumphant taunt Blake had used about how he had been gentle with her, Charlie tossed her head in his direction, as she deliberately provoked him. "Perhaps, if he hadn't been quite so gentle with me---then I might…"

As Blake's arm swung at her, the remaining words failed to emerge, but while her sneer had generated the expected violent reaction, Charlie had not anticipated that as an added bonus--albeit a perverse one--his hand might contain the butt of the gun, so that as it crashed against the side of her head, it knocked her sideways.

In fact, if Shaw had not grabbed hold of her she would have fallen again, but with everything around her becoming blurred, Charlie felt the warm, moist sensation as blood began to ooze from the impact wound, and because it was vital at that crucial moment that she did not lose consciousness, she struggled to bring his face back into focus.

At least her scornful remark had brought a definite understanding to Shaw's weathered features, as he began to fully appreciate that if she had never been capable of standing on her own two feet, then she was unlikely to be able to perform the more intricate task of dressing herself.

In his eyes, she recognised the lethal mixture of disappointment and infuriation because now, they would either have to waste time dressing her themselves, or alternatively, they would have to take her out of the house with her nakedness barely concealed, and to be sure that there was no doubt in his mind about what she had achieved, Charlie mumbled, "You can't expect to win all of the time…"

Although the words were slurred Shaw understood, and because Charlie was ready to risk everything--including her continued existence--in the form of an unwelcome suggestion she levelled a valid criticism. "Perhaps, if you had let me move sooner…"

Until that moment, Shaw had been careful not to go too far, but albeit on a temporary basis she had seized control of his game, and from his crouched position, as soon as the killer instinct materialized, his fingers closed around her throat depriving her of oxygen and yet, despite wanting to strangle her, his dispassionate control returned, and as he eased the pressure on her throat, allowing Charlie to gasp for breath, he addressed his associates.

"Although we're going to have to leave her behind, Mrs Daltry needs to appreciate the seriousness of her situation. So why don't you both go downstairs and make sure everything's ready for a clean exit and I'll join you in a few minutes?"

Until this contracted killer had acquired, what he had been commissioned to retrieve, Charlie knew that he would not risk premature execution, but when she saw Blake pass her husband's gun to Shaw, there was always the risk of further violence, and because this man had demonstrated how he was enthralled by terror and terrorization, which meant that he despised any kind of weakness, as he lowered the gun until she felt the barrel nestling against her knee cap, Charlie managed to maintain eye contact.

If he intended to carry out his earlier threat, then she was not going to afford him either the satisfaction of hearing her beg for non-existent clemency, or provide him with the gratification of knowing she would be watching his finger as he squeezed the trigger.

"I pride myself on never underestimating anyone," Shaw began to explain. "And if I do Mrs Daltry, they rarely live long enough to enjoy their moment of triumph. However, you've exceeded my highest expectations, and because I have admired your---oh, I'm not sure how best to describe it---but I suppose that it could have been your fearlessness, I've decided not to leave you with a poignant reminder of our visit…"

Feeling the pressure on her knee cap ease sent a wave of relief surging through Charlie and quite spontaneously, her eyes closed long enough to necessitate remedial action, but as soon as Shaw's fingers closed around her throat for the second time, threatening to deprive her of oxygen, Charlie's eyes snapped open.

Immediate subservience was greeted by a cruel smirk, and after Shaw eased his vice-like grip to enable Charlie to yet again gasp for breath, setting to one side the poignancy, he began to outline her unfavourable position. "It's a shame we were so rudely interrupted, but then sometimes things aren't destined to go according to plan, and at least we've reached an understanding, because unlike my associates, you and I know that there are good reasons why you've never been able to tell anyone the truth about your life, and since those particular reasons remain the same, I'm confident that you will be reluctant to divulge to anyone the real reason for our early morning visit…"

As Charlie listened to him outlining her supposed understanding, she knew that despite believing she had been free for the last three months, as one word rested upon the next, Shaw was reconstructing the walls of the prison in which she had lived for the last seven years. However, since there had to be more, when he removed his hand from her throat, she maintained eye contact.

"Considering how bad things could have been, you might like to consider yourself to be a very fortunate young woman, and before the cavalry come charging up the stairs ready to rescue you, I suggest you take a few minutes to consider how you intend to proceed…"

Now, if Charlie Daltry was a fortunate young woman, and she managed to live long enough to pen her autobiography, after having been threatened by experts, it would be punctuated by ultimatum after ultimatum. However, while she waited for Shaw to add his contribution to the list, remaining fearful of yet more reprisals, she managed to stop herself from flinching when he began to rearrange her shoulder length hair around her face.

"Of course, if it transpires that you've tried to trick me, and even before it can be verified we cannot gain access to the merchandise, then we'll be forced to come looking for you, and if that were to prove necessary, you can rest assured that I will expect to be able to draw our negotiations to a more permanent conclusion." Hesitating, Shaw rose to his feet, before adding, "I trust we understand each other Mrs Daltry…"

Beyond any shadow of a doubt, they understood each other, and as if he wanted to highlight her ineffectiveness, he threw the gun down on the bed and yet, despite believing she had heard him thundering down the stairs, Charlie refused to accept that she was alone.

Perhaps it was another cruel twist in his sadistic game, and not wanting to disappoint Shaw, if he should change his mind about leaving, Charlie managed to pick up the gun so that she would be ready to draw their negotiations to a different--albeit no less permanent conclusion--because given the opportunity, she would not hesitate when it came to savouring the gratification of her finger squeezing the trigger.

Then, Charlie occupied her mind by counting the seconds, one and two, and three and four, until those seconds must have melted into minutes, minutes during which she did consider how she intended to proceed and yet, she could not begin to find any evasive answers to the inevitable barrage of unasked questions--much less divulge the degrading truth about what had taken place in the early hours of that morning.

In the meantime, the imminent danger had come to pass. As for the questions, for someone so well acquainted with what had, in reality become---*the potential deadly sound of her own silence*--playing for time should not pose too much difficulty and yet, it was perhaps ironic that thanks to that same silence, Charlie heard a car drawing to a halt outside and because the cavalry would soon be entering the house, before beginning to move from room to room, as they gravitated upwards towards the only light which was visible, and having regained a profound respect for her vulnerability, Charlie reached for her discarded pure silk chemise, and after struggling to slip it over her head to conceal her nakedness, she toppled sideways, hitting the floor with a second, no less agonizing thud.

Finally, Charlie began to drag herself towards the corner, and although it was almost inaudible, she heard a soft click as someone closed one of the main entrance doors, which meant that nobody else could either enter or depart.

## JUNE 22   187 CHELTENHAM WAY   INCIDENT LOG 3957
### 3:45   Central Control handing over to Surveillance Centre at Special Operations

The first time Robert William Powell and John Bland had encountered Charlie Anne Daltry was three months ago, when their assignment had been a routine escort detail followed by a normal debriefing, and although the Case File in respect of the Paris Incident had never been closed--apart from the security status for 187 Cheltenham Way having been downgraded--there had been no reason for any further contact until the Police Officer had triggered the intruder alert, and since Commander Maddox had already issued orders via his

P.A. Sarah-Roxanna Retand for their immediate re-deployment, Incident 3957 had been passed to the impenetrable Surveillance Centre at Special Operations H.Q.

**JUNE 22   Special Operations Surveillance Centre--incident 3957--hand over complete**

Using the information at their disposal, like the Police Officer, the cavalry entered via the rear entrance, duly noting that someone must have had prior knowledge of the security code needed to release the integrated locking mechanisms, which controlled the front and rear entrances, while at the same time disarming the sophisticated silent alarm system.

Then, in order to allow the system to re-set itself, Powell clicked the door closed, so that nobody could either enter or depart undetected, and once Bland checked the Police Officer for any sign of life, working as if they were moving parts in a well-oiled piece of machinery, and gravitating towards the only visible light, they swept quickly and quietly from room to room,  and after establishing that the intruder or intruders were no longer present, the cavalry arrived at the door to the master bedroom, which was partially open.

**JUNE 22   187 CHELTENHAM WAY--INCIDENT UPDATE**

**3:59   Property secured--one confirmed fatality--intruder/s no longer present**

Satisfied that their weaponry was no longer required, the cavalry entered in a disarmingly hushed manner, and first impressions suggested that like the other rooms, the master bedroom was devoid of life.

However, first impressions often proved to be misleading, and because the room reeked of a lethal mixture of stale sex and its associated fear, they began to look for potential hiding places, and when Bland's attention was drawn to the small gap in the corner of the room, since they believed that they had found their assignment's refuge, using their non-verbal means of communication, Powell indicated his intention to step out onto the landing.

**JUNE 22   187 CHELTENHAM WAY--- INCIDENT UPDATE**

**4:10   Occupant located alive---until further notice---urgent communications only**

Minutes later, when Powell returned John confirmed that no matter how implausible it might seem, their assignment had somehow managed to squeeze herself into the narrow gap between the mahogany dresser and the wall, and not wanting to cause any undue alarm, before his hushed voice disturbed the silence, Bland crouched down.

"Mrs Daltry?"

After wedging herself in the narrow gap between the oversized dresser and the wall, Charlie had tried to convince herself that if she remained motionless and held her breath, perhaps no one would be able to find her and yet, the very idea was ludicrous, especially when finding people was a compulsory part of the cavalry's training programme. So irrespective of whether she was alive or dead, until they either located her whereabouts or they confirmed, through the use of thermal imagery that she was no longer on the premises, like a nasty habit, they would be going nowhere. Besides even though the voice sounded familiar, since familiarity can breed contempt, Charlie chose to bide her time, but then with a little more insistence, the same voice provided additional evidence as proof of his identity.

"Mrs Daltry, I'm John Bland and together with my partner, Bill Powell we first met three months ago, after Commander Philip Maddox assigned us to fly to Paris, so that we could escort you home in the Private Jet…"

Dear God, the recurring nightmares which forced her to relive the explosions, and the acrid smoke from the ensuing fires, before the horror of the final body count had made it impossible to forget, but while she remembered them, with the shock beginning to take its toll, Charlie was more unable--as opposed to unwilling--to offer a voluntary response.

In the hope that adopting a less formal approach might help, Bland tried to reassure her. "We've searched every room in the house Charlie, and because there's no one here except the three of us, it is safe for you to come out…"

Although it should have been inconceivable, Charlie tried to retreat further into the corner, but neither the slightness of her movement, nor the diminished light, prevented Bland from detecting the presence of a gun, and knowing how he handled the next few minutes would have a lasting impact when it came to re-establishing a meaningful rapport, he began to explain. "Having confirmed that whoever was in the house has gone, you no longer require the gun you're holding, and because we wouldn't want anyone to be injured--least of all you Charlie--if it was discharged by accident, I'm going to ease my hand into the corner, and when it covers yours, I want you to allow me to take control of the firearm…"

Considering the potential implications of a loaded gun in a shaking hand, the lack of urgency could have been questionable, but Special Operations was different from any other Agency, and thanks to their extensive training, unless the circumstances should change, the cavalry had an ulterior motive for wanting to proceed by taking one step at a time.

Nevertheless, if John failed to achieve the right result, then knowing that he and Bill would have to act simultaneously, he cast an upward glance at his partner, before he began to ease his hand into the corner.

Initially, it was almost as if their assignment was oblivious to either him, or the vice-like grip, she had on the butt of the gun and yet, when he began to unfurl her fingers, one at a time--using an intentional gentleness--until he was able to take possession of the lethal weapon, being disarmed drew Charlie's attention to his nearness and clearly alarmed, she tried to recoil again, which enabled John to determine that there was something in her left hand, and despite trying to tighten her grasp upon the small, cardboard packet, it slipped through her fingers and came to rest beside his knee.

Taking great care not to handle the gun more than proved necessary, Bland's first priority was to drop it into the open evidence wallet in Powell's hand and then, after picking up the oblong packet, he studied the label before passing it to his partner, and because it was time for the cavalry to draw Charlie's attention to the gravity of her predicament, he and Bill switched places, so that Powell could deliver the bad news.

"Although John and I can appreciate how difficult this must be for you, I need you to focus all of your attention on what I'm about to explain…"

Hesitating, Powell waited, but there was still no voluntary reaction. "As much as we would like to afford you as much time as you might need to adjust to our presence, the orders we were given are quite clear, and they do not include allowing either us, or indeed you, to play Russian roulette with your life. So initially, I want you to show me the palms of your hands, so that I can see whether you're holding any of the sleeping tablets…"

Yet again, Powell waited, before declaring, "We need to be certain Charlie. So if you don't do as I've requested, then regardless of whether you're holding any of the pills, we will be forced to rush you to the nearest hospital, so that the doctors can pump your stomach…"

"No…"

It might only be one word, but it was a beginning and yet, despite having opened her hands so that Powell could see they were empty, because John had indicated how many tablets were missing from the inner foil strip, he suddenly posed an unavoidable direct question. "Before we found you, how many pills had you managed to take?"

Clearly becoming distressed by his persistence yet again, their assignment tried to draw away from him, but it was far too important, and since Powell needed to achieve eye contact, he demanded, "Charlie I want you to look at me…"

Then, he waited until she lifted her head, before reiterating his initial warning: "I meant what I said--if you leave us no choice--we will rush you to the nearest…"

"No," Charlie gasped again. "I haven't taken any…"

It should have been enough, but after glancing at his partner, Powell still expected yet more clarification. "According to John, there are nine sleeping pills missing, but the date they were dispensed coincides with us escorting you home three months ago. Can you remember taking those tablets, in order to help you re-establish a more natural sleep pattern after we finished the debriefing sessions?"

Unable to be sure, Charlie shook her head. "Please, you have to believe me…"

Responding to her increased distress, Bland re-joined the exchange. "As Bill explained we needed to be absolutely sure, but I think we no longer have any concerns about the pills." Pausing, he waited while she absorbed the good news, before adding, "However, we do still need to confirm that you don't have any serious injuries, and we can't do that while you're wedged in the corner…"

It was a crucial moment and while Charlie came to terms with the fact that she had no choice, the silence lingered, until she offered her agreement. "All right, as long as nobody tries to touch me…"

Irrespective of how small, it was a breakthrough, and capitalising on their gain, Bland proposed a suggestion. "From what I can see, you have a head injury, but provided you appreciate that we will have to intervene, if we think there's a risk that you might sustain any additional injuries, why don't the three of us agree that you'll tell us if you need our help?"

It was a concession, and one which Bland hoped might begin to restore some of the control she had probably lost in the early hours of that morning, because if they were going to discover not necessarily what had happened, but more importantly the reason why it had occurred, then from the onset, without compromising their professional positions, and working as a team, they had approached this assignment knowing that irrespective of what had taken place, they needed to re-establish a relationship with Charlie Anne Daltry. But as an added bonus, with the sleeping tablet issue resolved, and the Police Officer beyond anyone's help, provided that they were careful not to disturb the crime scene, they could afford to give their assignment whatever time she might need, because there was no immediate rush to vacate the premises so that the Forensics Team could take over.

As far as Charlie was concerned, from the moment she had been disturbed by that suspicious noise at precisely 2:52 a m., her powerlessness during the ensuing sixty minutes, now necessitated that she prove to herself that she had some degree of control over what happened next and yet, for someone who had grown accustomed to being treated more like a valuable asset than a human being, she suspected that the concept of her being allowed to have any control whatsoever might be nothing more than a dangerous delusion.

Nonetheless, inch by inch she moved forward, until she was close enough to use the partially open, top drawer of the mahogany dresser, in conjunction with the wall to provide her with the leverage she needed to haul herself upright.

So, whatever dignity Charlie Daltry had left, it would seem she intended to retain, until she cast a downward glance at her pure silk chemise, which in its own right was revealing, but as a result of the physical exertion she had needed to expend, dragging herself across the floor it was drenched in perspiration, so that the material was clinging to the contours of her body. However, casting aside the negative in favour of the positive, instead of perspiration, it could have been drenched in blood and any concern over her modesty was unfounded, not least because hand-picked professionals like Bland and Powell would have no doubt witnessed, far more explicit sights throughout their memorable careers.

As for the cavalry, because it was vital that they did not contravene the terms of the negotiated concession, Bland and Powell chose to do what the cavalry were traditionally supposed to do and rode shotgun, while Charlie used the palm of her right hand to support her, as she inched her way along the wall towards the open bedroom door.

Even when she reached the doorway, Charlie somehow managed to move one of her shaking hands to the open door, but when she attempted to transfer her other hand, because the door was not a static object, her precarious balance became more unstable.

In that same instant, if Bland and Powell had not reached out, so that they could each catch hold of one of her upper arms, then their assignment would have landed in a crumpled heap on the floor, but then while Bland held the door steady to enable her to move into the doorway, as soon as Charlie re-established her somewhat dubious equilibrium, they honoured their side of their agreement by releasing her, albeit with a detectable degree of caution.

Once she was on the landing, the cavalry reverted to doing nothing, except continuing to monitor her progress, but then they could afford to be patient, because sooner rather than later their assignment would either run out of room to manoeuvre, or alternatively run out of wall to provide her with added support, and having indulged Charlie's need to do this in her own way, then this young woman would not only be prepared, she would also be willing to surrender herself into their custody.

Mercifully, the bathroom door was open, and because the cavalry were close enough to intervene, if they deemed it was necessary, there was minimal risk that she might fall, and having reached the wash basin, when Charlie grasped the cold porcelain, it was in the hope that it might distract her from the pain, because as much as she wanted to deny its existence, she had to acknowledge a deep-seated physical ache, which was growing in intensity.

Then, wanting to check the damage to her face, Charlie lifted her head until she could see her reflection in the mirrored cabinet. Fortunately, instead of a punch, the blow aimed by Blake--after she had spat in his face--had been open-handed and yet, the sight of the blood which must have run down the side of her face--after she had taunted him about his reference to having been *gentle with her,* and the butt of the gun had crashed against the side of her head, the flashback of the contempt on his face was about to produce an undignified result.

Edging sideways, Charlie used the top of the bath to support her while she eased herself down, until she was in the right position to start emptying, the contents of her stomach, and with such an overwhelming compulsion surpassing any need to retain her dignity, with her hands clutching at the porcelain, she continued to throw up over and over again until at last, the retching began to subside.

Although it would have been a damning disclosure, having been present at similar scenes, on more occasions than either John Bland or Bill Powell cared to remember, much less forget, they understood that now the transitional phase had begun, they should continue doing nothing, in case they stalled--or even derailed--its natural progression.

Now, with the reality robbing Charlie of any respite from the flashbacks, she was so disgusted at being able to smell--what she believed to be their foul stench on her body, she manoeuvred herself around, so that she could open the gold mixer tap, before trying several times and yet failing to unwind the plug from its resting place, until Bland chose to rescue it from her shaking hand. However, as soon as he had completed the task on her behalf, Charlie expressed her ingratitude by knocking his arm aside, and with the satisfying sound of the gushing water, she allowed herself to slump back against the bath.

"Since I don't have any serious injuries, there's no reason for you to stay…"

"So you think we should leave Charlie?" asked Bland, as he leant against the washbasin, and because his unrequested assistance with the bath plug had goaded her into re-establishing communications, he chose to pose a deliberate thought provoking question. "But even if we did leave, surely it won't make any difference, because pretending that none of this happened is no longer a viable option?"

"I'm fine," snapped Charlie. "I don't need your help..."

Standing in the doorway propping up the door jamb, it was time for Powell to once again make his own presence felt, and even though their assignment's statement was absurd, his tone of voice was soft and hushed, as he remarked, "From what we've seen since our arrival, we have cause to doubt that you can do this without having someone's help…"

Like his partner, Powell paused before suggesting, "And although we were deployed because of our connection with the Paris incident, if it would make this easier for you, we could always request that a female Operative be present…"

The very idea of having another representative from Special Operations present was ludicrous, but at least from what Powell was suggesting, Charlie understood that from the very beginning, they had never had any intention of leaving.

Sad, disillusioned, and feeling the impact of her aloneness, especially when there was one female who she trusted implicitly. Someone who would be willing to offer her unconditional support and yet someone Charlie did not dare involve for fear of thrusting her into the limelight when it might prove to be unnecessary. So left with no alternative she shook her head, as she offered an unconvincing excuse in order to mask the truth.

"I wouldn't want anyone to see me like this..."

"In that case," announced Powell. "You'll have to trust us to act in your best interests, and the only thing you need to decide--is how you want this to be done?"

Across the room, in the expensive, Italian floor to ceiling mirrored tiles which were surrounding Bill Powell, she could see more than her face in the reflection, and propped up against the bath, with her knees drawn up towards her chest, Charlie did not want to believe that the shattered, crumpled image could be an accurate portrayal of her.

If it was, then the answer would have to wait, because the water had stopped gushing into the bath and turning her head, Charlie realized that Bland had been presumptuous enough to turn off the mixer tap, and because she resented the audaciousness of his action, her snapped demand was delivered with an unavoidable directness.

"I want to have a bath..."

Still propping up the door jamb, Powell's deliberate negative body language was intended to assist him in his capacity as principle antagonist, especially when his loosely folded arms were accompanied by the elimination of any vagueness.

"You can have a bath later Charlie. First, we need to find you some clothes, so that we can get you away from the house…"

Charlie's breathing was becoming shallower, and because she suspected the real reason why she could not have a bath, and that reason threatened her right to retain some degree of control, her next direct question also demanded a direct answer.

"Will I have to see a doctor?"

Silence, but then Bill Powell released a resigned sigh. "The last thing either of us intends to do is lie to you, or mislead you Charlie. It would be counter-productive. Therefore, the answer is yes, you will need to be examined by a doctor…"

Now, Charlie understood that right from the start, it had always been whether the terms and conditions of her surrender were acceptable, and as she began to lose her emotional control, she snarled, "Nobody, not even a Doctor is going to touch me..."

Shaking his head, Powell pushed Charlie nearer the point from which there would be no return. "At the very least, you have a visible head injury, and because it's in your best interests, even if you have to be sedated, you will be…"

But Charlie interrupted him. "This has nothing to do with what's in my best interests, and if you insist on forcing me to do this, I'll say that I woke to find burglars in the house and they shot the policeman because he interrupted them. I'll even claim that, apart from the head injury, they never touched me…"

Since the matter remained non-negotiable, Powell continued to shake his head. "You can claim whatever you like after we arrive, but it won't make any difference to what happens next--because one way or another, we are taking you to the Mayfield Clinic…"

Finally, that particular Medical Facility had been introduced, and because Charlie resented even hearing its name, her surrender would have to be secured in exchange for a hefty ransom, but at least she had reached a decision about how she did not want this to be done. Hauling herself back up onto her knees, she began searching the shelf around the bath, and when her hands closed around the large ornamental shell, somehow she managed to find the physical strength she needed to ensure that she had a firm grasp, before picking it up and then, after aiming it with a wilful intent at Bill Powell, she hurled it across the bathroom.

Despite failing to hit her target, some of the expensive, Italian mirrored tiles which had provided her husband with so much gratification shattered on impact, and although the sound of breaking glass proved to be most satisfying, it was not enough to appease the simmering rage within her, and undeterred at having missed the first time, Charlie continued her frantic search for other objects she could use as potential missiles.

Passively observing, the cavalry saw no reason to intervene, not when they had worked as a team to restore Charlie's fundamental right to be able to voice her dissent, without the nature of that dissention incurring any reprisals. Besides, the mirrored tiles could easily be replaced, and until their assignment either ran out of suitable missiles, or they thought she was a danger to herself, they could continue to be patient for a little longer.

Then, after all that frenzied activity, suddenly Charlie was still, but while Bland had adjusted his position so that he was sitting on the edge of the bath, because touch and losing control seemed to be the predominate issues, despite moving a little closer, he sensed that it was too soon to risk touching her, as he asked, "Have you finished Charlie?"

Temporarily satiated, Charlie slumped back against the bath, before she admitted, "You have no idea what you're asking me to do…"

Ready to start picking up some of the pieces, Bland agreed, "Perhaps we don't, but from our professional experiences, we can appreciate far more than you might expect…"

As Charlie's tears refused to be suppressed and they started to escape, she could hear herself denying both of them access to the images, because they were far too ugly and far too deeply personal to be shared with anyone and yet, even if Bland could have heard her impassioned denial, having brought her this close to the edge of the imaginary precipice, there was little chance that he would be prepared to back away.

"We understand that it wasn't only what they did to you. It was the way in which they did it. How they looked at you? How they spoke to you? Even the way in which…"

"Please John," pleaded Charlie, as those few undisciplined tears threatened to dissolve into steady crying. "Please don't make me do this…"

Although it would never cease to be tempting to alter course, hearing their assignment address him by his Christian name urged Bland on, and as he eased himself down with a deliberate slowness, until he was on the floor behind Charlie, so that he would be in the right position to catch her as soon as she started to fall, he continued making his appeal. "God knows, you have every right to be angry and bitter, but you can't wash them away, and even if you smash every mirror in the house, it won't change one solitary moment of what happened during those fifty--maybe even sixty--minutes of your life…"

Then, having saved the best, or depending on how it was going to be received, the worst until last, he explained, "You're alive Charlie, and irrespective of how horrific it might seem, you have to accept that in addition to being physically attacked, you've also been subjected to a very serious sexual assault…"

Hearing those last two words caused more distress, than anything they had said or done since their arrival, but despite feeling Bland's fingertips brush against her shoulder, Charlie did nothing to stop him from tightening his grasp, as he added, "Believe me, from our experience of similar instances, if you don't acknowledge what's happened, then there's a possibility that it will go on haunting you, until it destroys you altogether…"

"No, you're asking me to somehow make it acceptable, and I can't…"

"That wasn't what I meant Charlie. It will always be unacceptable, but the young woman who we first met in Paris commanded our respect, because irrespective of the odds stacked against her, she turned out to be one of life's natural born survivors. So with the right kind of help, we know that you will be able to find a way to deal with this…"

Now, as Charlie was struggling to retain what was becoming a flimsy degree of control, she sobbed, "Perhaps if it had only been the threat of indiscriminate acts of violence, but being ordered to perform---made me feel as if I was someone who'd been paid to endure their derision while they subjected me…"

Sensing that something had changed, Charlie caught sight of Bland's expression and because she misunderstood the reason for his disapproval, she demanded. "What's the matter Mr Bland? Don't you approve of my description of the role I was forced to play? After all, you wanted me to acknowledge the reality of what happened---how this woman who had commanded your respect three months ago---had been powerless to stop them from not only disposing of my body, but also my mouth…"

Within each breaking heartbeat, Charlie recognized that the stakes in the game had become too high. But it was too late because the cavalry had managed to take her alive, and having dragged her back into their seedy world, shrouded in secrecy, a world perpetuated by its avaricious dependency on creating secrets, which once created needed protection in order to keep them safe from unscrupulous people, she was about to become a different kind of hostage, and after granting herself permission to lose control, in the days ahead Charlie would be unable to recall, whether she jumped or was pushed over the edge of the precipice, into the abyss below, as she sobbed, "No, I won't let you do this to me…"

Although the graphic depiction of Charlie's sense of despondency somehow suggested that she did not believe herself worthy enough to merit, the potential comfort of Bland's arms, at least he was in the right position to break her fall, and since he was afraid that her sudden movement might result in their assignment, sustaining additional injuries to her bare feet as a result of the shards of glass, which were strewn across the bathroom floor, as his arms came from behind her, his hands caught hold of her upper limbs.

"Please Charlie," He beseeched her, when she resisted his hold. "It's time to stop punishing yourself for events over which, you had no control…"

Despite her attempts to stop him, Bland somehow managed to ease his fingers down, until his hands were covering her clenched fists, before he drew her arms back so that they were crossed over her torso. Then, he did nothing, except continue to hold onto her until the tension in her muscles began to relax, and because it was safe to ease his oppressive grasp, which in turn enabled Charlie to surrender, and as she curled herself into his body, one of his hands was cradling her head, so that her face could remain buried in his shoulder.

Yes, amid the company of comparative strangers, without having compromised their professional position, despite Charlie remaining unaware, a unique level of trust had been established which in the days, weeks--and if necessary--even the months ahead, would enable the cavalry on behalf of Special Operations to uncover the reason behind what had taken place at 187 Cheltenham Way, in the early hours of that morning.

In the meantime, they listened in respectful silence to the sometimes inaudible, but no less disturbing content of Charlie's often deranged ramblings. Then, as soon as her soul destroying sobbing began to subside, Powell left the bathroom, so that their assignment would not overhear the relay of messages, as he updated H.Q. regarding the status of Incident 3957, prior to their imminent departure.

## JUNE 22   187 CHELTENHAM WAY---INCIDENT UPDATE
**5:12     Departure in fifteen minutes---premises ready for Forensics**

Physically exhausted and emotionally drained by the time Powell returned, the sobbing had ceased, and after taking the full length robe Bill had retrieved from the bedroom,

Bland draped it around her shoulders, but before attempting to help her onto her feet, his voice was gentle as he made his suggestion sound as if she had a choice. "If you're ready, I think it's time we found you some clothes, so that we can get you out of here..."

Fate! Sometimes no amount of extensive training or meticulous execution could prevent fate from casting its fickle hand over the best laid plans, and before Bland could scoop her up into his arms so that he could carry her over the fragments of shattered glass, without any prior signs, Charlie bent forward clutching her abdomen, and from the pit of her stomach she released an anguished cry.

However, from across the bathroom, it was Powell who first noticed the fresh blood which must have begun trickling down Charlie's legs while she was on the floor, and because it was time for them to once again start working as if they were moving parts, in the same piece of well-oiled machinery, the urgency of his request was directed at his partner.

"During the assault, Charlie must have sustained an internal injury, and because she's bleeding John---we need to get her to the Clinic as soon as possible..."

**JUNE 22    187 CHELTENHAM WAY---INCIDENT UPDATE**
**5:14    Injuries to occupant more serious than previously reported**
**5:35    Mayfield Clinic---emergency admission**

When it came to handling cases of sexual assault, it was not uncommon for objects to be used as if they were weapons, and because such instances did require urgent medical attention, the cavalry were a little bemused, when their assignment's excruciating pain seemed to have diminished during the short journey, between the Daltry residence and the Clinic. However, setting aside that phenomenon, if either of them had hoped that the next part was going to be any easier, then it would have been their turn to be labouring under a dangerous delusion, because after one of the Clinic's orderlies steered the wheelchair into Charlie's designated private room, she continued to express her feelings about her admission, in a most demonstrative manner.

Of course, Charlie did have two valid reasons why she was refusing to be coaxed, as if she were some badly behaved child, into swapping the wheelchair for the hospital bed. Firstly, as history would later prove, she had a good reason for resenting being admitted to this particular Private Medical facility and secondly, as she had stated before leaving the house nobody---not even the sympathetic female Consultant Gynaecologist---was going to touch her, much less subject her to any kind of internal examination.

Indeed, despite having exchanged one bedroom for another, Charlie had no intention of staying in this private room long enough to make use of the en-suite facilities, because even if there was anyone brave enough to try, then setting aside any other physical injuries, knowing that the flesh between her thighs felt as if it was on fire---nobody was going to subject her to that ordeal for a second time.

As for that excruciating pain, Charlie's ability to reduce it by bringing it down to a manageable size---so that instead of it controlling her, she could control its intensity---was only one of the unique resources at her disposal, but if she had unleashed any of them---either back at the house during her ordeal, or in that private room---then it had been her experience that the end result would be counter-productive. Instead, she exercised remarkable restraint, satisfying herself with lashing out, and hurling abuse at anyone who had the courage to approach the wheelchair, until the cavalry who had--together with that overly sympathetic gynaecologist---been lurking in the background decided that it was time for them to intervene, and since Powell had been the principal antagonist, before leaving the house, he lowered himself down, so that once he was face to face, Charlie could not avoid eye contact.

"What are you hoping all this will achieve Charlie?" He asked and then, not waiting for a reply, he explained. "Setting aside the pain---under that blanket, you're still bleeding and since your refusal to cooperate is irrational, what I told you back at the house remains unchanged---if necessary, I will have you sedated, so that Dr Wilson can examine you…"

Despite wanting to counter-challenge, Charlie had cause to consider her position, and having been admitted without her permission, her behaviour might be misconstrued as being irrational, and because she might lose what little control she did have---if Bill either had her sedated or restrained---albeit with reluctance she nodded her willingness to cooperate.

"Thank you. Now, since Dr Wilson needs to perform her initial assessment whether you like it or not, I'm going to lift you from the wheelchair onto the bed…"

Recognizing the immediate panic his suggestion had generated, Powell added, "But she only needs to feel your abdomen, so I give you my word that provided the situation isn't life threatening, we won't allow her to do anything else without your agreement…"

Although Charlie suspected the reason why she was bleeding, because she needed time to consider her options, she offered Powell no resistance as he lifted her onto the bed and, since his role had been enacted, he stepped back so that Bland was sitting in the chair beside the bed, while Dr Wilson examined Charlie, by skilfully moving her hands over her abdomen, before her question took the cavalry by surprise. "Prior to being attacked Mrs Daltry, did you know that you were pregnant?"

Uttering an anguished groan, Charlie rolled onto her side, and as if she was trying to protect her unborn child, she curled herself into the foetal position, as Dr Wilson added, "In my professional opinion, you must be at least thirteen---maybe even fourteen weeks…"

Learning that due to those events beyond her control, the bleeding meant that she was miscarrying, Charlie's tenuous grasp on the excruciating pain failed, and as it seared through her body like a red hot flame, her scream of denial was directed at Bland.

"Not my baby John. Please don't let them take my baby…"

Despite finding themselves faced with more questions requiring answers, Dr Wilson's next announcement, forced Bland and Powell to accept that those questions would have to wait, because fate's fickle hand had been cast for a second time.

"She's starting to haemorrhage---alert theatre staff, emergency D & C---as soon as we have the necessary paperwork---we're on our way down…"

Ah, the paperwork! Where would officialdom be without its protective paperwork, especially when it required a patient's signature? In any event, after a hefty dose of morphine had been administered Charlie was better able to consider her options, and perhaps the haemorrhaging might provide her with an unexpected window of opportunity, especially when her long term welfare had recently given her cause for concern and as a result, she had felt it necessary to ensure that all of her affairs were in order.

So, remembering Tony Shaw's reference to those---*good reasons*---if she were to bleed out, then in addition to them being more than adequately provided for in the financial department, despite their initial distress, her demise would also guarantee not only their safety, but also their continued anonymity.

As an added bonus, Charlie recognized a certain irony in knowing that if she did die, then the Mayfield Clinic would have to accept responsibility for the role it had played in her eventual demise. Yes, on reflection, perhaps it would be a most fitting way to end what had been started many years ago.

It seemed like a promising option but---oh dear, why does there always have to be an annoying but? Nevertheless, there was one technicality Charlie had overlooked, one reason why she could be prevented from executing her right to die with dignity and quite simply, having allowed herself to be taken hostage, her life was no longer hers to dispose of as she saw fit. So, when she was brought the consent form and---in a fit of pique---she ripped it up the cavalry were prepared to establish that unlike other people, Charlie Anne Daltry had never had any options whatsoever!

This time, because the urgency of the situation necessitated direct action, despite trying and failing several times, Charlie was unable to stop Bland's hands from covering her clenched fists, as she snarled at him accusingly. "You lied to me. Bill promised me that you wouldn't allow the doctor to do anything without my agreement…"

"Charlie, you're being unreasonable," argued Bland. "Because like everyone else in this room, you know that Bill never lied to you…"

Pausing, Bland waited, before he explained, "He gave you his word that we wouldn't allow Dr Wilson to do anything else, unless the situation became life threatening, and if this hasn't become life threatening, then everyone present would have…"

Raising her voice, Charlie interrupted him. "It makes no difference because I'm not signing the consent. Is that clear enough for both of you?"

Yet again, Bland had to counteract Charlie's attempts to writhe her hands free, so that he could regain eye contact.

"Oh believe me, we heard you loud and clear Charlie," he replied. "But since it's too late to save the baby, it won't make any difference to the outcome because one way or another, the termination is going to take place…"

Perhaps for no other reason than there was something sinister about Bland's choice of words, Charlie had stopped resisting.

"What do you mean by one way or another?"

Having sat down on the edge of the bed, it seemed most fitting that Powell should be the one to clarify their intent towards her. "It's quite simple. Our orders are to protect you, and that means protecting you from anyone or anything which might---in our professional opinion---pose a potential threat to your continued existence, and if necessary that includes protecting you from yourself…"

"It still doesn't make any difference, because I'm…."

As John's fingers touched the side of her face, his placidity silenced her protest. "Charlie, you weren't listening to what Bill was attempting to clarify, because if you refuse to give your written consent, then we'll be forced to assume that it's your intention to finish what our arrival at the house prevented you from doing, with the sleeping tablets…"

Even if Charlie had neither been listening nor hearing his partner, Bland had succeeded in regaining her undivided attention and if she was expected to trust the cavalry to act in her best interests, in what might turn out to be the difficult days, weeks---maybe even months---that lay ahead, then she suspected that it might be pertinent to discover how far they would be prepared to go, when it came to the execution of their professional duties.

"So if you don't voluntarily give your consent," John was explaining. "Because we cannot stand by and do nothing while you bleed out, you will leave us no choice---except to act in your best interest by requesting a psychiatric evaluation…"

Still sitting on the edge of the bed, Bill concluded the warning. "And if two doctors agree that as a result of recent events, you are incapable of making a rational decision, because the balance of your mind is disturbed---albeit on a temporary basis---then in order to guarantee your continued existence, we will not hesitate when it comes to having you sectioned for your own safety…"

Having discovered how far the cavalry would be prepared to go, as Charlie's gaze drifted between her alleged protectors, she hoped her stony expression would leave both of them in no doubt as to the depth of her revulsion at being blackmailed in such an insidious fashion, and after allowing the silence to linger, she delivered a thought-provoking declaration. "Believe me gentlemen, it's my experience that there's only one thing worse than having to make an unenviable choice, and that's finding yourself without the freedom to be able to choose. So if someone gets me another fucking consent form, then left with no choice, I will be forced to sign it…"

As soon as the paperwork was in order, combined with the morphine, the pre-med rendered Charlie decidedly light-headed. But as the powerful ceiling lights whizzed by overhead, she was aware that Bland was holding her hand on their journey to Operating Theatre, number two. Then, when the mask was about to cover her nose and mouth, she recalled Shaw's suggestion that she might like to consider herself to be, a *fortunate young woman* and if that were the case, while she was lying amid the nothingness of the Operating table, perhaps fate might decide that she was fortunate enough to never wake up again.

Some considerable time later, while still in the recovery room, Charlie thought that she could hear someone calling her name, but if she responded it would have meant having to exchange her warm, comfortable refuge---where she was neither dead nor alive---for a place where it seemed as if death had been all around her.

In reality, because those closest to her seemed to be under threat, when she responded to a more familiar voice, she woke up screaming, screaming about death, and if John Bland had not managed to illuminate that hellish darkness, Charlie suspected that there was a likelihood that she might have continued to scream forever.

Eventually, with Bland still riding shotgun, Charlie was returned to her private room, where Powell was waiting and while the nursing staff conducted the usual post-operative checks, the cavalry retreated to a safe distance, so that they could update each other without being overheard, before Powell detached himself from the scene of that particular crime.

As soon as he was alone, Bland made himself comfortable in the chair by the bed, so that until the remaining anaesthetic worked its way out of her central nervous system, he could watch over their assignment as she fell in and out of sleep, while at the same time, he could read the assortment of newspapers which Powell had left on the table.

Approximately four hours later, when Charlie stirred in a purposeful way, she found herself lying on her side in the standard recovery position, and focusing upon the top of Bland's head, she mumbled, "John…"

"Welcome back stranger," Bland announced, as he lowered the newspaper. "I was beginning to think you'd never regain full consciousness…"

After her unnatural sleep, Charlie was confused. "What time is it?"

Returning the folded newspaper to the side table, John glanced at his watch. "It's ten twenty-three. Once you were back in your own room, you've been falling in and out of sleep for a little over four hours…"

"My throat feels as if it's been scraped with a rasp. Am I allowed to have a drink?"

"Throughout the D. & C., you had a tube in your throat, but the soreness should soon wear off. As for you being able to drink, although the nurses have supplied me with some breakfast, and kept me awake with extra strong black coffee, until they're sure you aren't going to start throwing up, the only thing I'm allowed to offer you is some water…"

As Bland picked up the plastic beaker from the cabinet, Charlie remarked, "If there was any justice, I should at least be able to enjoy a pure malt whisky…"

"Oh, I think you should be thankful for small mercies, because if the food and drink police so much as overhear us mentioning whisky, they'll be in here confiscating not only your water, but also my coffee, before Dr Wilson subjects me to a full body search…"

In response to the image Bland had created Charlie laughed, and when John held the straw in the beaker steady, so that she could sip the water, because it proved to be far more refreshing than whisky, as soon as he rescued the straw she expressed her gratitude. "Thank you John---that was wonderful. Are you allowed to tell me what happened in theatre?"

After returning the beaker to its rightful place, Bland chose to disregard the normal protocol. "Although we should wait for Dr Wilson, during the D. & C. she did manage to locate the source of the bleeding, so there was no reason to perform a hysterectomy…"

Rolling from her side onto her back, Charlie groaned and as John elevated the top of the bed on her behalf, he offered her some advice.

"There's bound to be some post-operative discomfort. So why don't you try and take things one step at a time?"

"If the circumstances were different Mr Bland," Charlie replied. "Then for all the wrong reasons, you could turn out to be disgustingly good for me. However, I do seem to recall being even more badly behaved than I was before we left house and I think…"

Extending his arm, John placed a finger against her lips. "If you were about to apologise, then there's no need, because you did what any mother would have done in order to protect the life of her unborn child, and from the extent of the bruising that's developing on your torso and thighs, it was hardly surprising that you didn't want anyone to touch you never mind perform any internal examinations…"

Despite having severed eye contact, Charlie nodded her understanding, before choosing to change the subject. "I suppose we should tell someone I'm awake…"

"Since your routine observations aren't due to be updated for another thirteen minutes, you could choose to enjoy the peace and quiet for a little longer…"

"And what about those internal examinations, presumably they have been done?"

Bland nodded his agreement. "Yes, but as result of the bleeding, much of the evidence from the first swab might prove to be inconclusive. However, a second swab was more promising and it might even provide some DNA, and at least we did manage to photograph some of the physical injuries…"

"And can the rest be taken away from the Clinic?"

"Because we would prefer to get you away from the Clinic as soon as possible, and it will take several days for the bruising to fully develop, provided Dr Wilson is prepared to discharge you, any additional photographic evidence can be gathered later…"

"So if we dispense with the formalities," Charlie deduced. "Then there shouldn't be any reason why Dr Wilson cannot discharge me…"

Reaching up, John pressed the buzzer and within a matter of minutes, someone swiped their security pass through the automatic locking mechanism which enabled Dr Wilson to join them, and after acknowledging Bland's presence through a polite nod, she pulled the statistical chart from its holder at the end of the bed, so that she could check her patient's post-surgery observations.

"I was beside the nurse's station, when you buzzed," she explained, as she flipped the folder closed. "Apart from your blood sugar being a little low, I'm pleased with your progress. But the statistical data rarely tells me how much pain my patient is feeling…"

"Oh, on a scale of 1to10 it's somewhere between six and a half and seven…"

"That's hardly surprising, when you consider that in addition to the head injury, there's extensive bruising, not only to your hips and thighs, but also around the right kidney. So I've asked for a less strong and yet, faster working, form of liquid morphine be written up, and you can request some Oramorph every hour for as long as you feel it necessary…"

"Thank you, but I don't think my irrational behaviour, deserves such acts of consideration, especially when I knew that once the bleeding had started, my unborn child couldn't survive, and having asked John what happened, I'm grateful that you managed to locate the source of the bleeding so that you didn't have to perform a hysterectomy…"

Before proceeding, Dr Wilson cast a second glance in Bland's direction. "As your Consultant, I'm obliged to inform you that, in keeping with doctor/patient confidentiality, you are within your rights to request that Mr Bland wait outside…"

So despite the cavalry having been assigned to protect her, as she read between the lines, it would seem that she must not as yet be in---*protective custody*---but after her earlier performance, there was little to be gained if she chose to be obstructive.

"Since I'm not exactly a novice when it comes to procedures like this, I know that not long after Philip Maddox reads the official report, which you will have been asked to compile in respect of this morning's incident, he will pass whatever information he deems necessary to Mr Bland and Mr Powell. So while it's tempting to piss John off over a loop hole in the small print, I don't have any objections to him being present…"

At the prospect of seeing a Special Operative---*pissed off*---by one of her patients, Dr Wilson somehow managed to contain her own amusement. "That's fine Charlie, as long as you understand that at any time, you can change your mind about Mr Bland being present, then I'm happy to proceed…"

Pausing, Dr Wilson waited, until her patient nodded her understanding. "And you're correct about my having to compile a report and with things as they stand, not only with regard to your right to ask Mr Bland to leave, but also changes to the Data Protection Act which mean that I'm legally obliged to ask, whether you want to read the content. However, I must warn you that the file contains explicit detail, regarding what---in my professional opinion---caused the haemorrhaging, which then led to the termination of the pregnancy…"

At that precise moment, Powell's reappearance was announced by a soft click, as the door closed behind him and the security lock was reactivated and yet, neither the doctor nor her patient was distracted by the ill-timed interruption, and with Charlie's fingertips resting on the folder in the doctor's outstretched hand, she seemed to be undecided, and because Bland had updated his partner about the severity of the bruising, which in turn suggested that there had been an excessive level of violence, either before or during what seemed to have been a sexually motivated attack, the cavalry were hoping---in fact collectively, they were praying---their assignment would decide that she did not need to relive her harrowing ordeal so soon after the aggravated assault had taken place.

Then, after she took hold of the folder, it was as if time itself stood still, and not wanting to curtail the ensuing process, all the cavalry could do was hope that whenever normality descended, they had done enough to enable them to once again, pick up the pieces.

As for Charlie, when it came to that---*explicit detail*---because it had seemed important to acknowledge, the reality of the actual occurrence, instead of pure conjecture and within that heart-stopping moment, it had been too late to stop herself from being transported back to an earlier time--2:52 to be precise---when neither the Police Officer nor the cavalry were aware that she needed them to ride to 187 Cheltenham Way, so that they could rescue her from the clutches of Shaw and his associates, because a complete stranger's commanding voice had penetrated, what had become the deafening sound of her silence.

*"We're ready to do the re-run of the slaughter of the innocent one. So positions everyone—and quiet please--scene one---take two---roll cameras---and---action…"*

## JUNE 22    187 CHELTENHAM WAY
### 2:52    Incident commencing

*On that occasion, it had not been one of my recurring nightmares which had woken me from a light sleep. It had been a noise, undetectable by anyone in a deep sleep, but nevertheless an unfamiliar sound, and with the nightlight casting its illuminating ray across the floor to the door which this woman had never had any reason to close during the last three months, while I lay listening, I was hoping--correction--I was praying that the noise would turn out to be a figment of my imagination and yet despite the lingering silence, my unique inner sense was suggesting that everything was not as it should be.*

*Nothing specific, but somewhere, something was not quite right, and before I swung my legs out of the bed without making a sound, I reached into the half-open top drawer of the mahogany cabinet, which was next to the bed so that this adult could--as a precautionary measure--remove the gun I had kept in there every night, for the last twelve weeks.*

*After leaving the bedroom, there were two reasons why I headed towards the bathroom. Firstly, in the event that such a day did dawn, it was the one room in the house, which had a lockable door and secondly, having made sure that my affairs were in order, I undertook an advanced course in firearms training, so that if the need ever arose, I would be able to defend myself, and being the only child of Major William Charles Forsyth, as if I had been planning one of his military operations, because this strategist had devised two escape routes, one for downstairs, and the other for the upper part of the house, I knew that after climbing out of the bathroom window onto the ledge, I would be able to use the drainpipe to drop down onto the garage roof, thereby executing the perfect escape.*

*That had been the plan, and with one soundless bare footstep after another drawing me nearer to the bathroom door, this woman believed her objective was attainable. However, in reality, I was much further away than I could have imagined, because--in another heart-stopping moment, this woman knew--as only she could have known that there was at least one other person in the house, and that realization dawned--as it invariably did--too late to either change the past, or alter the future, because I failed to outmanoeuvre the arm which came from over my right shoulder before a hand covered my mouth. Then, from his concealed position in the bathroom, Tony Shaw stepped in front of me.*

*"It's a small world Mrs Daltry," he announced, as he snatched the gun from my hand. "And---day by day--hour by hour---yours has been getting smaller and smaller..."*

*"No---the scenes are far too ugly," I pleaded. "Please, don't make me..." But, as much as I wanted someone to ride to my rescue, it was only four minutes past three,* and back in that private room, everything would remain suspended until---*the director of the re-run uttered, the immortal word--CUT--but even then everyone would have to wait, while the rushes were being reviewed, before hearing the pronouncement. "Thank you, for your patience ladies and gentlemen that's a wrap..."*

### JUNE 22    187 CHELTENHAM WAY    INCIDENT UPDATE
### 3:05    Intruders present---urgent assistance required

*There was no need for a cue or a prompt to remind me how we ended up back in the master bedroom, and while Peterson was holding me Blake leant forwards until he was so close, I could smell his bad breath, as he almost whispered, "Although your nightdress is delightful, it isn't the kind of thing, we would expect any of the young women, we pay above and beyond the hourly rate to satisfy our diverse and demanding sexual tastes would wear and since you won't be needing it, perhaps we should reveal what's underneath?"*

*Then, with the kind of seductive slowness designed to provoke me, Blake began to slide the chemise up my thighs, and when it reached my hips, and Peterson eased his hold, so that he could attempt to transfer one of his hands to enable his associate to pull my chemise over my head, as much as I wanted to remain calm, when I saw the plastic tie in his hand, panic made me resist his hold, and although I did manage to break free, before I could reach the doorway my defiance was rewarded with a fist aimed in the region of my right kidney, which rendered me not only breathless, but also helpless and even more vulnerable.*

*However, I was prevented from falling to my knees, when Peterson caught hold of me around the waist, which enabled Blake to finish rendering me naked, before he used the plastic tie to secure my wrists tighter than was necessary and then, once I was on the king-size bed, Blake took the gun, and after lowering it, until the barrel nestled against my kneecap, Shaw issued me with a persuasive threat.*

*"Stupidity was not something I associated with you. So if you try to do anything like that again, I will be forced to allow my associate to squeeze the trigger..."*

Pausing, he allowed the silence to linger. "Now, in addition to not being stupid according to the profile I was given, you've been a very disrespectful young woman, but my colleague was right---we often do need a distraction, something to entertain us, and because it's my understanding that you don't mind if the sex is rough, and you enjoy playing games, we are going to have so much fun. Of course, whenever I do offer you the chance--but believe me you will have earned that opportunity--you will be able to either pause or even stop the proceedings by agreeing to surrender, what I've been commissioned to recover…"

"Please, I can't bear it," I begged my imaginary audience, who could not release me from the agony, but perhaps if I fast-forwarded the action, then the images might be less ugly? Yes, that's an excellent idea, because it might be nearer to the time when the Police Officer arrived to save me from the evil clutches of Shaw and his two associates.

## JUNE 22   187 CHELTENHAM WAY     INCIDENT UPDATE
### 3:13        Immediate Assistance required

Back in the master bedroom, I was telling myself that no matter what their intentions might be, nothing could be any worse than anything, this so-called consenting adult had experienced in the past, and after Shaw passed the camcorder to Peterson, so that there would be definitive proof of what had taken place, their game had commenced in earnest.

Sadly, unlike any of the prostitutes they might choose to pay more than the hourly rate to satisfy their diverse and demanding sexual preferences, when my legs seemed to be paralyzed, and I could not obey Shaw's initial order to my abject horror, I felt the cold metal against my thigh, and I realized that what Blake intended to do--was something far worse than I had been subjected to--at any time in my life.

Although I was terrified that my muscles might contract around the offending article, I did not believe that surrendering what Shaw had been commissioned to retrieve would change the pre-planned sequence of events, at least not until he offered me the opportunity. So I focused my attention upon the only positive aspect: Blake would not squeeze the trigger, because if I was dead, Shaw would not be able to collect the remainder of their agreed fee.

However, when Shaw repeated his order, with the proviso that it might be wise to obey him before Blake crippled me, somehow I managed to move my legs apart a little and yet, no amount of movement would have been enough to satisfy a seasoned sadist like Blake.

Oh my God, the pain was excruciating and yet, with Shaw's hand clamped over my mouth to prevent me from--disturbing my neighbours--as soon as the pain began to subside, he issued me with another direct threat. "Now you've learnt what will happen if you don't do whatever you're told to do, whenever you're told to do it, perhaps you'll be more cooperative from now on, because believe me, the two demonstrations of their ability to inflict pain, which you've experienced so far were somewhat tame…"

Then, without any further delay, I heard a metal fastener being lowered--undoubtedly the zip fastener on the Levi's Blake was wearing, and as he took hold of my hips so that he could drag me to the edge of the bed, as if it were a significant part of his curriculum vitae, he boasted about his sexual prowess.

"Up until now Mrs Daltry, nobody has lodged any customer complaints. So I don't think you'll be disappointed with my performance…"

**3:23** "Will somebody please shout cut!" Although it had only been the start, after the slaughter of the innocent one, I had recalled being tricked into responding, and because the images being generated were about to become even uglier, I had to stop the rerun.

Thrust back into the spotlight--albeit a different kind of limelight--in her private room the action had ceased to be suspended, and because Charlie no longer needed to read the conjecture contained within the report as the folder began to slip from her fingers--like a waterfall--the papers inside were cascading to the floor.

Mercifully, it was after the time when the cavalry could ride to her rescue, and since they had the same ulterior motive for wanting to sustain their control, when Dr Wilson's professional concern for her patient necessitated that she should attempt to intervene, Powell managed to steer her away from the bed so that his partner could start to pick up the pieces, and after John resumed his former position in the chair, in a calm tone of voice, he requested her undivided attention.

"Charlie, I want you to look at me…"

In response, their assignment seemed bewildered, but after John took hold of her trembling hands, she turned her head to look at him. "I don't know what happened John. At first, I thought that I could read the report, but then suddenly, I was back at the house and I remembered panicking and what happened when I had tried to run…"

As soon as the tremor in Charlie's voice confirmed that she was close to breaking down, John intervened. "But you're not at the house, and Dr Wilson did explain that she was fulfilling a legal loop-hole, so reading the content isn't mandatory…"

"You don't understand," argued Charlie. "For some reason, I hated myself, but couldn't remember why I felt that way…"

Tightening his hold on her hands, John interrupted her. "Before we left the house, I thought we'd established that whatever took place during those fifty--or maybe even sixty minutes of your life was beyond your control. In addition, from our experience of similar situations, with your continued existence under constant threat by the presence of the gun, you would have done whatever you had to do in order to guarantee your survival…"

Pausing, John waited for his explanation to be absorbed, before he suggested, "As for you reliving what happened, I think that with benefit of hindsight, you might agree that this is neither the time nor the place to conduct a post mortem. However, whenever that time does arrive, then with the guidance of a suitably qualified person, I know that you will be able to deal with everything that happened. But for now, I think we should focus upon making sure that you're well enough and strong enough, so that Dr Wilson will be able to discharge you as soon as possible…"

Despite casting a glance in Powell's direction, no words needed to pass between them, and because his partner understood that it was in everyone's best interest if he negotiated the terms and conditions of Charlie's discharge, after gathering up the papers, which still littered the floor, Bill passed the folder to Dr Wilson for safe keeping.

"Perhaps it might be best if we move to your Consulting room," he suggested, as he took hold of her elbow with the lightest and yet, at the same time, most persuasive of touches. "And then we can establish what medical criteria you need to see fulfilled, before you would be willing to consider discharging your patient into our protective custody…"

Initially, Charlie remained withdrawn, but then not long after his partner's departure, despite her initial certainty that she had had no intention of staying in her private room, long enough to make use of the en-suite facilities, with the last remnants of the anaesthetic having left her central nervous system, in a hushed voice she had expressed her need to go to the bathroom, and because John was eager to continue re-establishing a level of trust between them, he was willing to allow her the right to reassume some kind of control over her own destiny. So even though they had not sought the necessary permission, John agreed to help her, provided that they were careful, because if anything untoward did happen and she started bleeding again, then Dr Wilson would seize the opportunity to have his head surgically removed, so she could have it served up to his Commanding Officer on a silver platter for aiding and abetting her patient.

Although Charlie found the idea that a trained professional like John Bland could feel threatened by her slimly built Consultant unconvincing, with the help of his arm, she reached the en-suite without incident and then, knowing that Bland was hovering outside as an added safeguard, she left the door unlocked, in case anything did happen.

Meanwhile, although Dr Wilson had driven a hard bargain over her patient's discharge, after disarming the security lock Powell had taken advantage of Charlie's absence to update his partner--albeit in a hushed voice. "When I last requested an incident update, Forensics hadn't found any other weapons in the house, and the gun Charlie was holding, when we found her is the second firearm, which was registered to Mark Daltry. According to ballistics, the bullet recovered from the Police Officer was fired from that gun. However, as we anticipated, the only prints on it belonged to Charlie. and from trace elements located on the barrel, it has been confirmed that the gun was used…"

From inside the en-suite, when they heard the sound of running water, Bill hesitated but then despite the disgust which had registered on his partner's face, he focused his attention upon concluding his update. "Although the surveillance teams have been screening all communication channels, they haven't picked up any chatter in relation to any incidents which took place in the early hours of this morning…"

"And what about the entry system and deactivated alarm?" asked John, in a hushed voice. "Have Forensics managed to confirm whether they were bypassed?"

With the door to the en-suite beginning to open, Bill could only manage to shake his head and even though she had the benefit of two arms supporting her on the return journey, when every small tentative footstep caused the discomfort to register on her face, at least Powell could offer her some reassurance, regarding her pain threshold.

"Although the drugs administered after the operation must be wearing off, because Dr Wilson has asked for slow-release morphine sulphate tablets to be added to your prescription list they should afford you some relief until any residual pain or discomfort diminish. Once we get you back into bed, as well as arranging for the first tablet to be administered, I'll ask one of the Staff Nurses if you can have some liquid Oramorph, which should have an almost immediate impact on your pain level. In addition, in case you should experience any difficulties sleeping, Dr Wilson has also renewed your prescription for sleeping pills…"

Having reached their destination, it was a relief to be helped back into bed. "After achieving all that Bill, I'm almost too afraid to ask about my discharge…"

Powell sighed. "Now that did prove to be a little trickier. However, provided that there isn't any secondary bleeding, and you eat enough to raise your blood sugar level, so that it can be classified as acceptable, Dr Wilson is prepared to consider discharging you at approximately three-thirty, and since the time is eleven-fifteen, if you'll excuse my dreadful play on words, you'll only have to be patient for the next four hours…"

"When it came to negotiating on my behalf, it sounds as if you've done an excellent job and at least I can enjoy a cup of coffee…"

Bill extended his smile. "One of the Health Care Assistants, Tammy, is already organizing some toast and coffee, but if you don't increase the amount of water you're drinking, then you're risking a delay, because you'll have to be given fluids intravenously…"

Concerned about what was going to happen after three-thirty, Charlie asked, "After my discharge, where will we be going? Presumably, we can't go back to the house?"

Powell shook his head. "Firstly, our Forensic Team is still working inside the house and secondly, now that the property's security has been compromised, in the unlikely event that you wanted to return, it wouldn't be a viable option. However, without tampering with the crime scene, someone has been allowed into the property to organize some clothes and personal items you might need during the next few days. Then, after the Team vacate the premises, arrangements will be made for all your personal belongings to be packed up and transferred to your new home, as soon as it has been allocated...."

"You're right, I don't think I could return to the house," Charlie replied, but she was still curious to know where they would be going after leaving the Clinic. "But, you still haven't told me, where you will be taking me after I've been discharged?"

Bill released another sigh. "After delivering so much good news, I'm afraid that I have to deliver what might seem to be something less favourable. While negotiating the terms and conditions of your discharge, because of the amount of blood you've lost, Dr Wilson wanted you to stay in the Clinic at least overnight. In the end, we compromised and overnight we will be taking you to a safe house which is close enough to the clinic, so that we can get you back if anything untoward were to happen. Although it might not be an ideal solution, it was the best I could negotiate without having to discharge you against medical advice..."

Genuinely grateful, Charlie was smiling. "That's fine Bill, I'm sure you did your best and if we're going to fulfil the terms and conditions of my ransom, would one of you mind pressing the buzzer, so we can find out what's happened to my coffee and toast?"

### JUNE 22  INCIDENT UPDATE

### 15:38  Occupant discharged--en-route to overnight location
### JUNE 23  INCIDENT UPDATE

### 10:36  As per Commander Maddox--en-route to next rendezvous

Prior to their departure, Charlie had languished in a second hot bath, intentionally overflowing with bubbles, before she had joined the cavalry at the breakfast table, and despite having to be coaxed into eating, on the premise that the morphine sulphate tablet would be absorbed more effectively, up until Bill advised her that they had to leave the safe house at ten-thirty so that they could rendezvous with Major William Charles Forsyth, she had managed to swallow three--albeit small--mouthfuls of scrambled egg.

Of course, at the end of March, there had been no reason for Bland and Powell to be granted security clearance to access any Official Record, except the one that had come into existence as a result of Mark Daltry's marriage to Charlotte Anne Forsyth.

Perhaps, if they had been made aware of the other two Official Records, then the cavalry would have been forewarned that the relationship between Charlie and her father could at its best be described as volatile, and at its worst. downright acrimonious.

It would have also have explained, Charlie's last-minute attempt to postpone the face to face meeting by protesting that it was too soon for any kind of family reunion, and when the cavalry refused to consider postponement an option, if they had been in possession of the correct information, they might have understood why their assignment was sitting in the rear of the Jaguar wearing a rather sullen expression?

As he drove, John had been monitoring Charlie's expression through the rear view mirror, and mindful of how they were going to need her full co-operation without speaking, he prompted his partner to address the matter, and a few minutes later, despite being unaware of the reason for the hostility she felt towards this meeting with her father, Bill glanced over his shoulder, before he attempted to placate their assignment.

"Although you seem to feel it's too soon Charlie, surely you must be able to appreciate that Commander Maddox felt obliged to inform your father about the intruders at 187 Cheltenham Way---not only because of his connection with Mark, but also the sensitive nature of his current Military assignment...."

In the hope that he might be penetrating their assignment's inherent stubbornness, Bill waited and then, even though she continued to stare through him, he added, "Besides, it's only natural that his paternal concern necessitated that he ask Commander Maddox if the normal protocol could---on this occasion---be suspended so that this brief face to face meeting could take place. So why don't you try to relax?"

Since Bill was one of her protectors, Charlie found his naivety a little disturbing. "Obviously, you haven't attended many face to face meetings with my father, because if you had then you would know that few people--including my stepmother Helen--would risk relaxing when the Major takes time out of his busy schedule to attend a meeting…"

Then, Charlie severed eye contact, and because she suspected the reason why her father had risked suspending normal protocol, especially when he knew that if anything untoward were to happen, then the repercussions would resonate all the way to the highest possible Authority, she stared out of the window so she could attempt to prepare herself.

However, her preparations would have to wait, because after the Jaguar had left the inner city motorway in favour of a dual carriageway and then a winding lane, before Bland turned the car onto a farm track, Charlie was even more bewildered as to why this face to face meeting was taking place in such a remote location, until John steered the Jaguar onto an expanse of tarmac which Charlie knew had been used by small private planes before it had been decommissioned. In fact, although Charlie had not realized, because of their unconventional approach, it was the same airstrip she and her husband Mark had used, whenever Special Ops had needed their departure from---followed by their return to the U.K. without being detected---and after Bland brought the car to a halt some distance from the only structure, using high intensity heat-seeking binoculars, Bill seemed to be scanning the area surrounding the hangar. Presumably, he was checking that there were no signs of any inappropriate activity and yet, the interminable waiting lasted no more than a few minutes, before Charlie saw her father's armour-plated car approaching the domed structure, and when nothing happened, she vented her frustration.

"Oh my God, why does my father have to indulge in all this melodramatic nonsense? We're here, and the Major's chauffeur-driven car has arrived, so if this has got to be done, then can we please get this farce over with, as fast as possible?"

Casting a backward glance at Charlie, Bill offered her an explanation. "Clearly, patience wasn't one of the virtues you were blessed with Charlie. However, although we are confident that we weren't followed until we receive joint confirmation, from another Special Ops vehicle that your father's armour-plated car didn't attract any unwanted attention on its way here, we are obliged to wait…"

As soon as Bill finished speaking, John's hand moved to his right ear, so that he could deal with an incoming message, and after casting a nod in Bill's direction simultaneously, the cavalry and the Major's security officer emerged from their respective cars and yet, Charlie discovered that despite the central locking facility having been deactivated, when John pulled the key out of the ignition, the rear doors must have been child-proofed, because she was unable to leave the Jaguar until Bill opened the door from the outside.

Then, as they began to escort her across what resembled the equivalent of no-man's-land between the two cars, Charlie noted that Powell's hand rested on her arm, and although it might have been the tension of the moment her immediate---albeit inappropriate---thought was whether Bill's hand was there to prevent her from running away. Alternatively, if they were concerned about her safety, then why had they parked the car so far away?

In Charlie's experience, there would be a rational explanation, but she was about to come face to face with the Major, and before discovering if her father had undergone a metamorphosis during the last three months, it was time to switch from amber to red alert.

Given the circumstances, one would have thought that any concerned parent might have undergone some kind of metamorphosis, but the Major ignored his daughter, and despite it being ironic, in accordance with normal protocol, he opted to address her escorts.

"Mr Bland, Mr Powell, it was most reassuring to discover that Philip had re-assigned both of you. As we all know, continuity of care can prove to be expeditious and now, as agreed with your Commanding Officer, I need to speak with Charlotte in private…"

Without uttering a sound, Charlie was shouting at the Major---*damn it father, if everyone else calls me Charlie, then why can't you*---and yet, it was a waste of valuable resources, because she had failed to notice that like the cavalry, her father's security officer was retreating to a discrete place--somewhere neither too close, nor too far away.

Despite feeling as if there was no alternative based on previous face to face meetings, Charlie had cause to consider how many minutes this one might last, before her father would become so exasperated he would stop attempting to reason with his unreasonable daughter, and as if she were nothing other than an insubordinate subordinate, the Major would resort to issuing a direct order.

However, for a man renowned in the western world, for his Military prowess to make the mistake of allowing himself to be baited in such a manner would be a catastrophic emotional error on his part, because his order would enable Charlie to defy him, and although the Major was also her father, why should he treat his daughter differently than anyone else in the last nightmarish twenty-four hours?

Yes, as history had proved, because of the deep, hostile undercurrent that flowed between them, once they began to exchange angry words, her father would lose his temper, and resort to threatening his own flesh and blood.

Nevertheless, after taking hold of Charlie's arm, Major Forsyth steered them both into the hangar. Then, despite the fact that his driver had never left the car, and his security officer was loitering with intent at a discrete distance, as if he doubted the extent of his own extensive ability to demand complete privacy, he checked again that they were shielded from prying eyes and ears before he felt able to begin his explanation.

"In addition to telling me what had happened, Philip also informed me that although it must not have been confirmed until after you were escorted home from Paris--you must have been carrying Mark's child. Naturally, Helen and I were both shocked and gravely concerned for your welfare Charlotte, and while we regret that the pregnancy had to be terminated without breaching your right to the usual doctor/patient confidentiality, I understand that thanks to Doctor Wilson's expertise, there might not be any complications with regard to any future pregnancies..."

Having sold her soul to the secret manufacturing state when she had been too young to realize the life changing consequences, Charlie's immediate thought rested upon why anyone would be concerned about her confidentiality and yet, perhaps for no other reason than she knew that it would irritate her father, she dared to interrupt him?

"With all due respect father---since you seem to know so much about the last twenty-four hours of my life, I'm sure that even you might be able to appreciate that those hours have been somewhat traumatic. So why don't we dispense with the usual exchange of insincere pleasantries, and get down to business? Presumably, you must have had a specific reason for requesting that the normally inflexible protocol be suspended, or this--*touching family reunion*---would not be taking place?"

In disbelief, Major Forsyth shook his head. "I would have thought that was obvious Charlotte. After what happened in Paris, you were the only survivor, but when you were offered the chance to relocate, you chose to remain in the marital home. Then, four weeks ago at your own request, the security at 187 Cheltenham Way was downgraded, which means that there isn't any visual or audio intelligence to help determine either why this might have happened, or alternatively, the identity of your assailants..."

Nobody except her father could make an opening statement sound like a declaration of war, and because Charlie resented being made to feel as if she had in some way been responsible, especially if her suspicions proved to be correct and yet, until she acquired more corroborating evidence, she attempted to deflect what was probably inevitable.

"Before you start cross-examining me, because I've been somewhat preoccupied father, I haven't had time to consider why this has happened, or the…"

Suddenly, the Major was wearing, his---*don't you dare start*---kind of expression, and this time, it was his turn to interrupt. "Do you have to be reminded that in the early hours of June 22, a Police Officer died, a very young Officer whose premature death means that a young mother has to raise two children, who are under school age, singlehandedly?"

Taken by surprise, Charlie's harsh expression softened. "Although I remember a Police Officer being shot," she admitted, in a more subdued voice. "I had no idea that he was married, with young children…"

Finding the remorse in his daughter's voice reassuring, the Major was prepared to concede that there was no reason why his daughter should have been aware of the details. "Well, as you've explained Charlotte, you've had a tremendous amount of trauma to deal with, and unless someone told you, there's no reason why you should have known. However, now that you do, I trust you'll have a better understanding of how easy it is to hide from the reality when you don't have to deal with the more disturbing detail---such as a grieving wife and two young children who will have to grow up without their father…"

As the Major paused, his own expression softened. "Having visited grieving relatives on many occasions, I know that such matters need to be handled with the utmost diplomacy and although Philip wasn't obligated in any way, because the Police Officer died in a Special Operations property, he decided to accompany the Chief Constable, so that he could express his condolences for a brave Officer who was not only killed in the line of duty, but whose arrival might have saved your life…"

Then, the Major cleared his throat. "Nevertheless, I listed the sequence of events because I believe that there's a risk that they might be interconnected, and if there is a connection, then I have had to consider asking you how many dead bodies is it going to take, before you accept that it's time you told Philip everything?"

Having recovered her composure, Charlie was shaking her head, and despite knowing that she was being economical with the truth yet again, she tried to deflect the issue.

"There isn't any need to tell Philip," she tried to protest. "In fact, at this precise moment in time, I can give you my personal assurance that they're safe. Believe me, if I thought, for one moment that their anonymity had been compromised, I would have asked to meet with you, so that we could discuss our options…"

Major Forsyth released an impatient sigh. "And setting aside the truth, the whole truth, and nothing but the truth, what options do you think we have?"

Then, after a momentary pause, he started shaking his head. "I'm sorry Charlotte. In my professional opinion their anonymity might have been compromised. Furthermore, what you have to realize is that it's no coincidence that nobody except Mr Bland and Mr Powell have been permitted to have any direct contact with you. If there is a blessing, then perhaps we should be thankful that this incident did occur in a Special Ops property, because it necessitated that Philip was the first person to be told, which meant that prior to awkward questions being asked within the Ministerial corridors of power, he was able to secure an order that this matter was to be handled on a strict--*need to know*--basis…"

As her father had been enlightening her, Charlie was congratulating herself on solving the mystery of not only why the---*inflexible protocol*---had been suspended, but also why this face to face reunion was taking place in such an isolated location. Quite simply, there was to be no official record that it had taken place and yet, if it was deemed necessary that such extreme measures be taken, Charlie's insight only served to strengthen her resolve to remain vigilant.

"However," the Major continued to explain. "If the body count should continue to rise, Philip's position may well become untenable, and if that should happen, there's a strong possibility that this might not remain a matter solely for Special Operations and I think we both know the probable implications…"

Implications! Of course Charlie knew the probable implications, and when she considered how she had been forced to live her life, only too aware of the often painful consequences imposed upon her by other people's actions, she recognized a certain irony.

Yes, in this developing scenario, the potential implications for the Major were immense, and because this was his game, which they had all been forced to play by his rules, Charlie could not stop herself from turning her father's own words against him.

"And you father seem to have forgotten that when you were invited to visit me in Edinburgh, from the very beginning it was me who wanted to tell Philip everything…"

Trying to determine whether she was penetrating his armour-plating, Charlie hesitated, but ever the brilliant strategist, her father's expression was giving nothing away and yet, refusing to be intimidated, she remained undeterred. "Instead, you trapped us in this web of secrecy, and even you must realize that if I go to Philip now and tell him everything, then you'll be in the direct line of fire, not only because of the part you played in the cover up, but that prospective superstar you chose to protect, where would that leave him? Yes, that same person who has managed to scale the greasy ladder of success with an almost vulgar swiftness, until he secured the high profile career within the hallowed, upper corridors of power, where he enjoys all the perks that come with his prestigious position, unlike you father, he would lose everything…"

Although Major Forsyth had given his daughter a fair hearing, his professional instinct was telling him that immediate, remedial action needed to be taken, and sustaining eye contact--albeit later than expected--he added his own threat to Charlie's list.

"The killing should never have been allowed to start, and now preferably, before anyone else dies, someone has to bring it to an end. So you have seventy-two hours in which to talk to Philip. If he cannot confirm that you have either done so, or have agreed to do so by the end of that time, I will personally see to it that you don't have any option…"

Regrettably, at a time not too far ahead, if there could have been something offered in the Major's defence, it would have been that Charlie was too blinded by her outrage at being proved right, she had to retaliate in the most disrespectful and hurtful way imaginable, and after tossing her head back she uttered a derisory laugh, and because she no longer cared who might be listening, she dared to raise her voice.

"When it comes to threats father, there have been so many I've been forced to compile a list, and because I'll have to add yours to the bottom of that list, and for once in your illustrious career, you cannot pull rank, you will just have to wait your fucking turn…"

Irrespective of how many minutes the meeting had lasted, before the exchange of angry words brought it to an end, in that same instant nothing else mattered except for the disappointment and disillusionment Charlie felt for a man she had never been able to address as---*dad*---and because the Major believed any display of emotion to be a sign of weakness she turned away, so that he could not see the pools of liquid welling up in her eyes.

Yes, at that precise moment Charlie wanted to be anywhere provided that it was away from a man, who had never tried to understand her, and because his ultimatum would normally be the equivalent of a Military dismissal, she moved out of the hangar and headed towards Bland and Powell, who must have been concerned when they heard her raised voice.

However, because there was something else her father needed to add, the Major took his unreasonable and rebellious daughter by surprise, when he called after her, as she began to head across the remaining no-man's-land. "Charlotte…"

Unrepentant, his rebellious daughter continued to walk away, until her father's voice softened as he called after her again. "For once in your life Charlie, please don't allow the bad feeling between us prevent you from doing the right thing…"

Stunned, Charlie stopped in mid-stride. Perhaps hearing him call her---*Charlie*---had been a figment of her imagination and yet, despite the close proximity of Bland and Powell, it was enough to cause her to hesitate, and when she looked back towards the hangar, she could see her father standing by the car with his security officer holding the rear door open, in readiness for the Major to get into the back seat, and unless it was wishful thinking on her part, her father's expression seemed remorseful--maybe even apologetic.

Then, in the next agonizing ninety seconds, everything in her world was about to be turned upside down, because although Charlie had realized that instead of their relationship being irreparable, there was a chance of redemption, fate was about to rob her of that opportunity when she knew, as she had known in 187 Cheltenham Way at 2:52--with a sickening certainty that she was powerless to alter, amend, much less change, what was about to happen. Nevertheless, irrespective of how futile it might seem, Charlie refused to accept that the situation could not be adjusted to minimize the damage. So when she felt someone's fingertips touch her arm she brushed the hand aside, before turning around so that she could begin moving back in the direction of the hangar.

"If you remember, we made a deal," she announced, at the top of her voice. "And because I've kept my side of the bargain, this isn't going to happen--not here---not now---and beyond any shadow of a doubt---not like this…"

Initially, Bland and Powell were perplexed, until Charlie quickened her pace and when alarm bells started to ring it was Bill who reached her first, but as he tried to grab hold of her upper arms, she screamed out a heart-rendering warning, which seemed to suggest that somehow she knew what was about to occur seconds before it happened.

"It's the car Bill---they have to move away from dad's car…"

The upward fireball, followed by the ferocious undercurrent, blew all three of them off their feet, but after Charlie hit the ground, she was aware that someone was shielding her from any flying debris. Then, wanting to ascertain whether she had sustained any injuries, after Bill eased himself away from her, between them the cavalry helped her to stand up.

Within the immediacy of the aftershock it almost seemed to be surreal, until she looked back at the hangar and she realized that Bill was running towards the plume of smoke coming from the smouldering wreckage, while beside her, despite the ringing in her ears making it difficult to hear, she was aware that John was summoning assistance.

Although Charlie was too far away to determine whether there were any bodies on the ground, the frightened child within her needed to believe that the explosion might have blown them clear---and even if they had sustained life-threatening injuries, she was telling herself that since the medical profession was capable of performing miracles, then there had to be a glimmer of hope and after John's attempt to stop her failed, she began stumbling towards the hangar and the remnants of her father's armoured-plated car.

Satisfied that Charlie had not sustained any physical injuries, John chose to multi-task by coordinating the relay of messages from various different sources, while at the same time sprinting back to the Jaguar so that they could get their assignment out of sight as soon as possible. Besides, since Bill was heading back across no-man's-land, John was confident that his partner would intercept Charlie long before she got anywhere near the hangar.

Unable to avoid a collision with Bill, although Charlie attempted to outmanoeuvre his outstretched arm he somehow managed to encircle her waist, before curling her into his body, so that her feet were barely touching the ground. However, his successful interception was met with passionate resistance, which was orchestrated by screams of denial.

"Please Bill--we have to do something to help them…"

Despite her constant struggling, with comparative ease, Bill maintained his hold until the Jaguar reached them, and as John left the driver's seat, he updated his partner. "The helicopter's ETA is three minutes, but the arrival of the other Emergency Services will take seven minutes. In the meantime, since we don't have the slightest idea how this could have happened, before we find ourselves any more over-exposed, let's get her in the car…"

In response to John's suggestion, Charlie's attempts to writhe herself free once again intensified, and while Bill was forced to counter her resistance, she was pleading with them. "But you don't understand. I've lived my entire life, in the hope that I would hear my father call me---*Charlie*--- and because that's what he did, you have to let me go…"

"It's out of the question Charlie," Bill interrupted her, and because neither of the two men could find a more favourable option, apart from preparing Charlie Anne Daltry for the worst possible news, together they yet again countered her resistance, and as soon as Bill achieved eye contact, he explained, "Having been as close as any human being can possibly get to the car Charlie, it's my professional opinion that taking into account the ferocity of the fireball---mercifully---none of them would have survived the initial blast…"

Even if Charlie had heard him, it was perhaps predictable that she was not prepared to listen. "But my father and his security officer weren't inside the car. So you could be wrong, and while we're standing here doing nothing, they could be lying on the ground…"

Driven by desperation, Charlie started pummelling Bill's chest with her tightly clenched fists, but instead of releasing her, he raised his voice. "That's enough Charlie…"

This time, his sharpness rendered their assignment motionless, which enabled Bill to elaborate further. "For the last time, you aren't going anywhere near the hangar, never mind the car, and if you don't calm down, you'll leave us no choice, but to get you out of here, without waiting for the arrival of the Emergency Services…"

The threat of immediate detachment from the scene proved to be persuasive, and while there was a brief unresponsiveness, the cavalry acted upon the long overdue opportunity to get their assignment into the car, and with the assistance of John's guiding hand, on top of Charlie's head to ensure it did not collide with the upper rim around the door, the speed of their action left her little choice, except to get into the rear of the Jaguar.

Considering the traumatic events of the last thirty-three hours, the cavalry shared the same concern that this additional grief might push Charlie into emotional overload. However, in the aftermath of such a horrific incident, they also knew that wherever possible, before rushing someone away from the scene, an important part of that same grieving process was witnessing that everything had been done to rule out any and all signs of life, and because of the uproar this incident was going to cause, especially when normal protocol had been suspended, Bill joined their assignment in the back seat of the car.

Despite the child-proof locks, Charlie tried the door several times before resigning herself to perching precariously on the edge of the seat, and as if it was going to produce a better outcome, her eyes tracked his partner's movements as John coordinated the start of what Bill anticipated would turn out to be, nothing more than a retrieval operation.

So initially, Powell did nothing, apart from observe their assignment, and when the shock began to manifest itself as a physical reaction, Bill removed his jacket and yet, totally immersed in her pursuit of that better outcome, he doubted that she even noticed him placing it around her shoulders in the hope of alleviating the involuntary shivering, and although Charlie's ramblings did not seem to be making a great deal of sense---setting to one side what the cavalry had seen and heard with their own eyes and ears, which could only be described as uncanny---if their assignment had been aware of the impending explosion, then why had she not been able to do anything to prevent it?

During their extensive training, Bland and Powell had learnt not to take anything for granted, and to approach everything with an open mind. So, after John had confirmed that there were three fatalities, because Bill no long needed to monitor the constant relay of updates, he disconnected the microphone in his ear so that nobody could eavesdrop, while he used a hand-held, digital recorder to capture their assignment's ramblings.

Of course, while Charlie was tracking John's progress, she remained oblivious to what was coming out of her mouth. However, from what Bill could decipher, it sounded as if she was re-running, some of the conversation which had taken place during that last reunion--the same reunion, she had done everything in her power to avoid having to attend.

Eleven minutes later, John returned to the car, and as he got into the driving seat, his partner discreetly passed him the digital recorder with the headphones attached, which meant that Bill would have both hands free so that he could deal with Charlie's reaction, as John fired the engine, without offering one of the rear seat passengers any explanation.

"But I can't leave yet."

Despite understanding that since their last meeting had ended, with the Major and his daughter exchanging angry words, she was not ready to leave her father behind, both men remained silent, even when he resorted to begging. "Please John---please stop the car..."

At that crucial moment, it was vital that John did nothing, except carry on gradually increasing the car's acceleration, as Bill reached out until his touch drew her attention away from his partner. "If there had been even the merest sign of life, then the helicopter or the ambulance would have left the scene long before now. But they haven't, because together with his driver and his security officer, the explosion must have killed your father instantaneously. So there's no reason for us to delay our departure any longer..."

Finally, the teardrops which--twenty minutes ago--would have been a sign of weakness, were free to overspill, and after Bill encouraged her to move towards him, and John heard the kind of weeping associated with a healthy grieving process, it was safe for him to glance in the rear view mirror, so he could receive Bill's nodded agreement, and although Charlie would never forget how her father had died, with the headphones in place so that he could listen to what Bill had recorded, at least the right time had arrived for John to detach their assignment from the scene of Major William Charles Forsyth's assassination.

## JUNE 23  INCIDENT UPDATE
### 11:43   Departure Imminent---en-route to Headquarters
## JUNE 23
### 12:19   Arrival at Headquarters

By the time John turned the car into the underground parking facility the weeping had long since subsided, and while they waited for Security to verify the vehicle's identity before granting them access to the second, more secure part of the car park, with Bill's arm draped around her, Charlie seemed content to remain cocooned against him.

Of course, after parking the Jaguar in its designated space, there was always the risk that moving Charlie might spark a reaction, but it was almost as if she had been rendered numb, which meant there was a smooth transition into the five-storey, inner-city building.

In order to protect everyone who worked, within the hallowed walls of H.Q. certain procedures were never bypassed for any reason whatsoever. So when they reached the Security checkpoint, the cavalry used the palm prints of their respective right hands' not only to verify their identities, but in the unlikely event of something untoward happening, it also established that along with the other occupants, they were somewhere in the building, and while John organized a photo sensitive visitor's permit for their assignment, Bill was able to escort Charlie--who had remained unresponsive--to one of the guest suites.

Although the purposely designed state-of-the-art suites lacked a bedroom, some of their other amenities such as the motorized leather recliners and the selection of entertainment including, television, radio, magazines, and newspapers were a vast improvement on Charlie's overnight stay at the rudimentary safe house. In fact, for the benefit of short stay guests, these suites even provided their own version of room service.

A few minutes later, when John caught up with his partner, although the cavalry were eager to dot the i's and cross the t's on the official paperwork, after witnessing what they believed would be documented in the Military's archives as the date of Major Forsyth's assassination, combined with the additional matter the cavalry needed to address, before they could move their assignment to their final destination, they understood that there was a need to approach both matters with patience and diplomacy.

When room service arrived, there were two mugs of extra strong black coffee and a coffee pot in case refills were required, and there was a selection of sandwiches and an assortment of biscuits, plus a pot of tea, small jug of milk and a bone china cup and saucer filled with hot sweet tea to raise their assignment's blood sugar level.

After placing the bone china cup and saucer on the coffee table, as one might expect from anyone working in Special Operations, the young man introduced himself. "Hello Mrs Daltry. My name's Peter and I'm a member of the Administration Team…"

Charlie sipped from the cup. "My last hot drink was when we had breakfast, so the tea is most welcome Peter, and there's no need to address me as Mrs Daltry…"

"Of course, if that's what you would prefer," Peter agreed, with a warm smile. "And for as long as you're a guest at Headquarters, if there's anything you want, simply press the buzzer by the recliner, and provided that it's within my power to fulfil your request, I will be happy to oblige…"

Once Peter disappeared, although Charlie could not be persuaded to eat anything, the cavalry took full advantage of the extra strong, black coffee and sandwiches, but even after she finished her tea, she sat cradling her head in her hands. However, it was time to begin dispensing with the formalities, and while it seemed to come as a welcome distraction, when John used the offer of another cup of tea, in order to coax her into joining them at the desk, as she sat down opposite Bill, her confusion was genuine.

"I don't understand why you've brought me here?"

After opening a file which contained two sheets of paper, Bill replied, "Since we can't move you out of the city, until the official paperwork has been completed Charlie, we didn't have any choice, except to bring you to Headquarters…."

Turning the file around, Bill slid it across the desk, and because his partner had crouched down beside Charlie, John explained, "Yesterday evening, a High Court Judge granted Special Operations a Protective Custody Order, which names you as the person requiring protection. We are obliged to advise you to read the content carefully and then, once you've signed and dated it---since Bill and I have been exclusively assigned to protect you, in order to make it official, we will both need to countersign beneath your signature…"

Dutifully, Charlie read the content, and then as her gaze drifted between the two of them, she seemed even more perplexed. "Surely this isn't necessary? After all, if I'm here and I have no objections to you protecting me, then why do we need to make it official?"

"Because recent events have caused us to share the same reservations," John continued to explain. "There are good reason why we'd prefer to make it official. However, until we reach our final destination, it's in your best interests that we don't elaborate any further at this precise moment in time…"

Once again, Charlie's gaze drifted between them before she posed an unavoidable direct question. "And what will happen if I refuse to sign?"

Having bided his time, Bill was ready to lay the foundation upon which his partner would build their captivating case. "If you refuse to sign, then we'll have to upset a different Judge by dragging them away from the golf course, so that you can attend a hearing in open court, where you can enjoy your fifteen minutes in the spotlight..."

Then, John delivered the compelling bad news. "And once we're sworn in so that we can give evidence under oath, when the Judge asks us why Special Operations requested the Protection Order, we will be obliged to tell the truth, and after providing evidence regarding what's happened, he or she will be even more aggrieved--not because of anything we've done or left undone--but more than a little pissed off with you, for wasting the Court's valuable time, not to mention a flagrant misappropriation of tax-payers' money. So we would defy any Judge not to suspect that at best, those events must have rendered you a little crazy, and have you sectioned for your own safety, or at worst, that you must have some kind of death wish and sanction the need for Protective Custody even without your signature…"

Dejected, Charlie was staring at the papers. "You keep telling me that I'll have to trust you to know what you're doing, but as you will discover throughout my lifetime, I have ended up paying a high physical, mental, and emotional price, whenever I've trusted people who claimed to be acting in my best interests…"

"But I thought we'd established that we're not like other people," argued John on their behalf. "In fact, we'd ask you to consider, whether we have at any time acted in a way that was less than in your best interests, and it was because of our concerns over your past which caused us to ask Commander Maddox to obtain the Protective Custody Order…"

In all fairness, there were no grounds upon which Charlie could base a counter-challenge, but while it was a welcome relief for the cavalry once the document was signed, countersigned and dated by all three parties, what they needed to deal with next was a more delicate matter, and after clearing his throat, Bill began by issuing an apology.

"I'm sorry Charlie, but there's another matter we need to address…"

Although Charlie shook her head, she made no attempt to interrupt Bill as he explained, "Until forensics has had a chance to determine what caused such a powerful explosion, we can only speculate. However, we have received confirmation that like any other Military vehicle, the Major's chauffeur-driven car was swept for explosive devices at six fifty-five this morning, which suggests that whoever is responsible must have had--not only means of accessing his car, but they also must have known its most vulnerable point?"

When Charlie severed eye contact, Bill paused, but it was a momentary hesitation, before he delivered the last part their evidence. "In addition, they must have had some means of tracing his whereabouts, especially when very few people knew that Special Operations had decided to re-commission the airstrip…"

Even though Charlie's expression remained unchanged, so that there were no obvious signs that she had heard him, he finished by issuing a direct appeal. "Because it's our professional experience that there are no such things as coincidences, then there has to be a common denominator which connects the incident at 187 Cheltenham Way and what happened at the airstrip---and despite not having any firm evidence---we suspect that the common denominator could be you Charlie…"

Then, without referring to the recording his partner had made, John added his own contribution. "And working on the premise that someone does have inside information, if there's anybody else who could be at risk because they have a connection with either you or Mark, then we feel that it's vital that you tell us Charlie…"

As if she was preparing herself fleetingly, Charlie closed her eyes. "Neither of you has any idea how difficult this is for me, but the truth is…"

Clearly struggling, when the right words refused to emerge, Charlie was forced to hesitate, but when both men remained silent, she managed to explain. "Once you start delving into my past gentlemen, you're going to discover, why I've had no choice, except to learn to live within the confines of my own silence…"

Pausing, her gaze drifted between them. "However, because I am concerned that nobody should find themselves at risk, as a result of their connection with me, there are two people who would benefit from being moved to a safer location, and provided there aren't any objections, perhaps Special Operations could arrange for that to take place…"

Like his partner, John had already identified the more serious implications, and when she seemed reluctant to share the details, after he pushed a notepad and the pen towards her he was perhaps sharper than necessary, as he insisted, "Irrespective of the reason why anybody might be at risk, if it makes it any easier, then would you please write down, not only their full names, but also their current whereabouts…"

"All right, but I wouldn't want your arrival to cause any unnecessary alarm, so it might be best if I accompany you…"

Instead of telling an outright lie, John convinced himself that he was being economical, with the truth. "That decision is above our pay grade. When Bill updates him, it depends what Commander Maddox is prepared to sanction. Now, for the last time would you please write down the names and locations, so that I can plan the best route?"

Finally, Charlie wrote down the required information, but as soon as John picked up the notepad, he and Powell were heading towards the door---hesitating long enough---for Bill to glance back at their assignment.

"Whatever happens---we will be back to collect you…"

## JUNE 23    INCIDENT UPDATE
### 13:35    En-route to the Clunnell property
## JUNE 23
### 14:12    Arrival at destination---O'Keefe en-route to rendezvous

Although Powell had expressed Charlie's desire to accompany them to the Commander, after being asked whether---*he and Mr Bland had taken complete leave of their senses*---as expected, Philip Maddox had issued a direct order confirming that their assignment was to remain in the guest suite, which mean the cavalry could focus their attention on the mysterious Lorna Clunnell, and prior to their departure, they had managed to ascertain that the house was situated in an affluent part of suburbia, and devoid of a mortgage or any kind of loan attached to the property, the Title Deeds were in the sole name of Mrs Lorna Clunnell. So after Bill turned the Jaguar into Trafalgar Avenue, he slowly cruised the car up, and then back down the road, checking for any suspicious vehicles before he parked on the--*strictly no parking*--side of the avenue which was opposite the mid-terraced house.

Then, even before they climbed the steps leading up to the black front door, they had noted that the property did not have a door entry system, which often made gaining access more difficult, especially if they encountered any kind of resistance. However, in this instance, as soon as Bill rang the doorbell, their arrival was greeted by the unmistakable excitable chattering belonging to a child, and because Charlie had not volunteered--and the cavalry had not requested--any additional information, they had arrived without any preconceived ideas regarding the ages of Mrs Lorna Clunnell and Bobby Clunnell.

Loitering on the doorstep highlighted their presence, but while John shared his partner's eagerness to be inside the house, they needed to be patient until finally they heard the inner lock being released, and a young woman who left the safety chain in position, opened the door wide enough so that Bill could ask, "Mrs Clunnell, Mrs Lorna Clunnell?"

"That depends who wants to know…"

Ignoring the flippancy, Bill opened his identification wallet. "Please try not to be too alarmed, but we are here on…"

Ignoring his suggestion, Lorna interrupted him. "But I don't understand. Who gave you my name, and how did you know where to find me?"

"We're a little conspicuous standing on the doorstep Mrs Clunnell," Bill appealed to her. "So do you think we can answer your questions from the other side of the front door?"

As if acting on auto-pilot, Lorna Clunnell closed the door so that she could slide the safety chain free, and as soon as the two strangers entered the hallway, through a polite nod, she acknowledged the identification John showed her before Bill, who was only too aware of the presence of a child asked, "Is there somewhere we can talk in private?"

Genuinely perplexed, Lorna Clunnell hesitated again, before gesturing down the hallway. "Of course, please come through to the living room…"

Only too accustomed to the uncertainty that their sudden arrival could generate, they understood her hesitancy, but as they followed her into the living room that same uncertainty was shared by the little boy who seemed to appear from nowhere, only to seek refuge behind Lorna Clunnell's legs, until John crouched down so that he was level with the youngster. "And you must be the man of the house, Master Bobby Clunnell?"

After giggling, the youngster's head emerged from behind Lorna's legs. "I do hope you haven't come to arrest Lorna because of her parking tickets…"

John extended his smile. "Oh, I think if Lorna were to check, she'd discover that she doesn't have any outstanding parking fines…"

From their identification, Lorna understood that there had to be something more serious connected to their arrival and after ruffling Bobby's hair, she made him a tempting offer. "Bobby, while I discuss some boring grown-up stuff with our visitors, why don't you go upstairs and gather together the things you'd like us to take when we go to the park?"

"Okay," Bobby agreed, but then as the man of the house, he remained unsure about the new arrivals. "But only if you promise that you'll shout if you need me for anything…"

"Of course I will," Lorna confirmed. "However, I'm sure that I will be fine, because these gentlemen happen to be the good guys…"

After the youngster scurried away, before Lorna sat down on the leather sofa, she gestured towards the matching armchairs. "Please take a seat…"

Concerned that young ears might hear them, John closed the living room door, and while he chose to remain standing, Bill accepted her invitation, and once he was sitting down, he dispensed with the formal introductions. "My name is Bill Powell and this is my colleague, John Bland. We were given your name and this location by Charlie Daltry…"

"Oh my God!" exclaimed Lorna. "Has something happened to Charlie?"

"Mrs Clunnell," Bill declared, and then without addressing her concern, he explained, "All of your questions will be answered in due course. In the meantime, all you need to know is that---of her own free will---Charlie has placed herself in Protective Custody. In addition, purely as a precautionary measure, she has requested that you and Bobby be moved to a more secure location outside of the city…"

Even before Bill finished speaking, John anticipated Lorna's reaction by stepping between her and the closed door as soon as she rose to her feet. "Before making any new arrangements involving Bobby--it might be wise to allow my colleague to finish his explanation. After all, none of us would want to create any avoidable confusion if the instructions you are giving him keep changing…"

Cautiously, Lorna sat back down on the sofa so that Bill could continue. "Because of the sensitive nature of this matter it is being handled, on a strict 'need to know' basis. As a result, nobody except the two of us and our Commanding Officer know about the situation Mrs Daltry now finds herself in or her connection to you, which is why we've come in person. However, another Operative, Patrick O'Keefe is on his way here, but until someone advises him of anything different he knows nothing except that--in accordance with the orders he has been given--he is to escort you out of the city to a prearranged location…"

"And presumably that's why you wanted me to wait before telling Bobby anything, because you wouldn't want him talking about Charlie once Mr O'Keefe arrives? But what about Charlie, will she be joining us at this prearranged location?"

Despite having to repeat his earlier statement, Bill's tone of voice remained soft. "As I've already stated, all of your questions will be answered in due course…"

While Lorna seemed prepared to remain perched on the edge of the sofa, John chose to clarify what was going to happen after their departure.

"Once the premises have been vacated, a member of staff from our Administration Team, accompanied by another Operative will come into the house, so that they can pack up whatever belongings you and Bobby might need during the next few days…"

Suddenly, it was as if Lorna had grasped the potential seriousness of their situation, causing her to remark. "You make it sound as if once we leave with Mr O'Keefe, we won't be coming back to our home…"

Although her gaze drifted between them, when it became clear that neither of her visitors was going to reveal anything, Lorna pulled her house and car keys from the pocket of her jeans, before handing them over to John.

"You seem to have come well organized," she remarked, "But, I suppose that without the keys, none of it can happen---and yet, from the sparse information, Charlie has been able to share about the more secretive side of her life---I suspect that even if you didn't have the keys, an organization like Special Operations would find a way to gain access…"

Then, as if she never expected a response, Lorna looked at John, before asking, "Is it okay if I tell Bobby that instead of the park, we're going on an adventure?"

"Of course," John replied, as his smile broadened. "But please try to keep it simple. It's in his best interest not to know too much, and as you said yourself, once O'Keefe arrives the last thing any of us would want is Bobby talking about Charlie Daltry…"

By the time Lorna reached the bottom of the stairs, she had decided how she was going to handle the situation. "Bobby…"

"Yes Lorna…"

"I'm afraid there's been a change to our plans and instead…"

"But you promised that I could play football today…"

"Excuse me young man, what have you been told about interrupting people?"

"Sorry Lorna--it was very rude of me, but I was so disappointed that I forgot…"

"Okay, so we'll let that lapse pass, because after dealing with all the boring grown-up stuff, it's been decided that you and I are going to embark upon an adventure…"

"Wow---that sounds pretty cool. Do you know where we're going?"

"For the time being that's a secret. However, because this is no different from when we go to stay with Uncle Colin, I want you to start gathering together some overnight things, as well as any games or gadgets and of course the book we're currently reading last thing at night. Then, because I know what you're like, I'll be up in a few minutes to make sure that instead of a suitcase, we can fit everything into two overnight bags…"

Pausing long enough to allow Bobby to absorb her instructions, Lorna asked, "Do you understand me young man?"

Silence, but then a smaller, less excited voice replied, "Yes Lorna---but not knowing where we're going makes it ever so difficult for me to decide…"

"Nice try---but it's still a secret…"

"Shucks," grumbled Bobby. "Sometimes you can be such a spoilsport…"

"I know, but I'm afraid it happens to be part of my job description…"

As Lorna re-entered the living room she physically jumped when the doorbell rang, but as John disappeared, pulling the door closed behind him, Bill offered her some additional reassurance. "It's okay Lorna, as I explained that will be Patrick O'Keefe arriving, so that he can take over…"

In the hope that she could camouflage her anxiety, Lorna attempted an unconvincing smile, and because Bill sensed that there was something more serious troubling her, he remarked, "You seem to be apprehensive. If you're concerned about Bobby, there isn't any need for you to worry, because when he discovers what car O'Keefe drives, he'll be so overwhelmed he'll be fine…"

"Oh I'm not concerned or worried about Bobby--it's…"

Prior to Lorna's words drifting away, Bill noticed her glancing at the living room door, so like his partner had done with Charlie, he chose to adopt a less formal approach. "Unless you tell me what's troubling you Lorna, I can't help…"

"It's silly really," she admitted. "You'll think I'm being stupid…"

"If there's something worrying you, then believe me it won't be silly, and from the skilful way you handled Bobby, nobody could ever accuse you of being stupid…"

Clearly encouraged, Lorna nodded, but Bill detected the hesitancy in her voice as she began to explain. "Although Charlie has always been guarded whenever it came to how much detail she could share about her life, it's because of that guardedness that I've always been aware that one day, something like this was going to happen. But irrespective of how crazy this might sound, despite my awareness, I seem to be more overwhelmed than you seem to think Bobby's likely to be over the mysterious car Mr O'Keefe drives…"

Yet again, Bill offered her some gentle encouragement. "That doesn't sound in the least crazy. In fact, as a result of too many similar experiences, how you're feeling is a natural reaction whenever we land on somebody's doorstep without an invitation…"

"Although that might have something to do with it, the sudden urgency to remove us from our home has left me feeling as if the life Bobby and I have shared is about to change forever while at the same time all the intrigue in Charlie's own life has reminded me that despite never having known much about the world, she seems to have been forced to inhabit the profound sadness, I'd sometimes see reflected in her eyes has often made me feel fearful on her behalf. So if that makes any sense at all Mr Powell, you must be able to appreciate, my concern for her welfare, and since I'm not asking you to divulge any state secrets then surely, you must be able to reassure me that at this moment in time Charlie is safe…"

Until the relationship between the two young women had been established, it was perhaps ironic that like their assignment, Bill knew he could not reveal any sensitive details and yet, at the same time, irrespective of how meagre it might seem, he wanted to offer this particular half of that equation some peace of mind. So he hoped that the door would remain closed a little longer, because it was his turn to be economical with the truth.

"Regrettably, without Charlie's express permission, I cannot divulge any personal information. However, when we confirm how the two of you are both safe, and as she requested---you're both en-route to a more secure location--I'm confident that she will be relieved---or at least that's what John and I are hoping her reaction is going to be…"

As Bill had hoped, Lorna managed to read between the lines, but before she could voice her gratitude, the living room door opened, and ahead of John Bland a tall, athletically-built gentleman entered the living room, and with his own Special Operation's identification clearly visible, he introduced himself. "Hello Mrs Clunnell, my name is Patrick O'Keefe, and as far as I'm aware you have been advised of the reason for my arrival…"

Having relaxed a little, Lorna acknowledged the identification through a more convincing smile. However, before she could offer the new arrival her confirmation, an over-excited youngster's voice demanded her immediate attention.

"Gosh Lorna have you seen the cool car, and I do mean--*the really cool car*--that's parked in--*the strictly no parking area*--across the street? It's not your average kind of a Jaguar, like the one our first visitors also parked opposite the house. This one is an all-time classic--*a British Racing Green Jaguar XJS*--which is number two on the list of my all-time favourite classic cars and I don't know how we're going to fit everything in--or whether you will be able to squeeze into the space, behind the front seats, despite knowing how strict you are about me always sitting in the back seat--which I do all the time--if this is supposed to be an adventure--would it be possible for me to sit in the passenger seat?"

As Lorna's gaze drifted between the three men, an even more convincing smile crept onto her face. "It would seem that as a result of your arrival Mr O'Keefe at least one of us doesn't have any reason to be apprehensive about our adventure..."

"Sometimes it does attract a great deal of attention," admitted O'Keefe. "But since the Special Operation's registration grants me a considerable amount of immunity, provided that you give yer permission, I guess yer wee man could ride up front, and if I put a bolster cushion on the passenger seat, he might even be able to see out of the windscreen..."

As if to prove that John had been right about the need to keep the living room door closed, so that inquisitive young ears could not have overheard their earlier conversation involving Charlie--the youngster, who had so far been responsible for nothing more than excited chattering must have been eavesdropping on the upstairs landing, because in sheer delight at what he had heard, the decibels increased as Bobby shrieked, "Did you hear that Lorna? If Mr O'Keefe says it's all right, please give him your permission..."

Only too aware of the need to avoid mentioning Charlie, after she considered that this opportunity might provide a useful distraction, Lorna announced, "Gentlemen, before everyone ends up deafened, perhaps I should go upstairs so that after giving Bobby the good news I can bring him back into the realms of reality. However, at least he knows that instead of us leaving in your average kind of Jaguar, we are going to be transported in an all-time classic---*a British Racing Green Jaguar XJS*---and because there isn't much room hopefully the only objection I will have to deal with are which non-essential items, he's going to have to leave behind. But even then, I can reassure him that if we leave all the discarded items together, then you can organize their safe delivery to our eventual destination..."

Then, despite heading towards the door Lorna hesitated, and as if it were an afterthought, she glanced over her shoulder. "After what Bobby said about not knowing where I was going to sit while you youngsters are sitting up front, and Bobby will no doubt be experimenting with all the car's gadgets, I presume that there is room for me behind the front seats, or should I prepare myself for being crammed into the boot?"

Appreciating her wry sense of humour, O'Keefe tossed his head back and laughed. "There might not be much room in the back Mrs Clunnell, but it shouldn't take us very long to reach our destination and at least you won't need a bolster cushion..."

"In that case, perhaps I should be thankful for small mercies," declared Lorna. "Now, if you'll excuse me, I'll get Bobby organized and then, after I throw some of my things into an overnight bag, we should be ready to leave in about fifteen minutes Mr O'Keefe..."

After throwing her another winning smile he waited until she reached the top of the stairs and then, as soon as he could hear the beginning of her skilful negotiations, with a more subdued Bobby, O'Keefe turned his attention to the cavalry, and clearly about to embark on some kind of fishing trip, he began to explain. "After John completed the hand-over, I told him about what's been documented at Headquarters..."

Hesitating, O'Keefe waited, but when Bland and Powell remained silent, he added, "And apparently, you've both been classified as *unavailable*, for an *unspecified period of time*, which not only suggests that you must have been given some kind of exclusive assignment, it would also explain why I was sent here to take over, at such short notice..."

After selecting his words with some considerable care, Bill curtailed the fishing trip. "Even if that's what been documented you know as well as us that we cannot discuss what we may or may not be doing---because if there was a breach in security, then it will not only be us, but also any third party or parties who will find themselves summoned to the Commander's office, so that he can tear us all apart limb by limb..."

As O'Keefe winced, he emitted a low, hissing sound from between his lips before offering his agreement. "Yer right, and unless there were any mitigating circumstances and I cannot think of any, I'm far too attached to my limbs to risk losing any of them..."

"Well, it's a relief to learn that we all value our limbs," announced Bill. "So I'm sure we can leave the Clunnell family in your capable hands, while we head off to do whatever it is we may or may not be supposed to be doing. My God--even I'm not sure anymore…"

**JUNE 23   INCIDENT UPDATE**
**14:50   Departure from Clunnell residence**
**JUNE 23**
**15:25   Arrival back at Headquarters**

After performing the same ritual using their palm prints to not only confirm their identities but also to establish that they were re-entering the building, once they were inside the hallowed walls, they were advised that Commander Maddox had left H.Q., and until further notice, he could be reached at his country retreat. Of course, apart from the cavalry nobody knew that he had left, so that upon their arrival at Manor Park, he would be able to greet Lorna Clunnell and the delightful--if a little excitable--Bobby Clunnell.

Moving beyond security, they were also advised that the Person of Interest they had been expecting in connection with the Paris incident had arrived, and in light of the exclusivity of their current assignment, Commander Maddox had issued a direct order that nobody except Bland and Powell were to be given access to that particular person.

As far as the situation with Charlie was concerned, they were only too aware that the damage had been done, and because they were about to be classified as--*unavailable*--they opted to make a detour to the less comfortable custody suites, so that they could Interview the aforementioned Person of Interest.

Approximately fifty--five minutes later, having copied the audio and video surveillance of their Interview, before taking the original with them they made another detour to the Commander's office, so that the copy could be deposited in his wall-safe.

Next, they went to find Peter, the Admin Assistant who been assigned to take care of Charlie during her stay at H.Q., and as they had anticipated, the update was not good. In fact, when they checked the incident log, after the fifteenth time Charlie had demanded and then, failed to acquire Peter's attention, as if it were some kind of weapon, she had resorted to keeping her finger on the button, and before the constant buzzing could drive everyone in the Admin Office crazy, following standard procedure, Peter had obtained, the necessary permission to disable that particular facility. However, being ignored made Charlie even more angry, and knowing that the guest suite would have both audio and visual surveillance, Charlie had made her intentions clear, and because Peter wanted them to appreciate why neither he, nor anyone else in the Admin Team, had been prepared to venture anywhere near the guest suite without the protection of armed Operatives, Peter replayed the surveillance recordings of Charlie's disruptive behaviour.

Indeed, when it came to some of the threats Charlie had been making, especially the ones, involving the more delicate parts of their anatomy--like O'Keefe--they winced, and while still considering their position, they checked the security monitors again, only to discover that like their Person of Interest who was already on their way back to Paris, Charlie was sitting bolt upright in the chair by the desk with her arms folded, and having run out of excuses to avoid the inevitable, they had no choice except to venture inside.

Armed with what they had discussed while en-route to the Clunnell property, and keeping to the script, as soon as they went through the door, Bill began to make what was intended to be a placatory, opening announcement on their behalf.

"No doubt you will be relieved to learn that Mrs Lorna Clunnell and Bobby have vacated their last known address, and they should be arriving at their intended destination within the next fifteen minutes…"

Silence--but it was different from anything they had ever encountered, and despite knowing that she was expecting them to fill the void, when Bland and Powell did nothing, without unfolding her arms, Charlie levelled her first valid accusation.

"Gentlemen--and I make that reference jestingly, because perhaps I misheard you, or maybe I was labouring under some kind of delusion, but to quote your own words---*you will have to trust us to know what we're doing* and then, as you were leaving, you announced, "*Whatever happens, we will be back to collect you,*" and yet, despite all of that, you decided to leave me, in this fucking hell-hole for over three hours..."

"Now Charlie," Bill attempted to explain. "We did try..."

However, determined to vent the full force of her disillusionment, Charlie interrupted him. "Of course, it wasn't until you had both disappeared that I discovered---like the rear of the Jaguar, with its child-proof locking system---I couldn't leave the guest suite, unless someone opened the door from the outside..."

Anticipating Bill's next attempt to silence her, Charlie eased her grasp on her arms, so that she could indicate by raising her index finger that it might be wise to allow her to finish, and when he remained silent, she proceeded to level her second valid accusation.

"As for the Protective Custody Order I signed of my own volition, when in fact, I only signed the damn thing to avoid having to appear in some Kangaroo Court, where all the evidence was allegedly stacked against me---quite amazingly it had disappeared---because if it hadn't, you can both rest assured, I would have gained tremendous satisfaction in tearing it up into masses of little pieces..."

Without giving it too much thought beforehand, John began to clarify why any such action would have been a futile gesture. "It wouldn't have..."

However, the instant Bill nudged his elbow, John fell silent, because enlightening her to the fact that the original had been taken, by the Commander to his country retreat could only serve to inflame an already inflammatory scenario. In fact, a far more sensible option was to allow Bill to bring the situation back under their control. "All right Charlie, because you've levelled two accusations, the least you can do is allow us the right to respond..."

Then, Bill paused, and when Charlie seemed willing to listen, he proceeded to tell their assignment the truth. "Believe me, we did plan to come back and collect you, but when I advised the Commander about our intended visit to the Clunnell property, after he implied that---*we must have taken leave of our senses*---he issued a direct order which confirmed that you were to remain in the guest suite..."

As Bill allowed his words to fade, he knew that his partner would be ready to provide additional support, and right on cue, John added, "Besides, if you had come with us and anyone had been watching the house, firstly, it could have suggested a direct link between you and the Clunnell family and secondly, it would have attracted even more attention to our presence, and I'm sure none of us would have wanted to place Lorna and Bobby Clunnell in any unnecessary danger..."

Unimpressed, Charlie's arms remained folded, but at least she was no longer glowering at them. "Presumably, you expect me to believe all that nonsense? For all I know, you could be making up a load of fucking bullshit..."

Having left him no choice, Bill raised his voice. "Yesterday, I told you that we wouldn't lie to you or try to trick you, and because we've done nothing to warrant your verbal abuse, while we take care of some paperwork which we should deal with before our departure, we could leave you here until you decide to stop behaving like a spoilt child who you didn't get her own way, or if you've finished hurling unwarranted, personal insults, you could decide to come with us, so that you can be reunited with the Clunnell family..."

Suddenly, Charlie found herself confronted by the reality of having reached the point of no return and yet, as the Major had tried to warn her, the stakes had become far too high, so there was no other way, and after unfolding her arms, she issued an apology. "I'm sorry, but without any news, those three hours felt like a lifetime…"

Then, after Bill acknowledged her apology, she added, "Presumably, our final destination is going to be Manor Park your Commanding Officer's country retreat…"

As the cavalry exchanged a curious glance, Charlie realized that her protectors knew even less than she had imagined, and as they headed to the door, she threw a casual remark in their direction. "For two people who have been assigned to protect me, there is so much you don't seem to know, but believe me, you should have been more careful when it came to deciding, what you were going to wish for…"

### JUNE 23   FINAL INCIDENT UPDATE
### 17:10   Departure from H.Q. en-route to Manor park
Like any of their other assignments, neither Bland nor Powell would be presumptuous enough to predict how this one might end. In the meantime, because they needed to ensure that nobody could see or hear anything that might suggest much less imply a connection between their assignment, and the Clunnell family or their Person of Interest, prior to them leaving the building, John gathered together all of the audio and visual surveillance footage amassed throughout Charlie Daltry's time spent at H.Q.

Yes, despite being unwilling to predict the end, at least they were confident they had acquired everything they needed to proceed with Operation Code Named Tigress.
### JUNE 23   OPERATION TIGRESS
### 18:12   Arrival at Manor Park
Along with its own helicopter pad, Manor Park also had many other special features including a heated indoor swimming pool. However, while they were waiting at the main entrance for their identities to be verified by the twenty-four hours a day CCTV monitoring system, Bland and Powell acknowledged two of the four Class A marks-persons who were patrolling the perimeter of the estate, and until they were issued with a new directive they would continue working as part of a hand-picked team of sixteen marks-persons.

Beyond the gates, Bill followed the road up past the lake until they approached the refurbished Manor, with its cascading steps leading up to the double front doors, and because the scene which greeted them was so unexpected, initially the cavalry were left speechless because after they had been hand-picked by the Commander to join the Special Operations team, neither Bland nor Powell had ever had any reason to consider that, because of his dedication to his work, he would have any inclination whatsoever to indulge in frivolous activities and yet, Lorna Clunnell was sitting on the steps encouraging Bobby, who was firing his beloved football at the makeshift goalposts, while Commander Philip Maddox was acting as goalkeeper--albeit a goalkeeper who seemed---much to the youngster's delight to be failing to prevent the occasional ball from passing between the goalposts.

Wanting to gauge Charlie's reaction, John glanced at the rear view mirror, but despite everything she had been through, she was smiling, and what he found most reassuring was that her smile radiated genuine warmth, which suggested a profound affection.

Although Philip Maddox knew who was about to emerge from the Jaguar when Bill brought the car to a halt, as Lorna's encouragement had ceased, Bobby had stopped playing football, and because the blackened rear windows made it impossible to identify anyone in the back seat, it was clear they were curious to learn who was inside.

Now there was no need for the child-proof facility and yet, after the first tell-tale clunk confirmed that the central locking had been deactivated---and a second click confirmed that the child-proof facility had been disarmed Charlie seemed reluctant to vacate the back seat, leaving them no choice except to exit the Jaguar so that John could open the rear door.

"Is there something wrong Charlie?" John asked, in a hushed voice. "Because unless we've misjudged the situation, sooner or later you will have to come out of the car…"

At last, Charlie began to emerge, and despite the cavalry believing that there could be no more surprises, what happened next surpassed all previous expectations. For a moment, as the silence was left hanging, the suspense increased, until Lorna brought it to an end by summoning the youngster's attention.

"Bobby," pausing, Lorna waited for him to look at her. "Although we're among strangers, the three of us are in the same place at the same time, so I don't think that we need to pretend anymore…"

Like Charlie, the youngster seemed reluctant to move, until she confirmed what Lorna had told him. "Lorna's right Bobby, we don't have to pretend anymore…"

At last Bobby's fixed expression melted into a broad smile which seemed to beam from ear to ear, and as he broke into a run heading in Charlie's direction, he was shouting, "Mum, Mum where have you been, I've missed you so much?"

Dumbfounded, the cavalry expected their Commanding Officer to share their amazement, but his expression suggested that he knew enough not to be surprised much less shocked at discovering that instead of Lorna Clunnell---Charlie was Bobby's birth mother.

Conscious of the injuries sustained during their assignment's harrowing ordeal, Bill managed to intercept the youngster before he could collide with his mother. However, before he could start protesting, as soon as Bill swung him up in the air he passed him into Charlie's waiting arms, and as she hugged him, and kissed his forehead repeatedly, she confirmed her own sadness at their separation. "And I've missed you so much Bobby---but there were good reasons why it wasn't possible for the three of us to be together…"

Given the benefit of hindsight, the cavalry realized a significant clue should have been the way in which Bobby addressed his other mother by her Christian name, and considering that there was so much they did not know about Charlie Anne Daltry, her earlier warning that they should have been more careful what they had wished for seemed almost prophetic. Of course, what their Commanding Officer gave with one hand, he found a way to snatch something back with the other, and after they had requested the Protective Custody Order, he had also given them free licence to do whatever might prove necessary in order to uncover the truth, and when it came to the technicality of how they intended to achieved that objective, they were going to need Security clearance, so that they could gain access to all of the Official Records--past and present--in connection with their assignment.

In the meantime, although both of them expected Commander Maddox to be watching the reunion, he was at the top of the steps and was about to disappear inside the Manor, and refocusing their attention on Charlie, Bobby and not forgetting the mysterious Lorna Clunnell and the role she must have played in all this, as soon as Charlie allowed Bobby to slither to the ground, the two women were able to embrace.

"When these two reprobates arrived on the doorstep, I knew it had to be serious, and because they wouldn't give me any information, I've been out of my mind with worry…"

Despite being less concerned about Bobby and Lorna, because the cavalry were aware that regardless of the marks-persons, their assignment was yet again overexposed, John brought the reunion to an end--albeit a temporary one.

"I'm sure Bill would agree that the last few days have been exhausting for Charlie, so perhaps you should continue updating each other inside the Manor…"

"Oh no!" exclaimed Bobby. "Does that mean I won't be able to play football?"

This time it was Bill who ruffled the youngster's hair. "Not necessarily Bobby. After spending the last two days with your mother, we can appreciate how exhausting they must have been for her. However, as far as the football is concerned…"

Pausing, Bill steered Bobby away from the remaining adults so that it would seem as if they could not hear him. "If I tell you something, do you think you can keep it between you and me, because if the Commander finds out, I will be in serious trouble?"

"Yeah, I think so," Bobby replied, a little guardedly. "Unless it's something bad, like something a stranger who approaches me might say, because if that happens, then I have to tell one of my teachers or either of my two mothers straight away…"

"Oh, if I was a stranger, then that's exactly what you should do, but when we arrived at your house, and you were suspicious, Lorna did describe us as being the good guys…"

Wanting to be sure, Bobby glanced at the remaining adults, and when both women nodded their approval, he whispered, "Yes Mr Powell--it's all right…"

"Well--because Commander Maddox has a very important job involving National Security, he might not be in a position where he can play football with you every day. However, while we might not be as good as our Commanding Officer, I'm sure that one of us, or maybe even both of us, will be able to find some spare time to play football…"

For a moment, Bobby looked pensive, but then still in a hushed voice, he asked, "But won't you and Mr Bland have to help the Commander with his important work?"

Supressing the urge to smile, Bill replied, "Oh since we've been assigned to look after your mother for the next few days, we'll be staying around the Manor…"

As if all his Christmases had come on that day, Bobby exclaimed, "Wow, one of you would be--sort of--cool--but both of you would be a million--zillion--times cooler!"

Then, as he began marching up the steps, he conceded, "Gosh, I was wrong, this isn't going to be a boring, grown-up place with nothing for little people to do after all…"

# PART TWO

# JUNE 29

# THE INTERVIEW

# Let the Battle Commence

**JUNE 29**

*On the basis that everything runs in a circular motion then you, my invisible audience will be pleased to learn that we now find ourselves back at the place, where you first became aware of not only my existence, but also the gravity of my present situation because* within the present tense of my Godfather's study, I'm standing by the window staring out across the lake, and amidst the calm before the approaching storm, some of the words from one of my favourite songs seem to aptly describe the scene as it will be unfolding, throughout the evening. *"Treachery and treason there's always an excuse for it, and when I find the reason I still can't get used to it."*

A little to the left of me, Bill Powell is checking the equipment laid out on the table, which is situated between the window and the centrally placed desk, where John Bland has finished removing his short leather jacket before laying it on the desk, no doubt in readiness for our confrontation.

Ouch--that twinge of discomfort seems to have manifested itself, as a result of my reference to--*confrontation*--because I, Charlie Anne Daltry cannot as yet, provide any corroborating evidence for either my inner child's fear of being confronted, or this woman's sense of entrapment.

Provided that you have been paying attention, then you will know that I did not need to be dragged kicking and screaming into this room, especially when one considers that, despite having to remain within the confines of the sizeable Manor, this absentee mother has been able to enjoy several days, in the company of Bobby and Lorna.

At least that was the case until today, when I had known--as only I could have known that my carefree time was destined to be disturbed, and because my past was about to collide with what might constitute our future, mid-afternoon I ignored Bobby's impassioned pleas and excused myself, so that I could retreat to the sanctuary of my palatial en-suite bedroom to spend, yet more sleepless hours lying on the king size bed. Then, after taking a shower I had dressed, before our communal evening meal, which has been timed to fit in with what was supposed to be Bobby's normal evening routine within the Clunnell household, when a gentle tap on the door heralded the arrival of the cavalry to confirm that they had finished their preparation, and provided I felt sufficiently recovered, they were eager to proceed with operation code named Tigress.

For my part, although their arrival had proved that my instincts could be trusted, it was one of those moments we have all experienced, at some time in our life. Despite knowing something unpleasant will happen when it arrives, the initial impact is very similar to a blow being delivered which causes an involuntary tightening of the stomach muscles.

Nevertheless, rather than prolong the torment, I had confirmed that I was also eager to proceed, and after negotiating a deal over the events that took place, in the early hours of the 22nd of June, I had added that because of Bobby, Lorna and anyone else who might be implicated, as result of my testimony, then the evidence I would give would--to the best of my ability--be the truth, the whole truth, and nothing but the truth.

Through the reflection in the bullet proof glass, I have been watching as John slipped off the less visible shoulder holster, which the cavalry have both taken to wearing, since our arrival at Manor Park, undoubtedly so that my inquisitive, and as we have all discovered excitable son would not have any reason to bombard them with awkward questions.

Then, after hooking the gun and shoulder holster on the side of the chair, so that both items are dangling loosely, he picks up his jacket from the desk, before draping it around the back of the chair, which means that the weapon of mass destruction is concealed beneath it, and when I glance over my shoulder, John gestures towards the comfortable Executive chair, belonging to my Godfather, which is on the opposite side of the desk.

"Why don't you sit down and make yourself comfortable?"

If my invisible audience will excuse a dreadful play on words my immediate thought was--*how disarming.* However, please do not allow yourselves to be fooled by his laid-back invitation, because as the evening progresses it will prove to have been misleading.

Despite my earlier willingness to bare this woman's soul, even though I knew it would necessitate paring away layer after layer of resilient flesh until nothing remains, except brittle bone grinding against brittle bone behind me the door is ajar, and suddenly the vulnerable child within me has an overwhelming urge to collect Lorna and my son, so that even before it has been committed, we can flee the scene of the impending criminal act.

Perhaps I should clarify my reference to my vulnerable child. Having undergone extensive Person Centred Therapy, I am aware that we never completely lose our inner child who remains lurking in our consciousness waiting to materialize, whenever an occasion warrants it. Furthermore, I have the capacity to become the protective mother, this young woman and of course this adult who is grown-up enough to appreciate that even if we did manage to flee the scene, before the crime can be admitted as evidence, my protective parent knows that--albeit in disjointed fragments--too many pieces of the puzzle have been slotted into their rightful place. So even if there were a means of escape, I know that there would never be a safe--much less secure--hiding place for any of us.

Accepting that there is no alternative, this adult instructs my legs to propel this young woman back towards the desk, and when the preciseness of each step echoes a lack of enthusiasm, before he sits down John throws me an encouraging smile.

"At the prospect of talking to us about your life, you seem to be a little apprehensive Charlie," he suggests, but I'm aware that he has not finished, so I continue to study his face, until he adds, "When there isn't any need for you to feel anxious, especially when whatever you tell us should automatically identify anybody else, who like Lorna and Bobby might have played a significant role in your life story…"

Oh my God, he makes it all sound so simple, so neat and tidy when in reality, having been borne out of womanly weakness as I stated at the beginning, this script will reveal all the ugliness in my life, and believe me there's been far too much ugliness.

At the prospect of having to share all that unsightliness with my invisible audience yet again, I doubt this woman's ability to bare her soul with any dignity, but standing by the desk, staring at John's benign expression, this adult appreciates that I would not be in this room, if this young woman thought for a solitary moment that I could obtain a fairer hearing, or receive better treatment from a more sympathetic Agency, and after easing the Executive chair away from the desk, I finally sit down.

Then, with the desk separating us like an empty stage the principal players have assumed their opening positions and yet, despite the scene appearing to be set for the curtain to rise, I find my thoughts being monopolized by Bobby.

Wherever the beginning middle or end might be, everything I have done or failed to do, or might still be prepared to do has been, and will continue to be in the belief that Bobby should be allowed to grow up, living his life free from this illusory world, we now find ourselves forced to inhabit. A world which is built upon deceit, and the kind of manipulation which in turn leads to the corruption of those who should be incorruptible.

However, is that not the way it's supposed to be? Once the ill-prepared child within us bears a child of its own, do we not fulfil somebody else's notion of duty by living our life for that child, without seeking reward or recompense? Oh despite the fancy protestations by the feminists we remain, as we have remained for centuries, accountable to ourselves in the motherhood not only of future women, but also of future men.

Placing my lighter and packet of cigarettes beside the large robust glass ashtray, which ever since I was a child I have known to be reserved for the ash from my Godfather's daily cigar, my introduction of the Commander prompts me to look at John.

"Apart from two days ago when I was summoned to his study, so that he could dispense with some unfinished business, although my Godfather has managed to find time to join you whenever you play football, he has been conspicuous by his absence at mealtimes. So I can only assume that discovering I have a son has left him displeased..."

Of course, once we begin in earnest I suspect that there will be no room for assumptions, and even now while he is considering how he intends to word his reply, John's expression is revealing nothing.

"As far as we're aware your Godfather isn't displeased about anything, and if you had wanted to see him, then you could have asked either me or Bill. However, in his capacity as our Commanding Officer, when one serious incident triggers a second, even more serious incident, we tend to share the same concerns, but then it's our experience that none of us is ever surprised by what people eventually reveal to us about their life..."

How diplomatic! Coming from my principal male, such a prologue had all the right ingredients to leave my vulnerable child feeling a little threatened by his indirect reference to my revelations. Like life, this is not a rehearsal, and dressed to combat the sultry heat of this June evening, in a sleeveless cotton top with its cut away shoulders and low neckline, this woman feels improperly dressed for such an auspicious occasion, especially when I am beginning to realize that this will be a unique public performance.

A one-night stand for which a demure black dress with short sleeves and discreet neckline would have been a far more fitting costume, and because my thoughts have made me aware that I opted not to wear a bra, my vulnerable child feels the need to cover-up my nakedness, and without giving it any conscious thought, I loosely fold my arms.

Then, when John reaches for the insulated coffee pot and he seems preoccupied with pouring the murky liquid into the bone china mugs, which are neatly arranged on a solid silver tray, while he remains distracted my protective parent inspects the rest of my Godfather's inner sanctum. Although the walls are devoid of any mirrors, there are other ways of being unobtrusively observed, which I have learned to my personal cost during the last three years. However, when my protective parent's inspection reaches the floor to ceiling bookcases, while I'm scanning them John's perceptiveness startles me.

"There aren't any hidden cameras..."

Then he waits, until I look at him and as if he knows I do not believe him he explains, "Because of our misgivings, we took the liberty of ensuring that you will remain as anonymous as possible, and apart from the recording equipment, which will be under Bill's control, you can rest assured that there isn't any other audio--or visual--surveillance equipment being used, and as negotiated by the Commander, before receiving the seal approval from the highest possible Authority--in this instance--there's nothing and no one, except for the three of us and the machines…"

How cosy, how intimate, almost too intimate to be classified as official, but while he has omitted to mention the select bureaucrats who on a strictly need to know basis will be granted access to this exclusive performance, it would be naïve if not downright dangerous for this adult to pretend that this one-night stand is solely for the benefit of such an intimate audience. However, since no amount of dispute will win me an adjournment, I glance over my shoulder at Bill and the recording equipment.

"It still looks very formal…"

"On the contrary," John corrects me. "Although the equipment and files laid out on the table might seem oppressive, the proceedings will be far less formal than usual…"

As Bill joins us and he selects a bone china mug and saucer, his own eagerness to dispel my preoccupation with the machinery confirms that despite appearing to have been preoccupied, he has been absorbing every word of our dialogue. "Normally, official proceedings do take place, using unobtrusive surveillance equipment over which we have no control. However, because we have been assigned to protect you, that responsibility afforded us some considerable leverage, when it came to agreeing the terms and conditions surrounding this Interview and yet again, we took the liberty of deciding on your behalf that you might feel more relaxed, in familiar surroundings, and less intimidated if you could be sure, there was nothing sinister or underhand about the proceedings…"

Like his partner in crime, Bill hesitates long enough to throw a careless smile in a downward direction. "So, why don't you do as John has suggested---and try to relax. Then twenty minutes from now, I can give you my personal guarantee that you will hardly notice that the recording equipment is even present…"

Between you and me, there's so much concern for this woman's comfort. Perhaps my protective parent should be asking her vulnerable child to be impressed and yet, somewhere amidst the lesser intimidation of the relaxed performer, I suspect that this woman might have failed to grasp the most significant detail, and when Bill takes his coffee and he returns to the chair by the table, I seek the support of a dramatic prop.

Often beaten into submission and presumed dead, but never beyond being resurrected it's a habit this woman abhors and yet, despite the increasing social disapproval, my reliance on nicotine has often provided me with a useful prop in times of crisis.

As this consenting adult pulls a cigarette from the packet, I fail to notice John rising to his feet, but after I click the lighter and I inhale the smoke deep into my lungs, so that the nicotine stimulates dulled brain cells, I realize that it's all too damn comfortable.

In reality, it's not neat and tidy, and because nobody could describe my life as having been simple, the scene is far too intimate for any actual relaxation. But while the headstrong child within me is reconsidering the running away option, a soft click confirms that John has closed the door, and deprived of our only escape route, this woman is still assessing the loss, when he returns to the desk and as he sits back down, despite hearing the gentle purring coming from the table, I do not glance over my shoulder as Bill introduces the scene for the benefit of our wider audience.

"It is 18:33 on the 29th June. Present are Special Operatives John Bland and myself, Robert William Powell. Also present is Charlie Anne Daltry, nee Charlotte Anne Forsyth who has agreed to participate of her own free will. As negotiated by Commander Philip Maddox with the highest possible Authority, before these proceedings were subsequently granted the Royal Seal of approval during this particular Interview, we do not intend to use any other kind of audio or visual surveillance equipment…"

Then, with the impressive introductions completed nothing disturbs the silence, except for the gentle purring from the machine, but when I check out how I feel this woman is confused. However, it would seem that the curtain has risen and after tapping the first spent ash into my Godfather's virginal ashtray, I glance across the desk.

"If this has got to be done, then I suppose we should get on with it…"

A smile accompanies an appreciative nod, and having been foolish enough to deliver the opening line, in the absence of any verbal guidance, this amateur performer feels obliged to fill the void. "So, where would you like us to start?"

In no rush to respond, Bland lifts his own dramatic prop, and sips his coffee before delivering a vague suggestion.

"We would invite you to start anywhere you like Charlie…"

Not only vague but also perplexing, especially when this adult considers the kind of assistance my vulnerable child has enjoyed, during previous encounters--albeit three months ago. Instead of asking the questions, this woman is here to provide the answers, so I venture to ask a more direct question. "How far back do you want me to go?"

Still in no rush to reply, John hesitates. "Perhaps, you should start whenever you believe the beginning to be…"

Although more precise, it is another imprecise suggestion and somehow this is wrong. This is not what my inner child, protective parent or this woman expected. Daunted by the prospect of unlimited time and space in which to perform, my dramatic prop excuses my silence. Guess one could call it biding my time and yet, that extra time affords me, an opportunity to consider that while this woman did agree time and venue, and she negotiated her special deal, she omitted to negotiate the role play between the principal players. But before the three of us entered this room, what did this adult expect?

Interrogation, intimidation or had I hoped for nothing more taxing than chivalrous questions, which would have enabled this woman to limit the damage. If she did then it was not a conscious preference, because in all honesty I did not explore what our expectations should be. Instead, I assumed the manner in which the proceedings would be conducted and like everything else in this woman's life, I assumed too much. Having accepted that it is time to establish how John intends to enact his role, I exhale the smoke from my lungs, and once again tap the spent ash into the glass ashtray.

"Am I right in assuming that you simply want me to talk?"

"Yes," replies John and when he throws me another reassuring smile for future reference, I'm duly noting the lack of any hesitation, as he adds, "One of us will soon tell you, if you either haven't given us enough, or we want you to move time on…"

Damn it. Can things get any worse? In addition to unlimited time and space, I have been awarded complete freedom of speech, and my protective parent is warning this woman that without any boundaries, this performance will be both daring and dangerous. More importantly, amidst so much freedom, it will be harder for me to fulfil such an alien role with any dignity, and because I doubt that this woman has the skill--much less the courage--to strip myself naked, before the cavalry begin to pare away those layers of resilient flesh, I mentioned earlier, I venture to enter an admission regarding my lack of preparation.

"This isn't what I expected…"

Now John has reverted to being in no rush to reply, and while he sips from the bone china mug, I find myself pacing him---one and two--and three--and four--then at last, he poses the obvious rhetorical question.

"And what did you expect Charlie?"

At least it is a question--albeit the wrong one--and although this woman has admitted that she did not explore her expectations, I dare not declare a predilection for unchallenging questions. "I didn't give it much thought…"

An abstract answer, but while John is still revealing nothing which means that I cannot be sure, whether or not he believes me, I am grateful when his partner fills the void by introducing himself in his role as self-appointed arbitrator, and his opening declaration is made, without so much as a hint of accusation.

"During past encounters, despite what seems to have been our professional inadequacies, we aren't ready to give up on you--at least not yet. So whether you choose to believe it or not we are here to listen…"

Oh my God, they have been labouring under the misapprehension that they must have failed, when neither success nor failure was the issue. As stated at the beginning, the truth was always waiting to be uncovered and yet, somehow they never managed to pose the right questions. But at least I now have confirmation that having failed to ask the right questions, they intend to ask as few questions as possible, until the vulnerable child within me has led them to all the answers, and as I extinguish my cigarette, this adult offers Bill a somewhat feeble excuse for my actions.

"As God is my witness, I never lied to either of you…"

Although Bill nods his appreciation it would seem that I was right and my feeble excuse is less than satisfactory. "Nobody is accusing you of being untruthful Charlie. However, in light of recent events, we think you might agree that during those previous encounters, it must have required a tremendous amount of resourcefulness on your part to achieve such a level of economy when it came to the truth…"

How diplomatic! Reaching out Bill's fingers touch one of the three buff folders, which are resting on the corner of the table, and despite being indistinguishable from the other two, my protective parent suspects that it contains the information compiled three months ago, after they escorted me home from Paris, and because the evidence will later prove to be damning, my vulnerable child is not only trapped, but also consumed by guilt which is the only emotion we are all born incapable of feeling. In fact, guilt or being made to feel guilty has to be learnt with the lesson being taught during childhood by an adult. In my case, the adult responsible for teaching me was my father Major William Charles Forsyth.

On reflection, I could have chosen to tell the cavalry everything and yet, it should not have even needed to be a consideration. However, in accordance with the prophecy issued by my father--minutes before the car exploded killing three people--while I have chosen to maintain my precious silence people around me have continued to die, but despite the anticipated guilt that negative feeling proves to be a by-product rather than an intended result.

"Even though this isn't what you expected Charlie," Bill declares, bringing the silence to an end, before he offers me a suggestion. "Taking into account our expertise in such matters, perhaps you'll have to trust us to know what we're doing, and because you are in our Protective Custody that we are acting in your best interests…"

In case one of us should forget where we are in this saga let's recap. While performing in unlimited time and space with complete freedom of speech, Bill has reintroduced the issue of my being expected to trust them. As you my invisible audience will come to understand as a result of what will be proven, before this Interview comes to an end, the harsh reality is whenever I have trusted people, my trust has been betrayed, and turned into some kind of weapon in an attempt to control me. But if we can set aside that particular issue, then because my inquisitors have misunderstood my reticence, this woman enters a second more plausible excuse.

"You don't understand. It's very similar to my reluctance to divulge Lorna and Bobby's whereabouts. After keeping my own counsel for so long, I was forced to learn how to live within the sound of my own silence. So the very idea of having complete freedom of speech presents itself as being inconceivable…"

Sounds plausible enough, but do they believe me? It is the truth and this time, my fears are unfounded, when I am rewarded with John's encouragement.

"There's a first time for everything, and despite freedom of speech seeming to be inconceivable, we would invite you to try it. You might even start to enjoy it..."

Then, while he maintains eye contact his smile becomes reassuring, as he adds, "After all, being the good guys, the three of us are supposed to be on the same side..."

Like complete freedom of speech, it is another novel concept and yet, as they did after what happened in Paris, although they have remained close by my side during the last seven days, this adult is not quite as naïve as Bland and Powell might imagine this woman to be, and recognizing the irony my vulnerable child laughs.

"In the past John--the idea of us all being on the same side has turned out to be an illusion. Indeed, after you've heard everything, you'll realize that by my side, might not be a very healthy place to be standing in the days, weeks or even months ahead..."

John extends his smile. "Somehow--I think we'll take our chances..."

What can this adult say--except that they probably will, especially when they have been assigned to protect me, while at the same time uncovering the truth. But it has been a long time, since anyone dared to take this woman's part--or as John so quaintly stated--dared to be on my side, and the images from the past are beginning to stir.

"My God, it must be at least twelve years," this woman admits. "Since anyone dared to be on my side, while at the same time holding back the bureaucratic vultures who were circling overhead, each one of them waiting to devour their particular pound of my flesh..."

"At the Mayfield Clinic..."

So it would seem that John has rehearsed some of his lines--albeit from a different script. Unlike our most recent visit, his reference is in connection with a different department of the Mayfield Clinic. In any event, his studiousness merits being documented for the benefit of the official record, and I trust you will note my formal means of addressing him.

"You've obviously done at least some of your homework Mr Bland..."

"Naturally, as part of our preparation we've both had access to the contents of the Forsyth file, so we do know that after spending seven months, as a voluntary participant in a Category 'A' Research Programme on behalf of the Military, you were not only discharged from that Programme, but also categorized as being an unsuitable candidate for any similar kind of Research in the future..."

When John pauses, it seems to be stage managed--almost as if he is expecting me to fill the void, and because I'm hoping that he will divulge how much they do know about my admission to the Clinic for once, it is this young woman whose expression is revealing nothing and yet, knowing that for as long as they are centre stage, the principal players timing is crucial once again, I'm silently counting and as soon as I reach eighteen seconds, my patience is rewarded, when John provides the necessary information.

"Eleven months later you were admitted to the Mayfield Clinic, and since that seems to have been a relevant turning point in your life, I wonder whether that might be an acceptable place for you to begin exploring your new found freedom of speech..."

How intriguing! So far back in time, but unless John is holding something in reserve, it's not far enough to include any specific details, relating to my discharge from the Category 'A' Research Programme, which makes me wonder whether these highly trained and multi-disciplined professionals have been denied access to Classified information.

No doubt time will provide the answer, especially when everything runs in a circular motion, and while this might not be the place at which we need to begin, if my inquisitors are as clever as they imagine themselves to be, they must have realized that when we reach the end of my journey, we will find ourselves back at the place where we should have commenced the story of this woman's life.

Safe in the knowledge that as the plot unfolds everything will be revealed, my protective parent has been fast forwarding through the images generated by John's suggestion, but after scanning them for damaging revelations or emotional pitfalls, which might need to be addressed, when they come full circle I am prepared to make a commitment.

"It was a long time ago, so I fail to understand how it can be relevant to recent events. Besides before anyone can appreciate the circumstances surrounding my admission to the Mayfield Clinic, I would first need to clarify a few things with regard to what it was like being the only child of Joanna Mary and Major William Charles Forsyth…"

Then, affording John the opportunity to challenge my suggested deviation from the chosen route, it's my turn to hesitate, but after he nods his approval I begin the story of my life. "As I've already explained, the Forsyth's were only blessed with one child, and after six miscarriages instead of the son my father yearned to hold, he had to make do with a daughter. But despite being a disappointment, throughout the latter part of my childhood and into my teenage years everything was geared towards me fulfilling, some kind of role in keeping with the family's strong Military tradition. When I was growing up my mother had been my ally, and because she would have protected me--when she died--I lost…"

Despite my earlier scanning for emotional pitfalls, my own deviation finds me overwhelmed by the last crystal clear image I have of my mother, when she was alive.

*Frozen in time immemorial in true Military tradition, because age can no longer wither her, nor the years condemn, she remains as breathtakingly beautiful as I remember my mother to be as she stood in the hallway, saying goodbye on what was destined to become Judgement Day for two members of the Forsyth family.*

On the other side of the desk, John has allowed the silence to linger, but when it becomes evident that the remaining words are refusing to emerge from between my lips, he demonstrates his willingness to offer this young woman some assistance with her new found freedom of speech.

"According to the Forsyth file, your mother died two months before your seventh birthday--which is almost the same age as Bobby--and if she was your only ally in the Forsyth household, then at such a young age her death must have been devastating…"

Despite being grateful for the assistance how else could one describe it, except by stating that John seems to have an uncanny knack of understating the understatement? But at this precise moment, because they are coming thick and fast, it would also seem to be the case that the images from my own deviation cannot be put back into the Pandora's Box, I have opened without first managing to gain some kind of control over them.

*So down in the hallway of the Forsyth home, a member of staff from my father's Security detail had arrived to escort my mother to her pre-arranged appointment, so that she could address the families' of soldiers about how best to manage their sense of helplessness, during their loved ones' tours of duty, and while this is a routine occurrence on this occasion an excitable child was protesting, because she does not want--her beautiful mother--to leave the house on that day in particular.*

*Of course, despite being blissfully unaware of any unique abilities, with my face pressed up against my bedroom window I maintained a vigil, and while I was watching and waiting, I longed to catch sight of my father's car turning into the driveway, but it was not until a different, more official car had arrived that even before I had been summoned to my father's study, somehow I knew and yet, in that same heart-breaking knowledge, I was incapable of comprehending, how I could have known that the car containing my beautiful mother would never be making the return journey, up the gravel driveway.*

*Responding to the summons, I delivered myself to the Major's inner sanctum, where there was a different man from his Security detail, and accompanying my father's Superior Officer there was a complete stranger, and* even today, this young woman can still recall the face of that female Officer, *as she guided me to a chair before she crouched down, so that she could explain how the car taking my breathtakingly, beautiful mother to her appointment had been involved in a head on collision.*

*In what was to become a life changing moment, that same excitable child was protesting even louder than before her mother's departure. "Don't you dare say it, because if you don't say it, then it cannot be true--can it?"*

*Ignoring my protests, the female Officer tried to explain that after a van had careered across the central reservation at high speed, not only my mother, but also her Security Officer and their driver had died instantaneously, but that information had been no consolation to the bereft little girl, who ran from the study, so that my tears--which were forbidden in the Forsyth household--could be allowed to turn into uncontrollable sobbing.*

**October 22** *The day of my mother's funeral and dressed in a black coat and hat, my new minder, who was masquerading as my nanny had a firm grasp on this little girl's hand, as we stood beside my father at the front of our parish church and then, instead of giving her the chance to rise like a Phoenix from the ashes, the congregation moved to the place where they intended to entomb my mother. Then afterwards, I watched my father standing to attention and with his stiff upper lip intact, he accepted the handshakes and condolences from both his peers and his Superior Officers. But, as if I was invisible, nobody bothered to acknowledge either my existence or the emotional trauma I was experiencing.*

*Of course, it did not matter, because throughout that difficult day as if I was one of his subordinates, I had managed to behave in accordance with the orders I had been given.*

*Yes, that broken-hearted child had soon learnt that nobody must have chosen to hear her--much less considered offering her any comfort--when she cried herself to sleep every lonely night after the accident, until she was forced to accept that life was destined to be devoid of cuddles or kisses, from a father who was incapable of responding to any of his child's unique requirements, and to appease her sense of aloneness, she created a secret place--a place which was too special to be visible to the naked eye and yet, at that time I had no perception of how special* this woman was destined to become, and as if to prove that this adult has--and perhaps will continue to have--no control over the images, as quickly as they had arrived, they seem to be falling through the cracks in my mind.

Since the human brain is the most efficient hard drive ever created, for reasons which will become clear as this Interview progresses, despite attempts to replicate its interactive qualities, thankfully nobody has as yet managed to harness and therefore exploit its power.

Meanwhile, in the here and now of the present tense, my protective parent appreciates that while the images must have lasted no more than a few minutes, despite being unsure how much I might have shared with our wider audience, John's voice attracts my attention.

"Charlie are you okay? Although you seemed to be a little distracted, we were talking about how your mother's death must have been a devastating loss..."

"I'm fine--having introduced being the only child in the Forsyth household, it is important that everyone understands, not only what life was like after my mother died, but also the impact it had on my future. So I was merely trying to assess the full implications..."

Clearly satisfied John smiles, and until he either has something pertinent to say or one of them wants me to move time on, he seems willing to allow me to continue uninterrupted.

"Although death and destruction were occupational hazards for my parents, because both of them were also only children I didn't have any Aunts or Uncles, and my Grandparents lived hundreds of miles away, so I had never experienced anyone close to me dying, and despite the fact that I was broken-hearted, any display of emotion was frowned upon by my father. Consequently, even at the funeral I had been ordered not to cry..."

As this woman pauses, I drink the remaining lukewarm coffee from my bone china mug. "But after that fateful day, my life changed forever. Obviously, not prepared to risk losing another member of his immediate family, my father removed me from my private school, so that I could be tutored at home. In fact, after the accident the Major never let me go anywhere, unless it was in an unidentifiable vehicle with a two man armed escort..."

"You must have felt very isolated," John speculates. "Perhaps even abandoned..."

Pause--rewind--because in addition to John's ability to understate the statement, it would seem that he also has an uncanny ability when it comes to stating the obvious.

"Like any bereft child, I felt abandoned by the one parent in the Forsyth household who was not only capable of giving me hugs and kisses, my mother also defended my right to behave like a child. Simple things such as giggling or being excitable, and to offset my horrendous sense of aloneness, I created my own secret world--a world in which I first learnt to how to live within the confines of the deafening sound of my own silence..."

In the politest possible way, John interrupts me. "In the Major's defence the head on collision--that killed, not only your mother, but also her appointed Security Officer and their driver--occurred after your father had been given his first United Kingdom based Special Assignment on behalf of the Military, which led us to consider whether you ever knew about the in depth investigation into the accident..."

Investigation--this is indeed something I knew nothing about and yet, because I sense that this revelation might bear some disturbing similarities to a more recent event--relating to cars--I choose to do nothing, except listen as John continues to enlighten me.

"With the aid of DNA testing, which was backed-up by what we describe as Intelligence chatter, the Official Investigation concluded that the white van was being driven by a political activist who was on a suicide mission, and because your mother was occupying, the actual armour plated car the Major used, she was not the intended target. In addition, your father was not responsible for the decision to protect you from all conceivable threats. It was a direct recommendation handed down by the highest possible Authority..."

In light of the aftermath of this revelation, I hoped that later--my God could explain to me, why he chose to rob me of my loving mother, instead of a cold unfeeling father. But right now, I have to respond to another as yet unanswered request for my confirmation.

"No--I was never made aware of any investigation. However, you have to remember that when it came to his actions, my father wasn't accustomed to providing explanations, least of all to a heart-broken little girl he never found the time to even notice..."

As John nods, I think I'm beginning to detect a pattern emerging, but then he chooses to not only change the subject, he also draws my invisible audience's attention to something I regard as being inconsequential. "According to the Forsyth file, as well as being an accomplished musician, your list of academic qualifications is most impressive and by the age of fourteen, you had amassed fifteen GCSEs and six 'A' levels, followed by two degrees the first in applied mathematics and the second one..."

"Thank you, Mr Bland," This woman snaps. "Because I am well aware of what I regard as my worthless qualifications, there's no need to embarrass me by listing them all..."

Then, when John's expression confirms that he stands corrected, I elaborate further. "As I have already explained, throughout my childhood and into my teens, while strengthening his own reputation, I knew that my father wanted me to concentrate on fulfilling his ambition, and for the first and last time, I did gain his approval at the age of twenty-one, when I became not only the youngest participant, but also the most qualified candidate to be selected for the Research Programme..."

Opposite me, there is a detectable hint of anticipation in John's eyes. Perhaps he is hoping that I will elaborate further, but he must realize that when it comes to unlimited time and space and complete freedom of speech, this woman is a novice, and until directed or ordered by my Godfather to provide Classified Information, in connection with the Research Programme, my vulnerable child will continue to perform, with all the hesitancy of a badly rehearsed amateur at her first audition.

"So after I was discharged in virtual disgrace, and categorized as being an unsuitable candidate for any future programmes on behalf of the Military, I returned home to a disapproving father who had to accept that instead of his own craven image, I had been created in my mother's, and I know the reason why she would have been so proud of me..."

Like me, John has finished his coffee, and after checking the insulated pot, he gestures in my direction, and knowing that the caffeine will help me to remain focused, I'm grateful for the offer. Then, after he replenishes our bone china mugs, I afford Bill the time he needs to leave his neutral position, so that he can also have a refill. But as soon as he returns to his appointed place, I continue with my explanation.

"As for me, I was back in the same Ivory Tower, and because I had been wrapped in cotton wool and protected from everything, I had never been able to develop friendships, or experience the highs and lows of having a boyfriend, so my world began to fall apart..."

At last, we have reached the point at which my deviation comes to an end, and this adult is preparing to introduce my admission to the Mayfield Clinic. "I suppose my file states that I tried to kill myself, but like most things in your records that was only half--albeit the official half of the story. However, the truth is that upon my return home, I was prescribed tranquilizers and sleepers, and when they didn't kill the emotional pain, they pumped me full of anti-depressants. In the end, there were so many pills at my disposal, it would have been easy for anyone to forget how many they had taken, and because my father and his second wife, Helen were ill-equipped to handle the situation, irrespective of the fact that what happened with the pills was an accident, the Major chose to exaggerate, so that he could have me admitted to the Psychiatric Wing of the Mayfield Clinic..."

Then, this adult falls silent, and while I'm asking myself whether my father had exaggerated I drink some coffee from my mug. Perhaps, it was not accidental, and maybe this woman has adjusted the memories to make them acceptable? Does it even matter? After all, this is the story of my life, and I never professed to be a word perfect kind of performer.

Besides, whilst sustaining his impartiality, a trained professional like John will always ensure that this performance maintains a balanced perspective, and as if he has read my mind, there is another matter, he needs to bring to my attention.

"According to the Forsyth file, because you'd lost twenty kilograms in weight, which is approximately three stone---you were a very sick twenty-three-year-old..."

"That's what they told me," I hear my protective parent admitting. "However, you have to bear in mind that because I had never once--during those twenty-three years--been on any kind of diet, the weight loss was never intentional. It was something that happened at a time, when I must have been a very unhappy human being..."

Unhappiness or happiness! Both are abstract concepts, and while everyone knows when they are unhappy, I find myself questioning whether this woman has ever been happy? Indeed, if they were asked to do so, could many people even define happiness? Maybe, a fleeting moment during someone's lifetime--or perhaps nothing more than an illusory state of mind. In any event, after being sectioned for my own safety, in accordance with the provisions of the Mental Health Act, it seems to be a little ironical that being made aware of my unhappiness meant that happiness presented itself, as being an unattainable achievement.

"Naturally, I resented being incarcerated, so I admit that I was verbally abusive, and whenever there was due provocation, I was also guilty of physical retaliation. In fact, I was so uncooperative that by the end of the third day, I had lost so many--*privileges*--I wasn't even allowed out of bed without a member of staff being present..."

Behind me, I detect the slightest of movements, and because I suspect that as John stated at the commencement of this Interview, I might not have given them enough, I fall silent, until my diligence is rewarded with a response from our self-appointed arbitrator.

"For the benefit of the recording Charlie," Bill announces. "Can you confirm that your recovery programme was based on some kind of reward system?"

"Yes it was--upon my admission--I was given a list of things we all take for granted every day. Basic things, such as unrestricted access to television, radio, newspapers, or magazines. They were regarded as--*privileges*--and they included not being able to get out of bed whenever you wanted. So instead of having the freedom to use the en-suite, you had to buzz for a bedpan which would never seem to arrive in time…"

"So that there can be no misunderstanding Charlie, instead of a system where a patient would be able to earn them, everyone was given a list of things regarded as privileges, and every time someone was deemed to be uncooperative, one of them was taken away…"

"That's correct, it was as if the staff didn't want people to recover…"

"And because the weight loss wasn't the only reason for you being sectioned, can you describe what happened with regard to the prescription drugs, you had been taking?"

As the memory presents itself, I release a somewhat satirical laugh. "Although they might not have been the same uppers and downers, similar drugs continued to be prescribed, and because they were mandatory and not some kind of optional extra, you ticked on a daily menu sheet, despite being able to voice your objections, because the wardens needed to keep the inmates as docile as possible, if you refused to swallow…"

Without any prior warning, what must have been a supressed memory of a young woman curled into the corner of the room overwhelms me and yet, before any more images can escape from Pandora's Box, John attempts to save me. "Because we understand that this might not be easy for you, feel free to take whatever time you might need…"

However, it's too late to stop the images from revealing, their destructive outpouring.

*Ironically, in my private room containing a bed and a locker, there was no room for any privacy, because even if you were allowed out of bed, in order to minimize the risk that someone might be disposing of any evidence, if you wanted to use the toilet, you were not allowed to flush it.*

*Of course, the indignities were not confined to using the en-suite, because if you refused to swallow your pills--fifteen minutes later--the ward Registrar would arrive, armed with a loaded syringe, and two of the male nurses who were so proficient, they must have been awarded lifetime memberships' at the same misogynist's country club.*

*"I'm so disappointed Charlotte," The Registrar would announce, while keeping a9safe distance between us. "Because yet again, you've refused to take your meds…"*

*What an unenviable choice? The pills or the needle and with Marcus and Peter--the male nurses--manoeuvring themselves into position, I'm trying to avoid them, as I make my choice--albeit in a slurred voice. "I keep--telling you--the pills aren't--helping…"*

*Naturally, when it came to your dissension, after voicing your objections, the only thing you could do was offer token resistance, while the male nurses tried to immobilize you, so that the Registrar could empty the contents of the syringe into any available part of your anatomy. In my case, after they had tried to hold me down on the bed, and I had used my legs as if they were offensive weapons, they had started pinning me up against the wall.*

*Immediately afterwards, the Registrar would beat a guilt ridden retreat, leaving his victims at the mercy of the nurses who on the premise that they needed to ensure nobody injured themselves, while the drugs surged through our central nervous systems like out of control express trains, and as if being robbed of your basic human rights was not bad enough, patients had to endure the nurses' derogatory remarks and sick innuendos.*

*Things such as if we'd just take the damn meds whenever they were offered, none of the rough stuff would be necessary. That was usually Marcus, and because you could hear the relish in his voice, one could imagine what he fantasised about when he was off duty.*

*Next, Peter would embark upon, what I suppose was meant to be a therapy session, during which he would suggest that perhaps I wanted to be punished, because I was abused as a child. Apparently, it was the most common excuse for getting off on the rough stuff.*

*Then, Marcus would add to the torment by asking whether it was physical or sexual abuse and was the perpetrator my father, mother, brother, or the all-time favourite, someone I was told to address as my Uncle, and because they'd heard it over and over again, I was a poor little rich kid locked up in the Mayfield Clinic, so the family can avoid a scandal--and by then--I would have said anything if it meant they would leave me in peace.*

Struggling with the vividness of those poignant images, out of sheer necessity, my vulnerable child forces me to pause and yet, although my head remains bowed, so that I cannot see my worthy opponent on the other side of the desk--on this occasion--neither John nor Bill deem to offer me any assistance, opting instead to wait in respectful silence, until my protective parent re-emerges, and after swallowing hard this woman finds the fragile stability she needs, so that I can conclude--whatever I have shared--using my own words.

"After finding myself curled into the corner of the room on the planet Zog--talking to the Zargonians, whilst at the same time, not only praying that the misogynists would get bored and leave, but also hoping that the Registrar might have given me, an accidental overdose, so that I would at least be allowed to die with some dignity, I was forced to accept that my life would be less painful if I agreed to swallow the damn pills and then, serve the remainder of my sentence residing in La-La Land..."

During those ordeals, I had the power to cause absolute mayhem, in the same way that I could have created chaos either in the early hours of the $22^{nd}$ of June, or upon my most recent admission to a different part of the Clinic. However, if I had unleashed that kind of pandemonium, then my perpetrators would have been able to persecute me with a renewed vengeance. But at least I am confident that it's safe for me to lift my head, and when I achieve eye contact with John, it would seem that my revelations have brought a detectable distaste to his normally neutral expression, and still ensuring that my performance maintains a balanced perspective, the next observation, he has been waiting to bring to the attention of our wider invisible audience is destined to evoke another powerful image.

"Surely *the rough stuff*--as you described it--and the verbal abuse must have come to an end, once Professor Morgan took over your case--because you did respond to him..."

*Wow, hearing his name conjures up a strong image of a man, perhaps in his mid-fifties who arrived with one of his hands stuffed into the left hand pocket of his crumpled white coat, which seemed to match his overall dishevelled demeanour.*

*Between you and me, when it came to Psychiatrists Professor Kenneth Morgan was destined to be different from any of his predecessors. Like this young woman, he turned out to be a reprobate, while at the same time he proved himself to be a worthy adversary, especially when one considers that somehow he seemed to manage to snatch his patients from the edge of oblivion, and by the time we were returned to the harsh realities of the outside world--if anyone attempted to manipulate any of us--having become members of the Morgan Survivors Club, then at least we would be able to identify the reason for our unhappiness and take whatever remedial action might prove necessary.*

That memory of his first appearance, prompts my rebellious child to release a quite spontaneous laugh. "During the first two weeks there had been a multitude of Shrinks. In fact, once my appalling reputation started to precede me they began to arrive two at a time, but none of them managed to survive the second onslaught of verbal abuse…"

Opposite me, I find it encouraging that John's smiling again, and having realized that his distaste was probably the direct result of him being unable to neither condone, the undue force used to administer drugs, nor the ensuing verbal abuse from the staff, I'm certain that both of my protectors will enjoy hearing what happened, when the opportunity for retribution presented itself.

"Oh there can be no doubt that the Professor was different. Despite resembling a pathetic, wasted young woman--unlike the others--he never once threatened me with Draconian measures such as the equivalent of force feeding either via a nasal tube, or through a temporary peg inserted into my stomach. It was as if it would have been an admission that he had failed, which like the Major might have damaged his impeccable reputation. Nevertheless, one day not long after the staff had delivered the lunch trays to their inmates, Professor Morgan risked life and limb by choosing to visit me in my cell…"

Pausing, I utter a second even more spontaneous laugh, because there are more images looming on the horizon, which I am happy to share with my wider audience.

*"Good afternoon Charlotte." The Professor announced as soon as he came through the door with a smile on his face. "I'm Professor Kenneth Morgan, but it sounds so pompous, my staff and my patients call me Prof--and provided you have no objections, I'm going to address you as Charlie…"*

*Considering that I had good reason to have become suspicious of anyone who came through the door, especially a stranger who arrived with a smile on his face, and yet unlike any of his predecessors, he did not remain standing at a safe distance, and because I had managed to lose all of my privileges, the Professor plonked himself down on the edge of my bed, so that we were not only facing each other, he had also managed to achieve eye to eye contact with his captivated audience.*

*This was something different from anything I had ever experienced, but despite being out of my comfort zone, I knew that before swiping his Security pass through the locking system to gain entry to my cell--sorry I did mean my private room--he would have been watching the security monitors which were installed throughout the Psychiatric Wing.*

Forgive me for digressing, but I can imagine what you might be thinking and you would be correct. *It was more like a prison than a private Clinic, and because he would have witnessed my attempt to make the food in my plastic container disappear using the plastic knife and fork, which were given to all patients with anorexia or bulimia, in case we were greedy enough to try and add self-harming to our individual portfolios, instead of the usual tut-tut sound, this interloper proceeded to pick up the cutlery from my lunch tray.*

*"After I was asked to consider adding you to my patient list Charlie, I found your case notes intriguing--and would you like to know the reason why you fascinated me?"*

*Then, in between mouthfuls of congealed mashed potato and something masquerading as chicken breast drowning in watery gravy, plus overcooked carrots and peas, which could be described as two of the recommended portions of fruit and veg a day, except that the other three were never destined to arrive, this stranger continued delivering his monologue.*

*"Despite my extensive experience of working with patients who have eating disorders, you didn't display any of the normal characteristics, and since the one thing I cannot resist is a fresh challenge, I'm afraid we're going to be working together…"*

*Even before my brief residency, I had never been confronted by what turned out to be the suggestible sight of someone eating. However, experience had also taught me not to be too trusting, so when someone released the locking mechanism, and Marcus arrived with my assortment of uppers and downers, after he handed me the small plastic cup, because I had identified an opportunity to counter-challenge this interloper, without severing eye contact I placed the container beside my lunch tray, as I suggested, "Since you seem to have enjoyed the main course, perhaps you'd like to sample the dessert..."*

*Out of the corner of my eye, I noted that Marcus was still lurking with a sense of menace, as if he was furious while at the same time almost salivating at the prospect of being able to subject me to more of the rough stuff, but the Professor stole his thunder by throwing his head back and roaring with laughter, before delivering his response.*

*"Thank you for such a tempting offer Charlie, but I'm afraid I have to decline..."*

*My immediate thought was that he was no different from any of his predecessors, until he added, "Because I'm on a strict diet, I'm not allowed to indulge in desserts..."*

*Touché--and for the first time in longer than I could recall I laughed out loud, and it felt as if he had released the steam from a pressure cooker, but the Professor had not finished taking his new captive by surprise. "Upon checking your chart Charlie, I noticed that in the past, you regularly refused to take..."*

*Much to Marcus's delight, I dared to interrupt the interloper. "Because I don't have any desire to eat, I keep trying to make them understand that the drugs aren't helping..."*

*Then, the silence hung between the three of us, until it was the Professor's turn to risk incurring the wrath of the nurses, when he asked, "If that's the case, then I would invite you to consider, whether or not you want to continue taking the pills inside this plastic cup?"*

Opposite me, John has extended his smile, and despite the tension in my own personal prison cell, if I were to glance over my shoulder, I'm sure this woman would discover that our self-appointed arbitrator is doing the same, but while they might appreciate the irony of the image I have re-created for them, because of the need for their impartiality, only my rebellious child's amusement will be heard by our wider invisible audience.

Then, after finishing my remaining coffee, which as a result of neglect is lukewarm, I return the bone china mug to its saucer, and because I suspect that I might need an intake of nicotine, once I have admitted falling prey to another worthy opponent, I reach for the packet of cigarettes and lighter. "When it comes to considering the consequences of my actions, I'm afraid that everyone is going to discover that I have an abysmal track record..."

*Because when I asked myself about the pills, it had seemed like such an easy decision to make, and since this newcomer had earned the right to be addressed by his proper title, whilst continuing to maintain eye to eye contact, I announced, "When it comes to the drugs Professor, I can only reiterate what I keep telling the staff--that they should stick their pills in the same orifice I keep telling them to stick their food..."*

*"So are you telling me that you don't want to take any more of these pills..."*

*"Yes that's precisely what I'm saying ..."*

*"That's not only courageous, but also a most commendable decision. You have my personal guarantee that these pills will not be written up again. As for the food, if this was an NHS facility that meal would be disgusting, but for a Private Clinic it's so repellent, I wouldn't want to eat it either, so I'm not in the least surprised that some of the clientele have eating disorders. However, if you were given the chance to select something that might tempt you to eat Charlie, even if it is only a few mouthfuls, what would you choose?"*

*Then, as my gaze drifted towards an outraged and yet, uncharacteristically speechless Marcus, the Professor delivered an unexpected bonus. "Don't be concerned about Marcus or Peter, because now that you're my patient, nobody will dare to undermine my authority. So is there something that might tempt you to eat?"*

In that instant, I felt like a small child in a sweet shop with ten pounds to spend on anything I wanted, but it was soft jelly and cold ice cream which leapt to the forefront of my mind, prompting me to reply. "Some strawberry jelly and vanilla ice cream…"

"No doubt, you can appreciate what I meant by not considering the consequences of my actions, especially after I told the Professor what he could do with the drugs, without first taking into account that I was going to be catapulted from one extreme to the other…"

Appreciating my dilemma, John has extended his smile still further, but his tone carries an air of solemnity, as he once again states the obvious for the benefit of our wider invisible audience. "Although withdrawing the drugs was a little extreme, it was the quickest way of guaranteeing complete control not only of your mind, but also your body which is something all of his predecessors had failed to achieve…"

After flipping open the packet I remove a cigarette, but it does not reach my lips because without giving my action a second thought I am turning my lighter, so that it is almost replicating my heartbeat as it taps the desk during its circular motion--as if it is symbolic of the fact that what went around was destined to come back around.

"Not long after the Professor's departure, a small dish containing strawberry jelly and vanilla ice cream did arrive, and having been trusted with a grown-up metal spoon--much to my own amazement--I managed to eat several mouthfuls. Of course, by the time the Professor rematerialized, there could be no doubt that he had gained control of my body, mind and spirit, and since the shaking was so widespread like any self-absorbed addict, I would have done anything in exchange for something to ease the physical symptoms of the withdrawal process, and since my scrawny body wouldn't have earned me much money standing on street corners touting for trade, I would have sold my soul to the Devil himself for some kind of quick fix. Dear God, I felt more dead than alive, and if I had been capable of standing upright without falling over, I might have attempted to kill the son of a bitch, but even then that still wasn't enough to satisfy him…"

In complete disbelief, this woman starts shaking her head because despite all those qualifications, my vulnerable child failed to prevent this from happening. However, there are more compelling images, some of which cannot be revealed to either the cavalry or for the benefit of the recording--at least not until we reach the appropriate time--but until that moment arrives, I am happy to share what turned out to be my payback for having acted, without first considering the consequences of my own actions.

As I've explained, *when it came to the drugs, I would have even been prepared to beg Marcus or Peter to negotiate on my behalf for something to assist me with the physical pain. However, instead of conceding defeat, I chose to suffer in stoical silence and by the time Professor Morgan rematerialized--albeit for a different reason--I had regressed to being curled into the far corner of the room, and shaking so badly I seemed to be incapable of consuming the coffee in a plastic beaker--the kind a mother would give to a toddler, with a push on lid, incorporating a drinking spout to minimize the risk of accidental spillage--and despite having gained control of my body, mind and my free spirit, the Professor seemed determined to prove--beyond all doubt--that he was different from any of his predecessors.*

*Firstly, casting aside his professionalism, he chose to sit down on the floor in front of me, so that whenever I was ready he could achieve the same eye to eye contact he had obtained earlier, and secondly, in a soft tone of voice, he began what sounded like a heart-rending Doctor/Doctor intervention.*

*"After being prescribed that particular combination of drugs for the last seven months, if you'll pardon an inappropriate play on words--nobody in their right mind would suggest that stopping them with any kind of suddenness was going to be easy Charlie--that's why your decision was so courageous, I had to commend you for making it…"*

*Ashamed of my weakness, I tried to avoid eye contact. "I don't think I can do this…"*

*In response, the Professor removed my beaker, and after placing in on the floor beside us, he took hold of my shaking hands, and because his unexpected touch startled me, I lifted my head--and having achieved eye to eye contact, he reassured me. "Charlie I promise you that working together, you will come through the withdrawal. It's my experience that the worst of the symptoms will come to pass--in no more than, seventy-two hours…"*

*Then, he pressed the buzzer, and although I was expecting either Marcus or Peter to release the locking mechanism, a young nurse, I had never seen before came through the door, carrying a glass in one hand, and in the other a small plastic container, the kind of cup which I knew was used to dispense drugs, and as she approached the corner of the room, the Professor performed the formal introductions.*

*"Charlie this is Susanna Thomson. As a Specialist Nurse in Mental Health issues, she's currently working in my Private Psychiatric Clinic…"*

*Like the Professor, Susanna crouched down. "Hello Charlie, instead of Marcus or Peter, from now on my colleague Debra and I will be looking after you…"*

*Amidst the throes of the withdrawal it seemed to be surreal, until the Professor explained, "At my request, Susanna has brought you two Diazepam, which should take the edge off the withdrawal symptoms to enable us to talk for a short time, after which I have already prescribed something stronger so that you can get some much needed sleep…"*

*After being imprisoned within an oppressive regime, which was based on depravation everyone was being so kind, it was hard to believe that what was happening could be real. Nevertheless, after Susanna handed me the plastic cup, I was grateful when she held the glass steady, so that I could swallow the pills.*

*"Thank you…"*

*"You're very welcome Charlie." Susanna replied, before she ventured to suggest. "I'm sure that neither you, nor the Professor must be very comfortable sitting on the floor, and because you've started shivering why don't we help you get back into bed?"*

*As soon as I was beneath the flimsy bedding, Susanna disappeared again, and when she returned she was carrying two blankets and two cups of fresh coffee, one of which contained a straw, and while we waited for the Diazepam to work its way into my system, after elevating my head and shoulders, she made sure that I was warm and comfortable.*

*In the meantime, while the Professor drank from his own cup, he held the other one steady, so that I could sip the fresh coffee, until he was satisfied that I was relaxed enough to be capable of participating, in a meaningful doctor/client intervention.*

*"Thank you Susanna," He stated without a hint of superiority. "I'll buzz when it's time for you to bring me the heavier sedation I've prescribed for Charlie…"*

Finally, we have reached the aforementioned images, the ones which cannot as yet be shared with either the cavalry or the Official recording, because until we have travelled full circle and we find ourselves back at the place, where we should have begun the story of this woman's life, these images can only be shared with a more intimate audience--and in case this woman decides to ask questions later, I trust that you will be paying attention.

*Admittedly I was impressed, but I still harboured misgivings that anyone could put me back together again and yet, from the onset Professor Morgan confirmed that since his time was so precious, he had no intention of squandering a solitary second.*

*"Having read the existing Case file, it would seem that your life began to unravel approximately eight months, after you were discharged from the Research Programme…"*

*Even before the Professor paused, he seemed to have anticipated, my need to interrupt him. "But it was a Category 'A' Research Programme on behalf of the Military*

*Professor, which meant that I've never been able to talk about what went on at the Research Facility or reveal anything that happened, during those seven months of my life…"*

*"When I agreed to become your Consultant Psychiatrist," The Professor began to explain. "I insisted that I should be able to do, whatever I deem necessary in order to assist your recovery. In addition, although I have established a Case file, it is designed so that I know we're heading in the right direction. However, after you've been discharged, anything in connection with the Research Programme will be redacted, so that the only notes left in my Case File will relate to your struggle to overcome the many obstacles you will face during your Recovery, along with a notation that if anyone should require any additional information, then a formal request should be forwarded to the highest possible Authority…"*

*"After my mother died, I was protected from all outside influences, and mentored specifically, so that I could participate in something like the Research Programme. But nobody warned me that if you exceed everyone's expectations, then they would be prepared to go to extreme lengths in order to undermine one's capabilities. It was as if they were trying to take me apart piece by piece…"*

*"And presumably, that's the real reason behind you being discharged?"*

*"It was because I didn't understand why he would have given them permission…"*

*Suddenly the pain broke through the barrier formed by the Diazepam, and before it could gain momentum, I heard my vulnerable child pleading. "I'm sorry, but I haven't been sleeping, and because I'm exhausted the pain is threatening to become uncontrollable…"*

*Reaching up, the Professor pressed the buzzer. "There's no need to apologize. At least we've managed to lay down the foundation upon which we can build our working relationship, and you have my personal assurance that I have no reason to try and take you apart piece by piece…"*

Back in the present tense of my Godfather's study, while I attempt to recall how much has been revealed, and with whom I have shared what information, I remain silent because between you and me, despite trying not to complicate things, I seem to have managed to complicate what should have been uncomplicated, until John rescues me.

"So after the Diazepam took the edge off your withdrawal symptoms presumably, you and the Professor must have been able to talk?"

"Yes we did, and when the pain in my muscles broke through the barrier formed by the tranquillizers, the Professor did give me something stronger, so that I could sleep…"

At some point, my fingers must have stopped the lighter from making its circular journey, and when I yet again remain silent, as if I'm acting on auto pilot, the cigarette reaches my mouth, and in order to maximize the impact of the nicotine surging into my blood stream, after I spark the lighter into flame, I inhale as deeply as possible, before exhaling the spent smoke in a long, steady stream.

"That's why I didn't want you to embarrass me by listing all of my qualifications. In fact, for someone who was supposed to be super intelligent, I must have omitted to attend the classes which taught pupils basic common sense, because if I had been present and paid attention, I might never have ended up in such a dire situation--or at least--that's how it felt after my mother died, and within the Forsyth household, I lost my only ally…"

Although I had hoped that the cavalry might have grasped the more profound meaning behind those last words, John chooses not to seek further elaboration, opting instead to draw my attention to something else, I did not know about myself.

"Upon your admission to the Clinic, standard medical tests were undertaken, and the results confirmed that you were running the risk of sustaining irreversible damage to vital organs, and while the Professor's methods might have been unorthodox, and nobody in their right mind would suggest that going through drug withdrawal would have been easy, it was a significant turning point in your life, because not only did you respond to him, you entered into a voluntary contract, so that you could be pro-active in your own recovery..."

How naïve! In fact, too naïve for a professional like John. Maybe, he is affording me the opportunity to enlighten our wider invisible audience, and without the least hesitation, my protective parent corrects him. "Although I did agree to become one of the Professor's patients, the incident over the drugs wasn't the actual turning point in my recovery..."

Opposite me, John stirs and since the glint in his eye smacks of anticipation for no other reason than I suspect that the cavalry know that there is a different turning point, this woman tilts her head to one side. However, after his sudden death last year, as a result of a massive coronary, I was one of the mourners who attended the funeral of Professor Kenneth Morgan, so that we could celebrate his life, and because it's too late for any revelations to be misinterpreted as breaches in National Security, I see no reason why I cannot be honest.

"Once the physical symptoms of withdrawal began to subside, even I could recognize that there was something resembling a human being beneath the emaciated, drug crazed gibbering idiot," Hesitating, I tap the ash from my cigarette into my Godfather's ashtray, before I continue. "And when the Professor enlightened me about some of the harsher realities of bearing the Forsyth name--minor details--like the legal technicalities, behind my admission to the Psychiatric Wing of the Clinic--now that was the actual turning point..."

Far from silencing me, or redirecting the proceedings John proposes what must be the obvious conclusion. "To avoid any misunderstandings, are you telling us that Professor Morgan confirmed that you had been Sectioned for your own safety?"

"When it came to the issue of my safety Mr Bland, considering my revelations regarding how things were done prior to the Professor's arrival, whether I had been sectioned to safeguard my safety was questionable. But after providing my adversaries with the ammunition they needed, in the metaphorical sense my rebellious child had shot herself in the foot." Pausing, this woman yet again taps the ash from my cigarette. "It amounted to the same thing, I was not at liberty to discharge myself. Furthermore, because I could be subjected to any treatment deemed necessary--including E.C.T. one could say that it was one of the more levelling moments in my lifetime..."

John nods his understanding "This seems like an appropriate time to clarify that prior to June 22, there was no reason why the two operatives, identified by my partner at the commencement of this Interview, needed to be granted access to any Official File, except the one that came into existence, when Charlotte Anne Forsyth married Mark Daltry. As a result, it was not until our reassignment granted us access to the other two Official Files that we understood why Charlie expressed her revulsion, when we were forced to draw her attention to the fact that, if she continued to rip up consent forms to enable the termination of an unsustainable pregnancy to take place, then not only did we have the power to have her Sectioned for her own safety, we would not hesitate to use it..."

Taken by surprise, this woman is lost for words. How ironical that for once in my life and within my Godfather's study, the deadly sound of my silence might be for all the right reasons and yet, while I'm searching for the right words, it's even more ironic that when John fills the void--like the Professor--he continues to sustain his eye to eye contact.

"In fact, the only differentiating factor between the two instances is by the time Charlie found out about the first, the Sectioning was a fete-accompli, which meant she didn't have any choice, except to strive to achieve a discharge. This caused us to consider whether her discovery made her feel betrayed or resentful or maybe--at the very least--outraged..."

"Instead of outraged, I think a more apt description would be disillusioned, especially when you consider that although it had taken the mandatory two doctors to agree that I was endangering my own life, they had been influenced by my father and Philip Maddox who had decided that it was in my best interests to be Sectioned, but then I should have known better than to expect anything else from either of them…"

Spoken without a trace of bitterness or contempt, my protective parent congratulates this woman and yet, from John's expression it would seem that he remains unconvinced, and when the silence is left hanging, after exhaling the smoke from my lungs I elaborate.

"Up until then, there had never been any reason for me to consider the power and influence, other people could hold over my destiny, and I entered into a voluntary contract, because I knew how hard it would be to regain control of my own life, and between us we established an achievable Recovery Programme, which could be revised as my treatment progressed. For my part, I would cooperate fully and in exchange, when the Professor was satisfied with my progress, he'd convince everybody who needed convincing that I was capable of resuming a normal life. If indeed anyone who needed to be convinced was capable of defining what constitutes--*a normal lifestyle…"*

If my jibe jangled the nerves of the Special Operatives' security consciousness, then John declines to comment, but as I lean forward to extinguish my cigarette, I'm thinking about the termination and in all fairness, I feel that I should repay his compliment.

"For the benefit of the Official Recording, there is something I need to clarify about what happened on the 22$^{nd}$ June. With the benefit of hindsight, I can appreciate that I wasn't capable of rational thought, and once I started haemorrhaging, if Mr Bland and Mr Powell had not acted in my best interests, I would have bled out, and if that had been allowed to happen, I would not have been able to enjoy the last few days, in the company of two persons who mean the world to me, and because my behaviour in the early hours of that morning was atrocious, I would like to apologise for being downright disrespectful…"

Severing eye contact with John I glance over my shoulder, but after Bill acknowledges my rare public apology, our arbitrator has a revelation of his own, he needs to share--in what seems to have turned into an impromptu team building session.

"As one might expect, Professor Morgan was a busy man with a long waiting list. Having been granted access to those Case Notes, which weren't redacted we also wondered whether he explained that it was Philip Maddox who not only persuaded him to add you to his list, but also make you a priority. Then, after the Professor made him aware of the inappropriate practices, the Commander acquired Ministerial approval to turn the Clinic into a Special Operations Private Medical Facility, which meant that every member of staff who had used physical restraint, when it came to administering drugs, or who had chosen to make remarks of a degrading, or humiliating nature could be dismissed, and with their Licences revoked, the Disclosure process of the Criminal Records Bureau should have ensured that they would not be permitted to work with people deemed to be vulnerable ever again…"

This revelation has the potential to change everything, not least because it might enter a plea of mitigating circumstances on behalf of a Commanding Officer--who will later be revealed as a Godfather--who failed in his duty of care. However, in the meantime, I will continue to tell the story of this woman's life in light of the evidence at my disposal.

"Like the investigation into my mother's death, and the potential damage to my vital organs, nobody ever told me why Professor Morgan swept into my life. Perhaps some authoritarian figure must have decided that--on a need to know basis--I didn't need to know or maybe you should ask your Commanding Officer…"

Then, as my gaze drifts from Bill back to John neither of them comments upon my suggestion, and after a brief silence our arbitrator declares his willingness to conclude our dealings with my visit to the Psychiatric Wing of the Mayfield Clinic.

"Despite the circumstances surrounding your admission to the Clinic, it must have been worthwhile, because when you were discharged five months later, you were heading towards making a full physical and emotional recovery…"

Taking a few moments to gather together, my fondest memories of pitting my wits against such an excellent opponent, I cannot hide the warmth of my smile.

"Of course it was worthwhile. If nothing else the Professor taught me that despite the weight of my responsibilities, I could be a survivor or maybe I should describe it as how he taught me to survive in the secretive world our invisible audience inhabit…"

Having realized the irony of what will be revealed later causes my inner child to laugh. "However, once you've heard the entire story of my life, I suppose it could be argued that if the Professor hadn't taught me quite as much as he did about how to survive, I might not be sitting in a room like this talking to people like you…"

Placing his elbows on the desk, John rests his chin on his clasped hands, but while his curiosity seems to have been aroused as far as Professor Kenneth Morgan is concerned, I must have given them sufficient because it's time to move time on.

"Judging by the reports that follow your discharge, it would seem that the time you spent as Professor Morgan's patient gave you a new perspective on life…"

Recalling all those hours in therapy, so that my rebellious child could earn either a pardon or parole who could blamed her when she started to have some fun, and with her confidence growing day by day, she had been eager to experience all the things she had never been allowed to enjoy--such as experimenting with relationships and yet, despite being     a child I was playing in the grown-up's playground, so I  cannot determine any reason why I should be ashamed, if my naïve inner child made some mistakes.

"Because of my sheltered upbringing, I had a great deal of catching up to do, and like most kids when they are growing up, I made a few mistakes along the way…"

"According to the Forsyth file Charlie, it could have been far more serious than *making a few mistakes*…"

Now isn't that just typical? Maybe John has forgotten what it was like to be young and free--if indeed he allowed himself to be either of those two things.

"Perhaps it could have been. But since my father had embarked upon a personal crusade--a secret Military mission to make sure that I was introduced to the right people, I was playing with a hand-picked, select group of like-minded persons and it was fun. Dinner, dancing, parties, a different escort every evening, and although I was a slow starter--no doubt thanks to my worthless qualifications--I proved to be a fast learner. It was during those crazy nine months, I began to smoke and I acquired a taste for alcohol--but only in moderation…"

John is studying my face, and because we both know where this is leading I fan the flames. "As for the smoking, like many young people at that time, I explored smoking a little something extra blended with the tobacco…"

"There was one occasion, when the police became involved. So--*your alleged exploration*--could have got you busted, which would have led to a criminal record…"

Ouch, so accusing! So judgemental! Right on cue, my protective parent leaps to my defence. "For the benefit of the recording, Mr Bland's statement is absurd, because an individual can either be busted or not busted and as far as I am aware--*could have been*--is not admissible in a court of law." Pausing, I note a definite hint of disappointment, but it provokes my rebellious child into goading him. "Surely, there's no reason to look quite so serious Mr Bland. After all--strictly for personal use--it was nothing more than the occasional few drags on a shared spliff…"

Now, my playfulness has caused his disappointment to turn into outright disapproval, and holding my hands up, this woman enters a defence on behalf of her rebellious child.

"All right, I admit that there were occasions when I could have been busted. But on the evening to which you are referring, I can assure you that I had neither smoked, nor been in possession of any illegal…"

"But that didn't alter the outcome," John interrupts me. "Because four people at the same party were charged with possession, and two with intent to supply, which meant that everyone had to be hauled down to the nearest police station for routine processing…"

"Although everyone was taken to the police station, there were no grounds to hold the rest of us, and because in the literal sense, our family connections made us--*potential embarrassments*--after surrendering an assortment of bodily fluids for analysis, before being returned to our respective keepers, we were all issues with verbal warnings, not that the reference to--*mitigating circumstances*--made any difference to my father…"

Up ahead, I can see more images looming on the horizon, but I continue with my descriptive testimony. "Because of the Major's additional responsibilities on behalf of National Security it didn't help my situation, when the police insisted upon escorting me home, at three in the morning in a---marked---police car. The only things that could have made me more conspicuous would have been the flashing lights and blaring siren…"

Now, the images are so close that as soon as I finish setting the scene, they will have to be addressed. "Needless to say the Major was waiting to thank the Police Officers for my safe return, but once inside the house, when I tried to beat a retreat to my bedroom--instead of his daughter who would have been twenty-five in eight weeks--as if I was one of his insubordinate subordinates, he ordered me to join him and my step-mother in his study…"

*With no chance of escaping from the rear of the police car, I had tried to plan a strategy that might help me deal with my father, but when I followed him into his study, and I was greeted by the inadequate step-mother Helen, who looked even more sheepish than usual, I accepted that during this dressing down, there might not be any room in which to manoeuvre. Indeed, although one might have imagined that out of his uniform--instead of a Military man--the Major would be like an ordinary father, but as I studied him standing there, bolt upright with his hands clasped behind his back along with his tapping right foot, all that negative body language did nothing to assuage my initial fears.*

*"Have you taken complete leave of your senses young woman?"*

*As he delivered his opening declaration of war, the Major turned and marched six paces to the right before turning again, so that with me counting each precise step, he could proceed to march six paces back, until he reached his starting position.*

*"What did you think you were doing Charlotte?" My father roared, as he repeated his six pace marching drill in the opposite direction. "Or was this another classic example of you not considering the long term consequences of your actions?"*

*"As you suggested father I was having fun," I dared to offer what I should have realized was an ill thought out reply, but it was too late to stop myself. "Enjoying myself with the friends you selected--the ones you thought might be a good influence…"*

*Naturally, the Major was suddenly static. "And might I ask how you think facetiousness and mockery will help you in your present predicament Charlotte?"*

*"Of course they won't father. I'm sorry, but it's been a long day and I'm tired…"*

*For a lingering moment, he remained standing in front of his desk, but then he started shaking his head in dismay and the Major's next bellowed accusation made not only me, but also the timid second wife flinch. "Drinking alcohol and taking recreational drugs?"*

*Now as you will discover later, at this point in the proceedings I could have dug up a family skeleton from its shallow grave and hurled it at him, but since it would have enflamed things further, I chose a more placatory option. "During their search of the premises, the police found nothing, except for a small amount of cannabis…"*

*Disregarding my defence, the Major thundered on. "That's not the point Charlotte. Do I need to remind you that because you were a participant on a Category 'A' Research Programme, you have an open Security File which cannot be closed?"*

Suddenly, being able to hurl that old family skeleton at him was yet again tempting, but the Major had no intention of stopping. "What if someone took advantage and you ended up out of control through drink or drugs, and you divulged Classified Information?"

Having failed to enter an acceptable defence, I chose to remain silent while I waited for him to run out of steam, but then the Major added insult to a lifetime of injury, "And worst case scenario--what if the press had found out what had taken place?"

Wow, light touch paper and take a massive--albeit figurative step back. Angry, oh I was enraged, because yet again it would seem that the only thing the Major cared about was his precious reputation, and because I wanted to hurt him--in fact for having failed in his duty of care as a father the ache within me was so extensive I needed to wound him, and for once I had the ammunition at my disposal--a silver bullet which I knew would tear a hole through even his cold, dispassionate heart.

"Firstly, I'm well aware of my responsibilities, so there's no way I would ever allow myself to be out of control as the result of either alcohol or recreational drugs, and secondly, because I have not smoked any substance whatsoever, or drunk any alcohol, during the last few weeks, I can assure you that your reputation remains intact…"

"And do you expect me to believe that at a party raided by the police, you had not indulged in any recreational drug, or consumed any alcohol?"

"Since you don't believe me, perhaps you should check the toxicology results when they come back from the Laboratory…"

"Naturally, while we were waiting I dictated a note for my P.A. asking for a copy…"

"In that case, I would respectfully suggest that before you review them, it might be wise if you were sitting down…"

"If you're telling the truth, then why on earth would I need to be sitting down?"

"Because the results will confirm the reason why I have been abstaining from nicotine and alcohol…"

It was one of those touching father/daughter moments, and as I watched the realization dawning, the anger seemed to dissipate, before he answered his own question. "Are you trying to tell me that you've been irresponsible enough to get yourself pregnant?"

"Yes father" I confessed. "However, because it takes two people to make a baby, I can only be guilty of fifty per cent of the irresponsibility. Nevertheless, in approximately seven months and three weeks, you'll be a Grandfather…"

Suddenly, the image belonged to a Military man--a brilliant strategist whose empty eyes and ashen face were confirming that he had been wounded by the child, whose only crime was being born the wrong sex, and who the Major believed had been snatched from him by one of the trustworthy playmates, he had made it his mission to select on my behalf.

As the image of my father begins to fade, between you and me--that was what the Major chose to believe--but back in the here and now, this woman realizes that she has severed eye contact, and because my hands have started to tremble I clasp them together.

Retrospectively, I suppose my rebellious child must have imagined that I would achieve some kind of inner peace, if I hurt him as much as he had hurt me--when he failed me as a father after my mother died. But that wasn't how it happened…"

When my feelings start to shift and change, there is a wave of sadness developing. Perhaps, back in the Major's inner sanctum, during the following ten speechless beats, the preciseness of my youth was lost forever, because after that night nothing was destined to be the same between a father and his only child and yet, instead of abating, the sadness seems to be gaining momentum.

Clasping my hands tighter, a tremor has crept into my voice. "No matter how rebellious I might have been until the early hours of that morning, I'd never known my father to raise anything, except his voice to me and when he did lash out it was as if he'd been waiting ever since my mother died in that head on collision. Then, when the impact of his hand seemed to restore his ability to speak my father called me a whore, and before ordering me out of his sight, he made it clear that after he informed my Godfather--which was necessary because of my open Security File--then regardless of whatever romantic notions I might be harbouring, I would be getting rid of the baby…"

Without warning the tidal wave of sadness belongs to a different image, but while I'm hoping John will jump off the fence and fill the silence, it is allowed to linger, until I clear my throat, so that I can issue another apology. "I'm sorry, but talking about my father doesn't seem right somehow, especially when he's in no position to enter any kind of defence…"

Despite remaining on the fence, John offers me some encouragement. "I'm sure he'd understand, and since there's no immediate rush, take whatever time you might need…"

"Thank you, but until this part has been concluded we can't move on, and I suppose that regardless of how difficult things had been between us, once I was old enough to understand him better, we did share some kind of a relationship. However, after that night nothing was ever the same. It was almost as if my announcement…"

My God, it was nothing to do with the baby. Ever since the airfield there's been so much to distract my mind, when in reality I've been using my reconciliation with Lorna and Bobby as an excuse to deflect my sadness. In fact, it must be the reason why John has declined to offer me his assistance. He must have suspected where this was leading, but now that I've made the connection as I glance down in what seems to be a symbolic gesture, I must have unclasped my hands before lengthening my fingers, so that the tips of each one are touching as if this woman was about to start praying, and for the first time, I hear this adult acknowledging what happened at the airfield.

"After planning strategies throughout his Military service, which must have saved the life of countless people, my father didn't deserve to die as a result of such an act of cowardice," Pausing this woman waits before adding. "Back at the airfield, it wasn't like Paris, and because my father wasn't inside the car why did you…"

"Charlie…"

As if we are still in the rear seat of the Jaguar the cautioning voice belongs to Bill. However, during this performance there will be times, when this leading lady will refuse to be separated from her principal male, and this is the first of them. "If you had driven us to the hospital John--then it might have made it easier to accept…"

Silence--and yet like me--John must know that this is one piece of unfinished business, which needs to be dealt with, before we can move time on, and despite the slight shake of his head, the tone of his voice remains soft and steady, as he replies "Nothing ever makes it any easier to accept Charlie--and considering what you had witnessed--yet again, because you weren't capable of thinking rationally…"

Although hearing him deliver his words with the same kind of control, I have experienced in the past suggests that he can explain his decision to ignore my needs--or at least ignore what this young woman thought she needed while we were back at the airfield, I still feel that I have to challenge him.

"That's not good enough John--because no matter how bad it might have been, I still had a right to see him…"

Unperturbed, John's gaze never leaves my face, but now this woman has left him with no alternative, except to ratify my accusation.

"Yes Charlie, you had--and indeed still do have--the right to see your father. However, if you recall the actual incident in the aftermath of the explosion, Bill had managed to get as close to the hangar and the wreckage, as anyone could have achieved, and regardless of whether it was right or wrong, we acted on your behalf by deciding that you might not want the last memory of your father to be reflected by such a cruel misrepresentation…"

Somehow, this adult has omitted something. Something this woman did not see, or something my frightened child was prevented from seeing, and because I am not that child and John's image is imaginable while at the same time, its grotesqueness should necessitate that it remains unimaginable which means that I am unable to stifle a sickened groan.

"I'm truly very sorry Charlie," John is apologising even though he has done nothing wrong. "At no time did we intend to deprive you of your rights, and before the Major's funeral you will still be asked, whether you want to see him. Together with your Godfather, perhaps we all hoped that being better prepared, you might decide that with the passage of time, you wouldn't need to subject yourself to yet another harrowing ordeal…"

When John finishes speaking, Bill attracts my attention. "Because this is something you don't need to decide right now, why don't we discuss it at a later time?"

Isn't hindsight a wonderful thing? If only we had the benefit of it, before we make a mess of things, and as I allow my gaze to drift between them, I offer them an explanation.

"Because I hadn't considered the full implications until a few moments ago, I think I might have done you both an injustice for which I apologise. Besides Bill's right and although my father's funeral is unfinished business, we don't need to decide what's going to happen this evening. So perhaps we should continue with the story of my life?"

"Only if you're sure…"

"Yes I am Bill, but because it's so humid this evening, would it be possible for me to have a glass of sparkling water, and some ice to keep it chilled?"

"Of course…"

Then, without pausing the recording equipment Bill moves to the cabinet, so that he can fulfil my request while John resumes the Interview.

"According to the file, forty-eight hours after you told your father about the baby, you were admitted to the Gynaecological Department of the Mayfield Clinic, and in accordance with the copy of the consent you signed, the pregnancy was terminated…"

After expressing my thanks--albeit silently--while I regroup my thoughts, I sip the ice cold water. "Once the Major made up his mind about something, I knew that nothing would change it. So when my Godfather arrived the next morning, instead of offering any resistance I agreed that it would be best if the pregnancy was terminated. Then, with the Major providing the military escort, I arrived at the Clinic and subsequently, my father departed clutching the signed consent as proof that his mission had been accomplished…"

"Since your son is an excitable youngster who is about to celebrate, his seventh birthday presumably, something must have happened to make you change your mind?"

Reaching for the packet of cigarettes, my protective parent nods. "If the doctor had used the wording on the consent things might have been different, because terminating a pregnancy would have made it less personal, but being asked whether I understood that I would be--*aborting my baby*--made it seem so cold and callous--almost as if I was about to become a premeditated murderer. Then, when I realized I was doing what was best for other people, I knew that on that particular day I couldn't go through with it…"

Pausing, I cast John a mischievous smile, "I guess all those hormones surging through my body could have been responsible for my heart overruling my head. However, despite being aware that anybody can be traced, because the one thing I needed was a breathing space, so that I could decide what I wanted, I discharged myself. But since I needed to bankroll my--*running away from home, and flying solo adventure*--I went to my own bank, and withdrew £5,500 from the account into which the monthly interest was paid from the trust fund I had inherited when I turned twenty-one, before maxing out the £9,500 limit on my credit card, and apart from buying a few items of clothes, with the remainder I purchased things with a good re-saleable value--such as jewellery…"

John's head is tilted a little to one side. "And presumably, you had to work as fast as possible, because the minute your bank became concerned about the level of activity on your credit card, someone might have rung the land line number at the Forsyth house to ensure that you were the person responsible for those purchases…"

"Although my father wasn't due to contact the Clinic until after midday, and I had told my bank about my intended spending spree, if someone had rung the house the timid second wife Helen would have contacted him, and with the kind of strings the Major could pull, my adventure might have been over, long before it had even started…"

Pausing, I spark the lighter into flame, so that I can light my cigarette. "Along the way, I had the wherewithal to buy a pay-as-go mobile with a new number, before I used the old one to contact my father one last time. Of course, since the Major had rung the Clinic he knew I hadn't followed his orders, and sacrificed the unwanted Grandchild…"

"Considering how he felt that must have been an interesting conversation…"

Ever one for understating the understatement, I forgive John because I know his assistance was for the benefit of the recording. "What can I say, except that it was a fete-accompli and at least I was honest with him, when I explained that I had options, and until I'd made my own decision about my baby's future, I wouldn't be coming home. As you can imagine, after gentle persuasion failed to change my mind the Major started yelling, and when that also failed to achieve the desired result, and he resorted to issuing threats I cut the call. Naturally, when I took a taxi to King's Cross I knew that I had to run away as far as possible, and to someone my father didn't even know existed…"

"And that must be how Lorna Clunnell became involved--firstly with you and then after he was born with both you and Bobby…"

"While she concluded some outstanding family business, Lorna was staying in Edinburgh and I knew that when I arrived on her doorstep with nothing, except for one suitcase, and an overnight bag, she'd take me in without asking any awkward questions…"

Opposite me, a curious expression has materialized on John's face. "Although we didn't know Lorna Clunnell existed until the 23rd of June, as you would expect, we have done the usual background searches, but there are certain…"

Way ahead of John, this woman interrupts him. "As I have explained Lorna was finalizing some family business, and because her personal life prior to my arrival had nothing to do with the reason why we are in this room, her past is none of your business…"

"Perhaps not," argues John. "However, you have an open Security File and throughout the last seven years, Lorna Clunnell has not only concealed Bobby's true identity, it would seem that with your consent, she has brought him up as if he was her own son…"

Now, this woman is infuriated. "And what gives you the right to go rampaging through other people's private life without their permission?"

"Charlie," Bill announces, with sufficient sharpness to render me silent. "Before you interrupted him, John was about to explain that during our routine background checks, there are some periods of time and associated events we haven't been able to verify…"

When he pauses, I continue to stare through him, and because the images remain private and confidential I cannot stop myself from adding a degree of sharpness into my own voice. "I can only repeat that prior to my arrival in Edinburgh, any details in connection with Lorna's private life remain none of your damn business…"

Despite nodding his understanding, Bill is prepared to issue me with some leverage. "While we appreciate your reticence, we were hoping that you might be able to enlighten us. However, if you'd prefer not to betray what you deem to be a confidence, then we could invite Mrs Clunnell to provide us with the missing information…"

Between you and me, it is a persuasive lever, especially when such an undertaking might re-open old emotional wounds. So it's time for me to explore my negotiating abilities.

"I don't believe it's relevant to recent events, but if you're prepared to give me your word that you will not question Lorna about her personal life--or her private business—prior to my arrival in Edinburgh, I will do my best to tell you what you need to know…"

Bill's smile broadens. "With all due respect Mrs Daltry, I don't think you're in any position to bargain. But provided that Mrs Clunnell has done nothing more than act as some kind of surrogate mother, there should be no reason for Special Operations to do anything, except offer both Lorna and Bobby Clunnell the same level of protection…"

Does this woman have no bargaining power? Possibly not, but my rebellious child could make things difficult by withdrawing this adult's co-operation and yet, knowing what lies ahead of us, while at the same time understanding that at this juncture, any such defiant gesture might only serve to cause a loyal, and trusted person who is more than a friend considerable embarrassment, this woman opts to admit a gracious defeat.

"All right, since you seem to suspect that Lorna might pose some kind of threat to National Security, and you've left me no choice, I will endeavour to dispel your fears…"

Allowing my gaze to drift back to John, it is noted that far from belonging to a man who has emerged the victor from our first stalemate, this woman cannot find the slightest hint of triumph in either his eyes or in his tone of voice.

"So this is what we already know--born in Edinburgh Lorna's maiden name was McCardle. She has one sibling, a brother and after their mother died as a result of ovarian cancer, they were raised by their father. Subsequently, Colin McCardle qualified as an accountant, and because he had been offered a lucrative job in one of the big Brokerages, he moved to London, while Lorna continued to live at home, and work part time for her father's law firm until she married Bryan Clunnell and also moved to London…"

When John pauses, I suspect that he is waiting to determine, whether I will either correct him or elaborate of my own volition, but I think that by now you might have grasped that this woman finds this kind of voyeurism not only vulgar, but also despicable. So in order to avoid having to divulge anything, except the least amount of personal details, I will not speak until I have heard everything that the cavalry have discovered.

"In addition, when you were admitted to the Psychiatric Wing of the Mayfield Clinic, Lorna Clunnell was listed as a patient, and after it became our Medical Facility, because no existing resident was obliged to move to another Clinic, after your initial meeting your relationship must have developed, until Lorna was discharged six weeks before you…"

As John falls silent, I'm enjoying the role reversal so much I take my time, before filling his silence. "I'm somewhat disappointed Mr Bland. I was expecting something spectacular, but your discoveries are nothing more complex than routine detective work…"

"You seem to have missed the point Charlie." John corrects me, as if he's one step ahead. "Since medical records are covered by Doctor/Patient privilege and Mrs Clunnell is very much alive, we will either have to ask her permission to gain access to her Psychiatric Records, which we suspect that by their very nature, might stir up unpleasant memories or alternatively, you could provide us with the missing details on Lorna's behalf…"

If this was despicable a few moments ago, then it's becoming grubbier by the second, and as if it might make what I'm being asked to do more palatable, by creating a smoke screen I inhale deeply, before exhaling the spent smoke in one slow smooth breath.

"As soon as Clunnell joined her father's legal practice, Bryan didn't bother to hide his feelings towards Lorna. Of course, Andrew McCardle was suspicious, especially when Lorna had far more to contribute than Bryan, but when their relationship became more serious, and her father tried to discredit him, it proved to be a mistake because the less appealing her father attempted to make Clunnell appear, it had the opposite effect on Lorna and then, one evening she came home wearing an engagement ring, and announced that Bryan had asked her to marry him, and she had accepted his proposal…"

Leaning forward, I tap the ash from my cigarette. "Her father went ballistic, he even threatened to disown her if she married Clunnell, but by the time one of the Senior Partners discovered some financial irregularities it was too late, because Lorna believed Bryan when he claimed he was innocent, and since her father was trying to drive them apart, Lorna didn't need much persuading, when it came to running away with Clunnell to London…"

Yes--I am aware that my distaste is causing me to rush. "Four weeks later, they were married in Chiswick Registry Office without any friends or family present, and for the first eleven months everything seemed fine, until the day Clunnell came home packed his bags and left the marital home. For her part, Lorna had never suspected anything was wrong, she had assumed he was going to work, in his new firm of solicitor's every day---which he had, but in addition to having an affair with one of the Partner's wives--unbeknown to Lorna--he'd been gambling. So when he vanished, he left Lorna with an eight-week old daughter and a mass of bad debts…"

Opposite me, John seems perplexed. "There wasn't anything to suggest that Lorna and Bryan Clunnell had any children…"

Although it would seem that my inquisitors did not have access to this basic information, I suppose it's possible that the relevant documents might be housed within Lorna's Psychiatric Records. Makes no difference to the outcome, because this still feels as if I'm talking about someone who trusts me implicitly--behind her back and without her permission. So this adult is eager to dispense with this matter, and leaning forward again this time, I stub my cigarette out using excessive force.

"The Clunnell's had a daughter, Jessica and after Bryan disappeared within a matter of weeks, Lorna was evicted from the family home. However, having re-established contact with Colin they moved into his flat in Ealing. Then, things seemed to be improving, and because Lorna found herself a part time job and a child-minder, she was holding things together, until she woke one Friday morning long after Colin had gone to work…"

Remembering the group therapy session forces me to hesitate, because Lorna's recollection of what happened would be every mother's idea of a self-perpetuating hell on God's earth. "Although it was ten o'clock, Jessica hadn't woken…"

When I falter again, John offers me some assistance, by finishing what I had intended to divulge. "Presumably, Jessica had died in her sleep, and because there was no warning she would have been classed as a casualty of Sudden Infant Death Syndrome…"

"If she had lived, Jessica would have been eighteen months older than Bobby, and despite rarely talking about her daughter, I know that Lorna treasures the photos and a few special items, she chose to keep. Like any mother, the hardest part was not having any rational explanation for Jessica's death and yet, as I have discovered throughout my own lifetime, sometimes when life's going to kick you in the teeth it does a thorough job, and when Colin told Andrew McCardle that the Granddaughter, he was supposed to meet--for the first time in fourteen days had died--the shock caused him to have a massive heart attack, and because death was instantaneous that was when Lorna reached breaking point…"

"On its own Jessica's death must have been horrific," John speculates, as I sip from my glass. "But having to bear the additional burden of her father dying--while at the same time knowing that it was too late to set the record straight between them--would have generated more grief than any one person could safely handle, which must have had something to do with Lorna being admitted to the Psychiatric Wing of the Clinic…"

After nodding my agreement, there is a genuine sadness in my voice. "If Colin hadn't come home from the office in the middle of the day, so that he could collect some documents, the overdose Lorna had taken would have proved fatal. Perhaps not in an immediate sense, but nevertheless eventually, as a result of irreversible liver damage…"

Then, in order to determine, whether John intends to imply that I have not given them sufficient I pause, but since his impartiality suggests that the cavalry are satisfied, I volunteer the remaining information, so that we can dispense with this matter.

"Much to Lorna's amazement her father hadn't cut her out of his will, and because she had inherited half of everything, and Colin was so busy working she had volunteered to return to Edinburgh, so that she could finalize matters relating to the Legal Practice, before selling the family home. They say there's no such thing as a coincidence, but at the precise time, I needed a place to hide--someone who I had allowed to become close to me was prepared to provide me with a hideout, at least until the house was sold. For Lorna's part, she didn't seem in the least disturbed that I was pregnant. In fact, she seemed relieved to have someone around, while she laid the ghosts to rest…"

Suddenly, John's expression is suggesting that he knows, what might be around the next corner, prompting him to remark. "For the benefit of the recording, I think we should clarify the nature of the relationship you share with Lorna Clunnell…"

Since there is no reason why--*we need to clarify anything*--taking my time, I drink the remaining sparkling water in my glass, which forces John to elaborate. "After all, we wouldn't want anyone jumping to the wrong conclusion, especially when it would seem that you and Lorna shared a unique relationship. Indeed, the kind of friendship…"

Now, I'm so outraged, I have to interrupt him. "Mr Bland if you are about to imply that Lorna and I share anything, except for a relationship based upon friendship, then that would be rather like someone challenging the close relationship you share with Mr Powell…"

Opposite me, although my suggestion has brought a smile to John's face, it remains tinged with dubiety. "In fact Mr Bland, so that there can be no misunderstandings for the benefit of our invisible audience, I would like to set the official record straight by confirming that--*throughout the last seven years of my life, Lorna and Colin are the only people, I have been able to trust*--and despite loving and respecting them both, I can assure you that when it comes to the three of us, there's never been anything sexual about our relationships…"

Casting a backward glance, like his partner Bill is smiling, as he expresses his gratitude on their behalf. "Thank you for your clarification Mrs Daltry, and provided that John his satisfied, perhaps we should continue with you having run away to Edinburgh?"

After nodding his satisfaction, John quickly continues. "Even though your father knew nothing about Lorna Clunnell, considering the extent of his power and influence, if he had wanted to do so, surely the Major could have easily discovered your whereabouts?"

"That's correct and in theory, there should have been nowhere I could have hidden, but while Lorna and I searched for a resolution to my dilemma, because she was more level-headed and emotionally detached, she persuaded me to contact my father once a month, using a disposal mobile phone, so that I could reassure him that I was safe and well, and since he was pompous enough to assume that I intended to do what he regarded as the sensible thing and have the baby adopted, I did nothing to dispel his belief…"

"I'm impressed Charlie," John compliments me. "Because allowing the Major to believe what he deemed to be his preferred solution meant that he kept his distance…"

"For my part, I chose to believe that even if the Major used his influence to have me traced he knew that his rebellious daughter would keep disappearing. However, six weeks before my delivery date, since Lorna had found a buyer for the house, I agreed to invite my father to visit us, so that I could tell him that I wasn't going to have my baby adopted…"

"And by the time the Major arrived, you and Lorna must have reached an agreement that after Bobby was born, she would raise him as if he was her son…"

"Until his arrival we hadn't risked finalizing anything, but from the onset my father approved of Lorna. In fact, he thought she had been a good role model…"

Suddenly this adult is overwhelmed by anger and yet, I know that anger masks hurt. How could my father have done such a thing to his daughter and Grandson? Surely, he must have realized his deception would trap us in his world--and once imprisoned--the adult within me was destined to never experience the same level of freedom, during the next seven years.

"During those months in Scotland, I had been happier than any one person could have dared imagine, and however irresponsible it might have seemed, I had made plans for after Bobby was born. Of course, once I discovered that not only had my father covered up my sudden disappearance, with a plausible explanation--an extended trip to Europe--he had also permitted the signed consent to make its way into the Forsyth File, which had allowed my Godfather to believe that the matter had been resolved, when in reality…"

Yet again, the words fail to emerge, because there is something missing. Something my protective parent is avoiding, and when it comes to the plot thickening, it will be a vital ingredient, but John's impartiality remains intact, and because he seems unperturbed by the real reason for my father's deception--as if it's insignificant, I shrug my shoulders.

"I suppose my father's actions were the result of him believing the matter would be resolved to his satisfaction, when I had my baby adopted by complete strangers…"

"And since that was never what you and Lorna had intended, you had no choice, except to convince him that your hypothetical solution could be made to work…"

"When it came to the monetary side of our arrangement, Lorna's inheritance meant that she was financially independent, and although she intended to move back to London, she had no idea what she wanted to do with the rest of her life. As for me, my own sizeable trust fund enabled me to offer considerable financial support to our project…"

"Financially, it sounds plausible Charlie," John declares, as he continues to read my facial expression. "But from an emotional perspective, it can't have been easy…"

More sadness and tears of regret as this daughter tried to reason, with an intransigent father whose arguments sounded logical, and because the child within me, still yearned to regain his approval, in the end I agreed to his compromise.

"No, it wasn't," this woman confesses. "But then, nothing worthwhile is ever easy, and I should have never allowed my father to trap us through his deceit, especially when the only thing I wanted was to allow my son the right to grow up free from any kind of deception. However, at least with Lorna acting as his mother, I knew that I would be able to maintain some kind of meaningful relationship with Bobby…"

There is still something missing. Something my protective parent is avoiding. If this woman knows it, then John must be aware of it, and if I thought for one moment that he would permit such a vital ingredient to remain concealed, then this adult was wrong.

"What about Bobby's father? You've never mentioned him Charlie…"

"That's because there's nothing to say…"

At least that is my official stance, and because there is nothing this woman needs to say--correction there is nothing this adult wants to say--my principal male has every reason to counter-challenge this misleading leading lady.

"Being an unmarried mother with an open Security File shouldn't have posed any real threat to National Security, and despite reading the content of the file several times, we couldn't find any logical reason why Major Forsyth could not have told Commander Maddox the truth, either when you first disappeared or after Bobby was born…"

"I can assure you Mr Bland that the information you require was documented for the benefit of the official record…"

Tilting his head, a little to one side, which is something I've learnt John does whenever he's holding the winning cards in his hand. "That's correct and you told

Commander Maddox that you'd slept with so many different partners around the time of conception, it was impossible to determine whose sperm had fathered your baby…"

Pausing, John throws me a triumphant smile, before he adds, "In fact, what was documented is as follows, *"Numerous DNA tests can only reveal a multitude of red faces, in the upper corridors of Ministerial power*." For the benefit of the recording Mrs Daltry, could you please confirm that those were the exact words you used?"

Such fearlessness or alternatively, it could be described as my foolhardiness and yet, the passage of time changes nothing, because if my rebellious child were faced with the same adversity in this present tense, then she would have behaved with the same recklessness.

"Did I really say that? What an incredible act of bravery on my part…"

Unseen by our invisible audience yet again, John extends his smile, but at the same time, his voice maintains a serious overtone. "That is what's documented in the file, but then that same file also confirms that you had the pregnancy terminated, and as we now know, despite the consent form you signed and dated that's not true either…"

Between you and me, if the cavalry are concerned over one minor discrepancy, plus one irregularity within the Forsyth file, then once we reach the content of the Daltry file, which is littered with deceptions and untruths, they will come to appreciate that as this Interview progresses, the missing ingredient is destined to grow in importance.

"So I exaggerated," this woman admits. as I shrug my shoulders. "But in all fairness I think my father and Godfather would have preferred it to be true, because a multitude of one night stands would have been less damaging than one dangerous…"

Than one dangerous liaison and all this talk has manifested a new image, an image my protective parent has never needed to recreate, until the arrival of this moment.

If you will pardon another unfortunate play on words, *despite it seeming inconceivable, I had reached my early twenties with my maidenhead intact, and because my experience in sexual matters was non-existent, my rebellious child was looking for someone with the maturity to teach me everything I needed to learn about intimacy.*

*So along with twenty-five other guests, I was at Bradford Manor late one evening, and across the room, my rebellious child knew he was watching her, and he seemed so different from the younger men who were competing for her attention. Perhaps, he was destined to become the chosen one because as his eyes were following me, while I flitted from room to room, he was noting every move, every smile and each and every gesture and yet, the rebellious child within me evaded him, until he had the wherewithal to trap me on the stairs.*

*Unable to go up or down--or move to the right or left of him--this young woman was captivated by his warm, mature smile, and those strong hands as he had whispered, what he intended to do to me, if I were willing to give him my permission.*

*Such sweet memories of those intoxicating youthful moments, when the consequences had seemed to be inconsequential, but in the event of this woman losing her virginity, my rebellious child was robbed. In fact, it was nothing less than daylight robbery, because in and out of bed, he proved himself to be boring. Yes, without question, he was undemonstrative, uninteresting, possibly even weak and spineless--and because that young woman became disillusioned and pregnant, it will have to be admitted as evidence.*

When my protective parent realizes that I have chosen not to share those images with either the cavalry or our wider audience, and there has been a time lapse with an inexplicable sharpness I lift my head, and find myself making excuses on behalf of that spineless, pathetic specimen of male adulthood.

"Because I was inexperienced in sexual matters, he was fifteen years older than me and our liaison--if it could be described as a liaison--lasted no more than six weeks and it ended because we weren't honest with each other. On my behalf, I omitted to tell him about my open Security File, and although it could be argued that I should have asked, he failed to mention his devoted wife and two children…"

"So that there cannot be any ambiguity Charlie, for the benefit of the Official Record could you please confirm that Bobby's father was the reason why the Major had allowed the consent form you signed to be added to the contents of the Forsyth file?"

"That's correct--as one of my father's protégés--he was destined to achieve great things. So any indiscretion could have sorely damaged his career prospects…"

It's a familiar story--and one which John understands. "And since your father had chosen to assume that you intended to have the baby adopted by complete strangers, he couldn't risk having you traced in case the search aroused suspicion, and in order to avoid any further investigation into the paternity of your son, the Major had also chosen to perpetrate a misinterpretation of the truth…"

This adult utters a cynical laugh. "After they had lunch at the Major's Exclusive Club he decided I was his protégé's first and last indiscretion, and because all I wanted was to have my baby, it could also be argued that my rebellious child let them get away with it…"

As if I never cared about my own feelings, this woman shrugs her shoulders, but before I confirm upon which side of the morality line, I had chosen to stand, I momentarily sever eye contact. "Besides, because his wife was pregnant with their third child, the scandal would have wrecked his marriage as well as his career prospects, and since we had used each other and it had never been my intention to have any kind of permanent relationship with him--at that time it didn't seem fair to ruin him…"

Casting a glance at the opposite side of the desk, John is wearing his impartiality, but since we both know that he cannot avoid the substance of that missing ingredient forever, this adult is not surprised by the arrival of his next statement.

"Although we've now established that instead of multiple possibilities, only one man could have been responsible--surely you must realize that we do expect you to provide us with his name Charlie?"

"I know," I admit, but then my protective parent attempts to steal the show by entering another defence on behalf of my son's absentee father. "I've only heard from him once in the last seven years, and that's a long time to pretend that someone doesn't exist…"

"It's far too long Charlie…"

Decisive, emphatic John's response is a simple declaration of fact, However, while Bobby might have benefitted from the love and attentiveness of two mothers, he has grown up without any knowledge of his powerful and influential father. Suddenly, the consequences of our affair are not only consequential, they could be damaging to my son.

"You don't understand…"

Despite my stammered beginning, John makes it clear that this matter is non-negotiable, "In view of recent events Charlie, there's nothing to understand…"

Perhaps John is right and yet, far from my being unwilling to divulge his name, I remain reticent. In any event, I am grateful when our arbitrator intervenes on my behalf.

"When it comes to your life story Charlie, we still have a long way to go, and since I suspect that as this Interview progresses, you might feel less protective towards him, we can come back to his name later…"

Although I'm grateful for the reprieve--albeit on a temporary basis, I remain unsure whether his partner will permit such an important ingredient to be deferred. However, John rises to his feet, and after choosing to detach himself from his leading lady, he picks up my empty glass and moves to the cabinet, and while it might be a cosmetic exercise, he pours three glasses of sparkling water, before putting ice in each of them, and then after delivering one of them to his partner, he brings the remaining two glasses to the desk, which causes me to consider that if John is prepared to abide by all of our arbitrator's decisions, then there is more than one reason why I should express my gratitude.

"Thank you…"

Without responding John sits back down, which seems to be the cue Bill has been waiting for so that he can re-direct the proceedings. "Let's move time on Charlie. Why don't you tell us about Mark Daltry? From the documented sequence of events, we estimated that Bobby must have been almost three and half years old when you first met Mark…"

Despite my nodded agreement, I am aware that my relationship with Mark needs skilful handling, and while I am vetting my own recollections, I take several sips of water from my glass, before commencing. "Because of his political background, my Godfather had hand-picked Mark to become an International Negotiator and Trouble-shooter on behalf of Special Operations, and since Commander Maddox liked his prospective new recruits to be vetted by my father, Helen organized one of her tedious dinner parties, at which my presence was mandatory, and my immediate impression was how gallant Mark seemed to be…"

Yes, gallant was an excellent description of Mark Daltry, *when he had arrived on that fateful evening accompanied by his mentor, Commander Philip Maddox.*

*"Good evening Charlotte," announced my Godfather, as he entered the living room. "I'd like to introduce you to Mark Daltry who will be joining Special Operations…"*

*Extending his arm towards me, I noted his confident handshake and when Mark had to stoop a little, so that he could greet me with the customary light brushing of his lips against my cheek, after regaining his full height, he seemed to tower above me as he made what would turn out to be his opening declaration of war.*

*"After hearing so many good things about you from your Godfather, if you'll excuse my terminology it's a pleasure to meet you in the flesh. May I call you Charlie?"*

*Fair hair, blue eyes, intriguing smile,* and because he asked if he could call me Charlie, I admit that if the circumstances had been different, then his request might have earned him bonus points. *However, instead of being delighted to meet him, in or out of the flesh for no other reason than his connection with my Godfather, I needed to dislike him.*

"Despite my attempts to coax him out of his comfort zone, Mark Daltry confirmed that he was yet another self-opinionated, whizz kid who had been tempted to leave his mundane desk job at the Foreign Office, by the lure of more power and greater influence…"

Unseen by our invisible audience, John's impartiality has been replaced by a knowledgeable smirk. "Obviously, you must have met his type before Mr Bland. Arrogant, self-centred, and because people like him have an unhealthy determination to achieve success--regardless of the casualties along the way--they seem destined to be rewarded…"

"If that was how you felt, then Mark must have managed to change your mind…"

Taking my time, I continue to sip from my glass, before reaching for my cigarettes. "Eventually, Mark did turn me into one his conquests, but that first evening, the conversation at the dinner table would have deterred any woman from wanting further contact with him, and when he asked me if the two of us could go out to dinner the following evening, I declined his invitation. However, the next day when I came down to breakfast later than usual, there was a bouquet of roses waiting for me, accompanied by a note asking me to reconsider, and after I kept refusing he sent me roses every day, until I ran out of excuses and I was so embarrassed by my discourteousness, I felt obliged to accept his invitation…"

Back in the past tense, *Mark Daltry was asking me, what had made me change my mind, and when I told him that we had run out of vases, his laughter proved to be infectious, and the self-imposed barrier, which my protective parent had placed between me, and any member of the opposite sex--ever since the birth of my son--had begun to crumble.*

"It had been my intention to deter him by acting like a spoilt bitch at the restaurant, but away from the political arena, Mark was charming, intelligent, witty and beneath the layers of bureaucratic starch, I discovered that he had a genuine sense of adventure..."

Oh dear, the return of adventure and being adventurous and yet, despite my past misdemeanours involving men who have strong hands, between you and me, there are no excuses I can offer, except that someone like me should have foreseen the potential risks.

"After the meal, I had anticipated him suggesting that we go back to his place, where I would be invited to pay fifty per cent of the restaurant's bill, by having consensual sex with him. Instead, he took me home, and without even attempting to kiss me on the lips, before he drove away from the house, Mark asked me if I would do him the honour of accompanying him to the theatre. Then, over the next few weeks, he seemed to have an uncanny knack when it came to being in the right place to fulfil, the needs of any occasion and all times, Mark remained respectful, until he began to resemble an adoring, significant other person..."

Between you and me, Mark had been a resourceful adventurer who had toyed with a rebellious child's adventurous disposition, until the consequences of him not fulfilling a woman's needs to be wanted yet again, became too consequential to be ignored, and considering that he was the first man, I had allowed to penetrate my self–imposed barrier, what I failed to comprehend was why he had not initiated any kind of sexual activity. However, since my reference to intimacy has manifested memories of my first visit to Mark's--I was going to say his home--but there's a vast difference, between a house and a home, and because 187 Cheltenham Way, lacked the kind of warmth that comes from being lived in, until three months ago it could never have been described as a home.

On the premise that Mark had wanted to demonstrate his culinary skills, we had shared a wonderful home cooked meal, but then while we were savouring coffee and brandy in the living room, Mark's unexpected confession left me stunned.

*"Since we were introduced, you have been monopolising my thoughts. In fact, I've even been dreaming about you, and because I've never felt this way about any woman what I'm trying to tell you--Charlie Anne Forsyth--is that I've fallen in love with you…"*

*Strictly off the official record as I found out to my cost, according to the lyrics of the song--what's love got to do with it--but I admit to dressing with the sole intention that the pure silk, navy blue Victorian corset, with its hook and eye fastenings at the front, and laced up back, set against spray tanned skin would push him beyond the limits of his restraint, and after he lowered his head, and his lips touched mine when he started to kiss me, his demand responded to my demand, until irrespective of whether it was alive or dead I craved to be taken not by any man, but by this prototypical specimen of masculinity.*

*Reaching behind me, Mark began to unzip the navy blue dress I was barely wearing, before he encouraged me to stand up, so that he could ease it from my shoulders, until it cascaded to the floor around the matching six inch stilettoes, and because he wanted to appreciate the trouble I'd taken dressing for more than dinner, Mark took a step back.*

*"Like the instantly recognizable aroma of Chanel No 5, if you will excuse my forthrightness, you also have exquisite taste in underwear Ms. Forsyth…"*

*"Our aim was to please you Mr Daltry…"*

*"Indeed w hen it came to you deciding what to wear to best please me, it must have taken a great deal of effort--in fact…"*

While delivering his response, Mark's hands had started to define the contours of my upper body. "In fact, with your waist nipped in, and those well-presented breasts, believe me you have pleased me…"

By now, Mark's fingers were unhooking the front fastenings, so that he could caress and then massage those well-presented breasts, until he leant towards me and I could feel the warmth of his breath against my ear, as he asked, "Why don't you start showing me, what a naughty young lady you were planning to become, by moving your feet apart?"

In response to such a polite request, I was thinking that if my upper body had pleased him, then only God himself knew, what additional pleasure Mark would gain when he discovered that the matching Victorian thong had a split crotch, and although I had fantasised over dinner about Mark making love to me on the snowy white sheepskin rugs littering the solid oak floor, more adept in the art of memorable seductions than I had anticipated, he continued to exercise that same remarkable restraint.

"What's the rush, Ms. Forsyth? Sometimes procuring the right end result takes time, and I think you would agree that our first experience should be special for both of us. So do you think you could manage to move your feet further apart?"

Another supposed polite request, and satisfied with my additional movement, Mark lowered himself, until his lips and tongue were working between my legs, with such proficiency, I was forced to grasp hold of his shoulders to stop myself from falling, and as he had promised his own expertise in the art of memorable seductions procured what I was destined to discover would be the first of several orgasms.

Like an addict, Mark had me hooked and I was beginning to believe that unlike any previous sexual activity--instead of boring--this was proving to be demonstrative, imaginative, perhaps even erotic--until Mark distracted me by rising to his feet, so that he could place my hands against his Levi's and when it came to oral sex, I did have some experience--albeit limited. So without severing eye contact I began by tightening his belt, so that I could slip the notch free, before unbuckling it and then, after sliding his zip down I lowered myself until I was sitting on the edge of the sofa, but when I started using my lips and tongue, Mark wanted to enhance my basic experience.

"Would you please lift your head up Ms. Forsyth and then, tilt it back?"

Initially fearful of the unknown, when I pulled back in an attempt to sever contact it had been a spontaneous reaction, but Mark interlocked his fingers, so that his grasp on the back of my head tightened, as he chided me. "For future reference, it would be unwise to attempt pulling away from me ever again, and since I can assure you that there's nothing to fear, please continue with your head tilted all the way back…"

Despite my initial fear that I might not be able to manage without gagging, especially when Mark was growing longer and wider--much to my eternal damnation--I was becoming so aroused, I found myself allowing him to pull back, before starting to push forward a little deeper with each inwards motion, until Mark was making full use my mouth, while at the same time, he was offering his pupil some encouragement.

"Didn't I reassure you that there was nothing to fear Ms. Forsyth? I'm afraid you'll have to learn how to indulge my little idiosyncrasies, because either later tonight or perhaps tomorrow morning I will expect a repeat performance, and when I climax--even if it threatens to choke you--my hands will hold you locked in this position, while you provide me with the added satisfaction of not only hearing you, but also watching as you learn how to swallow every last drop…"

In a perverse kind of way, being kept in that position somehow made me feel as if I was being forced to fulfil his requirements, until I found myself hoping that he would climax, so that I could find out whether I was able to overcome that choking reflex. Instead, Mark *pulled out of my mouth--only by then my arousal necessitated that I beg him to lower the limit of his customary restraint.*

*"Prior to this evening, no man has aroused me like this, and because this young woman wants you to fucking screw her so badly, I need you inside of me…"*

*Instead of agreeing, Mark seized hold of my upper arm, and even though his vice like grip caused me to cry out, he forced me to accompany him into his own inner sanctum.*

*"There's a vast difference between being a naughty young lady who has exquisite taste in perfume and underwear than the kind of cheap slut who uses--F--words and refers to being--screwed--as if it's acceptable behaviour. Wouldn't you agree Ms. Forsyth?"*

*After my first transgression, it could be argued that I should have learnt from it, but as we all know when it comes to the consequences of my actions, I have an appalling track record, which meant that I made an even bigger mistake when I remained silent.*

*"I'm waiting Ms. Forsyth--and I should warn you that I detest the casual usage of the--F--word so much that until I receive an answer from you, I cannot decide what level of chastisement your vulgarity merits…"*

*Prior to my self-imposed celibacy having led such a boring sex life, because the reference to chastisement appealed to the inquisitive and adventurous sides of my nature, especially when I had never indulged in this kind of erotic foreplay, I found myself offering Mark yet another inappropriate reply.*

*"I'm sorry--I thought…"*

*"What you don't seem to understand is that this situation has arisen, because you didn't think before speaking, but the fact remains that when you chose to arrive dressed in such a provocative outfit, you intended to seduce me. Isn't that correct Ms. Forsyth?"*

*"Yes Mark I did---but…"*

*"Oh dear, what you have also failed to understand is that there aren't any--buts…"*

*Releasing me, Mark headed towards the impressive--if rather oversized--mahogany desk and then, as if to prove that his perfectionism was not the result of a mental health issue, such as Obsessional Compulsive Disorder, using a single sweeping movement across its surface he sent everything crashing to the floor, before he issued his first direct order.*

*"Come here…"*

*Then, when I continued to hover in the doorway, he chided me with another verbal warning. "It would also be unwise Ms. Forsyth to tax my patience…"*

Although I was curious about where this role playing might be heading, I had arrived with a fantasy of my own that after dispensing with the foreplay, we would be face to face, and because I hoped Mark would incorporate my needs into to his own role playing, when I reached the desk I leant against it, so that we were facing each other.

*"Close your eyes…"*

*Wanting to avoid taxing his aforementioned patience, I closed my eyes and then, I heard what sounded like Mark sliding one of the filing cabinet drawers open, and even when it was closed with a resounding bang and I jumped involuntarily, I never considered what he planned to do next, but with my eyes still closed, as the back of his hand brushed down my right arm, combined with my heightened sensitivity the lightness of his touch sent a shiver running up and down my spine, as he almost whispered his second direct order.*

*"Turn around," Pausing, Mark yet again waited, but when I failed to obey him, he issued his first veiled threat. "I warned you about not taxing my patience. Now, either you turn around, or you will leave me no choice, but to teach you the error of your ways…"*

*"You don't understand…"*

*After uttering an irritable sigh, Mark turned me around, before applying enough force to ensure that the side of my face was trapped against the surface of his desk.*

"There's nothing to understand Ms. Forsyth, and because it has been noted that you also seem to be incapable of controlling what comes out of your mouth, unless I require an answer I suggest you keep it shut. Do we have an understanding?"

Then, when I failed to provide him with an immediate answer, Mark uttered a second even more disagreeable sigh, before issuing his second veiled threat.

"I can assure you that your refusal to cooperate will end in tears, before your bedtime. Furthermore, although I had made a decision about what level of chastisement your vulgarity merited, if you refuse to confirm that we have reached an understanding over your silence, then I will be forced to consider what additional action needs to be undertaken..."

Much to my shame, I have to admit that because chastisement had reared its head again, and being in such a defenceless position was for some reason liberating, especially when it would exonerate me from any responsibility for whatever level of corrective action, Mark had decided to use in order to teach me the error of my ways. In fact, I was so intrigued that in the full knowledge I would be breaching our aforementioned understanding, in a hushed, submissive tone of voice, which was intended to mislead him, I admitted defeat. "If that's what it takes to satisfy you Mr Daltry, then we do have an understanding..."

"Oh whenever I'm ready Ms. Forsyth, I can assure you that whether you like it or not you will more than satisfy all of my varied needs..."

With one of Mark's hands keeping my torso pressed against his desk, I continued to be both intrigued and enthralled, until I heard a clinking sound, and because I could not identify its origin, I tried to prevent him from seizing hold of my forearm.

"As much as feistiness can be an endearing quality in a naughty young lady, in this instance since I'm taller, faster and stronger your resistance is a futile gesture..."

Of course, he was right and as soon as I grew still, Mark jerked one of my arms, behind my back, so that he could secure what--in my lack of experience--felt like some kind of metal bracelet around my wrist. Then, after forcing my arm towards the top of the desk, he snapped the other half of the ensemble around the raised corner, before proceeding to do the same with the other wrist.

Clearly pleased with his handiwork, Mark uttered a more agreeable 'hmm' sound, and in an attempt to ease the discomfort of the metal around my wrists, I grasped the corners of the desk and until Mark took hold of my hips, and he extended my arms and torso to their maximum length, by easing me back towards him, the additional strain on my arm muscles was so unbearable, it caused me to cry out and that's when I made my third--or was it my fourth mistake--by daring to lodge an objection.

"The handcuffs are secured so tightly. Can't you at least slacken them?"

"If you don't stop whining, I might decide to restrain each of your ankles..."

"No please, I swear I'll do..."

"Ms. Forsyth," Mark declared with such an authoritarian overtone, it rendered me silent. "When you agreed that we had reached an understanding, can you tell me why that particular request proved to be necessary?"

Of course, unbeknown to me, beyond that evening my ability to maintain my silence would be destined to become a significant factor in our relationship, but in that instant I could only speak the truth.

"You suggested that unless you required an answer, I should keep my mouth shut..."

"That's correct, and in addition to being prepared to grant you some degree of clemency, I was willing to overlook the first verbal transgression. However, since you seem determined to tax my patience, I'm afraid you've left me no choice, except to carry out the other part of my threat, by rendering you silent as well as restrained..."

Since my immobility had become a fete-accompli--amid a mass of contradictory emotions I found myself so mesmerized, by this erotic role playing that when I heard Mark *moving away from the desk--for the first time in this woman's mundane sex life--if I was asked after the event, I would have to admit to being so aroused by the prospect of being gagged as well as restrained, I could no longer prevent my second orgasm from overwhelming every inch of my body.*

*A few seconds later when Mark returned, his disapproving muttering suggested that having noted my climax he was even more displeased, and when this captive compounded that displeasure by twisting my head, until I could clearly see the gag in his hand--and like everything else it appeared to be larger than I had anticipated, so my lack of experience led me to try and dissuade him, by refusing to open my mouth.*

*"There's nothing to be gained by being difficult, especially when you're powerless to stop me forcing your mouth open Ms. Forsyth. Indeed, your non-compliance may well leave me no choice, but to select a far less comfortable gag from my varied collection..."*

*My God a collection of gags! Considering that I seemed to be caught up in a--*damned if I do, and damned if I don't kind of scenario--*I had cause to wonder, whether this kind of eroticism played a regular part in Mark Daltry's nocturnal activities.*

*"Ultimately the choice is yours Ms. Forsyth. However, if I were in your current position I'd open my mouth, and allow myself to be gagged--rather than--having to face the more severe consequences of my flagrant disobedience..."*

*Erring on the side of caution I conceded defeat, but after he drew the ties around the back of my head, so that he could fasten them, and the gag dug into the corners of my mouth causing me to release a muffled yelp, there was a menacing overtone in his voice, as Mark drew my attention to the additional error of my ways.*

*"Although I admit it was flattering--since you didn't have my permission to climax for a second time and then, you refused to accept the gag, I trust you'll remember how your rebellious streak caused you to pay a far higher price than should have been necessary..."*

*Not expecting any response, Mark chose to focus on more important things, and despite being groomed to become an International Negotiator and trouble-shooter, he would have undergone routine training not only in the use of fire arms, but also unarmed combat, so that in an unavoidable crisis he could handle himself, and applying those skills to the captive in front of him, he used his foot to nudge my legs into a more disarming position.*

*Then, as if conducting a body search his hands moved over my torso, until they reached the Victorian split crotch thong, where I knew he would discover that this particular prisoner who--in addition to being at his mercy--was also a soaking wet captive who could do nothing, except whimper while he undertook a cavity search firstly, using one finger, then two fingers, perhaps even three.*

*"As I suspected, despite the exquisite taste in perfume and underwear, like any run of the mill slut, you're dripping wet Ms. Forsyth. It can only be in anticipation of the punishment you deserve, not only for your vulgarity, but also your disobedience..."*

*As Mark taunted me his fingers continued working between my legs, while I did my best to grind my hips back to meet them, and when he suddenly withdrew, and I dared to release a dissatisfied--albeit muffled groan--he left me in no doubt that he was in control.*

*"Oh I've no intention of allowing you to climax for a third time, unless you have my permission. Do you understand me Ms. Forsyth?"*

*Initially, I uttered another frustrated groan, but then fearing further consequences, I gave him the satisfaction of hearing my muffled understanding, and as Mark leant over me, crushing me against the desk, he whispered in a precise threatening tone of voice.*

*"As I recall, you wanted me to and I quote--*fucking screw you--*and that's exactly what I'm going to do Ms. Forsyth. I intend to give you what you wanted, so that by the time I'm finished--you won't be able to sit down for at least the next three--hopefully even four days--without being reminded that in future, it might be advisable to either select your words*

*using the kind of decorum befitting a young lady, or be prepared to suffer the punishing consequences of your actions..."*

*In the meantime, recalling how much bigger things had been in this fantasy, including when this man had been in my mouth I braced myself, and when Mark dispensed with the usual formalities of a gradual entry, opting instead for a more forthright approach, and he thrust himself all the way into me, and he heard my sharp intake of oxygen, my captivity seemed to spur him on, until each powerful thrust was penetrating deeper than the last.*

*For my part, only too aware of Mark's warning, I was struggling to contain my third climax while at the same time with every thrust, my pelvic muscles were contracting around him and then relaxing in the hope of quickening his own climatic finale.*

*Then, without prior invitation one of his fingers strayed to the place which--thanks to my unadventurous sex life--remained unexplored territory. However, when I squirmed and from behind the gag I tried to voice my protest, Mark seemed prepared to save me from that particular threat.*

*Of course, any relief was short-lived, because Mark proceeded to conduct a second more thorough cavity search, and when he forced first one, then two fingers into me in response to his painful intrusion, I tried to scream an alarmed denial, and no longer caring about the strain on my arms, or the damage that might be inflicted by the metal encasing my wrists, I writhed against my restraints. But as if Mark had hoped to achieve that reaction from this captive, he climaxed and while he remained inside me emptying his sperm in shorter, pulsating spurts, this captive no longer cared whether I had been given permission, because I could no longer suppress my third climax, which to my eternal shame surpassed anything I had experienced in my lifetime.*

*In the afterglow, with the gag removed and freed from the restraints, Mark carried me to the comfort of his bed, where he begged me for my forgiveness.*

*"Charlie Anne Forsyth how can you possibly forgive me? I should never have been so rough and insensitive, especially when it was the first time we enjoyed each other. Somehow, the outfit and your perfume seemed to drive me to distraction, I hope I didn't..."*

*They say that ignorance is blissful, and wanting to silence him, I twisted myself around, so that I could place two of my fingers against his lips. "There's no need to apologise Mark. After all, we both know that I received what I duly deserved..."*

*Appreciating the pun, Mark uttered a small laugh as I offered him a more in depth analysis. "Like everyone, I've acted out run of the mill fantasies in my head, but I've never enacted any kind of erotic fantasy, and much to my shame I found that being speechless and immobile was so liberating it heightened my pleasure as well as the strength of my orgasms. Indeed, three in one session was unprecedented--a potential world record..."*

*Lying there in the comparative safety his arms--even now--I can still hear him telling me over and over again, how much he loved me. So I would have challenged anybody not to believe that it had all been so believable.*

*Oh in case anyone might later have cause to wonder---the answer is yes. The following morning, when Mark expected a repeat performance which necessitated me on my knees, when he demanded that I lift my head before tilting it back as far as it would go, although disobedience was tempting--on that occasion--instead of having to face the consequences of my rebelliousness I chose to obey him.*

*During that debut performance thanks to his encouragement, I did manage to take him a little deeper with each of his downward thrusts, until he emptied his sperm into my throat--in short yet prolonged spurts which did choke me, but since his intertwined fingers on the back of my head kept me locked in position, I was unable to pull back as I began to learn how to breathe beyond the gagging, until I managed to swallow--perhaps not every single drop, but enough to satisfy Mark Daltry.*

All things considered, it had been a memorable seduction, which in my naivety had been destined to change the course of my life and yet, this trip down memory lane has also been a lengthy lapse in concentration.

Especially when one considers that within the present tense of my Godfather's study, there are more pressing matters--such as the definitive details, which are going to require my full attention, and a little alarmed, I lift my head to discover that while he has been waiting John must have been watching me, and in a rush to excuse my absence I blurt out, what is intended to be the beginning of an apology.

"I'm sorry--I was…"

Remembering---my God have I been so absorbed during my trip down memory lane I've misplaced my rightful mind, especially when I'm unsure how much I have shared. Of course, on the one hand I'm praying that John will not ask, while on the other hand my inner child is hoping that this adult's cheeks have not flushed with that tell-tale reddish tone, which would provide evidence to support my embarrassment.

"There's no need to be alarmed Charlie," Bill reassures me. "Although you seemed to be somewhere else as we have explained, unless one of us tells you otherwise, you can take as much time as you need and then, whenever you're ready we can continue…"

Despite being aware that my hand is still covering my cigarettes, after glancing at John it would seem that like his partner, he intends to behave as if he is a perfect gentleman. Then, while my protective parent is re-grouping my thoughts into less revealing images, I flip the packet open, so that I can remove a cigarette, and because I believe that I'm ready to re-join the performance by resuming my rightful place, under the spotlight at the centre of the stage, despite picking up the lighter, my dramatic prop remains unlit.

"We must have known each other for at least six weeks, before I was invited to spend an evening at 187 Cheltenham Way where Mark surprised me, not only with his culinary expertise, but also by announcing that before being introduced to me, he had never felt the way he did about any woman, and the following morning when I woke up in Mark's bed, it had turned into something far more serious--than a casual fling…"

"Because you realized that you felt the same way about him…"

There are no excuses and at first, it was nothing more than unadulterated sex and then, more sex and yet, this woman is not too ashamed to confess her womanly weaknesses.

"It was Mark who introduced love into the equation, and when I let my guard down, I discovered that I shared his feelings. However, when he asked me to marry him in what seemed to be indecent haste I had no choice, except to refuse…"

"And presumably, Bobby was the reason why you declined his proposal?"

"Mark argued that if we loved each other, then there should be no reason why we couldn't get married? However, I felt it wouldn't be right to marry anyone, without them knowing that I had given birth to another man's child, and because he was so insistent he left me no alternative, except to bring the relationship to an abrupt end…"

"If that's how you felt, then something must have happened to change your mind, because if our calculations are correct, then approximately fifteen weeks after you were introduced by your Godfather, you did marry Mark Daltry…"

Clearly, John has grasped that the plot is about to thicken, which is further confirmation that although we have left the Forsyth File--albeit for the time being--the cavalry have done their homework and yet, I sense that there is something else--something they have uncovered, which is not documented in any of the Files relating to me.

In any event, in the present tense when I recall that while my rebellious child might have committed the original sin, this mother had been prepared to serve the life sentence, but once the damage was done, I am reminded that unbeknown to me I was about to exchange one kind of captivity for another. So my voice is hushed as I make my admission.

"Mark found out that I had a son…"

"Did you tell him?"

"Absolutely not," I hear this woman protesting. "As God is my witness, until I had no choice but to tell you, I'd never told another human being about Lorna and Bobby..."

"In that case, how did he find out Charlie?"

A little disconcerted, not only by the emergence of questions, but also their swiftness and directness, my protective parent cautions me and yet, when I recall that before we began in earnest, questions had been my original preference--as if what happened is irrelevant, I shrug my shoulders before I cast aside my concerns.

"My father thought Mark would make an ideal son-in-law. I suppose he represented the next best thing to the son, he had always wanted---and after deciding to replicate what he had done with Bobby's father, he invited Mark to lunch at his Exclusive Club, where he exercised his paternal prerogative to indulge in---one of those man-to-man conversations about his daughter's indiscretions…"

"Did you know what your father intended to do?"

"If I had known, or even suspected Mr Bland, then I would have challenged him…"

In need of my dramatic prop the cigarette reaches my mouth, and after clicking at the lighter I inhale deeply, before exhaling the spent smoke in a long steady breath--perhaps in the prophetic sense towards the opposite side of the desk, before I venture to elaborate.

"As far as I was concerned, although Mark was finding it difficult to accept my decision, I had already severed all contact…"

There is no reason why John should disbelieve my revelation and yet, he does have another question. "And did you find out how much Major Forsyth told Mark Daltry?"

"For obvious reasons, he avoided the identity of Bobby's father, and anything relating to the Research Programme. As far as I was aware, he told Mark that because of the delicate nature of his work, and my close encounter with the Vice Squad over the drugs incident, I had an open Security File, and as result of my rebellious years, I had a child with whom I maintained discreet contact…"

Although the consequences are not yet visible--for the time being--the plot thickening is complete, which enables John to reach the obvious conclusion.

"And once Mark knew about your son, there was nothing to prevent you from reconsidering his marriage proposal…"

"Naturally, I was furious with my father for having yet again interfered, but Mark insisted that because he didn't care about my misspent youth--nothing had changed…"

Pausing, I tap the ash from my cigarette into the ashtray, before casting an unconvincing smile towards the opposite side of the desk in readiness for my next admission.

"Mark wasn't only offering me the chance to be with the man I loved, he was also affording me the opportunity to escape from the past, because once Commander Maddox sanctioned the marriage, I would become part of the Daltry File, and although any other files held elsewhere could never be closed--over time their importance would diminish…"

More naivety, and because I knew that one day--as they did on 22$^{nd}$ June--my past and present would be involved in a head on collision with my future--I'm so disturbed by the nearness of less pleasant images with an alarming swiftness, I make eye contact with John, but it is too late to avoid staring into the murky depths of the abyss.

"While we were doing our preparation Charlie, we had cause to wonder if the same level of respectfulness and adoration continued after the wedding and whether, in accordance with the vows you exchanged, Mark did love, honour and cherish you…"

Stunned by my own complacency, I continue to stare not at John but through him, because I sense that his choice of words is connected with, whatever they must have uncovered, which might not be documented within any of my Files. With the benefit of hindsight, I can now appreciate how I have allowed myself to become too confident, and perhaps even too comfortable in my surroundings and now--albeit a little late--I understand that my earlier disconcertion was not caused by John's questions, but by my answers, which I had failed to notice were leading me towards the edge of this abyss. Beyond this moment, if I am going to prevent every image from illuminating the ugliness in my life, then this leading lady needs to play for more time, so that I can prepare an evasive strategy.

"Since you're the expert on the file Mr Bland---why don't you tell me?"

Suddenly, the impartiality has vanished and yet, maintaining the same smooth controlled delivery this leading lady finds his willingness to play her game disturbing.

"According to your psychological profiles, you were a perfect match. In fact, it would seem that you were the above average, happily married couple…"

As he pauses, John does that thing where he tilts his head a little to the right, before he adds. "But the file only reflects your relationship in public, and we would like you to tell us what married life was like when you were, behind the privacy of closed doors…"

More voyeurism! As Mark would say--*unnecessary vulgarity*--and irritated by the prospect of being defeated at my own game, my rebellious child has changed her parent's mind, and because this is not how my silence is destined to end, it's my turn to pose an unavoidable direct question.

"How much do you know already?"

"Enough…"

So my challenge has prompted his counterchallenge and yet, having learnt from a grand master, it is far from being enough to satisfy this leading lady.

"And how much is enough?"

As if he is deliberating the quantity John hesitates, before delivering his scripted reply, "Enough to suspect that Mark gave you reasonable grounds for wanting a divorce…"

Vague and indefinite, yet revealing enough to antagonize my rebellious child, and in light of the disturbing images which are looming on the horizon, if this young woman is to stand any chance of protecting the flesh covering these brittle bones, then every self-defence mechanism is demanding that I turn challenge, into outright confrontation.

"If that's the case, then why do you need to hear it from me Mr Bland?"

Silence---but unlike me, John does not need to justify his actions, and when his level-headed silence causes my petulant child, even more irritation her parent, forces me to snap my head around, so that I can involve our self-appointed arbitrator.

"What good can this do now? Since nothing can change what's happened, I don't believe that delving into the intimate details of my relationship with Mark is necessary…"

Like his partner in crime, Bill does not need to justify himself, and when he greets my demand with more silence, I'm determined that they will not take me alive without my putting up a fight to the death, and because my inner child knows that we cannot win, after taking one last fix of nicotine, I stub the cigarette out with a wilful intent, before re-directing my angry glare, until it locks onto my principal male.

"Well Mr Bland--if you know all the sordid details, then why don't you tell our invisible audience, what kind of sick satisfaction you can possibly gain from watching me bleed to death, all over your precious Commanding Officer's expensive Persian carpet?"

"All right Charlie," I hear our arbitrator conceding. "That's enough…"

Even sharper than my own, Bill's voice renders me silent. Far from being enough, my petulant child had barely taken off--much less reached full flight--but at least the strength of my aversion has won me an intervention, and because that intervention might lead to some kind of negotiation, I am prepared to listen to his explanation.

"I'm sure that everyone can appreciate the depth of your distaste, and whether you believe it or not from our vast experience, we can empathise with how you might feel…"

How can they comprehend, what this wounded human being is feeling? From my own vast experience, nobody ever bothers to ask me. Instead, people make assumptions about my feelings, but before I can challenge him, Bill has risen to his feet and he's walking across the study towards the cabinet as he continues to deliver his explanation.

"And you can rest assured that neither of us wishes to cause you any undue embarrassment or emotional distress…"

From the selection of bottles, which like everything else in my Godfather's study are neatly arranged on the cabinet, Bill selects the malt whisky bottle, and begins to pour healthy, or perhaps that should be unhealthy measures into two crystal glasses, before raising the bottle, so that he can gesture in his partner's direction, while he concludes his clarification.

"And lastly, despite your diversionary strategy, neither of us is seeking to gain any kind of satisfaction from examining the relationship you shared with Mark Daltry…"

Having poured a third overgenerous measure of whisky, Bill returns the bottle to its rightful place, as he adds, "However, I think you would have to agree that your relationship is relevant to recent events, and since we both felt it's important that everyone appreciates your point of view, this is a vital part of the proceedings…"

Now, any hope I harboured that this intervention might lead to any kind of negotiation has been dispelled, and while this leading lady should be impressed by their concern over the quality of my performance--in sheer disbelief--I am shaking my head.

"You don't have any idea what you're asking…"

Unmoved, Bill places one of the crystal glasses in front of me. Then, without either of them acknowledging my statement, John accepts the second malt whisky, leaving Bill free to return to the cabinet with a deliberate slowness, so that he can collect the remaining glass.

Damn that silence--waiting to be filled--only now, in addition to staring down into the murky depths of the abyss. I have to find a way to tackle their inflexibility.

"Surely, there has to be another way…"

Pleaded without daring to glance at John, my protective parent cautions me for having displayed such weakness, and as my fingers close around the crystal glass, I am so disillusioned and dejected out of desperation I find myself seeking divine intervention.

"My God, this is disgusting…"

"Yes it is disgusting Charlie," Bill agrees, in a soft tone of voice, and because he has returned to his designated place, I cast him a backward glance. "Perhaps it might make this a little easier, if you knew that because of some new information at his disposal Commander Maddox visited your step-mother, Helen yesterday afternoon, which means we're unlikely to be surprised, or shocked by anything you reveal to us…"

As I fail to stifle an exasperated groan, I'm damning my imperfect step-mother. Although it's true Helen had suspected that in the Daltry household, things might not be the epitome of marital bliss, which had led her to pose a few leading questions, how dare she interfere and yet, I know I'm being too harsh, because amidst her grief she would have been vulnerable, and therefore easily persuaded to air a few family skeletons.

Curiosity prompts me to glance at John, but lounging in the chair, savouring his malt whisky, he looks like a man who knows it all, when in reality he knows nothing and yet, it makes no difference to the outcome, because my protective parent will not allow me to provide them with the performance they expect from this leading lady, and as regrettable as it might be I have reached a final decision.

"I'm sorry--but I can't do this…"

Silence--followed not by immediate words, but through a well-timed demonstrative action, as John finishes his remaining whisky in one decisive mouthful.

"That's a load of crap Charlie," he announces. "There's no such thing as can't and if we're going to avoid any misunderstandings, I think it's time we clarified your position…"

How dare my principal male upstage his leading lady? More importantly, my protective parent thinks I have been misunderstood, and she wants me to protest my innocence, but having succeeded in gaining my full attention, John has no intention of being careless enough to afford me such an opportunity.

"Before dinner, you vowed to tell the truth, the whole truth, and nothing but the truth. In fact, if you remember rightly, it was part of a deal and although you did state that there may be times, when you might find it difficult--such as this issue over your marriage to Mark withdrawing altogether is not an option that's open to you…"

At last, I am able to protest. "I never said I wanted to withdraw…"

In response, John throws his leading lady what turns out to be a pre-emptive smile. "Although we are well aware that you haven't threatened to withdraw as I've explained, for future reference, I'm clarifying your position on behalf of us both…"

As if he is tempting me to fill his momentary silence John pauses, before delivering an unwelcome suggestion. "So while you're savouring your pure malt whisky, I strongly suggest that you think very carefully, before making any more sweeping statements about what you CAN'T--correction--WON'T DO…"

Of course, my principal male is right. How many times have I heard Lorna telling Bobby there's no such thing as CAN'T--and feeling like a child who has been reprimanded, I do as John suggested and yet, after sipping from the glass, because I still find myself facing that same abyss with unlimited time and space, and complete freedom of speech, the prospect of my delivering, an undignified account of my marriage remains abhorrent.

However, the pure malt whisky does help to clear my head, and it is not a question of my cooperation, but the manner in which they expect me to deliver my evidence. Perhaps if this was handled in a different way then I might be able to limit the damage to my dignity, which leads me to offer my agreement--albeit with a certain proviso.

"All right, but there has to be another way to do this…"

Behind me, Bill releases a wearisome sigh. "Of course, there's another way to do this Charlie. However, as you might expect from Special Operatives who have been trained in the techniques of psychological warfare, when it comes to asking and then re-asking, the same unavoidable direct question, until we acquire the correct response, you can rest assured that you wouldn't find the process any less disgusting…"

Considering that a few minutes ago, I found the swiftness and directness of John's questions disconcerting, my protective parent can appreciate his partner's warning.

"But there are two things you need to take into consideration. Firstly, having been assigned to protect you, we do have specific reasons for wanting to conduct this Interview our way, and secondly, our unsavoury talents in the interrogation department are normally reserved for people who are suspected of being involved in subversive activities, which might for example contravene the Official Secrets Act…"

Whatever Bill stated before he cited that example faded into obscurity, because between you and me, having been married to Mark, I never doubted their psychological training and yet, I still cannot find anything to justify this kind of voyeurism, until Bill robs me of the right to seek justification, as he hits me with another unconsidered consideration.

"However, before deciding whether you would prefer to enjoy our continued support, or subject yourself to our unremitting opposition, I think you ought to consider that while this is the first obstacle we've encountered, there will no doubt be similar sensitive or difficult issues we will need to overcome, before this Interview comes to an end…"

More threats or are they promises, and because it's hard to determine the lesser of the two evils yet again, curiosity prompts me to glance at John who responds by passing the edge of his hand across his throat in a swift severing motion, and when I can no longer hear the gentle purring of the recording equipment, I realize that in response to his partner's gesture, Bill must have depressed the pause button. Then, as if I have become invisible John   makes a strictly--*off the record*--suggestion directed at his partner, regarding how uncomfortable the proceedings could become for his leading lady, if she chooses to subject herself to their unremitting opposition.

 "Before dinner, we were undecided whether certain intelligence at our disposal might be useful. However, we did opt to bring the Interview into the study. Perhaps, this impasse might be an appropriate time for Charlie to hear, what the person of interest in connection with the Paris incident had to tell us about her loving, adoring husband…"

In abject horror, I'm shaking my head. Can this possibly get any worse? But, without needing to glance over my shoulder, I know that not even my sickened groan will prevent our arbitrator from endorsing his partner's suggestion.

"Although it's a relatively tame demonstration of our less savoury talents, I'm afraid that I have to agree with John, because after you've heard what was revealed to us, you might decide not only what your priorities should be, but also where your loyalties should lie …"

If there is any consolation to be found, at least the mystery has been solved as to not only why there are two pieces of recording equipment present, but also why I sensed that something had been uncovered and yet, when I can only detect the gentle purring sound from one of the machines, there is some solace to be   gained from the realization that my humiliation will not be made public, and until I hear John's voice, I'm telling herself that nothing can be revealed that I do not know, and because the hurting ceased a long time ago, the creation of these different images will not cause me any residual pain.

*"Okay Michelle, so after Mark made it clear that he had information he was prepared to sell to the highest bidder, did the man you refer to as his Sponsor agree to meet him?"*

*"Finalement..."*

*"How many times Michelle--English?"*

*"It's not always good—mais oui –finally..."*

*"And then once a Handler was appointed, did the deal go ahead?"*

*"Oui autant que je sache---err--how do you say--as far as I understand?"*

*"Not good enough Michelle--and we know you can do better..."*

Although we have never met, on the one hand we have shared a person of interest, shared the traitorous secrets of Mark's alternative existence and on the other hand, as Bill has enlightened me, perhaps worn down by having been asked unavoidable direct questions, which might have occurred, before the recording had been paused, there is a detectable irritability as the young woman barks her retort.

*"Que voulez-vous me dire? I can only repeat ce que I have told you--recouvrent et recouvrent, I am an administrateur, an organisateur--parce que ma réputation tend à proceed me, wherever I go, I am only told ce que je suis besoin de savoir--err-- no Handler's identite or their faces.  It's best for me to never attend any rendezvouses..."*

*"How did you know Mark wasn't setting you up?"*

*"Comment pouvez-vous dire cela dans English---feminine intuition?"*

*"If you continue to piss us off--perhaps you should consider that you cannot be returned to Paris, until we decide this Interview is over, and if you were delayed for too long, people might start asking questions about your disappearance. The kind of questions you might not find any easier to answer than ours..."*

Then, after a short pause, I hear a somewhat weary, yet resigned sigh---immediately followed by the young woman's admission.

"Both parties' offered---des garanties. The Sponsor would reveal son identite to Daltry, and in return, Mark would provide recorded evidence, which in the wrong hands would have ruined his---how do you say---his good negotiating reputation, and his credibility, not only with votre organization, but also with any other organization..."

"You mean---you---and your dubious reputation went to bed with him?"

As Bill warned me, his partner's responses are swift and direct. Instead of an interrogation it sounds as if he's conducting some kind of business transaction, and despite the starkness of his sexual innuendo, I'm still telling myself that nothing can be revealed, I do not know, and because the hurting ceased a long time ago, although the person of interest laughs at his suggestion, and I know the reason why she's amused, I console myself in the knowledge that over the years, I have built up an immunity to any emotional discomfort.

"Compte tenu de la possibilité--mais oui---given the opportunity, I would not have kicked such a man like Mark Daltry out of mon lit..."

"Yeah, yeah---we don't need a translator to understand. Perhaps we should add whore to the lengthy list of activities attributed to you, within our computer system..."

Not hurt, nor pain, but I was mistaken. Something is stirring, something that will not be supressed, and because my hands have started to tremble, my fingers tighten around the crystal glass, in anticipation of what is about to happen.

"Mon Dieu---one of your own people, and you never suspect him..."

"Isn't it remarkable how your English has improved Michelle? What do you mean, we never suspected? Never suspected what exactly?"

Despite the young woman's amusement being gained at my expense, because my hands which were trembling have started to shake, I find myself wanting my torturer to bring my misery to an end, by admitting the loathsome truth about the treasonous husband who was supposed to remain respectful and adoring after the wedding.

"The only personne que voulait que Mark in son lit, was a fair haired seventeen-year-old, who was well paid by the Sponsor, so that he could undertake sexual health screening, including HIV testing, before he spent quarante huit heures losing his virginity, in the Penthouse Suite at the hotel where Mark was staying..."

Silence--then John replies "You're obviously enjoying your moment in the limelight, so please don't hold back on our account why don't you carry on entertaining everyone?"

"What---même si vous ne me croyez pas, because neither of them was camera shy, there's a recording of everything that took place, during those two days, and that seventeen-year-old was worth every last euro. Mark's thing was inflicting punishment, and it is difficile de s'opposer, when you are bound and gagged--and forced to perform anywhere and everywhere, and during the oral sex, Mark was almost choking him, but he would have been--err--how do you say--doing him a favour parce-que afterwards, his life would have been over..."

In this woman's defence, I have listened in silence but now the glass can no longer conceal my shaking hands, and because I find myself not only wounded, but I also have a physical aching as a result of the sheer weight of my humiliation. So after swallowing the remaining malt whisky in one mouthful, as if I want the crystal to shatter into symbolic shards, I slam the glass down onto the desk, before rising to my feet.

"I don't have to listen to any more of this…"

"Yes you do…"

Since the damage has been done to this leading lady--albeit too fucking late--Bill must have depressed the pause button, so that he could silence the offensive dialogue, while on the other side of the desk, John remains seated and unperturbed that I'm standing, as I embark on what will turn out to be a vitriolic attack.

"Why John? Haven't I been subjected to enough humiliation?"

Then, when he continues to remain unperturbed and he makes no effort to defend himself, I launch my verbal onslaught. "I hate to disappoint you, but that attractive fair haired, seventeen-year-old virgin wasn't the first, and since young virgins were Mark's preference he wasn't the last, and if listening to that kind of crap provides you with some kind of sick sexual gratification, then I can provide you with the names of a few others..."

Perhaps he was unwilling to be drawn into time consuming clashes, but since I've brought the performance down to a personal level, I was guaranteed to achieve a reaction.

"When we returned from the Clunnell residence Charlie, you were warned about being verbally abuse, especially when it's on a personal level, and although you might have good reason to feel aggrieved about what has been revealed to us, in connection with your marriage that does not give you the right to hurl insults at either of us..."

Yes, this woman remembers. After being tricked into staying at H.Q., I had hurled so much abuse at the surveillance equipment, nobody was prepared to risk venturing into the guest suite. Then, when the cavalry had rematerialized I had vented my rage on them for having abandoned me and yet, I have to admit that I'm angry with the descriptive content of the dialogue instead of either of them, but as soon as I release John from my angry glare, he chooses to add his own personal insult to my original injury.

"Now, having felt obliged to introduce this other Interview, there is a valid reason for wanting you to hear some more. So if you've quite finished behaving like a disillusioned sixteen-year-old virgin, instead of an attractive young woman, perhaps we can continue..."

"And since I'm not a disillusioned sixteen-year-old virgin, do I have a choice?"

"No I'm afraid you don't--so sit down and listen..."

Ouch! Time to recap and it would seem that we have established three things. Firstly, this woman does not have any bargaining power. Secondly, I cannot make a dramatic exit, without appearing to withdraw, and thirdly, despite having unlimited time and space, and alleged complete freedom of speech, it would seem that there will be times when I will not have any choice, except to perform to order. But if my continued co-operation were to become an overriding issue, then that would make things difficult, and without considering the potential consequences of my action, I hear this woman issuing the ultimate challenge.

"And as an attractive young woman, what if I refuse to sit down and listen?"

Despite expecting another immediate response from John, he continues to remain seated and staring up at his leading lady's face, and because it's time for Bill to exert his authority, I hear him utter yet another wearisome sigh.

"Charlie if you refuse to sit down and listen, you will leave us no alternative, except to withdraw from this assignment, and if that should prove necessary, everything will have to be suspended, so that the Commander can assign other Special Operation's personnel who will need time, in order to familiarise themselves with the proceedings..."

Something else this adult had failed to consider. Time to recap the aforementioned recapping, because while I am not at liberty to withdraw from the proceedings, the two Special Operatives assigned to protect me are free to withdraw at any time. But perhaps more importantly, when this woman recalls that I would not be in this room, if I thought for one moment that I could obtain a fairer hearing--or better treatment elsewhere, and given the unsavoury alternatives, I elect to concede defeat and yet, as soon as I re-seat myself in my Godfather's chair, our arbitrator has the audacity to congratulate me, before he releases the pause button so that the offensive dialogue can continue.

"Thank you Charlie..."

*"C'est donc sans-err—is not relevant, because Mark is dead ..."*

*"Perhaps but what about Charlie Daltry--presumably, Mark did tell you that he was a married man..."*

"Bein sur--from what Mark described, his marriage into the Forsyth family made her a most valuable asset and afforded him la respectabilité, votre organisation required ..."

"And are you aware of what happened at 187 Cheltenham Way, during the early hours of 22ⁿᵈ June..."

Then, after another short silence, I hear John demanding, "Come on Michelle, the clock's still ticking..."

"Mais oui..."

"In that case, how much do you know and what do you know about the assailants?"

During the exchange, I have been staring at the desk, and in keeping with my sense of helplessness, I'm avoiding eye contact, because my humiliation is not yet complete.

"The Sponsor and Handler, they are---as I think you say---thorough people and because they want her dead, the Contract was issued to a freelancer and his two-man crew..."

" Why would anybody want her dead?"

"Je ne Sais pas--but maybe they think she knows too much about Mark's other--how do you say---his other life..."

Although I'm expecting another sharp retort from my principal male, Bill's somewhat less aggressive voice joins the exchange.

"This Contract could have been executed at any time during the last three months Michelle, but it wasn't..."

Yet more silence--and I must admit, it is somewhat disconcerting to learn that death could have come knocking at my door, any time during the last three months and yet, since Bill has not asked a direct question, the young woman chooses not to fill the silence, which leads him to persist with his line of enquiry.

"Then, once the freelancers were in the house, we now know they were present for at least fifty--possibly even sixty minutes--before being disturbed, but they still did not eliminate their primary target, and when it comes to a professional hit man and his two associates, who would have been eager to have the remainder of their money paid into the same pre-arranged account as their initial retainer, it struck us as odd---unless of course, the original Contract involved more than a basic elimination..."

"Pourquoi ne demandez-vous pas Mme Daltry..."

"Oh we will Michelle, but in the meantime we're asking you..."

"Je vous ai déjà dit maintes et maintes fois ..."

"Yeah, yeah," I hear John's cynical voice announcing "And we heard you the first time, but there still has to be more..."

"Elle est une belle femme---all I have heard is that they became distracted, and decided to have some fun..."

Then, in the next breath I hear the anger in John's voice, as he declares. "Fun---is that what you call having fun..."

"Peut-etre ---as you say--- perhaps she got what she deserved..."

"You malicious little bitch, Charlie Daltry was three months pregnant..."

Although I am impressed by the disgust in John's voice, as ironical as it might seem, I find myself wanting to hear her response and yet, because Bill has once again depressed the pause button silence has descended, but there is more. Perhaps it is something this woman does not know or maybe something they do not want me to hear, and because I will not be deprived as I snap my head around to look at Bill, I exercise this woman's prerogative to change my mind.

"Don't I get to hear the rest?"

Still more silence, and the expected is greeted by the unexpected, because now it is Bill who is detached and impartial, which can only suggest that it must be something my principal male does not want his leading lady to hear and yet, when I look back across the desk, so that I can confront him, John casts an affirmative nod in his partner's direction, and once the pause button is released the dialogue continues.

*"Tough shit, so it's a cruel world--how do you say it--ah oui--get over it..."*

Capitalizing on John's disgust, their person of interest in connection with the Paris incident has dared to antagonise him, not only through the haunting refrain of her laughter, but also her next unscripted suggestion.

*"Peut-etre, you should consider adding---WHORE---to the list of attributes she has in your computer records..."*

Amid the tension of the exchange, my naïve inner child had not anticipated that the moment of triumph would be overtaken by what sounded like a scuffle, but when a startled exclamation is followed by the young woman gasping for breath I lift my head, so that I can make eye contact with my principal male. Then, while we are both listening to Bill as he attempts to defuse the volatile situation, John's eyes never leave my face.

*"Although strangulation might seem like an apt way, in which to make the world a better place, there are two reasons, why you can't dispose of her---at least not yet? Firstly, like her filthy mouth, you don't know where the rest of her has been, and you wouldn't want to risk catching a transmittable disease, and secondly, now that she's known to us, we can have her picked up anytime we choose, and since she'll be more use if she's back on the streets of Paris, I'm afraid we'll have to return her in the same condition, as when she arrived..."*

In the next few intense moments, I find myself holding my own breath, until I hear the young woman gasping for air, but while John must have eased the hold around her throat, allowing her to breathe--confident that he will not kill her--she remains unrepentant.

*"Vous pouvez faire tout Ce que vous voulez me, but it won't change anything, because the freelancer and his two man associates have an exclusive Contract to fulfil and nobody not even you can..."*

Suddenly, the words are overtaken by another even sharper gasp than the last, and because John's fingers must have tightened around her throat for a second time, he repays the compliment by issuing a threat of his own.

*"As regrettable as it might seem my colleague's right. However, you might like to consider why the career path you've chosen, doesn't come with a pension plan, and when the day dawns that someone younger and more ambitious than you, decides they want to take your place as an administrator and an organiser, I hope that I'm present, because after they finish amusing themselves at your expense, and preferably before someone brings your misery to an end on a permanent basis, I'd like to ask you what it felt like to have had that much FUN?"*

In the next instant, when I hear the young woman's sharp intake of oxygen John issues her with a final demand. *"Okay--for the time being Michelle, I think we're finished with you, and since you must have had plenty of practice, unless you would prefer one of us to use reasonable force to achieve the same result, I suggest you turn around and place the palms of your hands against the wall..."*

After hearing the familiar clinking sound, which is followed by a half-stifled and yet, no less audible exclamation, John suggests, *"Oh my apologies if I've snapped the cuff closed a little tighter than usual. Ahead of our next encounter--and there will be a next time--why don't you think of it as a poignant reminder of our first face to face meeting?"*

Next--there is brief pause, and from my own experience I'm anticipating the second cuff being snapped closed, and as it produces a less audible pained gasp, John adds. *"Besides, if you were too comfortable, during the return flight to Paris, you might not learn the error of your ways, and we wouldn't want you to risk coming back into the country Michelle unless of course, it is at our invitation..."*

Clearly not expecting a response, I hear a tell-tale buzzing sound which as I recall from my time at H.Q. meant that someone else's presence had been requested inside the

Interview room, and since John had neutralized any potential threat from the young woman, the next voice belongs to Bill.

*"For the time being, we're finished with her, so you can get her out of here, but before she leaves this room make sure she's hooded, and since she has a filthy mouth over which she seems have no control, if she so much as utters a sound during her return journey, you have our permission to gag her..."*

In the present tense of the primary performance, the two principal performers are still maintaining eye to eye contact, and even though the secondary performance has been concluded, there is a noticeable respectfulness in John's next direct question.

"Have you heard enough Charlie?"

"Yes thank you..."

With a resounding click, the secondary performance is brought to an end, and because I need time to re-evaluate my position, I remove another dramatic prop from the packet, and yet, having now heard more than enough, I have to admit that there seems to be three reasons why John was adamant that irrespective of how degrading or humiliating the revelations might be, I should sit down and continue listening.

Firstly, the cavalry needed to establish, what information they had in their possession about Mark's sexual predilections. Secondly, having been assigned to protect me, because there could never be any justification for what had happened in the early hours of June 22, they wanted me to hear how they had defended my reputation. Then, last but by no means least in third place--between you and me--I think you would agree that despite being told numerous times, how I will have to trust them to know what they are doing until now, there has been no evidence that they are acting in my best interests, but as an added bonus, through my determination to hear, the remaining exchanges after Bill had paused the play-back my protectors have provided me with some proof as to their trustworthiness.

Sparking the lighter's small flame, the cigarette reaches my lips before being lit, and I'm thinking that nothing can alter the fact that in addition to the unfulfilled Contract, I am facing that same abyss, and yet of all the characters in this travesty of justice, this adult is the only person who can colour all the grey areas with the absolute truth--albeit an ugly hideous truth--and if they know so much then why am I so reticent? Indeed, in all honesty, it is not only the humiliation over Mark's sexual preference, and because this woman knows that there are even darker, more chilling images lurking around the next corner, and as Bill has cautioned me, they will create more obstacles which we will need to overcome.

Having reviewed all the evidence in private, you have helped me to reach a decision and after exhaling the smoke from my lungs, I shrug my shoulders in a casual way, before bringing the silence to an end. "Everyone regarded my husband as being incorruptible, and because nobody suspected that he was a fraudster, Mark used and abused not only my trust, but also the trust of anyone who could be of value to him, and while I'm still not sure, whether I can do this your way--at least not without some support I am willing to try…"

This leading lady's submission has not been won without considerable difficulty, and when John acknowledges my decision through a single respectful nod, I tap the ash from my cigarette, and as Bill explains the reason for our unscheduled intermission to our wider audience, I begin collating my disjointed memories.

"The time is 19:55 on the 29th of June. The same persons are present and no other surveillance equipment is being used. After a ten-minute recess, Charlie Anne Daltry, nee Forsyth has had an opportunity to consider, how she wants this Interview to proceed. As a result, she has decided to continue exercising her right to complete freedom of speech. In addition, as previously requested, Charlie has now agreed to disclose in her own words, the intimate details of the marital relationship she shared with Mark Daltry…"

It would seem that when it comes to being economical with the truth I am not alone, and having noted how Bill has made no direct reference to the existence of the other recording, with the silence being disturbed by nothing except the gentle purring from the equipment, this adult is as prepared as anyone could be to recommence the story of her life.

"After the wedding, I became everything Mark expected his wife to be, and from the beginning, I accepted that his work as an International Negotiator and Trouble-shooter on behalf of Special Operations would take priority over everything else…"

"Were you happy Charlie?"

Spontaneously, a light-hearted laugh escapes. "I suppose that everyone's definition of happiness would be different Mr Bland. However, after our whirlwind romance, we seemed to be consumed by the desire to discover new things about each other that during the first twelve months, Mark never gave me any reason to doubt that he loved me--or I don't think he did--until things began to change between us…"

Aware that my next statement could be misconstrued, there is a momentary reticence on my part. "Having grown up in the Forsyth household, I took it for granted that four out of every seven nights, Mark's work commitments meant that he couldn't sleep in his own bed. Of course at that time, I wasn't aware that he was sleeping, in someone-else's bed--or to be more precise, those beds occupied by fair-haired, virginal young men or even boys…"

Considering the recent evidence presented to me my decision to side-step, what kind of action had been taking place in our marital bed was deliberate, but if I had thought John would permit me to evade the issue, then I must have been delusional.

"And what about the sexual side of your marriage?"

Pinned down, I have to behave like an adult and blurt out the shameful truth. "For my first visit to 187 Cheltenham Way, I had dressed with the sole intention of seducing him, and because I had never experienced any kind of eroticism I found it exhilarating, until I later learnt that when it came to crime and punishment, he favoured the hard core variety, with Mark making sure that he was the one delivering the chastisement…"

Opposite me, I'm grateful when John does nothing, except nod his appreciation. "Naturally, although Mark's sexual preference might have been for young men, whenever it suited him, and with certain provisos, he would participate in straight sexual activity…"

"You stated that you'd never had any reason to doubt that Mark loved you, *until things between you changed*, for the benefit of the recording, can you be more specific?"

It is as if John knows that those changes will lead to the aforementioned chilling images lurking around the corner. Nevertheless, I'm determined to maintain eye contact. "Being honoured and cherished until death us did part weren't vital ingredients, but like any woman, I did have some expectations over the loving and caring part of the relationship, and when I sensed that Mark was distancing himself from me, there was a rapid decline…"

"Did you try to discuss it with Mark?"

In a perverse kind of way, I find his naivety fetching. "Really, Mr Bland--I would have thought that both of you would know that along with the expressionless poker face necessary to become a successful International Negotiator and Trouble-shooter, Mark also had to be mean, moody and magnificent. So he was an expert when it came to disregarding anything he thought was irrelevant, but when I kept questioning my role in his life, he seemed to become more possessive, until that possessiveness developed an unhealthy curiosity about my previous relationships with men…"

From John's expression, it is obvious that he knows where this is leading. "Apparently someone from my misspent youth had not only congratulated my husband upon his marriage, but also advised Mark about the rumours that had circulated regarding my liaison with a rising political superstar, which had supposedly left me pregnant. However, in order to avoid the scandal of multiple DNA tests, after telling the top secret brigade that I'd slept with so many men I couldn't identify the culprit, I'd agreed to have a termination, before being shipped off on an extended vacation…"

"And presumably Mark wanted to know about the rumours?"

Tapping the ash from my cigarette, I nod my agreement. "Of course Mark was curious, and because I thought it might alleviate his concerns, I assured him that I was never promiscuous, and up until that brief relationship I had been a virgin and then, after the baby was born I had chosen to remain celibate, until that evening at 187 Cheltenham Way…"

"And was that enough to satisfy Mark's unhealthy curiosity?"

Remembering my frustration at being worn down, I utter a third--albeit cynical laugh. "Instead of healing the rift, it only made things worse and usually, after Mark's third generous pure malt whisky as we were about to go to bed, he'd start to ask more direct questions. Questions like--why hadn't Bobby's father wanted to marry me? Was it because he had a wife? Did he have a family--and let's not leave out--had he been good in bed?"

Momentarily fearful, I hesitate again, before continuing, "Casting himself in the role of the aggrieved husband, enabled Mark to give an award winning performance. He was blaming my sexual relationship with another man for the rift between us, and because I remained unconvinced that answering his questions would clear the air, I kept reminding him that after my father had explained that I had a son, with whom I maintained discreet contact, Mark had assured me that despite my past indiscretions, he still wanted to marry me…"

"Did you consider separation or divorce?"

"Blissfully unaware of Mark's dual sexuality, there wasn't any reason why I should have considered divorce, and until I received a text message from Lorna's brother, concerning a letter he had received, I hadn't given any serious thought to separation…"

There is something missing, something else I should have clarified. "As God is my witness, I never expected anything from Bobby's father. However, the Major had felt it necessary to advise him of my decision not to terminate the pregnancy, and once he knew the baby was being adopted by a close friend, instead of complete strangers, then provided his anonymity remained intact, he intended to support his son, and until I received that letter, every six months a banker's draft had arrived at Colin's office…"

Leaning forward, I use excessive force to extinguish my cigarette. "But his letter confirmed that having reneged on our agreement, he regarded any obligation he had to--*the child*--as having been fulfilled, and he was withdrawing his financial support…"

"You sound angry Charlie---but it's our experience that anger masks hurt…"

"Oh I had bypassed being angry and moved straight to being fucking furious. Thanks to the interest from my trust fund, and Colin's careful administration of Bobby's affairs, my son has never wanted for anything. So the last thing he needed was his father's conscience money. In fact, those banker's drafts were deposited in a high interest savings account to fund his University education. However, I was so infuriated--and yes I admit that on Bobby's behalf I was hurt that his father should think he could make us suffer by withdrawing his money, I gave Colin specific instructions that if any more banker's drafts did arrive, then accompanied by my written response, they were to be returned to the issuing bank…"

"And did the letter from Bobby's father make any direct reference which would have implicated Mark?"

"No, but there's no such thing as a coincidence, and prior to Mark asking those direct questions there hadn't been any difficulties, and when I challenged him, Mark didn't even have the decency to deny it. Of course, he tried to brush it aside by telling me, he would reimburse me for any financial losses, but that wasn't the point, and because I suspected that he had used my son in some underhand way, I refused to let the matter drop…"

"Did Mark explain how he had discovered the identity of Bobby's father?"

"In all fairness, I never asked him," I admit. "But then my overriding concern was his motivation, because for someone who was supposed to be squeaky clean, he must have had an ulterior motive for contacting Bobby's father…"

"And after you discovered his ulterior motive, it stands to reason that you must have learnt the truth about Mark's alternative lifestyle…"

"Yes," I agree, before I attempt to avoid the intimate details by adding. "Eventually, I did learn the truth…"

"That's a little vague Charlie. Do you think you could be more specific?"

Now, those darker and more chilling images have drawn too close for comfort, and despite this woman choosing to remain silent, I know that John will not be deterred. "Well Charlie--how and when did you find out the truth about Mark's double life?"

In sheer desperation, I attempt to answer his question with a question of my own choosing. "Isn't it enough for you to know that it was Mark who told me?"

More silence, but not of my choosing, and for as long as the principal performers continue to stare at each other, my protective parent wants to believe that John might be prepared to accept my admission of guilt as being more than enough. However, this adult has overlooked that one important factor. In his appointed role, our arbitrator has the power to uphold, or overrule any decision or redirect the proceedings whenever he chooses.

"I'm sorry, it isn't enough Charlie," Bill announces, and when I turn my head to look at him, he picks up his somewhat old fashioned, notepad from the desk. "When asked, you confirmed that you hadn't given any serious consideration to divorce or separation, because you were unaware of Mark's dual sexuality, and until you received the letter from Bobby's father you didn't have anything to support your suspicions  However, until three months ago because you continued to live together as husband and wife, we feel it's in your own…"

If you will pardon my unfortunate play on words--determined not to be beaten--I hear myself snapping. "Yes Mr Powell, despite being aware of what might be in my best interests, the fact remains--Mark was my husband--so why do I need to justify…"

As Bill utters one of his wearisome sighs, it silences me in mid-sentence. "You don't understand Charlie. In your case, there had to be a reason--a damned good reason--why you would choose to remain in an empty, loveless marriage, unless you had no choice. At the very least, we believe you must have put up some kind of resistance…"

Returning to that unfortunate play on words, I suppose my protective parent did put up some kind of resistance, but being taller, faster and stronger, it was nothing more than the token kind because once we understood Mark's power and my pain threshold, those two parameters brought a dynamic new understanding to an ailing relationship.

As for my inquisitors, their tenacity is proving to be remarkable enough to warrant a backhanded compliment, and as my gaze drifts between them there can be no avoiding, the depth of my resentment at the unreasonableness of their expectations.

"My God, I thought I'd met more than my fair share of insensitive bastards, but within this unequal and imbalanced scenario, I suspect that since the odds are stacked, two to one against me, you might surpass all of your predecessors…"

Considering that I have been cautioned twice about levelling personal insults, I have cause to wonder whether my compliment might generate another reprimand, but there is no rebuke and since my inquisitors have clarified my position regarding withdrawal, I risk rising to my feet because if this has got to be done their way, then this adult is so consumed with shame at what I am being forced to disclose, I need to put some distance between myself, and my principal male. So with a deliberate slowness I turn away, and start to walk the length of what is beginning to resemble a prison cell, until I reach the large Victorian window, but despite the spectacular view across the lake the bullet proof glass, serves as a reminder that like everything else in my life the peacefulness is contradictory.

Feeling no less ashamed of what took place between husband and wife especially when I could have brought the degradation to an abrupt end. But if I had utilized my own unique resources, then Mark would have discovered something far more valuable than the identity of the man who had fathered my son.

Outside the daylight is beginning to fade, and soon the remaining story of this woman's life will be shrouded in darkness, and as if it will afford me some kind of moral support, I lean against the wood panelled recess. However, when my protective parent believes that I am as prepared as I will ever be to commence my narrative, one of those darker--more chilling images has ceased to be suspended, and in the hallway of 187 Cheltenham Way, I am heading

*Towards the front door with the sole intention of leaving. However, in the next few minutes, two alleged adults were destined to play a different game. Nevertheless, with my overnight bag clutched in my left hand and my house and car keys encased in the other, I was oblivious to the fact that not only during the remaining hours of that night, but also those leading into the new day yet again, my existence would be turned upside down.*

Strictly off the official record, it is important to acknowledge that I was not acting on a whimsical notion. My decision had been based on the premise that I was free to leave, whenever I chose to do so, and because once again, Mark had refused to engage in any kind of dialogue about the approach he had made to Bobby's father--*if you will pardon a subtler play on words*--I had left my husband in his study nursing his third, generous measure of pure malt whisky, while I had gone upstairs to pack. *But before my hand could touch the door handle, coming from behind me, Mark posed a question of his own choosing.*

*"It's late and because it's dark outside, where do you think you're going Charlie?"*

*Although his question caused me to hesitate in my naivety, I heard myself issuing, what I believed to be a valid ultimatum. "You don't seem to understand that since my son's anonymity is priceless, until you're willing to explain why you took it upon yourself to approach his father I'm going to stay with my father and Helen. Even though I suspect it's too late to rekindle, any fondness you once felt towards me--perhaps if we spend some time apart, my absence might make you value my presence…"*

*"Because that man--if indeed he could be described as a man--deserted you, apart from defending my wife's reputation, what other reason would your husband need, and before things get out of hand, why don't you put the bag down, because we both know you aren't going anywhere?"*

*"Please Mark, if I've told you once, then I must have told you a thousand times that it was me, and not Bobby's father who ended the affair, but that's not the point. Surely, you must be able to see that we're going round in ever decreasing circles?"*

*Choosing to challenge him, I reached out, but the minute my fingers touched the door handle, Mark delivered what I later realized was his first veiled threat.*

*"I'm afraid I cannot allow you to go anywhere, least of all permit you to go running back--as if you were a spoilt brat--to daddy's house so that you can tell tales of woe and misery in the Daltry household…"*

*Unable to move forward or back, I remained frozen in time and yet, Mark was so close, I could smell the whisky on his breath. "As I've explained Charlie, before things can get out of hand would you please put the bag down?"*

*"And what if I refuse?"*

*As his hand seized hold of my left arm, Mark exerted enough pressure on my wrist to cause me to cry out, and despite trying to maintain my hold on the overnight bag it seemed to slip through my fingers, until it landed with a dull thudding sound at my feet, but it still*

wasn't enough to satisfy my husband, and in an intimidating tone of voice, he added, "And since you don't need your house or car keys anymore, I want you to give them to me..."

Only too aware that they were my only means of escape, as my grasp on the keys tightened, in sheer desperation my voice was raised, as I gasped, "No Mark--this is ridiculous, you can't keep me here against my will--I have every right..."

Regrettably, because Mark had clasped his hand over my mouth the rest of my protest failed to materialize, and having silenced me, he explained, "I'm afraid, I also can't allow you to disturb anyone else, in case it triggers a security alert, especially when we're about to embark upon a night of adult passion and if you don't give me your keys Charlie, you'll leave me no alternative, except to take them by force..."

Although Mark was holding me pinned against him with his hand clasped over my mouth, I still tried to writhe myself free. However, against someone with his Specialist training my resistance was overcome with comparative ease and then, not content with prising the keys from my hand, Mark ignored my frustrated groan, and once again tightened his hold which rendered me motionless, so that he could offer me an unpleasant opportunity.

"Despite the fact that you don't seem to appreciate the gravity of the situation you have created, if you give me your word that you won't do anything stupid, like shouting or screaming, I am prepared to release you. Do I have your agreement Charlie?"

Left with no alternative I nodded, but as soon as he loosened his hold, Mark turned me around, and after seizing hold of my arm he jerked me towards him.

"What we seem to have encountered is a basic lack of understanding," Mark declared with a menacing overtone. "To be more precise, your failure to understand that there will be no trial separations, or any ridiculous talk about divorce, because this marriage will only be over, when I decide that you have outlived your usefulness..."

"My usefulness--what do you mean?"

"Surely, someone with your array of impressive--albeit underused--qualifications, must have worked it out by now Charlie?"

In all honesty, I had never thought that there was anything to work out, but in that same horrific instant some of the jigsaw pieces slotted into place, and staring up at him, this woman realized that this monster bore no resemblance to the man I had married, the same man who--not so long ago--had told me over and over again how much he loved me.

No, standing in front of this woman was a complete stranger, and with a sense of fearfulness I tried to pull away, and when his vice like grip prevented me from gaining my freedom, without considering the consequences of my action, I lowered my head and raised my arm, so that I could sink my teeth into the back of his hand, but having overlooked the fact that nothing begets violence, except more violence, although Mark released me, there was no time to capitalize upon my freedom, because reacting without any premeditated thought, Mark's uninjured right hand was being propelled towards my face, and as it reached its target, he exclaimed, "You malicious bitch!"

Despite his penchant for erotic games, until that moment none of them had involved actual physical violence. So initially I was too shocked to react, but then as if it might help soothe the burning flesh, I placed the palm of my hand against the side of my face, causing Mark to issue me with an advance warning about his intentions.

"That was a stupid mistake, because in order to ensure that you understand how acts of violence on your part will not be tolerated, I'll have to make you pay a high price..."

Then, as I watched him storming into the living room, I realized that whatever price he was going to make me pay, clemency would not be a consideration when it came to calculating the amount, and when Mark rematerialized, carrying what I knew from one bitter experience was a three-inch leather collar with a central bulldog clip, despite hating my display of weakness, I pleaded with him.

"I'm sorry Mark--please don't do this…"

"It's too late to be sorry Charlie. If you'd only had the wherewithal to learn your place in my life and then, known how to keep it none of this unpleasantness would be necessary. So as part of the price you have to pay you're going to wear the collar, and all you have to decide is whether you want us to do this the easy way or the hard way?"

Naturally, since this monster would have preferred--us--to do it the hard way, I chose to rob him of the satisfaction by turning around, and lifting my hair of my own volition, so that he could encircle the collar around my neck, and when he ordered me to place the palms of my hands on the wall to enable him to achieve the degree of resistance he desired, while he buckled the two straps, much tighter than was necessary, from the bottom of my heart I hoped--correction--I prayed that my obedience would cause him the maximum amount of frustration, especially when Mark used his body weight to crush me against the wall, so that in readiness for his intended punishment, he could whisper in my ear.

"After tonight, you'll appreciate that it would have been healthier if you had also learnt how to keep your mouth shut. But if I am ever going to achieve any lasting peace from your incessant whinging, then I suppose your questions need to be answered. Firstly, the reasons why I cannot permit you to go running around telling tales of woe and misery, and secondly that you understand what kind of behaviour I expect from my wife…"

"Whatever those expectations might be Mark," I dared to answer back, as he turned me around. "I promise you that they will have to be fulfilled over my unresponsive body…"

Tossing his head back, Mark laughed. "Why do you always have to indulge in your amateurish histrionics? But I suppose that once you've outlived your usefulness, it might be possible to arrange something involving--your unresponsive body…"

Having shared that unhealthy insight, Mark went back into the living room, and minutes later, when he returned carrying the bottle of malt whisky, as if it were in retaliation for robbing him of that earlier satisfaction, he subjected me to the final humiliation by clipping the leash onto the bulldog ring, so that as if I was a dog, he could lead me upstairs into the master bedroom, where I was instructed to strip in a slow and provocative way.

Although my trembling fingers made it difficult I somehow managed, but as soon as I was naked, Mark ordered me to wear a sleazy peephole bra and cheap split crotch knickers and then, dispensing with any lubrication or foreplay, while he subjected me to the first non-consensual and yet, conventional sexual activity between husband and wife, as if I was a prostitute who had been paid to satisfy him, he taunted me by describing his wife's shortcomings in the bedroom department. But that was only the beginning, and by the time it came to an end, I understood the reasons why I had no choice, except to maintain my silence, and within the prison my husband had constructed for me I had not only learnt my place, but also knew why I had to keep it, and when the whisky finally rendered him incapable of any further physical or emotional abuse, Mark had shared the intimate details about his alternative lifestyle, including his sexual preference for fair-haired, virginal young men, and of course the real reason why he had chosen to marry not only any woman, but this particular specimen and believe me love had never been a consideration.

What does love ever have to do with anything anyway? Back in the study, this latest lapse in concentration has been briefer than the last--not that it would cause any difficulties, especially when we have established that I can take whatever time I need whenever it's needed, and as if the gesture will help protect me, I wrap my arms around myself, before admitting in a hushed voice. "I'm sorry, I seem to be struggling with what took place…"

Like my husband, Bill's voice comes from behind me. "There's no need to apologise. Perhaps it might help, if you knew that like your first visit to the Daltry house--albeit fragmented--you have voiced some of your recollections about what happened between you and Mark on the night you intended to commence a trial separation…"

Help me--and how is that supposed to help me? Instead of helping, I'm mortified at having spoken out loud, not only for the benefit of my inquisitors, but also our wider audience, and in the vain hope that the increasing darkness might swallow me up, I continue to stare out of the window. while Bill is delivering his exposé

"Summarizing your recollections, this is what you brought to our attention: -

1. That night Mark prevented you from going to stay with your father and Helen.
2. To make sure, he relieved you of your house and car keys.
3. After biting the back of his hand Mark reacted by using disproportionate violence.
4. Then, after securing…."

"Please Bill," I beseech him suddenly, but then without thinking it through to the end, I rush my attempted explanation. "I can't bear to hear anymore, because it's too…"

Despite being fragmented and recapped as impersonal bullet points, it remains too damn graphic, which makes me afraid to look over my shoulder in case I might discover their piteous expressions, because the last thing this woman deserves is to be pitied. In fact--albeit three years and eleven months too late--what I need is an escape strategy and yet, the rest will have to be revealed, but maybe Bill wanted me to realize that in their daily life, since this ugliness must constitute routine procedure, the cavalry are not in the least embarrassed or mortified by my revelations, and because I have found the words I need to express my feelings, they enable me to disturb their continued respectful silence.

"Since it's my understanding that it's in my best interest to make everyone aware of my point of view by telling my own story, I am willing to continue doing this your way, as long as you appreciate that some parts might be too sensitive, or too painful for me to…"

"Charlie," Bill interrupts me. "Any fears you might have are unfounded because if we think you can't continue, then having been assigned to protect you, it's our responsibility to ensure that you don't fall. Furthermore, if by accident you should do so, then you can rest assured that one of us will catch you long before you hit ground zero…"

Still unable to look back, I'm thinking that once they know everything, their collective desire to catch me if I'm falling might be short lived and yet, inch by painful inch, I know that somehow I need to keep moving towards the end of this woman's life story.

"After Mark took me and the bottle of pure malt whisky upstairs, not content with expecting me to strip in a slow and provocative way, he made me wear seedy underwear more befitting a prostitute than his wife and then, he forced me over to the dressing table where he--I'm sorry--during an ordeal which lasted over three hours, I was going to describe what Mark did using the politically correct terminology, because when it started it was non-consensual regular husband and wife sexual intercourse. But that is an inadequate description what took place and--during those hours--he repeatedly raped me…"

When I hear the resentment that has crept into my voice, it causes me to pause long enough to re-establish my equilibrium. "Whatever might have presented itself as enthralling and exciting between two consenting adults before those hours, when it came to delivering my punishment, using restraints and gags, and I discovered that my husband did have a varied collection of gags--some of which were more comfortable than others--only on that night Mark wasn't in a comfort giving frame of mind, and yet regardless of the copious amount of whisky he consumed, he still managed to indulge in his erotic fantasies. But he saved the best, or the worst until last, and after telling me how he preferred fair-haired young men who were virgins--despite being the wrong sex--I cannot deny that I was a virgin…"

Perhaps for no other reason than I feel overwhelmed, by the depth of Mark's depravity, the correct words fail to emerge and yet, without putting his words into my mouth,

Bill offers me some assistance "It's okay Charlie. You don't need to be more explicit, we accept that on that night, Mark must have introduced you to full penetration anal sex…."

Now that it has been admitted as evidence, I find the courage to glance over my shoulder in Bill's direction, as I offer him my confirmation. "It was his grand finale…"

As my gaze drifts from Bill towards my principal male, I'm greeted by a rare display of emotion, and in addition to shaking his head, John's expression confirms his disgust at my last revelation. However, like their pity, sympathy might cause me to remove the finger which I have--in the metaphorical sense--lodged in the crack in my imaginary dam, because if I allow the flood gates to open, I might become inconsolable. Instead, I redirect my gaze back out of the window, as I continue to explain. "Eventually, Mark released me. Bruised, battered and bleeding from his grand finale, I found myself curled in the foetal position on our marital bed, but while the whisky had robbed him of the ability to perform any further sexual assaults until he passed out, I was forced to listen to his drunken verbalizations, which were designed to rob me of any remaining dignity. Nevertheless, Mark told me why he had married me, and as I had come to suspect love had never been a consideration. Since his dual sexuality could have proved to be problematic if he found himself in a compromising situation, Mark had decided that what he needed was the façade of a heterosexual relationship. So I'm afraid a marriage of convenience was the self-sacrifice, my loving and adoring husband had been willing to make…"

Pain, sorrow, regret or perhaps a mixture of all three, in any event without removing my finger from that crack in the dam, two stray tears overspill from the pools of liquid welling up in my eyes. Brushing them away, I am relieved that the cavalry cannot witness my display of weakness, but I must have allowed the silence to linger or maybe on a subconscious level, I was testing our arbitrator further, because not to be proven lacking, and delivered in a quiet, yet concerned voice, Bill enquires, "Are you all right Charlie?"

Am I all right? Between you and me, one has to wonder what our wider audience might conceive rightness to be. On a personal level, thanks to the people around me, I suspect that I have never been all right in my entire life. However, it seems safe to leave my safe haven, and after unfolding my arms I turn away from the window, and begin the slow walk back across what is beginning to feel even more like a prison cell and yet, it's not until I reach the desk that I am able to achieve eye contact with John, and as I reseat myself in my Godfather's chair, he poses the obvious question.

"During his drunken verbalizations, did Mark tell you the real reason why he had approached Bobby's father?"

Oh why did everything connected to my husband have to be so damned intricate, and after sighing, I attempt to explain. "You have to bear in mind that Mark divulged some information during that night and then, over an extended period of time, he revealed more details about his life, and once he had the backing of the Forsyth name, it had increased his bargaining power, which meant he was more influential at any negotiating table. Then, after approaching Bobby's father it had started with the occasional piece of--insider--information, such as proposed Parliamentary changes to Foreign Aid, or Defence contracts. However, having grown up in the Forsyth household, I understood that like my father, Mark must have been approached regarding possible advance warnings, which could give certain parties an unfair advantage during negotiations…"

Reaching out, I touch my cigarettes. "But unlike my father, once Mark came to appreciate the financial rewards, if he started putting the right piece of information into the wrong hands, or the wrong piece of information into the right hands that's when he decided to betray everyone who trusted him, including Special Operations and his country…"

At some point I must have been too ashamed of my husband's treachery that I've severed eye contact with John and yet, when I realize that up until this moment in the story of my life--apart from maintaining my silence--I have done nothing wrong, and after lifting my head, I cast a weak smile in his direction. "In keeping with acts of treachery, it was very subtle, and Mark was clever enough to ensure that his security systems were as infallible as possible. In fact, considering the regular security screening we both had to undertake, Mark must have been a proficient traitor to be able to hide his dual sexuality, and his decision to fund his own private pension plan, because until the early hours of the 22$^{nd}$ June, nobody had any reason to doubt, either his truthfulness or his loyalty…"

"Clearly, discovering the devastating truth had a big impact on you Charlie. However, if you had…"

Believing myself to be way ahead of him, I dare to interrupt. "If you're about to imply, or even suggest that I should have done the decent thing, then I would draw your attention to the following--firstly, I was not my husband's keeper and secondly, he was taller, faster and stronger than me, and in third place for the benefit of the recording, I would like to state quite categorically that when it came to the financial side of my husband's treachery, I never benefitted from any ill-gotten gains, because in an attempt to conceal, its final destination any money would have--no doubt--passed through many accounting facilities, before being deposited in some obscure off shore bank account…"

Not witnessed by our wider audience, John is smiling. "Although I'm confident, everyone will be reassured by your clarification, I was only going to confirm that if you had been able to approach Commander Maddox, then Major Forsyth would have been obliged to resign his command for having conspired to conceal, the identity of Bobby's father who would have also been forced to tender his resignation. In addition, together with Mark the three of them would have been arrested and charged, not only with attempting to pervert the course of justice, but also with conspiring to commit offences in accordance with the Official Secrets Act and the Prevention of Terrorism Act…"

Oops! I guess that's what happens when one jumps into the pool without ensuring that one's water wings will stop them from sinking like a stone and yet, I'm so impressed, I cast him a congratulatory nod, before remarking, "When you put it like that Mr Bland, it seems to be a great pity that we cannot resurrect the death penalty in respect of treasonous acts which endanger the life of innocent people…"

Then, I pause long enough for the strength of my position to be acknowledged. "But you're right Mr Bland. Even if I had been in a position where I could have gone public, it would have been a mess, and my main concern had been that Lorna and Bobby didn't end up as a headline in the newspapers. However, learning that my husband was a lying, cheating, traitorous, scum-bag did prompt a few rash threats to emerge, but while I understood that further violence was a constant risk, Mark knew that he wouldn't have to resort to anything quite so drastic to guarantee my continued silence…"

"Because you had your own fair-haired young man who together with Lorna needed your protection…"

As I am remembering, my protective parent causes me to clench my fists. "Yet again, you have to appreciate that for a long time--no matter what happened--it was always as if Mark was one step ahead of me. Naturally, I didn't keep anything relating to Lorna or Bobby at 187 Cheltenham Way. At least nothing personal that could have identified them, but when I started making rash threats about involving my father, Mark showed me some photographs, he had in his possession. They proved that he knew what kind of car Lorna drove, and which private school Bobby attended. Then, Mark took great delight in describing, not only the psychological problems, but also the pathological disorders of the people, he had hired to trace the Clunnell's, so that the photographs could be taken…"

In need of a dramatic prop at last I remove a cigarette from the packet, but my hand is trembling, and when I click the lighter, and it refuses to spark into flame, not once, not twice, not even at the third attempt, without asking permission, John has the audacity to reach across the desk and when his hand covers mine, I'm startled by his touch.

As I remember from when he caught me as I was falling in the bathroom, back at the house, despite having strong hands his grasp is warm and gentle, and when my eyes find his face, I allow him to retrieve the lighter from between my trembling fingers, and as if to annoy me, it sparks into flame at his first attempt. Then, with his hand covering mine, John steadies the trembling and keeps the flame motionless, so that I can light my cigarette.

During those few moments, something passed between us, but whatever it was, it is neither up for debate, nor explanation, and as John returns the lighter to its rightful place, for the benefit of the official recording, he expresses what appears to be an innocent observation.

"When Mark showed you the photographs he had commissioned, the implied threat towards Bobby and Lorna would have been any parent's worst nightmare…"

Having hoped that neither of my inquisitors would dwell upon my feelings, I inhale the smoke deep into my lungs, so that the nicotine can subdue the lethal mixture of anger and distress, before I feel confident enough to offer John a response.

"It was a most persuasive deterrent, especially when Mark reminded me that if push were to ever come to shove, then nobody could protect the three of us forever…"

Although I expected a further reaction from John, it is our arbitrator who requires some additional clarification.

"Despite Mark's threats, you're here now Charlie--albeit a few years later than might have been advisable--and as you have stated, because you've spent your entire life, eating, breathing, even sleeping in a world where regular security screening and secrecy has been routine procedure, surely you must have known that sooner or later, you would end up in a room like this talking to people like us?"

Now, strictly between you and me--provided that you have not lost the will to live, and that you have continued to concentrate, you will recall that I have recently made a reference to--*albeit three years and eleven months too late*--and as for Bill's inference, then to save you from having to return to the prologue, if you are unable to remember, I referred to and I quote--*my ending up trapped in a room like this, talking to comparative strangers like John Bland and Bill Powell.*

However, I have no excuses to offer in my defence. "Yes, I probably did, but I think I've also made it clear that I'm not doing this out of any sense of duty. In fact, I'm here because after what happened on 22$^{nd}$ June, followed by the incident at the airfield I was left with no alternative. Besides, one can never go beyond the place at which one has not yet begun, and in the story of my life, you're way ahead of yourself Mr Powell..."

Pausing, I wait and then, when Bill's expression remains questioning, I utter one of his wearisome sighs. "At that time, Mark had all the power. He set the game up, which meant that we were forced to play by his rules. As for me, as you yourself have brought to everyone's attention, irrespective of whether it is in this room with people like you, or with Mark during the last three years and eleven months, bargaining power was non-existent, but nature often has a nasty habit of re-balancing the force, and over a period of time, a change in our circumstances earned me more freedom to be able to bargain…"

So mystery blended with a hint of triumph, offers enough intrigue to suggest that the plot thickening is far from complete, especially when I add, "Indeed, once you've heard everything, I think you'll have to agree that despite appearances the balance of power couldn't be more evenly distributed…"

If we cannot go beyond the point at which we have not yet reached, then this is hearsay, and instead of circumstantial evidence, John is eager to remain focused on the point we have reached.

"Obviously, Mark's threat or threats must have been persuasive and no doubt, he was satisfied with the outcome, but what about you Charlie?"

"Although accepting the restrictions placed upon me by other people has been part of my life for as long as I can remember as my track record has confirmed, and will continue to confirm Mr Bland, I have never accepted any restriction without some kind of struggle…"

Leaning forward, I tap the spent ash from my cigarette. "And because Mark's terms and conditions of my surrender were no exception, after listening to him that night, I was so disgusted--so repulsed--that the very idea of having to live with him in any capacity other than as his housekeeper, presented itself as being obscene…"

"So presumably, Mark expected more than a marriage of convenience in which you fulfilled the role of his housekeeper?"

How absurd, even more absurd than I have found his attempts at naivety. "On that night, while we were still in the hallway, when Mark had mentioned his long term expectations, I had told him that--*Whatever those expectations might be, they would have to be fulfilled over my unresponsive bod*y, but Mark didn't see any reason why anything should change between us, and for as long as I remained living at 187 Cheltenham Way, and I had a credit card with a five figure limit, so that I could buy anything I wanted, then despite preferring young men, he expected me to fulfil all of my marital obligations, whenever he chose to demand them. For my part, I vowed that my reference to--*unresponsive*--would in the literal sense mean that I would never reach for him, touch him, or kiss him, because being the Devil incarnate who I suspected had no soul there was no way, I was going to allow that depraved monster to contaminate mine with his filth…"

Much to my embarrassment in an unguarded moment, my overwhelming sadness permits, two more stray tears to overspill, and after brushing them away with my left hand, I reach forward, so that I can excuse the lapse by extinguishing my cigarette, and taking advantage of the silence in a quiet, respectful tone of voice, John expresses what appears on the surface to be yet another innocent observation.

"You must have hated him Charlie…"

"Hate is a dangerous emotion Mr Bland," I hear this woman reply, without any premeditated thought. "But that night, I hated him so much I wished that he were dead…"

"And what about after the night, did you continue to hate him?"

Suddenly, what appeared to be a superficial observation feels less innocent, and since John seems determined to fixate on hatred and hating, I choose to antagonise him. "During the induction period, I found it hard to adjust to what Mark expected, but while he made it very difficult for me, I tried not to hate him all of the time…"

Then, before John can respond, a combination of his professional training, and my unique abilities causes both of us react to a barely audible, singular clicking sound, which for once does not come from the recording equipment.

As implausible as it might sound, it would seem that someone has been eavesdropping on the other side of the door, and when the handle completes its revolution and the door creeps open, we can see my son's face.

Framed against that tousled fair hair, an endearing expression is enhanced by a natural cuteness, and admiring my son's courage, which is masked beneath an appealing coyness, this mother's biased smile broadens.

"Hello young man, I would have thought it was past your bedtime…"

Responding to the warmth in his mother's voice, Bobby sidesteps through the narrow gap, so that we can see his favourite Spiderman pyjamas, and while he waits to discover, whether his presence will be tolerated he hovers by the door, and his small voice is hesitant. "Because I've been playing chess and backgammon, Lorna let me stay up later than usual…"

Every day since our arrival although the cavalry have managed to find some spare time so that they can play football with Bobby, as he pauses his curious gaze drifts between the two men, before he adds, "Lorna said that you were very busy and I shouldn't disturb you, but I wanted to say goodnight…"

The last thing this mother needs is for a young and fertile, overactive imagination to suspect that there is anything odd about the scene, and in an attempt to distract him I push my Godfather's chair away from the desk.

"It's all right Bobby. You can come in--but only for a few minutes because it's very late, and you wouldn't want to get into trouble…"

Not needing a second invitation, Bobby rushes across the study, and disregarding any residual pain from my bruising I lift him a little, so that I can hug him, and when I lower him to the floor, he admits the real reason for his interruption. "I'm sorry--I was so angry with you but until Lorna explained how--even though we are all here--you still have important work to do--I didn't understand why you couldn't play chess with me…"

Perhaps I should explain that when John and Bill had told me they were ready to begin, I had decided that we should start after our early evening meal, which meant reneging on a promise to play chess, or backgammon with Bobby, and his disappointment had led to a rare outburst. However, since it had been nothing more than a breakdown in communications, this forgiving mother lowers her head, so that I can plant a kiss on his forehead.

"It doesn't matter Bobby. We're still friends, and although I had to let you down because of work I had hoped that Lorna would offer to play…"

"Oh, it wasn't Lorna. You and I know that no matter how hard she tries--her strategy is always the same, which makes her easy to beat. It was Uncle Philip who offered to play some games with me, but despite being an improvement on Lorna--nobody seems to be a better opponent than you…"

As you will discover later, hearing my son talk about Commander Philip Maddox in such a familiar way should have evoked instant contempt and yet, this mother suspects that not only my son, but also Lorna might have good reason to rely on him in the difficult days, weeks, months, or even years ahead, and without any trace of resentment I hear myself praising my son's achievement, using the same familiarity.

"Because Uncle Philip has such an important job looking after people--like the three of us--I have no reason to doubt that he would be a worthy opponent…"

"Yeah, he's good," Bobby replies, with more confidence in his small voice. "But after he got checkmate in the first game, because I began to understand his strategy I won the next, and the two backgammon games were the same--Uncle Philip won the first and then, I won the second…"

Pausing, my son strains his neck, so that he can inspect the desk, before he demands, "You promised me that you would give up smoking…"

"I'm sorry Bobby, although I had stopped--like many addicts--I relapsed…"

Capitalizing on his victory, Bobby looks up at me, and over his head this adult can see John's appreciative smile as the small voice announces, "Well, you know what we smoke busters say about cigarettes…"

Curtailing his reprimand, this admonished mother interrupts her son. "Yes, I know you've told me often enough---*people who smoke will eventually choke…"*

As Bobby nods his satisfaction, he reaches up, and when his fingertips touch my cheek with a genuine concern in his voice, he asks, "Why have you been crying mum?"

What a dichotomy? Do I tell Bobby a lie, or do I risk causing that same fertile, overactive imagination undue concern? All things considered, I opt for choosing my words with the benefit of hindsight. "I haven't been crying Bobby. On two occasions, I was talking about something very sad, and by accident a couple of tears managed to escape…"

Tilting his head a little to one side Bobby seems confused, which means that one question generates another. "You mean--sad--like when Lorna and I got up on that terrible morning to find Sid the most--VICIOUS--white rat in the whole wide world--dead in his cage, and I cried--and cried. Was it that kind of sad mum?"

Unsure about the analogy between my sadness and Bobby's white rat dying, this mother attempts to avoid the smirk on John's face, and ever the diplomat I find a truthful comparison I can use, which might be enough to avoid revealing more than one occasion.

"I suppose it was like that kind of sad. We were talking about my father dying, and because I know how proud he would have been of his Grandson, I was sad that you never had the chance to spend some time with Major William Charles Forsyth…"

When Bobby heard his Grandfather's name, my son's eyes seemed to grow larger and larger in amazement. "Gosh--Major--William--Charles--Forsyth--with a name like that he must have been a very important man. Was your dad as important as Uncle Philip?"

"Yes Bobby, he was an important man who had a brilliant military career…"

As I have previously stated this is my son, my reason for having clung to the belief that dead would not be a better option, and although he has a power inside of him, which far surpasses my own abilities, if anyone were to discover his true value, I would never forgive myself. Then, because Bill must have believed that it might be of benefit to our wider audience, I'm suddenly conscious that he has not paused the recording equipment, and while this mother could detain her son indefinitely, when the gently purring reminds me that we still have a considerable distance to travel, before we will find ourselves back at the place, where we should have begun, I attempt to bring the interruption to an end.

"Okay young man, because we still have some more work to do, one more kiss and then, you had better get yourself upstairs, before Lorna discovers you're absent without leave, and she has to come looking for you…"

"Too late," a voice declares from the doorway. "I'm afraid Lorna's realized he's missing, and she's found him in the one place where he knows, he's not supposed to be…"

Despite the serious overtone, Lorna is smiling, and when Bobby's giggling proves irrepressible, and he throws himself at me in a playful way, Lorna's gaze drifts from John to Bill. "I'm sorry about the interruption. I'm afraid, I fell for one of the oldest tricks in the book, which went something like this--*Lorna, I think I must have left my computer game in the living room, and if I wake up early I was going to practice. So I'll pop downstairs and see if I can find it. It'll only take me a few minutes…*"

More of an explanation than an apology, and when Lorna's gaze falls upon me, this adult recognizes her genuine concern for my welfare. However, even if my visual appearance confirms that I am as weary as I am beginning to feel, it is not Lorna's responsibility to save me from myself, and re-focusing my attention on Bobby, when this mother cuddles him he is squirming and shrieking with sheer delight, as I am demanding information about the nature of his punishment for having disobeyed one of Lorna's specific instructions.

"All right, I did try to warn you, but now that you've been caught in the act, what might I ask is this week's punishment for such flagrant disobedience?"

"I don't know…"

"Oh, I think you do," this mother teases him. "Aren't you supposed to be beaten to within an inch of your life, or have your football confiscated for the next five days?"

"Anything except my football, if Lorna has to do something, she can beat me, but I'm very sorry and I promise it won't happen again…"

"An unlikely story, especially when that's what you said the last time, but I suppose we could plead mitigating circumstances, and then Lorna might decide to spare you…"

Unseen by our son as I look up, Lorna's expression has turned into outright disapproval, which has nothing to do with Bobby's misdemeanour. Unlike him, she suspects that the scene in the study is odd--perhaps even sinister--and whatever is happening, it's taking its toll on her closest friend. However, in the story of my life, this woman has gone beyond the point from which there can be no return, and because nothing can change the course of my destiny, this protective parent lowers our son to the floor.

"Okay young man, now I suggest you go off to bed, before either of your mothers can change their collective minds…"

Still standing in the doorway, Lorna's disapproval, which I'm sure would not have gone unnoticed by Bill who has had a clear view of her suddenly vanishes, and when Bobby hesitates as an encouraging gesture, she holds her hand out as she suggests.

"Come along Bobby. You know better than to try to push your luck too far…"

With a deliberate slowness, Bobby crosses the study, and when he takes hold of Lorna's outstretched hand she bends a little, so that she can whisper something into his ear. Then, as if our son has remembered his manners--like a practised performer--Bobby half turns to face his expectant audience.

"Good night Mr Bland. Good night Mr Powell. Thank you for playing football…"

"Goodnight Bobby," the cavalry announces in stereophonic unison, before Bill adds, "And don't forget, it's your turn to be in goal first tomorrow morning…"

Spoken without any trace of relief that the interruption is coming to an end, and because the broad smile on my son's face as a result of him knowing, what tomorrow is going to bring is the last thing this mother sees. But even after he vanishes, I continue to stare at the door, and although it is unnecessary, I find myself explaining the reason for the interruption.

"Whenever it was safe enough for me to find some time, so that we could all be together, it was far too precious to be squandered on cross words, and after what happened earlier, Bobby needed the reassurance of knowing we were still friends…"

Opposite me, John is wearing an appreciative smile as he delivers what seems to be another innocent remark. "Considering how difficult it must have been to achieve a workable balance, Bobby is a credit to both of his mothers. You must be very proud of him?"

Although you might not remember the declaration I shared with you earlier, it's time for me to set the official record straight. "Of course I'm proud of him. Bobby has been my whole life, and everything I may or may not have done, after I married Mark has been and will continue to be, so that he and Lorna can retain their freedom and their anonymity…"

Even if my inquisitors have not yet grasped where this is heading, this matter is too important to be delayed, and after pausing so that I can take a steadying breath, I continue safe in the knowledge that one of them will stop me, if I am in danger of falling into the abyss. "Please don't misunderstand me--my priority is Lorna and Bobby. For my part, I'm not as naïve as you'd prefer me to be, and although nobody has made any reference to my long term future, I'm realistic enough to know how this might end for me…"

Since I have crossed over into enemy territory, without either of my protectors feeling the need to save me, their attentiveness encourages me to introduce the final frontier. "For as long as the contract remains unfulfilled, despite your expertise there are no guarantees that you will be able to protect me. Alternatively, regardless of the fact that Commander Maddox is my Godfather, after he has heard the remainder of my life story he might decide that I deserve to be thrown to the lions so that they can rip me apart limb by limb…"

As my instinctive need to protect Bobby intensifies, I am forced to hesitate. "But, since my son is innocent of all and in fact any charges, which could be levelled at him, he should not be held responsible for his birth mother's transgressions…"

"We understand Charlie…"

Of course, this time there can be no doubt that they do understand, especially when I have recognized that there was nothing innocent about John's enquiry, and despite having initiated this scene, I cannot find any reason for him--on the cavalry's behalf--to employ either evasion or deception when offering his leading lady his full response.

"Firstly, thanks to your own diligence, since it would seem that few people know about your son's existence, much less know his identity, despite a possible change of surname and having to be relocated, we're confident that affording Bobby and Lorna protection should not pose Special Operations any difficulty..."

Too perfect in the present tense to be unscripted, and his soliloquy has been rehearsed. "And secondly, when we gathered together not only the Official Files, but also every last piece of information, so that we could prepare for this Interview, because we suspected that events, involving your son might be of a delicate political nature, Commander Maddox took the liberty of seeking some kind of guarantee, from the highest possible Authority..."

When John pauses, I sense that this has been written into his soliloquy, so that I will grasp the dramatic significance of his next revelation. "Then this afternoon, when we confirmed that we had finished our preparation, Commander Maddox advised us that during the Interview, if the issue of Bobby's future arose, then using our own discretion, he authorized us to inform you that irrespective of anything that might have happened in the past, or may well happen in the future, your son has had the Royal Seal of approval bestowed upon him with regard to his safety and continued anonymity..."

Suddenly rendered speechless by the mixed emotions, which have been generated by the length's my Godfather has undertaken to ensure my son's future freedom. However, once everything has been revealed, it might not be quite so easy to fulfil such a vast commitment during the initial furore when everyone will want their particular pound of flesh and yet, this protective parent understands that what has been achieved surpasses anything, I had hoped might be achievable, and feeling somewhat humbled my voice is hushed.

"Thank you for clarifying my son's position. It is most reassuring to know that Commander Maddox has managed to achieve something which exceeds my expectation..."

Having dispensed with my concerns, Bill has what seems to be a once in a lifetime offer to tempt me. "If we're all going to stay the distance I'd better rustle up some more coffee, and because I'm sure you'd like to freshen up Charlie, why don't we take a fifteen-minute break?"

Until this Interview is over the last thing I expected was to be offered, the opportunity to escape from this room, and in sheer disbelief I am staring at him, but Bill is smiling, and this mother has not misunderstood his intention.

"Besides, before we continue, I'm sure it would put your mind at rest, if you knew that Lorna has managed to settle Bobby for the night..."

Strictly between you and me, having read between the lines, it is my belief that Bill is confirming that he did not fail to recognize Lorna's concern for my welfare. But despite that issue, when it comes to my response to the offer--like my son before me--I neither intend to push my luck, nor do I need to wait for a second invitation.

"Thank you Bill, I'd like that very much..."

Stepping beyond the study, no sooner has the door clicked closed behind me than I am tempted to stand there listening, but like my son before me, it would be unwise to the found loitering with intent to eavesdrop in a place where I am not supposed to be and yet, as I move towards the staircase, it strikes me that perhaps for no other reason than the incessant chattering from an excitable almost seven-year-old has ceased--at least for the rest of the night--amid the silence, the Manor is shrouded in an eerie almost spooky stillness.

At the top of the sweeping staircase, I head down the upper landing until I reach my son's room. Then, I hesitate outside the door, which has been left ajar so that one of his mothers can respond if Bobby should wake before morning. Although I have to confess that since our son has been taking advantage of his busy schedule by enjoying all of the things he has missed because he did not have a father, he has never needed either of us and even now, Bobby is lying on his side with his face turned towards the door, and there is nothing to suggest that he is not sleeping.

If he is asleep, then it would be selfish to disturb him and yet, because a stray arm is dangling over the edge of his bed, I am unable to suppress the urge to rescue it. So this birth mother tiptoes into the room, but when I lift his arm using the lightest of touches, so that I can place it beneath the lightweight duvet, Bobby's eyelids flicker open.

"Shush Bobby," I whisper. "Go back to sleep…"

"Before I closed my eyes, I was planning the things, I'm going to do tomorrow…"

"But you won't have the energy to do anything," I whisper, as I brush the mass of unruly hair from his face. "Unless you get a good night's sleep…"

"And then before I did fall asleep, I was thinking about how cool it is when we don't have to pretend. Do you think we'll ever be able to be together like this forever and ever?"

In light of the last bombshell dropped downstairs in the study, I somehow manage to the muffle the sound of this mother's breaking heart at the realization that for the three of us, there might never be a happy ever after. "I don't know whether it will be possible Bobby. I suppose we'll have to wait and see what Uncle Philip manages to arrange…"

"Having you and Lorna and sometimes Uncle Colin has more than made up for not having a dad. Do you have any family photos of your mum and dad?"

"Yes I do, but right now you need to get some sleep, so close your eyes…"

Leaving the door as I found it, I head down the landing to that palatial en-suite bedroom, and by the time I hear a gentle tap on the door, I'm sitting at the dressing table, repairing the make-up I first applied before dinner, and because Lorna knows that there is no need for an invitation she enters the room, and after sitting down on the bottom of the king-size bed, so that we can see each other through the mirror, she makes her announcement.

"I was packing some washing away, when I heard you come upstairs…"

Then, she pauses, before posing a direct question. "Are you all right Charlie?"

As I did with Bobby, I opt to take what I hope will be the less damaging route. "Apart from being a little tired I'm fine Lorna…"

"Have you finished the work you had to do with John and Bill?"

"Not yet--we're taking a fifteen-minute break, so I could freshen up…"

Through the mirror, I can see that same disapproval Lorna displayed downstairs in the study, and while she has the right to demand some answers about what the hell is going on, she will not pressure me. However, Lorna does deserve some kind of an explanation, and through the safety of the mirror, I confess, "After Bobby was born things happened over which I had no control, and I fooled myself into believing that nobody would ever uncover the truth, but I was wrong and I'm so sorry Lorna…"

Unperturbed, Lorna is smiling at me. "You must have had your reasons, and after the Major visited us in Edinburgh, I suspected that your life must have been littered with undisclosed complications, because if it hadn't, then you wouldn't have needed me…"

After everything has been revealed and her life is turned upside down, I can only pray that Lorna will remain this understanding, but my overriding concern is for the time, especially after taking into account, the few extra minutes I spent visiting my son's room, because not only is there not enough time to deal with the complexities of those complications, like my son I also would not want to be accused of being absent without leave.

"Lorna I have to go and finish what someone else started a long time ago. But like Commander Maddox, it's time you knew the truth, the whole truth and nothing but the truth, and because there are some important matters connected to Bobby we need to decide together--tomorrow or the next day--we need to talk…"

Lorna shrugs her shoulders. "Of course, whenever you feel that the time is right I'll be waiting, but as far as I'm aware we aren't going anywhere, so maybe you should give yourself some time to recover from whatever you're doing downstairs…"

Perhaps Lorna's encounter with her own mortality explains why nothing seems to disturb her level-headed perspective. However, as Bill has discovered nobody should ever doubt that she sees and hears everything, and because she would fight to protect the people she loves, after I rise to my feet, Lorna continues to watch me, as I prepare to leave the room.

"Are you sure you're okay Charlie?"

"As soon as this Interview comes to an end, I promise I will be…"

Having reached the door, I know that Lorna will release me, but not before she voices her outright dissatisfaction with the scene downstairs.

"From what I saw, whatever is going on down in--*Uncle Philip's study*--the odds seemed to be a little uneven, and if you need any help--or you would like some moral support, then you know where to find me…"

"Thanks Lorna--for now it is best if I do this alone, but once we come full circle and we find ourselves back at the place where we began, I might need your assistance…"

Comforted by Lorna's genuine offer I cast one last smile in her direction, before heading along the landing. Then, lost in my own thoughts about what lies ahead of me, I'm descending the staircase, when someone comes out of the study carrying an assortment of files, and since it's too late for me to retreat we are destined to collide.

Bearing a striking similarity to my father, Philip Maddox is tall with flashes of white streaks in his hair from bearing the burden of his extensive responsibilities, and I'm sure every eligible woman would describe him as handsome. But his only partner has been--and will continue to be--his command and right now, unplanned by either party this brief encounter cannot be avoided without causing embarrassment.

"Good evening Commander…"

How formal and yet, how befitting such a sombre occasion, and when the Commander looks up at me, he is unperturbed by our close encounter.

"Good evening Charlie…"

Sharing the same sombreness, but at the same time the seriousness of this occasion my Godfather watches me, as I descend the remaining stairs and yet, without any awareness of my subconscious motivation, I halt my descent a few steps from the bottom of the staircase, because I want to preach from the advantage of the moral high ground.

"Bobby was telling me how earlier this evening, you were indulging his love of chess and backgammon…"

"For his age he has a remarkable gift, but then as I recall his mother was also that gifted. You have every reason to be incredibly proud of him Charlie…"

Caught off guard I recall those happier times, when my Godfather used to come and spend the weekend with my father and mother, and he was the one who taught me, how to become a brilliant strategist, when I was only five years old and yet, despite the fondness of the memory, I have to remind myself, when and where did it all begin to fall apart?

"Yes Lorna and I are very proud of him," this mother boasts. "My only regret is that my father never had the chance to meet his Grandson…"

"I'm sure that Major Forsyth would have relished getting to know him…"

Our exchange is polite and personal, but somewhat superficial because in addition to being his Goddaughter, I'm also an assignment--or to be more precise his assignment, which means that when there is nobody else present, we must keep some distance between us.

"We're only supposed to be taking a fifteen-minute break Commander--and if don't get back, Bill might think I'm absent without leave and send out a search party…"

With a somewhat paternal smile, Philip Maddox nods. "Of course Charlie…"

Then, as if he's about to head in the direction of the living room, the Commander turns away but when this Goddaughter completes her descent, and we are sharing the level low ground he looks back at me.

"Re-assigning Bland and Powell was never coincidental Charlie. Of all the Operatives, they are my most proficient team and thanks to their multi-disciplined training, they were the most qualified to deal with the suspected complexities of this situation…"

As he pauses, I recognize that same paternal concern for my welfare, and it seems genuine, as he asks, "I trust they're treating you with respect Charlie?"

"Considering those complexities," I hear this Goddaughter reply. "Apart from the occasional skirmish they are treating me, as well as can be expected… "

"That's a relief. Let's hope it stays that way until you reach the end…"

At the study door I hesitate, and because this protective parent would like to thank her Godfather for what he's done to secure Bobby and Lorna's safety and anonymity, I look back towards the living room, but my Godfather has vanished, which leaves me with no choice, except to accept that this intermission has come to an official end.

# PART THREE

## JUNE 29

# Hell Hath no Fury

## like

# A Good Wife Scorned

In my absence, the scene has been reset and relit, so that the study is bathed in a high intensity light, which mimics daylight, and my principal male is standing staring out of the window. However, when John hears the door click closed behind me, he returns to the desk and places his crystal whisky glass next to the silver tray so that from the insulated pot, he can pour coffee into the two remaining bone china mugs.

Sitting at the table Bill smiles, and as I ease my Godfather's chair away from the desk, he acknowledges this protective mother's safe return.

"Was everything okay Charlie?"

"Yes it was. In fact, once I reached my own bedroom Lorna joined me for a few minutes, but only after my son--whose eyes had been closed--had managed to ambush me, because when I tiptoed into this room, instead of being asleep, Bobby had been lying planning all of the things he intends to do after his football practice tomorrow. On behalf of his two mothers, I cannot thank you enough for having managed--every single day since our arrival--to take some time out of your schedule to indulge our son's passion…"

Having read between the lines, Bill was extending his smile. "It must be a relief to know that everything was all right," he declares, acknowledging my reference to Lorna's earlier concern and then, when the smile turns into an impish grin, he explains, "And there's no need to thank us, especially when you take into account that most of our assignments don't involve spending days at Manor Park, and since we rarely have the time to indulge in frivolous pursuits, I'm sure that together with our Commanding Officer--whenever he is available--we're enjoying being able to play football as much as, if not more than Bobby…"

As I sit down, John places one of the coffee mugs in front of me, before he resumes his position on the other side of the desk, but there is something missing, and having noted that Bill also has a crystal whisky glass, I issue my principal male with a direct question.

"Don't I get another pure malt whisky?"

As John shakes his head, he replies, "For the time being, you'll have to be satisfied with another mug of coffee and a glass of sparkling water, which has some ice in it…"

"That seems to be a little harsh…"

"Based upon these observations, our decision is a precautionary measure," John enlightens me. "Instead of taking one of the sleeping tablets Dr Wilson prescribed, it has been noted that you prefer to stay awake for most of the night, and when it comes to the issue of food--for example this evening--although one would have thought it impossible, you somehow managed to eat even less than on any other day, since our arrival at the Manor…"

Is there no end to the cavalry's intrusiveness? While on the one hand, it makes me feel protected on the other hand, it is as if I am living my life under a microscope, but I can plead that there were mitigating circumstances. "Considering how subdued everyone was at dinner, it felt more like the last supper than a pleasant evening meal…"

A plausible excuse, but not one which will influence the outcome, and after John finishes his whisky in one decisive mouthful, I seek solace in my own addiction, and when I pull a cigarette from the packet, I notice that in my absence, my Godfather's glass ashtray has not only been emptied it has also been washed, and when I click at the lighter and it sparks into flame, I hear Bill re-introducing the scene for the benefit of our wider audience.

"The time is 21:12 on the 29th of June. After a fifteen-minute recess this Interview is recommenced, with the same three persons present--and as negotiated by Commander Philip Maddox--no other means of surveillance is being used…"

Then with nothing, except the familiar purring from the equipment disturbing the silence, this adult exhales the smoke from my lungs, before glancing at John.

"If we're going to continue, then after all the excitement I think I need a cue…"

John is stirring his coffee, and as one would expect, such a talented performer does not need to refer to the script. "We were talking about how much you hated Mark and how difficult it was for you not to continue hating him, after the night he told you not only about his dual sexuality, but also his betrayal of both you and his country…"

Of course we were, and while I'm gathering my recollections, this alleged adult spoils the cleanliness of the ashtray with spent ash from my cigarette?

"After that night, Mark didn't treat me like a human being--much less a woman--and in the privacy of 187 Cheltenham Way, despite being allowed to express my true feelings, outright contempt was rarely tolerated. For Mark's part, behind those same closed doors he seemed to thrive on the constant hostility, especially if he managed to push me into responding with derision, which warranted remedial action. But in public, I was expected to fulfil the role of his adoring dutiful wife, and bearing in mind that every time he touched me, I wanted to throw up, Mark still demanded a perfect performance…"

Pausing, I take a steadying breath. "In the end, I wasn't eating or sleeping, but for Bobby and Lorna I knew that somehow I had to find a way to adjust to my situation. So one day while Mark was abroad on an assignment, I went to the beach in the early hours of the morning, because I needed to watch the dawn breaking…"

Now, provided that you have been paying attention, you will remember me describing that day in the '*Prologue',* which preceded the story of this woman's life.

"And while I searched my heart I released the tears, I had refused to give Mark the satisfaction of seeing me cry, and after the crying turned into inconsolable sobbing, unlike when we were in the recovery room after the termination--perhaps because nobody could hear me I started screaming, and by the time I couldn't scream anymore, the sun was rising on the new day, and I vowed that if--correction--once I regained my freedom nobody would ever take me alive again, but it was nothing more than another dangerous delusion…"

Like that day, two tears dare to escape. "But since Mark didn't want to lose such a valuable asset, he opted to lure me with the promise of my eventual freedom…"

It had been something to cling onto, but despite the fact that I might be digging my own grave because it could also be regarded as complicity, I have no choice except to proceed. "Mark didn't suggest anything civilised like divorce or separation, but he did assure me that at some point, his extra curriculum activities would necessitate his disappearance, and when that day arrived, he gave me his word that I could have my freedom…"

"From what I'm hearing Charlie, it sounds as if you didn't believe him…"

Between you and me, would you have believed a pathological liar like my husband? Yet again, John's naivety can only be for the benefit of the Official Recording. "At that time Mr Bland, it was the one ray of hope I had to cling onto, but even if I had believed him I wouldn't have trusted the son of a bitch, and when I considered the implications of his intended disappearance, I suspected that I knew far too much to be left in the firing line, in case people started to ask awkward questions…"

With his impartiality intact, John is assessing my facial expression, and because he senses that the plot is about to thicken, he encourages me to divulge more information.

"And presumably, that's when you must have stopped hating him?"

"The realisation that I might not live long enough to enjoy my freedom provided me with the incentive I needed, and somehow I had to find a way to give myself some bargaining power, so that I could protect all three of us and at the same time secure my freedom…"

Pausing, my inner child casts a mischievous smile in John's direction. "As it turned out finding a way to play Mark at his own game, proved to be easier than I had expected, especially when he had never considered that I might be capable of using my brain. But the hardest part for me was finding an acceptable way to rebuild some degree of trust. However, when I began to recognise the irony of Mark finding himself trapped--preferably by the balls in his own deception--I started to enjoy myself. In fact, after everything he did to me, it seemed like a most appropriate way in which to end our unfortunate relationship…"

"Hell hath no fury…"

As a woman scorned? Yes, I was a woman scorned and in my innocence, I laugh. "Well, I suppose that's how it was meant to work. However, we wouldn't be here now, if I hadn't made a few mistakes, but the fact remains that whenever Mark decided it was time to retire from public life, I was confident I had done enough to secure our freedom…"

Without warning John's impartiality has become clouded by a professional pensiveness. Perhaps he disapproves of revenge, or maybe he preferred his leading lady, when she was cast in the role of the victim.

"You obviously disapprove," my mischievous child encourages her mother to chide him. "But I'm afraid it happens to be the truth Mr Bland…"

As John's pensiveness is replaced by the kind of concern, I recognised in Lorna's eyes, this leading lady is confused, and because this is not the reaction I had anticipated, I am a little afraid, but before I can explore the reason behind my fear, Bill attracts my attention.

"Before we go any further Charlie," he announces, as I turn to look at him. "I think there's something we need to clarify…"

Relieved that my confusion is going to be dispelled, and unaware of any impending danger, I offer my agreement. "Of course Mr Powell, after all that's the reason why we are undertaking this Interview…"

"From what you've explained, it would seem to be the case that you somehow found a way to protect not only yourself, but also Bobby and Lorna, so that whenever you suspected that Mark intended to retire from public life, you had a means of securing your freedom…"

"Naturally, there were some risks involved, but as I have already stated, I was confident that I had done enough to secure our lifelong freedom…"

Despite having responded to his request for clarification--in Bill's eyes--I can see that he shares John's concern, and even more confused my gaze drifts between them.

"I don't understand…"

Opposite me, John stirs and ready to re-join the performance, he places his elbows on the desk and clasps his hands, so that he can rest his chin on them. "It quite simple Charlie. Although we haven't heard everything, nothing can alter the fact that fourteen hostages, including your own husband and his P.A. died during what turned out to be his last assignment. In fact, by the time we arrived in Paris to help Henri Retand--in the literal sense to pick up the pieces--you were the only survivor, and I think you'd have to agree that Mark's death would have been a convenient way in which to end your relationship…"

"Oh I see…"

Releasing him from my gaze, my protective parent leans forward, so that I can extinguish my cigarette and my overriding feeling is disappointment. Now, my Godfather's non-coincidental reason for re-assigning Bland and Powell seems to be most apt, because after affording me with enough rope to hang myself, I was right to harbour misgivings that the Commander's study was turning into a prison cell.

How could they suspect that this mother could be capable of such an act, which could only be described as mass murder? Oh how foolish this leading lady has been for having allowed herself to grow too comfortable in her complacency.

"Congratulations Mr Bland," I declare, as my icy glare falls upon him. "If I'd known I was on trial, then I would have chosen my words with more care…"

Then, I snap my head around, but before I can level a similar accusation at our arbitrator, it is as if someone other than Bill has depressed the pause button, because the action in the study has been suspended, and from the past there are more images. Images which have formed the content of my nightmares for the last three months. But as much as I want to prevent this from happening, I do not have any choice. So the best I can hope to achieve is that I can make this a brief summary of what happened on that last day.

*To ensure that the political, wheeling and dealing did not attract too much attention to the delegates, who were assembling to represent several Governments, there was minimal security and yet, when we flew to Paris for that long weekend at Jacques Foray's purposely designed residence, which was close to the banks of the River Seine, the negotiations were important enough to necessitate that Mark's twenty-eight-year-old Personal Assistant Anthony accompany us in the Special Operation's Private Jet.*

*For my part, together with the only other female present, who was the American delegate's wife Anne-Marie--after shopping until we dropped by day--we were expected to lighten the tedium of the after dinner conversations with innumerable anecdotes and yet, this particular female had been more alert than usual, because although I did not know how, or when or even what was going to happen--approximately forty minutes, before the three of us were due to return to the private airfield--that happening occurred when I heard raised voices, followed by a small explosion on the ground floor. But despite the plume of smoke which began drifting upstairs, the fire must have been extinguished with amazing swiftness.*

*Then, I heard someone screaming before everyone, including Jacque's household staff were forced to assemble in the conference room, and with my husband chosen to act as an intermediary on the behalf of the masked gunmen who I assumed were terrorists, the interminable waiting had begun in earnest.*

*Every hostage knew the policy of no negotiation, and because the terrorist's first and only demand--that they be given some kind of guarantee that the American delegate would return to the residence--did not receive any response--as they had threatened, after selecting Mark's P.A they executed their first hostage. However, that single bullet into the back of Anthony's head meant there would be no more communicating, and when an exchange of gunfire shattered the glass in the first floor window, one of the gunmen took me with him and after falling together, we landed in the garden at the side of the building.*

*With a leg injury sustained from the shattered glass, I could have been a liability and yet, this frightened woman represented that young man's one chance of bargaining, and after giving me the choice of a bullet from the gun he was aiming at my head--or somehow managing to haul myself onto my feet, I opted for the latter. However, before I could avoid his grasp, he hooked his arm around my neck, and used his teeth to pull the pin from a grenade. Of course I knew enough about weaponry to understand that his hand keeping the lever clamped down was the only thing stopping us from raining down in little pieces. So after he forced me to accompany him out of the garden and into the street, I had no choice* except to relay his demands to Henri Retand, who was the person Commander Philip Maddox had appointed to be in charge of the Paris division of Special Operations.

"Henri, he wants you to remove the marksmen from the surrounding rooftops..."

Silence, but in his naivety, although his demand might have sounded reasonable as my husband had taught me, while at terrorist college, he must have skipped some training.

"The marksmen aren't going anywhere Charlie..."

In response to Henri's refusal, I sensed my captor's slight movement, and even before the pain seared through me, I suspected that he was going to aim his foot at my leg injury, so that I would cry out and yet conscious of the grenade, I was struggling to remain upright, as I heard Henri delivering his declaration, which I understood was intended to save me from further random acts of violence.

"Since the entire area has been sealed, there's no media entourage observing anything that's happening, and he must be an amateurish imbecile, if he imagines for a single moment that anyone in this street would allow themselves to be influenced, by his ability to cause his hostage pain. Now does he understand what I've explained Charlie?"

Silence--more bloody silence, then I heard the young man whispering his reply, and like any good intermediary, I relayed his message to Henri.

"He says he understands Henri..."

"Okay, so what's it going to take in order for him to release you?"

"He wants a car to take us both, beyond the sealed area..."

Initially, I heard Henri utter an incredulous laugh, and because I did not need to be reminded about the negotiating policy, as the arm around my neck tightened, I was so afraid that when I heard my captor promising to release me, I pleaded on my own behalf.

"Please Henri, with my leg injury I'm not sure how long I can remain upright, and once we're beyond the sealed area, he's promised he'll release me, but if he doesn't get what he wants I frightened, he'll turn himself into some kind of martyr, and given the choice I would rather gamble with my own life, than die here and now like this on the street..."

Silence--yet more fucking silence--but then amidst the tension, Henri's voice announced, "All right Charlie, because we wouldn't want him to develop cramp, and drop the grenade by accident--try and stay calm. The car is on its way..."

A few moments later, when the car drew to a slow halt Henri was in the driving seat, and despite being comforted by his nearness, something about the scene was not quite as it should be, and in that terrifying moment of realization, I understood that it had all been too easy, because a man in Henri's position would never be in the driving seat, except to afford me some degree of reassurance, even though it might turn out to be misleading.

Befitting the occasion, the street was shrouded in what I suspected was about to become the deadly sound of silence, and there was an uneasy stillness among the specialised spectators, especially the marksman who were still visible. But it was not until my captor left me no choice, except to accompany him as he stepped away from the wall--and move towards the rear of the car--that all my alarm bells seemed to start ringing at the same time.

In that same instant, I understood that somehow I had to stay both strong and calm, but when he ordered me to reach down, so that I could release the rear door of the car, there was a tell-tale click, and I realized why I had been right to speculate about the possible misleading reassurance afforded by Henri's presence, because despite my precarious position, he had never intended to allow this amateur to leave the scene. However, before my fear dissolved into hysteria, this helpless hostage heard the distinct recoil from a high velocity weapon, and as the bullet headed towards its target, it coincided with my scream of denial, because it would seem that none of us were destined to leave the scene.

Even in death, the young man's arm stayed around my neck as he took me to the ground with him, and unable to do anything to help myself, I watched as the grenade rolled *out of his lifeless hand, and despite hearing what I hoped was Henri scrambling over the bonnet of the car--like my heartbeat--the seconds were ticking away.*

*Seven, and six, and five, and four, and three and then, I heard myself beginning a final prayer.* "Our father who art in heaven. Hallowed be thy name. Thy kingdom come, thy will be done." *But not it would seem on that day or on that street, because I later discovered that Henri had managed to scoop up the grenade, and after throwing it over the high wall which surrounded the garden, he shielded this hostage from any flying debris.*

*Unsure whether I was alive or dead for a lingering few seconds, the stillness and silence made it impossible to determine fact from fantasy, but when Henri eased himself away from me, before removing the limp arm from around my neck there was a flurry of activity, and we were surrounded by armed Special Operatives, who seemed intent on ensuring that my captor could not pose a threat to anyone ever again.*

*It had been a calculated risk, and since Henri could have killed us both, I should have been screaming and yet, when I raised my arm towards my face, the blood on the hand did not belong to me, and because my captor had been unmasked, and Henri did not want me to look down and see the face of the young man who could have been my executioner, he lifted me off the ground, and as if speed might in some way erase the memories of such a close encounter with my own mortality, he turned both of us away, so that he could rush me to a waiting ambulance.*

*Then, during what must have been a sedated sleep darkness had descended, and I awoke five hours later to find myself in Henri's home. At some point, John Bland and Robert William Powell must have arrived, but the introductions proved to be nothing more than a fleeting distraction, because not having received any up to date information, I was demanding to know what had happened to my husband?*

*Silence and yet, the answer was lying within Henri's expression, and as if this wife did not want to hear it confirmed, I was shaking my head as he expressed his condolences.*

*"I'm truly very sorry Charlie, but it's my understanding that two hours after you left the scene, Mark's body was recovered from the ground floor of the building..."*

*Pausing, Henri waited and then, as if this widow might not have heard him, he asked "Do you understand what I'm telling you Charlie?"*

*"Yes Henri--my husband is dead..."*

*In Henri's guest bedroom, I was somehow managing to remain on my feet, but after Henri's hand guided me into the chair next to the bed, even in the event of his death, this wife will behave with dignity, and because I needed to know about the remaining hostages, this widow posed another question.*

*"Once everyone was assembled in the conference room, apart from the masked gunmen--and including Jacques and three members of his household staff, I counted fourteen hostages, how many of them?"*

*"Charlie," Henri interrupted me. "Dealing with Mark's death is difficult enough and this is something that can be dealt with later..."*

*"No it can't wait Henri. After the gunman took both of us out of the first floor window, I need to know what happened to those remaining hostages..."*

*Then, Henri released one of those resigned sighs, people tend to release around me whenever they are about to deliver bad news, and as the words left his mouth it was as if I were lip reading, so that I could somehow make his words more acceptable.*

*"Dear God, surely there has to be some kind of mistake Henri?"*

*"I'm afraid there's no mistake Charlie. You are the only survivor..."*

As the images fade into the background, I feel as if I have been betrayed by the very persons who made me believe that I could trust them and yet, with the pause button released,

I am free to level that suspended accusation at Bill. "And as our self-appointed arbitrator Mr Powell, do you think I had something to do with what happened in Paris? That I could have been responsible for the deaths of those innocent people…"

Like his partner, Bill will not rise to my challenge, and until this hostage provides an outright denial, which should be accompanied by an adequate defence, their assignment remains, not innocent until proven guilty, but guilty as charged--albeit by default.

Could my rebellious child have had the power and influence to reap such devastation? On reflection, if it were not for the abhorrence of the deaths, then because it would have required not only intricate premeditated plotting, but also perfect predetermined execution, I would be flattered instead of aggrieved.

Despite my belligerence as the forecast suggested, the tension is eased by a distant rumbling of thunder. "Sounds as if there's a storm coming, but at least the rain will help to lower the temperature," Pausing, I wait and then, responding to a fond memory I explain, "When Bobby was very young, he used to refer to the rain as--*plutting*--and he would ask either one or even both of his mothers, what could have made the sky so sad that it was crying. In fact, I think that's an apt description of how I feel at this precise moment…"

Of course, while I remain accused nothing will penetrate their collective solemnity, and when my inner child prompts me to laugh, her parent tries to issue an apology.

"I'm sorry, but you both look so serious, and…"

"That's because this is very serious Charlie," Bill interrupts me and then, as soon as this parent contains her inner child's exuberance, he explains, "Although you appear to be aggrieved by our professional concern--on several occasions throughout the evening, you have referred to the possible consequences of your involvement, and I'm afraid that those references make our suspicions reasonable…"

"For the benefit of the recording, as previously stated to the other half of this dynamic duo in future I will endeavour to select my words with more care…"

Thoroughly enjoying myself, this leading lady intends to prolong this scene for as long as the cavalry will indulge me. However, as I rise to my feet, so that I can execute a triumphant move to the window, my departure is prevented when John reaches across the desk and as his hand closes around my forearm, his demand confirms that their indulgence has reached its limit.

"Sit down…"

While the audacity of his touch might have caused me to be still I do not obey him, and as one might expect from a leading lady, my eyes remain locked on John's restraining hand for several seconds, before lifting my head until I achieve eye contact.

"Come on Charlie, you've had your fun. So would you please sit down?"

The politeness is accompanied by the removal of his hand from my arm, but while my rebellious child is free to persist with her disobedience, her parent understands that since failing to respond to such a polite request might be misconstrued, it would be wise to resume sitting in my Godfather's chair--albeit in stoical silence.

"Thank you. Now for the benefit of the recording, I would invite you to put everyone out of our collective misery, by confirming that although you were anticipating Mark's early retirement, you had nothing to do with what happened in Paris…"

Whatever happened during that exchange, it would seem that we have moved beyond the point at which John held the lighter steady on my behalf and something had passed between us--to the intimacy of his restraining hand, and because his suggestion is tinged with irritation, it tempts me to goad him. But when I reach for my cigarettes, his arm sweeps across the desk for a second time, so that he can snatch the packet from beneath my fingertips, as his raised voice snaps at me. "Damn it Charlie--stop pissing about…"

Whilst anger is a response to which I'm accustomed John has not reached the point at which his irritation would force me to relinquish my right to remain silent, but then much to my own annoyance, Bill elects to execute one of those executive decisions.

"John's right," he declares, as he switches off the recording equipment, with a singular dull thudding sound. "We don't have to put up with this childish behaviour…"

Despite having gained my full attention, Bill's action also does not guarantee that I will relinquish my right to remain silent, as he explains, "I thought we'd established that we will either do this our way or not at all, but it would seem I was mistaken. However, before you do or say anything, you might have cause to later regret, the circumstances have changed and considering everything we've heard up until now, if you leave us no alternative, except to withdraw from this assignment, then we would endorse our recommendation to the Commander that you should be transferred to H.Q., so that you can be Interviewed by M I 6 in connection with suspected offences in accordance with the Prevention of Terrorism Act…"

As Bill pauses, I am too stunned to react, especially when the goal posts must have been moved during my absence, but then Bill confirms what would be any mother's worst fear. "Of course, Bobby and Lorna would stay at Manor Park, and until proven guilty, you would remain under the protection of Special Operations. But after what you've told us about Mark and Bobby's father, combined with everything connected with the Paris incident, the Commander is confident that M I 5 and M I 6 would be most eager to talk to you …"

Setting to one side that this could be nothing more than an empty threat, as far as my Godfather is concerned, I find it disturbing that in my naivety, I failed to take into account that every good deed has to have a catch, and after going to such great lengths to secure Bobby's safety and anonymity, Bill is confirming that the Commander would be prepared to separate this mother from her son and his other mother, so soon after our reunion and feeling disheartened and thoroughly dejected, I'm staring at the floor until our arbitrator continues, in a softer and more amenable tone of voice.

"But it's irrelevant, isn't it Charlie? After all, you're intelligent enough to know the alternatives, and because we don't believe you'd be here now, if you thought you could negotiate a better deal elsewhere, in my capacity as arbitrator, I don't think you had any intention of being either obstructive or uncooperative…"

Pausing, he waits until I glance at him. "Isn't that correct Charlie?"

"Yes," I hear this woman conceding. "If I thought I could obtain a fairer hearing or better treatment from any other agency, on behalf of not only myself, but also Lorna and Bobby then I wouldn't be in this room, and because you have been tolerant, and understanding, I can only apologise for my disrespectful behaviour…"

Then, I glance across the desk. "It never occurred to me that you might think me capable of such an horrific act, and your suspicions made me doubt your motives…"

Over by the window, Bill must have switched the recording equipment back on because I hear him re-setting the scene. "This Interview is recommenced at 21:24 on the 29th of June with the same persons present. After giving it some reconsideration, Charlie Anne Daltry, nee Forsyth has agreed to clarify the position regarding her personal involvement in the Paris incident three months ago…"

Thrust back into the limelight. and aware that delivering my soliloquy will be fraught with further pitfalls, my self-destructive inner child is telling this parent that she needs to feed her addiction, but the packet remains resting under John's hand, and because I should not have ended up in the position of needing to ask, I resign myself to the fact that my disobedient child has sealed our fate and begin my unrehearsed dialogue.

"Before the three of us were due to fly to Paris, Mark made it clear that having led a double life for far too long, he was getting ready to retire. But as God is my witness, I never knew what Mark intended to do, or how he planned to do it? As for your suspicion that I arranged for my husband to be killed--because it would have been a convenient way in which to end our relationship--any accusation arising from it would be unfounded, especially when I have every reason to suspect that Mark isn't dead…"

Aware of an even greater need for a dramatic crutch to prop me up, I am hoping that the plot has thickened enough to enable John to release the contraband, he confiscated from my over-exuberant inner child and yet, despite such a damning revelation, it would seem that he does not intend to release his hostage without further clarification.

"I think you'd better explain what you mean Charlie?"

"When the masked gunmen took control of the building--like everyone else--it was the last thing I expected, and because Mark had never revealed any details about the plans he had made, I didn't know what the hell was going on. As you can imagine, the rest of that afternoon was a living nightmare, and after the first intermediation failed, and they carried out their threat to execute a hostage…"

The flashback is so horrific it causes me to falter, which prompts Bill to offer me some assistance. "Would it help Charlie, if I confirm that according to the autopsy, Anthony died instantaneously as a result of a single execution style bullet into the back of his head?"

Since it is in my best interest that I clear my own name, I'm grateful for the support. "Thank you, but as one of them executed Anthony they made the other hostages watch and as long as I live, I will never forget Emilie's terrified shrieking. However, within minutes that single shot seemed to cause all hell to break loose, and after the glass shattered, one of the young masked men and I were falling out of the first floor window. Then, once we were on the street, Henri pulled his crazy stunt with the grenade, and before I could do or say anything, I was being rushed to a private Clinic, where I was sedated while they patched up my leg injury, and by the time the sedation had worn off, you had arrived and when I asked him, Henri informed me that Mark's body had been recovered from the ground floor. So nobody had any reason to suspect that he was alive…"

"Except you, and it would seem that you chose to maintain your silence…"

"It wasn't like that…"

Angered by John's accusation, my protective parent's defence was rushed and quite spontaneous, but he remains uninfluenced by hearsay.

"Perhaps it wasn't, but did you know that Mark was alive?"

"No!" I exclaim, as I am becoming flustered. "Since I had not been given any updates between leaving the building and waking up at Henri's five hours later, how could I have known, what had happened to Mark and the other hostages?"

"All right, I will rephrase the question. Did you suspect that Mark was alive?"

Feeling undeniable discomfort, because the aforementioned pitfalls now mean that anything I say can--and no doubt will--be used against me and yet, there is no definitive reply to John's accusation. "Surely, you must be able to appreciate how learning that I was the only survivor left me so shocked, I wasn't capable of knowing what to think, much less suspect? But for the benefit of the recording, what I can confirm is that I never told any lies, and when I was asked to make the provisional identification, I told the truth Mr Bland. There could have been no mistake…"

There had been no reason to doubt, and the realization that I'm not the only person, who could be held accountable generates more images from three months ago.

So after the accusations of complicity, levelled in the present tense of the study *there is comfort and a sense of control, because with that horrific day ended, and a new one about to begin, it was the early hours of the morning.*

*After I had been reminded that there were legal formalities, which needed to be concluded, before John Bland and Bill Powell could escort me home, despite being exhausted and conscious of my emotional fragility with Henri driving and accompanied by my escorts, I* suppose my vulnerable child should have felt over-protected, by such an impressive entourage, but when we arrived at the hospital the formalities, which needed to be concluded were not what my protective parent had prepared me to face.

Indeed, while I had not requested any detailed explanation, it would seem that this newly widowed wife must have been labouring under a misapprehension, because due to the extenuating circumstances, instead of being greeted--as one might expect--by a corpse, we were being ushered into a bleak, sparsely furnished room, by an official who was carrying a large manila envelope and a buff folder.

"My name is Andre Deploise," The official stated in almost perfect English, as he placed a digital recorder next to the mysterious manila envelope and buff folder, before he offered me his condolences, "I'm very sorry for your loss Madame Daltry…"

Having undergone extensive therapy, it would never cease to amaze me, how people refer to someone's death as being a loss, because Mark was not lost--my husband was dead.

"Once it was safe to enter the premises," Andre Deploise began to explain. "Several bodies, including your husband were recovered from inside the Foray residence. Could you please confirm, whether Mark Daltry wore any jewellery?"

Initially, my bewilderment left this widow lost for words--and yes, in this instance the use of loss is appropriate--until he repeated the question. "Did you understand Madame? I need you to confirm whether your husband wore any jewellery…"

"Only his wedding ring," I heard this widow replying, and then I was touching the gold band on the third finger of my left hand, as I explained, "Our rings are not only identical, but also inscribed with our initials together with the date of our wedding…"

"Thank you…"

Now, without giving it any conscious thought, I had begun to twist my wedding ring. "Since I've come to identify my husband Monsieur Deploise--surely, this is irrelevant?"

However, he had emptied the contents of the envelope onto the desk, and it was the cigarette lighter that drew my attention, prompting me to open up a different dialogue as I picked it up. "Yes, there can be no doubt that this lighter is mine. Although my husband never approved of me smoking, Mark bought me the lighter as a birthday present, and he had it engraved with my initials--and before two of the masked gunmen found us in the bedroom, I remember Mark pushing it into one of the inside pockets of his jacket…"

As I had been speaking, I noted that in addition to the digital recorder, Andre Deploise was making notes and with genuine regret, he apologized. "Although your comments are duly noted, I'm sorry but it is not enough, I still need you to formerly identify the wedding ring…"

Irritated by his persistence, my inner child was making it hard for her parent to sustain my dignity, but left with no alternative I picked up the ring, and despite the strong sensation that ran through me, I refused to be overwhelmed and remained focused upon the evidence. "There is no doubt whatsoever that this is my husband's wedding ring…"

Then, Andre Deploise gathered up the lighter and the ring, before he sympathized with this inexperienced widow. "This must have been very difficult for you Madame Daltry, so I am grateful for your co-operation…"

There had to be more, and because my request came from the depths of a heavy laden heart, it was sincere, "As I explained earlier, I came to identify my husband…"

"Charlie," Henri interrupted me. "After the harrowing events of the siege, you aren't thinking rationally…"

Outraged, this widow was prepared to stand her ground and argue in my own defence, "Henri I am in complete control, and I want--no--I demand to see my husband…"

"With all due respect, you don't seem to have understood that you were asked to make a provisional identification…"

*Silence, but this time I was responsible, because I was struggling to determine the difference between provisional and formal identification, and when I felt Henri's hand on my shoulder, I was grateful for his clarification. "There is something you don't know. Something I should have clarified, before things got this far, and I'm truly sorry Charlie. However, not long after the shooting started, there were two more explosions on the ground floor, which meant that some parts of the building were extensively damaged by fire…"*

*Then, Henri crouched down beside my chair, before he continued, "And since Mark's body was found at the epicentre of those explosions, we asked you to make a provisional identification--based on personal effects--because the conclusive proof from the DNA analysis could take some time…"*

*"My God," This widow gasped, "Learning I was the only survivor was horrific, without finding out that there isn't enough of my husband left for me to identify…"*

*"As much as I would like to tell you something different, I'm afraid I can't…"*

*In that instant, I wanted to be anywhere as long as it was away from that room. However, I was shaking, and too afraid to stand up in case I collapsed, but determined to maintain my dignity, with Henri still crouched beside me, and in a barely audible voice, I whispered, "Henri I don't think I can stand up. Could you please get me out of here?"*

*"Of course, we'll get you back to the house and then, provided you've recovered enough to travel, John and Bill will escort you home in the Private Jet later today…"*

Evidently, during the early hours of that day in that cold, dismal room, I had not been alone and thanks to those memories, which confirm there had been no reason to have suspected, never mind know that my husband was alive, John Bland is out of order.

"For the benefit of the Official Recording, as I recall both of you accompanied me, when I made the provisional identification, and since everything identifiable would have been documented, in our Special Operations' Personnel Files, including our personalized wedding rings, there was not the slightest possible doubt that Mark's ring, and my cigarette lighter were in his possession when the siege commenced…"

There is something I have missed and yet, I'm too blinded by my desire to turn John's words against him to be able to capitalize on anything else. "Especially when one considers that his death would have been a convenient way in which to end our marriage, and if the treacherous son of a bitch had had the decency to stay dead, then none of us would have ended up in a room like this talking to each other. Wouldn't you agree Mr Bland?"

Unperturbed, John continues to monitor my facial expression, and it is Bill who distracts me. "Of course, in addition to us all being present at the provisional identification, if the DNA analysis hadn't confirmed Mark's identity, then alarm bells would have been ringing at Special Operations long before now. However, in my capacity as self-appointed arbitrator, my overriding concern is for what's best for you, and because of the complexities of the situation, I think that irrespective of how tedious it might seem, we need to proceed with extreme caution, and by taking one gradual step at a time…"

Having remembered--albeit too late--what I had failed to capitalize upon, I am somewhat frustrated at being beaten to the accusation over the DNA. "Oh I wholeheartedly agree Bill that--*it is in everyone's best interests*--if we proceed with extreme caution…"

In response, Bill throws me an appreciative nod, which confirms our collective understanding. "Okay, now if you believed Mark was dead when we escorted you home from Paris, then your assurance, and I quote--*especially when I have every reason to suspect that Mark isn't dead*--those words suggest that during the last three months, you must have heard from him Charlie…"

"Yes, I believe that I've heard from him," I reply, but then afraid that any ambiguity might be misinterpreted, I quantify my statement. "But only on one occasion…"

Silence, but opposite me, John resembles a bloodhound who is about to dig an old bone-it had buried earlier--back out of the ground--if you'll pardon my unfortunate analogy, and having picked up the scent, he pursues his prey with nothing more sinister than two-word demand. "When Charlie?"

Having read between the battle lines drawn up by our arbitrator, and aware that when it comes to my best interests, it is not only a matter of when I heard from Mark, it is also whether in some way I was guilty of conspiring in his retirement from public life.

"Surely, the question should be, how long have I known my husband was alive?"

In that slow precise manner, I have come to recognize as dogged determination, John shakes his head. "No, I specifically asked, when you had heard from Mark?"

Such a talented performer knows the answer, and my vulnerable child is trying to avoid having to make an outright admission.

"Recently…"

"Damn it Charlie," snaps John, as he grows more exasperated. "Would you answer the question?"

Left with no alternative, with a detectable caginess, I reply. "A few days ago…"

Opposite me, when I dare to glance at him, John now resembles a bloodhound with an old bone, it should have left buried, but at least his impartiality has been replaced by a professional distaste, as he answers his own question with an implied suggestion, which requires my corroboration. "In the early hours of the $22^{nd}$ of June…"

Suddenly, the principal players have drawn close to the edge of the danger zone, and surrounded by monstrous images yet again, this leading lady severs eye contact, but while I dare not explore the content, especially when I am so afraid that my protective parent might not be able to contain the images and yet, for all the wrong reasons, when it comes to a man in pursuit of his prey, my hesitancy proves to be unacceptable.

"Well Charlie," John demands. "We need you to confirm whether Mark was at 187 Cheltenham Way in the early hours of the $22^{nd}$ June?"

Such terror remains inconceivable, and I have sustained my sanity by keeping the events locked away in a twilight world, and provided you were paying attention, you may recall that I referred to a deal, I had made with the cavalry before our evening meal. For my part, I vowed to tell the truth, the whole truth and nothing but the truth, and in exchange we would not discuss anything that happened during those sixty minutes of my life. So all I can do is hope that John will honour their side the bargain and yet, because it remains complicated, I attempt to keep my admission as concise as possible.

"No Mark was not at the house…"

"Charlie!" exclaims John, as he is becoming more exasperated. "You cannot avoid the issue indefinitely. Sooner or later you have to confirm how you heard from Mark…"

In my heart, I know my principal male is right, and irrespective of the complications, it is in my best interests to offer some kind of explanation. "You have to bear in mind that because of the flashbacks I experienced at the Mayfield Clinic--out of sheer necessity--I have blocked out the images of what took place during those sixty minutes of my life. However, after our arrival at Manor Park, because I have become more conscious of a sequence of connections, at first I couldn't be certain, but after what happened at the airfield…"

Having sensed some kind of change, I lift my head in time to witness the knowledgeable glance, which passes between my inquisitors, and although I do not understand the significance, my gaze drifts between them. "Other than the explosion did something happen at the airfield that I should know about?"

More silence, but then Bill offers me something resembling a response. "At this precise moment, it isn't important Charlie. I've made a note to remind me, and if it's relevant we will come back to it later. For now, let's concentrate on taking one cautious step at a time, and you were about to clarify something connected with the incident at the airfield…"

Of course, having reached this pivotal point in the story of this woman's life, I have to trust them to be acting in my best interest, and after regrouping my thoughts, I am ready to proceed. "After we returned to H.Q., and we dealt with the Protective Custody Order, you expressed your concern that there seemed to be a pattern forming, and how the person or persons responsible for the explosion must have had access to information, not only about my father's daily routines, but also the most vulnerable places on his car…"

"And presumably, marrying into the Forsyth family," suggests John "Mark would have acquired enough information, so that if someone were to gain access to the Major's car, then they would be able to plant an explosive device…"

"Yes, I suppose it was something similar to that," this leading lady agrees. "But I swear to God, it has only been during the last couple of days that the pieces of the puzzle have begun to slot into place…"

"Charlie," Bill interrupts me. "Taking into consideration that in our area of professional expertise, it would be far too dangerous for us to allow ourselves to be influenced by such things as mysterious coincidences, but we do have some up to date information in connection with the incident at the airfield…"

Intrigued by his reference to coincidences, Bill holds my attention "Two days ago, the Forensic report on the Major's car arrived, and the team managed to ascertain that the explosive, which had been disguised and placed near to the fue l tank was a device never seen before, and it was so sophisticated it could have been planted weeks ago, because it could not have been detected, until it was armed by remote control, which could have been only minutes before the explosion. Consequently, even though the car was swept for suspect devices on a daily basis, none of them would have prevented what happened at the airfield…"

For my part, there is a certain irony within Bill's choice of words, especially when we are nearing a time and place, where their perception of some things will need to be redefined, because within the reality of my world, everything happens for a reason. However, for the moment I am grateful for the update. "Thank you, it's comforting to know that there was nothing anyone could have done to alter the outcome…"

Turning away from our arbitrator, I discover that John remains a man with a mission to fulfil and why would his leading lady disappoint him? "Then, earlier this evening, after hearing what your Person of Interest had to tell you about the Contract caused me to remember that before they left the house, Shaw asked his associates to wait downstairs, and once we were alone he reminded me about--*the good reasons, why I'd never been able to tell anyone the truth about my life*--and since nobody except my father; Bobby's father, and of course Mark knew about Lorna and Bobby, it could have only been my husband who must have issued the Contract in order to tie up some loose ends between us…"

As every woman will be able to imagine that admission was not an easy one to make, and my self-destructive inner child has not ceased telling her parent that she needs to feed her addiction, while at the same time, being able to hide behind a smoke screen.

Since fortune is supposed to favour the brave, my gaze drifts across the surface of the desk, until it confirms that the confiscated contraband remains resting beneath his hand. However, my principal male seems stunned by the realization that my husband must have despised me so much, he had granted them free license to have some fun, and because the silence is left dangling, I feel obliged to offer John, yet more elaboration.

"Mark was a bad loser, and because he hates loose ends he must have waited, until I was foolish enough to believe that for first time in seven years, Lorna, Bobby and I were free, before sending Shaw and his associates to conclude our unfinished business…"

Now, without any added discussion, the cavalry knows sufficient and in disbelief John is shaking his head, as he asks, "And did they conclude that unfinished business?"

"No," I admit, with an even greater reticence. "Which is the only reason why I am still alive…"

Ever since they found me in the early hours of that morning, the cavalry have never exerted any pressure regarding what took place, but whenever this adult feels able to unburden the horror of those images, I will be afforded a safe environment and professional help. In the meantime, apart from releasing a longer disapproving sigh, since it would seem that John is prepared to honour their side of our agreement, after shrugging my shoulders in a nonchalant manner, my requests are deliberate attempts to lay the matter to rest.

"May I have a cigarette now?" I ask in a hushed, respectful voice. "And because my mouth's very dry, could I also have another glass of iced sparkling water?"

Behind me, I hear Bill rising to his feet, and while he is moving to the cabinet, as if John has forgotten he glances down at the contraband underneath his hand, and after uttering another longer derogatory sigh, he slides the packet across the desk.

"For someone who is about to move from six to seven-years-old, your son has a very wise head on his young shoulders, and since you smoke far too many cigarettes, I'm afraid I share his disapproval. So perhaps it's time you quit altogether…"

"Of course, I'm aware that it sets a bad example to Bobby," I admit and then, making eye contact with John I take a huge risk by counter-challenging him. "However, I think you'd have to agree that there's a certain irony in her Majesty's Government warning me that smoking might damage my health--perhaps even kill me?"

Touché, but yet again I have failed to consider the repercussions of my actions, because when I flip the packet open and pull out a cigarette, I had not realized that my delivery of those difficult admissions has left me trembling, and despite having picked up the lighter with the intention of sparking it into flame, John reaches across the desk and as his hand covers mine, it would seem that what passes between us has grown stronger than the first time. In fact, as the feeling flows through me, it's strength seems to confirm that although we are on opposing sides of the desk at the end of this day, and the dawning of the next, I can trust this man to be acting with my best interests at heart.

With my cigarette lit, I note that John places the lighter, so that either of us can pick it up, and with tmy self-destructive child pacified, when Bill fulfils the other half of my request by placing a glass of iced sparkling water in front of me, after exhaling the smoke from her parent's lungs, I express my gratitude. "Thank you Bill…"

Then, once he is back in his appointed place, he explains, "Because of the complexities of your situation, I've devised a route map so that we can reach our destination without needing to back-track, but things might not seem to be in the correct order

"That's fine Bill--I will be guided by your judgement…"

"Okay, with regard to Mark's retirement, we have established that as a direct result of his extra curriculum activities, he managed to convince everybody, including you that he was dead, and because he was prepared to compromise his successful disappearance, by contracting Shaw, Blake and Peterson to tidy up the loose ends, I think the time has arrived, where you should tell us, what you did to necessitate that level of unwanted attention?"

Oh dear, so the time has arrived for me to reveal the whole truth, and I'm aware that it might be wise to err on the side of caution before confessing, how this scorned wife added her own devious ingredient, which complicated the aforementioned complications, whilst at the same time further thickening the plot.

"Of course, but I don't think you'll like it any more than Mark…"

Now it is Bill's turn to sigh in a knowledgeable way. "If it was worth Mark taking such a monumental risk, then my professional instinct is telling me that we won't, but at least our disapproval should not exceed the boundaries of colourful expletives…"

Having duly noted the--*should not*--my protective parent begins her somewhat guarded explanation. "When I was growing up, my father taught me to disregard anything I might see or overhear in connection with his work. However, in Mark's house we played a different kind of game, and because I knew too much to be left running free after his retirement, there seemed to be no harm in knowing even more…"

Such proficient, multi-disciplined operatives must have a reasonable awareness of what the rest will be, but I am conscious of John's damned impartiality and after tapping the ash from my cigarette, my protective parent continues to proceed--with extreme caution.

"In fact, because it had struck me that knowing as much as possible about his alternative lifestyle could be beneficial, once H.Q. gave me the necessary clearance, so that I could accompany Mark whenever he thought it appropriate, for the best part of thirteen or fourteen months, I noted every detour we made from the agreed schedule, and once inside unapproved venues such as clubs or restaurants, I observed every strange face, and mentally noted every name. Sooner rather than later, they all began to emerge--people like Marty Schreiber, Arthena Yentranue, Toni Devires, Arnovich Timento, Adriane Pertona…"

Both of my inquisitors must have recognized at least some, if not all of those names, but there is still no reaction prompting this woman to ask, "Do I need to list any others?"

"No," John replies. "I think you've given us sufficient …"

Bewildered by his remarkable calmness, I consider that perhaps it might have something to do with the recording, until Bill's tone expresses more concern. "Although John's right Charlie, I suspect that there has to be more…"

As I dare to glance over my shoulder, Bill's expression is too sombre not to reflect their collective disconcertion. However, since they were the ones who demanded to know, I should have nothing to fear, except fear itself. "Thirteen months is a long time, and because I was trying to find a way to protect the three of us, it went further than observing and listening--I'm afraid that I decided to keep a written record of anything that seemed significant such as names, dates, places and subsequent events…"

"Jesus…"

Since my eyes have been fixed upon the desk, I would have expected the blasphemy to have come from Bill, but when my error causes me to glance at John, despite his blasphemous expletive--somehow he is managing to sustain his impartiality, as I attempt to enter a hurried defence in respect of my action.

"Nobody ever knew--and before we went to Paris, I burnt the notebooks." this scorned wife states, but there is still no indication that either of my inquisitors are relieved, and because they seem unimpressed by my defence, I remind them about my admission. "I did tell you that you wouldn't like it any more than Mark…"

"Well you were wrong Charlie," Bill contradicts me, with an alarming immediacy. "Because if you burnt the notebooks, then there still has to be more, and if that's the case, I think we're going to like it even less than Mark…"

"All I was trying to do was find a way to convince Mark that if anything untoward happened to either me, Lorna or Bobby, then there would be no hiding place from either Special Operations or his Handler and ultimately his Sponsor…"

"From what you've revealed, you obviously succeeded," Bill snaps back cuttingly. "So I suggest that you stop procrastinating and tell us how you did it?"

Reaching forward, I extinguish my cigarette, and after sipping from my glass, when another rumble of thunder, heralds the nearness of the approaching storm, I have no choice, except to admit the absolute truth. "Before I burnt the notebooks I selected certain names, dates, times and places. Then, using some actual facts I created a piece of literature, which in anyone's hands would have been enough to discredit him beyond redemption…"

"Like I said earlier," John states for his partner's benefit. "Hell hath no fury…"

As this woman scorned? With his damned impartiality remaining intact, John continues to stare at me, but then he rises to his feet, and after picking up his empty glass he gestures in Bill's direction, before walking away from the desk and yet, despite his detachment from the scene, there is still no reprieve because Bill seeks even more elaboration, which I suspect he hopes might lessen the damage to my position.

"Charlie, is it safe for us to assume that the names you selected from the notebooks, included at least some of the names you've already listed?"

"Yes, but I'm afraid you'll have to add your Commanding Officer to the list…"

"Wonderful…"

By the cabinet, with his back turned towards his leading lady, John had been pouring the whisky, but since my last admission must have penetrated his impartiality, his derisory mutter is followed by the return of the malt whisky bottle to its rightful place, using an unreasonable degree of force, which causes me to flinch. But in all fairness, neither of them has the right to be angry, and as I am sure that you would be prepared to bear witness on my behalf, despite the cavalry wanting to know, now they do know the absolute truth--perhaps it is a stereotypical male thing--but instead of being grateful, they wish they had never asked. However, I must reiterate that neither of them has earned the right to be angry.

As he leaves the cabinet, I sense John walking to the table no doubt so that Bill can take a glass from him, but then John returns to the cabinet, before approaching the desk and when he places a crystal glass containing some pure malt whisky in front of me, without daring to look up at him, I remark, "I thought I wasn't allowed another drink…"

Silence--but then with a wounding cynicism, John replies, "Oh since we have the rather daunting responsibility for trying to keep you alive, I've changed my mind. In fact, after hearing how you've compromised, some of the most dangerous, not to mention most influential Persons of Interest in our computer database I think you deserve it, and since from this moment the going is destined to become a great deal tougher, than even we had imagined, if I were in your position I'd drink it, because you're probably going to need it…"

Now we are back to promises or threats, and I think everyone would agree that was a definite threat. However, considering that I never expected, much less asked anyone to accept--*the rather daunting responsibility for trying to keep me alive*--I could challenge John and yet, my dignity will not permit me to be goaded into responding.

Refusing to look at him, as my free hand closes around the glass he chooses to detach himself from the tension between us, by taking his own glass with him, when he walks away from the desk towards the window, leaving Bill to resume control of the proceedings.

"Before we move time forward Charlie--for the benefit of the recording--I'd like to make sure that there can be no misunderstanding, by doing a quick review…"

Casting a backward glance at Bill, I can see John standing by the window, as our arbitrator commences his review. "As Mark's wife you had access to certain privileged information, including details relating to his extracurricular activities, and because you were trying to find a way to protect, not only yourself, but also Lorna and Bobby Clunnell, you kept a written record of any information that might prove useful, such as dates, places, names. Then, after selecting certain pieces of information, you destroyed your written record and replaced it with a fictitious piece of literature, which you intended to show to Mark, whenever you suspected that he was preparing to retire from public life…"

"That's correct, but I'm not a complete idiot and what I showed Mark were photocopies of some of the more damaging pages…"

Raising his hand, Bill silences me. "A few moments ago Charlie, I did explain that after making a route map, some events might not seem to be in the correct order, and if you don't have any objections can we leave the how and when you told Mark until later?"

"Of course, I don't have any objections Bill. It was rude of me to interrupt...."

"That's not a problem Charlie," Bill confirms, as he casts an understanding smile, in my direction. "Earlier you told us and quoting your own words--*not long before the three of us were due to fly to Paris Mark made it clear, he was getting ready to retire*--could you please clarify the way in which Mark made it clear?"

"All right, but you have to take into consideration the way we lived day by day in 187 Cheltenham Way, because once the honeymoon period came to an abrupt end, we never sat at the same table to eat our meals, or slept in the same bed, unless we were away on an assignment for Special Operations and we never shared intimate or personal conversations. In addition, when it came to the sexual side of the marriage, although it wasn't very often if and I suppose when Mark wanted the gratification of entertaining himself, with my unresponsive body, then we had sex..."

Out of the corner of my eye, I note John's slight movement, which seemed to coincide, with my mentioning the sexual side of our marriage, but my priority must lie with containing the images my reference has generated, and because faking it was a vital factor of that dirty job, but somebody had to do it, after sipping from my whisky glass I fix my gaze on the desk, so that I can focus my attention on the present tense within the here and now of my Godfather's study.

"About four weeks before the Paris trip, Mark told me that he required my presence during that long weekend and then, I realized that the negotiations must be important, because Mark and Anthony spent every day of the week before our departure, working together at H.Q. Then, one evening Mark came home particularly pleased with himself and when he suggested that we should celebrate by going out to dinner, I was intrigued--perhaps even a little suspicious--and because I wanted to know more, I accepted his invitation..."

Despite the distance John has chosen to put between us, I sense that he is watching me, but I will not look back, not even in response to his disagreeableness. "Over dinner, Mark was different--he was upbeat and wanted to reminisce. It resembled a farewell gesture, some kind of swansong and by the end of the evening, two bottles of wine had been consumed, and because I needed a shrewd way in which to extract more explicit details, after we got back to the house I made..."

When the words fail to emerge, I'm hoping that the cavalry cannot sense my mortification over what my rebellious child encouraged her parent to do, and since containing those explicit images has become a struggle inside of my head, I have to keep repeating the same refrain--*it was a dirty job, but in case it was the last time, somehow I had to do it...*"

"Charlie," Bill enquires, in a softer tone of voice "Are you okay?"

"I'm sorry, but throughout this Interview of all the admissions I've had to make this next one feels as if it's the worst, and that's the reason why the words refused to emerge. However, Mark had drunk more of the wine than me, which meant he was mellow, and susceptible to flattery, and because I needed to massage his oversized ego, so that he would divulge more details about why he was so pleased with himself, which I suspected might be connected with his intended early retirement from public life..."

Behind me, I sense John stirring again, and my muscles contract in anticipation of his intention to steal the words, before they can come out of my mouth. "Presumably, what you're trying to tell us is that instead of being unresponsive, you became proactive by instigating, some kind of sexual activity between you?"

Definite derision has crept into his voice, but I refuse to be baited into retaliating. "Yes Mr Bland, it was a dirty job, but somehow I had to force myself to do it..."

Pausing, I sip some whisky from my glass. "But I can assure you that it was straight sexual intercourse and after massaging his ego, with all that sycophantic nonsense, before we fell asleep in our marital bed for the first time in over twelve months, Mark told me that he had negotiated the kind of lucrative deal, he had hoped might arise one day, and although he would miss me, especially when I had proved to be, not only his most valuable asset, but also a special kind of beautiful woman, who had been capable of arousing him and exciting him sexually, out of sheer necessity I would soon have the freedom, he had promised me…"

"And this lucrative deal," demands John. "Did Mark tell you anything about it?"

With his derision beginning to wear me down, this time I cannot stop my irresponsible child from making her parent take the bait. "Considering that I had to set aside my unresponsiveness, so that I could do what we women do, when it comes to lying back and thinking of England, while we're faking our participation, although I was good in bed Mr Bland, I would have needed to undergo a sex change to extract that kind of detail…"

Silence, but while I'm considering how much I preferred the scene, when my principal male was opposite me, so that I could attempt to read any change in his body language or his mannerisms, John's next demand causes me to flinch again.

"And having--*extracted*--what you wanted to know--when and how did you tell Mark about your so called fictitious piece of literature?"

Now it would seem to be the case that enough, will never be enough to appease John's underlying resentment, and because he seems to believe that he has earned the right to be judgemental, my protective parent waits, until my silence prompts him to glance over his shoulder, before fanning the flames from the spark he has kindled.

"What exactly have I done to merit your disapproval Mr Bland? Perhaps you would have preferred me to remain cast in the role of the victim, instead of a woman whose underhand methods suggest, I've spent the last two years of my life, whoring to be free…"

Then I pause again, so that my deliberate choice of words can heighten John's disapproval. But it is the truth, and because that side of Charlie Anne Daltry is something my invisible jurors need to take into consideration as we head towards the finish line, and the end of this part of my life story. However, within the present tense of my Godfather's study, I will continue to fan the flames.

"But irrespective of whatever you perceive it to be Mr Bland--it happens to be history and since it cannot be rewritten I suggest you get over it, so that we can move on…"

"In the case, why don't you answer the damn question…"

Yet more derision, so I continue to antagonize him. "Forgive me if I misunderstood, but that was what I was prepared to do a few minutes ago, but Mr Powell asked me if--the when and how I had told Mark--could wait until later…"

"Since it happens to be later answer the damn question…"

Having maintained eye contact throughout our exchange, and knowing that I have dented his armour plated impartiality, I use his own terminology in an attempt to admonish him. "Your underlying resentment seems to suggest that there is a more serious difficulty, and if it concerns the Protective Custody Order, Commander Maddox foisted upon both of you, then if--you remember rightly--after Bobby's unscheduled visit disrupted the proceedings, I expressed my concern over my son's future. However, since I made it clear that I was not as naïve as you would like me to be and therefore, I know how this might end for me. So I would respectfully remind you that I never expected--much less asked, you or anyone else to accept--now, how did you describe it? Ah yes, and I quote--*the rather daunting responsibility for trying to keep me alive*…"

As this leading lady had intended that direct hit has further weakened the armour of his impartiality, and because John remains a highly trained, multi-disciplined operative, assigned to fulfil what is beginning to resemble an impossible task, this time his discomfort causes him to stir, but before there is any real danger of him taking a step back towards the desk, so that we can slug this out, through challenging sentence being met by counter-challenging sentence--like any competent referee--Bill keeps us in our respective corners of our imaginary ring, by extending his right arm sideways with one finger raised in the air.

"That's enough…"

By the window John hesitates, but along with my irresponsible child, we have no choice, except to endure the frustration of acceding to another executive decision, and when John turns away and he stares back out of the window, Bill focuses his attention upon me.

"Before things can get any more out of hand Charlie, would you please do what John has asked, and answer his damn question…"

Another threat--but now that they seem to be arriving thick and fast, I'm contemplating that having been threatened for most of my life, those issued by the cavalry are growing emptier, and therefore less intimidating, until Bill demands, "Well Charlie…"

"Gosh Bill--how stupid of me to have been labouring under the misapprehension that I had unlimited time and space, and complete freedom of speech…"

"Charlie!"

Yes, as we have established this performer can be tiresome, but having penetrated John's armour, and working on the premise that what goes around will come back around, he will remain aggrieved about whatever offended him, and since I can afford to be patient, after turning away and sipping at the remaining whisky in my glass, I make a genuine appeal.

"As you said Bill, it's been a long day and every time I feel threatened by either of you, I lose my ability to focus, and because I have to gather together my recollections, so that I can regroup my thoughts, I would be grateful if you could be more patient with me…"

More silence, but then after I suspect the cavalry have exchanged furtive glances--in a softer tone of voice--Bill requests my attention. "Charlie would you look at me please…"

Albeit with a noticeable reluctance, I look at him. "Please accept my sincere apologies. I'm sure we can both appreciate that after achieving a great deal this evening, you must be getting tired and if you would prefer it, we can end this Interview now, and then pick up where we left off tomorrow morning, which would enable you to get some sleep?"

Having read between the battle lines, it would seem Bill might be concerned that the sniping between the two principal characters could escalate, until it reaches a point at which, not even our arbitrator might be able to call the proceedings to order, because John and I will have issued a formal declaration--confirming that we are at war.

As far as sleep is concerned, although the offer is tempting I doubt my ability to achieve any more sleep, than I have been able to achieve, since our arrival at Manor Park, especially with the added weight of the content of this Interview, rerunning inside my head, in conjunction with what I will be facing tomorrow morning.

"Thank you for the offer Bill," I hear this leading lady state, in a calm level headed voice. "But now that we've reached this point, I'd prefer to continue…"

Over by the window, John casts a cursory glance in my direction, before he offers Bill his own endorsement, and although I doubt that either of us can guarantee that the cease fire will prevent us from undertaking, three falls, two submissions or a knockout, we have left our arbitrator no choice, except to afford us his own agreement.

"All right Charlie, provided you're sure that's what you want…"

"Yes, I'm sure and the answer to John's question is that I never did tell Mark, what kind of insurance policy I had organized in order to secure our freedom, after his intended early retirement…"

Out of sheer necessity, I clear my throat and I can only pray that I do not create the wrong impression, which might incite further sniping. "Working on the assumption that something might be going to happen in Paris, before we left the house to go to the airfield, I put some of the photocopied pages from my fictitious piece of literature, inside an A4 envelope, before placing it in one of the magazines I carried onto the Private Jet…"

Aware that there are more images, and this time, there would seem to be no reason why I cannot share them not only with the cavalry, but also our wider audience.

*During the flight between the decommissioned airfield and its equivalent in Paris, it was perhaps fortuitous that Anthony--who had worked until the early hours of the morning to finalize some last minute amendments and adjustments--had excused himself and in the hope that he would be able to catch up on some sleep, he had gone to the rear of the Jet.*

*It was an unexpected window of opportunity, because it afforded me the privacy and safe setting I needed, and once we were airborne, having vowed that whenever I began to turn the pages of that particular magazine, as soon as I stumbled across the envelope, without the slightest hesitation I would hand it to my unsuspecting husband.*

*In theory, the plan had seemed clear cut, except for the fact that Mark who was sitting beside me, was engrossed in Anthony's last minute alterations, and knowing how much he hated to be interrupted, when I reached the penultimate page I faltered. However, it remained a dirty job, and because I was the only person who could do it, I could not allow a last minute touch of cold feet to prevent me from completing my mission. In fact, if I was going to stand any chance of protecting the people I held closest to my heart, I had no choice and after turning the page to reveal the envelope, I leant a little towards my husband, and attempted to bring the sacrosanct silence to an end with a whispered summons.*

*"Mark…"*

*In response, my husband uttered a--hum--sound, and because it proved to be an anti-climax, even before I cast him a sideways glance, I suspected that his attention would have remained fixated upon the revisions Anthony had prepared and duly collated.*

*"It's important Mark…"*

*Since the second attempt was delivered a little louder and with more resolve, it proved to be an irritation which necessitated, a disapproving sigh and yet, this wife had dared to disturb his concentration, which also guaranteed a sideways glance.*

*"After our recent conversation, I was wondering whether your early retirement from public life might have something to do with these negotiations…"*

*"Charlie I don't have time to deal with this," Mark replied, in a hushed, irritated voice, but after checking whether there was any danger that Anthony, or a member of the flight crew might be within earshot, he added, "If everything goes according to plan, then this might turn out to be my last assignment on behalf of Special Operations…"*

*So with no excuses for backing out of what needed to be done, my fingers closed around the envelope. "In that case Mark, there's something you need to read, and for once it won't wait until next week, next month, or even next year…"*

*Clearly annoyed, Mark's gaze drifted down to the envelope, and he was shaking his head, in that certain way that was quite a unique part of his personal persona. "This is neither the time, nor the place to indulge in one of your childish games Charlie…"*

*"Oh, believe me this isn't a childish game…"*

*Despite his scepticism, Mark took the envelope, and after removing the photocopied pages, as I had witnessed on numerous occasions, he skimmed through the first page to determine, whether the others merited a more in depth inspection, and having discovered that the content warranted his due consideration, when he returned to the beginning of that first page, and began to reread the transcript, my heartbeat began to race.*

*Ever since I decided to trap Mark in his own deception, I have visualized this moment, and this scorned wife had longed to see her`husband's face and yet, instead of my victory* leaving me elated, I was consumed by a strange emptiness, because in keeping with the persona of an adept negotiator his expression revealed nothing at all.

At last, Mark returned the pages to the envelope, and without looking at me, he asked, "Is it safe to assume that there are more than those few photocopied pages?"

"Yes, there's more…"

Whispered, restrained, polite the exchange was almost surreal, especially when Mark complimented me. "Since the quality of your disinformation is quite unprecedented, you must have been watching, listening, and documenting over a lengthy period of time…"

Unsure whether Mark expected to receive any confirmation, when he paused, I opted to wait and then, still without looking at me, he enquired, "I trust you've taken the necessary precautions to ensure that they cannot find their way into the wrong hands…"

"Having learnt from a Grand Master--the crème de la crème--my security is as infallible as your own…"

"I'm flattered and that's comforting to know, and what do you intend to do next?"

After taking a steadying breath I told him the truth. "I don't intend to do anything Mark. You can regard it as an insurance policy, because after your retirement and taking into account a respectable adjustment period, I never want to see your face, or hear your name ever again. Now I trust we understand each other's position…"

With a deliberate slowness, Mark turned his head, so that he could make eye contact, before whispering, "Blackmail is so grubby, so unbecoming Charlie, it doesn't suit you…"

Now this good wife was finding his calmness disquieting, but having gone beyond the place, where I should not have begun, although I might have been walking through the valley of death, I had told myself that I would fear no evil, and without severing eye contact, I offered him more reassurance that he was not under any immediate threat.

"Ever since you told me about your extra curriculum activities, I have sustained my silence, and I would have nothing to gain and perhaps everything to lose, if the truth about your alternative lifestyle, and your treasonable deeds were to be revealed…"

Severing eye contact, Mark released a congratulatory laugh. "I taught you well Charlie, perhaps even too well, and it would seem that you have considered all of the implications. However, you do realize that you deserve far more than your freedom…"

This scorned wife should have been afraid, but then I reminded myself of the reason, why I undertook these precautions, and if I did know more than was healthy, then I had been right to be fearful that I might not live long enough to enjoy my freedom.

"While I'm aware that I might deserve more than my freedom, if anything untoward were to happen to me--or Lorna or Bobby--then arrangements have been made for an uncensored copy of the fictitious piece of literature to be delivered to Commander Maddox. It would therefore be your first and last mistake Mark…"

As Mark released a second small laugh he reached down, so that he could pick up his briefcase. "That's incorrect Charlie, I made my first and last mistake, when I never considered that my breathtakingly beautiful wife might be capable of such a betrayal…"

Then, with a resounding stereophonic click Mark opened his briefcase, and after thrusting the envelope inside, he whispered, "Although you and my credit cards might be able to enjoy yourselves at my expense, I have the best part of forty-eight hours ahead of me Chairing these negotiations. So if you've quite finished playing games, then I would like to continue my preparation, by incorporating Anthony's alterations into my schedule…"

Surely, there had to be more, and because he knew I was watching him, after closing his briefcase Mark lent towards me, before turning his head, so that he could once again achieve eye contact, as he offered me more reassurance. "There's no need to look so concerned Charlie…"

*Pausing, as any skilled negotiator would do, he waited before delivering his punch line. "Having made your position clear, you have guaranteed your freedom. In the meantime, perhaps you should pray that your security system is as infallible as you seem to believe it to be, because if what you've done should become common knowledge, then I would have cause to doubt that either of us will be alive long enough to tell anyone the truth…"*

*Mesmerized by the strange glint in my husband's eye, his wife was unable to stop him, when he lent towards me until his lips could brush against mine--in a rare--public display of affection, and because I could smell the muskiness of his aftershave, the same aftershave, I had first bought for him, in what now seemed to be too many moons ago, my heart was pounding faster than I could have imagined humanly possible.*

*This was everything I had wanted and yet, because I had loved him with my whole heart, and maybe still loved the man who--during our last time together--had managed to set aside, his sexual preference for young male virgins in order to make love to me with a tremendous tenderness, there was a sense of trepidation, in realizing that because of my betrayal, when his lips had brushed against mine, not only had my husband instigated divorce proceedings, in the very nest instant, he had granted me, my Decree Absolute.*

*Of course, with the benefit of hindsight the irony of our situation was obvious. In the crazy parallel universe Mark inhabited, if he could have set aside the fact that I had proved to be a valuable asset*--then Mark Daltry would have realized that from the very beginning, he had loved, and maybe still loved Charlotte Anne Forsyth with his whole heart.

Back in the study, it would seem that my revelations have heightened John's incredulity. "Surely, you weren't naïve enough to expect Mark to believe that your piece of literature was meant to be nothing more than, some kind of insurance policy?"

"After living with Mark's terms and conditions for a considerable period of time Mr Bland, he had no reason to doubt that I would not continue to maintain my silence…"

"Well, I happen to agree with Mark's description of blackmail--*it's so grubby, so unbecoming*--it rarely suits anyone least of all an amateur like you Charlie…"

Ouch! Now that one hurt, not only because of John's choice of words, but also the sharpness in his voice? If it's time, then this adult is prepared to undertake the aforementioned three falls, two submissions or a knockout and yet, clearly convinced that we cannot be trusted to play nicely together, Bill's interruption manages to keep us in our respective corners of the imaginary boxing ring.

"And what about after you arrived in Paris Charlie? Presumably, at some point Mark must have mentioned the incident again?"

Casting a glance in John's direction, I'm aware of an increased need to deliver my dialogue in a calm, precise manner. "By the time I woke in the morning, Mark and Anthony were already engrossed in the alterations from the previous day, so that my husband could continue Presiding at the negotiating table, and because I was asleep when Mark came to bed, the only time we came face to face was during the pre-scheduled meals…"

Pausing, I reach for my cigarettes and pull one out of the packet. "But it was obvious that even more than the American delegate's wife, I was nothing more than a decorative accessory, and whenever his hand touched mine I sensed an increasing contempt for my betrayal, but all I could do was hope that whatever he had planned, my insurance policy had convinced him that somehow he had to keep me alive…"

After clicking at the lighter, I look back at my inquisitors, and John is shaking his head. "Did you never stop to consider that there might be worse things than dying Charlie? In fact, it's our experience that when it comes to people who have found themselves in similar positions, they soon discovered that when it comes to their continued existence, dying would have been the easier option…"

Of course, he is preaching to the converted because growing up in the Forsyth household, I became aware that if an injured casualty of some obscure military conflict could have been given a choice, between enduring a slow tortuous road to recover half of the physical person they used to be, or being afforded the opportunity of choosing an instantaneous death on the battlefield, then dying might have been the easier option. However, I now have cause to suspect that John might not be aggrieved with anything I have done. Instead, he could be peeved because the cavalry failed to ask the right questions, and after exhaling the smoke from my lungs, I opt to deliver an inflammatory suggestion.

"In that case, you will be relieved to learn that I did get what I deserved Mr Bland. Only Mark saved that particular privilege, until the last day…"

"Yes I remember," John retorts, with a backward glance. "But when Bill commented upon the bruising, I also recall how your response led us to believe that one of the masked gunmen was responsible for inflicting them…"

"Ding, ding, seconds out," Bill announces, signalling the end of round one and then while John and I continue to stare at each other, he explains, "Since Bobby's better behaved than either of you, if you continue behaving like children, then you can expect to be treated like them. So before we proceed, do you both understand me?"

For his part, John casts his partner an affirmative nod, and when I turn away, so that I can tap the ash from my cigarette, it is sufficient for Bill to express his gratitude.

"Thank you…"

Risking a sly backward glance, I note that Bill has picked up one of the buff folders from the desk, the same one I suspected contained the information compiled during the debriefings, which were undertaken three months ago.

"Okay, this seems like an appropriate time to recap on what happened, inside Jacque Foray's residence on that last day…"

If you'll pardon an inappropriate pun, since this had been done to death, this weary adult groans at the prospect. "Surely, we don't need to go over it again?"

But for my benefit, John snaps, "Oh yes we do Charlie…"

Since the brusqueness of John's confirmation seems unnecessary, it prompts an ill thought out protest to emerge, which I direct at our arbitrator. "But after you escorted me home from Paris, during the subsequent debriefing sessions Bill, we went through it over and over again, and everything I told you was the truth…"

Determined to steal the words from out of his partner's mouth, without looking over his shoulder, John declares, "We don't doubt your truthfulness Charlie. However, I think you'd agree that there's a vast difference between the truth, and the whole truth…"

Touché, but in response, my protective parent swoops down to enter the defence I had been holding in reserve. "Perhaps you never asked the right questions Mr Bland…"

Still behaving like children, the principal contenders find themselves batting innuendos, back and forth across our imaginary net. However, despite finding it more difficult, Bill manages to seize control, by confiscating our invisible toys.

"Although we went through it repeatedly at the end of March, for the benefit of the recording, I think it's in your best interests, if we went over some of it again Charlie…"

"And this time," John interjects, from his safe haven. "Irrespective of how trivial or insignificant any detail might seem we need you to tell us everything…"

Opting to concede defeat--albeit with reluctance--I behave like a grown up. "If there's any danger that it might make you more agreeable Mr Bland, then we'll go through it again, and since you know everything, why would I have any reason to omit any details?"

Pausing, my gaze drifts back to our arbitrator and with a detectable degree of disrespect, I ask, "Are WE going to start from when I woke up, on that last day Bill?"

"No that won't be necessary Charlie. Unless you have any objections, I would like to begin from around the middle of the last day…"

Then, after my weary child lodges no objections, Bill flips open the buff folder, and starts to read from the typewritten text. "So this is what we documented from the recordings of the debriefing sessions. Firstly, the negotiations were concluded to everyone's satisfaction by 11:00. Secondly, a light lunch was served at midday, during which the American delegate was advised by his Personal Assistant about an urgent telephone message. As a result, the three of them left the building, one hour earlier than expected. Thirdly, after their departure you made your excuses and went upstairs to finish packing, and although you could not be sure of the exact time, after hearing raised voices you left the second floor bedroom, so that you could investigate…"

As Bill pauses, I tap the ash from my cigarette, before casting him a backward glance, which prompts him to ask, "Is that an accurate account of the events Charlie?"

"Yes it is, apart from the fact that as a result of our conversation on the Private Jet, I was aware that something was going to happen, and when I first heard the raised voices, I was thinking that in forty minutes, we were scheduled to return to the airfield, and if that was Mark's last assignment, then I would have gained my freedom…"

After documenting the amendment on his rather old fashioned notepad, Bill continues, "So that would set the time, when you went to investigate at approximately 13:15 and presumably, once you reached the landing, it must have been a couple of minutes later, when you first saw Mark standing outside the conference room?"

Since Bill's recollection has conjured up a new image I close my eyes, and when I reached the end of the landing, and I looked down, behind the present tense.

Below me, in the past tense, *as the image comes into focus, Mark was not alone. Someone was standing beside him, but in the next instant, I was distracted by a small explosion on the ground floor, and as the smoke from the ensuing fire began to rise up the stairwell, I heard a woman screaming, and from the accent it sounded as if the female was Emilie, Jacque Foray's housekeeper and then, my husband must have sensed that someone was observing them, because both men looked up,* and back in the present tense.

Since I do not want to address the wider reaching repercussions in my Godfather's study, I suspend the image, so that I can glance at Bill with a clear conscience, and because he knows me well enough to be able to read my actions and reactions he is waiting, perhaps even anticipating, the arrival of some piece of missing information, and left with no alternative, I confess my unintentional indiscretion.

"Everything was happening so fast, I don't know how I failed to remember, but when I reached the landing and looked down, Mark wasn't alone. He appeared to be engaged in a heated discussion with another man…"

Unlike his partner, Bill reveals neither disapproval nor disappointment, and he sustains his level-headed control, as he asks, "Did you recognize this man Charlie?"

Too afraid to release the image, it remains frozen in the past tense. "No I'd never seen him before that last day…"

"And while you were inside the building, did you see him again?"

"I don't understand Bill, what are you hoping to achieve with these questions?"

By the window John's temporary detachment comes to an end, when he glances over his shoulder, so that he can repay my earlier compliment by directing his words, with a detectable degree of disrespect. "Surely, someone as INTELL!GENT as you should not need to rely upon your degree in applied mathematics to work it out Charlie…"

Then, knowing that my principal male will be more than willing to enlighten me, I maintain eye contact, until he volunteers some clarification. "Earlier you indicated that once you were all assembled in the conference room, you counted fourteen hostages, and together with the five masked gunmen, there would have been a total of nineteen people. Then, when their demand that the American delegate be returned to the building failed to receive a response and Anthony was executed, which in turn triggered more gunfire, after one of the masked gunmen took you with him when he jumped out of the window, including Mark there would have been sixteen living persons and one dead body left inside, and because seventeen bodies were recovered, why don't you describe this mysterious stranger for us?"

Of course, John's right and I do not need to apply my worthless degree to work it out. Suddenly, I'm struggling to keep the image from coming into focus, as I enter what is supposed to be a defence. "But I only saw him for a moment…"

That's correct I had no reason to consider the long term implications, and since I do not want to remember, although the image remains suspended, when it comes to a multi-disciplined professional like John, his leading lady's reply was too rushed and too defensive.

"He must have been standing beside your husband, and even if you only saw him for a moment I'm sure that compared to Mark, you can at least give us some idea of his height, and build, maybe even his colouring…"

"I don't remember…"

"Coming from someone who had spent, at least fourteen months noting every place, and name, and watching every strange face that's not good enough, and I think you can do better Mrs Daltry…"

Having heard John level a similar accusation at a different leading lady, how dare he compare me with that Person of Interest in connection with the same incident, and because I'm exasperated with either being accused or held responsible, provided that Bill does not prevent us, I am more than willing to undertake, the aforementioned three falls, two submissions or a knock out.

"This isn't fair Mr Bland," I declare, as I snap my head around, so I can confront him. "After that moment on the landing, I never saw him again, and as I explained earlier because the pieces of the puzzle did not begin to slot into place, until a couple of days ago when I first started to suspect that Mark was still alive--I wouldn't have had any reason whatsoever to make any connection between that mysterious man, and my husband…"

"Possibly not," John fires back at me. "But I'm not asking you to justify why you failed to mention this man three months ago? If seventeen bodies were recovered from the building, all I'm trying to establish is whether that man could have been the owner of the unrecognizable remains, we buried in your husband's grave on that miserable rainy day in April, and since life isn't fair only you or Mark can provide us with the answer…"

The image remains distorted, but even though my gaze drifts to our arbitrator, there will be no reprieve, as Bill adds his own endorsement. "I'm afraid I have to agree with John. Since everyone known to be in the building not only before, but also during the siege was accounted for after the bodies were recovered, it's important because if we did bury this man in your husband's grave, then we're going to need an Exhumation Order, before we can verify the DNA results…"

Exhumation order! My God, this surpasses anything I could have anticipated, and suddenly that image in the past tense is neither suspended nor blurred.

*Below me on the landing, when Mark sensed that someone was observing them, and both men looked up, although such an uncanny coincidence should not have been possible, compared with my husband, this other man was the same height, same build but different colouring,* and in the present tense it will have to be entered as previously undisclosed evidence, and barely able to hear my own words, I admit

"Only Mark can tell you for certain whether this man somehow took his place, which would have enabled my husband to leave the building, but since his height and build were very similar, I think it could have been possible…"

At last, this adult has stated the whole truth and yet, there is something I need to clarify. "Given the benefit of hindsight, if I had suspected that he intended to fake his own death, then taking into consideration that Mark was an only child, side by side there was an uncanny resemblance, but in the next instant all hell broke loose when the small explosion occurred on the ground floor…"

"Sorry for interrupting Charlie," John silences me. "But during our preparation Bill, I seem to remember that there's something documented in Mark's file about how Mr and Mrs Daltry became eligible to adopt, after numerous attempts at IVF had failed…"

For is part, Bill is thumbing through the appropriate folder, so that he can confirm his partner's observation. "Apparently, when Mark was first vetted on behalf of Special Operations because his birth mother had a child who was on a Social Service's at Risk Register, before he was born she agreed to have him fostered, and when she did not contest the subsequent adoption, Mark junior became the only child of Mark and Alison Daltry who had been unable to conceive a child of their own…"

Whilst this might be very interesting for the cavalry, I fail to make the connection. "But that still doesn't explain how the result from the DNA analysis, confirmed that my husband was dead?"

"That's why we need to acquire an Exhumation Order, because we won't be able to determine whether Mark managed to plant more than your cigarette lighter and his wedding ring on this man, and since it's our experience that nothing is impossible, the Commander will have to ask his P. A. to appoint people from one of our Administration Teams to go back to Mark's birth, so that the adoption can be examined in more depth…"

Feeling a little less intimidated I manage to offer Bill a fleeting smile, prompting him to explain. "Before we can move beyond that last day in Paris, it's in your best interest if we finalize the outstanding details, and unless you have any objections, I suggest that we continue taking one step at a time…"

"Of course, but I'm concerned that the wrong impression is being created, and as a result, I could be blamed or even held responsible for the fact that so many people died…"

"Although ambiguities and innuendos might be suggesting otherwise Charlie," Bill declares, as he directs his remark in his partner's direction. "Nobody has any grounds whatsoever for holding you accountable for anyone dying on that last day…"

As he pauses, our arbitrator waits until John accepts the subtle reprimand through another backward glance, before Bill proceeds. "In fact, Mark's elaborate plan was quite ingenious, because there can be no doubt that your husband, somehow managed to arrange and then, orchestrate the siege, so that he could escape undetected from his double life, and leave everyone believing that along with the hostages, he had died inside the building…"

Over by the window, John stirs in a more meaningful way. "And, if he hadn't either underestimated his wife or as Charlie said herself--*if he'd had the decency to stay dead*--then Mark might have pulled off the greatest escape in the history of Special Operations…"

As my principal male was delivering his line, there was something about the way in which he was staring at his leading lady, but this seasoned performer will reserve her right to be flattered, in case it was meant to be a back-handed compliment, which leaves Bill free to begin concluding any unfinished business.

"Charlie can you remember what happened to the envelope, and the photocopied documents, Mark had taken from you during the flight to Paris?"

For my part, not wanting to be found guilty of giving any more incorrect or misleading details, I excuse my delay in responding by checking that the cigarette, I had left in the ashtray is extinguished and yet, in the past tense Bill's question has generated a new image of my husband's profile. What an apt choice of words?

*Downstairs, I could hear more raised voices, not shouting in French, and Emilie had started screaming, when Mark came rushing up the stairs, and after he grabbed hold of my upper arm, he forced me to accompany him into the bedroom, and because the usual calm debonair negotiating persona had disappeared, I was fearful of the unknown.*

*"Whatever is going on downstairs Mark, is it something to do with the early retirement you've been planning?"*

*Ignoring my question, Mark was conducting a visual scan of the room, and when he did not find whatever he was looking for, he demanded, "Where's your cigarette lighter?"*

*"It's in my shoulder bag…"*

*Snatching my bag from the bedside cabinet, Mark went to the dressing table and turned it upside down. Then, after rummaging among the contents, until he found the lighter with that tell-tale stereophonic click, he opened his briefcase and removed the envelope I'd given him during the flight to Paris, before taking both items into the adjoining en-suite.*

*In less than forty minutes, we were due to return to the airfield, and if this was to be his last assignment, then I would have gained my freedom. Instead, I watched my husband sparking the lighter into flame, so that he could set alight to one of the corners of the envelope. Then, using his thumb and index finger, while Mark held it above the sink in the en-suite, he confirmed that my worst nightmare was about to turn into a reality.*

*"That small explosion suggests that we are about become pawns in a hostage situation, and since it's standard procedure for the building to be searched room by room, we might only have ten minutes Charlie, before they reach us…"*

*It all seemed unreal, and because Mark needed to be certain that I had heard him, he raised his voice. "Are you listening to me Charlie?"*

*"Yes Mark," I replied, with an obvious sharpness. "I heard what you said…"*

*"Before you were granted clearance, so that you could accompany me on my assignments, can you remember the basic instructions you were given in case we ever found ourselves in such a situation?"*

*"Of course, I should do whatever I'm told to do, whenever I'm told to do it, and in addition to speaking only when I'm spoken to at all times, I should endeavour to avoid making eye contact, especially if any of the assailants admit to being terrorists, but if this is something connected with your plans Mark, then I have a right to know…"*

*Still no response and yet, as I continued watching him, I realized that his normal calm persona seemed to be returning, and it struck me that perhaps the envelope and its content had given rise to some serious misgivings, but then during our flight Mark had warned me that if anyone found out about my insurance policy, then he doubted either of us would live long enough to tell anyone the truth,* but in the present tense.

"Charlie…"

Back in the study, Bill's request for my attention causes me to freeze the image of my husband in the adjoining en-suite. "Beyond any shadow of a doubt are you certain that Mark burnt both the envelope, and its contents?"

Since there's no doubt whatsoever, my response is immediate. "If you're worried that other people might have read or even had access to the content, then I can assure you that the envelope was the only thing Mark took from his briefcase, and he must have been concerned about anyone finding them, because he went to extreme lengths to eradicate any trace of their existence by rinsing the charred remnants down the sink…"

Outside a louder clap of thunder from the storm, which has been growing nearer seems appropriate, as John states the obvious. "And I don't suppose that in your naivety, you also never stopped to consider that during those remaining few minutes, your husband might want to know not only, what provisions you'd made in the event of such a situation arising, but also the whereabouts of the original fictitious piece of literature…"

"With all due respect Mr Bland," His leading lady almost barks at him. "You've never taken into consideration that like my husband, you might be underestimating my capabilities, because in an attempt to avoid receiving, what Mark thought my betrayal merited, I didn't need to rely on my right to remain silent. Instead, when the question arose, I told Mark what he wanted to know. However, as one can imagine, for a man like my husband with his perfectionism and oversized ego, it was the last thing he wanted to hear…"

Startled by my admission--perhaps even a little alarmed--I had seen Bill look up from the file and as soon as the opportunity arose, he sought some clarification. "I'm sorry to interrupt you yet again, but did I hear you confirm that you told Mark the whereabouts of the original document?"

How delightful it is to discover that when it comes to the issue of naivety, it is not a quality unique to me or John "Don't you think you're being a little naïve Mr Powell?"

Then, without affording our arbitrator the right to reply, I confirm my own demise. "Since we are all grown-ups, we know that I would have been dead a long time ago, if I had told Mark the absolute truth and then, none of this would have been necessary. Instead what I told my husband…"

*Inside the en-suite, as Mark rinsed every last remnant of ash down the sink, he asked, "During the flight, we never discussed what provisions you had made in case this kind of situation should arise, and it might end with people dying?"*

*"If either you or both of us were to die today Mark--then nothing would happen, because there wouldn't be any reason why anyone would need to know what I've done…"*

*Pausing, I waited for him to turn the tap off, before adding, "However, using this situation as an example, if anything untoward were to happen to me, and you survived, then we would be dealing with different kind of scenario, for which I have taken the necessary precautionary measures…"*

*With his calmness remaining undisturbed, Mark half turned to look at me. "Now that is a shame Charlie, because it means we do have a difference of opinion…"*

*Unbeknown to my husband, while he was still preoccupied in the en-suite, I had lifted his handgun, back out of his flight bag. The same gun which I had removed from the place, where he had concealed it upon our arrival, and when he began to move into the bedroom, I was holding it in my right hand, but with my arm extended down the right hand side of my body, so that it was partly concealed behind my upper thigh.*

*"Since we only have a few minutes left," Mark stated, as he took another step towards me. "In which to resolve our difference of opinion, while at the same time concluding some unfinished business Charlie, we can either do this the easy way or the hard way…"*

*Raising my arm so that I could grasp his gun with both hands--as if I was a professional--was enough to prevent my husband from taking another step in my direction. "As you can see, there is something else you failed to consider your breathtakingly beautiful wife might be capable of doing, and now that we understand each other's point of view, I don't think we need to do this--either the easy way or the hard way…"*

*Tilting his head a little onto one side, Mark congratulated me. "Although this seems to be something else I underestimated, the gun is only a meaningful deterrent if the person aiming it is prepared to pull the trigger…"*

*In order to prove that this was not some kind of whimsical gesture, I disengaged the gun's safety catch, which caused my husband to raise his hands a little as if he was surrendering, while I afforded him an explanation.*

*"Of course, having grown up in the Forsyth household Mark, ever since I was a child I've known something about firearms. However, after you told me about your betrayal of not only me, but also your country for my own protection, I completed an advanced course in firearms training, and if you give me a reason, then make no mistake, your body will be one more casualty of whatever is happening right now inside this building…"*

*"Since I estimate that you have no more than four or maybe five minutes before they reach this end of the landing, although you could continue to hold me hostage, sooner or later, you need to make a decision about what you intend to do next?"*

*"Oh I don't intend to use the gun Mark," this wife replied. "At least not unless you give me a good reason. Presumably, you're keen to discover the whereabouts of the flash-drive which contains the entire piece of fictitious literature, and since I'm opting to do this the easy way, it is in a safety deposit box back in the United Kingdom…"*

*Beyond the door, I could hear activity further down the landing, but I was not about to be silenced. "Furthermore, about twelve months ago, in anticipation of your retirement, I had the foresight to finalize my personal affairs, and because I have appointed my Godfather, Philip Maddox not only as the administrator of my estate, in the event of my disappearance, but also as the Sole Executor of that same estate, in the event of my death. I'm afraid that somehow you have to find a way to keep me alive Mark…"*

*Momentarily distracted by the slamming of a door on the landing, Mark seized the initiative and grabbed hold of my hands. Then, after he severed my two-handed grasp on the gun, he twisted my arm behind my back, so that he could take possession of the weapon and as he held me crushed against him, he put his free arm around my neck.*

*"It would seem that thanks to your meddling in things beyond your comprehension, all that remains is for you to appreciate what might happen, if we both survive and you fail to maintain your silence…"*

*Despite the confined space, as Mark released me I tried to keep some distance between us, but when it came to limiting the damage, my self-defence abilities were nothing compared with my husband's trained capabilities, and when it came to the level of pain Mark could inflict with fewer and yet, more well placed blows, he exceeded my expectation.*

*Then while I was writhing on the floor in absolute agony, retching and clutching my stomach, regardless of how odd it might have seemed, when the door opened I was relieved because the arrival of the two masked gunmen saved me from any further violence. Besides, my husband could not have risked beating me to death,* and back in the present tense.

As if it might make the level of violence acceptable, I shrug my shoulders as the approaching storm, which has continued to rumble on towards Manor Park, produces a more pronounced clap of thunder. "Like my husband's plan it was ingenious, except that once the formalities were concluded there was nothing more that Mark could do, other than make me appreciate what might happen, if I decided not to maintain my silence…"

Although I had hoped that my revelations might make John less disagreeable, his dissatisfied mutter suggests otherwise, but no doubt fearing an escalation in hostilities between us, Bill rides to my rescue.

"Irrespective of the agreement we reached before dinner Charlie, I'm afraid that the introduction of the gun means that I need to ask you to confirm some details relating to the events of the 22nd of June…"

It is a daunting request, but I trust him. "That's okay Bill. After I began making connections a couple of days ago, there are some things I don't mind talking about…"

"Although that might be the case, if you're struggling, then please raise your hand so that we can pause while you recover your composure…"

Finding Bill's contingency plan comforting, I cast him a gentle nod, before he begins to read from a different file. "In our written report, we documented how we had found you in the master bedroom at 187 Cheltenham Way on June 22 at 4:10. However, after somehow managing to squeeze yourself into the small gap, between the dresser and the wall, John ascertained that you were holding a gun so tightly he had to unfurl your fingers, one at a time. Since we now know you underwent a course in firearms training for the benefit of the recording, and using your own words, could you please tell us about that gun?"

As a louder clap of thunder disrupts my train of thought, it gives me the opportunity to freeze an image of Blake, while I explain. "When they were interrupted, Shaw realized that if I couldn't stand up without falling over, then there was little chance of me getting dressed. So he took Mark's gun from Blake, and he placed it against my knee, while he threatened me with what would happen, if I didn't maintain my silence and then, as if he wanted to prove my helplessness, he threw it down on the bed. So, I picked it up and if any of them had come back up the stairs, especially Shaw, I swear to God that the young Police Officer would not have been the only fatality…"

"Thank you Charlie. Unless there's anything else you'd like to add, I think that clarifies everything regarding the second handgun registered to Mark Daltry…"

Behind me, even before John utters a sound, I sense that he has been watching me. "Despite being trained how to aim and fire a gun, while you were in Paris, you must have realized that up against a man like Mark, who had undergone basic unarmed combat training, when it came to relieving you of his gun, it must…."

"But if the gun had not bought me some extra minutes," I dare to interrupt him. "Then the bruises Bill commented upon would have been far worse…"

Silence, as incredible as it sounds, if you will excuse another dreadful play on words, there is an almost deadly silence, until another even louder clap of thunder rolls across the sky. Then, when I hear John's muttered dissatisfaction, because we have almost come full circle, and we are about to find ourselves back at the place, where we should have begun the story of my life, this adult believes I am more than prepared to undertake the aforementioned three falls, two submissions or a knockout, with the kind of determination not to be thwarted by our arbitrator.

"All right Mr Bland," this leading lady announces, as I swallow the remaining whisky from my glass in one decisive mouthful. "I think you've provided our invisible audience with enough disagreeable muttering, and disapproving tutting not to mention, more than your fair share of facetious remarks and subtle innuendos. But surely, within our almost incestuous threesome enough must be more than enough for any Interviewee?"

"Charlie…"

Well now, guess who? Shucks guess it was too easy, but nothing will stop this scorned woman, when I've got her mind set on doing something my way.

"Up until now Mr Powell," I declare, in a strong positive voice. "With the exception of a few skirmishes, I think you would have to agree that to the best of my ability, you have enjoyed my co-operation. However, after journeying this far, there are some vital pieces of information missing, and if you dare to intervene I will make things very awkward, by withdrawing that co-operation…"

Distracted by a spectacular flash of forked lightning, which seems to suggest that God, our Heavenly Father is affording the three of us, some kind of Divine intervention, I hesitate, before I continue. "And before you start making intimidating waves about MI5, I suggest that you check the file again, because that threat was made, before you discovered, what kind of insurance policy I had created, Furthermore, because of the names in that piece of fictitious literature, I suspect that if you were to ask your Commanding Officer--who in turn would need to consult the highest possible Authority, because in order to avoid any further embarrassment, he would be seeking approval for Special Operations to be granted the opportunity to clean up the mess, my husband has left in your own backyard…"

Like any well-rehearsed leading lady, I pause for a few seconds, before delivering the final part of my soliloquy. "Of course, now let me remember how your partner described it? Ah yes and I quote, "*Blackmail is so grubby, so unbecoming and it rarely suits anyone, least of all an amateur like you Charlie.*" unquote and since we have established that blackmail is one of my specialities we could always pause, while you check with Commander Maddox how he wants you to proceed, in his--*own best interests…*"

Then, when Bill chooses to remain silent, which is bliss to my ears--as another flash of forked lightning lights up the study--my gaze moves to his partner.

"Well Mr Bland, provided that we agree to abide by some basic guidelines, which our arbitrator can lay down, isn't it time you had the decency to clear the air between us?"

After casting me a complimentary nod, John picks up my imaginary gauntlet. "Subject to our arbitrator's approval, it will be a pleasure Mrs Daltry…"

Not only blackmailed, but also outvoted it is Bill's turn to utter a disapproving mutter and because he suspects that this will end badly for one of us, he is shaking his head, as he announces for the benefit of the recording. "How can I possibly refuse? However, if you insist on behaving in this infantile fashion, then there will be no biting, scratching, hair pulling or head-locks, and whenever I tell you to break, you will disengage and before John can continue to clear the air, you will wait until this referee finishes the official count…"

Allowing us time to absorb his words, Bill hesitates, before adding, "But let there be no mistake, if things get out of hand, and either of you should give me cause to regret this, I will halt this Interview, and even though it might mean that we cannot proceed until tomorrow morning, I will seek the necessary guidance from the Commander. Now, having made myself crystal clear, I hope that you can be trusted to play nicely together?"

For a lingering moment, the two men continue to stare at each other, and although I sense there's a reason why I need to understand, I fail to grasp the significance. How intriguing, but then my speculation has to come to an end, when John turns away from the window, and after walking to the cabinet, so that he can return the empty glass he has been nursing to its rightful place beside the pure malt whisky bottle, he returns to the window, so that he can place a respectable amount of distance between us--at least enough distance to satisfy our arbitrator.

"All right Mrs Daltry," John states, before he begins to clear the air between us. "After your father took it upon himself to interfere, not only in respect of Bobby's biological father by allowing the consent to reach the Official Record, but also three years after Bobby was born, when he fixed it, so that once Mark Daltry knew about the existence of your son, there was nothing preventing you from marrying him. For the benefit of the recording, as incredible as it might sound, I don't have any difficulty whatsoever accepting, how you had no choice, except to learn how to live within the confines of your own silence…"

Strictly off that same Official Record at this point, I was thinking so far so good, until another flash of lightning is followed by an immediate clap of thunder, which seems to roll out across the heavens as the storm passes directly over Manor Park. Then, when the heavy raindrops begin to pound against the bullet proof glass, it is perhaps prophetic that their arrival should coincide with John continuing to deliver his deductions.

"But once you learnt the truth about Mark's alternative lifestyle and you discovered, how he had been blackmailing Bobby's father, what I cannot comprehend is why you maintained your sanctimonious silence and then, after choosing to follow Mark's example by producing your fictitious piece of literature, you decided to meddle--with amateurish incompetence--in matters way beyond your comprehension or your control…"

As John pauses, I suspect that he is far from finished defending his disagreeableness, and since I am aware that it would be a negative sign, I manage to maintain eye contact, while he catches his breath, and when he proceeds his voice becomes lower and less sharp,

"But having spent your entire life surrounded by all this Charlie, what I find incomprehensible is why you of all people would have believed, that you possessed some kind of God given right to be able to break the rules--the rules we all have to abide by--and expect to get away with it?"

At least John has reverted to addressing me by my Christian name, which suggests that perhaps his brain has reconnected with his mouth, but I know he is right, because I would have to admit that as a result of any action, there will be an equal and opposite reaction, and after meddling in things beyond my comprehension or my control, there would have always been consequences and yet, in all fairness, this adult had never believed that I could break any of the rules and expect to get away with anything.

"Perhaps, I was desperate Mr Bland…"

"I'm afraid that I have to disagree with you Mrs Daltry…"

Wrong again, and after taking one step forward, we have jumped two steps back, and having reverted to using the formal means of addressing me, it enables John to detach himself from any kind of personal connection, while he continues his rampaging.

"Obviously, you weren't desperate enough or you would have realized that the sensible solution would have been to seek the right kind of support, and having scrutinised the contents of the Forsyth File, unless we're missing something fundamental, we couldn't find any reason whatsoever why you would not have received a sympathetic hearing, if you had decided to approach Commander Maddox…"

Of course, there is something fundamental missing and having come full circle, we have arrived back at the place, where the story of my life should have commenced and it would seem that my earlier assumption was correct. The cavalry have never been granted the security clearance required to access any Classified Information from the Research Programme. If they had, then they would have discovered that despite Philip Maddox being my Godfather, my vulnerable child would only have approached him, in the unlikely event of hell freezing over.

"As I've tried to explain, there were other people who needed to be considered so it would have meant wrecking …"

Anticipating the end of my statement, John's raised voice silences me. "If you had approached the Commander, then the ensuing furore over the role the Major had played when he concealed the identity of your son's father, despite having tendered his resignation, because he never knew the truth about Mark, his Military Directive would have been reinstated. As far as Bobby's biological father was concerned--after contravening the Official Secrets Act he didn't deserve to remain in his privileged position. However, for some inexplicable reason, you felt unable to make an approach to your own Godfather …"

It would seem that Bill was correct. This is going to end badly for one of us, and with John winning line by unscripted line, it would seem it's a foregone conclusion it's destined to be me. However, since I also remain accountable, in accordance with potential offences in pursuance of the Official Secrets Act, this is not a line of enquiry, I am willing to pursue.

"Like everyone else, I believed Mark was dead…"

"Irrespective of whether Mark was alive or dead," argues John, "As our Person of Interest in connection with the Paris incident suggested, if Mark's Sponsor and Handler were thorough and they suspected that you knew too much, then all anyone needed to do was wait for three months, before *issuing a Contract to* three freelancers. However, if you had asked for assistance, either when you first discovered the truth about Mark or during our debriefing sessions after we escorted you home, you would have gained proper protection, not some ill thought out childish insurance policy, but professional protection…"

Only too aware that every contribution, I have attempted to make has failed to quell John's disagreeableness, I choose to remain silent, until he is finished. "Protection not only for Lorna and Bobby, but also for your father, his driver and his Security Officer…."

Wounded by his succinctness, I sever eye contact and then, believing that he is finished, I make the innocent mistake of daring to ask him. "What do you want me to say Mr Bland? I have no defence to offer, except that I knew the risks…"

Whoosh--light touch paper, before taking a big step back. Regrettably, it is perhaps predictable that having chosen the wrong words, John's reverberating pronouncement would be immediate. "That's a load of bullshit. In fact, don't ever try to give me that kind of crap, because I was there and from what I saw with my own eyes, your understanding of those risks was somewhat conspicuous by its absence when we found you at 4:10 on the 22$^{nd}$ June in the master bedroom of 187 Cheltenham Way, clutching the gun in one hand, and a packet of sleeping tablets in the other, which even you admitted you would have swallowed if it hadn't been for your unborn child…"

"Please…."

It was meant to be the beginning of a heartfelt plea because earlier, I thought John had been prepared to abide by the agreement, we had reached before dinner, but when he takes a step away from the window, I'm too overwhelmed and too fearful that he might trigger the images from the events of that horrific Thursday morning, I cannot find either the right or wrong words, which might prevent him from approaching the desk.

"What's the matter Charlie?  Surely, you can't still be denying that it happened, because it did--and I don't believe that a respectable middle-class lady like you had any idea of the kind of prolonged terror, you could be subjected to in your own home?"

Having reached the desk, I sense John's hand moving towards my face and yet, after what happened when he held the lighter steady, I have nothing to fear from his touch. Unlike his words, his hands would never harm me, and because those words will only release the images if I allow them to do so, I do nothing to prevent him from raising my head, until he can see my face.

"Don't you dare cry?"

Despite the pools of liquid threatening to well up in this leading lady's eyes, I will not give my principal male, the satisfaction of witnessing their escape.

"I can assure you that I wasn't going to cry…"

"Oh I'm pleased to hear it, because if you dare do that thing you women do, whenever you get overemotional, I might be tempted to take a leaf out of your husband's book and beat the shit out of you…"

Still staring up at him, once again this scorned wife reminds herself that she has no reason to be afraid, because despite having played this scene with another leading lady, John is a different kind of man to the one I had the misfortune to marry.

Is it over? Has his brain finally gained control of his mouth? Although my vulnerable child cannot be sure her parent decides to test him, by venturing to pose an unavoidable direct question. "Would it make you feel any better?"

"I doubt it…"

Releasing my face, John moves to the other side of the desk, but despite the rumbles of thunder suggesting that the storm is moving away from Manor Park even after he reseats himself, John's sigh confirms that this is not yet over.

"Considering everything you've told us Charlie--you must have been more than desperate to have placed yourself in such a position. In fact, for some reason, you must have been blinded by contempt or you would never have behaved in such a reckless way..."

This remains a line of enquiry I am not at liberty to pursue, and because John's persistence has caused two stray tears to escape I rest my elbows on the desk, so that my hands are covering my face, but there is no respite from this level of professionalism.

Reaching across the desk, John draws my hands away from my face, and I continue to avoid eye contact, while he levels even more thought provoking questions. "Oh the bruises might have started to fade, but do you have any idea how long it will take, before you can look at yourself in a full length mirror or allow any man to touch your body, without you being reminded of what took place during those sixty minutes of your life?"

"Please don't," I attempt to reiterate my plea. "Please don't do this..."

Suddenly, my principal male is deceptively calm. Calm enough for the preciseness of his words to inflict maximum damage, as he ignores my plea for some degree of clemency and chooses to describe, what he believes could have been an end game scenario.

"And once Shaw, Blake and Peterson were inside the house, if the elderly lady at 181 Cheltenham Way hadn't been disturbed, by the sound of a car engine, and she hadn't reported her concerns to the police, you would have told Shaw everything he wanted to hear. Believe me, irrespective of any ideas you might have harboured about holding out, you would have told him, and if Shaw had succeeded in getting you away from the house..."

"John..."

Out of control, John disregards his partner's summons. "While they waited for the merchandise to be verified, as if you were an animal, Shaw would have kept you gagged and chained, and to alleviate their boredom in addition to a constant stream of verbal abuse--on a daily basis, they would have raped, sodomised and forced you to perform oral sex..."

After Bill's attempt failed to spare both me, and our invisible audience from his partner's graphic description of my hypothetical fate, while John remains unstoppable, as if it might help protect me from the verbal onslaught, my head is cupped in my hands.

"And--by the time the remainder of Shaw's fee had been paid into some obscure off-shore bank account, you would have been begging him--believe me, you would have begged him to put you out of your misery..."

"Please John--you gave me your word..."

Silence, a blessed deadly silence has descended, until John dares to excuse his behaviour. "You were the one who wanted me to clear the air between us. Besides, if you remember rightly when I--or should I say we--gave you our word, we only agreed that we would not ask you to describe, what took place on that Thursday morning..."

"You bastard," I hear this scorned leading lady announcing. "You unmitigated bastard, you have managed to turn this into some kind of personal persecution..."

Lifting my head, I achieve eye contact, before adding, "But you can afford to be a smug bastard, because I did tell Shaw or at least I surrendered the bank details..."

Persecution and justification, two opposites of the equation, especially when one considers that it's too late to stop the images from escaping, but with regard to my denial John is also right because unlike when we were at the Mayfield Clinic, I can no longer pretend that I am an actress playing a biographical role in a film or a television programme.

Regrettably, not only was it real, the actual events were autobiographical, and if for no other reason than it might make John Bland feel uncomfortable, then to the best of my ability I will attempt to share them with our wider audience.

### JUNE 22     187 CHELTENHAM WAY     INCIDENT UPDATE
### 3 13a m   Urgent Assistance Required

Time to recap--*while Blake had used the barrel of the gun to bring about, what I later discovered was the cold-blooded murder of my unborn child, keeping one hand clamped over my mouth, Shaw had been recording the proceedings on the hand held camcorder. However, as soon as the excruciating pain began to subside, he eased his hand away from my mouth, before issuing me with that persuasive verbal threat.*

*"Now you've experienced what will happen, if you don't do whatever you're told to do, whenever you're told to do it, perhaps you'll be more cooperative during the rest of our visit, because believe me, those tame demonstrations of my associate's ability to inflict physical pain were only the beginning..."*

*Then, without any further delay I heard the tell-tale sound of a metal zip fastener being lowered, undoubtedly the zip on the Levi's Blake was wearing, and with Peterson still holding my arms pinned above my head, after grabbing hold of my hips, Blake elongated my torso, by dragging me down to the edge of the bed, and because he had bragged about his sexual prowess as if it were an essential part of his curriculum vitae, I remember thinking that although I might not be at liberty to lodge any customer complaints, the very least I could do was everything in my power to rob this habitual rapist of the sexual performance, their paymaster--whoever that person or even persons might be--was hoping to watch from behind the safety of the camcorder replay.*

*"Now, isn't she a sight for a man's sore eyes?" Blake remarked and then, as his hands moved over my body, and he began massaging my breasts in a futile attempt to arouse me, he added, "And if they were adorned such firm breasts would look magnificent..."*

*After Peterson took control of the camcorder, Shaw began to tell me about their paymaster's expectations. "This contract came with some specific requests. So for the benefit of the recording, I want you to provide my associate with his optimum position..."*

*Although Blake had lifted my legs, they were shaking, and when I hesitated, Shaw grew impatient. "If you don't start becoming more cooperative, I'll have to consider, whether you require a little incentive--such as using the clamps to adorn your breasts, before being secured using metal screws and since we have six of them, I'm sure you can imagine where the other four would go. Is that what you're going to force me to do Mrs Daltry?"*

*At the prospect of such a delightful incentive my legs moved, and because I knew what he expected, once my feet were on Blake's shoulders, Shaw acknowledged my subservience. "Now that's a small improvement because you are beginning to resemble someone working in the sex trade who's being paid to do, whatever my associates want, whenever they want it, and for as long as I allow them to do it..."*

*From bitter experience, I understood that my undignified position would provide Blake with the extra leverage he required as he thrust himself into my body and yet, having anticipated the renewed surge of pain, I stopped my vulnerable child from crying out by digging my fingernails into the palms of my hands, and while I should have been kicking, screaming, begging--maybe even pleading with Shaw that I would do anything and everything in an attempt to avoid the inevitable, knowing that any meaningful resistance would incur further reprimands, I chose to fix my gaze on a particular point on the ceiling.*

*Of course, having perfected the art of how to be unresponsive from the crème de la crème, I was trying to detach myself from his gratuitous presence, and thanks to the slow beat from one from my favourite songs I had been listening to on the stereo system before I had drifted into my usual light sleep, I was telling myself that for as long as I could continue to chase the words around in my head, my body would not respond to his incessant demands for its participation.*

*Oh how naïve, especially when I had not taken into consideration that this was a game, which Blake must have played on many previous occasions, and when he adjusted his rhythm, skilfully altering his tempo, my rapist was violating my delicate flesh powerfully and deeply, in a deliberate attempt to cause prolonged discomfort.*

*Adjusting my breathing with each inhalation becoming more even and then, every exhalation growing longer, my vulnerable child tried to offset the impact and yet, the precarious balance of my self-imposed isolation had been disturbed, and in an undesirable moment of reality, I realized that I was breathing in unison with my rapist, and when my muscles began contracting before relaxing again, I released a frustrated groan, and because I was thoroughly disgusted with myself for having been tricked into responding, I could not stop myself from trying to expel him from my body.*

*But, without needing to look at him, I knew it was too late and because I had provided him with the gratification he needed, within a matter of seconds Blake ejaculated with one final triumphant thrust.*

*In that same instant this female was motionless, and because his satisfaction filled me with revulsion, I was imagining my fingernails, clawing down his face, and from the pit of my stomach I was screaming abuse at him and yet, despite aching to do those things, instead of rewarding him with any kind of reaction, I opted to do and say nothing.*

*Then, staring up at him, my eyes remained devoid of all emotion, but as he slid out of my body, and he began to reorganize his clothing, Blake dared to smirk as he began to congratulate himself on his sexual expertise.*

*"Didn't I promise you that I've never had any customer complaints Mrs Daltry?" Pausing, he tightened the belt around his Levi's, before uttering a light laugh. "Perhaps, I should come with my own satisfaction guaranteed certificate?"*

*Lying there, I continued to stare through him as if he did not exist, while he persisted, "With powerful muscles like the ones between your thighs, if you were working in the sex trade, then you could earn someone a decent income. In the meantime, since that was one the best screws I've had in a long time, once I'm sure you've learnt some proper manners, I might decide to use you again--perhaps from behind or maybe..."*

*Despite remaining silent while Blake had been speaking, as an indication of my disinterest, I had turned my head to one side, but using his body weight to crush me to the bed, his finger and thumb forced me to look at him, so that when his lips brushed against mine, I could smell the foul stench of his bad breath.*

*"I don't think that's an appropriate way in which to express your gratitude Mrs Daltry, especially when I went out of my way to be gentle with you..."*

*Tempting me, Blake's tongue began to inch its way into my mouth, before he had a change of heart, and when he released my face I was still staring into his eyes. Then, without giving the consequences of the action any consideration, my rebellious child prompted her parent to retaliate, by spitting in the direction of his eyes, and while I remained defiant and impenitent--with a misleading calmness--Blake wiped his face.*

*When the first backhanded blow struck, because it was propelled with the expected force, Shaw clamped his hand over my nose and mouth but mercifully, he prevented Blake's swinging arm from reaching its target for a second time, by intercepting it in mid-air.*

*"That was very impolite Mrs Daltry," Shaw cautioned me. "Indeed, it was downright rude, and such a flagrant act of disobedience merits some kind of punishment. So along with the other pieces of information I was given as part of your profile, it's my understanding that you have perfected the art of how to perform mind blowing oral sex..."*

*As one might expect, Shaw did not fail to notice how I had closed my eyes for the briefest of moments, when the stench of Blake's breath had brought to mind his dubious personal hygiene, and how I would need to overcome the urge to throw up, and because Shaw was not about to relinquish his power, he capitalized on my weakness.*

"When we're working on a retrieval contract, which requires the eventual elimination of the primary target, nothing escapes my attention Mrs Daltry. Not a smile, or a frown, or the anticipation of something less palatable and from what I witnessed, the idea of performing oral sex, during which I don't doubt that your lips and tongue would do an excellent job did not appeal to you…"

As Shaw paused, and he eased his hand away from my mouth, I heard the tell-tale sound of another zip being lowered, in readiness for more sexual activity.

"Of course," Shaw continued. "Until you've learnt how to behave, nobody would risk using your mouth. After all, we wouldn't want any mishaps with those pretty teeth of yours. Now would we Mrs Daltry?"

Unsure whether Shaw expected a response from me I remained silent, until he uttered a disapproving sigh, before demanding, "Whenever I ask you a direct question, I expect you to provide me with a response Mrs Daltry. Do you understand me?"

"Yes I understand…."

"Good, then we might be making some progress and since we always come prepared, in case we need to silence someone, so they cannot disturb any third parties in this particular instance there is one gag, which might suit our purposes…"

Miraculously, Blake produced a bag, and after rummaging inside Shaw pulled out what appeared to be some kind of metal contraption.

"As you can see this gag," Shaw began to explain, before changing his mind. "No perhaps it would be best if I allow my colleagues to demonstrate its benefits…"

With Peterson no longer holding my arms above my head, Blake seized hold of the plastic tie around my wrists, and pulled me up, so that I was sitting at the bottom of the bed, and despite being aggrieved that his earlier physical chastisement had been curtailed when Shaw had intercepted his swinging arm, at the renewed promise of not only further sexual gratification, but also retribution for my rebellious child having dared to spit in his face, he was almost salivating, as he took the metal contraption from Shaw's outstretched hand, before once again tempting me, by bringing it close to my mouth.

"There are two ways we can do this, and if I was given a personal preference, then after what you did, I would choose the hardest, but whichever way you decide you would like this to be done, I guarantee that you will open your mouth, so we can demonstrate the benefits of using this gag on anyone who needs to be taught how to control, whatever comes out of their filthy mouth…"

Despite being given a choice when I hesitated, without giving me to opportunity of choosing the easy way, Peterson grabbed hold of my hair and yanked my head back.

"It's my turn next," he snarled at me, as he passed the camcorder to Shaw. "And I'm growing impatient. So if you don't do what you've been told to do right now, then once we're finished with you, I'll make sure that you die a slow and agonizing death…"

What a perfect gentleman, but with my head tilted back I opened my mouth, and for the benefit of the camcorder, Shaw's took great delight in providing the commentary. "The principal benefit of this particular gag is that it's similar to a horse's harness and tackle. It even comes with a metal bit to keep the wearer's tongue clamped in place…"

This was something not even my husband had used as a punishment for one of his concocted misdemeanours, and because being compared to an animal made me fearful, I tried to pull away, but Peterson twisted my hair, before whispering in my ear. "There's no point in trying to resist and if you continue testing my impatience by being uncooperative, then I might not be responsible for my own actions…"

Clearly satisfied with my subsequent cooperation, Shaw continued his commentary. "And once the bit is clamped in place, using the screws the other metal part--which you will note is attached to straps, similar to reins, forces the mouth to be kept open, and so we can demonstrate that spitting will not be tolerated, the screws are being secured tighter than usual, but Mrs Daltry only has herself to blame. If she hadn't been impolite and downright disobedient, then none of this unpleasantness would have proved to be necessary…"

Pausing again, Shaw waited until Peterson released my hair, so that Blake could take control of the straps--correction reins--and then, moving the position of the camcorder to the best possible angle, he carried on with his descriptive commentary. "And once someone's teeth cannot pose any threat, anyone can screw the disarmed subject, without them being able to assist the process, which prolongs the user's enjoyment, while at the same time teaching the recipient that they run the risk of being asphyxiated…"

As soon as the commentary ceased, Peterson wasted no time commencing the practical demonstration, but then without any explanation he pulled out of my mouth.

"I suppose everyone deserves a second chance, and provided that you've learnt your lesson and you're prepared to guarantee that you've got control over your mouth, if you give me your nodded agreement, then I might be willing to dispense with the gag…."

In another moment of weakness, I conceded defeat but no sooner had the vile contraption been removed than Peterson left me in no doubt about what he expected, "Since your reputation precedes you, then for your own sake I hope that you can live up to it…"

Having noted that my defeat had begun to harden him, despite hating myself, I was hoping that my willingness to cooperate would make him climax as soon as possible, especially when he was congratulating me on my performance. "I'm pleased you decided to control your mouth, because your capabilities far exceed your reputation…"

Then, Peterson curtailed my plan by pulling out of my mouth, and as he stared down at me, a lewd smirk crept onto his face. "Now as if you're a bitch on heat I intend to take you from behind, so I suggest you turn around and lie face down over the pillow, my associate has placed behind you, and since we've been asked to provide a visual record of your newfound willingness to cooperate, we need you to position your face, so the camcorder can capture every single change in your expression throughout your participation…"

At first, I did not want to envisage anything worse, except more degradation, and after I turned around, and bent over the pillow, Blake seized hold of the plastic tie, between my wrists, so that he could drag my arms up towards him and then, Peterson must have removed the belt from his Levi's because I felt him threading it between my hips and the pillow before buckling it, so that it would provide him with more leverage. However, it was not until Shaw took over the commentary that I understood what a naïve idiot, I had been for not having realized, the nature of Peterson's intended violation.

"Naivety can be so becoming Mrs Daltry, but surely you must have worked it out because according to the profile, although you might be the wrong sex, you do have some experience when it comes to anal penetration. In addition, since my associate is making you a very rare exception, he has no intention of being gentle with you, and as an added bonus, thanks to the introduction of a vibrator, we're hoping that as you did for his colleague, dual penetration will provide the recording with the satisfaction of seeing you climax…"

In that instant, it would have made no difference because gentle or rough, all bets were off the table, and with Shaw's hand yet again clasped over my mouth, it took three pairs of hands to keep me still, but as soon as I felt the barrel of the gun, nestling in a different orifice I stopped struggling, which enabled Shaw to resume his control of the commentary.

"It never ceases to please me, whenever a gun barrel brings about instant obedience? However, earlier I did state that I would afford you, the opportunity to either pause or even halt the proceedings, if you agreed to surrender, what you know I've been commissioned to recover. So Mrs Daltry, is there something you would like to share with me?"

After nodding my agreement with a degree of cautiousness, Shaw eased his hand away, so that I could reveal what he believed would direct him to the flash drive.

"Downstairs, in what used to be my husband's study in the large mahogany desk, underneath the third drawer down there's an envelope…"

Even before I finished my directions I heard a flurry of activity, and because Blake was no longer holding the plastic tie around my wrists he must have left the bedroom, so that he could retrieve the envelope.

Beside me, Shaw remained seated on the edge of the bed, but in the aftermath with the threat of the gun barrel no longer present, my continued stillness seemed to be unreasonable, and after unclenching my fists, I flexed my hands in the hope that I might be able to restore at the very least an adequate blood supply, and a few minutes later, when I heard the missing rapist return, and Shaw seemed to be pre-occupied with the contents of the envelope, I attempted to ease the horrendous aching in my shoulders, by inching my arms down the bed, but as Shaw had promised, since not even the slightest of movements would escape his attention, he placed a restraining hand on my back.

"You haven't been given permission to move, and unless you want to make me angry Mrs Daltry, I suggest that you stay where you are…"

"But I've given you what you wanted…"

"Charlie…"

"Although you had no choice but to give Shaw what he wanted, did it stop him?"

Initially, I'm unsure which one of my inquisitors has drawn me out of the master bedroom at 187 Cheltenham Way and my graphic revelations of what took place on that Thursday morning, and although I had not realized at some point I must have started to cry.

As for my principal male, John is no longer on the opposite side of the desk. Instead, he is crouching beside my Godfather's chair, but at least he has not risked trying to touch me, and when I wipe the tears away, before sniffing in a most unladylike fashion, although it might seem perverse, like Blake with his bag of gags--as if by magic--John manages to produce some paper hankies. However, because he caused this to happen by reneging on their part of our agreement, even when I take some of the hankies I refuse to look at him.

Then, despite having determined that it was Bill who drew me back into the present tense of my Godfather's study, I know that as soon as I answer his question, I will have to finish what John started, so I am also unable to look at our arbitrator.

"Of course, it didn't stop Shaw and after he had acquired what he wanted, the only thing I could do was pray that something would happen to save me…"

### JUNE 22   187 CHELTENHAM WAY   INCIDENT UPDATE
**3 40 a m   Urgent assistance no longer required**

"And who gave you permission to speak?" Shaw chastised me. "Anyway, in order to fulfil this contract, what I'm expected to retrieve is more than just bank details, which is most regrettable Mrs Daltry, because it means that you haven't given me enough…"

For the second time, I had been tricked and after watching Shaw slide the envelope containing not only the bank details, but also the key I would need to access my safety deposit box into one of the inside pockets of his jacket, as if he was a man, who had unlimited time and space to do whatever he wanted with this woman's body and mind, he was smiling, as he tried to provoke me by running his fingertips up and down my spine. Then, he heightened my belief that dead was going to be a better option. "Besides, before we vacate the premises Mrs Daltry, it won't do you any harm if you're taught the kind of lesson, which I can assure you from similar instances, you're not likely to forget in a hurry. It will give you a chance to reflect upon how much rougher the games are going to become, if the four of us should arrive at the bank only to discover that the safety deposit box is empty…"

"Do you want her gagged?" I heard Blake ask. "It might be the wisest option…"

*In response, Peterson released a sickening laugh. "Since we're going to use dual penetration, let's increase that to a threesome, especially now that the spoilt bitch has learnt some manners, so you shouldn't have any difficulty getting her to cooperate…"*

*Time for a fear and alarm check and firstly, Shaw was right, despite being a little out of practice--having been married to Mark--anal penetration was not something to which I was unaccustomed, and secondly, although I had never been anything more than a wedding or funeral type of Christian, as I prayed for some Divine intervention, perhaps even a minor miracle, as if God had heard my prayers, before Peterson could begin teaching me that lesson I would never forget in a hurry, I swear I heard a different voice speaking my name.*

### 3 39 a m   Occupant identified as Mrs Charlie Daltry
### Checking Property status and D.V.L.A. registration

*"Mrs Daltry?"*

*In the master bedroom silence descended, prompting the stranger's voice to elaborate. "I'm an officer with Thames Valley Police Mrs Daltry. The back door was unlocked and the alarm has been deactivated. Is everything all right?"*

*Despite the hand, which Shaw had clamped over my nose and mouth, out of the corner of my eye, I caught sight of someone taking a step towards the door, and wanting to warn the Police Officer, this captive dared to resist his hold and yet, one step ahead of me, with Peterson's help, Shaw managed to yet again render me motionless as well as silent, leaving Blake free to deal with the interloper.*

### 3 44a m   Special Operations downgraded property--Operatives deployed
### Proceed with caution

*Sadly, the instruction to proceed with caution had arrived too late, but there could be no doubt that if the Police Officer's death had not been in vain, then I had to survive.*

"Charlie…."

Soft and appealing the calm, persuasive voice once again belongs to Bill, but with my crying threatening to dissolve into sobbing, when I glance down at my sleeveless cotton top, with its cut away shoulders and revealing neckline, there are two damp patches, where my tears must have been rolling down my cheeks, before trickling onto my top, and having chosen to undertake this Interview, with the added freedom to tolerate the almost oppressive heat of this June evening--by not wearing a bra--those same dark patches are now making my nakedness even more evident.

Resting my elbows on the desk in a hushed voice, I hear this leading lady admit, "The accusations John levelled about my naivety cannot be substantiated. In fact, if you check the Daltry file, after the debriefing sessions came to an end, you will find that Commander Maddox offered me the chance to relocate. However, being aware that either Mark's Sponsor or his Handler might not want any loose ends--or alternatively--they might think that I knew too much, I chose to remain at 187 Cheltenham Way because if anything did happen, then at least I was occupying a property assigned to Special Operations…"

When I sense John's hand nearing my shoulder without looking at him, I dare to raise my voice. "Don't you dare touch me Mr Bland--because if you do--then I swear to God, I might not be responsible for my own actions?"

"I'm sorry Charlie, after reliving what they put you through, the fact that you're sensitive about being touched is quite understandable…"

Now I'm thinking that John has a damned nerve. Not only has he reverted to addressing me by my Christian name, he's made an outrageous assumption.

"Since you had the decency to clear the air between us, the very least you can do is afford me the opportunity to respond to all of the accusations you have levelled at me. Furthermore, for the benefit of the Official Recording, although it might come as a disappointment Mr Bland, the only person I do not want touching me is you!"

"Of course, please accept my sincere apologies…"

Oh my God, now John's trying to be polite and considerate, but I think you might agree, it is a little late for either of those qualities to put in an appearance.

"As for Mr Bland's vivid depiction of what my fate might have been, taking into account my background, and my own graphic description of what they put me through, far from being some nice, respectable middle-class lady who was harbouring any illusions, or labouring under any misapprehensions, I knew that if Shaw managed to get me out of the house, then he would have kept me gagged and restrained, so that whenever they chose to amuse themselves, Blake and Peterson could continue torturing me sexually, until…"

When the remaining words fail to emerge, I attempt to conceal my lapse by reaching for my cigarettes, but my hands are shaking so badly that I cannot even flip the packet open. Releasing a frustrated groan--in a fit of pique--I thrust it to one side, but then John risks making me even more angry by picking up the discarded packet.

The last thing this woman wants is a sign of his remorse, but as much as I want to remain angry, as if he has done it on numerous occasions, not only does John flip the packet open, so that he can remove a cigarette, after placing it between his own lips, he clicks the lighter and then, without inhaling the smoke into his lungs, he lights it on my behalf.

Now I'm faced with a dilemma. Do I attempt to take the cigarette from him, or deprive my brain of its much needed nicotine fix, by declining his offer? But it's irrelevant, because having overlooked that my shaking hands are incapable of holding the damn thing, as one might expect, John can propose a sensible compromise. "At the risk of getting my head in my hands, why don't I hold the cigarette on your behalf Charlie?"

Time for a quick review, having reverted to addressing me by my Christian name, while showing signs of remorse, not only is John being polite and considerate, he's using my addiction to demonstrate his contrition. Forgive me, but it's almost too good to be true and yet, despite drawing the line at affording him a verbal response, when I nod my head with his help, I inhale the smoke deep into my lungs, and after the nicotine hits my brain in ten or maybe twelve seconds, after I exhale in a long, slow even breath, I am able to continue.

"From the moment Shaw had the bank details, along with the key for my safety deposit box, I knew that somehow I had to find a way to slow the proceedings down, and I will be eternally grateful that the elderly lady living at 181 had the foresight to contact the Police, after she was disturbed by the sound of that car engine, because despite praying for some Divine intervention, may my God forgive me for doubting that my prayer could be answered in time to save me, from having to take drastic action…"

As the image of the Police Officer who sacrificed his own life, in order to save mine comes into focus, I am forced to hesitate, but I sweep the fresh flood of tears aside and with John's assistance, I manage another sharp intake of nicotine. "And I deeply regret that the Police Officer died, and after my father told me about his wife, and two children under school age, you have to believe that if there was any justice, then since his family needed him, and Bobby has Lorna and Colin, I wish that he and I could have swapped places…"

Suddenly, it's as if my heart is breaking with the sheer weight of the repressed grief, but as my entire body becomes racked by sobbing, having extinguished my cigarette John disregards my earlier warning, and since he has risked stretching his arm across the back of my Godfather's chair, when I feel his fingertips touch my shoulder, because I need someone to break my hypothetical fall, I begin moving in his direction until I slump against him, so that he can hold me, until I'm able to bring my sobbing back under control.

"As we did earlier Charlie, would you look at me?"    Pausing, Bill waits before adding, in a polite, but more insistent tone of voice. "Please--it is important…"

Despite looking back towards the table, I avoid making eye contact with Bill. "It required a tremendous amount of courage to share in explicit detail, some of the abuse you were subjected to on that Thursday. However, bearing in mind that this is the first time you've acknowledged being sexually assaulted, and taking into account the depth of your distress, then in my capacity as arbitrator, I feel it would be in your best interests to postpone the remainder of this Interview until tomorrow, so that overnight you can recuperate…"

While Bill has been speaking, John's hand was tightening on my shoulder, and he is prepared to add his own encouragement. "Because Bill and I had never attempted to conduct an Interview in this manner Charlie, what we set out to achieve was a feat of mammoth proportions. As a result, all three of us have come full circle, and having arrived back at the place where we began, I have to agree with Bill that it's time for you to get some rest…"

It is tempting and yet, there is one flaw. "Thank you, but since the last time this issue was raised, nothing has changed--I still don't think I could achieve any meaningful rest, never mind get some sleep, until this Interview is over…"

Then, when neither John nor Bill chooses to fill the ensuing silence I do have an alternative proposition. "But I must look a frightful mess. Would it be possible for us to take another break, so that I can have a quick shower and get changed?"

"Of course Charlie," Bill replies. "Feel free to take as much time as you need and then, after you've had the chance to freshen up, we can review the situation again…"

As I push my Godfather's chair away from the desk, and I rise to my feet--in addition to the shaking--I have also overlooked that my balance might be unstable, and as John's hand catches hold of my arm, his concern is genuine. "Are you all right Charlie?"

My God, what does my principal male expect me to say? No his leading lady is far from being all right, but if I'm left in peace for a short period of time, I might manage to recover my composure.

"Since the damage is nothing worse than a few tears Mr Bland," I reply as I retrieve my elbow from his light grasp. "Perhaps I should be grateful that you didn't carry out your earlier threat to take a leaf out of my husband's book and--*beat the shit out of me*…"

Clearly unsure whether I'm being serious, John continues to study my face, until I throw him a good-humoured smile. "Relax Mr Bland. Since all is supposed to be fair in love and war, there's no need to be too concerned, especially when I'm not going to do anything stupid with my son asleep upstairs…"

Then, with as much dignity, as any leading lady can hope to achieve when departing from the glare of the spotlight on the centre stage, I move away from the desk, but as I head towards the door, I know that my principal male is watching each unsteady step.


Undeniably relieved at having escaped from the study, my vulnerable child is praying that we can reach the sanctuary of my bedroom, without having to produce one more explanation, which in my fragile state of mind might push me, beyond the point of redemption, and as if I am afraid of awakening the ghosts I mentioned earlier--the ones who must inhabit a Victorian building like the Manor--using the softest of touches I click the door closed behind me, before  removing my sandals, so that as I climb the sweeping staircase in my bare feet, I can avoid any creaking floorboards,.

# PART FOUR

## June 29

## Co-conspirators

Having reached the upper landing without being intercepted by either my Godfather, or Lorna, I hesitate outside my son's bedroom. More than anything else seeing Bobby would help me focus upon something other than my own sense of despair, but after his reaction to my earlier distress, it would be selfish of me if he should discover how much more distressed I had become once he and Lorna had left the study.

Instead, I seek the solitude of my own room, and once I am sitting in front of the dressing table with my facial image staring back at me, the dark smudges under each eye confirm that I do look a frightful mess. Perhaps for future reference, if the script necessitates playing scenes super-charged with emotion, then waterproof mascara should be a primary requisite in any professional make-up artist's bag.

After pouring a small amount of eye make-up remover onto a cotton wool pad, as I begin to wipe away the smudges, I realize that once Shaw's orchestrated cacophony of abuse came to an end, and as he had predicted the cavalry came riding to my rescue, it had been too easy, especially for someone like me to keep the images locked away in the tailor-made dungeon, which I had constructed in my mind, and having deprived them of light and oxygen, they had to remain trapped within a vacuum, so that I did not have to dwell upon the possible longevity of the mental, physical and emotional damage.

With all traces of my smudged mascara eradicated, this other mother rises to her feet, and our rebellious child leaves a trail of discarded clothes in our wake, as her parent heads towards the en-suite, and by the time I turn on the power shower, I am examining how I'm feeling, and several disparaging adjectives spring to mind, including dirty, tainted, impure and then, as if it were only yesterday when the foul stench of Blake's breath is blended with the smell of urine, as Peterson had neared my mouth, they prove to be a potent cocktail, but unlike the previous occasion, when I was on my knees, clutching the porcelain as I had thrown up repeatedly, this time the retching is short lived and yet, by the time I am standing in the shower, with the warm water cascading down through my hair and onto my skin, instead of soothing me, the water does nothing to appease the vividness of the images.

Resting my head on the cold tiles, my crying once again gives way to sobbing, and I realize that I never had the chance to finish responding to all the accusations levelled at me, especially when John had demanded to know whether--*I had any idea how long it would take, before I could look at myself in a full length mirror, much less allow anyone to touch my body without my being reminded of what took place during those sixty minutes of my life?*

Setting to one side the issue of allowing anyone to touch my body, although it might be too soon after the images were granted access to the light and oxygen they needed in order to make their first public appearance, strictly between you and me, if I am honest, then it would seem that nothing has changed.

In fact, since that Thursday morning my naked body has offended me so much, I have avoided catching sight of its reflection in any full-length mirror, but now it must disgust me to the extent that acting on auto-pilot, after pouring shower gel onto my body brush, what begins as having a quick shower must have turned into something more sinister.

Unless Lorna Clunnell found herself confronted by a Catch-22 situation, she would never deem to interfere in Charlie's personal life--or meddle in her private affairs, and because the sound of running water in the adjoining room suggested that Bobby's other mother was in the  shower, at first there seemed to be nothing out of the ordinary, until the unmistakable sound of retching was followed by crying, which in turn dissolved into the kind of heart-rending sobbing, Lorna could never have imagined humanly possible.

Mindful of their earlier discussion, and the reference Charlie had made to undisclosed complications, taking into consideration how their similar experiences at the Mayfield Clinic had enabled Professor Morgan to turn them both into survivors, irrespective of whatever had been going on down in--*Uncle Philip's study*--those undisclosed complications had somehow managed to drag a strong, dignified young woman like Charlie Anne Daltry into the depths of the most sorrowful distress.

But when that pitiful sound had drawn Lorna into the adjoining bedroom, once she was standing outside the closed en-suite door, she found herself confronted by the sound of something far more disturbing than either the retching or the sobbing, which did necessitate some kind of intervention on her part.

Curbing the spontaneous urge to open the en-suite door, Lorna left the bedroom and headed down the sweeping staircase, but as she neared the study and she could hear voices, she slowed her pace, before announcing her presence by tapping on the partially open door, and when the voices inside fell silent she eased it open.

"Oh I'm sorry Commander, I didn't expect to find you in the study…"

"I'm afraid I took advantage of the pause in the proceedings to come and collect even more documents, which my P. A. has flagged as being worthy of my attention..."

"I didn't mean to intrude, but might I have a word with John and Bill…"

"Certainly, if you'll excuse me, I'll leave you in their capable hands…"

Despite beginning to move around her the Commander hesitated, and as if it were an afterthought, he looked back at the three of them.

"Tomorrow, I don't have any appointments scheduled until after midday. Since my driver isn't picking me up until 11:45 and provided nothing urgent requires my attention, I can spare an hour, or maybe even ninety minutes to play football…"

"That would be very kind of you Commander…"

"Despite having allowed the first formal address to go without being corrected," Philip Maddox began to chide her. "How many times do I have to ask you to call me Philip?"

"I'm sorry, somehow it seems disrespectful to address someone in your position in such an informal fashion, but in future I will try to remember Philip…"

"I sincerely hope you do Lorna, especially when few people are invited to address me by my Christian name," Pausing, the Commander turned his attention to his subordinates. "And if Mr Bland and Mr Powell can also set aside some free time, the three of us should be able to indulge Bobby's passion by enjoying something resembling an actual football match, especially if Lorna acts as our unbiased referee…"

"Of course we will Sir…"

After their joint confirmation, Lorna waited until the Commander disappeared, before levelling her first demand. "Throughout the last eight years, I have never had any reason to interfere in Charlie's private affairs--or any justification for prying into her personal life, but now I want to know what the hell has been going on in this room?"

"Earlier Lorna I did notice…"

Disregarding Bill's attempt to appeal to the more reasonable side of her nature, Lorna interrupted him. "I'm not stupid Mr Powell, and unlike Charlie, I haven't been worn down as a result of being trapped in this room for far too long, especially if I wasn't eating or sleeping, and since there was a marked difference, between the first time Charlie came upstairs, and this second break in your so called proceedings, I'm not asking--I'm demanding to know--what the hell has been going on?"

Silence, until Bill dared to pose some obvious questions. "Presumably, something must have happened to necessitate your intervention? Can you give us some indication as to why you need to know what we've been doing?"

"Perhaps you didn't hear me the first time Mr Powell. Since I'm not stupid, I wouldn't be here unless something has happened and at first, when the sound of running water in the adjoining room suggested that she was using the shower, there seemed to be nothing out of the ordinary, until Charlie's retching was followed by crying, which dissolved into the kind of heart-rending sobbing, I could not have imagined humanly possible. But after I was drawn to her bedroom and I was standing outside the closed en-suite door--I heard something far more alarming…"

As if it was somehow going to make her next revelation more palatable Lorna closed her eyes, for her briefest of moments. "During our earlier--albeit brief discussion--Charlie referred to some undisclosed complications, which occurred after Bobby was born, and for my part I had made light of the situation. But what I overheard was so alarming I found it distressing, and since we've only encountered it once, throughout our shared experiences, and in that particular instance, it was as if it was eating that person alive--piece by piece--until it consumed them altogether, and that's the reason why I need to know right now, what the hell has been going on to manifest this kind of behaviour…"

Even before she had finished her explanation, after casting a nod in his partner's direction John disappeared, but when Lorna attempted to follow him, Bill moved between her and the doorway, so that he was blocking her exit.

Initially perplexed, Lorna's response was perhaps predictable. "What do you think you're doing?"

Then, when her question remained unanswered, she declared. "I'm not asking you Mr Powell, I'm insisting that you get out of my way…"

"I'm afraid I can't do that because for as long as Charlie remains in Protective Custody, it's in your best interests that you allow us to handle the situation on your behalf…"

"Handle what situation?" demanded Lorna, and now Bill could hear the exasperation in her voice as a result of his silence. "At least tell me whether I'm right to be concerned…"

For the second time, her demand for information was left unaddressed, prompting Lorna to declare. "This is outrageous. First, you refuse to tell me what has been going on and then, you expect me to allow both of you to handle the situation--whatever that situation might be--when for all I know it was the pair of you who created it in the first place…"

Along with Lorna's increasing exasperation came the likelihood that her raised voice might wake Bobby, but when Bill once again tried to reason with her, and he reached out to touch her, she stepped away from him. "Please Lorna, if you're going to grasp the significance of what I'm about to explain, then I need you to calm down…"

"I can assure you," snapped Lorna. "I've never been calmer in my entire life…"

"So why don't we move to the desk? You'll be more comfortable sitting down…"

After Philip Maddox had received the briefest of updates regarding the status of the Interview, despite being detained a little longer than intended by Lorna Clunnell's arrival, he had taken the additional documents, and returned to the living room. However, having left the door ajar, when he had caught sight of John Bland climbing the stairs two at a time, his haste combined with Lorna's raised voice had drawn him back to the study so that he could lend whatever support his seniority might afford his remaining subordinate.

"Mr Powell…"

Without glancing over his shoulder, Bill Powell acknowledged the arrival of his Commanding Officer. "Yes Commander…."

"Since my departure have you encountered some kind of difficulty?"

"No Sir," Bill replied and yet, aware of the importance of maintaining eye contact, while at the same time not giving Lorna the chance to challenge his negative reply, he added, "What we seem to have encountered is a conflict of interests…"

"In that case, might I suggest that we keep this conflict down to a dull roar, because if the raised voices were to disturb anyone else, then I suspect that one particular young man might have good reason for feeling aggrieved, if he's too tired to take advantage of being able to play football for a full ninety minutes after breakfast tomorrow morning…"

Such an adept tactician was worthy of Bill's admiration, especially when the introduction of a third party had provided Lorna with, an additional conflict of interests, and when her pretty features softened, he was able to add his own confirmation. "I'm confident that Mrs Clunnell understands how unfortunate it would be if Bobby was disturbed…"

"Good--now would you please update me about this conflict of interest?"

"Of course Commander. As you already know, before I make a final decision regarding whether the remainder of this Interview should be postponed until tomorrow, we decided to take another break, so that Mrs Daltry could have a shower and get changed. In the meantime, when Mrs Clunnell overheard Charlie retching and sobbing in the en-suite, naturally she was alarmed, and because I suspect that she believes we are in some way responsible, she wants to know what we have been doing in your study…"

Pausing, Bill waited and when neither the Commander, nor Lorna filled his silence, he finished his update. "And when you arrived Sir, I was about to explain our difficulties whenever it comes to sharing confidential information…"

"Thank you Mr Powell," Philip Maddox announced, as he stepped into the study, so that he could also achieve eye contact with Lorna. "During the last few days, I've come to appreciate the uniqueness of the relationship you share with my Goddaughter, and if I had overheard her vomiting and sobbing then like you, I would have been alarmed. However, I'm in the fortuitous position of having been able to select the Operatives who would be responsible for taking care of my Goddaughter, and since Bland and Powell are experts when it comes to protecting anyone from harm, even if it might be self-inflicted, then unlike you at least I would have had that added reassurance…"

Lulled into a false sense of security by the Commander's slow, smooth delivery, Lorna was no longer agitated, and when her lips parted, her voice was lowered to below the suggested dull roar. "Of course you're right Philip. If I had been in your position, then I might not have been quite so alarmed, I suppose the most disturbing aspect was overhearing what sounded like scrubbing. It was almost as if washing herself wasn't sufficient…"

Before proposing what was destined to become a winning suggestion, Philip Maddox sighed. "At this point Mr Powell, I'm reminded that sometimes second guessing can lead to more alarm than is necessary, and when it comes to the issue of divulging personal data, since you are trained how to deal with such matters, in this instance you have my permission to use your discretion over how much detail you share, in order to quell this tidal wave of speculation, before it can turn into a Tsunami…"

After acknowledging his understanding through a sideways glance, using the lightest of touches, Bill's hand closed around Lorna's elbow, before he repeated his earlier suggestion. "While I try to answer at least some of your questions, I still think that you'd be more comfortable, if you were sitting down…"

At first Lorna seemed hesitant and yet, she did nothing to prevent Bill's hand from guiding her towards the desk, and as soon as she was seated in the Commander's Executive chair, he crouched down in front of her, and aware that Philip Maddox had resumed his former position in the doorway, Bill began exercising that aforementioned discretion.

"Until tonight, although there hasn't been any need for you to know, as I suggested a few moments' ago, John and I have been acting in your best interests…"

"Is that because of Bobby?"

"Partly, but it's important that you appreciate, we are acting on behalf of both of you, and like Charlie, I'm afraid you will have to trust us to know what we're doing…"

Initially, Lorna did nothing, but then she started shaking her head. "And what about the scrubbing I heard inside the en-suite? If you weren't responsible, then did it have something to do with the life experience Charlie and I shared?"

In the hope that Lorna might reach her own conclusion Bill waited, before replying, "I'm sorry Lorna, but without Charlie's specific permission, I'm not at liberty to divulge any personal information. However, although any such scenario might seem to be unpalatable, if that were the case and I hadn't prevented you from following John upstairs, then there would have been a strong likelihood that regardless of the uniqueness of your relationship, coming at a time, when more than ever before she might need your support, if Charlie wasn't ready, your presence could have driven a wedge between you…"

"Oh my God…"

"Perhaps now you can appreciate why it was best to allow John to assess the immediate situation on his own?"

Oblivious to anything that might be giving cause for concern beyond my palatial bedroom, once I had fooled myself into believing that I must be all cried out, and I was satisfied that there could not be an inch of my naked body, which in my state of denial I had not brushed clean, taking great care to avoid catching sight of myself in the full-length mirror, I had exchanged my wet towel for the fluffy white robe, which had been hanging on the hook beside the washbasin, and by the time I heard the first gentle tap on the en-suite door, with my knees draw up close to my chest--this alleged adult was sitting on the floor, propped up against the bath, while listening--if you'll pardon the unfortunate play on words, but nevertheless I was listening to the sanitised sound of my own sanctimonious silence.

Besides, after what happened in the study, there had been no point in responding, especially when any request for privacy would be disregarded, and then with an almost irritating predictability--albeit a little louder--a second tap on the door announces the imminent arrival of my visitor, and as it begins to open and John starts to appear, not only is he looking sheepish, he is also wearing a butter would not melt in his mouth expression.

"May I come in?"

After paring away layer upon layer of my resilient flesh, until there was nothing left, except my brittle bones grinding against brittle bones, because this man has seen it all, this leading lady doubts she has anything that she needs to hide, beneath the virginal white robe.

"Since you and Bill have confiscated the keys to every lockable door inside the Manor, I fail to see how I could stop you from gaining access?"

"May I join you?"

Now John is gesturing to the vacant space next to me, and still hugging my knees, I shrug my shoulders, but as he eases himself down onto the floor beside me, if I had admired his sheepishness upon his arrival, then despite sensing that there might be an ulterior motive, his cautiousness seems to merit my acknowledgement.

"Because time has moved on John, and I've been re-running what happened after you found me on that Thursday morning, I stopped wanting to tear you apart, limb by limb approximately ten minutes ago…"

"I'm pleased to hear it…"

Casting him a sideways glance for the first time, I notice that he has nice eyes. Dark and deep, those eyes must have witnessed far worse misery than mine and yet, considering my dubious track record when it comes to selecting partners, there is strong likelihood that if the circumstances were different, then he would make a suitable future conquest, and since the idea conjures up a new image, this leading lady remarks, "But if I was in your position, I wouldn't allow myself to become too complacent about my overall safety, because I haven't finished assessing how much the human race might benefit from your castration?"

From between his lips, John emits a low hissing sound, and as I cast him another more furtive glance at the thought of his manhood--or to be more precise--the possible lack of it, he wears a pained expression, until I add a qualifying observation.

"However, like the keys, it has been noted that all sharp--or if I were given a preference--then all blunt and serrated instruments have been placed well beyond my reach in case I should attempt to damage myself or any third party…"

"That's a relief…"

Upon his arrival, although John had noted that the brush was hanging upside down on its hook, in the hope of determining the extent of any damage as a result of Charlie having used it to try and scrub herself clean, before joining her on the floor, he had been checking, every inch of visible flesh, but there was no evidence to suggest that it had been used as if it was an offensive weapon. However, within our shared present tense, when the silence threatens to become protracted, and it prompts this assignment to glance in his direction, he responds by throwing his leading lady one of his warm persuasive smiles.

Considering that this is another intermission, and beyond the study--and our adversarial roles--there is a joint understanding, perhaps unprofessional, but nevertheless it reminds me of a similar instance. "We've enacted this scene before Mr Bland…"

"And as I recall Mrs Daltry, it was quite memorable…"

"I suppose memorable is a worthy adjective to describe what happened, but while I still can't recollect everything that led up to that scene, I have a vivid memory of throwing up, until there was nothing left, except for the hollow sound of retching, and with the benefit of hindsight you were a formidable double act, and when I was outraged because you had turned off the mixer tap, it seemed to be Bill's cue to start pushing me, nearer and nearer to the edge, so that you could catch me as soon as I began falling…"

When I hesitate, John does nothing to disturb the silence, opting instead to determine whether I am able to continue dealing with the after-effects. "And I remember Bill telling me that I couldn't have a bath until later. Then, when I almost screamed at him that nobody was going to put me through it again, he was adamant that if I refused to cooperate, then acting in my best interests, he would have me restrained and sedated, so that a sympathetic female Doctor could examine me…"

Following the sequence of events, the next image proves to be empowering. "Oh my God, I was so angry with him, I can still see my flailing arms, as I searched the shelf above the bath for potential missiles, and although you could have brought all that frenzied activity to an end, you chose to do nothing…"

"It's our experience," John explains, in a hushed voice. "That in instances of prolonged physical or sexual abuse, it's important to establish a level of trust, and for as long as you were in no immediate danger, working as a team we needed you to feel as if you had at least some control over the proceedings, and when I did nothing to stop you from expending all that energy, and your hands closed around the large ornate shell, your eventual success didn't only bring about your immediate stillness, it made you feel empowered…"

Ah empowerment after being subjugated, but we seem to be mirroring each other, and the image John has created makes me laugh. "That large ornate shell--which quite ironically, my husband bought for me on our honeymoon is quite heavy. So how on earth did I manage to hurl it across the bathroom in Bill's direction?"

At Bill's expense John and I share the same laughter, before he explains, "Sometimes when people have been trapped with their assailants, it's not unusual for them to somehow manifest superhuman strength. However, in your case after you launched it across the bathroom towards the doorway, and it shattered some of the floor to ceiling mirrored tiles, if Bill had been in any immediate danger, then like the multi-skilled professional he's supposed to be, I'm confident that he would have ducked in time…"

In response to the image of me forcing a professional like Bill to duck, we share more of the same laughter and in keeping with the replaying of events, John extends his arm along the bath, and after I inch myself around so that it can move across my upper body, he uses his hand to draw my torso back until I'm leaning against him.

This leading lady has to admit that her principal male is not only warm, he is also comfortable, and within what might seem to be the irony of these few intimate minutes spent in each other's company, despite whatever came to pass between us down in the study, encircled by his capable arms, I am confident that regardless of our differences I am in the safest possible hands, because I can still trust him to be acting in my best interests.

"As an added bonus John, now that we have finished slotting all the missing pieces into their respective places, considering that Mark loved those Italian mirrored tiles--more than he ever loved me--if I had realized the significance at the time, then the sound of the glass shattering would have been even more empowering…"

In response John's hand tightens a little and as if his confirmation should also be more significant than I realize, I feel his cheek brushing against the side of my head, before it ends up resting on my damp hair.

"Of course Bill and I had the benefit of knowing, there were three things at our disposal. Firstly, the tiles could easily be replaced. Secondly, since the property had been compromised, unless it should prove necessary for therapeutic reasons under no circumstances would you have been allowed to return to the house. Thirdly, although you did not realize the symbolic interpretation, there was one other reason why you needed to shatter those mirrored tiles?"

Despite suspecting that John is right, I cannot recall any other reason than Bill's intransigence. "Before I started searching for missiles, I couldn't believe that the reflection in the tiles belonged to me. Does that have something to do with the third reason?"

"Oh I think it's important that you work it out for yourself Charlie,"

Then, before I can cross-examine him further, my principal male diverts my attention with an unexpected explanation.

"Although working as a team, we were prepared to afford you as much time as you needed, when it came to compiling our official report on what happened after we found you on that Thursday morning, we have documented that during this rescue and retrieval assignment, when it came to the terms and conditions of your surrender, we had never conducted an intervention in which we had encountered anyone with your level of dogged determination, not to accept our protection…"

Wow, as my son would gasp what can this leading lady do except to thank John for the compliment? "Coming from two professionals with many years of experience, I have to admit that I'm flattered…"

Hesitating, I wait to determine whether John needs to add anything else, before lightening the mood. "But because Bill demonstrated the same dogged determination with the benefit of hindsight, perhaps I should have taken a little longer, before launching that shell across the bathroom?"

Then, after sharing yet more simultaneous laughter, I state what is obvious. "You do realize that if we don't stop meeting like this, our close encounters in bathrooms could be misconstrued Mr Bland, they might even cast doubts on your professional conduct…"

As John's hand squeezes my shoulder, there is a detectable degree of triumph in his voice. "Somehow I don't think there's much danger of you lodging an official complaint on the grounds of my gross misconduct, in any bathroom or en-suite Mrs Daltry…"

Touché! Why does this man have to be right all of the time? Of course, he must know that even if I were to lodge an official complaint, there is nobody who could be trusted to handle it, but at least he does not intend to gloat.

"But if it's any consolation, because Bill blames me for pushing you too far, instead of lodging an official complaint about my misconduct, he has read me the riot act…"

"Is that the real reason why you came looking for me, so that you can placate the other half of your dynamic duo?"

But without any hesitation, John replies. "No, I came to see if you were all right…"

"In that case, given the circumstances, I think that all things considered this assignment happens to be as well as anyone could expect her to be…"

The image from 187 Cheltenham Way is starting to fade, and having relived those events in the safety of the here and now, I free myself from John's arms. This is not over and as soon as I return to the study, so that we can resume our roles as the principal performers, because I might still need to respond with hostility or resentment, unlike in Mark's bathroom where I was in the company of comparative strangers, I dare not become too complacent, and tilting my head onto one side, I re-establish eye contact. "There wasn't any need for Bill to read you the riot act John--unless of course, your pushing me too far meant that I couldn't divulge what you were hoping to hear?"

John's gaze remains fixed upon my face, and in those dark deep eyes I can see the aforementioned admiration he holds for this particular adversary. "Now as I recall prior to that unstoppable ranting you made a declaration--something along the lines of--*how I must have been blinded by anger and contempt not to seek the right kind of protection…*"

Pausing, my rebellious child smiles, and content in the knowledge that we are talking strictly off the official record, her parent adds, "Strictly between you and me. I think you hoped--possibly even expected that I would drop my guard, and deliver an emotive outburst directed at a man who in addition to being your Commanding Officer is also my Godfather, and because you didn't get what you wanted that's why Bill has read you the riot act…"

Reciprocating my smile, although John will not commit himself, he acknowledges my astuteness through a decisive nod, before he explains, "Taking into account that you're a natural born survivor, and while you might not weigh much, as we discovered on that Thursday morning, you're tougher than you look…"

"I'll take that as a compliment," Hesitating, this woman tilts her head back onto one side. "Besides, before we're finished, I might get the chance to repay the compliment…"

Suddenly the sheepishness has returned. "That might be a little difficult, especially now that Bill has decided that you've been through enough for this evening, and in his capacity as arbitrator, as soon as you come back downstairs, irrespective of how you might feel for the benefit of the Official Recording, he intends to suspend the Interview…"

Unsure whether I believe him I continue to stare at John, until it is obvious that he does not intend to drop his own guard and give something away. "Although I can accept that Bill has read you the riot act, knowing how vital the missing pieces of information have become to Special Operations, I have every reason to suspect that his displeasure stems from the fact that after you brought your tirade down to a personal level, and it pushed me over the edge, I was left too distressed to continue…"

Affording my principal male, the chance to reply I hesitate and yet, his expression continues to give nothing away. "However, now that I've had a shower I feel rejuvenated, and since I only need to get dressed, would you please express my gratitude to Bill over his concern for my welfare, but as we've established I'm tougher than I look, and in a few minutes, when I return to the study I'm determined to finish what we set out to achieve. Besides, it's my experience that if things are left to their own devices for a few hours, then they have a nasty habit of gaining a new perspective, and in the cold light of the new day this sharp adversary might have turned into a somewhat dull blunt opponent…"

Having turned the tables on my principal male, it is his turn to be unsure whether he believes me, but after John hesitates, he re-establishes eye contact. "Because we have managed to achieve far more than we envisaged, as an added consolation Charlie, you're doing better than anyone could have expected…"

Without warning those dark, deep eyes are once again smiling at me, as John adds, "Now in case Bill is growing concerned that you might have discovered the whereabouts of the blunt and preferably serrated objects, I'd better get back to the study before he becomes concerned for my welfare and sends out a search party…"

"Of course John…"

Meanwhile in the study throughout his subordinate's absence, Philip Maddox had chosen to hover in the doorway so that he could listen to the exchange of dialogue inside his inner sanctum, and when John reached the bottom of the sweeping staircase, despite slowing his pace, as if his Commanding Officer possessed the gift of second sight in a hushed voice, he acknowledged John Bland's arrival without needing to glance over his shoulder.

"The prodigal operative has returned. After listening to Mrs Clunnell's description of what she overheard, I trust that upstairs in my Goddaughter's bedroom everything is now in order Mr Bland?"

"For the time being everything seems to be as one would expect Commander…"

"*Seems to be* is too ambiguous for my liking, would you please elaborate?"

"Of course Sir," Bland replied respectfully. "Having made an initial assessment over the next few days the situation needs to be monitored and if necessary, we will plan an intervention. However, I think Powell would agree that as Mrs Clunnell has demonstrated this evening, there's an existing risk that the situation could become volatile, and because I'm sure that none of us would want the balance of a young impressionable mind to be disturbed if he were to overhear his two mothers challenging each other, we need to build in some kind of contingency plan…"

"Oh I quite agree and although I might be a little rusty Mr Bland, I dare say that making sure Bobby's removed from the Manor, via a single clean and quick action shouldn't pose someone like me too many difficulties…"

"Thank you Sir. Hopefully, we will be able to give you some advance warning…"

Casting his subordinate, a sideways glance, Philip Maddox maintained his hushed voice. "As you know, I've chosen not to read your report until after you conclude this Interview, but taking into account her father's death and how Charlie and her stepmother Helen have never shared a close relationship, despite us needing to rebuild a few bridges, it would seem that I'm the nearest thing Charlie has to a close relative, and since Mrs Clunnell was demanding to know whether the abuse was physical or sexual, before listening to the content do I need to prepare myself for what I'm going to be hearing Mr Bland?"

What a dilemma? However, his Commanding Officer's assessment was correct. Since Charlie had few people she could rely upon, except Lorna and Colin McCardle, John elected to select his words with a degree of diplomacy.

"If it were a female member of my family Sir, then considering everything that's been revealed, before I listened to the playback, I'd want someone to suggest that perhaps I should savour one--or even two--generous measures of pure malt whisky and then, in case I need some additional support, it might be wise to keep the bottle close to my right hand…"

"You seem to have inherited one my vices John. Have you finished the Interview?"

"No, but as I've explained to Charlie, throughout this evening we have managed to accomplish far more than we had envisaged, and although it has taken its toll on your Goddaughter, she remains determined to conclude the proceedings tonight…"

Despite the smile which crept onto his face, Philip Maddox sighed. "Reckless seems appropriate, especially when I've never known a time Charlie wasn't behaving recklessly…"

"In the latter part of the recording Sir, I think you'll find that being reckless, and behaving recklessly are words you will hear being used repeatedly, but if it's any consolation, apart from having to overcome some instances of reluctance, Charlie's been most cooperative, and I think Powell would agree that we only need to tie up a few loose ends…"

Casting his subordinate another quick glance, Philip Maddox nodded his approval. "It was perhaps most fortuitous that Special Operations were alerted about the intruders at 187 Cheltenham Way and then, thanks to you having escorted Charlie home from Paris, as a personal favour to me, the highest possible Authority afforded us the opportunity to clean up, whatever mess had been left in our own back yard. However, before I have to start fending off the take-over bids, which will come from other agencies once the rumours start to circulate, is there something constructive I can be doing, so that I'm better prepared, prior to my having to begin negotiating on my Goddaughter's behalf?"

Relieved that he could offer something positive, John's reply was quite spontaneous. "Actually Sir, before tomorrow morning, there are a few things which could benefit from your organizational skills. After living with the sound of her own silence for the last seven years, although everyone suspected that it might be complex, in light of what Charlie has revealed whatever was complicated, those complications caused even more complications, until nothing in your Goddaughter's life was as it seemed to be on the surface…"

"Throughout her entire lifetime," the Commander remarked. "I've never known Charlie to do anything by halves, so that doesn't surprise me in the least…"

Despite the seriousness of the situation the two men exchanged a wry smile, before John explained, "Firstly, on the grounds of fresh evidence having come to light, we are going to need a High Court Judge to grant us an Exhumation Order in respect of the remains in Mark Daltry's grave, and secondly, because it might have been a grey area when he was vetted before joining Special Operations, someone needs to be assigned to begin a more thorough investigation into his adoption by Mr and Mrs Daltry…"

"It sounds as if there's some doubt about Daltry's death three months ago…"

"Regrettably, when you referred to the mess in our backyard, you didn't have any idea how accurate you might be, but nothing can be proven, until the DNA tests are double checked, and cross referenced with any new information from the adoption investigation…"

Despite his Commanding Officer's curious expression, when John heard Lorna's raised voice making unreasonable demands on his partner he fell silent, and because it provided him with a valid excuse to avoid any unavoidable direct questions, he suggested, "With your permission Commander, I think it's time I rescued my partner…"

"Be my guest," Philip Maddox replied, and then as if it were an afterthought, he added, "And John, thank you for not only being honest, but also for the sound advice…"

"It was my pleasure Sir…"

Then, wanting to have the added reassurance of knowing that Lorna was not about to drive that wedge between herself and his Goddaughter, Philip Maddox loitered out of sight of the open door and yet, as he had been trained to do, John Bland was prepared to bring his own gentle persuasion to bear on Lorna Clunnell, as she focused her attention on the prodigal operative. "Thank God you're back John. Did you see Charlie and was she still trying to scrub herself clean?"

Although no words needed to pass between the two men, rising to his feet, Bill allowed his partner to assume his crouched position, beside the Commander's executive chair. "By the time I reached the en-suite door Lorna, I couldn't hear either any sobbing or scrubbing, and once inside, while we talked about our last encounter in a different bathroom, I was able to check out Charlie's skin, but there was no evidence that she had been overly zealous when using the brush, so I chose not to challenge her…"

"But surely if someone doesn't challenge Charlie, then the scrubbing will continue?"

"Possibly, but now that we're aware of what's happening, I give you my word that we will be monitoring the situation on a daily basis, and if necessary we will intervene…"

Pausing, John allowed the silence to linger, until Lorna's lips parted. "In fact Lorna, a few moments ago, when Commander Maddox asked me for an update I explained that we might need to plan an intervention, and if that were to prove necessary, because none of us would want a young impressionable mind to be disturbed, he has agreed that he will take steps to ensure Bobby is removed from the Manor. Believe me, we do appreciate how hard this must be for you, but have we done enough to convince you that ever since we first landed on your doorstep, we have been acting in everyone's best interests?"

For a few tense seconds, Lorna did nothing, but then at last, she offered her agreement. "As long as you understand that if it does continue, and you fail to act I would find it difficult to stop myself from intervening, then I will leave the matter in your hands…"

Upstairs in my room, it is time for a change of costume before we enact the final scenes, and because my personal belongings from 187 Cheltenham Way arrived two days ago, and my Godfather's housekeeper Margaret has been kind enough to organize my clothes in the walk-in-wardrobe, I select a pair of figure hugging black leggings.

Next, I start flicking through the clothes on the rail, until my attention is drawn to the oversized tee-shirt, sporting an image of the original rebel without a cause James Dean. This is one of Bobby's favourites, but only because of its association with another of the cars on my son's top ten list--a classic racing car--which turned the actor into a living legend when he died, after a head on collision while driving his new Porsche 550 Spyder at over 100 mph.

Sliding the tee-shirt off its hanger I slip it over my head, before choosing a pair of comfortable sandals with a wedge heel, and if you'll pardon yet another dreadful play on words, my costume is a--*marked*--improvement on the designer clothes and expensive shoes, I was expected to wear in my capacity as Mark Daltry's wife. However, with my shoulder length hair, blown almost dry and swept back from my face, so that my features are defined, by nothing more alluring than a light dusting of grey eye-shadow, and the merest hint of waterproof mascara, the image for the final scenes in this performance will be casual, while at the same time camouflaging my inherent rebelliousness.

Although it might seem to be ironic, having come full circle to find ourselves back at the place where John chose to begin the story of my life, I'm reminded that it was Professor Kenneth Morgan at the Mayfield Clinic, who first made me believe that this was the person who could emerge by the time I was discharged and yet, the person other people would not allow me to remain--at least not until now--because having been granted unlimited time and space and complete freedom of speech, despite my initial abhorrence this reluctant leading lady realizes that if anyone were to ask--*would the real Charlie Anne Daltry, nee Charlotte*

*Anne Forsyth please stand up*--then having forgiven my transgressions over the last seven years as my God who despises nothing he created had intended, and for as long as he intends it to be so, this is the Charlie Anne Daltry he created in his own image.

Checking my face in the mirror one last time, I am a little pale, and I have done nothing to attempt to conceal the darkening shadows under each eye, which stand as a testimony to my inability to achieve any worthwhile rest. But at least I am refreshed after my shower, and when I click the study door open, only to discover that John is lounging in his chair, with his feet propped up on the corner of my Godfather's desk, in the kind of disrespectful fashion, which would merit a brusque order from his Commanding Officer delivered in a sharp tone of voice, something like, *"Feet Mr Bland..."*

As for our arbitrator, Bill is standing by the window, and as he glances over his shoulder, I note that they both seem somewhat taken aback by my complete metamorphosis.

Of course, apart from the two most important pieces of the puzzle, in my innocence, I believe that there is nothing left to reveal about my life, and because the worst must have come to pass, I click the door closed behind me, before approaching the desk with a naïve sense of calmness.

Those dark, deep eyes are still smiling at me, and when John swings his legs off the desk, and he gestures towards my Godfather's chair, there is nothing concealing his personal appreciation for my metamorphosis. But as he had forewarned me, Bill voices his concerns. "It's my professional opinion that you've been through enough Charlie, but despite the fact that my partner helped you to fall over the edge of the abyss, John has expressed your determination to conclude this Interview tonight. However, if we..."

"Please Bill..."

Raising his hand in the air, Bill silences me. "Would you please give me the chance to explain Charlie?"

"I'm sorry--it was rude of me to interrupt..."

Lulled into believing that he is back in control, Bill expresses his gratitude. "Thank you--as I was about to explain--if we proceed--then it's my duty as arbitrator to warn you that we will reach a point at which our professional obligations will necessitate that none of us leave this room, until we know every last detail..."

Ah, the aforementioned missing pieces of the puzzle and yet, I understand that the next time those questions are asked, no doubt with a professional directness, then irrespective of how tired or how distressed I might become, until I have provided them with the answers, there will be no more intermissions or unscheduled breaks.

"It's okay Bill, I understand, but it doesn't change anything. As I explained to John, since I doubt I could sleep until it is over, I still want to finish this tonight..."

Albeit damaged and battle scarred, this adult is supposed to be of sound body and mind, and after uttering a somewhat displeased sigh, Bill leaves the window and begins to approach the desk.

Thanks to long suffering Margaret, during this woman's absence, yet more fresh coffee and a light supper of sandwiches, and home-made shortbread biscuits have been provided, and because John has finished pouring coffee into the bone china mugs, Bill slides one of the saucers across the desk, so that the mug is in front of my Godfather's chair. Then, after repeating the process with a bone china side plate and knife, he picks up the sandwiches and biscuits and having re-seated myself, he invites me to select something to eat.

"No thank you, I'm not very hungry..."

Perhaps not, but Bill remains persistent. "Since it's been a long and often arduous evening Charlie, you could at least humour me by attempting to eat something..."

"Do I have a choice?"

"Because Special Operations is obliged to act in accordance with the rules laid down by the Geneva Convention, and your pathetic attempts at eating are beginning to resemble a hunger strike, it would be wise to humour me or I might decide to send you to bed, without hearing the rest of your life story…"

Then, when I look across the desk in the hope of getting some support from my principal male, John's eyes remain locked on my face, and irrespective of what happened prior to our intermission, or what passed between us in the privacy of the en-suite, he is prepared to confirm that he and his partner in crime are united on this issue.

"Bearing in mind Bill's dogged determination, if I were you I'd humour him, especially when you're in Protective Custody and he has the power to have you force fed…"

Yes, it might be wise to humour Bill, and after taking a sandwich and a shortbread biscuit, from the plate in his hand using the knife, I cut the half of the sandwich, so that it makes two quarters, before I take the smallest possible bite. Not much of a gesture of goodwill on my part, but it would seem to be enough to satisfy our arbitrator, because after picking up his own coffee and sandwiches, Bill returns to the table leaving behind a poignant remark, which I suspect is directed more at his partner than me.

"It's comforting to know that despite events prior to our intermission, I do still command some kind of control over these proceedings…."

Under the pretence of drinking some of my coffee by the end of the second bite, the quarter of my sandwich is left lying on the plate, and with the principal players back in their appointed places for the commencement of the final act, when I hear the gentle purring from the surveillance equipment, Bill reintroduces the scene.

The time is 22:28 on the 29th June. Present are John Bland and myself Robert William Powell. Also present is Charlie Anne Daltry, nee Charlotte Anne Forsyth who has requested that we conclude these proceedings tonight, even though she has been offered the opportunity to postpone the remainder of this Interview until tomorrow morning. There is nobody else present and as negotiated by Commander Philip Maddox and then, sanctioned by the highest possible authority no other visual or audio surveillance equipment is being used…"

If you will forgive another Freudian slip, then nobody knows better than me that there can be nothing more off-putting than being expected to perform to order, and because John is not observing his leading lady, it is the sandwich which holds the focus of his attention, despite managing another even smaller bite, when I hear Bill reopening the proceedings, I am grateful for the added distraction.

"Prior to our second intermission Charlie, you described some of the things which happened, before our arrival at 187 Cheltenham Way. With regard to what's been recorded, is there anything you would like to add, or even alter in connection with the abuse?"

"No, I think I've said everything I wanted or needed to say on the subject…"

Then, instead of delivering his next line, Bill remains silent. How appropriate, especially when it affords me the opportunity to start repaying John for having reneged on their side of our agreement, and as I glance over my shoulder, I deliver my declaration of war. "If I'm not mistaken, this is where you pick up from the last notes you documented on your notepad, a few moments before John's ranting pushed me over the edge. Despite having referred to the fact that neither of you could find any reason, why I could not have approached my own Godfather, John suggested that *I must have been blinded by contempt or I would never have behaved in such a reckless way…"*

As I had anticipated, it is as if time has stood still, until I hear Bill rising to his feet, and without disturbing the silence, he moves to the desk and lowers the notepad, so that John can read what he had written before his partner began his unstoppable ranting. Then, without making any reference to what they have both witnessed, Bill returns to the table and sits back down, before moving time on by adjusting, the words to his next question. "In that case

Charlie, if I give you my word that John will remain on the other side of the desk--with his mouth shut--is there anything you would like to say about that particular allegation?"

After handling such a sensitive issue with the utmost discretion, I cast a congratulatory backward nod in Bill's direction, before my gaze drifts between them, and because they both understand that if what they have witnessed was to become common knowledge, then it would double the value of the existing Contract--opposite me--those deep brown eyes cannot hide the admiration John has for his adversary, as I reply, "No Bill, I think John said more than enough for both of us…"

Is that punishment enough? Perhaps, but while I am wondering when I first noticed the colour of John's eyes, I test the limit of the boundaries my inquisitors have imposed, by pushing the remainder of my sandwich to one side, before sipping from my coffee mug and then, knowing that Margaret's home-baked shortbread biscuit will provide me with a sugar rush, I dunk it into the hot liquid, before satisfying their apparent fixation over my eating.

Next, I push those same boundaries to the maximum limit by rising to my feet, and when neither of them risks challenging me over the discarded sandwich--taking my coffee mug and the last remnants of my shortbread biscuit with me--this adult dares to move towards the window, as Bill chooses to fill the silence.

"For the benefit of the Official Recording, in my capacity as self-appointed arbitrator, I think it's in your best interests to reiterate the following. Throughout this evening, if not immediately then eventually, irrespective of how difficult it might have seemed, whenever asked to do so, you have found a way to elaborate upon issues, which were of a sensitive nature, including what took place in the early hours of that Thursday morning…"

Pausing, like any good arbitrator should--Bill waits, before delivering the bottom line. "Is there anything else we should know about your life Charlie?"

Leaning against the wood panel in the recess of the window, while I am considering whether there might be something I have--in all innocence--forgotten, after dunking the remainder of my biscuit into the coffee, I multitask by excusing not only my silence, but also continuing to satisfy my inquisitors desire to see me eating and then, because I cannot find any significant omissions, I bring the silence to an end

"No Bill, with the exception of the two missing pieces of information, I cannot think of anything…"

"There is one thing that you've never mentioned Charlie…"

There was a familiar air of superiority in John's voice, and perhaps I should have known better than to presume we were nearing the end of our journey. Is there something I have forgotten to mention? Something important enough to warrant a challenge, and as I turn my head to look at him, John seems eager--perhaps even too eager--to enlighten me.

"With the exception of a few unavoidable references in connection with the termination, you've never mentioned the baby…"

"That's because there's nothing to say…"

After the murder of the innocent one, may my God forgive me for speaking in such a dismissive way. But since John knows I wanted to have my baby so much that I even risked being Sectioned for my own Safety when I refused to sign the consent, there has to be something lurking behind his suggestion.

"Possibly not," John is speculating, with his deep brown eyes smiling at me. "But while your pregnancy seemed to be the most natural thing before your revelations, I think you'd have to agree that it now seems strange that you would conceive the child of man, you had every reason to hate, a man who--in your own words--*didn't treat you like a human being--much less a woman*…"

"I don't understand…"

Liar--you bare-faced, shameless liar--I understand where John's innuendo is leading us, and despite having injured my vulnerable child before our intermission, this adult realizes that he now intends to add insult to that injury. Opponents so soon? Sooner than expected and as I begin to walk back to the desk, each slow step is significant.

"I would have thought it was obvious Charlie," John continues with his explanation. "After all, you're an attractive woman and being trapped inside an empty, loveless marriage to a man like Mark must have been intolerable…"

"And is that how you both see it?"

Ignoring my question, John remains so superior and so confident that he must be right, he has a long way to go, before he will finish daring to add insult to his original injury.

"And taking into account your husband's sexual preference, you can't blame us for doubting that when we escorted you home from Paris, the child you were carrying was Mark's baby. However, if you were involved in a sexual relationship with somebody else, we wouldn't want them to end up dead--or badly injured. Would we Charlie?"

"How dare you?" I hear this woman protest, before my gaze drifts between the two of them. "How dare both of you?"

Oh but the man who has been sitting opposite me throughout this evening, he dares in particular, and because I'm outraged by the condescending overtone in John's voice, having reached the desk, after this woman returns the mug to its saucer, my eyes never leave his face, as John finishes adding his personal insult to my former injury.

"It's not an unreasonable assumption, and nobody could have apportioned any blame Charlie if you had sought consolation within an extra marital relationship…"

"You," this leading lady begins to utter, but now the right words I need to express my feelings remain trapped in my throat, and when they refuse to emerge--like an imbecile--I keep repeating my initial uttering. "You…"

With those brown eyes smiling at me, John seems to delight in delivering the missing words on my behalf. "I suspect that the words you're searching for might be, and I quote Charlie--*you supercilious bastard…*"

Oh how accurate and yet, the words would not do justice to my injury, and because my reaction will speak louder than any amount of words, without giving any premeditated thought as to the possible consequences, this leading lady's right arm is swinging towards the side of my principal male's face.

Like the breaking glass in Mark's bathroom, as my hand collides with its intended target, the sound of the impact is gratifying, but while it might have been cathartic, I am horrified that I dared to even consider striking him--much less managed to deliver the blow. In fact, I'm so disbelieving that as if my arm is frozen, it remains suspended in the air, until a smirk creeps onto John's face, ahead of him posing an unavoidable direct question.

"Did that make you feel any better?"

Are there no depths to which this man will not sink? Using my own words to taunt me, and because I still want to wipe that smirk off his face, for the second time my arm is being propelled towards the side of his head with a deliberate intent of inflicting some serious damage, and it remains on target until John's hand suddenly intercepts my arm in mud-air which demonstrates how easy it would have been for him to avoid the first blow.

Yet again, it is as if time has stood still, but then with his hand around my forearm, those deep brown eyes are looking up at me, and his supercilious overtone has been replaced by the commanding professionalism, this adult has come to expect from him.

"Although there could be no doubt that I deserved the first, I can assure you that once is a rare privilege afforded to few people and then, only in certain circumstances. However, since twice would be an indulgence for anyone who might find themselves pinned in your current position Charlie, it might prove to be the kind of luxury, you cannot afford…"

Calm, precise and delivered with the kind of perfect control necessary to leave my rebellious child and her parent, in no doubt that we have been warned and yet, I remain no less infuriated at being expected to perform to order, and after snatching my arm free from John's grasp, this adult's gaze drifts between my two inquisitors, and when neither of them has the decency to intercede, as I start to move back to the window, I make my feelings clear.

"No doubt I've said this before, but who the hell do you people think you are?"

Silence--but between you and me, since neither of them has any defence to offer, although it might seem ironic, it's their turn to sustain their own sanctimonious silence and yet, at the same time with this scorned wife's loyalty and integrity challenged, both of them expect me to defend my sexual conduct. This is outrageous, so outrageous my rebellious child feels that it is appropriate to add her own somewhat more explicit expletive.

"And what the--FUCK--would either of you know about it anyway?"

No less outraged, this woman turns away from the desk, but my arms are folded as I move back to the window, and my angry glare continues to drift between them. "In case either of you has failed to notice, I am over the legal age of consent, and although both of you must have had to sell your souls when you joined Special Operations, I do not have to be accountable to your Almighty Commanding Officer. So the last time I checked, I have been free to sleep with whomever I want, whenever I choose to do so…"

"Nobody doubts it Charlie…."

At last the false prophet--in the guise of our arbitrator--has deigned to re-join the proceedings, and despite his tardiness his tone is soft and placatory.

"But it's all hypothetical isn't it?" Pausing, Bill once again waits and then, when I refuse to give him the satisfaction of filling the silence on his behalf, he is forced to qualify whatever that--so called hypothetical is--by adding. "Because you didn't have a sexual relationship with anyone except Mark, did you Charlie?"

"As I have previously stated, it's none of YOUR FUCKING BUSINESS…"

As my breathing is becoming shallower and more rapid, I'm unsure whether I'm angry at their assumption that I must have been unfaithful, or aggrieved because this scorned wife remained faithful to a man who--as John has reminded everyone--never treated me like a human being, much less a woman.

"My God," I hear my protective parent beginning her protest. "Under the pretence of what's in my best interest, throughout the course of this evening not only have you publically HUMILIATED me, you have also COERCED me into describing all of the sordid details in connection with me discovering the corruption and treasonable offences committed by the man, I had the misfortune to marry…"

When my rapid breathing forces me to hesitate, I inhale a deep, steadying breath into my lungs, before releasing it slowly and evenly. "Regardless of whatever your precious files might say about me, I'm only human--a flesh and blood kind of humanoid--but not content with having pared away layer upon layer of resilient flesh, until there's nothing left except brittle bone grinding against brittle bone, you now want to rob me of my remaining dignity, but I do not--I repeat DO NOT intend to relinquish it without a fight to the death gentlemen. So I trust that you understand the seriousness of my position?"

"Of course we do Charlie…"

Despite their simultaneous confirmation from their respective places, I'm aware that my inquisitors are watching me, and because it's my belief that if they had any defences to offer, then they would have declared them by now. So it would seem that the centre stage is mine to command, which leaves me free to deliver the remainder of my soliloquy.

"Did you never consider how I must have yearned to have a relationship with someone who was capable of treating me like a woman? Or how I could only imagine what it would be like to have a man make love to me, instead of using me whenever he wanted?"

Behind me the silence continues, but now I am sensing that it has nothing to do with neither of them having defences they can offer. It is more out of the respect they have for this Interviewee, which somehow makes it easier for me to make the kind of admission, no woman should be forced to make at any time throughout their existence.

"But after I knew about my husband's alternative lifestyle, and while I was waiting for him to grant me my freedom, Mark left me in no doubt that if I was ever foolish enough to stray into anyone else's bed, then in addition to the damage he would inflict on the other party, he'd punish me by making sure that for as long as I was alive, nobody would want to look at my face--much less touch my body…"

Since anger invariably masks hurt, some of my rage seems to be abating, but since it was such a damning admission, as if my protective parent wants the darkness to swallow me up, I stare out of the window, until my rationalization prompts me to utter an incredulous laugh, before I cast a backward glance at John. From his expression, it is obvious that he remembers the last accusation he levelled, during his unstoppable ranting, and because I had promised him, before he left the en-suite that if such an opportunity did arise, then this woman would repay the compliment, I choose to turn his own words against him.

"Yes Mr Bland, I thought you might make the connection to that same accusation you levelled at me, before our second intermission…"

Suddenly, there is a rare display of regret, but I believe you would have to agree, it is too late for a demonstration of compassion--much less concern--and after fixing my glare upon Bill, his partner's leading lady admits to what should be inadmissible.

"So while I hate to disappoint both of you, there aren't any more even grubbier skeletons lurking in the family closet, because you're right Mr Powell. With the exception of enjoying the innocent attentions of someone who found me interesting, and dare I be so bold as to suggest attractive, although I hate to admit it, I was faithful--no, let's not give any more cause for misrepresentation--in light of what we now know--until the early hours of the 22$^{nd}$ June, when my husband turned me into a cheap whore, I had never been unfaithful…"

Turning away from the window, my protective parent fixes her icy glare on a more subdued adversary. "As for you Mr Bland, yet again you are way out of line, because beyond any doubt it was Mark's baby…"

"Neither of us actually believed that you had been unfaithful Charlie. However, for the benefit of the Official Recording, we needed to eliminate all possible doubt…"

Perhaps they did, but there are more diplomatic ways in which to achieve the absolute, and no less angry with my principal male, this woman is walking back towards the desk, and with my arms still folded, I decide that it is time to add insult to his injury.

"Relax Mr Bland, I understand that when it comes to assignments like these, this is nothing more than routine procedure for two highly trained and multi-skilled professionals like you, and I'm sure that when he listens to the playback, your Commanding Officer will be most impressed with your performances…"

Touché, and John appears to be wounded, but his acceptance of my derision through a gentle nod, allows me to proceed. "Although Mark isn't here to explain, I think you can appreciate why children were not one of his priorities, and since it's clear that neither of you studied biology, perhaps it's fortunate that I can pinpoint the exact occasion…"

"It must have been when you undertook that dirty job but someone had to do it…"

Having reached the desk, as I reseat myself in my Godfather's chair, I congratulate John upon having recalled the incident. "That's correct--it was not long before we were due to fly to Paris and I needed to massage his oversized ego, so that he would tell me why he was so pleased with himself. So after dinner when the taxi dropped us back at the house, without any of the usual crime and punishment nonsense, Mark turned into the man I'd married, and after taking me to bed, we had straight sexual intercourse, and because it was the first time in longer than I could remember, I had stopped taking any precautions. It was such a memorable occasion, especially when we woke up in our marital bed. Having explained all this is there anything else you require as proof of my faithfulness?"

"No Charlie," Bill replies. "You've given us more than enough…"

"I'm pleased to hear it, because if you had wanted diagrams, then I would have grounds to suggest that the pair of you need to spend more time indulging in carnal pursuits, but preferably not with each other, because that might be regarded as being incestuous…"

Turning my head so that I can focus on Bill, I announce, "It's supposed to be a woman's prerogative to change her mind, and because I've taken all I'm going to take from either of you I'm afraid that I've changed mine and now, there is something I would like to clarify about the place where the story of my life should have begun…"

With Bill lulled into a false sense of security for a second time, he gestures in the air, with his open hand. "Be my guest Charlie…"

Tossing my head back, my rebellious child prompts her parent to laugh. "I'm not sure whether Commander Maddox will like what I'm about to say, but since you have the rather daunting responsibility of keeping me alive--no doubt you'll stop me--if I go too far…"

Without knowing what I intend to do or say, Bill acknowledges the advance warning through a positive gesture and opposite me, despite his earlier moment of triumph followed by his display of weakness, John's expression has reverted to revealing nothing. Perhaps there are no winners or losers, and maybe what I am about to say is not relevant to the proceedings, but after reaching for my first cigarette since our intermission, I pull one from the packet and yet, after such a pronounced metamorphosis, it remains a habit I abhor so I lay the cigarette in the ashtray, which has been emptied and washed for a second time during my absence

"Although I cannot deny that some of the accusations levelled by Mr Bland are valid, and because of my upbringing, I should have known better than to allow myself to be caught up in other peoples' deceptions. However, it's important to document that learning to live with the sound of my own silence, didn't begin when my father allowed the consent, I had signed at the Mayfield Clinic to reach the Forsyth File, or after he meddled in my life yet again, with eventual dire consequences by telling Mark Daltry that I had a son with whom I maintained discreet contact…"

"For anyone who is authorized to hear the content of this Interview Charlie, it's clear that your entire life has been punctuated by a series of events, in which other people have played a part without your prior knowledge--or your consent…"

"That might well be the case Mr Powell. However, when Mr Bland referred to a mishandled past, I think it's only reasonable that anyone listening to the recording should appreciate that this began, while I was a willing participant on the Research Programme…"

Anticipating Bill's forthcoming disquiet, I choose to digress "There's no need for you to be concerned Mr Powell. Earlier this evening, when it was first mentioned, I assumed that despite being granted unlimited access to the Forsyth and Daltry Files when it came to the Research Programme, because your Security Clearance only gave you access--on a need to know basis--neither of you are aware of its purpose…"

"That's correct Charlie…"

Then, before Bill can elaborate this woman turns her head, so that our arbitrator can see the genuine warmth in my smile.

"Although you might think I need to be saved, you couldn't be more mistaken Mr Powell. Indeed, after all the years of living in devout silence, you can rest assured that since nobody understands better than me about the probable consequences, if I should contravene, the Official Secrets Act, no classified information will be recorded. However, if you choose to prevent me from making the highest possible Authority--appreciate my position--then you would be denying me my constitutional right to enter a valid defence…"

If I say so myself that was a winning declaration, and since Bill cannot deny me the right to defend myself, with a detectable reluctance he nods his approval, so that once I cast a courteous glance at my principal male who is smiling, because he knows that since this woman has turned into a butterfly--albeit one with fragmented wings--which need time to fully develop, I am about to seize control of the moral high ground.

"Despite being a source of disappointment to my father, from an early age it became evident that I had been born with some unusual abilities, and after my mother's death, my sheltered upbringing meant that those talents could flourish, without either control or restriction, so that by the time I was invited to become the youngest participant on the Research Programme, I seemed to be in a category above the other seven candidates, and with Commander Maddox acting as one of the official observers who were monitoring the welfare of the participants, despite finding those seven months a tremendous strain, my Godfather was available whenever I needed some moral support..."

Acting on auto-pilot, I reach for the cigarette, which is lying where I left it in the glass ashtray, but holding it seems to be sufficient, so I don't pick up the lighter. "Perhaps it was naïve of me not to consider that having a test score of 99.15%, would mean that someone might want to determine whether such a success rate could be reduced, but I swear I never considered it--and up until--someone authorized the introduction of lysergic acid diethylamide together with amphetamines, everything had been fine..."

Succumbing to every addicts need for the relative safety of a nicotine fix, I reach for the lighter, but I'm aware that my inquisitors are waiting in respectful silence, and since Bill has not yet felt it necessary to save me from myself, I do not spark it into flame.

"At first new phenomena emerged, and my responses were not only faster, but also more accurate and yet. it was so exhausting, it felt as if my unique abilities were draining all of my energy, and because I couldn't sleep I became overanxious, and when I developed acute paranoia, it must have been decided that I should be told the truth, and as it transpired that truth meant that yet again, I had been tricked by people I thought I could trust..."

Opposite me, it is John's turn to stir. "Since mind altering drugs were being mixed with amphetamines, it's hardly surprising you couldn't sleep Charlie and presumably, because of the family connection, Commander Maddox must have been chosen to tell you?"

"Yes, but my Godfather didn't come alone. He arrived accompanied by the Major, and after the Commander told me what they had done to me without either my knowledge or my consent, I didn't utter a sound. Instead, I left the Interview room, and after making sure that that they couldn't follow me by using my mind to lock the door, I entered one the laboratories. However, before we deal with, what I did and how yet another half-truth made it impossible for me to approach Commander Maddox..."

Hesitating, I glance over my shoulder. "The folders on the edge of the table Bill, the one relating to the debriefing sessions, are the documents in chronological order?"

"Of course..."

"Good, that's what I was hoping, but first I would like both of you to focus your attention on the floor to ceiling book shelves and in particular, from the top to bottom--on the third and fifth rows, books--three, five, seven, eleven, and thirteen and then, on the seventh and ninth rows, books--two, four, six, eight and ten...."

"Charlie..."

Please forgive me, but since my mind is made up, it is too late to save me from myself, and after closing my eyes, I visualize the folder containing the contents from the debriefing sessions, which I know I have chosen because it's going to pose a little more difficulty, especially when the folder is on the bottom of the pile. Nevertheless, since my inquisitors are focusing on the book shelves, in my mind I'm aware that Bill has failed to stop the folder from leaving the desk, so that the documents are strewn all over my Godfather's expensive Persian carpet, prompting Bill to yet again attempt to save me--or perhaps this time, he is choosing to try and save them from any further inexplicable chaos.

"Charlie…"

This woman was right, Bill's demand for my rebellious child's immediate attention is more forceful, but this kind of parlour trick should never be interrupted, especially when I have to make them appreciate that the first demonstration was not some kind of freak accident. Besides, despite their advanced training, what could they do to stop me from using my mind? Closing my eyes again, I refocus my attention on the neatly ordered books on my Godfather's shelves, and because this requires less concentration, I can hear the nominated books, falling one after the other off their designated shelves.

Then, when I open my eyes between you and me, the three of us could have heard a pin drop, not least because the gentle purring from the recording equipment has long since ceased, which prompts me to dispel any fears Bill might be nurturing.

"There's no need to be alarmed Bill. On your behalf, I took the liberty of suspending the surveillance equipment, so that nothing deemed Classified could be recorded, and before you ask, the answer to your next question is--yes, at any time during this evening, I could have paused or stopped the recording. But I didn't because it would have proved to be counter-productive, especially when you take into consideration that if I had used any of my abilities while I was married to Mark, or in the early hours of June 22, then my husband would have never allowed me to gain my freedom, and if Tony Shaw had discovered my potential financial worth, then we would have been long gone before you arrived…"

Despite my hesitation, when neither of them seem to want to pass comment, I add, "Although I've demonstrated my ability to move objects using my mind, if you need any further examples, I could show you more of my unique abilities. Such as my total recall, and what I did with your notepad, my cognitive powers would prove invaluable, if they fell into the wrong hands--and I can speed read and then repeat every word I've read. However, since I think longsuffering Margaret has more enough to deal with, while we are all guests at Manor Park, I would be disinclined to perform any further cheap parlour tricks…"

"On behalf of both of us," I hear Bill state from behind me. "The exactness of your ability was one of the most impressive displays of telekinesis we've witnessed. In fact, when we were at the airfield, we noted that it was as if you knew, the explosion was going to happen, and once you and I were in the rear seat of the Jaguar, although you didn't realize what you were doing, I used a hand held digital recorder to capture word after word while you were rerunning, the details of what had passed between you and the Major…"

"But Bill," I interrupt him. "That ability isn't a blessing it is a curse, especially when you consider that despite seeing the image of the explosion, like too many other occasions, I cannot alter, what other people's life expectancy are predestined to be, or change the course of history, and because that ability is worthless, it seems to reinforce the existence of a God, or when it comes to the sceptics, some kind of higher power or energy giving force…"

Laying the unlit cigarette back down in the ashtray, as I place the lighter beside the packet, John fills my silence. "You told us that you were discharged from the Research Programme, because of something you did Charlie. Since we're talking strictly off the Official Recording can you possibly elaborate for us?"

Tossing my head back, I laugh. "Using my mind, I sealed the door to the lab, so that nobody could stop me, and after embarking upon a destructive spree, in less than two minutes all the debris was piled in a pyramid like structure in the centre of the room…"

After the cavalry share the same laughter, John suggests, "I suppose that was one way to guarantee that several high ranking Officers might be a little pissed off with you…"

"Oh that wasn't the reason why I was discharged in disgrace," I state as I am basking in the limelight. "But are you quite sure you want me to divulge any more Official Secrets?"

Silence, and although I had doubted that they had ever been young and rebellious, they allow their inner children to emerge. "Oh we're both positive Charlie..."

"All right, but you were warned," I caution them again, before I admit. "While I was still in the laboratory, I managed to breach not only their alleged impregnable main frame firewall, but also the firewall that lay hidden within the first two..."

"Oh my God," I hear Bill announcing. "Surely you didn't Charlie?"

"I'm afraid I did, and still using nothing, except my mind I didn't only erase all of the audio and visual research data, I searched for the back-up discs and any flash drives, so that I could also wipe out any record that neither the other seven participants, nor I had ever been present. So those are the precise reasons why the file relating to the Research Programme contains nothing, except for the details of my dishonourable discharge, and why I was categorized as an unsuitable candidate for any further research..."

Strictly between you and me the enormity of my capabilities, and the potential for their misuse, not only Bill, but also my principal male seem to be lost for words, and because I want to alleviate their fears, in a hushed voice, I explain, "All I intended to do was ensure that any similar Research Programmes would be handled in the right way, so that nobody else could be mistreated, and because I'm not accustomed to living with the sound of your silence and it's beginning to unnerve me, would one of you please say something?"

Behind me, Bill clears his throat. "As I've already confirmed we have encountered telekinesis several times, but the strength of your abilities is so unique, neither of us has witnessed a phenomenon of this enormity, and you're right Charlie, in either the wrong or the right hands, the potential for its misuse is monumental..."

"And if I were to hazard a wild guess, despite all your extensive training, you cannot conceive how you would contain anyone with my kind of abilities. In fact, after I unsealed the doors to the Interview room and the laboratory, with a deliberate suddenness two M. P.'s ended up sprawled across the floor, but since I knew the protocol, I was already on my knees with my interlocked fingers keeping my hands clasped behind my head, and by the time the Commander and my father joined us, there was a gun aimed at the back of my head..."

For a few moments the silence lingers, until Bill calls the proceedings to order. "Thank you Charlie, your descriptive testimony has been most helpful. Before we recommence the Interview, are there any other submissions you would like to add?"

"But you don't seem to have grasped the full implications of my discharge from the Research Programme. Surely, you must have realized that my reputation precedes me, so that when it comes to the rather--*daunting responsibility for keeping me alive*--like my unique abilities the risk factor has grown in its enormity, which is why the only thing I was concerned about was Bobby and Lorna's long term safety and anonymity..."

"With all due respect," Bill states, sharply enough to render me silent. "Although you might be a mouthy little upstart, who has demonstrated that she's got more balls than most of the men we've encountered over the years, our being reassigned wasn't a coincidence Charlie. So if anything were to pose a threat to your continued existence, you can rest assured that since we take our obligations seriously, we don't intend to allow anything to damage our 99% success rate..."

In view of Bill's description, this mouthy little upstart laughs, before John adds, "Perhaps this might seem incredulous, but until the Protective Custody Order is rescinded by a High Court Judge, even if the highest possible Authority were to come through the study door carrying a gun, we would seek to neutralize the potential threat to your life..."

As John pauses, I remain silent, which forces him to continue. "From what you have shared with us regarding the enormity of your abilities and taking into account that Commander Philip Maddox--who also happens to be your Godfather--must have been aware of your reputation when he reassigned us, I can give you my personal guarantee that our

Commanding Officer has no intention of giving up on you, and since there is more likelihood of us all dying as a result of old age, can we please conclude this damn Interview?"

For a lingering moment, I continue to study John's features, but behind those deep brown eyes, there is nothing concealing the depth of the additional admiration he holds for this mouthy little upstart, who found the courage to turn them into co-conspirators.

"Of course John," this leading lady replies, with a warm smile. "But please don't touch the pause button Bill, because before I demonstrated my telekinetic abilities, I suspended the surveillance equipment. So if we're going to avoid any kind of detectable lapse in timing, then it might be wise to allow me to reverse the process and then, you can pick up from the last thing that was recorded, and I'm quoting my own words--*now, before we deal with what I did and how yet another half-truth made it impossible for me to approach Commander Maddox*--unquote…"

After Bill nods his agreement, I release the suspended recording, and as soon as the gentle purring fills the study, Bill asks, "And what about the half-truth you mentioned--if that was the reason why you felt unable to approach Commander Maddox, so that you could achieve the right kind of protection, could you please elaborate for us?"

*June 27 15:15 Two days ago, Bill had been dispatched to advise me that I had been summoned to my Godfather's inner sanctum.*

*When it came to my son's love affair with football, although whenever possible Commander Maddox has found the time to join the cavalry, so that they could indulge Bobby's passion, it would take more than one gesture to convince me of my Godfather's metamorphosis, especially when he has been conspicuous by his absence at our communal meals, which was the reason I had come to suspect, he had been avoiding me and yet, suddenly when he requests my attendance in his study, he expects me to grant him an audience. Sounds unreasonable, too damn right it was unreasonable.*

*So when we reached the closed door, not only did I not bother waiting to the announced, I also entered without bothering to knock and it came as no surprise to discover, the other half of his dynamic duo lurking inside.*

*"Good afternoon Charlie," Commander Maddox announced, as he turned away from the window. "Thank you for agreeing to join us, I do hope my request for your presence, didn't disturb you if you were trying to rest?"*

*Small talk! Surely, my Godfather did not summon me because he wanted to make polite conversation. "No, I wasn't resting Commander. However, since I was about to play backgammon with my son, could we please make this as brief as possible?"*

*"Of course," My Godfather replied, and having reached the desk, before sitting himself down in his Executive chair, he suggested, "Please take a seat…"*

*As if it were a defensive gesture, I chose to remain standing, so that if necessary I would be towering above, and looking down upon a man who believed himself to be above reproach and yet, when it came to the family skeletons, since nobody knew better than me where their remains lay buried, I refused to be intimidated by the Commander's stature, or his apparent limitless power.*

*Disregarding my blatant contempt, the Commander addressed his subordinates who must have been a little bewildered. "While Mrs Daltry and I discuss a private and confidential matter, would you please wait outside for a few minutes' gentlemen?"*

*"Of course Sir…"*

*Then, as soon as the door clicked closed behind them, my Godfather explained, "Charlie in light of recent events, I have every reason to believe that what happened at the Military Research Facility will need to come under closer scrutiny…"*

"And what would you like me to say? It was a mismanaged catastrophe, and nothing has changed. I still do not regret what I did, and if it were necessary I would do it again..."

"Please Charlie," The Commander appealed to the more tolerant side of my nature, having not yet realized that when it comes to this issue, I do not have a more. tolerant side. "Something arose, which at the time, presented itself as a necessary half-truth, but since the circumstances have now changed, I have been granted the authorization, so that..."

Too prejudiced against anything connected with the Research Programme, as I turned away from the desk, I was demanding, "And what part of--I don't regret my actions---did you not understand Commander, unless you'd like me to give you a repeat performance?"

Having reached the door, I opened it and despite being prepared to deal with Bland and Powell from behind me, the Commander's voice delayed my departure.

"I have proof Charlie. Written proof about something on that last day, when the Head of the Military Research Programme had no choice, except to discharge you..."

At least he had succeeded in regaining his Goddaughter's full attention, and as I turned around, he was sliding the top drawer of his desk open, and confident that curiosity would be my downfall, as I was gravitating back towards the desk, the Commander produced an envelope, which he proceeded to hold in the air, so that it was grasped between his thumb and index finger, while he once again addressed his subordinates.

"It's all right gentlemen. You don't have to leave. Now that Mrs Daltry understands the full implications, I don't think she has any intention of doing, or saying anything that might contravene the Official Secrets Act. Isn't that correct Charlie?"

Refusing to afford him an answer to his question, using one swift, disrespectful upward movement, I lifted the envelope from between his thumb and index finger, as he issued a subtle warning, "Sometimes the truth hurts Charlie, and as much as I regret what happened, if there is a way forward, then you do need to confront the half-truth..."

By that time, my only clear thought was what the hell? Surely, after all these years, the contents could not harm me, and after picking up the letter opener from my Godfather's desk I slit the envelope open, before sliding out the contents, while the Commander provided a more detailed explanation.

"For obvious reasons, those three pages are copies. However, there can be no mistaking the signature and the seal of office on the second page, and the date coincides with your departure from the Research Facility..."

Calm and in complete control, the palms of my Godfather's hands were touching so that his chin was resting on his fingertips as he added, "Along with that letter, its accompanying declaration were placed in the Research Programme file, in case there came a time when you needed to know the absolute truth..."

For some inexplicable reason my hands had begun to tremble, and when Bill came to my rescue and he eased the chair away from the desk, so that I could sit down, before he retreated to a discreet distance I was grateful for his assistance, and with some trepidation I started to read the first page, but soon I was wishing that my Godfather had not tempted me, especially when it came to the paragraph relating to the use of mind altering substances, in conjunction with amphetamines, and how Philip Maddox had not known in advance. In fact, when he was told he had been so enraged, he demanded to know why he had not been summoned long before it had become evident that prior to me developing acute paranoia, I had begun to experience bouts of severe disorientation.

Then, with an even greater trepidation, I started to read the second page, which confirmed that after it had been agreed, I should be told about the drugs, because of the strong bond we had built between us--during those seven months--my Godfather had been asked if he would attend the forthcoming Interview.

*"But you were there Commander," this protective mother heard her vulnerable child protesting. "In fact, it was you who delivered the news, and because I thought you had tricked me into believing you could be trusted that's why I reacted in the way that I did..."*

*Opposite me, Philip Maddox maintained his calm persona. "I'm afraid it is the truth. As the letter explains Charlie--for fourteen days--I had been on a special assignment, which meant that it had been so easy to keep us apart, but then in the hope that the situation could be redeemed, I agreed to attend that Interview, and because of the relationship we had built over the previous seven months, you assumed the worst--that I was to blame..."*

*Genuinely perplexed, and in my naivety I ventured to propose an obvious question. "That doesn't make any sense--why would you allow me to assume it was you, and if you weren't responsible, then who gave them the necessary authorization?"*

*This time my Godfather chose to remain silent, which in turn left me no choice, except to read that third and final page. Of course, since the only other person present was my father, I should have been suspicious and yet, because this daughter found it inconceivable that his lust to bask in my Military success had enabled him to disregard that the drugs could have killed me, I read each word of the Major's admission of guilt not once, but twice and then sickened by the harsh reality I lifted my head, so that I could achieve eye contact.*

*"This is bullshit," I snarled at the Commander. "And I don't believe a word of it..."*

*With the palms of his hands still clasped together, and his fingertips touching his chin, my Godfather delivered his reply without the slightest hint of alarm. "Don't believe it Charlie? Or is it that you either don't want--or would prefer not to believe it?"*

*"It makes no difference," this protective mother heard her injured child protesting. "These three pieces of paper are copies, and since we all know that documents can be doctored or manufactured, so that they can appear as if by magic at a convenient time, especially when the Major cannot enter a defence against this kind of crap..."*

Between you and me, I know that when my Godfather listens to the surveillance footage, he will come to appreciate why yet another half-truth had robbed me of the ability to approach him, so that I could have acquired the right kind of protection for the three of us

*Needing to express myself in a disrespectful way--in a fit of pique--I started to tear up the contents of the envelope, and after rising to my feet firstly--as if it were confetti—I dared to scatter the pieces not only over the desk, but also the Commander and then secondly, I turned away and although I could only sense his hand gesture, he must have confirmed that neither of his subordinates were to do anything to impede my departure--much less prevent me--from leaving his inner sanctum without being dismissed, because in his infinite wisdom my Godfather understood that it would take time for the healing process to begin.*

*Instead of returning to Lorna and Bobby, I climbed the sweeping staircase, so that I could seek the privacy of my own room, where I hid in the en-suite, and because the deadly sound of the silence imposed upon me, by other people's half-truths, deceptions, and misrepresentations had not only robbed me of the opportunity to trust my Godfather--for her part--Lorna had been robbed of the chance to pursue a life of her own choosing and yet, by far the biggest loser was my son, because while he has been growing up, he has been robbed of the chance to spend more time with his birth mother, and satisfied that nobody could see or hear me, I allowed my tears to flow without fear of either censure or restraint.*

*"Oh, what a tangled web we weave, when at first we practice to deceive."* How beautifully Sir Walter Scott's words describe deceit, and back in the present tense, our arbitrator offers me their agreement. "In your case, it's a perfect quotation, especially when your life had begun to fall apart after your discharge. Indeed, it now seems ironic that as a result of an accidental overdose of the legitimate drugs, which you were being prescribed, you ended up in the Psychiatric Wing of the Mayfield Clinic. However, after Professor

Morgan took over your case as I recall, since what had happened at the Research Facility was addressed Charlie, what I don't understand is why the issue of culpability never arose?"

In all fairness, I can appreciate Bill's dilemma. "Although I can't remember every last detail of the recovery programme Professor Morgan devised for me, when he was satisfied that I had made sufficient progress, he was going to convince anyone who needed convincing that I could be trusted, and because I was being discharged to the Forsyth house, there would have been nothing to be gained, and perhaps everything to lose, if I had discovered at that particular time that instead of the Commander, the Major had been responsible. Besides, like you, I doubt the Professor's client/doctor confidentiality would have granted him access to what meagre information was contained, within the file…"

After Bill nods his appreciation, John chooses to enhance the limitations of my initial defence. "And presumably, until the 27th of June. your belief that your own Godfather had been responsible must have been the actual reason, why you couldn't approach Commander Maddox, and if you couldn't seek the right kind of protection, then you were left with no choice, except to find an alternative way to ensure not only your freedom, but also Lorna and Bobby safety, which is why you created your fictitious piece of literature?"

"That's correct," I agree, but then referring to our recent en-suite scenario, I add. "But then I'm sure that both of you must have suspected that there had to be an underlying reason behind the hostility, I felt towards my Godfather…"

"And in my capacity as arbitrator, during the years we've been partners, I've never been present at an Interview, or an Interrogation, where John has had to work quite so hard to penetrate, what seemed to be the impenetrable. So, for the benefit of the Official Record, its commendable how Charlie withstood the repeated recriminations for as long as she did, and when I referred to her as a mouthy little upstart who has demonstrated that she has more balls, than many of her male counterparts who have found themselves in similar positions, my description was a gross understatement, because when it comes to offences, in pursuance of the Official Secrets Act--instead of condemnation--the highest possible Authority should be proud of Charlie Anne Daltry, nee Forsyth because unlike her treasonous husband and her son's father, she has proved herself to be an exceptional credit to her country…"

Hearing Bill repeat his description merited another spontaneous laugh, and although this mouthy little upstart is flattered, as I glance over my shoulder, our arbitrator announces his intention to move time on. "Setting aside what happened at the Research Facility is there anything else, you would like to comment upon, which is not necessarily in connection with what we have discussed during this evening?"

"Oh please Bill," this leading lady groans. "Surely, there cannot be a single thing, I haven't mentioned, discussed, explained, or elaborated upon. But it's been a long evening, and because my weariness is threatening to consume, every aspect of my physical being, including my ability to rationalize my thoughts--even if I can't sleep--I would like to attempt to achieve some meaningful rest …"

In response, Bill throws me one of his reassuring and yet, at the same time I suspect it to be a misleading smile. "We're almost finished…"

If we have almost finished, then it's time for this leading lady to deliver, her most revealing dialogue lines and as Bill rises to his feet, I look back at John as I state the obvious in a hushed voice. "Oh I see, and I suppose you want me to disclose the identity of Bobby's father, and the location of the flash drive?"

Having reached the desk, Bill places his old-fashioned notepad and pen, a short distance from my right hand. "It's our experience that if a piece or indeed pieces of information have been locked away for any length of time, then as we did with Lorna's whereabouts--it's often easier to write the details down--instead of voicing them …"

As Bill pauses, he waits until I look up at him, before running his finger across his throat, indicating that after turning them into co-conspirators, he wants me to use my mind to pause the recording equipment, so that there will be no discernible time lapse, and as soon as I oblige him, and the gentle purring ceases to disturb the silence he heads back to the table, and reseats himself, before clarifying the reason behind his silent request.

"On my behalf Charlie, I wanted you to pause the surveillance equipment, so that I could reiterate that this has been a successful Interview, and you might do yourself a grave injustice, if you were to create the wrong impression..."

"But I've never said..."

As it has done on previous occasions, Bill's raised right hand brings my intended interruption to an abrupt end. "And while we are well aware that you have never refused to disclose, either of those two details, when the issue of Bobby's paternity first arose, and you were reluctant to reveal his identity, on the grounds that when it came to your life story, we still had a long way to go, I agreed that we would leave his name until later, because you might not feel quite so protective towards him by the time we reached the end..."

"Which I don't think I do ..."

"Possibly not, but after safeguarding Bobby's anonymity for the last seven years, it would be quite understandable that you might have doubts about acknowledging the connection, between this man and your son, and if you didn't harbour at least some reservations, then you would have moved the notepad and pen closer to you..."

Damn their psychological profiling and yet, finding myself outmanoeuvred, I am left with no alternative, except to explore my initial reservation. "Hypothetically, I suppose that for as long as we remain in this room, what has passed between us has stayed between the three of us. But once I confirm his identity, then by tomorrow lunchtime my own name will be infamous in the upper corridors of power, and because I know that such damning notoriety will result in numerous, nervous bureaucrats running around like headless chickens--with each one of them--demanding their particular piece of this young woman's body, preferably served up to them on spectacular solid silver platters..."

"But why should your name be infamous?" Bill asks, before he answers his own question. "If it were any other agency Charlie, then that might be the case. However, because our objective is to clean up the mess left in Special Operation's back yard by your husband, this situation will be handled with the utmost discretion..."

For my part, I remain sceptical, and because I cannot share Bill's confidence, I'm shaking my head. "But I'm not sure how that circumvents the issue of my name..."

"It's easily done Charlie, and on the grounds that some incapacitating health issue is going to make it impossible for him to continue, in his prestigious position with deep regret, the highest possible Authority will accept his resignation and then, in exchange for his written admission that he has committed offences, which have contravened the Official Secrets Act, along with his willingness to afford Special Operations, his fullest cooperation as to the disclosure of those contraventions--both past and present--his immediate family will be spared the ignominy of discovering that this husband and father chose to betray not only them, but also his country. In addition, during his lengthy absence, the Commander will ensure that his wife and children do not suffer any undue financial hardships..."

In my naivety, I had not considered the enormity of the repercussions. "If that's the case, then you're asking me to destroy a man's entire life..."

Ready to re-join the proceedings, opposite me John stirs and as one might expect, my principal male remains unsympathetic. "He destroyed himself..."

Then, when I glance at him, he explains, "Like you Charlie, he did have a choice, but then unlike you--he was in the fortuitous position, where he could have chosen not to allow himself to be compromised by Mark Daltry..."

"The last time I checked John, two wrongs never made anything right…"

"Oh I wholeheartedly agree," John fires back at me. "But his motivation was self-preservation, and because he wanted to avoid a scandal, apart from withdrawing his financial assistance, he never gave you or Bobby a second thought. So right now, you cannot afford to consider anyone, except yourself and your son, plus anyone else who has found the courage to stand by you, throughout the last seven years. Trustworthy people, like Lorna Clunnell and her brother Colin McCardle…"

Of course John's right, and perhaps for no other reason than I know there is no alternative, subconsciously my hand is moving to the right, until it comes to rests on top of the notepad and pen. "All right, I accept that if things are handled in the way you have described, then in the upper corridors of power my name will not be infamous, but what about M I 5 and M I 6? As I recall earlier in the Interview Bill stated that sooner or later they would have to be informed…"

"That's also correct," Bill agrees, without the least hesitation. "Eventually, Commander Maddox will advise the Heads of both M I 5 and M I 6 that perpetrated by Mark Daltry, Special Operations has experienced a breach in its own security…"

"But surely as his wife they will want to Interview me?"

"Probably, in fact because of the steps we have taken, I think John would agree that we would be a little disappointed, if they didn't want to conduct an Interview…"

"Now you're not making any sense at all Bill…"

"Once again Charlie, it's easily explained. Are the following statements correct? Firstly, you came into this room of your own volition, and once you were inside, after being granted unlimited time and space, and complete freedom of speech, is it not the case that you have told us in your own words, the story of the significant events, which have constituted the last seven years of your life?"

"Yes…"

"And secondly, is it also not the case that each and every one of those words has been the truth, the whole truth, and nothing but the truth and for the benefit of any persons who need to know, at the request of our Commanding Officer have we not recorded, the whole truth, so that all of the grey areas have been coloured by your testimony?"

"Of course Bill--but…"

"What you fail to realize Charlie--is that there aren't any buts," Bill perseveres, "Because if we have fulfilled the terms of one half of our assignment and the evidence has been recorded, then why would any other agency need to conduct another Interview?"

"You make it sound so easy. Perhaps even too easy, because knowing how things work in the upper corridors of power, I don't believe that you have the power to stop them…"

Opposite me, John attracts my attention. "And what makes you think that we don't possess the power needed to stop another agency?"

Pausing, my principal male waits, until he can achieve eye contact. "Recently, Bill had cause to confirm that our being reassigned by Commander Maddox--who also happens to be your Godfather--wasn't a coincidence and then, after we advised him that we needed to acquire a Protective Custody Order, when he prepared the application to the High Court, instead of the order being assigned to Special Operations--in an unprecedented move--and at our personal request, he specified that it was to be assigned to Special Operatives John Bland and Robert William Powell…"

"Yes as I recall, although it might have seemed incredulous, you explained that until the Protective Custody Order was rescinded by a High Court Judge even if the highest possible Authority were to come through that door carrying a gun, you would seek to neutralize the threat--but surely neither M I 5 nor M I 6 will be posing a threat to my continued existence?"

"You're missing the point Charlie. The terms of the Protective Custody Order state that we will protect you from anything or anyone who might, in our professional opinion, seek to cause you physical, emotional or mental harm, and if necessary that includes protecting you from yourself…"

"Like at the Mayfield Clinic, when I wouldn't sign the consent for the termination?"

"Yes but our principal objective was to ensure that without our specific consent, nobody else had the right to gain access to you…"

As John pauses, it's as if he's affording me time to absorb the full impact, before he explains, "So irrespective of whether a request were to come from M I 5, M I 6 or even Special Branch, when it's declined on our joint behalf by Commander Maddox, an appeal would then have to be lodged in the High Court. But they would be required to prove, beyond all shadow of doubt that Bill and I have been negligent, and because we have taken extreme care to dot all the 'i's and cross the 't's, we're confident that our legal team would be able keep any appellant wrapped up in red tape--long enough--for things to be resolved…"

Tilting my head, a little to one side, this leading lady has an admission to make. "Okay, I have to admit that in theory, it sounds impressive, but…"

"Of course," Bill interrupts me. "The sudden resignation is bound to create some initial speculation. However, as well as being named on the Protective Custody Order for almost eight days, we've been classified as being--*unavailable for the foreseeable future.* In addition, we've taken extreme precautions, so that nobody can link you with Lorna Clunnell, and we've also ensured that there is no record of the time you spent at H.Q., and that includes any audio or visual surveillance footage, we're also confident that the last place anyone would expect to find either us or you--is hiding in plain sight--at Manor Park…"

Having absorbed each persuasive word, I'm forced to accept that the way in which the cavalry have orchestrated this entire affair is not only clever, it is also a brilliant demonstration in the art of forward planning, and because Bill's somewhat old fashioned, note-pad is still beneath my right hand, I slide it across the desk, until it is resting in front of me, but as my fingers touch the pen, this mother has another reservation.

"As Bill stated because seven years is a long time, I wouldn't want Bobby to discover the identity of the absentee father who turned out to be such a disgraceful role model…"

"Unless either you or Lorna should choose to tell him," Bill reassures me immediately. "I'm confident that the Commander will be willing to confirm that you have our word that there's no reason why Bobby should ever find out…"

Finally, I do the grown-up thing and yet as I pick up the pen, knowing that there is no other way fills me with an inexplicable, but no less profound sadness for his family. "When I first met him, he was a lowly Private Secretary. Now as far as I'm aware, he's a Principal Private Under-secretary, with a wife who probably worships the ground he walks upon, and three sons of his own who must look up to him…"

Unimpressed by my display of sentimentality, John's statement suggests that he has misunderstood my motivation. "If that was meant to be the beginning of some kind of defence Charlie, then it's not quite correct…"

Then, after a dramatic pause, he declares, "He has four sons, and it's about time that he was forced to acknowledge the existence of the remarkable young man who is asleep upstairs--no doubt dreaming about playing football tomorrow with the three of us…"

Like so many previous occasions, this leading lady's surrender has not been won without a struggle, and while I am searching for any more reservations, the silence is allowed to remain undisturbed and yet, like my valiant protectors, I know that this mother has exhausted all of her excuses, and because I cannot any longer avoid the inevitable, I write the name on the notepad. Then, after nudging it across the desk towards my principal male, John picks it up, and because I have not been asked to restart the surveillance equipment for the benefit of his partner, John states the name of Bobby's father.

"Robert Lloyd Reece-Milliner, I suppose the double barrelled surname adds a certain *old school tie* kind of above reproach trustworthiness and loyalty…"

Glancing over my shoulder, Bill seems to be checking what I suspect is a schedule of names. "According to the list, Reece-Milliner is assigned to the Foreign Office, and since he has direct access to the Minister, he must have been in an ideal position to gain prior knowledge of anything Daltry might have found useful to help fund his private pension…"

After listening to the exchange, I feel doubly guilty when Bill fixes his gaze upon me. "And what about the flash drive, I cannot risk asking you to restart the recording, so that we can conclude the Interview, until you divulge its whereabouts, plus any duplicates along with the details of the bank--if indeed, there ever was a bank with a safety deposit box?"

At the prospect of losing her insurance policy, my vulnerable child prompts her mother to pose a question. "My God, I hope you both know what you're doing?"

Then, when neither of them answers, I confess. "I didn't do anything exciting with the flash drive, and because there is a safety deposit box, containing a fake flash drive, and the details inside the envelope, I surrendered to Shaw would have led him to the bank…"

Opposite me, John has started shaking his head. "And if they had managed to get you out of the house and then, taken you to the bank what the hell would you have done?"

"Considering that on June 22, I engineered the situation, so that they couldn't take me with them, then what might have happened next is nothing, except conjecture. But hypothetically, Special Operations would have been searching for me, and for my part, I would have assumed that I had nothing left to lose, and because the alarm needed to be raised, if we had reached the bank, then once we were inside the vault, I would have been able to use my unique abilities, and while the three of them were bewildered as to how several boxes close to mine were opening, and spilling their contents onto the floor, amid the confusion, I would have used the intercom to alert the security staff that I was being held hostage, by the three men with whom I had arrived, and by the time the vault was reopened, using the gun Shaw would have taken with him, all three of them would have been dead…"

"Congratulations," John states, but since I suspect that it's a backhanded compliment, I wait for him to add. "You bring a whole new meaning to the definition of reckless endangerment Charlie, but it's comforting to know that in a hypothetical sense, if you'd reached the bank, you would have executed the kind of back-up plan, which took into account that there would be no security cameras inside the safety deposit vault…"

"All right," Bill declares, with an increased determination. "If you didn't put the actual flash drive in a safety deposit box Charlie, then what the hell did you do with it?"

"After writing down my precise instructions along with the flash drive, I placed them inside an envelope, which I put into a lockable briefcase. Then, after giving the briefcase to the one person I have been able to trust implicitly, in the event that something happened to me--either my sudden disappearance or rumours about my demise--I told him that he should open the briefcase and follow the instructions inside the envelope…"

Opposite me, like his partner, John has reached a conclusion, and as he casts a glance at Bill, they make a simultaneous announcement.

"Colin McCardle…"

"Since Colin has handled all of Bobby's financial affairs, he was the obvious choice, and although it might not seem like a secure place, although Mark knew about Lorna, he never considered that there would be someone like Colin and as far as Lorna was concerned, she knows nothing about either the flash drive or the briefcase…"

As I have been delivering my confirmation, Bill has been rummaging in one of the pockets of his jacket, and having retrieved his Radio Transmitter, he directs his next suggestion at his partner. "Because Lorna agreed that she would stay awake, in case we needed her, I think it's time we asked her, if she wouldn't mind joining us…"

Initially I'm confused, prompting me to ask, "I don't understand, when did Lorna agree to stay awake in case you needed her, and why do you want her to join us, as I've explained apart from being Bobby's surrogate mother, I've protected her, by ensuring that she knows nothing about the last seven years of my life. You also gave me your word…"

0Having disregarded my protest, John has disappeared, leaving Bill to placate me. "Relax, we have no intention of cross examining her Charlie, and the reason she agreed …"

Then, before Bill can finish his explanation, someone who must have been on the receiving end of the Radio Transmitter demands his immediate attention

*"Did you want something in particular Powell, or was your summons in case I'd become so bored I'd fallen asleep?"*

"Well, it doesn't do any harm to make sure you're conscious O'Keefe, and if it's safe to assume that you found the right location, can you update me on the present position?"

*"After Mr McCardle returned home without incident at 18:32, there was a delivery of Chinese food, at 19:41 which was followed at 19:45, by the arrival of an attractive young woman, and I'm sending you an image to yer phone, so that someone, somewhere can do a facial recognition to confirm her identity…"*

"I'm impressed by your diligence O'Keefe, but since we're talking about two occupants--instead of one--is there anyone who could come and join you?"

*"Well Morton does owe me a favour and I dare say he can be here in ten or maybe fifteen minutes at the most. Sounds as if this surveillance is important Powell, does it have something to do with why you've both been classified as being unavailable?"*

"You're fishing O'Keefe, and if I answered that question, I'd probably have to shoot you myself, but it's important enough for one of us to visit Colin McCardle tonight…"

While Bill has been engaged in his dialogue with a man with a smooth Irish accent, I have been thinking that if I ever felt in control of my own destiny, then through the surrender of those two pieces of information, it is ironic that my fate now rests in other people's hands.

Then, as Bill shuts down the Radio Transmitter--albeit on a temporary basis--John returns accompanied by Lorna, and she appears to be relaxed and quite comfortable with the surroundings, and despite acknowledging Bill's polite nod, which is accompanied by a warm smile, she seems to be more concerned with my shattered appearance than the papers littering the floor, or the gaps on the book shelves, and when John gestures in the direction of his former chair Lorna sits down, before voicing her initial observation.

"You look even more dreadful Charlie than you did the last time we came face to face upstairs in your bedroom…"

"Thanks," I mutter under my breath, but when Lorna continues to stare at me, this alleged grown-up feels obliged to offer her a reason. "As I explained at the time, I had to come back down to the study to finish what someone else started a long time ago…"

Discounting my excuse, Lorna's angry glare drifts from John, who is leaning against the cabinet, towards Bill who remains sitting beside the table.

"Gentlemen, while I don't doubt the importance of whatever you have been doing," She states, with a misleading calmness. "What I cannot understand is why some of the work you have been doing couldn't have waited until tomorrow?"

Neither of my protectors has any defence to offer. There are only mitigating circumstances and in his capacity as arbitrator, Bill makes it clear that he does not intend to justify those circumstances. "Unfortunately, after being offered the opportunity to leave the remainder of our work until tomorrow Charlie decided that even if it meant continuing into the early hours of the morning, she wanted to conclude her previously undisclosed life story in one session…"

Once again, Lorna's gaze falls upon me, and as if she does not want to believe that the image opposite her belongs to her strong, capable best friend, she begins to shake her head and yet, because it's beginning to feel as if I have lived and died, in order to be reborn in my Godfather's study--in desperation--I make a direct appeal. "Please Lorna, I'm all right…"

Whoosh, it proves to be another one of those moments, when I should have stepped back, before lighting the touch paper, because now Lorna has grounds to challenge me.

"During that first break Charlie, you also claimed that the restrictions placed upon you by other people, led to complications, during the last seven years, but now from what I can determine, there is sufficient cause for me to doubt that for some inexplicable reason, you've never been treated like a flesh and blood kind of human being in your entire life…"

Oh, how accurate and this is the reason why Lorna has made an excellent second mother to my son, and because I suspect that she has not finished expressing her displeasure, when she pauses, I choose to remain silent, which prompts her next challenge.

"Do you have any idea what you look like?" She demands, before allowing her angry glare to drift between my inquisitors. "And if Philip Maddox assigned both of you to protect Charlie, then who the fuck is supposed to be protecting her from you?"

"Please Lorna," I hear this woman beseeching her. "You don't understand…"

Responding to the increased desperation in my voice, Lorna raises her hands in the air, before she apologises. "I'm sorry Charlie, but I couldn't believe that Philip Maddox, your own Godfather would have allowed them to do this to you…"

Then, after Lorna shifts her gaze until she can focus on Bill, she announces, "According to John, there was a specific reason why you wanted to see me?"

Leaving his position at the cabinet, I watch as John moves to the table, so that he can retrieve the mobile phone from his partner's hand, before he brings it to the desk.

"As a precautionary measure," Bill explains. "We've had someone shadowing your brother ever since he left his office. Although he is at home, he has a female visitor, and from the image sent a few minutes ago, can you identify her for us?"

After glancing at the image on the mobile in John's hand, knowing that Lorna hates this kind of voyeurism almost as much--if not more than me, and because she will regard this as an unjustified intrusion into her brother's private life, her response is predictable.

"Why don't you ask Colin?"

Placing my elbows on the desk, this exhausted leading lady rests her head against my cupped hands, and before either of my protectors can issue Lorna, with any kind of a warning—much less an outright threat, although it's beyond logical reason, I find myself making an appeal on their behalf. "If you know Lorna, then for God's sake tell them, or we'll still be here at breakfast time…"

Conceding defeat, while she is studying the image on Bill's mobile, Lorna takes her time, before she confirms the young woman's identity. "That's Christine McPherson. She works in a rival firm of accountants and they've known each other for years…"

"Thank you Lorna. Your cooperation is much appreciated…"

Still with my head resting in my cupped hands, once Bill expresses his gratitude I hear him clicking open his Radio Transmitter.

"O'Keefe…"

*"Yes Powell…"*

"What's the status regarding Morton's assistance?"

*"His E T A. is within the next five minutes…"*

"Good--the young woman is Christine McPherson, and after what has been brought to our attention, instead of observing from across the street, Bland and I would prefer you to be inside the house…"

After Bill pauses, this woman lowers her hands when I hear him add, "Oh and all the usual restrictions apply--no landline or mobile phone calls or any text messages. Plus--no visitors, and under no circumstances are either of them to leave the house, until I arrive and my own E T A. should be between the next forty or maybe even forty-five minutes…"

*"No problem Powell, we'll look forward to your arrival…"*

As soon as Bill shuts down the Radio Transmitter, this leading lady turns her head so that I can see him, and when I achieve eye contact I reiterate Colin's innocence.

"Apart from keeping the briefcase safe, Colin's done nothing wrong. So why are you treating him, as if he is some kind of criminal?"

Instead of our arbitrator, John chooses to try and placate his leading lady. "The restrictions are standard practice Charlie, and they are intended to ensure that Colin's rights are observed, because I'm sure that nobody would want him to do anything rash, like opening the briefcase, which would create untold additional complications…"

"At least let me talk to him…"

Having moved back to the desk, John is shaking his head. "It's important for us to demonstrate that everything is done in accordance with official procedure…"

Across the desk, Lorna appears to be assessing the situation, but her continued silence seems to suggests that she is beginning to grasp the seriousness, as my protective parent turns her attention to Bill. "If I can't talk to him, then at least let me come with you, because if you go charging in there demanding that he hand over the briefcase, Colin's unlikely to surrender it without some kind of struggle. But if you take me with you, then I can explain…"

"No…"

"Please Bill, he deserves some kind of an explanation…"

Of course in my heart, I doubt our arbitrator will change his mind. "I'm not sure what part of NO you don't understand Charlie, but you are not coming with me…"

"Why?"

Crouching down by the side of the desk, John attempts to rescue his partner. "Setting aside that we have gone to elaborate lengths to make sure that O'Keefe cannot make any connection with either you and Lorna and Bobby, or you and Colin McCardle you are exhausted, and despite your stubbornness, the remarks Lorna made about your appearance are not only astute, they are also accurate…"

"I'm fine…"

Naturally, John's laugh bears a certain degree of incredulity. "Charlie you can't expect us to believe that you're fine, especially when you consider that despite your regular attendances at the communal meals, your ability to manoeuvre food around a plate, without it ever reaching your mouth should be classified as an art form in its own right, and instead of doing the sensible thing and opting to take advantage of the sleeping tablets Doctor Wilson prescribed, since our arrival at Manor Park, the amount of sleep you must have managed to achieve every day cannot be more than two--or maybe three hours--at the most…"

Embarrassed by this leading lady's conspicuousness and my principal male's accuracy, I sever eye contact as he continues to list my shortcomings. "In fact, unless you start eating and sleeping on a regular basis, Bill and I are concerned that you won't make it through the next few days, without needing to be readmitted to the Mayfield Clinic, and since we're sure that's the last thing you would want--for once in your life--you're going to start listening to the people who care about what's happening to you, and whether you like it or not, you are going to start doing, whatever you're damn well told to do…"

Pausing, John waits until I look at him, before he asks an unavoidable direct question. "So Charlie, have you grasped the precariousness of your present situation?"

"Yes and I'm sorry--I never meant to be difficult--and since it would separate me from Lorna and Bobby, the last thing I would want is to be readmitted to the Clinic…"

As far as Lorna's concerned, she has finished assessing the seriousness of our situation, and because the level of care shown by my protectors towards me, means that she might have misjudged them, she chooses to endorse what John has been telling me.

"Charlie I have to agree with John. In all the years we've known each other, I've never seen you so downhearted and setting to one side that since our arrival, you haven't been allowed to venture outside the Manor, I don't think you could go anywhere, until you get some sleep. Now I don't have any idea what's going on, but if it will afford you some reassurance and it proves to be an acceptable compromise, then I don't mind accompanying Bill. However, I wouldn't expect that my presence would be in any capacity other than as someone whose presence might help to placate my headstrong brother…"

Without waiting for Bill's response to Lorna's generous offer, I cast a weak smile across the desk. But I cannot expect her to do any more than she has done up until tonight. "Lorna, this is far more serious than Special Operations discovering the identity of Bobby's actual father, and even if it's possible, then it would be unreasonable of me to expect you to become any more involved than you already are…"

Tossing her head back Lorna laughs. "After posing as your son's mother for the last seven years Charlie, how much less involved would you like me to be?"

This time, I manage a more convincing smile, prompting Lorna to congratulate me. "That's better, your exhaustion seems to be clouding your judgement, because if you take away their weaponry, then like the rest of us, these two are nothing more than the flesh and blood type of reprobate, and provided it's what you want, I will accompany Bill and then tomorrow morning, I will be able to confirm that when we left Colin and Christine, everything in the McCardle house was fine…"

"Yes I'd like that very much," I hear this other mother reply, before offering her an explanation. "After I realized that I needed to put my affairs in order along with instructions about what he should do if I went missing, I gave Colin a locked briefcase…"

Of course, neither of us has stopped to consider my protector's position, until Bill's voice silences us both. "Excuse me ladies, but your plans haven't taken into account that it would be most irregular for either of us to allow any third party to compromise their own safety at least not without gaining the Commander's approval…"

Yet again, John disappears and knowing that he has gone in search of my Godfather I proceed with due caution. "Provided that the Commander approves, on my behalf, would you explain to Colin that he has to allow Bill to take possession of that briefcase, but the three of us are all safe, and being afforded protection by Special Operations, and would you also tell him that knowing how much he safeguards his privacy, I'm so sorry that he didn't have any prior warning that this was going to happen..."

"Of course I will Charlie. But I'm sure Colin will understand that there must be a valid reason why this visit couldn't have waited until tomorrow morning…"

With the same impeccable timing, I have come to expect from my principal male, John returns and without saying a word, he moves to the table, so that he can give Bill a piece of paper and then, for a few tense moments the silence continues, until Bill releases a deep sigh, "Okay, since it's up to us to decide, I don't see why you can't accompany me Lorna…"

"In that case Bill, do you want to leave immediately?"

"No we can't leave, until we've dealt with an outstanding formality…"

Curious to know more about this--*formality*--I glance over my shoulder, in time to watch Bill pulling an A4 manila envelope from amongst the remaining files on the corner of the table. Then, he waits until his partner takes it from his hand, and as John moves back to the desk Lorna remarks. "That sounds a little ominous Bill…"

Despite Lorna's misgivings, John has removed the contents from the envelope and together with the pen, which is still resting beside the notepad he places the sheets of paper in front of her, before he adds his own instructions. "For legal reasons, we are obliged to inform you that it's in your own best interests to read the content thoroughly, and once you're satisfied, you need to sign and date it and then, since the main document specifies our full names, we will need to countersign it..."

Of course by now, I suspect that the document must be a Protective Custody Order and without touching the pieces of paper, Lorna is skimming through the written text, and when she lifts her head, so that she can look at John, she confirms my presumption.

"From its content, it would seem to be the case that if I sign this document, then Bobby and I will be in Protective Custody, which has been granted to Special Operations by a High Court Judge, but then assigned to both of you..."

"That's correct," John agrees. "Obviously, Clunnell is the surname on Bobby's birth certificate, and because he's a child, he isn't legally permitted to sign a separate Court Order, so we had to request one on behalf of you both..."

"But I don't understand. Surely that was the point of us being brought here?"

"Ever since you arrived at Manor Park," Bill explains. "There has been an indirect need for you both to require protection. However, as a precautionary measure Commander Maddox requested the High Court Order, and after what Charlie has revealed about her life, it's time we turned our inferred requirement into something more official..."

"Surely, there has to be some kind of catch?"

Between you and me, provided you have been paying attention, we know that there is a catch, and before either of my inquisitors can make light of the full implications, this Interviewee summons her best friend's attention.

"Of course there is Lorna, but isn't there always some kind of catch?" I announce before I enlighten her. "And despite the masses of red tape, if you agree to sign, then neither you nor Bobby will be able to leave whenever you choose to do so, and if you refuse to sign, then these two reprobates as you so aptly described them, will afford you your fifteen minutes of fame during a hearing in a court of law..."

"Charlie," Bill interrupts me. "Since the three of us know that's a gross exaggeration of what happened, please try to be reasonable..."

Thoroughly enjoying myself at their expense, I have no intention of being reasonable. "Surely, you're not trying to suggest that when I wanted to know what would happen if I refused to sign was an exaggeration? How you'd threatened to haul me in front of a different High Court Judge, and after you provided the Court with all the evidence to support, why I was being unreasonable--presumably, you also didn't warn me that the Right Honourable, him or her would offer me one last chance, and if I still refused to sign the Protective Custody Order, then I would find myself being sectioned for my own safety which..."

"That's enough Charlie," Bill attempts to silence me. "You've had your fun, and there are far more serious matters, requiring Lorna's attention--namely her brother..."

From Lorna's expression, there can be no doubt that it came as a relief to discover that the real Charlie Daltry has only been beaten into submission by exhaustion, and keeping up the momentum, she tilts her head to one side, before she asks, "Since you've known them longer than me Charlie, can I trust them?"

"In their defence," I admit using a more serious tone of voice. "I can confirm that despite the inevitable skirmishes we have encountered throughout this evening, as we neared the end of the untold story of my life, I came to appreciate that at all times, John and Bill have been acting in my best interests, so that irrespective of whichever agency, Special Branch, M I 5 or even M I 6 should make..."

"Oh my God," Lorna interrupts me. "Although I had my doubts about your marriage to Mark Daltry, whatever you've done Charlie, it must be very serious if it has been brought to the attention of Special Branch, M I 5 and M I 6..."

"That's why earlier this evening, I did warn you that regardless of how disturbing it might be, because there were some things connected to Bobby we needed to discuss, it was time you knew the truth, the whole truth and nothing but the truth. But right now, I need you to remain focused upon my explanation, regarding the Protection Custody Order you are being asked to sign in respect of our son…"

Pausing, I wait until Lorna nods her head, before proceeding. "In the event of any other agency making an application to Interview me, or they attempt to remove me from their protection, although I doubted their motivation, John and Bill have not only conducted this Interview, so that nobody can prove that they have been negligent in their duty of care, it also means that I will get a fair hearing from those who would seek to judge me. In addition, prior to my coming upstairs for the first intermission, when I expressed my concern over Bobby's future, Commander Maddox had authorized John and Bill to confirm that after his approach to the highest possible Authority, the safety and anonymity of my son, which will include you, has been granted the Royal Seal of approval…"

Despite Lorna's stunned expression, she picks up the pen so that she can sign and date the Protective Custody Order. Then, after John countersigns, he takes it to the table, but as soon as Bill adds his own signature, he is forced to respond to a summons from his R.T.

*"Powell are you able to confirm what time you will be arriving?"*

"If you're having to ask O'Keefe, then there must be some kind of difficulty, which despite your extensive and very expensive training you and Morgan cannot overcome…"

*"Do you want the good or the bad news first?"*

"O'Keefe it's been as long day and I'm too tired to indulge in childish games. So whatever it is, would you please put John and I out of our misery?"

*"Okay, but don't shoot the messenger. The good news is that we are inside the house, and neither of the two occupants has attempted to leave the property…"*

Then, when there is a deliberate delay, Bill snaps "And the bad news…"

*"Both occupants know a great deal about their human rights, and although we have taken possession of their mobile phones, unless Mr McCardle receives some kind of explanation, he's demanding that he be allowed to contact his solicitor. Is there anything you can give us that might calm him down, because if you can't, we'll be forced to cuff him?"*

"Tell him that we have received intelligence data, suggesting that he's in possession of material, which falls within the provisions of the Official Secrets Act…"

Hesitating, Bill casts a smile in Lorna's direction. "And you can also advise him that his sister Lorna Clunnell will be accompanying me. Since it's imperative that neither of them involve any third party, if that doesn't calm him down, then split them up, and if it should prove necessary, you have our permission to physically restrain, not only Colin McCardle, but also his partner Christine McPherson…"

*"Will do Powell and I do hope that the very attractive Lorna Clunnell is listening, because she was such a good sport when she waived the rules so that yer wee man Bobby could be driven up to Manor Park in one of his favourite classic cars, while sitting on a bolster cushion in the passenger seat. I'm so glad our paths are destined to cross again…"*

Instead of that smooth Irish blarney O'Keefe, perhaps you should concentrate on this assignment, because if there's any unnecessary complications , then I doubt the Commander will be taking any prisoners. It's 23:22 and because we'll be leaving in the next ten minutes I reckon we should reach you by 00:14

*"Since none of us would want to be on the receiving end of the Commander's sharper words, I suppose we should concentrate on containing the situation until you arrive…"*

"I'll fetch my jacket," Lorna declares, as Bill shuts the Radio Transmitter down, but when she nears the door, she looks back at me. "Although I know the reason why you despise any kind of drugs on this occasion, in what seems to be extenuating circumstances, I think you should seriously think about taking one of the sleeping pills John mentioned…"

"I know you mean well Lorna, but earlier I did explain that it would be such a relief to finish this Interview, I thought that I might be able to get some proper rest…"

For a lingering moment, Lorna remains in the doorway, but aware of the pressing need for an immediate departure, she resists the urge to challenge me further. Then, as soon as she disappears, John reseats himself in the chair on the other side of the desk, and although I attempt to rise to my feet, Bill chooses to delay my own departure.

"Before you leave, there are a couple of technicalities which need to be resolved…"

As I reseat myself, John turns the Protective Custody Order around, before nudging it in my direction. "In order to cater for all eventualities as Bobby's actual birth mother, we would like you to countersign…"

Too exhausted to raise any objections as requested I countersign, not only in the name, Charlie Anne Daltry, but also my maiden name, and as soon as I nudge the Protective Custody Order back across the desk, Bill presents me with the second technicality.

"As you might recall at my request, you suspen0ded the recording. Would you please reverse the process, so that John and I can conclude the proceedings?"

Having forgotten about the surveillance equipment, this leading lady does as she has been asked, and when the gentle purring once again fills the study, opposite me those deep, brown eyes never leave my face, and for my part I do not sever eye contact, while John is delivering his declaration.

"Thank you Charlie for affording us, your full cooperation. When it comes to parting with sensitive information it's never easy, especially when personal details might have far reaching consequences, such as your son's continued anonymity. However, having overcome your reticence, we're grateful that you have written down, not only the identity of Bobby's father, but also the details regarding the location of the bank…"

Then, when John pauses, it is our arbitrator's cue to deliver his scripted lines on behalf of this dynamic duo. "And after Commander Maddox has listened to the recording, and we recover the flash drive, I'm confident that he will be able to seek an agreement, which will produce an outcome in everyone's best interests. So unless there's anything you would like to add or amend, I would like to formally terminate this Interview…"

As the relief flows through me, its intensity is so unexpected, it causes me to hesitate, before I reply, "Thank you Mr Powell, but there's nothing I want to add or amend..."

"For the last time, it is still the 29th of June. Present are Special Operatives John Bland and myself Robert William Powell. Also present is Charlie Anne Daltry, nee Forsyth and with no other audio or visual surveillance equipment having been used throughout this entire evening, this Interview is terminated at 23:12…"

Despite my exhaustion, I have to confess that my protectors devised a smooth exit strategy, especially when the reference to the bank details will avoid Colin coming under close scrutiny for anything, except his handling of the Clunnell finances.

In addition, for the benefit of the recording, Bill has made a subtle adjustment to the timing in order to build in a degree of leeway, so that any discrepancies throughout this evening cannot be detected, unless someone uses not only a stopwatch, but also extensive time and motion techniques while they are rerunning the entire Interview.

On reflection, my protectors have worked hard to cater for any--or indeed all eventualities--but the relief when Bill had made his statement about wanting to terminate our Interview is now forcing me to acknowledge that my exhaustion is manifesting itself as physical pain, which runs throughout my body, and without waiting to be dismissed I rise to my feet, but as I move towards the door, yet again John's concern is genuine.

"What about Lorna's suggestion Charlie? There are extenuating circumstances and it's our experience that whenever we have been working on an assignment for any length of time, which requires us to work what we call, overnight vigils of perhaps two or three hours staying awake and then, grabbing two or three hours sleep, we find ourselves caught up in something our extensive training taught us to acknowledge as sleep deprivation, which in turn makes it even harder to re-establish any kind of normal sleep pattern…"

Pausing, John waits and when I fail to look at him, he adds, "Although we appreciate that you don't have direct access to the sleepers Doctor Wilson prescribed, I can arrange for you to have a sleeping tablet so that you can get some much needed sleep…"

In the hope that my protectors will respect my decision, I glance over my shoulder. "Despite what I told Lorna, it's an even greater relief to have concluded this Interview than I had first imagined, so I would prefer to find out whether I can fall asleep without resorting to any kind of chemical solution…"

Then, without waiting for John to counterchallenge, with what must be the last remaining ounce of dignity, this leading lady exits from the centre of the stage, without taking a bow, and once outside the study, because there is no longer any need to eavesdrop on my protector's hushed exchange of dialogue, this flesh and blood kind of human being, heads for the sweeping staircase and when I reach the upper landing, Lorna is heading towards me in readiness for her imminent departure.

Despite having turned not only her life, but also Colin's life upside down, through making them complicit, as Lorna embraces me, her whispered words are reassuring me that none of this will change the fundamental basis of the relationship we all share.

For my part, as I watch Lorna rushing down the staircase, I am reminded that if it had not been for the love and support of two devoted friends, then I could not have journeyed this far or clung onto my continued existence, even when I have had reason to consider that dead would have been the more preferable option.

## JUNE 30   2:15

As much as I hate to admit it, when I last checked the clock on the bedside cabinet it was two o'clock, and because I suspect that my protectors are right and my exhaustion is preventing me from closing my eyes, so that I can be swept beyond consciousness on the king size bed, I have resorted to sitting in the comfortable armchair beside the window.

Of course, in the early hours of the morning when every second seems like a minute and every interminable minute feels like an hour at first, when I heard someone outside the bedroom door, I succumbed to the temptation to close my eyes, so that I could pretend to be asleep, but I soon realized that while one can fool some of the people some of the time, one should never attempt fooling someone, if that person happens to be a trained Special Operative, who has arrived with the intention of entering my bedroom.

"And you can cut out the closed eyes crap," John announces. "Because I've been checking on you and Bobby every thirty minutes, and it would be a minor miracle, if you had fallen asleep, in the last eighteen minutes and forty-five seconds…"

Opening my eyes, I almost bark my demand at him. "Do you have any idea, how damn annoying it is when someone is right all of the time?"

Daring to ignore me, John moves to the chest of drawers, so that he can place the tray he's carrying on a secure surface, but since I'm eager for an update, while his back remains turned towards me, and in softer tone of voice, I risk posing a less inflammatory question.

"Is there any news about Bill and Lorna? I've been so worried I think it's been…"

With a detectable scepticism, John replies, "Nice try, but we both know that isn't the reason why you can't sleep. But at the McCardle residence everything went according to plan and after Colin handed over the briefcase, as a precautionary measure Bill managed to persuade both of them that it might be judicious, if they moved into a safe house, where we can provide round the clock security until this is over…"

"Although it's starting to feel as if this can never be over that's a huge relief, because as one might expect, Colin is so protective towards the three of us, so I was afraid that he'd end up, having to be restrained, before Lorna and Bill arrived at the house..."

Turning away from the chest of drawers, John crouches down by the armchair. "All this negativity is the result of not sleeping and for our mutual benefit, I've brought one thermal mug containing extra strong black coffee and the other one contains an age old remedy for sleeplessness--hot--well by now, it'll be more like warm milk…"

Glancing at the tray, this woman is curious to learn more about the third item. "And presumably the crystal glass contains some whisky? Is that for your benefit or mine?"

"Yes it does contain some pure malt, which is for your benefit and not mine, but I also rescued your cigarettes and lighter from the study, and despite your determination to quit--on this occasion--while you drink your pure malt, before moving onto the warm milk, I thought that you might like to be thoroughly decadent, and enjoy one last cigarette…"

Tilting my head, a little to one side I am considering that this seems to be too good to be true, prompting me to ask, "Presumably John, there has to be some kind of catch?"

### *JUNE 30    1:59*

*After fast forwarding through the surveillance footage, so that he could highlight the untold secrets of his Goddaughter's life, by the time his personal reflections were disturbed by a gentle tap on the closed study door, having taken his subordinate's advice, Philip Maddox was savouring the remnants of the second pure malt whisky, which like the first he had poured from the bottle, which he had strategically placed close to his right hand.*

*However, when the door opened, instead of longsuffering Margaret, whom he had omitted to inform that since they could manage, without any further assistance, she had his permission to go to bed, Bland appeared carrying a tray, containing what seemed to be an unexpected and yet, most welcome assortment of refreshments.*

*"After completing my routine thirty-minute check on Charlie and Bobby," John began to explain, as he used his foot to nudge the door, until it clicked closed. "When I came back down, I noticed that the study light was still on, and because about an hour ago, I managed to persuade Margaret that if she went to bed to get some sleep, before tomorrow morning we were capable of fending for ourselves, I thought you might appreciate a pot of Earl Grey Tea Sir…"*

*"Thank you John that's most considerate…"*

*So that Philip Maddox could lift the teapot and accompanying bone china cup and saucer onto the desk, John lowered the tray and then he waited until his Commanding Officer finished pouring some tea into the cup, but after he added a dash of milk from the accompanying jug, he ventured to ask a direct question.*

*"Excluding the time spent warming up at the beginning and then, at least forty minutes, spent winding down at the end, because the substance of the Interview must have lasted approximately four hours Commander, surely you can't have listened to everything?"*

*"Good gracious no!  In the interim, I heeded your subtle warning, and after pouring myself an unhealthy measure of pure malt whisky, once I knew how Bobby's anonymity came about, I fast forwarded to the point at which Major Forsyth yet again interfered in his daughter's life, so that  Charlie could marry Mark Daltry, and while I listened to the most significant, but at the same time, the most disturbing highlights of the life, my Goddaughter had to endure, my revulsion at what I was hearing was to some degree anesthetised by a regular sip of pure malt whisky…"*

"I'm sure that I speak for not only me, but also Powell, in confirming that during the intermissions, because some of the testimony is very disturbing, it's hardly surprising that Charlie often had to be coaxed into revealing what she would have preferred to keep hidden. However, when it came to attempting to protect not only herself, but also Lorna and Bobby, despite taking the law into her own hands, if I might be so bold as to voice a personal opinion, then if Charlie were my Goddaughter, her amazing resilience and her unquestionable resourcefulness would have made me immensely proud…"

Tilting his head, a little to one side, a smile began to crinkle the corners of the Commander's mouth. "That's an interesting personal observation and I have to admit that I did feel a sense of pride, especially when this Godfather neared the end of the recording and I poured myself a second pure malt whisky, so that I could toast my Goddaughter because from the documents strewn across my Persian carpet, and the books, which have been selected with obvious care, before being removed from the floor to ceiling book shelves, I realized that although nothing is revealed on the recording, Charlie must have demonstrated at least some of her unique abilities…"

Pausing, the Commander sipped from the bone china cup, before posing an unavoidable direct question. "Is it safe for me to assume that my realization is correct?"

For a lingering moment while he chose his words with care, John remained pensive. "As much as I would like to deflect the question with an evasive reply, not content with demonstrating some of her unique abilities, as far as the Official Secrets Act is concerned in the end, your Goddaughter managed to turn us into co-conspirators. However, earlier when Charlie had told us about her insurance policy, we deemed it important to discover, whether there was at least some kind of defence, and because I had kept pushing her, until she revealed what happened during those sixty minutes on the 22$^{nd}$ of June the damage I had inflicted was enough for Charlie to eventually reveal, the reason why she had harboured so much personal resentment and hostility towards you Commander…"

"Yes," Philip Maddox agreed. "The words Charlie quoted from Sir Walter Scott's poem--Oh, what a tangled web we weave, when at first we practise to deceive--seem to be a most appropriate way in which to describe a life story punctuated by half-truths, misrepresentations and misinterpretations…"

Pausing, Philip Maddox once again sipped from his cup, before changing the subject, by requesting an update on his partner's whereabouts.

"Have you heard from Mr Powell?"

"Yes Sir, his arrival back at Manor Park with Mrs Clunnell and the briefcase is estimated at 2:45. Although it's taken longer than expected, as a precautionary measure, Colin McCardle and Christine McPherson have both agreed that provided there are no difficulties with their respective employers, they should move into a safe house with round the clock security, until any threat has either been neutralized or eliminated…"

"Excellent, and from Companies House, Sarah-Roxanna can get me a list of people who are on the Board of Directors, so that I can use my privileged position to ensure there are no difficulties with their respective employers. When I reassigned you and Powell, while I never doubted that you'd do a thorough job, your decision to afford my Goddaughter, unlimited time and space, and complete freedom of speech was nothing less than a brilliant manoeuvre, because it left Charlie without any place to hide from the truth…"

"Thank you Sir, I'm glad you approve of our methodology…"

"First thing tomorrow morning," Philip Maddox continued to explain. "On the grounds that something urgent requires my personal attention, I intend to request that my lunchtime appointment be rescheduled, and while we're waiting for the results of the exhumation, and the in depth search into Mark Daltry's parentage, I can concentrate on listening to everything and then, after using the notes I've made during the significant *highlights, by the time I approach the highest possible Authority, there will not only be nothing left to chance, I will also be able to present a plan of resolution, which will redistribute the balance of power in favour of ourselves..."*

*Hesitating, Philip Maddox swallowed the last remnants of pure malt whisky, in his crystal glass, before he gestured towards the items on the tray. "Since there is nobody else here except you and me, presumably one of the thermal mugs is for you and the other for my Goddaughter, but what about the whisky in the glass?"*

*"I'm afraid I have to admit that the whisky is a precautionary measure Sir. Since our arrival at Manor Park, Charlie hasn't been eating and when that's combined with the fact that her inability to achieve, any meaningful sleep has now pushed her into sleep deprivation mode, Bill and I are concerned that she might not make it through the next few days, without experiencing, some kind of physical collapse. So one of the thermal mugs contains heavy duty black coffee to keep me awake and the other one contains hot milk and although the glass does contain some whisky, it also contains..."*

*Alarmed by his subordinate's reference to a physical collapse, Philip Maddox interrupted him. "Since any kind of hospitalization at this juncture could prove to be disastrous, especially when we all agreed that it's vital that we keep not only Charlie, but also Lorna and Bobby Clunnell hidden from prying eyes in the most secure place for as long as possible, I suspect that what you're about to confirm is that the glass also contains a crushed sleeping tablet..."*

*"Yes Sir, at eleven forty-five, when the issue of taking one the sleeping tablets was discussed, on the basis that it was such a relief to conclude the Interview, Charlie wanted to determine whether she could fall asleep without using chemicals..."*

*"And presumably, she's still awake?"*

*"Although I didn't venture into her room Sir, the last time I did my routine check I could hear her moving around..."*

*"Under the circumstances, you have my permission to do whatever it takes in order to avoid hospitalization, and since I know how stubborn she can be, offer my Goddaughter one last chance, and if she refuses to take a sleeping tablet, then use some of your charm to get her to drink the whisky, before enjoying the hot milk..."*

*From his lightweight jacket pocket, John revealed a packet of cigarettes and lighter. "Since I rescued your Goddaughter's cigarettes, after she left them in the study Commander, I have the ideal incentive to get her to accept both. Of course, Bill and I suspect that the reason why Charlie stops herself from falling into a deep sleep is because she's afraid that if she's not in complete control of what's happening, then the nightmares might break through, which is why I'll be watching over her Sir, throughout the night..."*

*After turning away, John clicked the door open so it was ajar, before he looked back towards the desk. "Speaking of charm Sir, there were a few occasions throughout this evening, when there was good reason for suspecting that I might have..."*

*"Even if there was something wrong with my hearing, Mr Bland," The Commander rescued his subordinate, before he could incriminate himself. "Then, the last time I had my eyesight checked, I was deemed to have twenty-twenty vision. Besides, I've been fulfilling this role for far too long not to realise when one of my Operatives might be coming close to violating their professional code of conduct. Do you think your involvement could jeopardize the fulfilment of your assignment?"*

*"Not up until now Sir..."*

*Impressed by is subordinate's spontaneity, Philip Maddox selected his words as if he was speaking as a Godfather. "Considering that my Goddaughter is going to need all the allies she can find--for the time being Mr Bland--we'll leave things as they are..."*

*"Thank you Sir..."*

*"However, if I should fail to pull the right kind of white rabbits out of their respective political top hats, as my Goddaughter suggested, having accepted the rather daunting responsibility for keeping her alive, it would be a waste of an excellent Operative, if you should find yourself standing between Charlie Anne Daltry, and her destiny…"*

*Pausing, Philip Maddox allowed the silence to linger, before adding, "I trust you'll take on board what I'm telling you, not as a Godfather, but as your Commanding Officer…"*

### JUNE 30   2:23

"You haven't answered my question. Is there some kind of catch attached to the crystal glass and the cigarettes?"

From the inside pocket of his lightweight jacket, John produces the carton containing Doctor Wilson's pills, before enlightening me as to my forthcoming dilemma. "Two hours ago, we agreed that you could have one last chance to fall asleep, without resorting to chemical means, but since you're still awake I'm hoping you'll take a sleeping tablet…"

"Why can't we see whether the whisky and warm milk send me to sleep?"

"And like the closed eyes routine," John fires his first accusation at me. "You can wipe that butter wouldn't melt in your mouth expression off your face, because we both know that if nothing has worked up until now…"

"Please John--I'm positive that if you're here, then I will be able to fall asleep…"

Of course unbeknown to me, John knew that there was a catch, but he intended to make it seem, as if I had convinced him, and after moving to the chest of drawers he picks up the crystal glass, before he crouches down in front of the armchair.

"All right, but if this fails you have to promise me that without any further discussion, you will take one of the sleeping tablets. Do we have a deal?"

Blissfully unaware, I am so exhausted I cannot latch onto either John's thoughts or his feelings behind his own butter would not melt deep brown eyes and yet, it's the kind of bargain no leading lady, much less this one should refuse.

"Of course we have a deal John…"

Handing this assignment the crystal glass, when I swallow the first mouthful and it burns the back of my throat, it causes me to cough and splutter.

"For God's sake John!" I exclaim. "This glass must contain at least three measures of my Godfather's pure malt whisky…"

"Do you ever stop complaining Charlie? Since we struck a deal, I expect you to drink every single drop…"

Despite wanting to argue, John has moved back across the room, so that he can collect the two thermal mugs, and when he places them on the bedside cabinet, without making eye contact, he states. "If the whisky's going to work, then it needed to be triple strength…"

Dutifully, this woman manages to swallow the remaining whisky in one decisive mouthful, and as soon as my protector retrieves the crystal glass, like he has done previously, John places a cigarette, between his own lips and then, after sparking the lighter into flame, I watch as he does not inhale the smoke into his lungs. Instead, as John offers me the cigarette, he expels the smoke from inside of his mouth, and despite having vowed that I would quit smoking, I take that first inhalation of smoke deep into my lungs.

Then, as I exhale in a long smooth breath, and the nicotine hits my brain, John hands me the thermal mug containing the warm milk, and I have to admit that it tastes better than I had anticipated. "And do both of you use this old fashioned remedy for sleeplessness?"

"Although it might seem odd for two trained professionals, whenever exhaustion pushes us into sleep deprivation that's our first line of offence. But if it fails, then because of our responsibilities, we don't have any qualms about resorting to chemicals…"

Suddenly, I feel comfortable enough to allow the silence to linger, so that I can enjoy alternating between my cigarette and the warm milk, but then static items in my room seem to be blurring around the edges and in my naivety, I have cause to wonder whether either this old fashioned cure for sleeplessness is working, or maybe that malt whisky was far too strong. It makes no difference, because as this leading lady requests her principal male's attention, there is a degree of alarm in my voice.

"I don't feel very well John. In fact, I think I'm going to throw up…"

In response, John is rescuing the half smoked cigarette from between my fingers, so that he can stub it out in the makeshift ashtray, before retrieving the thermal mug from my hand, and although his voice seems to be distant, I can hear him reassuring me.

"If you don't fight it Charlie, you won't be sick…"

Then, it's too late because as the reality dawns on me, I hear this woman beginning to slur her accusation at someone who is supposed to be acting in my best interests. "You lying, cheating--son of a bitch--you tricked me. It was--the whisky--I hate you. Are--you--even listening--to--me? I--said--I hate--you…"

"Oh believe me I heard you, but let's try to look on the bright side, shall we? After you've had the benefit of at least five hours uninterrupted sleep, you'll be able to hate me with a renewed vengeance tomorrow morning. In the meantime, why don't we make you more comfortable by getting you into the bed?"

As far as his leading lady was concerned, when it came to John's underhand methods, there was no--*WE*--about anything, but as much as I wanted to resist, I can do nothing to prevent him from lifting me out of the chair, and after placing me in the recovery position, he covers me with the lightweight duvet. Then, he moves the chair closer to the bed, so that he can hold one of my hands, while at the same time allowing the fingertips of his other hand to brush the stray stands of hair from my face, using the gentlest of touches.

In the past tense, we must have enacted a similar scene, but my mind is succumbing to the hypnotic effects of the sleeping tablet, and John is right--when I awake refreshed--I will be able to hate him with a renewed vengeance. So lying on my side, the last thing I will recall seeing are those penetrating brown eyes, and the last thing I will remember hearing is his soft tone of voice reassuring me that he intends to remain by my bedside, so that he can watch over me throughout the remainder of the night.

### JUNE 30   3:11

Before propping his feet up on the edge of the bed, John had removed his trainers, and until his negative thoughts had been distracted by the sound of the Jaguar, heralding his partner's return at 2:51, he had continued to sit in the armchair while he had been contemplating the warning his Commanding Officer had delivered.

Over the years, having learnt to live day by day, and if necessary hour by hour, the issue of personal involvement had never arisen, but even if he had crossed that forbidden boundary by turning his involvement with Charlie Daltry into something personal, John had never had any reason to consider that a man like Philip Maddox, who was renowned for his unique negotiating skills might not be able to find a resolution, which would prove to be satisfactory to all parties.

However, the issue was nothing more than circumstantial evidence, and to offset the monotony of an overnight vigil, during which John would afford himself the luxury of dozing, it came as a welcome relief, when Bill had made a detour, but as soon as he had provided John with an update, which was delivered in a hushed voice, he disappeared again, so that at least one half of their partnership could achieve a few hours uninterrupted sleep.

### JUNE 30   4:14

Of course, in the early hours of the morning tempting fate was a recipe for disaster and at first, John's dozing was disturbed by the slightest of movements, and in the hope that his assignment might find herself slipping back into a deeper sleep, he chose to do nothing, except observe and listen, until the rapid eye movements beneath Charlie's eyelids quickened, and because she was growing more fretful, John prepared himself in case he needed to react, if she could not bring about a satisfactory resolution to her dreaming.

*There is snow on the ground and ye, as my bare feet leave a trail of footprints behind me, I have no awareness of the cold at least not until I hear a voice call out to me. "Where do you think you're going Charlie? Don't you know it's dark outside?"*

*How did my husband get inside my head and why is he asking me hose questions? The same questions from the past tense when I had tried to leave him, and because I need him to be figment of my imagination yet again, I defy him.*

*If you had wanted everyone to believe that you were dead Mark, then you could at least have had the decency to stay dead..."*

"Charlie..."

*It is a different voice, but amid the escalating urgency to start fleeing from my husband, I could not identify its owner, and because I am prepared to defend myself, when a hand touches my cheek, and my eyes shoot open someone catches hold of my arms.*

"Look at me Charlie..."

Then, back in the present tense when I realize that the hand belonged to John, I stop resisting, and as he releases my arms with a degree of caution, he offers me some clarification, which he must be hoping will help to dispel my confusion.

"You were dreaming Charlie, but that's all it was just a dream and together with Lorna and Bobby, you are at Manor Park with not only me, but also Bill..."

Courtesy of the sleeping tablet, mixed with the triple strength pure malt whisky, as one might expect, I am experiencing some disorientation. "But there was snow on the ground and using my footprints, someone must have been following me, because a voice called out, and I swear to God that it belonged to Mark So what your Person of Interest told you was right, and until the terms of the Contract have been fulfilled, Shaw and his two associates will never stop looking for me..."

At some point the tears must have overwhelmed my normal self-control, and as the full extent of my distress causes me to breakdown, I admit "I'm so afraid that Lorna or Bobby might get caught in the crossfire, the only way they can ever be safe is when I'm dead..."

After being disturbed by the sound of John's voice, after checking that Lorna and Bobby were still asleep, Bill entered Charlie's room in time to witness his partner moving to the other side of the bed, so that he could lie down beside their assignment before putting his arm around her. Perhaps familiarity does breed contempt, but if their suspicions about the nightmares were accurate, then it was vital that Charlie slept through the rest of the night, and because of the chill in the early morning air without making a sound Bill made sure that until John chose to leave the bed, they were both beneath the lightweight duvet.

Finally, Bill sat down in the vacant armchair, so that he could listen in respectful silence, while John offered some much needed reassurance. "Because I'm going to stay right here, there's no reason for you to be afraid. So why don't you go back to sleep Charlie or tomorrow morning, you'll be too tired to hate me with that renewed vengeance?"

Biding his time, Bill waited until Charlie's breathing once again deepened, and once he was satisfied that his partner would not require any further assistance, without speaking Bill indicated that he would double-check that Lorna and Bobby were still asleep, before returning to his own room, so that at least one half of their partnership could finish catching up on his much needed sleep.

**JUNE 30   8:12**

By the time Bill delivered two bone china mugs of coffee to Charlie's bedroom, his partner was sitting in the armchair, and after he accepts one the mugs in a hushed voice, Bill updates him. "Provided that nothing else happens to upset the revised timetable, Margaret will be serving breakfast at nine-fifteen, and the Commander has advised me that because he wants to focus his attention on the surveillance footage, he has decided to reschedule his lunchtime appointment. So not only does the Commander intend to join us for breakfast, as he arranged with Lorna last night, if she can fulfil the role of our impartial referee, as well as being our goalkeeper, then the four of us can enjoy playing football…"

Pausing, Bill cast a glance towards the bed and their sleeping assignment. "Did you manage to get any sleep during the remainder of the night?"

"After you left Charlie didn't stir again," John whispered. "When I woke her up, she was dreaming, so I think we were right to assume that if she allowed herself to fall into a deep sleep, then she was afraid that she would have no control over the nightmares. As for me, I drifted in and out of sleep, until around five o'clock, and then I must have felt it was safe to fall into a deeper sleep, because I didn't wake up until ten minutes ago…"

"Almost three consecutive hours that's not too bad, and the Commander has explained about giving his approval for the crushed sleeping pill in the pure malt whisky. Presumably, that's the reason why Charlie wants to hate you?"

From the pocket of his lightweight jacket, John produced the carton of sleeping tablets, Doctor Wilson had prescribed. "Guilty as charged, but as we agreed, if I hadn't taken advantage of the opportunity, she was heading towards a physical breakdown…"

"Perhaps we should be thankful that despite joining Charlie on the bed, at least you managed to keep your clothes on, because I'm not sure our Commanding Officer would condone that kind of familiarity, between you and his Goddaughter…"

"Oh please don't you start Bill, because after persuading Margaret that we could manage without her--at around 2:11--I took the Commander a pot of tea, and I felt obliged to inform him that there were times when my professional boundaries came close to being compromised, and he delivered his text book speech about personal involvement…"

"Hello this is Charlie," I hear this woman snapping. "Not only am I awake, I can also hear every word, and I'm so pleased my Godfather gave you a hard time about you drugging me. In fact, I seem to recall that when it came to the deal we negotiated over a certain three items, you turned out to be a--lying--cheating--son of a…"

In mid-flow, Bill curbs my ranting. "Good morning Charlie. Since someone seems to have woken with a sore head, perhaps it's fortuitous that I've come prepared with a mug of coffee, and as God is my witness, I swear that it contains nothing except caffeine…"

Having rolled onto my back, as I am struggling to re-position the pillows, so that I can prop myself up against the headboard, Bill places the mug on the bedside cabinet, before he dares to offer his assistance. "Why don't you let me help you Charlie?"

Fixing my icy glare upon him, I issue a direct threat. "Unless you want my ranting to become physical as well as verbal Mr Powell, don't you dare lay a finger on me…"

"Gr-r-r-r…"

"And as for you Mr Bland--if that guttural sound was meant to imply that instead of someone code named Operation Tigress, you are comparing me with a grizzly bear--then after what you did to me you would be right.…"

Then, as I take the coffee mug from Bill, out of the corner of my eye I notice that without responding, John is about to beat a hasty retreat. "And where do you think you're going Mr Bland? We have some unfinished business…"

"Oh I don't think you're likely to let me forget, so you can hate me later. Right now, I need to have a shower and then get shaved before breakfast, and I do hope that after what Lorna had to say last night, you're going to make a concerted effort to eat something…"

"And after the deception over the sleeping pill, what do you intend to do as an encore, if I don't eat Mr Bland? Ask my Godfather whether you can start force feeding me?"

However, John will not be goaded into delaying his departure, and as he disappears, I almost growl at Bill. "Do you know what he did to me?"

"Of course, but I also know that when Lorna and I returned at 2:51, he was sitting in that armchair, and then at 4:14, after he had woken you, because you were dreaming, by the time I responded to the sound of his voice, I watched him joining you, on the bed, so that he could hold onto you, and since he promised that he would stay with you, prior to you waking this morning, John had undertaken an overnight vigil, during which he must have managed to achieve no more than three consecutive hours sleep…"

Feeling guilt ridden, while I'm searching for the words to excuse my bad behaviour, Bill continues to explain. "Because Lorna and Bobby are awake and Margaret isn't serving breakfast until 9:15, I suggest you have a shower and put some clothes on, and unless you want them to know that there's been another upset, perhaps you could attempt to be civil at the breakfast table." Pausing Bill waits until duly admonished, I nod my agreement, before he adds, "Irrespective of the reason behind our actions, we have only ever done what we believe to be in your best interests, and at least you had the benefit of five and a half hours sleep. So might I also suggest that you cut John a little slack, especially when your Godfather might regard his familiarity, as being too personal, and if that were to happen the consequences could be far reaching, for all of us…"

## JUNE 30   9:11

"Uncle Philip, Uncle Philip…"

In a rush to reach the ground floor, but mindful of the two verbal warnings issued for running on the stairs, my resourceful son climbed over the top the rail of the sweeping staircase, and by the time Bobby finished his descent, Bill was waiting at the bottom, so that he could lift the youngster off the bannister.

"All right young man, where's the fire?"

"Please Mr Powell--I have to speak to Uncle Philip…"

"Whatever it is Bobby you can tell me…"

"You don't understand. If anything worried me or I was upset by something Uncle Philip told me that it didn't matter how silly it might seem--and I don't think this is silly, then as the Commanding Officer who is in charge of everything that happens, he would be able to sort it out for me…"

"Yes Bobby," Philip Maddox agreed, as he emerged from his inner sanctum. "That is exactly what I told you and I'm sorry, I couldn't respond to the urgency in your voice. However, after breakfast, because I want to join Mr Bland and Mr Powell when they play football, I was using the special red telephone, which I showed you in my study, so that his Personal Assistant could reschedule a prearranged lunchtime appointment…"

When the Commander hesitates, Bobby glances at Bill. "You see that proves what I was saying, because if Uncle Philip can rearrange appointments as if it was an everyday kind of thing, which I'm sure it isn't and I don't think he would have said about wanting to play football--then he must be even more important than I had imagined…"

"Thank you Bobby--I think we've established my importance. Presumably, something must have happened to upset you?"

"Ever since we arrived at Manor Park Uncle Philip, because it will soon be my birthday, I've been trying to behave like a seven-year-old should by having my shower and then, putting some clothes on without Lorna having to check on my progress all the time, and although I couldn't remember whether I was supposed to brush my teeth, before or after my breakfast, when I went to tell her that I had even brushed them for the full two minutes, counting up to thirty on each of the four sides and from the back to the front, she wasn't in her room, but I could hear her voice and she was with mum and they were…"

Without even considering shortening the youngster's long-drawn-out explanation, having crouched down, so that he was on the same level with this remarkable almost seven-year-old, there was not even a hint of alarm in the Commander's voice as he chose to delve a little deeper. "And was it something they were doing which upset you?

"Mum and Lorna never disagree about anything Uncle Philip, so I have never once heard them get cross with each other. But after Lorna wanted to know something, which must have been something bad involving mum, and when she refused to tell Lorna, their voices were getting louder and louder…"

Remaining focused on Bobby, but mindful of what had been agreed the previous evening, Philip Maddox was prepared to offer the youngster a tempting proposition. "Of course you're right Bobby, and because I am in charge I think we should issue a direct order that Mr Powell--with Mr Bland's help--should find a way to resolve this disagreement…"

"Because they were very cross with each other that sounds like a good idea…"

"All right young man, why don't you issue Mr Powell with our orders?"

Momentarily bewildered Bobby hesitated, before seeking clarification. "Are you sure you want me to do it Uncle Philip?"

"Yes Bobby I did mean you…"

"Mr Powell your orders are to go upstairs, and together with Mr Bland, Uncle Philip and I want you to resolve the disagreement between my two mothers…"

Having never been issued with an order by anybody who was almost seven-years-old, Bill had to suppress a smile. "Of course Bobby…"

Then, as Bill headed up the stairs, Bobby could not contain his elation. "That was so cool Uncle Philip. If any more things like that happen, can I issue some more orders?"

"For the time being, I think we should concentrate on the successful completion of the first order, and while our best Operatives undertake, what could be a dangerous mission, especially when it might mean having to come between two disagreeing young women, so that I can show you another one of the surprises at Manor Park, why don't we go outside?"

"Gosh, until you allowed me to issue a direct order, which was even cooler I thought that the heated swimming pool in the extension was brilliant, and then the helicopter pad was so cool Is the next surprise better than all those Uncle Philip?"

"In order to gain access to this particular surprise, which is something personal belonging to me, we will need to go into the concealed underground garage…"

Rising to his feet, as Philip Maddox placed a paternal arm around Bobby's shoulders, Margaret appeared, carrying a tray containing serving dishes and their respective covers, but as if it was not unusual for things at Manor Park to be scheduled, and then rescheduled, before sometimes needing to be cancelled altogether, Margaret was matter of fact as she stated the obvious. "You don't need to explain Commander. You'd like breakfast to be served a little later. Fortunately, I haven't started on the eggs, and the grilled bacon and sausages can be kept warm in the oven…"

"What can I possibly say Margaret? Except that I can't thank you enough for your perpetual forbearance?"

Feeling a hand tug at his sleeve, Philip Maddox resumed his crouched position, so that he could listen to the youngster's hushed request. "It's been such a long time since I had my supper Uncle Philip, before Margaret returns them to the kitchen, do you think she might let me have two rashers of bacon to keep me going, until we can have our breakfast?"

Since the arrival of the three visitors, two of whom could be classified as extended family, Margaret had seen a different side to a man, who often seemed heavy-laden by the weight of his responsibilities, and without needing a formal request she brought the tray close enough, so that Bobby could select his two rashers of bacon and a bread bun covered with low fat spread, and despite needing nothing more rewarding than the delight on the youngster's face, as she handed Bobby two paper napkins--one for his bacon sandwich--and a second one containing a grilled sausage, he complimented her.

"Gosh thank you Margaret, the sausage is an unexpected extra, but I have to tell you that when you cook the bacon, until it's really--and I mean really, really crispy--around the outside edge that's exactly how I like it…"

"Whenever any of the guests at Manor Park pass a favourable comment about the food I prepare, it makes the effort worthwhile, and if the Commander is going to show you his pride and joy Bobby, I don't think you're going to be disappointed…"

By the time Bill neared Charlie's bedroom door, he could hear nothing, except the impassioned exchange between the youngsters' two mothers.

"We've been through so much together, and because I suspect that whatever happened must be bad Charlie, please don't shut me out…"

"You don't understand, it's so sordid, I'm too ashamed to share any of it with you…"

"Ladies, what neither of you seem to appreciate is that this isn't achieving…"

From the degree of desperation Bill could detect in his partner's voice, he recognized that the time for reinforcements to put in an appearance was long overdue, and because Lorna's presence was proving to be counterproductive, seconds ahead of John issuing him with an urgent request, as soon as Bill entered the room, he was heading in Lorna's direction.

"Get her out of here Bill…"

"No you can't force me to leave. So I'm staying until I have some answers …"

Of course, since there's no such thing as CAN'T, as soon as Bill's arm encircled Lorna's waist, he physically hauled her out of the room. Then, once they were on the landing, Bill exerted nothing more than minimal force to manoeuvre Lorna around, until he was able to use his body weight to keep her pinned against the wall, before placing the palm of his hand over her mouth so that he could stifle her non-stop verbal protests.

Never having considered that this man--the same man--who Lorna had accompanied in the early hours of that morning, might be capable of behaving in this way, as much as she wanted to resist Bill's hold, it had been a long time since any man--much less a virtual stranger--had been so close to her that she found herself compelled to remain still, while his hushed voice justified the reason why he had behaved in such an ungentlemanly fashion.

"On behalf of both of us, I apologise for having overlooked that this matter might need to be addressed sooner than we had anticipated. However, as we explained yesterday evening, because we were afraid that if you tried to intervene before Charlie was prepared to divulge what took place, then this might be the result. So I want you to stay here and regardless of what takes place you are not--I repeat--you are not going to interfere. Instead, you will be prepared to wait, until one of us comes to collect you, and so that there can be no mistakes do you understand what I've told you?" Pausing, Bill waited and then, after Lorna nodded her appreciation, while he began to put a more discreet distance between their bodies, he also eased his hand away from her mouth, before delivering one final ultimatum. "And I should warn you that if you cannot curb your instinctive need to lend your support, then whether you like it or not, you will be joining Bobby outside of the Manor…"

Meanwhile in the present tense of my room, although I could neither see nor hear Lorna, this so called adult did not presume to enjoy her fleeting moment of respite. Instead, I'm standing in the far corner of the room, and because I know that when Bill returns yet again, the odds will be stacked two to one in their favour. So despite John's attempts to reason with me, he seems to have overlooked that when it comes to the issue of my reasonableness, I have a tenacious ability to be unreasonable.

"Charlie--as soon as…"

With the same impeccable timing as his partner, Bill reappears in the doorway. "As you can see, there's nobody else here, and if I give you my word that Bill and I will remain on this side of the room, instead of standing in the corner, resembling a frightened rabbit caught in the headlights of an oncoming car, why don't you sit down in the armchair?"

Despite John's sleek delivery, I reserved the right to be suspicious, but with Bill in the doorway, and John sitting on the bed, it would not be possible to execute a clean exit anyway, and because the armchair is a safe distance from the bed, with a deliberate slowness I sidestep, until I can sit down.

"Is Lorna okay?" I ask, but then in the aftermath of our heated encounter, I voice a bigger concern. "And where's Bobby? Up until this morning, there's never been any reason for Lorna and me to disagree, so he would have been confused by our raised voices…"

"Like you, Lorna is supposed to behave like an adult," Bill scolds me. "But your son's fine. Fortunately, not long after your arrival at Manor Park, your Godfather made sure that Bobby understood that if anything upset him, then his--*Uncle Philip*--would deal with it on his behalf. So when he finished sliding down the bannister, shouting *Uncle Philip* at the top of his voice, after he told him about his two mother's exchanging cross words, with the Commander's permission your son issued me with a direct order, which stated that I was to come upstairs and then, together with Mr Bland, we were to resolve this disagreement…"

In the aftermath of his reprimand, if Bill is attempting to defuse the tension, then he is succeeding, because the image he has created causes this proud mother to laugh. "Of course you do realize that we're going to hear about him issuing that order, over and over again…"

"Oh I don't doubt that for a moment, but never having been issued with an order by someone almost seven-years-old, I had to suppress a smile. As for Bobby, he was so thrilled I overheard him telling the Commander--*that was so cool Uncle Philip. If more things like that happen, can I issue some more orders*---and the last time, I looked over the bannister, Margaret had appeared, carrying the breakfast tray, and because it had been such a long time since he'd had his supper, she gave him some bacon and a bread bun--plus a sausage--in a napkin to keep him going until breakfast, before the Commander escorted him outside, so that he could show Bobby his pride and joy in the underground garage…"

As Bill falls silent, it is John's turn to make me feel more at ease. "On behalf of those of us, for whom it's also been a long time since supper and who have not been offered either a bacon sandwich or a sausage, if we're ever going to be able to have some breakfast, then having received our orders, perhaps we should focus upon resolving this disagreement…"

Pausing, John casts a backward glance at his partner, before he explains, "And there seems to be three principal issues, starting with your son. Perhaps as a result of him growing up without a father, Bobby seems to regard his stay at the Manor to be an adventure, and I'm certain that none of us would want him to start asking awkward questions or become overly concerned about the future. Next, there's Lorna and we should clarify that during our second intermission, when you came upstairs to have a shower and get changed, Lorna was awake and after your retching followed by your crying, which dissolved into sobbing had drawn her into your room, she overheard you being--overzealous--with the body brush, and because you had both encountered a similar occurrence she came downstairs…"

"It was at the Mayfield Clinic," I interrupt John as I make the connection which causes me to ask. "And is Lorna aware of every sordid detail about the abuse, including what they did to necessitate the termination of what was deemed to be an unviable pregnancy?"

Of course Charlie's reference to the Mayfield Clinic was something Lorna did not know had been divulged about her personal life, and because Bill was still in the doorway, it seemed like the ideal excuse to cast a glance along the landing. But despite the exactness of his instructions, she was no longer standing with her back against the wall.

Instead, Lorna was sitting on the floor, and with her knees drawn up to her chest, it was as if she was starting to appreciate, why Bill had afforded her that one last chance to remain on the landing, because irrespective of how disturbing the content might be or how distressed Charlie might become, one of Lorna's hands was covering her own mouth, so that Bobby's other mother would not discover that she was listening to every word.

"Yesterday evening," John was explaining, as Bill resumed his former position. "When Lorna came downstairs, she was demanding to know whether it was physical abuse, sexual abuse or a combination of them, and because we could not divulge any personal information without your consent, Lorna does not know everything, and that brings us to the third issue. Your apparent compulsion to scrub yourself clean, and because it's an unhealthy psychological manifestation, it needs to be addressed…"

"But it isn't necessary," I hear this so called adult protesting. "Until yesterday evening, I had managed to keep the images locked away, but after you provoked me and I shared everything with you, including the fact that Tony Shaw used that hand held camcorder, so that he could provide definitive proof for their paymaster. So by the time I left the study, I felt used and discarded all over again to the extent that I could even smell them on my skin. But I swear that it was the first time…"

Silence, oh how I still loathe it, when the cavalry remain silent, and as if to prove me right, John asks, "And before I joined you in the en-suite--and I distracted you from your negative thoughts--were you satisfied that you no longer felt used and discarded?"

Sensing that his question might be tempting me to go somewhere, I might prefer to avoid, I respond with a question of my own choosing. "Was that the real reason, why you came to find me--because Lorna had come downstairs?"

"As I explained at the time Charlie, because Bill had read me the riot act for having pushed you too hard too fast--my principal reason was to see if you were all right…"

His principal reason is something I could turn against John, but when Bill stirs his movement attracts our joint attention. "Unless the pair of you want me to read you the riot act again, can we please focus on the third issue?" Pausing, he waits until we both nod our agreement. "Thank you, and because we seem to be encountering some avoidance, I'm re-establishing my role as arbitrator, and you haven't answered John's question. Were you satisfied that you no longer felt used and discarded?"

What did I say abou the odds being two to one in their favour? But before I can be accused of any more avoidance, I admit to having committed the offence.

"Okay, despite thinking that I had done enough I was wrong, but I swear it won't happen again…"

In the doorway, Bill is shaking his head. "I'm afraid that giving us your word isn't sufficient Charlie, because Lorna knows enough to have started jumping to conclusions, and we aren't prepared to risk that Bobby questions his belief that this is an adventure…"

Still sitting on the bed, John resumes control over the proceedings. "In the early hours of this morning, I expressed our concerns that your difficulties with eating and sleeping might mean that you're heading towards an unavoidable physical crisis, and your Godfather has given us his approval to arrange to have you readmitted to the Mayfield Clinic so that those two concerns--along with this new manifestation--can be addressed in a safe environment by qualified health professionals…"

"But if you do that, then for security reasons I'd have to be admitted to the Psychiatric Wing of the Clinic, and it would mean being separated from Lorna and Bobby at what might be a crucial time within our life together. Surely, there must be another way, especially when I've agreed with Bill that I will make an effort at mealtimes, and after last night's success, I'm sure we can reach a compromise over my use of the sleeping pills…"

"If you don't calm down Charlie, the only option will be hospitalization…"

In Bill's capacity as arbitrator, the sharpness in his voice is accompanied by his raised hand, and because I know better than to push him too far, not only do I opt to cease pleading, I also decide that when it comes to protesting--*me thinks this lady doth protest too much.*

"As I was about to explain," John continues, with those brown eyes reassuring me. "In the short term, we could attempt an intervention, but there are conditions attached. Firstly, irrespective of how challenging, it might become we will expect your full cooperation, and if you should fail, then there may be no alternative, except for hospitalization and secondly, even if you do manage to see it through to the end, we will expect you to start working on a one to one basis, with our resident Consultant Psychologist and Psychotherapist, who has the equivalent security clearance as your original mentor Professor Kenneth Morgan…"

If John is warning me that it might become challenging then as my son, who is prone to gross exaggeration would have stated, *it's going to get real scary*--and yet, compared to the alternative, it remains the lesser of the two evils.

"All right," I declare, without severing eye contact. "I accept those conditions and even if it does seem challenging, I will attempt to give you my fullest cooperation…"

Now, John's deep brown eyes seem to be congratulating me. "Late yesterday evening, when you shared many of the disturbing details from the prolonged sexual assault, because that outpouring occurred, as a result of my having pushed you too far, it's possible that you might have felt threatened all over again. Through visualization, we want to try and demonstrate that despite the negative self-image, we believe you were left with Charlie, there were some positive things that emerged--things which--we suspect you never considered possible. Do you understand the concept of visualization?"

"When Lorna and I were in the Mayfield Clinic, during group therapy sessions we would be asked to visualise a situation which had generated powerful responses--such as great sadness or extreme anger, and because both of those mask hurt, by revisiting the same situation from behind the security of a blindfold, it was hoped that we could learn how to turn those negative emotions into something more positive…"

From the bed, John nods his appreciation. "At least you've had some experience of the technique, and at this point it would be normal procedure for us to invite you to make yourself as comfortable as possible, before closing your eyes. However, if you would prefer to use a blindfold, then I'm sure Bill will be able to find something suitable…"

Despite having no reason to disbelieve that as they have done in the past one of them will catch me, if I should begin to fall, only too aware of the consequences, if I fail to do this I decide to proceed with caution. "If it's going to be challenging then I think that I would prefer to be blindfolded…"

"That shouldn't pose too much difficulty," Bill confirms. "But I do need to step outside of the bedroom for a few minutes…"

Then, while Bill's out of the room as John suggested, I make myself as comfortable as possible, by lifting my legs off the floor, and after I wrap my bare feet in my robe, I tuck them beneath me, before closing my eyes, so that I can clear the clutter from my mind.

"Charlie," Bill announces upon his return. "There was a silk scarf on the landing, which might have been the one Lorna was wearing, when I removed her from the room. Would it be acceptable if John leaves the bed, so that he can use it as a blindfold?"

Then, while I'm considering the implications, if John moves closer the silence lingers, but I dare not refuse what seems to be a sensible solution. "That's fine Bill…"

Although I'm unable to see the scarf, as John is tying it at the back of my head, despite my disagreement with Lorna, because I can smell her perfume, somehow I find it comforting. Then, when I sense that John is moving to the front of the chair, and he uses the lightest of touches to allow his fingertips to squeeze my shoulder--quite spontaneously, I find myself reaching up, so that I can reciprocate the gesture by touching the back of his hand.

"If you would prefer me to do so, I will move back to the bed," he states, in a calm hushed voice. "However, since some of the tension has been defused, and from experience you know that you can trust us to be acting in your best interests, would it be acceptable for me to remain by the armchair?"

Yet again, while I consider how comfortable I feel with him remaining so close during this intervention, the silence is allowed to linger before I tighten my hold a little on the back of John's hand. "Provided that you accept a slight revision to your terms and conditions, in so much as--if it becomes too challenging--and I ask you to back off, you should do so immediately, I don't see any reason why you should have to move back to the bed..."

"You have my word that I will respect any such request Charlie, but if at any time you think you're in trouble, all you need to do is raise one of your hands in the air, so that we can pause, while you determine whether you feel able to continue..."

Now I'm aware that he's either crouched by the armchair--or perhaps as I seen them do--whenever they are playing a game with my son, John could be sitting cross-legged on the floor, but either way he is holding my hand as his partner introduces the intervention.

"Although John has introduced the issue of the negative self-image you seemed to have been left with after you told us, what took place during those sixty minutes of your life. In my capacity as arbitrator, it sounded as if you thought you had failed in some way. So could we begin with you describing, what was the cause of that sense of failure?"

What a dilemma? But while I'm considering the repercussions if I dare to speak out against something--one half of the dynamic duo--brought to my attention, although it might seem to be a little ironic, I'm biding my time and yet, I cannot find any other way to avoid what seems to be the inevitable.

"Before John's unstoppable ranting pushed me over the edge," I hear this woman admitting. "He asked me, whether I had any idea how long it would be, before I would be able to look at myself in a mirror without being reminded of what had happened, and once I reached the en-suite, I realized that the miserable son of a bitch was right?"

"Oh crap Charlie, I'm so terribly sorry," the miserable son of a bitch apologises, albeit a little too late. "Because I was so angry with you for having placed yourself in such a dangerous position, I never even considered the lasting impact of my words..."

"But why would you, especially when you were describing what your professional experience must have been in similar instances..."

Ready to challenge my accuracy, Bill announces, "That's not correct Charlie, because you weren't like any other instance. In fact, I can confirm that we had never encountered anyone as unique as you, and that was the reason why I read the riot act to the same miserable son of a bitch. But setting that to one side, you do realize that you cannot avoid looking at yourself in a full length mirror indefinitely, and if we can overcome that obstacle, then the third issue relating to your sudden need to scrub yourself clean might be resolved..."

"But I've already agreed to work on a one to one basis with your resident Consultant Psychotherapist, and I'm sure the disagreement with Lorna can be settled..."

"That was a valiant attempt to avoid dealing with the third issue, but what do you expect me to tell your son?" Pausing Bill waits, before he explains. "More than anything else, Bobby needs some stability in his life, and although I made light of the situation this morning, all he had been trying to do was find Lorna, so that he could tell her that without her having to check on his progress every few minutes, he had been showered, before dressing

207

himself in the clean clothes, she had selected for him last night, and although he couldn't remember whether he was supposed to do it--before or after breakfast---but I think we can overlook such a minor transgression--because he had even brushed his teeth for the full two minutes--in the way he'd been taught--by counting to thirty on each of the four sides…"

Beneath the blindfold, through a muffled sob, this mother pleads. "Please don't…"

"What's the matter Charlie?"

After the sharpness in Bill's voice cuts me off, he continues to explain. "If the truth hurts, then it damn well should hurt not only you, but also Lorna, because that remarkable young man was so proud of his achievements, but instead of gaining any kind of recognition, Bobby heard his two mothers exchanging *cross words* for the first time in seven years…"

Between you and me, I'm so ashamed it feels as if my heart is breaking and yet, when I fail to stifle another sob, although Bill had hesitated, it is obvious that he has no intention of stopping, until he finishes reading me--*one of his notorious riot acts.*

"Both of you seem to have overlooked that Bobby has been resourceful enough to accept being removed from his family home, without him asking any awkward questions, and he's been so thrilled that since you arrived at Manor Park, the three of you haven't needed to pretend. In fact, until those *cross words* this morning, everything was fine. So I think you and Lorna might agree that nobody could blame him for being so perplexed, he came sliding down the banister, shouting at the top of his voice, so that he could tell your Godfather--who unlike you--he has never had any reason to distrust…"

Pausing, yet again Bill waits, and because his explanation has left me riddled with guilt, it forces me to remain silent, until in that softer more amenable tone of voice, which I've come to appreciate, he adopts whenever he needs to either gain someone's attention, or their cooperation, at last he concludes his dressing down. "Since John and I have no intention of going down to our late breakfast, knowing that we will have to tell Bobby that despite the order he personally issued, we have failed to resolve the disagreement between his two mothers. That's why it's imperative that all three issues are dealt with right here and right now, including the part that was played by Lorna in all this…"

At last, it feels safe enough for me to speak. "I'm so sorry Bill, although you might have to be patient with me, I'm willing to give you my full cooperation, and because you reintroduced Lorna, my initial feelings have changed, and I'm hoping that after you removed her from my bedroom, she didn't join Bobby outside of the Manor…"

Yet again, silence descends, but with John still holding one of my hands, perhaps his partner in crime is checking to determine Lorna's whereabouts. Then, when Bill brings the silence to an end, after measuring the distance between the chair and his voice using my unique abilities, I'm confident that he has resumed his former position in the doorway.

"Because we've never lied to you Charlie, I'm going to be honest and confirm that although she was free to run away, she has remained close enough to hear everything, including me laying the law down with regards to Bobby, and the last time I checked, she was still on the landing. However, Lorna has been warned that it's imperative she does not try to interfere. So if she should attempt to enter your room without an invitation, then she will be dealt with in the appropriate manner…"

"In a way it's a relief that she can hear everything, especially when we can't be sure what the consequences might be for me, and there are so many other things Lorna needs to know, it will help if these three issues can be resolved through this intervention…"

"That's a blessed relief, especially while there's still a fighting chance of John and I being able to eat some breakfast, preferably before we risk dying of starvation. So I suggest we start this intervention…"

"Of course, and if I do find myself struggling, instead of using the forbidden CAN'T word, I'll do what John has suggested and raise one of my hands in the air…"

"As long as you trust us," John reassures me. "Everything will be fine…"

"Yes Charlie, you have no reason to distrust us, especially when we have established what caused your negative self-image, and through this intervention, it's our intention to eliminate the negatives, beginning with how you found yourself trapped in the house, with three male assailants Tony Shaw, who had accepted the Retrieval, before Termination Contract, along with his two associates, who have now been identified, as Michael Blake and Paul Peterson. Is that a true reflection of the situation?"

"Yes it is, but I made some stupid mistakes--like when I tried to run…"

"Charlie!"

Naturally, Bill's exclamation necessitates that yet again, I have to issue an apology. "I'm sorry, my reference to--*stupid mistakes*--suggested that I had failed in some way, which was never the case…"

"That's an improvement. So while John was waiting for Lorna and me to return from our visit to the McCardle house, he had the foresight to prepare some affirmations and having had the chance to study them--if necessary I will be adding my own contribution…"

Before he begins speaking, John tightens his hold on my hand a little. "To the best of your ability, I would like you to repeat the following affirmations back to me--*after Mark Daltry blackmailed Robert Lloyd Reece-Milliner, so that they could both commit offences, which contravened the Official Secrets Act, and my husband told me about his alternative lifestyle, including his sexual preference for young male virgins, because I had been…"*

Although I reserve the right to remain sceptical over how this will help to change the perception, I hold in my mind of what God had created in his own image, until I feel overly challenged, I see no reason why I should not be a willing participant. *"After Mark Daltry used my son to blackmail his father Robert Lloyd Reece-Milliner, and they both knowingly committed offences, which contravened the Official Secrets Act and when I challenged him, my husband told me the truth about   why he'd married me and his alternative lifestyle, including his sexual preference for seventeen year old male virgins, with the sole intention of inflicting some kind of punishment, and   because I*--then, when the words refuse to emerge, I raise my free hand in the air, as I gasp, "I'm sorry…"

"Charlie this isn't a race," Bill affords me some immediate support. "And since there's no rush--take a few deep breaths--and then, whenever you feel able to do so, can you describe for us, what part of the affirmation seemed to overwhelm you?"

While I'm heeding Bill's advice, I'm considering the impact of my actions if I cannot do this, and because I know that failure is not an option, it provides me with the strength I need to be able to offer some kind of a description. "Knowing that Lorna is listening, and being aware that she never knew anything about my marriage, which arose in conjunction with the memory of how Mark was such a sadistic bastard, he used to take great delight in trying to goad me into expressing my revulsion--as he used to describe, what he did to those seventeen-year-old kids, and it sounded so gratuitously cruel, but like everything else in connection with my husband--as quickly as it arose--it has come to pass. So perhaps we should carry on from the last words John stated, which were--*because I had been…"*

More silence, but then John double-checks. "Are you sure about this?"

"Absolutely no doubt whatsoever…"

"At least you know you can pause Charlie whenever you need to do so, and the end of the affirmation is *because I had been resourceful enough and courageous enough to devise an infallible way in which to protect not only myself, but also Lorna and Bobby, although Mark might have used and abused my body, he never touched this woman's soul…"*

If for no other reason than Lorna and Bobby, who does need both of his mothers, I'm telling myself that perhaps I can do this. *"Because I had been resourceful enough to devise an infallible way, in which to protect not only myself, but also Lorna and Bobby and then, having been courageous enough to bide my time, until he decided to retire from his double life--having failed to take me alive--although Mark might have used and abused my body, this woman never allowed his depravity to contaminate my soul…"*

"Excuse me for interrupting," Bill apologises even though--like his partner--he has done nothing wrong. "But before John moves on Charlie, I think we should take a few moments, so that using the visual images generated, you can compare the two affirmations and then, share any differences with us…"

Having taken part in far too many therapy sessions, I can appreciate the cavalry's strategy, and instead of Bill making suggestions, he is allowing me to take control of my emotional well-being, and I have to admit that there were some marked differences.

"As I approached the end of the first, I was concerned that Lorna might think less of me for having stayed in a loveless, abusive marriage. However, during the second affirmation, I realized that until I could be sure that my insurance policy was as infallible as I could have made it, either Lorna or Bobby, and perhaps even Colin could have been at risk from acts of violence, similar to those demonstrated on the 22$^{nd}$ of June, and I'd forgotten that it had taken years to compile the information needed to guarantee that infallibility…"

"So you were successful," Bill announces, with a hint of self-satisfaction. "Because if you had failed Charlie, then by the time we arrived in Paris to assist Henri--instead of seventeen known fatalities--there would have been nineteen, and via DNA testing, the Forensics team would have been able to identify your body, which would have meant that we might never have known that Mark Daltry had orchestrated the siege, so that his past could not be revealed, because Special Operations believed he had also died on that fateful day…"

"Looking back, I am now prepared to admit that it was a reckless game, which had been fraught with dangerous pitfalls, and while it's hard to predict the--*what if this had happened, or what if that hadn't taken place*--in my case, maybe if there hadn't been quite so many untruths, half-truths and misinterpretations, then perhaps I might have been in a position, where I could have found a way to bring Lorna and Bobby--in the metaphorical sense--in out of the cold, without subsequently being forced to do so…"

"That's a valid criticism," John agrees, as he squeezes my hand. "However, as I mentioned earlier Charlie, when I took the Commander a pot of Earl Grey tea, I did have two ulterior motives, which were for the right reasons. Firstly, I wanted his permission to blackmail his Goddaughter, so I could drug her and secondly, since I knew he would have been listening to the Interview, I was hoping he would update me, and as expected so that he could highlight the significant stages, he had fast forwarded through the playback, and he confirmed that your quotation--*Oh, what a tangled web we weave, when at first we practise to deceive*--was an appropriate description, and because you did whatever you had to do in order to protect the only people you've been able to trust implicitly, as far as I'm aware he intends to use your quotation, when he's preparing his case in your defence…"

"In addition to Lorna and Colin, I suppose I've also come to trust you and Bill…"

"Perhaps there's someone else you need to add to that list…"

"Is there John? How intriguing?"

"And I'm afraid that particular intrigue will have to be pended until later," Bill curbs my almost pathological curiosity. "Because before we move on to the next affirmation, which deals with those sixty minutes of your life, so that you will be able to focus your visual images, I would like to refresh your memory about some of the things, you managed to overcome. Starting with--after Blake's inappropriate use of the gun barrel--which later led to the termination of your pregnancy, although the pain must have been excruciating Charlie, can you describe what you did while he was raping you?"

"How could I ever forget, and although I should have been kicking, screaming, begging--perhaps even pleading--I knew that it wouldn't change anything, and because I was determined not to give their paymaster or paymasters any satisfaction, after I reduced the pain down to a manageable size, I fixed my gaze on a point on the ceiling and then, I chased the words from a song around in my head, and as soon as Blake tricked me into responding, I deliberately contracted and released my pelvic floor muscles, so that his climax would turn out to be more like an anti-climax…"

"Despite being tricked into responding Charlie, surely being able to detach yourself from your rapist must have been a remarkable achievement?"

"Perhaps it was Bill," I hear this woman reply. "But then it was the crème de la crème who first taught me how to be unresponsive…"

"You're missing the point Charlie," Bill persists. "Instead of believing that you had the resources necessary, you seem to be labouring under the misguided impression that the only reason, you could achieve that kind of detachment was because of your husband…"

"I'm sorry, but I don't understand…"

"Maybe things will become clearer, after the next affirmation…"

Then, without any further delay John's smooth, calm voice assumes control. "Using the same technique Charlie--can you repeat the following affirmation back to me--*by the end of those sixty minutes on the 22$^{nd}$ of June, having been resourceful enough and strong enough to exercise the necessary physical self-control and emotional self-discipline, in order to prevent Tony Shaw from taking this woman alive, I orchestrated the ending, so that instead of being able to take me with them, he had no choice except to leave me behind…"*

Once again, despite recognizing my positive achievements, I reserve the right to remain a little sceptical, but having come this far, there can be no turning back. *"By the end of those sixty minutes of my life on the 22$^{nd}$ of June, because I had been resourceful enough and strong enough to exercise the necessary physical self-control and emotional self-discipline to orchestrate the ending to my own advantage, I managed to rob Tony Shaw of the ability to take this woman alive, which meant he was forced to not only leave me behind, but also without any strategically placed bullets*--my God that was almost…"

Although it makes no sense, when the right words failed to emerge, and the wrong words were threatening to overpower them--at some point--I must have raised my free hand in the air, because Bill's intervention is a blessed relief.

"Take your time Charlie," he reassures me. "As we've done in the past, take a few deep breaths, because they'll help you to determine, whether you want to try again--or if you would prefer to have some assistance from me…"

For someone who is supposed to be a lateral thinker, I remain unable to find the right words to describe what occurred. "Whatever took place, because it felt as if it was fundamental, but at the same time monumental, provided that it won't count against me, it might be best Bill, if you give me the benefit of your assistance…"

More silence, but then after no doubt conferring with his partner, Bill declares, "Of course it won't count against you, and while it might not be what you want to hear, in my capacity as arbitrator, I'd like to suggest what I believe created this impasse…"

Pausing, Bill waits and when I do not raise either any objections or questions, he continues. "In my professional opinion Charlie, while you were repeating John's affirmation, you identified all of your positive attributes. Is that correct?"

"As I stated a few moments' ago, I don't understand what you mean…"

"Yes you do," Bill persists. "So stop procrastinating and answer the question…"

"Okay, I admit that not only hearing, but also repeating how I had been resourceful enough and strong enough to exercise, the necessary physical self-control, and emotional self-discipline throughout those sixty minutes seemed to be overwhelming…"

"That's interesting, and since we have reached that particular point in the proceedings, before I continue, I'd like to stress that from now on--either John or I--will tell you whenever we want to make any changes to your participation…"

"That sounds a little scary Bill…"

"Not necessarily, especially when you've known from the onset, what we intended to achieve. So with John's help, I want you to get out of the chair and onto your feet…"

Lowering my feet to the floor, John takes hold of both hands, so that I can rise to my full height, and as he moves behind me, I can feel the warmth of his breath against my ear, as he whispers, "As long as you trust us to know what we're doing, I give you my word that everything will be fine…"

Feeling a little intimidated by an unknown factor, my heartbeat has started to race, and when I sense that Bill has moved from his position, as if John has picked-up on my fearfulness, he clarifies the reason for his partner's movement.

"Please don't be too alarmed, but Bill has left the doorway, so that he can move the free standing Cheval mirror in front of us, and once it's in position, before I remove the scarf, we suggest that at first, you might prefer to keep your eyes closed, until either one of us asks you to open them--or alternatively--you feel able to do so of your own volition. Do you understand Charlie?"

"Of course I do, but unless you want the damn suspense to kill me, can we please get this over with?"

"Sorry," John apologises, as he removes the scarf. "Okay, now that Bill is back in the doorway, he intends to afford you some guidance…"

"Charlie if you discount Mark Daltry and the role you believe he played, in the art of unresponsiveness, then isn't it conceivable that you must have acquired the ability to be resourceful enough and strong enough to exercise that level of physical self-control and emotional self-discipline, long before those sixty minutes of your life?"

"It's possible Bill, but is this some kind of trick question? Or even a multiple choice kind of thing?"

More silence, but then Bill rewards my patience. "To narrow your search down, perhaps you should be considering, the place at which we commenced your life story, as opposed to the place where you thought we should have begun…"

Although both occurrences arose hours apart during the Interview, because they share the same common denominator, my initial reaction takes me by surprise.

"All right, so now that I understand, before I give you my answers--for some inexplicable reason--I feel an overwhelming need to open my eyes…"

Coming from behind me, yet again I feel the warmth of John's breath against my ear as he suggests, "If you think it's appropriate, because you are partially dressed would you like me to loosen the sash on your robe, so that it falls open?"

Do I think it is appropriate? Perhaps do I have any choice might be more apt? Nevertheless, one way or the other this has to be done and I would prefer to maintain some degree of self-respect. "Yes John, would you please loosen the sash on my robe…"

Opening my eyes does add a different dimension, and having directed my line of vision towards my lower body, I can see my ivory, pure silk French knickers--plus, my legs and feet, but the remainder of my reflection will have to wait, until I'm feeling brave enough to look at the naked parts of my anatomy. However, between you and me did that thought suggest that I'm capable of overcoming my own saboteurs?

"Charlie," John's hushed voice enquires. "Are you okay?"

"Sorry--I was getting used to seeing the lower part of my body…"

"There's no need to apologise," John assures me. "In fact, because you've avoided catching sight of yourself in the full length mirror, can you describe how it feels seeing that part of your reflection for the first time since the 22$^{nd}$ of June?"

Once again, the silence lingers. "Because of its direct link to the sexual assault, although my reflection should be abhorrent, I think being partially dressed has made it easier. But I'll have to give myself a little more time, before looking at my entire reflection..."

"That's fine Charlie," Bill agrees on their behalf. "But what about the two instances I gave you. Prior to you opening your eyes you stated that you understood..."

Now I'm asking myself, should it be this easy? "Well, the answer to the first is that I was struggling with the concepts of unlimited time and space. However, since you had been granted Security Clearance to gain access to all the Official Records, including the Forsyth File, you knew that eleven months after I had been discharged, from the Category A Research Programme on behalf of the Military, I was admitted to the Mayfield Clinic, and because that seemed to be a relevant turning point in my life, John had wondered whether that might be an acceptable place to begin exploring my complete freedom of speech..."

Pausing, I regroup my thoughts, so that I can respond to the second instance. "But the place, where we should have started the story of my life was the reason why I had been dishonourably discharged from the Programme, and categorized as being an unsuitable candidate for any future Research, which was ludicrous, because my destructive actions had demonstrated what could happen, if a candidate with my unique abilities passed beyond, their stoppable potential, and needed to protect themselves from all conceivable threats..."

As my words drift away, I remain in complete control, and because the silence is almost sacrosanct, it's as if nobody dares disturb it. "Regrettably, it wasn't as easy as it is now to rationalize it, but when my life fell apart, and the mix-up with the prescription drugs occurred, it provided the Major with an excuse to have me Sectioned, and once I was admitted to the Psychiatric Wing of the Clinic things didn't improve, until the arrival..."

Suddenly, the feeling is so strong that yet again, I'm forced to pause, and as if to afford me some additional support, in case I should fall, I realize that John's fingertips are cupping my elbows, as I manage to gasp. "Oh, my God, Professor--Kenneth--Morgan..."

Once again, I feel the warmth of John's breath against my ear, as he confirms that this manifestation is not some figment of a fertile imagination. "Even though I did suggest that perhaps there was someone else, you might need to add to the list of people you had been able trust Charlie, you sound surprised..."

Temporarily rendered speechless, by the clarity of the image in my mind, John lends me some assistance. "If you would like to raise your line of vision, so that you can see his face, then I could hold the two halves of your robe closed..."

Between you and me, it should have been a tempting offer, especially when the image I am holding onto in my mind, confirms that the Professor is standing by the full length mirror, and with my viewpoint diminished, I can see nothing more than those brown corduroy trousers he used to wear every day, and the bottom of his crumpled white coat, but despite everything that he accomplished on my behalf, I remain reticent "I'm not sure..."

Naturally, for our newly reappointed arbitrator being undecided is not an acceptable option. "Since it was the Professor's recovery programme, which enabled you to acquire those unique levels of physical self-control, and emotional self-discipline, which you utilized during the prolonged sexual assault, what is there to be unsure about Charlie?"

Having realized that my reticence is in fact my fearfulness, my response is immediate. "Initially, I thought I might be a disappointment to him, but that's absurd. However, in my mind he's standing in the wrong position..."

Still dissatisfied, Bill demands, "What do you mean by in the wrong position?"

"During the recovery programme he devised for me," this young woman replies with no less immediacy. "Whenever my weight increased, and he wanted me to acknowledge the physical improvements, the Professor would be standing behind me, affording me the necessary encouragement..."

Pausing, it should be noted that our arbitrator remains silent. "Since I was unable to have one last look at the Professor's face before he died, and even though I will have to create an older version from my memory, this seems like a rare opportunity. So provided that John's offer is still open and initially, the two halves of my robe can be kept closed, until I feel comfortable enough to see my upper body then I'm..."

As John interrupts me yet again, I can feel the warmth of his breath against my ear. "That's not a problem Charlie, and if you would like some added reassurance, you can always close your eyes, while we do this..."

"Thank you, but I don't think that will be necessary..."

Then, as soon as I lift my head, the image that greets me is warm and comforting. "One of the Professor's hands is resting on his hip, which is how he would be standing if I was being more difficult than usual, and despite being in the wrong position, he is smiling at the three of us..."

"Do you mean that instead of me, he should be standing behind you Charlie?"

"Yes that's exactly what I mean, but his expression has changed, and although I could never be a disappointment to him, because he turned me into one of his survivors in his eyes I can see that he does disapprove of something..."

"Can you elaborate for us Charlie?"

At least Bill's tone of voice has lost its sharpness. "Having survived a prolonged sexual assault--which was part of the Contract my husband commissioned, and which would have culminated in my premature demise, it was ludicrous for me to imagine that I could pretend that it never happened, by either washing them away or trying to scrub myself clean, and since the Professor helped me develop the resourcefulness needed to overcome my fears, he would regard it as imperative that I reclaim ownership of my body, and if he were standing behind me, he would be encouraging me to find not only the strength, but also the courage to ask him to release the two halves of my robe..."

Silence, and then while I am considering my own admission, neither of my co-conspirators interferes, until the warmth of John's breath is directed at the back of my neck, as he almost whispers.

"So within the present tense of your bedroom, because I included the following proviso--*until you tell me to do otherwise Charlie*--although it's me instead of the Professor, are you strong enough to ask me to release the two halves of your robe?"

"When you referred to our present, although my past and present seemed to collide, I could not see what the future holds for me, but the Professor's image is fading, and because he would be telling me that there's nothing to fear, except fear itself, and I don't want him to leave without knowing that I could do this I suppose I don't have any choice..."

"Okay, then to make it a little less scary on my count, let's do this together--one, and two, and..."

Three, and lowering my line of vision it's far less scary than I had feared, and because his work is done, my mentor is using his raised hand, which was resting on his hip to confirm his departure, while he mouths the words, which were intended to dispel all of my doubts. "The Professor is reminding me that w*hatever the future holds, I am a beautiful woman who is in complete control of her own body, mind and spirit...*"

Suddenly, my legs seem to be incapable of supporting me and yet, somehow we manage to reach the bed, and with John holding onto me, I know it's time I apologised to Bobby's other mother. "If Lorna's still on the landing, then I need to tell her I'm sorry..."

As soon as Bill stepped out onto the landing, Lorna used her fingertips to sweep the tears from her cheeks, before she took hold of his outstretched hand and yet, as he helped her to rise to her feet, she was shaking her head.

"Because if the issues in my own life, I've been foolish enough to believe I could handle anything, but despite Charlie warning me about things that happened after Bobby was born over which she had no control, what I fail to understand is how…"

This was the rarely seen vulnerable side to Lorna Clunnell, but when Bill attempted to stem the fresh flood of tears caused by the mass of conflicting emotions, which had robbed her of the ability to finish her sentence, she tried to stop him from guiding her towards him. "Until I know whether I'm capable of doing this, I can't allow you to be nice to me…"

Having still not learnt that there is *no such thing as can't,* Bill ignored her protest and while he waited for her to regain control of her emotions, he heard the excitable chattering of an almost seven-year-old as Bobby and the Commander returned from their adventure, and relieved that together with John, they had fulfilled the youngster's order, he explained why Lorna was more than capable.

"Considering how difficult it must have been listening to the often horrific details Charlie has revealed, you could have chosen to leave the landing, but you didn't…"

As if it would make things easier, Lorna's face remained buried in his shoulder. "At least I now understand why Charlie reacted like she did, when I came into her room, demanding to know whether the abuse was physical, sexual, or a combination, because this isn't about me fulfilling some need within myself to be reassured that I didn't fail her…"

"And that's even more absurd Lorna, because like Charlie and the Professor, you know you've never disappointed her once--much less failed her in some way…"

"Perhaps I haven't," Lorna persisted. "But if she's going to be working with your resident Consultant Psychologist and Psychotherapist, then as far as my role is concerned, I can appreciate that I have to respect Charlie's right to divulge, as much as she needs to tell me, whenever she feels the need to do so, does that sound achievable or am I being naïve?"

"Although it sounds achievable, what you've overheard is a small part of Charlie's experiences during the last seven years, and because the kind of details, she might choose to share could evoke some powerful feelings, you will need to take care of your own emotional well-being, but then there's no reason, why you couldn't make use of the same service…"

"I'll bear it in mind, especially after listening to you and John this morning made me realize that as far as your work is concerned, it's more complex than I had first imagined, so I suppose that having a resident therapist must be vital…"

"It's not only vital it's essential, and irrespective of whether we have any unresolved issues all Operational Personnel, including John and me, and even the Commander's Personal Assistant are expected to undergo regular Psychological screening, in order to confirm our fitness to practice…"

Easing herself away from him, Lorna admitted, "It's been a long time since I trusted any man--least of all a virtual stranger--to hold me in his arms…"

"It was my pleasure," Bill replied and then, after Lorna used her fingertips to make sure there was no evidence that she had been crying, he stated, "Okay let's do this?"

In my room, even before John stirs beside me, I instinctively know that Lorna and Bill have entered the bedroom, but I wait until she reaches the bed, before I issue an apology.

"I'm so sorry Lorna, but our time together was always far too precious to waste a solitary second, because even when I thought dead would have to be a better option, it was both of you who gave me the strength I needed to carry on…"

After John and Lorna switch places, she takes hold of my hands, so that I can feel the strength pass between us. "And I also owe you an apology, but all that matters is that we find a way to get through this together, like we've done throughout the last seven years…"

Meanwhile on the ground floor when Philip Maddox and Bobby had returned from the underground garage, they were greeted by Margaret who was leaving the study, carrying an empty tray.

"Since Ms. Retand arrived five minutes ago your timing is impeccable Commander. She's in the study, listening to whatever you recorded on your machine, but her working day began at 5:12 and then, the car you ordered, picked her up at 6:30, which meant she didn't have time for anything, except a cup of instant coffee. So after she accepted my offer, I've taken her some toast and strawberry jam--plus, a pot of your favourite Earl Grey tea…"

Pausing, Margaret glanced down at the youngster. "And if you send Bobby down to tell me whenever you're ready I can start serving, what's rapidly turning into brunch…"

Then, as Bobby's eyes widened she bent a little, so that she could speak to him directly. "And did the surprise prove to be better than when you discovered the indoor, heated swimming pool, or after you heard that helicopter arriving, and you found out that Manor Park has its own helicopter pad?"

"When we first arrived at the Manor, I thought it was going to be a boring kind of grown-up place, with nothing for little people to do. Gosh, was I wrong because as far as surprises go, if there is such a thing, it was a million-squillion times better than the last one, especially when Uncle Philip let me sit on a bolster cushion, in the passenger seat, so I could see over the dashboard, and because there's more, I can't wait to tell everyone about it…"

For his part, although Philip Maddox had not been able to detect, his subordinate's whereabouts, or hear the two disagreeing mothers, without raising Bobby's awareness, as Margaret regained her full height, he lifted his arm in the air a little, before extending his finger towards the top of the sweeping staircase, and after she shook her head, he afforded the youngster something to satisfy his inherent curiosity.

"Thank you Margaret. After I've updated Ms Retand, I'll send Bobby down…"

"Gee whizz, Uncle Philip--does that mean I'm going to meet Ms Retand? If she's allowed to be on her own, in your private study with the special red phone, then she must be ever so important?"

"Sarah-Roxanna is my Personal Assistant, and because she knows where I should be and who I should be with twenty-four hours a day, she's a very important young lady…"

"Wow Uncle Philip--if she's that important are you sure you want me to meet her?"

"Why on earth would I not want you to meet her Bobby, especially when I don't have many visitors, never mind guests who stay for more than a few hours, and you've had quite an impact on my life. So I'm confident that she would like to meet you?"

As soon as they entered the study, before Sarah-Roxanna Retand vacated the Commander's Executive chair, she removed the earphones through which she had been listening to the notes and instructions, Philip Maddox had dictated late into the early hours of that new day. "Good morning Commander…"

"Good morning, Sarah-Roxanna--please sit back down. I'm afraid things have been a little topsy-turvy this morning, which means that we haven't as yet had any breakfast…"

Feeling Bobby's hand tug at his sleeve, the Commander corrected his oversight. "And this young man is Bobby who I'm sure is delighted to meet you…"

"Hello Bobby…"

"Hello…"

Overcome by a sudden charming coyness, Bobby's greeting had been hushed, and when the Commander felt the same tugging at his sleeve and he crouched a little, as if he did not want Sarah-Roxanna to hear him, Bobby used his hand to shield his mouth. "Uncle Philip, don't you think she's terribly young to have such an important job…"

"Trust me Bobby, since Sarah-Roxanna was destined to become my P.A., she has all the necessary qualifications, including being able to speak four foreign languages…"

"Whoa!" exclaimed Bobby. "Four languages, she must have started to learn them when she was my age, and she is so pretty Uncle Philip. Does she have a husband?"

"Why do you want to know Bobby, unless you're thinking about proposing to her?"

In response, Bobby giggled and still shielding his mouth, he dared to correct the Commander. "Don't be silly Uncle Philip. I don't think little people, even little people who are about to be seven-years-old are allowed to get married. Besides, Lorna and mum might be very cross with me, if I proposed to anyone without first asking their permission…"

Supressing his smile and yet, knowing from the unique bond between them that she would accept his challenge, Philip Maddox maintained eye contact with Sarah-Roxanna. "That's a shame Bobby, especially when my P.A. doesn't have a husband, and because she has to work such long and often unsociable hours, she doesn't get to meet many suitable young men. Isn't that correct Ms Retand?"

Resisting the urge to counterchallenge her Commanding Officer, Sarah-Roxanna chose to address Bobby. "Although working as the Commander's P.A. does necessitate that I work long and often unsociable hours, by the time I signed the Official Secrets Act, I had no doubts whatsoever about the seriousness of the commitment I was undertaking…"

Then, Sarah-Roxanna raised her line of vision, until she achieved eye contact with Philip Maddox. "With all due respect Sir, your breakfast will be delayed even longer, if we don't address the upshot of the voice mails you left on my machine at 3:12 this morning…"

"Of course…"

"So after preparing the Ex-Order you requested, it was delivered to the Chambers of Judge George Matthew Porter by one of our Couriers, where his P.A. acknowledged its safe arrival at 8:13. Judge Porter seemed like the best candidate, because not only has he handled similar requests in the past, he's also not due to preside in Court until this afternoon, which means that Special Operations should be in possession of the Order by lunchtime…"

"That's even faster than I had anticipated…"

After acknowledging the Commander's nodded approval through a polite smile, Sarah-Roxanna added, "And with regard to your second request Sir, from our Administration Team, I have assigned three people to conduct an in depth investigation into Mark Daltry's parentage, and his subsequent adoption into the Daltry household…"

Yet again, Philip Maddox felt that small hand tug at his sleeve, and after he crouched a little, Bobby explained, "Golly, if Sarah-Roxanna got up at FIVE O'CLOCK, and she did all of those things by HALF PAST SIX, then she must be almost superhuman…"

"Indeed she is Bobby, and while we finish discussing today's agenda would you go down to the kitchen, and tell Margaret that one way or another, we're ready for her to start serving breakfast…"

"Gee whizz, you bet I will Uncle Philip, but what's an Ex-Order?"

"Because it's a little complicated Bobby, I'll attempt to explain it later..."

Fortunately, the Commander and Sarah-Roxanna managed to avoid another request from Bobby for additional clarification, when a gentle tap on the open study door announced the reappearance of the missing subordinates, and because their arrival rendered the occupants inside silent, John opted to greet their Commanding Officer's P.A.

"Good morning Sarah-Roxanna, what a pleasant surprise…"

"Good morning boys, I do hope that while you're classified as being, unavailable for the foreseeable future you're managing to stay out of trouble…"

"What can I say?" replied John. "Except that it was destined to be a dirty job, but since someone had to do it, our Commanding Officer decided to reassign us…"

"According to the Commander that so called dirty job includes, improvised football matches, playing chess or backgammon, and board games like Twister, but then as you stated, I suppose somebody had to do it. Besides, your little secret is safe with me…"

Mindful of his manners, and what he had been taught about not interrupting anyone, Bobby waited until Sarah-Roxanna fell silent, before posing his question.

"Mr Powell, have you and Mr Bland managed to resolve the disagreement, which caused my two mothers to exchange those cross words?"

"Yes Bobby, although at times, it was a little tricky, John and I have managed to fulfil the direct order you gave me, so there should be no more cross words between your mum and Lorna…"

"Phew that's a relief. So while Uncle Philip finishes talking to Sarah-Roxanna, I could go upstairs to say hello and then, while we're having breakfast, I can tell everyone about the most AMAZING adventure, Uncle Philip and I have had this morning…"

However, when Bobby neared the doorway, John was ready to block his exit, while Bill dropped down onto one knee, so he could explain. "Your mum and Lorna need to discuss some boring grown-up stuff, so it might be best if we don't disturb them…"

"But aren't they going to have any breakfast, and what about Lorna playing football?"

"They will get some breakfast." John reassured the youngster. "Because we're going to ask Margaret, if she'll take a tray upstairs, and as for the football, there's no reason why the four of us can't play without Lorna…"

Initially, Bobby seemed unsure, but then he tilted his head a little to one side. "I guess it would be the first time the four of us would be alone, which sounds pretty cool, but when it comes to the football, although we don't know whether Sarah-Roxanna would be any good, I suppose that if she finishes her work, she might be able to come and join us…"

"Gosh Bobby," gasped Sarah-Roxanna, as she placed her right hand against her heart. "I'm flattered that you'd consider me to be worthy of such an honour, and if the Commander allows me to set aside some time, I'm sure that together, you and I might surprise those two reprobates. In fact, if you come over here I'll let you into a closely guarded secret…"

Without needing a second invitation, Bobby scurried back across the study, so that Sarah-Roxanna could whisper something in his ear, which caused the youngster to exclaim, "Golly gee whizz that's brill!"

"Now since this is going to be our secret weapon, I think it merits a high five don't you Bobby?" Hesitating long enough for their hands to collide in mid-air, Sarah-Roxanna added, "But first young man, you need to go and eat some breakfast…"

Then, when Bobby turned around, because his cheeky grin was beaming from ear to ear, for his partner's benefit, John remarked, "Don't know about you Bill, but I think that impish smile means that they are conspiring against us?"

"Oh no doubt it's some kind of strategic tactic, but before battle can commence, as Sarah-Roxanna suggested, we need to have some breakfast, don't we Bobby? Come on, we can go down to the kitchen together, and while I talk to Margaret you can wash your hands, before you sit down at the table--and that's not a request--it's a direct order…"

"Yes Sir," Bobby confirmed. "Isn't Sarah-Roxanna brilliant? As well as being clever she's so pretty, but when I asked, if she had a husband Uncle Philip thought I wanted to propose to her, which would have been silly, especially when I was thinking that unless the Commander has people staying, he must be a little lonely in the Manor with nobody to help him, except of course Margaret. So I thought it would be cool if…"

Before Bobby could embarrass anyone, Bill interrupted him, "Excuse me young man, since breakfast has been delayed for far too long, will you please hurry up…"

Precisely fourteen minutes later, when Philip Maddox joined them at the dining table, in between forkfuls of scrambled egg, and still more sausages and rashers of bacon, Bobby was describing his latest adventure to Bland and Powell. "Like Mr O'Keefe did when he drove us up to the Manor in the classic British Racing Green Jaguar, Uncle Philip put a bolster cushion on the passenger's seat, so that I could see over the dashboard…"

"And did the Commander take the Spyder Porsche for a spin around the grounds?"

"Gosh Mr Powell, since it's number one on my list of all-time favourite classic cars, I thought that I knew all the car's specifications, but no computer download could have prepared me for being driven, while I was in the passenger seat--or when…"

As Bobby's words drifted away, his gaze came to rest on his hero the Commander. However, since Philip Maddox knew that for as long as he remained at Manor Park, in addition to his--*Uncle Philip*--being available if anything were to upset Bobby, unbeknown to Charlie and Lorna there was something else, he had decided would be in that young man's best interests, and because there might never be a more advantageous moment, than the four of them eating alone, he chose to open up a window of opportunity for his subordinates.

"Despite asking you not to share our secret, I am prepared to give you permission to tell my subordinates what we did--provided that you start calling them--John and Bill and only address them by their formal names Mr Bland or Mr Powell, if something upsets you, and for some reason you are unable to locate my whereabouts…"

"So like the cross words this morning, they would know something was wrong?"

"Yes Bobby, that's exactly what I meant…"

"But if I tell them what we did, I wouldn't want you to get into trouble…"

"Because we were on private land I won't get into any trouble. But if you don't finish your breakfast, I might have to deal with some cross words from your two mothers…"

Having finished his sausage and bacon, while Bobby turned John and Bill into their co-conspirators, he resumed his routine of talking in between forkfuls of scrambled egg.

"Mr oops--silly me," Bobby corrected himself. "I meant to say John and Bill--so let's start again, when we reached the main gates Uncle Philip turned the Porsche around, and coming back down past the lake, and into the curving bit, which is like a chicane on a race track, the Commander let me sit on his knee…"

"Wow Bobby," John declared. "Did the Commander allow you to help him drive?"

"He did, and while Uncle Philip was controlling the pedals, even though there were four hands on the steering wheel, because I've read the Highway Code several times, I knew that mine were in the correct ten to two position, which meant that if anyone had been watching us, it would have looked as if I was driving the Porsche. As I told Margaret, it was a million zillion times better than when I discovered the indoor heated swimming pool, and the helicopter pad, but I guess you can see why mum and Lorna would be upset not with me, because I won't be seven, until another three weeks and one…"

Pausing, Bobby counted the remaining days on his left hand, by using his thumb to consecutively touch each one of the fingertips. "And two, three, four, five days and fifteen hours--but that's the reason why they would be very, and I do mean--VERY--cross with Uncle Philip, because he was the grown-up who was responsible for taking care of me…"

When Philip Maddox had first entered the dining room, because John and Bill had acknowledged his silent gesture, which each of them had been given--albeit at different times in the early hours of the morning--after managing to supress a smile at Bobby's reference to his Commanding Officer's responsibilities, when acting as an appropriate adult, as he had been instructed, Bill began to ease that window of opportunity open.

"As far as I'm aware nobody else, not even John or I have been invited to sit in either of the front seats--much less drive the Spyder Porsche…"

"But Uncle Philip, wouldn't that make me the first person to ever be allowed to drive your most prized possession?"

"That's correct Bobby…"

"Whoa--that makes this morning the very best morning I've ever had in my life…"

Taking into account that Bobby was only seven, or whenever it suited his purpose--in his own defence--he was capable of pleading that he was only six years three weeks, five days and fifteen hours old, this time it was Philip Maddox who found himself having to supress a smile, and because he needed to bring the youngster back into the realms of reality, he offered this remarkable young man an explanation.

"Perhaps I should explain Bobby that as far as those two are concerned, because I've had first-hand experience, not only with regard to their unique driving abilities, whenever the need for excessive speed should arise, but also some of their more risqué manoeuvres, I've never felt that I could trust either of them not to test the legendary capabilities of my prized possession, instead of treating her with the respect she deserves…"

Suddenly, Bobby seemed pensive, but then he confirmed that his knowledge extended way beyond the specifications of his number one classic car. "According to the legend, it was estimated that the film star James Dean must have been driving at between 110 and 120 miles per hour, when he lost control of his brand new Spyder Porsche. So are John and Bill allowed to drive that fast?"

In response to the Commander's affirmative nod, John opened that window of opportunity a little wider, by divulging more details.

"Yes we are Bobby. But in our defence, the incident to which the Commander is referring took place when there were four people in the Jaguar, including Sarah-Roxanna, and because we were due to fly to Rome, so that your *Uncle Philip* could preside at some negotiations, which were classified as Secret, Bill was driving us all to the airfield, when we intercepted a request from our Communications Centre on behalf of other Operatives in the same vicinity, who required urgent assistance in order to force a suspect vehicle to stop…"

When John fell silent, Bill finished divulging the remaining details. "After the Commander instructed me to respond, it was necessary to drive in excess of 115 M.P.H. and to avoid a collision with the suspect car, together with the other Special Operations driver we had no choice, except to perform very precise emergency stops…"

"Wow," gasped Bobby, as his eyes widened. "That must have been so exciting. Did the car you were chasing contain people who had done some bad things?"

Having finished his scrambled egg and yet, uninterested in anything, except for the answers to his questions, after Philip Maddox finished preparing a slice of toast with low fat spread and seedless strawberry jam, he had exchanged Bobby's breakfast plate with the clean side plate, and because all three adults knew that thanks to the inquisitive mind of an almost seven-year-old, the answer to each question would generate another question until they achieved their objective, and as if he was acting on auto-pilot, the young man picked up one half of his slice of toast, and while John answered his question, he took his first bite.

"In the rear of the suspect vehicle, there was one gentleman, and his female companion, who were both classified in our computer records as--*Persons of Interest*--and before they left the country the Special Operatives wanted to Interview them…"

Then, while Bobby was considering his next question, he took a second bite from his slice of toast. "But if it took a high speed chase in order to stop them, surely that must have made the people in the back seat even more suspect?"

"Although it would have made us more suspicious," John replied. "Because we didn't have any actual proof, we could do nothing more than Interview them informally…"

"And what about Sarah-Roxanna, I know that she can go with the Commander, because she told me that she has signed, something to do with secrets, but I can't…"

Ready to rescue the youngster, Bill explained, "It's called the Official Secrets Act, and it means that anyone who signs it, isn't allowed to either discuss or disclose anything about their work to anyone, unless they have the necessary permission…"

"So, does everyone who works with Uncle Philip have to sign it?"

"Yes, everyone who is selected by Commander Philip Maddox to join the Special Operations Team has to sign the Official Secrets Act…"

Then, as if to eliminate every last shred of doubt that anything was going to escape his enquiring mind, Bobby asked his next question. "Because he is the Commander, I know that Uncle Philip wouldn't have been worried, but what about Sarah-Roxanna? Surely, she must have found the high speed chase frightening?"

This time, all three men found it necessary to supress a smile, at the prospect of Sarah-Roxanna being frightened of anything or anyone, but sticking to their hastily prepared script, it was John who corrected Bobby's misconception.

"While I'm sure that Sarah-Roxanna would be flattered by your concern for her wellbeing Bobby, but there isn't any need…."

"But surely, she must have found it a little bit scary?"

Despite the seriousness of their primary objective, John's smile remained soft and understanding. "I'm sorry Bobby, but there's nothing about the incident she would have found scary, because together with everybody else who needs to carry out operational duties such as accompanying your Uncle Philip if his personal attendance is needed at negotiations like the ones in Rome--after he had selected Sarah-Roxanna to become his Personal Assistant, she had to undertake a course in unarmed combat and advanced firearms training to a standard, which was predetermined by our Commanding Officer…"

Suddenly, the atmosphere changed, and as if Bobby were considering the implications with the same disturbing calmness, Philip Maddox had originally detected in his Goddaughter, six months after her mother had been killed, her son swallowed his remaining toast, and drank the tea in his bone china mug before offering a response, which for once left his subordinates lost for words--albeit temporarily.

"So if Sarah-Roxanna knows how to use a gun, then that would explain why you and Bill have been wearing shoulder holsters, which you've tried to keep hidden under your jackets presumably, so that I wouldn't ask any questions before you were ready to tell me…"

While his subordinates were searching for what he knew would be, the right words, Philip Maddox chose to respond on their behalf. "How observant of you Bobby--and do you have any idea why the three of you are staying at Manor Park?"

"Although I might be a little person Uncle Philip, I'm not stupid…"

"Gosh, if I gave you that impression Bobby, then please accept my sincere apology, because the one thing nobody could ever accuse you of being is stupid…"

Having recovered from their temporary lapse, as soon as the Commander cast a glance in their direction, having found the right words, Bill was prepared to add the cavalry's own endorsement. "In fact, from the way in which you keep achieving checkmate in less moves, with every new game we play, it's obvious that you have the skill of an adult opponent, who finds themselves trapped inside a little person's body…"

"Am I really?" asked Bobby, before answering his own question. "But I suppose opponents don't realize that when one of them keeps challenging me, the reason why they don't win is because I've managed to work out, what Uncle Philip said is--*their strategy*…"

"For someone who's not yet seven-years-old that's a remarkable achievement," John congratulated him, before he asked. "But you still haven't answered the Commander's question about whether you know, why all three of you are staying at the Manor?"

Expressing his reticence, Bobby sighed, "Now this might sound a little creepy. Although I don't know, where it comes from sometimes I sense things are going to happen, before they do--but despite being aware that a bad man was going to hurt mum, because I didn't want Lorna to worry I never told her, especially when mum had explained how she wouldn't be able to contact us or see us for what seemed like forever and ever. Then, once we were all in the same place--like John and Bill with their guns--although mum has tried to keep the bruises on her wrists hidden, so that I wouldn't want to know what had caused them, they made me think about whether I had been right about the bad man hurting her…"

Confirmation that Charlie's pregnancy had not been terminated had led the Commander to consider, whether her son might have inherited if not all, then perhaps at least some of his mother's unique abilities. But since this was neither the right time, nor the appropriate place to examine Bobby's capabilities, Philip Maddox chose to overlook his revelation. "As Bill has suggested, despite being a little person you certainly managed to handle that situation better than many adults would have done…"

"But I still need to know whether someone did manage to hurt my mum…"

Irrespective of the eventual outcome, in addition to Bobby being able to trust all three of them implicitly, Philip Maddox needed to ensure that the misrepresentations--throughout his mother's lifetime--were not passed down to this recently discovered next generation, and after taking into account the challenge faced and yet, met by Charlie Daltry during the Interview, then to the best of his ability, it was the Commander's intention to speak the truth, the whole truth and nothing, except for the truth.

"As much as I regret it Bobby, someone did manage…"

Unlike his subordinates, who had learnt from the day they had been hand-picked to join the Special Operations Team, the cavalry watched in astonishment, as an almost seven-year-old dared to interrupt their Commanding Officer with his disillusioned outburst.

"As the Commander, you're supposed to have control over everything. But if that's true, how could you have let such a terrible thing happen?"

Despite detecting his subordinate's readiness to defend his impeccable reputation, from its resting position, palm down on the dining table, they needed no other indication of his intent, except for the slightest upward movement of the fingers on his left hand to prevent their intervention, which left Philip Maddox free to offer Bobby his truthful explanation.

"Sadly Bobby many years ago, a misinterpretation of a vital piece of information meant that your mother chose not to tell anyone about something sinister, which had been ongoing for the last three years of her life. So until I found out, I was powerless to protect my own Goddaughter …"

"Surely, there shouldn't have been anything," argued Bobby. "That mum couldn't tell you about Uncle Philip--unless of course--it was something secret…"

"While I'm sure your mother will explain what happened, since the three of us were either present during or have subsequently listened to what was recorded yesterday evening, I can confirm that it took a long time, and a tremendous amount of courage before my Goddaughter was in a position to be able to not only protect you and Lorna, but also why she felt it necessary to avoid having any direct contact during the last three months. However, at 3:49 on 22nd June, after Central Control passed our Surveillance Centre an intruder alert at the Special Operations property your mother shared with her husband, at 3:59 they advised Sarah-Roxanna of the position, and after she updated me without any hesitation, I reassigned John and Bill to not only investigate, but also to protect my Goddaughter…"

At last, the sharpness in Bobby's voice began to diminish. "Is that the real reason why John and Bill have been trying to keep their guns hidden beneath their jackets?"

"Yes Bobby," Philip Maddox replied. "Initially, they were assigned to escort your mother home from Paris three months ago, but on the 23rd of June, they advised me that via the High Court, they needed a Protective Custody Order in respect of my Goddaughter and then, late yesterday evening, Lorna also agreed that both of you should be protected by a different Protective Custody Order, which has been assigned in the name Clunnell…"

"Well, I guess being in Protective Custody sounds pretty cool and presumably, the bad man hurting mum had something to do with my two mothers exchanging cross words?"

Philip Maddox nodded his agreement. "That's right Bobby, but I think that now you can appreciate why I wanted you to know what you should do, if anything were to upset you and for some reason you are unable to find me…"

Tilting his head a little to one side, Bobby suggested, "But now that I know a great deal more Uncle Philip, if you sent me on one of those training thingamajigs and I learnt self-defence, and everything about guns I could find the bad man, and make sure that he couldn't hurt either of my two mothers ever again…"

For the second time, despite the Commander detecting his subordinates trying to suppress their smiles at his predicament, Philip Maddox managed to sustain, the same calm professionalism for which he was renown at the negotiating table.

"Of course that's a possibility, but what if there was more than one, and they turned out to be bigger and stronger than you, is there anything else you could do Bobby?"

Initially Bobby looked pensive, before he announced with the same boldness. "Now that we can talk about the guns, under their jackets, I suppose that after running to find Mr Bland and Mr Powell, I could issue them with another direct order to find the bad men and then, they could help me shoot them. Is that what you meant Uncle Philip?"

More than anyone, having found himself in a hole, Philip Maddox should have known when to stop digging, and before things could become even more complicated, he opted to alter his approach. "That's not exactly what I meant Bobby, although issuing my subordinates with a direct order to assist you would be a good thing, until you're old enough to become a Special Operative, I'm afraid you aren't allowed to shoot anybody…"

"Oh I hadn't thought about that Uncle Philip," agreed Bobby, with a detectable degree of somewhat disturbing disappointment. "But I suppose that unlike the driving, mum and Lorna would be very cross with me, if I was arrested for shooting someone…"

"Yes I think they might be a little cross with both of us," The Commander confirmed. "However, running to find Mr Bland and Mr Powell was an excellent idea…"

"Okay, as you suggested earlier, if I think something is wrong, and for some reason I don't know where you are, then I'll go and find John and Bill…"

Finally, the slight upward movement of the Commander's entire left hand was the signal the cavalry needed to add their contribution to the proceedings, and in an attempt to address Bobby's apparent fixation over shooting people, John explained, "Although there can be no doubt that the bad man--or even bad men--would need to be punished, like the people involved in the high speed chase, sometimes we do want to Interview Persons of Interest. So can you think of a reason why we would need to do that Bobby?"

At first, while Bobby was considering the various options his pensiveness seemed to be heightened, before he replied, "Well, I suppose you might want to Interview, whoever hurt my mum so you could find out why they did such a bad thing and then, in order to stop them from doing the same thing to anybody else's mother, you could shoot them…"

Accepting that in the short-term, nothing was going to dampen the young man's determination to shoot someone, Bill chose to concede defeat on their behalf. "Yes I suppose that if it were to prove necessary Bobby, we could shoot someone…"

"Okay, I'm glad we've sorted that out. Now I've finished my breakfast, and since I'm sure that I was supposed to brush my teeth after I'd eaten instead of before, if I promise not to disturb mum and Lorna when I go upstairs, please may I leave the table Uncle Philip?"

After their arrival Philip Maddox had noted that because his upbringing had been based upon traditional values, including civility and good manners, there could only be one answer to the politeness of his request. "Of course you can leave the table young man…"

"Thank you," replied Bobby, but after carrying his dirty dishes to the trolley Margaret used to transport things, between the kitchen and dining room he ground to a halt, so that he could ask one final question. "And is it also all right, if I tell Sarah-Roxanna that provided she's finished her work, we're almost ready to go outside and play football?"

Like everything else, while planning how best to ensure that Bobby would have a better understanding of why--for the vast majority of the time--John and Bill were wearing shoulder holsters, which contained real guns, every detail had been meticulously checked, but once all of his questions had been answered, it had been agreed that their meeting should end on a less serious note, and choosing to tease the youngster, Philip Maddox replied, "I'm afraid that isn't acceptable Bobby. Instead, you can tell Sarah-Roxanna that at a convenient point, she can stop what she's doing, so that she can come outside and play football..."

"Phew Uncle Philip for a moment you had me really worried, because I thought you were being serious..."

Then, before Bobby could escape from the dining room, John and Bill left the table, and once his partner was blocking the only exit, John explained. "I'm afraid we can't allow you to leave, until you tell us what Sarah-Roxanna whispered to you..."

"Because it's a secret," argued Bobby. "I can't tell you..."

"Firstly, since there's no such thing as CAN'T, what you mean is that you WON'T tell us, and secondly, you haven't signed the Official Secrets Act, and because we're experts when it comes to making people tell us things, we could threaten to tickle you and keep tickling you, until you can't stand it any longer..."

Despite Bobby's attempt to outmanoeuvre Bill, two strong arms caught hold of him and swept him off the floor and yet, the youngster was giggling, as he shrieked, "Put me down or you'll be sorry..."

Then, when it made no difference and John continued to approach them, Bobby sought the Commander's assistance by pointing out their disregard for the rules.

"This isn't fair Uncle Philip, because not only did they leave the table, without first asking your permission they also want to cheat by making me tell them what Sarah-Roxanna's secret weapon is going to be ..."

"Yes I can see what they're doing, and if they don't want to spend some considerable time sitting on the naughty step, then I must insist that my subordinates stand down..."

Pausing, Philip Maddox waited, and thanks to some rushed forward planning when Bland and Powell failed to obey his order, their Commanding Officer was in a position where he could sustain the pretence of their disobedience, "Gentlemen I'm growing impatient..."

Then, when Bland and Powell still seemed to be reluctant to release their captive, much to Bobby's delight, there was an intentional sharpness in his hero's voice, as the Commander declared, "THIS IS YOUR FINAL WARNING gentlemen. Now kindly put Bobby down and allow him to leave the dining room..."

"If you insist Sir..."

As soon as Bill allowed his hostage to slither to the floor, the young man beat a hasty retreat, but while the cavalry were gathering together the remaining dirty dishes, fortunately the three of them did not need to suppress their smiles, when they overheard the exchange of dialogue between Bobby and the Commander's Personal Assistant, which much to their relief did not contain a single reference to either guns or shooting people.

"Although they threatened to tickle me, even if Uncle Philip hadn't stopped them, I would never have told John and Bill about how you grew up with two older brothers, who forced you to join them whenever they played football, which means that like Lorna instead of being useless, you've actually had masses and masses of practise..."

"Gosh Bobby you were so brave, especially when I know how badly behaved those two Operatives can be, and you're right, if they had forced you to tell them under duress, they would have been cheating. So while you go upstairs and brush your teeth, I'll finish inputting the remainder of this letter on the Commander's behalf and then, by the time you come back down I'll be free to come outside, so that together we can beat our opponents..."

# PART FIVE

# Unfinished Business

# and

# Consequences

**July 3$^{rd}$  9:45**

Gee whizz, as my excitable son would exclaim in amazement at how far we have had to travel, in order to arrive at a place where I have to accept responsibility for the consequences of either my actions--or my inactions, which seems to have been the story of my life in so much as I have been damned if I did, and damned if I did not, and while I am not likely to admit it to anyone except you--my invisible audience, the cavalry would have good reason to accuse me of hypocrisy, especially when I was so opposed to the idea of re-entering into any kind of a therapeutic relationship on the grounds that it was unnecessary.

Now we all know the adage relating to *famous last words* and in my case, instead of being a waste of time, therapy is turning out to be a most efficient way in which to dispose of any other outstanding business, until all that will remain is the aforementioned consequences, but before I can get so far ahead of myself that I am unable to locate the place, where I first went astray--prior to my next session--perhaps I should simplify things by explaining the means, method and motive behind this phenomenal occurrence.

**June 30**

Having listened to the Interview, my Godfather had gone to H.Q., accompanied by Sarah-Roxanna, so that they could start to prepare for the forthcoming negotiations, and while we were assembled at the communal breakfast table, when Bobby queried their absence Bill had reassured him that his Uncle Philip would be back at the Manor in time for dinner.

Then, for their role in the ensuing conspiracy, the cavalry had arranged to distract my inquisitive son by taking him outside, so that together with Lorna the four of them could play yet more football, while for my part I was upstairs in my own room, trying to reason with myself through the reflection in the mirror on my dressing table, when a gentle tap on my door announced Margaret's arrival.

"Dr Thomas James has arrived Charlie. As you requested, together with his companion, they are waiting for you downstairs in the Commander's study…"

"Thank you," I heard this woman reply, but as I stood up so that I could look at myself in the full length mirror, I sought a second opinion. "Do I look all right Margaret?"

"You look amazing Charlie." Margaret replied, as she moved into the room, so that we could both see my reflection. "In my capacity as housekeeper, I'm responsible for the welfare of everyone who comes to the Manor, and since the three of you arrived, your presence has touched the lives of everyone here, including the Commander and even Mr Bland and Mr Powell. It's almost as if the three of you have put them in touch with something they had to sacrifice a long time ago…"

As Margaret paused, I did not even attempt to interrupt her, because they were not merely words, they were pearls of wisdom from someone who neither had anything to lose, nor anything to gain from sharing her observations with me.

"And while I've tried to pin it down, the only common denominator I can find is your son, and he needs both of his mothers, especially the one who must have been courageous enough to give birth to him without anybody knowing and then, keep his identity a secret for so long, which is why you have to go downstairs and do whatever is necessary to dispose of all the bad things, and because you're the closest thing he has to any kind of family, you have to trust that your Godfather will handle the rest on your behalf…"

This was not the first one to one talk Margaret and I had shared, and I was grateful for her frankness. "Thank you Margaret, as usual your insight is inspirational…"

"You're very welcome, and as you might expect from my primary role as housekeeper downstairs in the study, there's ample coffee and tea inside the insulated pots…"

A few minutes later, when I was approaching the study door, which was partially open I could hear two voices, and because one of them belonged to a female, and from somewhere in my past life, it sounded as if it should have been recognizable with a little less trepidation--like Margaret--my gentle tap on the door announced my imminent entrance.

As soon as I pushed the door open, I noticed that there was a tall, slimly built gentleman standing by the window, and from his profile I could tell that he was smiling as he watched, what I knew was my son and his decoy detail playing football, and I found it reassuring that even though he had not met him--from what he could see--he had an awareness of not only Bobby, but also Lorna and the special bond that will bind the three of us together forever, even if my forever might only be a few days, weeks, months, or maybe if I am a very fortunate young mother it might be years, and having reached that climatic moment a chinking sound drew my attention to the cabinet, and I had been right, the young woman was no stranger, and as she turned to look at me my response was immediate.

"Oh my God Susanna, what a wonderful surprise…"

"Hello Charlie, it has been a long time and from the background information, which accompanied the urgent request for Dr James to handle your case, it would seem that perhaps it's been far too long…"

Of course, between you and me we knew that it had indeed been far too long, but before I could offer Susanna my agreement, Dr James turned away from the window and began moving towards the two armchairs, which were separated by a small occasional table and angled, so that they were not directly facing each other.

"It's a pleasure to meet you Mrs Daltry, and since we're going to be working together, I trust that you have no objections to me addressing you as Charlie…"

"Since I have presumed that it would be acceptable to call you Thomas, I have no objections whatsoever to you addressing me by my Christian name…"

Having reached the armchairs, Dr James invited me to join him. "Why don't we make ourselves comfortable Charlie?" Pausing, he waited until we were both seated, before he began to explain. "Considering the level of discretion needed whenever we find ourselves dealing with sensitive issues involving, not only people such as yourself, but also a Special Operative who may need to work through something in connection with an assignment, for obvious reasons, we do not record sessions. However, I do need to be able to highlight significant events and notable points. So from the onset of our therapeutic relationship I would like to make notes, and since I do not want anything between us to be hidden at any time, you can ask to read anything I have written…"

As I had been listening, I was forced to admit that I was impressed, not only by his directness, but also his offer of complete transparency between us. So my smile was intended to reflect my satisfaction with the arrangements he had made on my behalf.

"As Susanna has no doubt explained, when it comes to considering the consequences of my actions, because I have an appalling track record, I think it's imperative that you do make notes…"

"I'm glad you approve Charlie. However, from Professor Morgan's notations, which are documented in his file and Susanna's confirmation, I'm aware of the circumstances, both prior to your admission and then, your subsequent discharge from the Psychiatric Wing of the Mayfield Clinic. So with regard to your alleged appalling track record, I'm reminded that given a certain set of circumstances, the reality often is that in order to produce the right results, sometimes people are forced to do the wrong things…"

As much as I appreciated what I perceived to be the equivalent of a defence for either my action or my inactions, I released a quite spontaneous laugh. "And I am reminded Thomas that *reality is an illusion--albeit a persistent one…*"

"Albert Einstein…"

Touché and now I was beginning to think that this Psychotherapist and I were well matched, and tilting my head a little to one side, I congratulated him. "I'm impressed Thomas, and because there is still some unfinished business, which needs to be addressed and in connection with that there are some dark areas, which need to be illuminated…"

"That's interesting, but if I might venture to introduce another quotation, then according to Henry Ford, *"No matter how fast the light travels darkness gets there sooner…"*

Surely nobody could have denied that to be true? In fact, when one considers that prior to June 22$^{nd}$, I have always been searching for the light, but every time there could have been an opportunity, I would discover that either my father--or the man I had had the misfortune to marry--had made sure that prior to my arrival, the darkness had descended.

Despite being temporarily lost in the past tense, neither Thomas nor Susanna deemed to disturb my rationalization process, until I lifted my head and attempted to apologise. "I'm so sorry, but your reference to the darkness always arriving before the light seemed to sum up so many things in my life…"

Over by the window, Susanna had been watching the football match, which was still taking place at the front of the Manor, but even before I finished speaking, she started moving back to the cabinet, so that she could collect two of the insulated coffee mugs, and when she placed them on the occasional table Thomas and I expressed our gratitude simultaneously, "Thank you Susanna…"

"Oh believe me, it was my pleasure," Susanna replied, as she returned to the cabinet, so that she could collect her own coffee, but after she picked up a sizable pile of folders without a trace of remorse, she admitted, "In fact, since I have run out of excuses to delay my departure, I have no choice except to retreat to the dining room. But I will be hoping that one of you might find a valid reason to rescue me from these case notes, which will either be indecipherable--or alternatively--open to misinterpretation…"

After Susanna's reluctant departure, Thomas explained that two years before Professor Morgan's sudden death, the Commander had decided that in addition to the Mayfield Clinic remaining a Special Operations Medical Facility, it should have its own Resident Therapist, and since Susanna had wanted to work alongside Dr Thomas James, I realized that it had proved to be most advantageous, because she had been able to expedite matters, not only in connection with the circumstances surrounding my admission to the Psychiatric Wing of the Mayfield Clinic, but also how my relationship with Susanna, and her colleague Debra had become a fundamental part of my recovery programme, until my eventual discharge back into the real world with an entirely new perspective on life.

Then, while we drank our coffee, we spent some time discussing his priorities, including dealing with the unresolved issues as a result of the prolonged sexual assault, in the early hours of the 22$^{nd}$ of June and the incident at the airfield, especially when the arrangements for my father's funeral had not as yet been finalized by my step-mother Helen, but Thomas was eager to confirm that nothing should remain hidden, and after returning his insulated mug to the table he extended his smile, before he began his explanation.

"It's my understanding Charlie that you have been advised that when Commander Maddox asked me to work with you, he granted me Security Clearance to access any Official File which might assist me, including what happened at the Research Facility. So I do have an awareness of your unique abilities…"

Pausing, Thomas waited for me to nod my understanding and yet, I declined to offer him any verbal confirmation, until he finished his explanation. "Then during a subsequent face to face meeting, your Godfather told me about the impact your son's presence has had on everyone at the Manor, including Mr Bland and Mr Powell…"

Despite opting to remain silent, the warmth of this mother's smile seemed to necessitate that Thomas write something down on his notepad, before he continued, "In fact, from the way Philip described playing chess and backgammon--or being able to participate in the improvised football matches, it was hard to differentiate between, your Godfather's enthusiasm for keeping Bobby entertained, and his own personal enjoyment, and from what I've seen this morning, it would seem that his enthusiasm is reciprocated by his subordinates, and because that young man seems to have somehow managed to put all three grown-up's in touch with their inner children--subject to your approval Charlie--I would like to meet not only Bobby, but also his other mother Lorna  Clunnell…"

At last, this mother was prepared to re-join the conversation. "Actually, if you hadn't suggested being introduced to my son, then I intended to do so Thomas…"

"That's also most interesting, because now I'm curious to know the reason why you wanted me to meet Bobby?"

Yet again, the image brought a warm smile to my weary features. "In order to answer your question you need to take into consideration that this morning, after we had finished breakfast for their part in the conspiracy, John and Bill had arranged to distract my inquisitive son by taking him outside, so that together with Lorna, the four of them would be playing football, before your arrival at the Manor…"

"Excuse me for interrupting Charlie," Thomas apologised. "But since you wanted me to meet Bobby, why was there such an elaborate plan to distract him?"

"As I was about to explain, during a recent opportunity for my Godfather, and his subordinates to spend some time with my son without anyone else being present, amongst other things, Bobby found out that he had been right and *a bad man--or even bad men*--had hurt me, which were his exact words, he has developed an overprotectiveness towards me. So if we are going to be working together at the Manor, it won't take Bobby very long to realize that his Uncle Philip--plus, John and Bill and not forgetting Lorna--are acting as decoys, and once that happens, my inquisitive son will start by asking a question, which will lead to another question and then another one, until he discovers exactly what's going on…"

With his head tilted a little to one side, Thomas's question took me by surprise. "Did anyone tell Bobby or even mention to him about what had happened to you?"

"Of course not, and if Bobby had asked anyone, then I would have been told…"

"In that case, surely it must have crossed your mind that your son might have inherited, at least some of your unique abilities?"

"Yes it has, but as a result of my own experience, I wouldn't want my suspicion to be tested, until I was left with no choice…"

"And if he were my son Charlie, I would feel the same way, and although his overprotectiveness towards you is most admirable, I want you to feel comfortable. So it might be best if I meet him as soon as possible, which could take place after breakfast tomorrow morning, and so that I can deal with any underlying fears or doubts, I want him to feel able to talk freely so I was going to suggest that perhaps his Uncle Philip with whom he seems to have developed a special bond could introduce us and then, after we've had a chance to talk, you can introduce me to Lorna…"

For a few moments, I allowed the silence to linger, before I chose to be honest. "At first I wasn't sure, but then my instinctive, overprotective mother moment came to pass, and provided it can be arranged with the Commander at such short notice it sounds fine…"

"Strictly between you and me, your Godfather has acknowledged that because this is a crucial time, which the three of you need to spend together, Philip has granted me permission to do whatever I feel necessary to ensure that you aren't separated from Lorna and Bobby. So if I need him to be at the Manor tomorrow morning, then I'm confident that he will ask his Personal Assistant Sarah-Roxanna Retand to rearrange his appointments accordingly…"

Having listened to everything, there was no reason to imagine that in the days that lay ahead of us, I would discover that assisted by the notes he had made during our first meeting, like John Bland and Bill Powell, Dr Thomas James would prove himself to be a multi-skilled, Person Centred Psychotherapist. In fact, despite my claim that additional therapy would be a waste of time, if you will pardon my unfortunate play on words--in the final analysis--I was forced to admit that like Susanna's initial ability to expedite matters, when it came to the unaddressed or unfinished business, working with Thomas proved to be a most expeditious way in which to dispose of them. However, I am getting ahead of myself, so please suspend that concept, while we deal with my son.

## July 1st  9:10

Yesterday evening Lorna and I had explained that I was participating in Psychotherapy, and so that Bobby could grasp the role of a Psychotherapist, the three of us had watched a DVD, which was used for training purposes.

Of course, when we had asked him whether he had any questions, my son had been far more interested in joining the cavalry who were waiting for him down in the living room, so that before he played chess with my Godfather, he could participate in his favourite game Twister, which he loved so much, because being such a *little person,* he would be giggling and shrieking, as he squeezed with remarkable ease either over, under, around or in between, the spaces and gaps created between John and Bill's arms and legs.

Then this morning, even my Godfather was conspicuous by his presence, when everyone gathered in the dining room, and as soon as my son finished his breakfast, comprising of two sausages, three rashers of bacon, and a generous helping of scrambled egg, which left sufficient room for a slice of toast with low fat spread, and his favourite seedless strawberry jam--plus a glass of milk and a bone china mug of tea--as he began to gather his dishes together, Bobby requested the necessary permission, before he vacated his chair.

"Please may I leave the table?"

"Yes you can Bobby," Philip Maddox replied, as silence descended before he explained. "But after you finish brushing your teeth there is something special, which you and I need to do, so would you make sure that you come straight back downstairs…"

After placing his dirty dishes on Margaret's hostess trolley, Bobby began to speculate. "If something's special Uncle Philip is it the same as being secret?"

Philip Maddox nodded his agreement. "Yes Bobby, what we need to do is secret, so I'm afraid I can't tell you, until you to come back downstairs…"

"But will we still be able to play football?"

"Provided that you don't allow yourself to become distracted, then as soon as we complete our special assignment, there should be enough time for us to join not only my subordinates, but also Lorna outside…"

Setting what must have been a new record for brushing his teeth, four minutes later, when Bobby took the quickest route between the upper landing and the ground floor, by sliding down the bannister, Philip Maddox was waiting for him, and after lowering him to the floor, my Godfather crouched down, so that he could achieve eye contact with my son.

"There's someone who has asked to meet you Bobby, and like Sarah-Roxanna Retand within Special Operations, this person has a very responsible role to fulfil…"

"Although it's a very long word for little people to remember, before I fell asleep, I practised saying it over and over again, and if it's no longer a secret Uncle Philip, are we meeting the Psycho--thera--pist who is going to be helping mum?"

"Despite being a long word, you're right Dr Thomas James is a Psychotherapist, and because he will be working with my Goddaughter, yesterday morning while you were outside playing football, he asked for your mother's permission, so that he could meet not only you, but also your other mother Lorna…"

As soon as the Commander eased the study door open, Dr Thomas James turned away from the window and started walking towards the two armchairs.

"Good morning Thomas," Philip Maddox announced, before he hastily added, "As you requested this is Charlie Anne Daltry's biological son--Master Bobby Clunnell…"

"Hello Master Clunnell, do you mind if I call you Bobby?"

"If I say that it's okay does that mean I can call you Thomas instead of Dr James?"

"Since all of my friends call me Thomas. I would prefer it…"

Despite being less reserved than his first encounter with Sarah-Roxanna Retand, when Philip Maddox responded to a familiar tug on his sleeve by stooping a little, the youngster's whispered observation forced both adults to supress a smile.

"Uncle Philip, don't you think that like Sarah-Roxanna, Thomas is far too young to have such a long word, attached to his name, and instead of proper shoes--like me--he's wearing his trainers?"

"Yes Bobby, but apart from his footwear, I can give you my personal guarantee that Thomas has more than enough qualifications to merit the title Psychotherapist…"

Having reached the armchairs, as Thomas sat down he added his own corroboration. "If it makes you feel any better Bobby, then in precisely eight days, I will be thirty-three years old, and the reason why I'm wearing my trainers is that like many of my clients, my number one priority is to be comfortable while I'm working…"

Yet again, Philip Maddox felt a tugging at his sleeve, but this time, he sat himself down in the vacant armchair, so that he could achieve eye contact with the youngster.

"Uncle Philip, since Thomas is wearing his trainers, don't you think it would be pretty cool, if he could join us outside and then, there would be enough time to not only complete our special assignment, but also play football?"

"Yes it would Bobby," replied Philip Maddox. "But before Thomas can join us, I think that he needs to talk to you in private…"

Thomas nodded his agreement. "Actually, since you have somehow managed to put not only Mr Bland and Mr Powell, but also Ms. Retand and the Commander in touch with their inner children, and I fail to see why I should not be allowed to have some fun, although I might be a little out of practice, I think that subconsciously, I was hoping that Philip would invite me to come outside, so that I could participate in one of your improvised football matches. However, your Uncle Philip is quite correct, and before we can enjoy ourselves, I would like us to spend about fifteen minutes talking in private…"

Precisely nineteen minutes later, as the Commander had requested, Lorna and I were waiting at the bottom of the stairs in anticipation of the study door opening, and when Bobby emerged closely followed by my Godfather, my son was wearing a broad smile, behind which he could barely contain his enthusiasm.

"Gosh, not only did Thomas turn out to be much younger than I had expected, even while he's working with people he's allowed to wear his trainers. In fact, he wears them all the time, and because Uncle Philip has said that when we go outside Thomas can join us, playing football this morning is going to be even more awesome than usual…"

After years of dealing with subtle inferences, Lorna's response was immediate. "But unlike you, Thomas doesn't have to wear the same school uniform as everyone else in his class, and as for him joining us, I suppose that you would like your mum and me to make sure that there's enough time to play football, before Philip has to leave the Manor…"

When it came to making my son reconsider his options, thanks to Lorna's expertise we can move time forward to the point, where working with Thomas proved to be a most expeditious way in which to dispense with, some of the unaddressed or unresolved matters, beginning with my father--Major William Charles Forsyth.

## July 3$^{rd}$ 9:35

As one might expect from someone with my unique abilities, even before the request was made, I knew that my presence was required in the Commander's study, where it came as no surprise to find the cavalry waiting inside, and once the door clicked closed behind us, it had been a relief to learn that like the head on collision, which killed my mother, what happened at the airfield had been officially recognized as being an act of terrorism, which had been committed by Contracted assassins.

Consequently, while similar arrangements were being made with the immediate family members of my father's driver and Security Officer, Helen had been working alongside the Military's advisors in order to finalize every last detail of my father's funeral.

Having always known that once the arrangements had been made, I would have to make a final decision and yet, despite accepting that my desire to see my father's remains had been irrational, because I do have conflicting feelings about attending the funeral--on my behalf--I asked my Godfather to request an urgent session with Thomas, so that I would not keep Helen waiting any longer than necessary.

## July 4$^{th}$ 10:12

Of course, since Susanna had accompanied Thomas, before being banished to the dining room, so that she could continue dealing with, the remainder of those client case notes, she had offered me the benefit of her reassurance that at least if I had conflicting feelings about the Major, then surely that must be a vast improvement upon the position, where I had felt nothing, except resentment towards my father?

Naturally, Susanna's insight proved to be invaluable, even before she added that with Thomas's guidance, she was confident that whatever conclusions I reached would be something, which *I would be comfortable enough to live with for the rest of my life,* and then as far as my son was concerned, she drew my attention to the fact that since Bobby never had the chance to develop any conflicting feelings, *he had every reason to be proud of his Grandfather's Military achievements.*

Delving into my past, I doubt that you will recall that after being Sectioned for my own Safety as their Specialist title had suggested--between my one to one sessions with Professor Morgan--either Susanna or Debra seemed to know, not only what needed to be said but also when I was in a frame of mind so that I was willing to listen to them.

Once my son had been added into the equation, it provided me with a different perspective of what could happen--as opposed to what should happen--at my father's funeral, and working together, it took Thomas and me almost ninety minutes to reach a satisfactory conclusion, and during that time we explored my feelings of resentment, and from the notes he had made at our first meeting, Thomas  reminded me that I first felt resentful, when my mother died in that head on collision while she was being escorted in my father's car.

At six years old that incident had changed my entire life, but as an adult I could appreciate that while death was a regular occurrence in my father's life, those deaths were impersonal, and since losing his beloved Joanna Mary must have given him first-hand experience, amid his struggle with a personal grieving process--finding it impossible to relate to a bereft little girl--instead of a Mary Poppins lookalike he had hired a minder!

So as much as I regret that the animosity between me and my father had made it impossible, on that fateful day at the airfield for me to give the Major a fairer hearing, it proved to be irrelevant, because as we later discovered once the device had been installed that explosion could have happened anytime and anywhere.

Like my mother before her, since my step-mother worshiped the ground my father walked upon, and knowing that she had loved him with her whole heart, I accepted that the funeral should be a lasting testament--something which Helen would be comfortable enough to be at peace with, for the rest of her life, and if I were to selfishly decide that I needed to attend, it would turn out to be a security nightmare. A fiasco which would, not only attract unwanted attention to my presence, but also disrupt the solemnity of such an auspicious occasion and yet, Susanna's observation about Bobby having every reason to be proud of his Grandfather's Military achievements, did need to be addressed.

So eighty-two minutes after we began--thanks to Thomas's guidance--I agreed that provided my Godfather could manage to put everything in place, and at the same time gain Helen's approval, I would like my son to represent me, but only during the church service and then, at the social gathering of the top brass, once the burial had taken place.

**July 7<sup>th</sup> 10:31**

May my God forgive me for having ever doubted that even at such short notice, the Commander in Chief of Special Operations might not manage to arrange everything. In fact, I have to admit that I was a little surprised that Helen should have advised my Godfather to inform me that she would deem it an honour to have her Step-Grandson, and his other mother Lorna Clunnell join not only her, but also Philip Maddox in the pew at the front of the church, which was reserved for immediate family members and their guests.

Of course this morning, the usual football match had to be postponed, but for once Bobby did not raise any objections, because he knew that Patrick O'Keefe would be arriving in an unmarked car at 10:55, so that he could escort the Commander, Lorna and my son to the church, where Helen would be waiting to greet them.

Considering the number of important people who will be attending the funeral, as we did with the Psychotherapist, Lorna and I have spent the last two days coaching Bobby, so that he knows what to expect, and when it came to finding him something suitable to wear fortunately, when their belongings had arrived at the Manor, Bobby's school uniform, including his black blazer and his shoes were amongst them. However, having safeguarded my son's anonymity for the last seven years, while it could be argued that after today, all of the aforementioned important people, including the highest possible Authority will know that Bobby is the legitimate Grandson of Major William Charles Forsyth, as one might expect such notoriety terrifies me, which is the reason why I wholeheartedly agreed that the Clunnell family did not join the rest of the mourners at the graveside for the actual burial.

In readiness for their arrival, I am staring out of the window, and as soon as I sense my son's nearness, I half turn to be greeted by Lorna and a little boy who--without a single hair out of place, and the knot in his tie expertly centred--could easily be about to have his school photograph taken instead of representing me at his Grandfather's funeral.

"All right Lorna," this mother demands. "What have you done with our real son?"

Unable to sustain his serious expression, Bobby starts giggling, before he attempts to correct me. "Don't be silly mum, I am your real son…"

While I continue to sustain the momentum, I'm shaking my head, but at the same time, I am trying to avoid catching sight of Lorna's expression. "Oh I'm not being silly, because whenever he dresses himself in his school uniform, his tie is never that straight and with his unruly hair, our real son has never looked this angelic…"

Since nothing is blocking my view of the doorway, unbeknown to Lorna and Bobby, I have noted not only John's arrival, but also what he is carrying, which prompts me to lower my line of vision, until I can determine my son's deliberate mistake.

"So if you are our real son, instead of an imposter, then presumably John and Bill, who are accustomed to attending Military funerals must have helped you to get dressed?"

Without bothering to consider whether there might be any pitfalls, Bobby's response is far too enthusiastic. "Of course they did. It was John who used some water, so that he could smooth my hair into place and then, because Uncle Philip let me borrow one of his black ties, after Bill knotted it the right way, he made sure that it was correctly placed, before issuing me with a direct order that the tie had to remain straight, until after the funeral…"

"Excuse me young man," John announces from the doorway, and although my son falls silent, he does not glance over his shoulder. "But haven't you forgotten about something very important which you agreed to do?"

Having being caught red handed, I feel an immense sense of pride that since Bobby's upbringing has been based upon traditional values, without needing to be asked, he does the right thing, by admitting that he has failed to fulfil his side of their agreement.

"Sorry John, but I hadn't forgotten altogether. I just thought I'd wait until Mr O'Keefe arrives to take us to the funeral…"

As John moves into the bedroom and he extends his arm in my son's direction, instead of any incredulity regarding Bobby's excuse for not having changed his shoes, his tone of voice is soft and gentle, as he begins his explanation.

"Although he hasn't arrived, we have received a message from his Radio Transmitter, which confirmed that his E.T.A. would be five minutes, so why don't you come and sit down, so that we can put your shoes on?"

Thankful that he has avoided a reprimand from someone he would like to model himself upon, Bobby takes hold of John's hand, but when they reach my king sized bed, instead of my son having to clamber up, with the kind of gentleness one would not normally associate with a man in his profession--John lifts Bobby up and places him, so that his legs are dangling over the edge of the bed.

Then, with John still maintaining his soft and gentle tone of voice, as he begins to remove Bobby's trainers, he finishes his explanation. "And as soon as we go downstairs Bobby, I will personally make sure that your trainers are placed in the British Racing Green Jaguar, so that while Patrick O'Keefe is driving you back to Manor Park, no doubt with you sitting on a bolster cushion in the passenger seat, so that you can see out of the windscreen, you will be able to achieve all that while you're wearing your trainers…"

By the time John pauses, he has finished securing my son's shoelaces in a double knot to avoid any mishaps. "All right young man, why don't you jump down off the bed, so that your mothers can confirm whether that's an improvement?"

But even when both feet are on the floor, Lorna and I choose to make him wait for our collective response, which forces Bobby to voice his exasperation.

"If you are both teasing me, then would you please stop it right now, and tell me whether or not I am good enough to represent my '*bio--logical*' mother at the Military funeral of my Grandfather Major William Charles Forsyth?"

Finally, after making our son suffer for as long as possible, even without needing to glance at his other mother, I allow my broad smile to express the collective pride Lorna and I must be sharing over Bobby representing me at my father's funeral.

"So you were both teasing me, which was a very naughty thing to do. Besides, how can I believe that I'm good enough, unless you actually say the words?"

Accepting that the reprimand--albeit from an almost seven-year-old is justified, in stereophonic unison, Lorna and I share the same apology. "Yes, it was very naughty of us and we're both very sorry…"

Then, after casting a sideways glance at Lorna, I continue speaking on our collective behalf. "In fact, you're more than good enough and although biological is another word which little people would find hard to understand without knowing its meaning, as your biological mother, I am honoured and deem it a privilege that you will be representing me at my father's Military funeral…"

"Phew that's a relief. It was John and Bill who helped me to find out what bio--logical meant, and before you gave birth to me because I grew inside of you, we share the same genes or something called…"

Growing a little impatient, Lorna interrupts him. "There will be plenty of time to finish the biology lesson when we get back, but right now we have a funeral to attend and presumably you can remember everything you have to do, not only while we are inside the church, but also at the social gathering afterwards?"

"Honestly Lorna," Bobby declares as he places his hand on his hip. "Since we went over it what must have been a million, trillion--or even a zillion times, how could I ever forget exactly what I'm supposed to do…"

Of course, with so many high ranking Military Personnel attending the funeral, everything was being recorded to ensure that any irregularity, irrespective of how insignificant could be swiftly dealt with, while at the same time enabling me to watch the proceedings. So long before Patrick O'Keefe drove my son back to the Manor, with his trainers on and him sitting on a bolster cushion in the passenger seat of the car, which up until now still remains number two, on his top ten list of classic cars--the British Racing Green Jaguar--I already knew that Lorna and Bobby had done more than enough to make me proud of both of them.

Now if you are wondering what happened to Lorna, then there was a valid reason why she had been spared the discomfort of having to squeeze herself into the cramped space, behind the front seats of the British Racing Green Jaguar.

After their departure, John had advised me that while every precaution had been taken, so that Bobby and Lorna were not over-exposed, as an added precaution, taking a different route, the Commander had requested that Matthew Morton should drive Lorna back to the Manor in a car, which was destined to necessitate that Bobby rearrange, his top ten list of classic cars, as soon as he found out about the Jaguar F-Type. But by the time I heard one of the double doors, opening and then closing again followed by Bill greeting Lorna, my representative had already raced up the sweeping staircase, so that he could begin delivering the minute by minute version of a day in my son's short life, which he would never forget.

Or that was the case, until my Godfather afforded all of us some relief, when he managed to persuade Bobby that perhaps we could postpone watching the highlights from the social gathering until after our evening meal. However, at 18:42 my son was faced with an even bigger dilemma because he also wanted to play Twister with John and Bill, before learning even more chess or backgammon strategies from his Uncle Philip, which meant that the highlights had to be edited to meet the needs of his busy social schedule.

Naturally, it was not until we started watching the shortened highlights that I began to appreciate that although my son might have been robbed of the chance to meet his Grandfather in person, with my own Godfather keeping a watchful eye on Bobby, so that he was close enough to perform the formal introductions to a Colonel, two Generals, one Field-Marshal, three Majors, and of course the highest possible Authority, without our seven year old son needing to be prompted or corrected, because we were able to watch him and hear him fearlessly addressing each and every one of his elders in the correct manner, meant that his two mothers were consumed by an even greater sense of pride at what two women had singlehandedly managed to accomplish.

Perhaps more importantly, after safeguarding Bobby's anonymity for the last seven years, I was relieved that having given my Godfather the necessary permission, he had made certain that each powerful and influential person knew that the youngster to whom they were being introduced was not only representing his mother Charlie Anne Daltry, he was also the legitimate Grandson of Major William Charles Forsyth.

## July 8th 13:11

When Thomas and I had conducted a quick review of our therapeutic relationship, we had established what unresolved matters still needed to be addressed, and considering recent events, it now seems to be a little ironic that one of the three contenders, involving ancestry strikes me as being most relevant, especially when it is connected with the actual owner of the remains, which we laid to rest in the grave reserved for my husband on that miserable day three months ago.

So I am hoping that you can recall how Sarah-Roxanna Retand had arranged for Judge George Matthew Porter to grant Special Operations an Exhumation Order, while at the same time, she had assembled an Administration Team at H.Q., to conduct a more thorough investigation into my husband's adoption by Mr and Mrs Daltry.

In addition, I have found recent events so physically and emotionally draining that every day after our light lunch, I have been excusing myself, so that I could retreat to my bedroom and when Margaret popped her head around the door, which was still ajar I had exchanged my clothes for one of my loose-fitting kaftans, so that through using one of Thomas' ruses, I would psychologically feel relaxed enough to be able to fall asleep.

At first, Margaret seemed concerned that she might have disrupted my new regime at a crucial moment, but as it transpired, provided that my bedroom door was not closed, she had been dispatched to advise me that together with Mr Bland and Mr Powell, the Commander would like all three of us to join him in his study.

## July 8th 13:21

Although I had asked Margaret if she would mind explaining to my Godfather that I would be downstairs in five minutes, ten minutes later I was standing outside the closed study door, wondering why I have always felt the need to pause and take a steadying breath.

Perhaps it has something to do with the fact that the completion of this chapter of my life story rests upon, whether Commander Philip Maddox can satisfy all the other Agencies, who no doubt want their particular pound of my flesh for what they perceive to be my complicity over my husband's alternative lifestyle, and while I had believed that my sole priority was to secure the life-long freedom and continued anonymity of not only Bobby and Lorna, but also Colin McCardle, and since that has been achieved, during the last fifteen or even sixteen days I think the three of us have all enjoyed being in the same place at the same time without having to pretend, and for my part I now find myself longing for this--albeit utopian scenario to continue and yet, irrespective of how implausible that might seem to be, would it be too much for any mother to ask?

Of course, I am not like any normal mother and like Joanna Mary Forsyth it would be heart-breaking, if history were allowed to repeat itself, so that my son is forced to attend his mother's funeral and yet, within the here and now of that present tense, I accepted that it was time to stop speculating, and deal with whatever was lying beyond that closed door.

So taking a bold step forward, I entered the study armed with a well-rehearsed apology for my lateness, and once inside there was only one item on the agenda, parentage or to be more precise, the rightful owner of the remains we buried in the grave reserved for my husband, because in conjunction with the exhumation, the Administration Team had completed their in-depth investigation into my husband's adoption into the Daltry family.

Three months ago, after I was forced to make a provisional identification using the personal possessions, which had been found beside the human remains on the ground floor of the Foray building--as Mark had intended--it was not until the DNA from those remains was confirmed as a match with the DNA sample held on the Official Record at H.Q. that everyone was satisfied that by the end of that day, I was the only survivor.

However, as revealed during the Interview, since recent events had led me to suspect that Mark was still alive, which could only have been possible if he either planted his own DNA on those remains--or alternatively--from the description I gave of a man I subsequently recalled seeing--albeit for no more than a minute--Mark must have had a twin brother.

So it was hardly surprising that the report compiled by the Group Leader of the Administration Team confirmed that Mark Daltry did have a brother. In fact, they were monozygotic twins, and because they shared the same DNA, either before or during the siege, my husband must have arranged for his twin brother to die instead of him.

As the investigation progressed, it also revealed that although Mark's birth mother Mary had never disclosed the names of any male partners, despite her mental health issues, she was managing to bring up one child who was under school age, and with whom she had a strong maternal bond. However, after her Social Worker raised concerns about the sudden introduction of two babies, it had been agreed that if Mary placed one of the twins into temporary foster care, then his brother could remain with her for a trial period, during which the situation could be monitored, in the hope that the entire family could be reunited.

Suddenly, the case notes had been redacted, which meant that the investigation ground to a halt, while the Commander found himself having to exert more than the usual amount of leverage in the upper echelon of the corridors of power, until the Government Department responsible, released the un-expunged Social Services report, and as the Admin. Team had suspected, after there had been a change in the Social Worker assigned to their case, although the older child had been placed on the Local Authority's, *At Risk register,* which meant that Mark not only remained in foster care, due to the loss of continuity, the family situation had also ceased to be monitored on a regular basis.

As a result, nine months after the birth of the twins, while Mary was experiencing a severe psychotic episode, the older child--who had been celebrating her fifth birthday--was rushed to hospital, where she had been pronounced dead upon her arrival in the A. & E. Department, and because of the circumstances the case notes had been redacted in what appeared to be a deliberate attempt to suppress the details.

Naturally, Mary's state of mind necessitated that in accordance with the Mental Health Act she had needed to be Sectioned for her own Safety, and although Mark's twin brother, whom she had chosen to call Paul had been placed into emergency foster care, as soon as Mary was deemed capable of making a rational decision, she signed the necessary documents, which meant that Paul and Mark were both eligible for adoption.

Then, the Administration Team focused their attention on Paul's own case notes as compiled by his Social Workers, and after spending his childhood and adolescence in and out of several Care Homes, which was perhaps predictable, considering what he must have discovered about his birth mother, and the suspicious circumstances surrounding the death of his sister, despite being eligible for Adoption his disruptive behaviour--which his Clinical Psychologist believed to be deliberate--meant that he never remained with any family longer than the trial period.

During that same period, Mr Daltry Senior's position in Corporate Finance had necessitated that the family reside in Germany, Switzerland and Italy. So being multi-lingual and armed with all the right qualifications, Mark had been destined for the Foreign Office, before joining Special Operations and then, knowing that he was adopted, after he betrayed everyone who trusted him via his alternative lifestyle, it would have been easy for him to trace his identical twin brother, and for his part--albeit a naïve one--considering his background there can be little doubt that Paul would have become an eager participant, especially if there seemed to be minimal risk in exchange for maximum financial gain.

**July 10<sup>th</sup> 12:27**

Throughout the last forty-eight hours, I have been experiencing a gradual awareness that somewhere, something significant is in the process of changing, and because there seems to be a heightened sense of danger, I need to prepare myself, so that whenever that potential threat materializes I will be able to deal with it.

So starting at 9:12 and continuing until we were interrupted, Thomas and I have spent this morning working our way through the unresolved issues, which we identified two days ago, but before we began it was agreed that whenever we both considered that we had dealt with something, then we would take a short break, before moving onto the next issue and then with Susanna banished to the dining room, so that she could continue working her way through that same back-log of client case notes, when the silence had lingered, it had prompted Thomas to invite me to select a place, where we could begin our lengthy session, and I chose the resolution of the Administration Team's investigation.

If you are wondering why I chose that starting point, then I admit that at first I was unable to provide Thomas with a reason and yet, after he drew my attention to the fact that the investigation had conclusively proved that there were no depths to which my husband would not have been prepared to sink, in order to convince everybody that he had died on that last day, it made perfect sense.

So working together, we established that once my Godfather had confirmed that the Administration Team had not been able to trace any extended family, who might have continued to hope that one day, he would be found and returned to them--I was and indeed still am--perplexed over the reason why I must have felt that Paul had earned the right to have his remains returned to the grave, which my husband had always intended him to occupy.

In defence of my initial bewilderment, I had maintained that the only connection between us was the fleeting glance, we had shared on that last day, when Paul had looked up at me, seconds before the first explosion occurred on the ground floor, which meant that we had both become victims of my husband's manipulative mind, but then Thomas suggested that it might be helpful, if we began to make some comparisons.

Of course with the benefit of hindsight, I realized that Paul must have been so grateful for his newfound sense of belonging that despite the sizable increase in his bank balance, he must have never questioned Mark's ultimate intentions towards him, and as far as I was concerned, while we were flying to Paris in the private jet, if I had not managed to find the courage to provide Mark with the evidence to ensure that if anything untoward were to happen during that long weekend--then somehow--he would have to find a way to keep me alive. Otherwise I would have shared the same fate as Paul.

So considering the next unresolved issue, it seems to be quite ironical that my insurance policy was the only reason why I am still alive. But at least Thomas and I both deemed the issue to have been resolved and as agreed, we took a short break, during which I chose to leave the study--albeit on a temporary basis.

Although the Commander's negotiations on my behalf was one of the unresolved issues we had highlighted two days ago--during my absence--I had decided that I did not want to waste time speculating upon hypothetical outcomes, especially when there was a piece of unfinished business involving John Bland.

Since you might not recall the incident, perhaps I should explain that during the Interview, as a result of what he regarded as my reckless behaviour, over that aforementioned insurance policy, John's brain managed to lose control over what was coming out of his mouth, and not even Bill's attempted intervention could stop his partner from demanding to know the answer to his question, and it was so scathing I am able to quote the actual words he used. *"Do you have any idea how long it's going to take, before you can look at yourself in a full length mirror, or allow any man to touch you, without being reminded of what took place during those sixty minutes of your life?"*

Even though the issue of the full length mirror was resolved when the cavalry performed an intervention, as a result of Bobby hearing Lorna and I exchanging cross words, I still need to find the answer to the second part of John's ranted demand, but then when I fell silent, Thomas made a direct request to know whether I had considered how far I was willing to go in order to achieve a satisfactory resolution, especially with regard to John Bland's professional position.

Within any therapy session such a request would be a rarity, and between you and me I was startled by its arrival, until I realized that some of the more intimate details might pose a conflict of interests for Thomas, but once we redefined our boundaries we were able to discuss my intended preparations, before we rehearsed not only some of my dialogue lines, but also how I would counteract every possible negative reaction from John to my unexpected arrival in his room.

Despite having started at 9:12 by 12:16 there was still so much more preparation we needed to undertake and yet, before I could push the limit of our revised boundaries by beginning to outline the explicit details of how far I would be be prepared to go in order to gain an answer, a tap on the study door announced the arrival of that interruption I mentioned earlier, when Susanna brought our therapeutic marathon to an end.

"Commander Maddox has asked me to apologise on his behalf Thomas, but something has been brought to his attention, and because he needs to discuss it with Charlie, preferably before lunch, as soon as it's convenient to do so, he would like you to suspend your therapy session, so that together with Mr Bland and Mr Powell the three of them can join his Goddaughter in the study

Considering the urgency attached to the Commander's request, I found it reassuring that even though it meant adjusting his schedule, Thomas was delaying his departure until after lunch, so that he would be available, if there was anything I needed to address, and approximately six minutes after the departure of my therapeutic team, when my Godfather and his subordinates joined me in the study, I was already sitting at the desk.

"Good afternoon Charlie…"

"As much as I admire your optimism, I'm not sure that there can be anything '*good*' about this meeting Commander, especially when it required the deferment of a therapy session, which had reached a crucial moment in the rationalization process…"

Bearing in mind the intimate content of that therapy session, perhaps it was most fortunate that I managed to stop my gaze from drifting in John's direction, by remaining focused on my Godfather as he sat down in his Executive chair?

"I'm afraid that the interruption was unavoidable, because early this morning an incident occurred, which necessitated that after Sarah-Roxanna and I finished compiling my official report, we had to prepare a carefully worded statement on behalf of the Minister. However, during the inevitable period of anticipatory silence leading up to the press office releasing it at 15:00 in case there is any media speculation, which can only be based upon nothing more than rumour, I wanted you to know what's happened as soon as possible…"

Taking into account my premonition, I was unable to mask the hesitancy in my voice. "What kind of an incident Commander?"

Suddenly, an awkward silence descended, but before I could question the reason for its arrival, my Godfather cast a glance in Powell's direction, and as if it had been prearranged, Bill began to explain on his Commanding Officer's behalf. "During the Interview Charlie, when the identity of Bobby's biological father first arose, on the basis that there was still a long way to go--and later--you might not feel quite so protective towards him, in my capacity as self-appointed arbitrator, I allowed you to postpone divulging his name..."

Between you and me, while I was reminding myself that having grown up with two mothers who have loved him with our whole hearts, and a surrogate uncle Colin McCardle who has been an excellent father figure and an ideal role model, because there has never been any reason for Bobby to know the identity of the absentee father who had denied his existence, I allowed Bill to continue explaining on my Godfather's behalf.

"And even when we neared the end of your life story, despite knowing that Bobby's continued safety and anonymity had been granted the Royal Seal of Approval, you still refused to write his name down on my rather old fashioned notepad, until you received a guarantee that whenever the time came to remove Robert Lloyd Reece-Milliner from his position, the matter would be handled with the utmost discretion..."

With my reservations threatening to indulge in some of their own speculative supposition, erring on the side of caution, I brought the explanation to an end. "Thank you Mr Powell, but I have managed to grasp that the incident, which necessitated that this meeting take place, must in some way be connected with Bobby's biological father being removed from his privileged position..."

Yet again, silence descended, before my Godfather uttered a dissatisfied sigh. "Once I knew about the blackmail, the matter was referred to Internal Affairs with the suggestion that they might like to focus their initial investigation on assignments, during the last twelve months for which Mark Daltry requested approval, so that you could accompany him..."

"And presumably you made your suggestion, because it was during those negotiations that as a result of what I saw and overheard, I managed to create my insurance policy?"

From the opposite side of the desk, my Godfather cast me a congratulatory nod, before he continued delivering the remainder of his explanation.

"In the proverbial sense, if I hadn't made the suggestion, then it would have been like looking for needles within haystacks. However, even after Internal Affairs identified four separate occasions where the successful outcome strongly suggested that Robert Lloyd Reece-Milliner must have provided Mark Daltry with information, relating to Foreign Office policy, it wasn't until six o'clock today that the highest possible Authority advised me, that I had been granted Ministerial approval to dispatch Operatives to the Foreign Office..."

Genuinely perplexed, I dared to interrupt him. "But I don't understand, because if it was supposed to be handled with the utmost discretion, then surely there shouldn't have been any need to prepare a carefully worded statement for the press office?"

As soon as the words left my mouth, I remembered that my Godfather had failed to clarify what kind of an incident had occurred, and as if all three of them were waiting for me to make the connection between--Operatives being sent to the Foreign Office--and the need for me to prepare myself, so that I could deal with the threatened danger, nobody disturbed my rationalization process, until the protective mother within me was ready to seek some specific clarification.

"Since we wouldn't be in your study having this meeting, unless something untoward happened at the Foreign Office--might I suggest that on Bobby's behalf--Lorna and I deserve to know--how disturbing the bad news actually is--so that we can be prepared?"

Over by the cabinet, despite detecting John's slight movement, I maintained eye contact with my Godfather, until he felt obliged to provide me with a response.

"It's disturbing enough to provide me with a valid excuse for asking Mr Bland, if he would be so kind as to dispense two generous measures of pure malt whisky, and while I use the contents of one of the crystal glasses to help cauterize my wounds for having failed to consider that there might have been risks involved, I'm hoping that the contents of the second glass will help you to decide whether or not--in this instance--which is of a personal nature, you might prefer to read my official report..."

Prior to my arrival at Manor Park, because of the misrepresentations, misinterpretations and half-truths, I had regarded my Godfather as an adversary, but now the polite nod of our heads, and barely detectable tight-lipped gestures constitute a display of our recently established mutual respect. However, I still waited until John had granted both of us with access to our emotional crutches, before voicing my decision.

"As much as I appreciate being given the chance to choose Commander, I cannot think of a single reason why I should need to corroborate anything you tell me..."

"That's fine, but if at any time--you should feel the need to do so--there's nothing preventing you from changing your mind..."

In all fairness to the Commander, he had already begun his explanation by the time his persistence struck me as being strange enough to warrant some additional clarification and I realized that instead of asking what kind of an incident had occurred, I should have queried the significance of this particular instance.

"Since I'm not obliged to reveal the identity of any Operational member of my staff, there was no reason for anyone to know that after assigning Patrick O'Keefe and Matthew Morton, they were dispatched to the Foreign Office, so that they could initially charge Robert Lloyd Reece-Milliner with the four instances, which had been identified by Internal Affairs as having contravened the limitations of the Official Secrets Act..."

Hesitating, my Godfather sipped from his crystal glass. "Naturally, the matter was handled with the utmost discretion, and to ensure that none of his own staff or any of his colleagues were aware of what was about to take place, as soon as the Minister was advised that O'Keefe and Morton had entered the building, he summoned Reece-Milliner to a private room, so that the charges could be read out to him and then, respecting his right to remain silent, until he had access to legal representation, they escorted him downstairs..."

At that precise moment from out of nowhere, I was ambushed by a new image, which I chose to suspend, until I could measure its emotional impact, but it was overwhelming enough to cause me what could only be described as an excessive degree of discomfort, and even though there was no evidence to suggest that I needed its contents, as the fingers of my right hand closed around the crystal glass, despite having no awareness of my action from its resting place on the surface of the desk, I must have raised some part of my left hand--albeit that it needed to be no more than a matter of inches, in order to render my Godfather silent and then, while he waited for me to decide whether or not I wanted to change my mind, the sound of the silence was deafening.

In the end, no words needed to pass between us, because for my part I raised the crystal glass, so that I could drink some of its contents, and without needing me to ask, my Godfather turned the buff folder containing his report around, and as he nudged it across the desk, so that I could assume the responsibility for reading it, I offered my audience an explanation for my actions.

"Although it was rude of me to interrupt Commander, I found myself overwhelmed by the appearance of an image, which belonged to an entirely different incident..."

"Presumably, it was connected with what happened while you were in Paris?"

This time when I drank from the crystal glass, it was because I needed its contents to reduce the emotional impact of my admission. "It was nothing more than a flashback of something that happened once the masked gunman and I had left the building…"

With the image still suspended, when I paused, silence once again descended, and despite considering that the time had arrived for me to read the official report, out of the corner of my eye I caught sight of Bill approaching the desk, and after handing his Commanding Officer a second buff folder, my Godfather began to explain. "According to the official report Charlie, you couldn't have found yourself in a worse position for two reasons. Firstly, you had sustained a debilitating leg injury--and secondly--the masked gunman had pulled the pin from a grenade, and with his arm around your neck, he instructed you to negotiate on his behalf with the Head of our French Division…"

Suddenly, the image was demanding to be set free, but before releasing it, I wanted my Godfather to finish setting the rest of the scene, as it had unfolded in that street. So I delayed my participation, by once again sipping from my crystal glass.

"Unless there's something missing Charlie, as far as I can tell, Henri Retand did everything in accordance with routine procedure. In fact, it wasn't until you made your impassioned personal request that Henri decided to back down over the gunman's demand for a car and a driver to take both of you beyond the sealed area…"

Of course, when that car arrived it was being driven by Henri--who would have never put himself in that position--unless he had no intention of allowing us to leave the scene. However, my Godfather was right, there was something missing--or to be more precise it was something we have overlooked--because the car and its driver were not the first demand that naïve young man had forced me to make.

"My God, how many more dead bodies is it going to take?"

Unsure whether the words had come out of my mouth, but at the same time needing to know the answer, I explained, "Minutes before the explosion added another three bodies to the total--that was what my father said--and they reminded me that in Paris, minutes before it led to his own demise, the car wasn't the gunman's first demand…"

After expressing his dissatisfaction through another lengthy sigh, my Godfather afforded me his agreement. "No it wasn't Charlie His demand for the car came after his attempt to have the marks-persons removed from the surrounding rooftops had failed…"

No longer able to control the image, as soon as it obtained its freedom, like my whisky glass with crystal clarity, I could see the gunman and me, and having vacated the driver's seat, because Henri knew the risks if the crazy stunt he was planning should fail, his expression was meant to instil within me, some kind of belief in his ability to succeed.

In the end, I was not given the luxury of a choice, which meant that in the study, my head was bowed, and my eyes were closed, as I found myself forced to re-experience the events, as the scene reached its deadly conclusion.

"Perhaps the advanced weaponry training I undertook made it possible--or maybe immediately after the discharge, I imagined hearing the recoil as the empty casing was ejected from the barrel, but even though the marks-person had ensured that my captor drew his last breath, he did not release me, so that once we were on the ground, there was nothing I could do, except watch the grenade rolling away from us, and while I might never have been anything more than a Wedding, Christening, and Funeral kind of a person, as I counted the seconds until its detonation I had started reciting the Lord's Prayer in case Henri did not manage to reach either me--or preferably the grenade in time …"

Finding myself ambushed, by the powerful emotions attached to the memory of that countdown, I was forced to hesitate, before re-establishing eye contact with my Godfather.

"Is it safe for me to assume that the presence of a marks-person was destined to become the connection between the two incidents?"

"That's correct Charlie, and although our Forensic Personnel are still in the process of conducting a fingertip search for any traces of DNA, which might have been left behind on the rooftop opposite the rear entrance, it's clear that someone must have been camped out long enough to have established Robert Lloyd Reece-Milliner's daily routine…"

Taking into consideration that I ended his brief extramarital fling, before I discovered that I was pregnant, then regardless of the wife who worshiped the ground he walked upon, and the three sons, whose existence he had chosen to acknowledge, so that he could use them to provide him with the level of respectability his position required, although I might not have needed any visual corroboration for the sake of all his offspring, especially his fourth son, I had earned the right to request additional clarification.

"I can only apologise if this seems selfish or ghoulish, but as Bobby's birth mother, I need to know whether there are going to be any repercussions for my son…"

For a few moments, the hollow sound within the silence was once again deafening, but then in an almost paternal tone of voice, my Godfather afforded me the benefit of his personal insight. "Having known you since you were a child Charlie, I can appreciate how many obstacles you must have had to overcome, in order to protect your son throughout the last seven years. So I doubt that anyone in this room would think that such a request was either ghoulish or selfish…"

Doubting his sincerity, I lifted my head so that I could achieve eye contact, but without him needing to say anything, his eyes were confirming that he was proud of the young woman I had become, as he added. "And I'm confident that on my behalf, Mr Powell will be able to fulfil your request for some additional corroboration…"

"Of course Sir…"

After moving to the desk, Bill rescued the buff folder containing the official report, so that he could respond to his Commanding Officer's subtle order. "As you are no doubt aware Charlie, until the Ballistics team complete their investigation no details will be released to the media. However, Morton has advised us that after the car arrived he was holding the rear door open, and during the four or maybe five paces, it took O'Keefe to escort Robert Lloyd Reece-Milliner, between the rear entrance of the Foreign Office and the Jaguar, the marks-person must have been making the final adjustments, so that by the time the trigger was squeezed, Bobby's biological father had been destined to die instantaneously…"

Ironically, within that same instantaneous moment involuntarily, my eyes closed and yet, the silence which followed provided me with the chance to make certain that once I had expressed my gratitude, my emotions would not cause me to sustain any embarrassment. "Thank you Bill. Regardless of what he might have deserved--at least his wife and his three sons will be relieved to learn that he did not suffer any more than was necessary…"

Suddenly aware of my planned reference to Thomas, once again I had to make a conscious effort to stop my gaze from drifting in John's direction. "Provided that there isn't anything else Commander, then in case there is any media speculation, I need to tell Lorna about the incident at the Foreign Office and then, because it had to be suspended, Thomas and I have a therapy session, which we have to reschedule…"

Although that was my intention, before I attempted to stand up, my Godfather prevented me from leaving. "Actually Charlie, as a direct result of this morning's incident, something else has arisen, which I think we should deal with before we adjourn for lunch…"

Despite the unfinished business, I have to admit that I was intrigued, especially when Bill moved back to the desk, and replaced the buff folder relating to the Paris incident with a third file, so that after my Godfather flipped it open, he could begin to explain.

"Naturally, I can appreciate your need to update Lorna, while at the same time rescheduling the interrupted therapy session, but I wouldn't have delayed your departure Charlie, unless there was a worthwhile reason…"

Now, I was even more intrigued. "In fact, our own arrival was delayed, because at my request Mr Bland made sure that--until you're ready to break the bad news in person--then thanks to Margaret's assistance, nobody will be able to gain access to any radio or television reports, which might reveal any details in connection with this morning's incident…"

Pausing, my Godfather seemed to be affording me the chance to comment, but since I was curious to learn what constituted being worthwhile, I chose to remain silent. "The last time we talked about the progression of my negotiations on your behalf, I explained that we were encountering some unexpected difficulties, but there has been a development, which suggests that one of the issues over which--all of the Agencies involved could not agree--can now be resolved…"

Having failed to grasp the relevance of Bobby's father within those difficulties, I raised my right hand, so that my Godfather would allow me to interrupt. "I'm sorry Commander, but if this has got something to do with my husband, then I would have assumed that his alternative lifestyle, which led to him blackmailing Bobby's father and ultimately, the betrayal of everyone's trust would have made him the greatest difficulty when it comes to finding a resolution, which will satisfy all of the Agencies involved, especially when each one of them must have their own agenda…"

"In theory that should have been the case Charlie, but during the Interview, you confirmed that after your return from Paris, you chose to remain in the marital home, so that if anything untoward did happen, then Special Operations would be the first Agency to be informed, which we were in the early hours of the 22$^{nd}$ June, and after I reassigned Bland and Powell at their request, a High Court Judge granted them a Protective Custody Order, on June 23$^{rd}$ which meant that subsequently, the highest possible Authority was prepared to allow me some time in which to clean up the mess, left by your husband in my own back yard…"

"And has it been cleaned up?"

"Fortunately, after two of Henri's Operatives managed to establish a means of dealing with his Handler and Sponsor, it would seem that irrespective of how reckless it might have been, the existence of your insurance policy--and Daltry's failure to retrieve it--has turned him into the kind of liability, which now poses a threat to their continued anonymity…"

Remembering how that recklessness had triggered the incident, when my principal male's brain had lost control over his mouth once again, I found myself having to make a conscious effort to stop my gaze from drifting in John's direction, as my Godfather continued with his explanation. "Consequently, Henri has been working towards securing a settlement, which will satisfy not only his Handler and Sponsor, but also this Commanding Officer and the highest possible Authority that Mark Daltry's early retirement will be far less financially rewarding and therefore, less comfortable than he had intended it should be…"

Naturally by now, I had realized the true significance of today's incident upon the difficulties my Godfather must have been encountering. "So presumably the development to which you were referring relates to the death of Bobby's biological father, and the fact that he has ceased being a liability?"

"That's correct Charlie and as a direct result, the highest possible Authority has already rearranged his own schedule, and because I have been summoned to attend a meeting at 8:15 tomorrow morning--after dinner--my driver will be taking me and Sarah-Roxanna to H.Q., so that while we are staying overnight in my penthouse apartment, thanks to her expertise, by the time I attend that meeting my presentation will be word perfect…"

Unaccustomed to being the recipient of such good news, I remained sceptical. "It all sounds promising, and while I'm sure that you will negotiate, the best possible deal on my behalf, I'm not harbouring any fanciful expectations, especially when M I 5 and M I 6 must be desperate to obtain their particular pound of my flesh, in respect of what they must deem to be my complicity…"

This time, it was my Godfather's turn to render me silent, by raising his right hand. "I was beginning to think that despite working with Thomas, you were never going to pose any questions about the concessions I have managed to gain--or perhaps more importantly--what agreements I have managed to negotiate on your behalf..."

"Oh believe me," this young woman admitted. "Despite appearances suggesting otherwise, it was more a case of being too afraid of the answers, if I did ask any questions..."

Opposite me a smile crept onto my Godfather's face. "In that case, let me offer you my personal assurance that the highest possible Authority has already agreed that none of the Agencies involved has any grounds to accuse you of complicity..."

Pausing, my Godfather waited for me to nod my acceptance, before adding. "In fact, it will no doubt come as an even greater relief that after having you excluded, from any of Mark Daltry's dealings with his Handler and Sponsor, between us Henri and I have established that our main objective is to ensure that there are no loose ends, which could lead to any unforeseen repercussions..."

Having read between the lines, in his capacity as his Commanding Officer, my Godfather is suggesting that although my husband has become a liability, it is not enough for him to be deprived access to his pension fund, but I would rather not consider how things might be resolved on a more permanent basis, so I chose not to pose any leading questions.

"Moving on to the unfulfilled Contract Charlie, because your insurance policy is no longer an issue, arrangements are being made through Daltry's Handler for the remainder of the money to be paid to Tony Shaw and his two associates by your husband, so that he can confirm that because the terms have changed, Shaw can consider that after the visit he made to 187 Cheltenham Way on the 22$^{nd}$ June, the Contract was deemed to be fulfilled..."

"It sounds straightforward enough, but can any of them be trusted?"

"Perhaps they can't, but I am in a position to also give you my personal assurance that once the balance has been paid, there will be no further action taken with regard to the Contract which your husband commissioned..."

Although there were no guarantees that anyone would abide by their side of such a complex deal--given the circumstances--it was better than I had expected, so I allowed my Godfather to continue uninterrupted. "Prior to your arrival at Manor Park, although I had never had the opportunity to observe the three of you together, despite the difficulties you must have had to overcome during the last seven years, what you and Lorna have managed to achieve is remarkable, especially when I take into consideration that Bobby told me how this is the first time, you have been able to spend such a long time together, which has been even more special, not only because he has been able to play football every single day, but the fact that you haven't needed to pretend..."

As this proud mother's eyes closed, my Godfather allowed me the time I needed to recover my composure, so that I could explain "Although Bobby's enjoying every minute of every single day, Lorna and I have prepared him for the possibility that the three of us might not be able to stay together, and because he's grown up with my professional responsibilities necessitating that sometimes we have to be apart, when that time comes he will be fine..."

Perhaps my son would be fine, but afterwards this mother would be an emotional wreck and yet, opposite me another soft smile had crept onto my Godfather's face. "Oh I don't doubt for a second that Bobby would cope, but there is something that you need to take into consideration, because as I recently had cause to remind one of my subordinates..."

Pausing, in his capacity as a Commanding Officer, he did nothing to prevent his gaze from drifting in John's direction, before he demanded, "Isn't that correct Mr Bland?"

"Yes Sir, there was something you needed to bring to my attention..."

"Good, I'm glad you can recall the incident, because I stated that even if there was anything wrong with my hearing, which I'm pleased to say there isn't, then the last time I had my eyesight tested, I was deemed to have twenty-twenty vision…"

Remembering the early hours of that particular morning, and how I had overheard the Commander cautioning his subordinate, it was my turn to yet again stop my gaze from drifting in John's direction, as my Godfather explained its relevance.

"So when it comes to you Charlie, from what I have seen with my own eyes, and the spontaneous laughter I have relished hearing--in my opinion--whatever you had hoped might be the eventual outcome your expectations have changed during the last ten days, and now regardless of the fact that you might not believe you deserve it, more than anything else, you would like to be granted the opportunity for the three of you to continue living together, as a family unit, which would of course necessitate some kind of monitoring…"

Suddenly, it was a relief that I was sitting down, because hearing my revised expectations expressed in words left this mother, incapable of either the ability to move or speak and yet, clearly not expecting me to do either of those things, my Godfather was sliding the top drawer of his desk open.

"That's what I am aiming to achieve, and to assist me I have what I suppose could be described as an insurance policy of my own, which I have not as yet introduced into my discussions with the highest possible Authority…"

As he produced yet another folder, I knew that it contained the sparse details relating to my discharge from the Research Programme. "On the day that I was persuaded, by the Major to allow you to assume that I was the person responsible for the introduction of Class 'A' substances, into the tests you were undertaking I underestimated your reaction…"

Despite the admission of guilt, I dared to challenge his perception of that underestimation. "As I remember it Commander, because I chose to use a combination of my abilities--together with my father--you were totally overwhelmed by their strength…"

Tilting his head to one side, my Godfather nodded his agreement. "Perhaps we were, but unfortunately, your determination to prove that the Research was flawed also provided definitive evidence of your powerfulness, and having robbed the researchers of the ability to sustain any kind of control, you also demonstrated that the only way anybody could have stopped someone with your capabilities was through their annihilation…"

Although the reference to my possible demise was disconcerting, when my Godfather paused, I chose to remain silent, so that I could learn more about my probable executioners. "As one might expect the Military's Top Brass were a little vexed, at the time and resources spent working with the other participants, only to have you highlight their inadequacies, by managing to erase seven month's research material in a matter of minutes…"

In that moment, I found myself wondering whether the Top Brass might have been less peeved, if I had given everyone an even more precise demonstration of my capabilities, by only erasing the research material relating to me. But with the disapproval beginning to resemble the kind of summarization, which would regularly appear at the bottom of my school reports, being facetious would only fan the flames, so I opted to be penitent.

"But as if the stigma of a dishonourable discharge wasn't enough Commander, I was rewarded with what turned into a prescription drug dependency, and a security file which was destined to remain open even after I married Mark Daltry…"

Raising his right hand, my Godfather's cautioning gesture, silenced me in mid-sentence. "Nobody can deny all of those things, but you're missing the point Charlie, because after witnessing the full extent of your capabilities and then, listening to the concerns raised by the Top Brass I was fearful for your long term safety. However, because I had been rewarded with the responsibility for monitoring your progress through that open security file, and I had the means at my disposal, I was able to establish an insurance policy, so that if the need ever arose it would afford you some protection…"

Thanks to the benefit of hindsight, I could appreciate the dilemma faced by my Godfather. "And presumably, you never told me because until now, there has never been any need for me to know about its existence, especially when my life seemed to spiral out of control after my discharge from the Research Facility, and as John and Bill enlightened me during the Interview, by the time you were advised of the situation, I was such a sick young woman you had no choice, except to endorse the opinion of two independent doctors that I needed to be Sectioned for my own Safety. But even after my admission to the Mayfield Clinic, it wasn't until you persuaded Professor Morgan to take my case that I embarked upon, a long and often traumatic road to my eventual recovery…"

At last, all traces of sharpness had left my Godfather's voice. "Naturally, Kenneth knew the steps I had taken in order to protect you, and in an attempt to repair some of the damage done to our relationship it was our intention that your father should set the record straight by telling you the truth. But since your recovery necessitated that you create an entirely new life, there never seemed to be an appropriate time or place to do so, without obstructing--or perhaps even damaging the healing process…"

Remembering the strength of my reaction, on the day when I had been summoned to my Godfather's study, because he suddenly felt that it had been the appropriate time and place to provide me with written proof that it was my own father, who had authorized the use of drugs and yet, even though I ripped up the letter, before showering not only the desk, but also my Godfather with the pieces, my anger had concealed my distress, because I knew how that first deception had started a chain reaction, which had been destined to eventually rob Lorna of the chance to have a life of her own choosing because Bobby--who had been the biggest loser--would have been able to grow up living with his birth mother.

Nothing can change the past, but within the present tense of this most recent summons to my Godfather's study, he has already declared that through his insurance policy, he wants to change my future, so that the three of us can continue living together as a family unit, and as if he can read my thoughts, his voice was soft and appealing.

"Having established that prior to your arrival at Manor Park, there were additional misrepresentations and misinterpretations, which caused you to doubt my trustworthiness, I'd like to propose that we focus our attention on the best outcome I can secure on your behalf?"

"Since neither of us can change anything that happened in the past Commander, your proposal sounds like an excellent idea…"

Flipping open the folder containing the sparse details of my discharge from the Research Programme, my Godfather removed a single document and then, perhaps for no other reason than he was anticipating my stunned reaction he turned it around, before sliding it across the desk, so that I could see the details without having to touch it.

"Because of its sensitive nature Charlie, this folder and its content are kept locked inside my personal safe at Manor Park, and up until a few days ago, when Mr Bland and Mr Powell were added to the list of people who needed to know, only the person granting the Royal Seal of Approval and I knew about its existence…"

For the benefit of the official record, my initial reaction was way beyond being stunned. In fact, even when I was able to speak, it was to state the obvious. "But surely there must be some kind of mistake Commander, because instead of my son this document relates to Charlotte Anne Forsyth?"

Over by the cabinet, despite detecting John's movement, I could not take my eyes off the details, and even when he poured some pure malt into my empty glass, before adding a little sparkling water, I doubt he could hear me expressing my gratitude, because my Godfather was confirming what should have been obvious.

"Because that document relates solely to you Charlie, there isn't any mistake…"

Still confused, I started to shake my head. "I don't understand…"

"On that day," Commander Maddox began to explain. "When I listened to the Top Brass expressing their fears over the kind of threat, the sheer strength of your unique abilities might pose to their cosy distribution of power, I politely drew their attention to the fact that they were missing the point, because the drugs had been introduced to determine whether your abilities could be undermined--or destabilized--or weakened--and on your behalf, I suggested that perhaps someone had decided that you needed to be told the truth, because you had discovered a plausible reason for the profound confusion you had been experiencing. In any event, you did prove that if your abilities were ever threatened, then you would automatically do whatever was necessary in order to protect yourself--while at the same time--you would afford any other friendly participants the same level of protection by safeguarding not only their own abilities, but also their anonymity…"

Operating on auto-pilot, I picked up the crystal glass, so that I could swallow some of its contents, before questioning my own actions. "But after I wrecked an entire laboratory, I erased everything Commander, including all the back-up data …"

"Oh I agree that your actions were a little extreme…"

When my Godfather paused, I lifted my head, but as I glanced across the desk instead of derision, I was greeted by a congratulatory smile. "But while the Top Brass would never admit it, they were actually embarrassed, because nobody had taken into consideration that when you discovered how you had been tricked, you might retaliate, by turning yourself into a weapon of mass destruction, and although they seemed to accept my submission that there was nothing stopping them from recommencing the Research, using the same participants, as I've explained, I remained fearful that you could be regarded as too much of a threat…"

Admiring his persuasive capabilities, I nodded my appreciation. "In fact Charlie, I have been granted two audiences. The first took place after your life fell apart and you had to be Sectioned for your own Safety. During that audience, I highlighted the fact that although your abilities were exceptional, as a result of what had happened--instead of a gift--you regarded your uniqueness as some kind of curse, and after providing the names of everyone who could associate you with the Research--or the Research Facility--it was agreed that any future access should be on a strictly need to know basis, so that when you were discharged from the Mayfield Clinic your anonymity would be guaranteed…"

Eager to learn what else I did not know about myself, when my Godfather paused, I posed an unavoidable direct question. "And what about the second audience?"

"As one might expect, when I was preparing for the first audience, I kept something in reserve, in case I should need it at some later date, and because of what you revealed during the Interview, I asked Sarah-Roxanna to request the second audience, as soon as I had heard everything…"

Of course, compared with the Research Facility, where I had only managed to upset the Top Brass, several other Agencies were going to be more than a little peeved with what I had done in order to not only gain my freedom, but also protect myself from my husband.

"During the second audience Charlie, I explained that in my professional opinion we would be deluding ourselves, if we failed to consider that around the world, there must be numerous people who had the same unique capabilities, and if they should ever pose a threat to our stability, then you would turn out to be a valuable resource, not only when it came to identifying any such threat, but also being able to neutralize it. So in addition to your guaranteed anonymity, it was agreed that as Commander in Chief of Special Operations, I should be responsible for securing your permanent protection from anything--or anyone--who might seek to cause you any physical, mental or emotional harm…"

Suddenly, it all made perfect sense, not only from John and Bill being reassigned after they had escorted me home from Paris, but also their subsequent request that the Protective Custody Order be obtained exclusively in their joint names--instead of Special Operations in general--and after swallowing the remaining whisky in one mouthful, I expressed my mixed emotions. "I don't know what to say Commander, except to extend…"

Anticipating my gratitude, the Commander interrupted me. "Although I intend to use the Royal Seal of Approval as leverage, there are no guarantees that the highest possible Authority will be able to persuade the other Agencies, what's in their own best interests. But since Mr Bland and Mr Powell obtained the Protective Custody Order exclusively in their names, if it should prove necessary, they will be able to legally break a few of the rules…"

While remaining in the background, it struck me that without seeking any recompense what this man has done for me throughout my lifetime, amounted to more than the duties of a Godfather, and despite my misguided animosity I was genuinely grateful.

"Although I have thoroughly enjoyed every single moment I have been able to spend with Lorna and Bobby, as if we were a proper family Commander, I have never lost sight of the fact that it might have to come to an end. But while I know that you will negotiate, the very best deal for all three of us, this mother wants you to understand that any extra time, even if it's only one day--would be a blessing…"

Aware that he would never commit himself to anything that he is not in a position to guarantee, I attempted to change the subject. "Now if there's nothing else, I think I should go and find Lorna and then Thomas, so that we can reschedule our interrupted therapy session, before Margaret wants us to assemble in the dining room…"

Perhaps he might not be able to commit himself, but yet again my Godfather attracted my attention. "Naturally, I have every intention of negotiating the best possible deal for everyone concerned, and like Lorna I do hope that at some point in the future, instead of Commander, you might feel that it's appropriate to address me as Philip?"

Appreciating my Godfather's subtle declaration that as far as he was concerned, failure was not an option, I extended my smile, before I delivered a declaration, which confirmed my true feelings.

"If we discount my step-mother Helen, then you're the closest thing I have to family, so I would like that very much, but until the negotiations come to an end, and there is a deal in place, it doesn't seem right to address you by anything other than Commander…"

Not expecting a response, I severed eye-contact, but as I rose to my feet, Philip Maddox addressed his subordinates. "Gentlemen, if I'm going to be unavailable until at midday tomorrow, then before lunch I think you should find not only Bobby and Lorna, but also Sarah-Roxanna, so that while my Goddaughter finishes her therapy session with Thomas, I can compensate for my absence by playing football later this afternoon…"

## July 10th  14:26

Having established on numerous occasions that Thomas is a gifted Person Centred Therapist, when we recommenced our interrupted therapy session--from the onset--he made it clear that he was not going to afford me any room to manoeuvre, and after casting nothing more than a cursory glance at his notepad, it was as if there had never been any interruption at all, but while he repeated his request with regard to whether I had considered, how far I would be prepared to go, in order to achieve a satisfactory resolution, especially with regard to John Bland's professional responsibilities--in all fairness--I had no idea what will happen, once I am inside his bedroom.

Indeed, I agreed that it might be enough for him to admit that when it came to those aforementioned professional responsibilities, he had acted in an irresponsible manner, because if he had not allowed his brain to lose control of his mouth, then he would never have expected an answer to those two demands.

Of course earlier, I had realized that the more intimate details might pose a conflict of interests for Thomas, so we did have to redefined our boundaries, so that we were free to discuss my intended preparations, which enabled us to rehearse not only some of this leading lady's dialogue lines, but also how I would counteract every possible negative reaction from my principal male in response to my unexpected arrival in his bedroom.

### July 10<sup>th</sup> 22:43

This is it! Since I have not changed my mind, then while my Godfather is staying overnight in his private apartment at Headquarters it has to be tonight, because he would neither approve of my intended action, nor its motivation.

So with Bobby and Lorna both sleeping, I have had a shower and brushed my teeth, before moisturising my body with a lotion, which will not overpower my favourite perfume, Yves St Laurent's Rive Gauche and then, wearing nothing except my towelling robe from the en-suite, I have been waiting for the familiar tap on my door, which will announce the imminent arrival of what should constitute John Bland's final appearance of the day.

Of course throughout the night, one half of the dynamic duo will perform a security check to ascertain that--preferably in their own beds--everybody is still sleeping, and after spending too many nights pretending to be asleep, I know the next one will occur two hours, after Bill hears his partner clicking the door closed, as he leaves my bedroom.

As his face appears through the small gap he has created, John is checking to determine whether or not I am still awake, before venturing into my bedroom carrying a crystal glass, which he places on the bedside table.

"I've completed the last security check Charlie, but before I go to my room and have a shower," he explains and then, even though the contents of the glass do not need any explanation, he adds. "Earlier today, while we were in the study, Bill and I suspected that although you managed to hide your true feelings, you were actually upset by the way in which Bobby's father died. So we thought that you might like an extra strong pure malt whisky, and in case you're still awake in the early hours of the morning, I've also brought you a sleeping pill…"

With John studying my face through the reflection in the mirror, my voice is soft and appreciative. "Although that was a very thoughtful gesture John, I wasn't in the least concerned about Robert Lloyd Reece-Milliner. However, I was upset on behalf of his wife, because she is going to discover, how difficult it is to raise her sons without a father…"

Having sat himself down on the bed, John empathises. "Perhaps it does seem to be ironic, but nothing can alter the fact that irrespective of whether your husband was alive or dead, it would seem to indicate that Mark Daltry had planned to eliminate anybody, who knew too much about his alternative lifestyle. So in case you should find yourself overthinking what happened, I'll leave the sleeping pill beside the pure malt whisky…"

As John disappears, I am hoping that there will be something even more significant, which I might have cause to be overthinking and then, while I unwrap the three full length pure silk chemises and their matching robes, which Sarah-Roxanna purchased on my behalf, for the arrival of such an occasion, because for the next step in the healing process to begin, I need to be wearing something which has no connection whatsoever with my past.

So after choosing the black chemise and its matching robe, both of which are edged with ivory lace, as I quite literally slip into them, this leading lady is practising those dialogue lines, which Thomas and I rehearsed--while at the same time--I am running and rerunning how I will counteract every conceivable negative reaction from a reluctant principal male.

Finally, it is time to bring that coincidental asset into play, but after picking up the crystal glass, I fail to show its contents the respect it deserves by swallowing the pure malt whisky in one defiant mouthful, before leaving my room as quietly as possible, so that in my bare feet, I can move undetected down the landing, until I am standing outside my primary target's bedroom door.

Then, my rapid heart rate necessitates that I pause, so that using my unique abilities, I can moderate the extra adrenaline being pumped into my blood stream, before I slip into his room, and as John emerges from the en-suite wearing his bathrobe, he is using a bath towel to remove the surplus water from his hair, but even though he casts me nothing more than a cursory glance, his apparent indifference does not weaken my resolve, especially when I have turned the key in the lock.

"This is a surprise Charlie," John remarks nonchalantly, as he begins to assess the situation, and because he still has not looked at me, I allow him to continue uninterrupted. "But it's a pleasant one--or it would be, except that I'm wondering why you've felt the need to lock the door, and there are three possible reasons? Firstly, you want to stop me from detaching myself from the scene prematurely, and secondly, you don't want anyone to disturb us, and since everyone else is asleep, Bill seems to be the most likely offender..."

For the benefit of my invisible audience, it should be noted that John still has not looked at me, but since I am eager to learn what constitutes his third reason, this leading lady chooses to remain silent, until he feels obliged to enlighten me.

"Or continuing with the premature theory--in third place--perhaps you're afraid that you might suddenly change your mind, and since the door is locked, you would have time to reconsider your decision to beat what would be a hasty retreat..."

As he stops speaking, John returns the bath towel to the en-suite, but when he reappears and he finally looks at me for once he seems to be lost for words, and after all my careful preparation, I choose to interpret his apparent reticence as indifference, which provides me with a convenient excuse to turn away from him, as I declare, "That's okay John, because even before I came into your bedroom, I knew there was a possibility that you might not be prepared to take me seriously..."

Since I have implied that he is to blame for my need to fulfil, his third prediction, after unlocking the door, I attempt to restore a more balanced perspective. "In light of what's happened, perhaps it might be in our best interests, if we pretend that I was never here..."

Absolutely mortified by what I perceive to be the mess I have made, all I want to do is escape, but despite managing to open the door, the palm of John's right hand reaches over my shoulder, so that--using the softest of touches--he can click it closed again, and despite being able to feel the warmth of his breath on the back of my neck, which makes me aware of his closeness--for what seems like an eternity--neither of us moves nor speaks, until I find the inner calmness to be able to enter a more rational explanation for my actions.

"During our therapy session this wasn't how Thomas and I rehearsed it. So if you don't have any objections I'd like to leave with whatever dignity, I can salvage..."

Without even allowing him to consider whether he has any objections, which he might like to raise, yet again I try to escape, but this time John manages to gain possession of his own valuable asset by locking the door, before removing the key.

"Please John, isn't it enough for you to have proved that your third prediction was accurate?" I hear this woman admitting. "And because this has been a monumental mistake, I'd like to return to my own bedroom..."

Despite my request, yet again nothing disturbs the silence for what seems like another eternity, until John's eventual response manages to ambush me.

"And as God is my witness, as soon as you give me the opportunity to explain the reasons for my initial reaction, I won't do anything to prevent you from leaving..."

Although John has turned me into a captive audience, throughout the ensuing silence, I continue to feel each of his warm breaths against the back of my neck, and I am aware that he is allowing me, the time I need to decide whether the terms of my continued captivity are acceptable and yet, as soon as the steady breathing ceases, my principal male issues me with an unexpected declaration in connection with his behaviour.

"If I was in your position then considering the mess I've made of this, I probably wouldn't want to even think about turning around, but if you were facing me, then you would be able to witness first-hand the sincerity of my apology for my ungentlemanly conduct..."

Taking into account that John has done nothing, which might convince me that if I do turn around, then I will not be running the risk of being subjected to more humiliation and yet, as if he never expected any kind of response, he continues with his explanation.

"In fact, while you were working with Thomas, because I can appreciate the obstacles, you must have had to overcome, before you could even begin the planning followed by the rehearsing, so that you would have the courage and the emotional strength you would need to be able to come into my room, only to end up feeling as if I wasn't taking you seriously, and that was unforgiveable..."

As John takes a steadying breath, since my position is beginning to change, I feel able to offer him some encouragement. "Despite appearances I am listening John..."

"After using the towel as a distraction, when I returned it to the en-suite, I knew I had run out of excuses to avoid doing more than simply glancing at you, and you looked so amazing I was speechless, but we're trained how to stop ourselves from acknowledging those feelings, especially if they should arise while we're working on a Protection Assignment..."

So there is another irony, because while I am listening, I find myself trying to avoid acknowledging my own feelings, but yet again, John seems to be unstoppable.

"Instead--*and preferably before we begin to consider acting upon them*--as soon as it's practical, we're supposed to request an urgent one to one session with Dr James..."

Fleetingly, I find myself wondering whether John has already had that one to one session, which might have posed a conflict of interests for Thomas. But having realized that at some point, the palms of his hands have come to rest upon my shoulders, amid a mixture of conflicting emotions, although my head is warning me that I am perilously close to having to make a commitment, my body is telling me something different, so that a combination of my willingness to respond to the almost exquisite lightness of his touch, as his hands tighten a little, inch by inch I am turning and then--albeit with my head bowed in order to avoid eye contact--I find myself facing my resurrected principal male.

Strictly between you and me, if I was honest about that one to one therapy session, after being repeatedly challenged over my belief that I had chosen John Bland, for no other reason than that moment when his brain lost control of his mouth--having saved the best until last--in the final analysis, Thomas invited me to compare the unstoppable ranting about allowing any man to touch my body without being reminded of what happened, during those sixty minutes of my life, with what took place, after the cavalry found my hiding place in the master bedroom at 187 Cheltenham Way.

Since those events occurred at the start of my life story, I would not expect you to recall them, but after my whereabouts had been located, John dealt with the gun and the sleeping pills, which I had been holding. Then, they had both been prepared to afford me, as much time as I needed to adjust to the permanence of their presence, until a battle of wills between me and Bill confirmed that certain conditions, relating to the terms of my surrender were non-negotiable, but since John had manoeuvred himself into position, as soon as I attempted to stand up, his arms had come from behind me, so that he could stop me from injuring my bare feet on the shards of glass which were strewn across the floor.

Until now, within the present tense of John's bedroom, I had failed to grasp the significance of being held pinned against him, because possibly for the first time--since my mother died--being unable to move meant that I had felt safe. A complete sense of safeness and yet, when that damning revelation necessitates that I mask the tears, which are threatening to escape and I close my eyes, John responds by reducing the distance between us, and after overpowering, what I must admit was a half-hearted attempt to stop him, he allows history to repeat itself by wrapping his arms around me.

Instead of any sense of fear, with one of his hands cradling my head, so that my face is resting against the exposed moist skin of his upper body, John seems to be prepared to wait, until I finish experiencing what feels like an identical sense of absolute safeness.

Eventually, John eases his hold a little and in a soft tone of voice. he explains, "Since I'm not a complete idiot, I suspect that after what happened as a result of me allowing my personal feelings to cloud my professional judgement over what I perceived to be, your reckless behaviour, although we have dealt with the first part of my demand, in order to move forward in the therapeutic process, you now need to discover whether or not, you will be able to allow any man to touch your body, without you being reminded of what took place at 187 Cheltenham Way…"

Finding his forthrightness almost unbearable when my muscles tense involuntarily, John hesitates, before he affords me some much needed reassurance. "As far as I'm aware, there isn't any urgency Charlie, especially with my Commanding Officer staying overnight at H.Q., and Lorna and Bobby are both sleeping, so the only person who could possibly disturb us is Bill, but since he isn't due to perform the next security check for approximately…"

Hesitating again, John eases one of his arms free, so that he can glance at his watch. "One hour and forty-six minutes, so I think we should be able to smuggle you back into your own room, before he finds out that you're missing. However, even if he should discover that you've been hiding in my room, I can assure you that he won't be too shocked, but because he's unlikely to accept a defence based upon the premise that you were holding me hostage, so that you could make improper demands of a sexual nature, apart from being obliged to read me, yet another one of his infamous riot acts, since we are a team, and like moving parts in the same well-oiled piece of machinery, we tend to be very discreet, when it comes to each other's implied or intended indiscretions…"

With my self-consciousness beginning to diminish, when I am unable to contain a quite spontaneous laugh, he continues to encourage me to feel more at ease.

"Before your arrival at Manor Park, although it was hardly surprising considering the circumstances, I had never seen you smile--much less heard you laugh--but after being reunited with Lorna and Bobby, it's as if you've become a little more alive with each day that's come to pass. But I feel that I must warn you that despite the fact that you are a very beautiful woman, if you're expecting me to pick you up and throw you onto the bed, so that I can ravish you, then you're going to be sorely disappointed with my performance…"

Since being ravished was not one of the options, which Thomas and I had considered, when its ridiculousness prompts me to release a more convincing laugh, John seems determined to eliminate any remaining tension between us.

"Besides, when it comes to the section in our Professional Code of Conduct, which is dedicated to dealing with wanting to ravish a beautiful woman, since I haven't had the chance to practice ravishing anyone during the last three months, I think you might agree that it's a relief that we can discount it as an option…"

Then, while he is still holding me as close as possible without any warning, he chooses to change the subject. "With regard to our present predicament, approximately five minutes ago, despite your half-hearted attempt to stop me, I managed to put my arms around you and since you haven't lodged any verbal protests, I'm wondering how it feels to be this close to a man who's wearing nothing, except a bathrobe?"

Gosh, what a leading question and yet, after discounting all of the alternative replies, I know it deserves an honest--albeit revealing answer--so I tell him the truth.

"For the second time in what seems to be a lifetime, I feel safe…"

"Now I'm intrigued Charlie, and curious to know about the first time…"

"It was while we were in the bathroom at 187 Cheltenham Way, and after managing to hurl that large ornate shell in Bill's direction, I had succeeded in smashing some of the expensive Italian mirrored tiles, and when I tried to stand up, you put your arms around me, so that I wouldn't injure my bare feet on the shards of glass strewn across the floor, but it wasn't until a few moment's ago, I realized that for the first time since my mother died, I had experienced an unconditional awareness of my absolute safeness…"

Suddenly overwhelmed by an image of my mother, John responds to the tremor in my voice by tightening his hold a little. "Having established that there isn't any rush Charlie, you can take whatever time you need to eliminate any doubts or concerns…"

Whilst doing nothing that might disturb that unconditional awareness of my safeness, I explain. "Considering that Thomas encouraged me to address my concerns--such as the preliminary results from the lab, which were encouraging--I felt even less apprehensive after Thomas explained that because of the risks involved, it would be standard practice for anyone working in a profession such as Special Operations to be screened on a regular basis…"

"That's correct Charlie, and in addition to being expected to undertake screening at least every three months, we are also provided with the most up-to-date information, so that we can protect not only ourselves, but also any consenting third party…"

So it would seem that John is confirming that neither of us would be at risk from any transmittable disease, and aware that for my part I am rapidly running out of excuses, I find myself releasing another ironic laugh.

"Taking into account that I came into your room expecting you to compromise, your professional Code of Conduct, you seem to be demonstrating remarkable understanding…"

"Well if it would make you feel any better, then I could suggest that it's about time you stopped behaving like a sixteen-year-old virgin, and started acting like the beautiful young woman you are, and begin by answering a leading direct question…"

Remembering the last time, he accused me of behaving like a sixteen-year-old virgin causes me to release yet another laugh, before I agree. "Since it cannot possibly make me feel any more embarrassed than I do right now--you can ask me whatever you want…"

"Do you trust me?"

Wow, out of all the possible options, the abrupt introduction of the trust issue was not something I had considered and yet, because there can only be one response within its next profound beat, my heart overrules my head.

"If I didn't trust you, I wouldn't be standing in your bedroom dressed like this," Pausing, so that I can catch my breath John remains both still and silent, until I am ready to add. "And despite threatening to take a leaf out of my husband's book, and beat the shit out of me in my heart, I know that unless it was to stop me from indulging in any additional reckless behaviour, you would never use your hands as weapons in order to secure your own way, not only when it comes to me, but also any other woman, because you would regard it as a sign of weakness…"

As I finish my explanation, once again John tightens his hold on me, and when his lips brush against my forehead for the first time, I find myself wanting more.

"Despite being honoured that you should feel that I'm trustworthy, I'm afraid that I have to agree with your assessment of the beating option, because if I were in your position, then I don't think I would allow myself to become too complacent, especially when you take into consideration that unlike the ravaging option, if you should decide to indulge in any additional reckless behaviour, beating the shit out of you remains a strong probability, …"

After releasing another even more spontaneous laugh, as I look at him I discover that he is wearing one of those butter would not melt expressions, and when I realize that I have finally run out of excuses and I can see the admiration, which is reflected in those deep brown eyes for the inappropriateness of my behaviour, I find myself making a direct suggestion.

"Before we take this any further, Thomas suggested that I should choose an escape word, and if you don't have any preferences which you might like to propose, then I think that it should simply be *STOP*…"

Now, those deep brown eyes are congratulating me for having made such a bold move, and if you will pardon a dreadful play on words, after tilting his head onto one side, my principal male rises to the challenge.

"That's an excellent choice Charlie, and if at any time, you should decide that you don't want to proceed, I give you my personal guarantee that I will never be so out of control that I will not be able to stop immediately…"

Oh my God, when I press my hand against his chest with each strong beat of his heart, matching my own, I know that John means every word, and despite the circumstances none of what is happening around me feels as if it is being engineered or manufactured, so that having reawakened something buried deep within me, I admit that for either all the right, or even all the wrong reasons I want this man. So when he lowers his head until he fulfils my desire for more, and his lips touch mine it's as if we both understand that using a level of gentleness, one would not normally associate with a man in his line of work, John is providing me with a further demonstration of his self-control.

Between you and me, although there is no sense of urgency or any demand for my reciprocation by the time it comes to a natural end, because I became a willing participant, I am aware that my cheeks must have reddened a little and yet, John allows the silence to linger, so that I can regain my composure, before his tone once again becomes serious.

"On 29th June as the evening progressed, and my role meant that you should gradually reveal more and more about your life, I found myself increasingly challenged by your habitual, and often deliberate dalliances with reckless behaviour, and as a result of being married to a man like Mark Daltry, you found me to be a worthy adversary…"

Remembering the inevitable challenges throughout that evening, and how my Godfather must have known that there were times when the atmosphere, inside his study must have been electrifying makes me smile and yet, I do not interrupt my principal male's recollections. "In fact, as the Interview progressed, there were moments when things passed between us, which altered the fundamental basis of our relationship, and although I'm willing to admit that until a few moments ago, I hadn't realized that I must have been waiting for a genuine excuse, so that I could kiss you, I need you to confirm that beyond all doubt that this is what you want, because once we cross that invisible line between professional and personal, we will have to face any resulting consequences…"

Wanting to be sure that there can be no doubt, as soon as John hesitates, using my toes I increase my height, and then employing a level of boldness one would not normally associate with a young woman in my situation, my lips touch his mouth, but despite having provided him with the confirmation he needs, John continues to demonstrate his self-control, by making sure that the delicacy of the second kiss is no less exquisite than the first.

Then he picks me up, so that he can carry me not to the bed, which would have been the obvious choice, but to the armchair by the window, and once I'm seated, he affords me an explanation. "Despite knowing that you have complete control, over everything that happens between us before we begin, I'd like to take a few minutes to try and create the most advantageous environment…"

Strictly between you and me, having awakened that something deep within me--in my eagerness to proceed--I cannot find a solitary thing wrong with the existing environment, but when John moves to the dresser, so that he can light the candles, before he chooses a CD from the selection in the rack, and he loads it into the machine, because his actions seem to be part of an established routine, I decide to regard my keenness as a private asset, especially when he dims the lights, before moving to the bed, so that he can slide the lightweight duvet, and its matching top sheet to one side, before he reorganizes the pillows.

In all fairness, even if John had not allowed his brain to lose control of his mouth, sooner or later I would have needed to know the answer to the same question. So if for no other reason than I trust him, not only with my body and mind, but also my soul, I'm glad that I seem to have chosen him, and with the first track almost finished, when he disappears into the en-suite, although it's an even bolder indication of my collusion, I leave the armchair, so that I can sit on the edge of the bed, as the next track from the C D starts to play.

Wow! Although the first track had a mysterious kind of sadness attached to it, the second is completely different, and when I close my eyes there is an image of the shoreline and the waves, as they are pushing forward and then, the current draws them back, so that the sea can achieve its high tide, before the entire process is reversed, and I find myself back at the very beginning, where unbeknown to any of the people who have played a part in my life story I had explained, why I was sitting on the beach in the early hours of that morning.

Of course, since the dawn has been breaking on that beach for millions, possibly even trillions of years, and we are here for such a short period of time, we could never fulfil all of our objectives within our lifetime and yet, with the reawakening of that something, which I must have buried deep within me, because it seemed to be unattainable, there is an awareness that if I grant it, the unlimited time and sufficient space it needs to reach its full potential, then in the present tense of John's bedroom, I can achieve the kind of transformation which might enable me to begin a new chapter in my life story.

Sensing John's return from the en-suite, I open my eyes and as he takes hold of my hands and encourages me to rise to my feet, I attempt to apologise for my boldness. "I'm sorry, but I felt compelled to come and sit…"

"It doesn't matter Charlie," John interrupts me, so that he can explain. "As far as I'm aware there aren't any rules. In fact, we haven't even established any guidelines, but since the rest of the world is beyond that locked bedroom door, there's only you and me…"

As John's fingertips ease the robe off my shoulders, and it falls to the floor, he allows the palms of his hands to run down my outer arms, and when I experience that familiar tingling sensation, I am unable to stifle an almost pained gasp at the tenderness of his touch, but irrespective of how delightful my discomfort must seem, after picking me up, John lays me down on the bed, so that my head and shoulders are resting on the pillows, before he provides me with additional proof that our success is dependent upon us doing this his way.

"And what about the tracks from the C D, do you think they're acceptable or would you prefer to choose something different…"

Curbing my boldness, I deliver my reply in a nonchalant fashion. "That won't be necessary John. In fact, I would like to hear them again, especially the second one…"

"Of course…"

But when John moves back to the dresser, I find myself seeking some additional reassurance. "Are you sure that we won't be disturbed?"

"If it'll make you feel more at ease, I can put a note on the other side of the door, confirming that you're not in any immediate danger and then, provided that Bill doesn't decide to try and rescue me, preferably before I compromise my professional position, I'm confident that our privacy will be guaranteed…"

As he pauses, John extends his smile, before he suggests. "So while I organize the note, all I want you to do is close your eyes, so that you can focus on the music, and as an officer and a gentleman, I give you my word that unless you tell me to *stop*, the progression of events will happen quite naturally…"

Between you and me, it did cross my mind that perhaps I should be honest, and admit that because my feelings have changed, my newly established escape word might have become irrelevant, but while I am lying there with my eyes closed, having accomplished his mission sooner than I had anticipated, when John returns on this next occasion, after his lips brush against mine, although the kiss begins with the same exquisite delicateness, it gradually becomes more impassioned, until I am being swept away by an indescribable wave of craving, and since my principal male has set the scene so magnificently, he has managed to arouse within me a growing yearning to discover what I can expect, once he is inside of me, and after experiencing a warm, moist sensation, during the delivery of the next no less passionate kiss, John seems to enter my body effortlessly.

Much to my dismay, even with the memories of my less pleasant sexual experiences trapped on the other side of the locked bedroom door, I am still too afraid to look at him, but while I am focusing on the music, I experience a sudden awareness that as he promised, this seduction is progressing quite naturally, and despite his enforced period of abstinence, as a result of the cavalry being assigned to escort me home from Paris, I now find myself imagining that those deep brown eyes are smiling at the prospect of the fulfilment, he will be able to enjoy, especially when he seems to be controlling my body as well as his own, so that as if my actions are involuntary, each time he pushes a little further forward, my muscles are contracting and then, when he draws back I am releasing them, and once our bodies are moving in perfect harmony, as part of that same progression, I feel a sudden need to become proactive, and as I bend my knees I bring my heels up towards my hips, and when I am confident that he cannot manage to escape I reach up, so that I can draw his torso down towards me, because I want him to hear me whispering over and over again *"Don't stop, please don't stop…"*

Not that John has any intention of stopping, not when he is confident enough in his performance to know that unless I use my escape word, he is managing to spark that equally indescribable sensation deep within me, and having ensured my full participation that feeling starts radiating, throughout my entire central nervous system, until it ignites every single nerve ending, and because John has not relinquished his overall control, he understands that even if its intensity verges upon being delectably painful on this occasion, when it explodes I need it to overwhelm me. So he knows when to push forward for the last time, and although I do not have any firm evidence, I also have nothing to disprove that we have not shared that wonderful moment, when two people climax almost simultaneously.

Unable to find a more adequate description, within the aftermath of such perfection having created an almost utopian environment, where my past and any future that we might have remain trapped on the other side of the locked door, John's arm continues to hold me, so that beneath the top sheet, which is barely covering us I am curled into his body, and with the C D still playing, it is as if time itself has been suspended, and while we are each processing what has passed between us, especially when it would seem that we have gone much further than merely crossing that invisible line, between what was my personal need to know whether this was possible and the boundaries of John's professional code of conduct.

According to the evidence, the only stimulation John seemed to need were those kisses, which started so delicately, before becoming more passionate, but there was none of the usual crass fumbling with any part of my body--least of all my breasts--and while his mission might have been to prove that I would be able to allow a man to touch my body, once he was inside of me, he managed to turn my pleasure into something more meaningful, so that even if John's climax occurred a few seconds after mine, I am immensely proud that together with his own performance through my own arousal, which turned me into an active participant, I made a worthwhile contribution towards procuring that phenomena. Although it also makes me appreciate that every single step, during this seduction was designed to be different and yet, my subsequent realization of what this man has done for me, causes tears to well up in my eyes, but when they threaten to escape, I manage to brush them aside fast enough to prevent them from moistening John's torso, but irrespective of how subtle it might have been, any movement would have been enough to cause John to react, and as that protective arm tightens around me, he brings the silence we were sharing to an end.

"Are you okay?"

Unaccustomed to feeling quite so liberated the silence lingers, until I find the right words. "I'm more than okay John. In fact, I've never felt this way in my entire life…"

Considering the threatened tears, I am aware that I was not being one hundred per cent truthful because initially, as he had promised me--with my eyes closed and the C D playing, I never once thought about anything that occurred in the early hours of that morning at 187 Cheltenham Way, but his achievement went much further than anyone could ever imagine, especially when I was fully focused upon, what was happening in the here and now of John's bedroom that this experience proved to be different from any of my previous sexual encounters. So different that while I have been processing what passed between us, I have become aware of another damning revelation which no woman should have to admit--least of all someone who has a seven-year-old son.

"When I said that I was more than okay, there's something I need to explain…"

"Believe me Charlie, you don't have to justify anything…"

"Oh but I do John," this woman protests. "Because I want you to know that for the first time in my life, I now know what it's like to have a man make love to me…"

In response that protective arm tightens again. "Then it was long overdue…"

Without needing to check, I know that John is being sincere, and not being able to see his face somehow makes it easier. "You made me feel so special…"

"That's because you are," John admits, in a rare moment of transparency. "In fact, you're more than special you are unique, an incredibly beautiful young woman who entrusted me with her body and mind and then, rewarded me with her willing participation, so that if you're unsure Charlie, then the answer is yes--although it was never my intention--it proved to be a welcome bonus when we both climaxed almost simultaneously…"

"Now that complicates things, especially when this was supposed to be a tactical exercise to determine whether I would be able to allow a man to touch my body…"

"Oh I think we managed to dispel any concerns you might have been harbouring…"

"That's very tactful John, but lying in the silence, I was thinking about how much I had wanted you. It reminded me of the words to one of my favourite songs. *"Yes, I need you tonight, and I'll show you a sunset if you'll stay with me until dawn…"*

"Judie Tzuke," John confirms the singer/songwriter, before he admits, "And for my part, instead of feeling any degree of discomfort at having disregarded my Professional Code of Conduct, I was lying in the stillness thinking how natural this feels, especially with the rest of the world trapped on the other side of the locked bedroom door…"

Now I think you might agree that this level of consideration is what makes John Bland everything any woman could ever want or need in their life and yet, because his chosen profession is fraught with too many uncertainties, the cruellest irony might be that he would find it difficult--if not downright impossible--to make any kind of a lasting commitment, but as far as I am concerned I can settle for what he has shared, and God willing whatever else he might be prepared to share with me.

Then, as he rolls onto his back he retrieves the arm, which has been holding me, as he announces, "If I'm going to do the next security check, I think I need to have another shower and after what's happened perhaps it should preferably be a cold one…"

Ignoring John's protestations as he leaves the bed, I note that he is still wearing his robe, and because I am curious to see more of him, I wait until I hear the water gushing from the shower faucet, before I slip out of bed and allow my full length chemise to fall to the floor around my feet, and after wrapping the sheet around me, I head for the en-suite, but without needing to turn around as soon as I enter, John reacts to my presence

"As a trained professional Charlie, I wouldn't be very good at my job if I didn't instinctively know when someone comes within six foot of me…"

When I choose to remain still and silent, John glances over his shoulder and groans, before quickly severing eye contact. "Would you please put me out of my misery, by confirming that you're not naked beneath the sheet…"

"I'm sorry if it complicates things, but for some reason I felt so hot and clammy in my chemise, I decided that I also needed a shower, although from the amount of steam, it would seem that you changed your mind about having a cold one…"

"Charlie," He beseeches me. "Please don't let that sheet fall to the floor…"

"In that case, you have a choice, either I take the sheet off and it remains dry, or I can leave it on and you will have to explain to Margaret, how you suddenly became incontinent in the early hours of the morning…"

Pausing, I wait until he groans again, before I select an option on his behalf, and after allowing the sheet to fall to the floor, there is an even greater wickedness, with which I want to tease him, but as soon as I am within his grasp, John catches hold of my arm and pulls me in front of him, before he transfers his grasp to my wrists.

"More reckless behaviour Mrs Daltry?" he asks, as he pulls me back against him and then, with the water cascading over both of us, he reminds me of the potential precariousness of my position. "You seem to have forgotten that I still reserve the right to carry out--the as yet unused threat--to beat the shit out of you…"

In response to what I deem to be an empty threat, I dare to release a lurid laugh, but by way of a counterchallenge John's hands start tormenting me, by smoothing the suds from his shower gel, all over my upper body, especially my breasts, and because it's arousing me, I hear this woman entering an admission, I had intended to introduce at a later time.

"I have a special request John…"

"And I don't suppose it has anything to do with me taking a leaf out of your husband's book and beating the shit out of you?"

After releasing an even more lurid laugh, I admit, "Well, I suppose it has something to do with my husband, but not quite as drastic…"

"So before you discovered that he was a cruel son of a bitch, it must have something to do with the erotic games you played with your husband…"

By now my legs have been parted by his hand, but I have to admit that's not quite how it happened, and strictly between you and me, it was more a case of my thighs parting in readiness for his hand to move between them, and as God is my witness, when this seducer ceased his exploration with the kind of cruel and frustrating swiftness, which was guaranteed to produce a pathetic moan--albeit muted--because I must have been at least twenty, but no more than maybe thirty seconds away from climaxing again.

"In accordance with my Professional Code of Conduct," John declares, as if he did not hear me. "I'm not at liberty to beat the shit out of you, until you act with reckless endangerment, so after giving it some initial consideration, your generous offer is tempting, but until you confirm that you're willing to accept that there are some things I would not be willing to do, I cannot make a final decision about how we need to proceed?"

After issuing a frustrated groan, I manage to gasp. "I'll accept whatever you want…"

"That's what I thought," John states, with a deliberate degree of smugness and then, after pressing my body up against the cold tiles, he adds. "So while I smooth things over with Bill, and we do the hand over, so that he can get some proper sleep, I want you to get yourself dried off and then, be back in bed by the time I return or you'll be in even more trouble…"

After John left the en-suite I was tempted to discover how much more trouble I could be in, but while I was using a bath towel to dry myself, I became aware of a mellowness, which like the liberation I had never experienced in my lifetime, and having noted that one of John's shirts was draped around the chair in front of the dresser, because I could smell his aftershave, I slipped my arms into the sleeves and then, after throwing the top sheet back across the bed, I lay down, before pulling the lightweight duvet over me, and for the first time in longer than I could remember, I found myself unable to resist the urge to close my eyes

So I did not have any idea that Bill had challenged his partner, over his own reckless behaviour, and oblivious to the length of time that had elapsed, before John came back to bed, although I did stir as he joined me under the duvet, the mellowness and liberation had dissolved into contentment, and after responding to the arm, which encouraged me to curl into him, I drifted straight back off to sleep.

Despite having every intention of coming back to bed, so that we could proceed from the point at which we had had to pause, John was content to do nothing, except hold me and while he was contemplating what Bill had suggested should be his partner's next responsible action, because he had left the door ajar to enable him to react to the slightest irregularity, approximately fifty-five minutes later, when it began to creep open and hesitantly, Bobby's head appeared, without jumping to conclusions John reacted in a hushed voice.

"Hello young man. Did something disturb you?"

"It was another bad dream…"

"Surely, not that man again?"

"Yes, but I think it was a different one, and this time he had a big gun. So I went into mum's bedroom to make sure that she was all right, and when she wasn't there, I was even more upset until I saw that your door was open, and the night light was switched on…"

"Although you did the right thing coming to find either Bill or me, you have to remember that not only your Uncle Philip, but also several other people are working very hard to make sure that there aren't any bad men coming after your mum ever again. But for now, would you like to come and join us?"

Curious to know who else was occupying John's king-size bed, Bobby moved even closer and after standing on the tips of his toes, he exclaimed, "Gosh, so this is where mum has been hiding! Did she have a bad dream too John?"

In response to the innocence of youth, an affectionate smile crept onto John's face, but after he helped Bobby onto the bed, so that the youngster could make himself comfortable beneath the lightweight duvet, he chose to be economical with the truth. "Yeah, I think it was something like that Bobby. Now like your mum, I want you to close your eyes and then, once you're fast asleep, I'll carry you both back to your own beds…"

A few minutes later, although it should have been an impossibility, Bobby somehow managed to snuggle himself still further into John's body, as he remarked. "Don't you think that the three of us sharing the same bed is pretty cool John?"

"Yes it is Bobby, and I guess that's what Bill is so concerned about because it feels so natural, almost as if was destined to be this way…"

Then, when the ensuing silence suggested that Bobby had fallen asleep, John dared to relax a little, until a small voice summoned his attention.

"John…"

"Go to sleep…"

"But it's important…"

"Okay, but make it quick…"

"I was wondering whether finding mum asleep in your bed, should be our secret?"

After taking a few moments to consider his response, John explained, "Until I've had a chance to explain what happened to the Commander, perhaps it might be best if we don't tell anyone…"

"I do hope that you don't get into any trouble…"

"Oh because I've already had to offer him a partial explanation, I'm hoping that he might be expecting to hear what I have to tell him…"

"Phew, that's a relief because I wouldn't want us to never be able to do this again…"

Despite his original insistence, John realized that he was allowing the exchange of dialogue to continue. "Right young man, even for someone with an enquiring mind like yours that's more than enough questions at this time in the morning, and you won't be able to concentrate when we play football tomorrow, unless you get enough sleep…"

Several hours later, when John scooped me up into his arms, I caught sight of the first rays of light and sleepily, I muttered. "The dawn's beginning to break…"

"Yes it is Charlie, and even though Bill reminded me of my professional responsibilities and obligations, I don't regret a single moment of what happened between us." Hesitating, John kisses my forehead, before he enlightens me about our visitor. "And I wouldn't worry too much about your son, because he thinks you were hiding in my room, after you had a bad dream…"

Having reached my own room, as John lays me down, the chill from my silk sheets causes me to experience a rational moment, which prompts me to ask. "Did you say my son?"

"Yes, but there's nothing to be concerned about because he thinks it's a secret…"

"In that case, unless I have another son who isn't called Bobby, then we are so busted, because he'll never manage to keep it to himself…"

Finally, John pulls the lightweight duvet over me. "Try not to worry Charlie, because having talked things through with Bill, I'm going to make sure that Bobby's inability to keep a secret won't matter…"

## July 11th

*Regrettably, after the previous night's eventfulness, it was not until the cold light of the next morning, before I gained possession of all the facts*, because during the challenge Bill had made with regard to his partner's reckless behaviour, it had been suggested that it might be best if John explained to their Commanding Officer, not only what had occurred, but also the reason why it had happened.

Then after Bobby had found me, not only in the wrong bedroom, but also asleep in the wrong bed, because John knew that it would be a disaster if the Commander learnt what had happened through a third party, especially an almost seven-year-old who was prone to gross exaggeration, he accepted that he did not have the luxury of a choice.

So by the time the chauffeur driven Jaguar had drawn to a halt in the driveway, at 7:16 the insubordinate subordinate was showered, shaved and dressed and yet, John Bland afforded his Commanding Officer and his Personal Assistant a further twenty-five minutes, before he headed down the sweeping staircase in time to hear Sarah-Roxanna Retand excusing herself.

"If there's nothing else Commander, I'd like to freshen up before breakfast and then, as soon as we've eaten, I'll make sure that the amended minutes from the final meeting are input onto the system, which will make them official…"

"Apart from that technicality, I think we have covered everything, and because events have been somewhat frenetic, I would like to thank you for providing me with an excellent alternate pair of eyes and ears, whenever we had cause to adjourn…"

"Oh I can assure you that watching you bargaining until you've achieved, the agreement you wanted, before the negotiations even started will always be a pleasure Sir…"

"While I appreciate the compliment, I'm also aware that in the last twenty-four hours, you've hardly had any sleep whatsoever, so I was going to suggest that since I intend to advise Mrs Daltry about the agreement that's been reached, which will no doubt be followed by my attendance on the make-shift football pitch, you might like to get some rest…"

"Thank you Commander…"

Having decided how he wanted to handle his admission of guilt, as Sarah-Roxanna left the study, John placed a finger against his lips, so that she would understand and then, he waited until she was almost at the top of the stairs, before he announced his presence through a respectful knock on the open study door.

"Good morning Mr Bland…"

"Morning Sir. I'm afraid there's a personal matter which I need to bring to your attention, preferably before breakfast…"

For a lingering moment, Philip Maddox did nothing, except maintain eye contact with his subordinate, before he released a resigned sigh.

"In that case Mr Bland, you'd better come in and close the door…"

Although it should have been an impossibility, something within that resigned sigh, seemed to suggest that Philip Maddox knew about the personal matter to which his subordinate was referring, and with his partner's poignant reminder that at the very least, he was guilty of gross misconduct, after closing the door, John Bland waited until his Commanding Officer sat down in his executive chair, and even when a hand gesture invited him to sit down on the other side of the desk, he declined the offer.

"If you don't mind Sir, I'd prefer to remain standing…"

"Oh dear, so this personal matter must be very serious…"

"I'm afraid it is Sir," John admitted, before he began to explain. "It's in relation to the early hours of June 30th, when you had been listening to the highlights from the Interview, and because I needed your permission to effectively drug your Goddaughter…"

Admiring John Bland's forthrightness Philip Maddox chose to interrupt his subordinate. "As far as I can remember Mr Bland, since I had failed to consider Margaret's predicament, not only on my behalf, but also on the premise that we could survive without her, you had managed to persuade her to go to bed, which is why you brought me a pot of Earl Grey tea and then, after gaining my permission to drug my Goddaughter--before you left the study--you drew my attention to the fact that during the Interview, there were occasions when you had come close to losing your professional objectivity…"

Upstairs, I had woken feeling rejuvenated for the first time in months and yet, despite the fact that I was wearing John's shirt, as if it had been a dream it took a few minutes for me to recall what had occurred in his bedroom, and after slipping my arms into my robe, I went to find him and when he was nowhere to be found, it was his partner in crime who enlightened me as to his whereabouts.

"John's gone downstairs Charlie, so that he can do what needs to be done, if we're going to stand any chance of not having to withdraw from this assignment…"

"Damn it Bill, since this was my fault why didn't you stop him?

Without waiting for response, I headed downstairs and by the time Bill caught up with me, much to Margaret's astonishment, I was blatantly eavesdropping outside of the closed study door, and when I heard my Godfather uttering the immortal words--*when your brain lost control*--that was my cue, and knowing that Bill would not prevent me, because his attempted intervention would complicate an already complex situation, after one single sharp knock on the door, I did not even consider waiting for an invitation to enter, and as I swept into the room, I dared to steal the words out of my Godfather's mouth.

"That's correct Commander, when Mr Bland's brain lost control over what was coming out of his mouth, and after he had demanded to know if I had any idea how long it would be, with regard to looking at my reflection, or allow any man to touch my body without me being reminded of what took place during those sixty minutes of my life..."

As I paused, I half-turned and as soon as I achieved eye contact with John, I challenged him. "After what happened last night, I thought we agreed that we would come and talk to your Commanding Officer together..."

Hesitating, I shifted my gaze, so that I could address the Commander. "Naturally, Mr Bland is trying to do the gentlemanly thing, but after working through everything else with Thomas, there seemed to be no other way of discovering whether I would be able to allow any man to touch me. So I waited until I knew that John was in the shower and then, I went into his room and after locking the door, I removed the key, so that I could confront him..."

Although my Godfather had raised his hand in the air, when I had failed to fall silent, there was a sharpness in his voice. "Charlie, you're prejudicing your own case..."

"But you don't understand..."

"Oh, it's because I do understand that it might be wise to stop *DIGGING?*"

Stunned by his sharpness, I whispered a sheepish apology. "I'm sorry..."

Then, confident that we were both listening, my Godfather enlightened us. "While your desire to defend Mr Bland's honour is most commendable, from his bedroom window which as you are aware overlooks the driveway a certain excitable, almost seven-year-old was eagerly awaiting the return of our chauffeur driven Jaguar at precisely 7:16..."

Between you and me, we know that there have been occasions in my life, when even I have wanted the ground to open up and swallow me, but standing in front of my Godfather wearing nothing, except for John's shirt and my robe, which was unfastened meant that they all paled into insignificance and yet, despite my sudden embarrassment at being improperly dressed, my Godfather had no intention of suppressing any detail from his explanation.

"According to Bobby, because he knows about such things thanks to one of his favourite teachers--Mrs Wesley--during my absence, he thought that something wonderful had happened, and until Mr Bland could come and talk to me, although it was meant to be a secret, since everyone was still asleep, he couldn't resist sharing it with someone..."

Oh my God, Mrs Wesley introduces the primary school children to basic biology, and it is her responsibility to make sure that the youngsters understand what constitutes appropriate or inappropriate behaviour between the boys and girls, as opposed to what happens between their mummies and daddies, and taking into account my son's propensity for gross exaggeration, I was dreading the remainder of my Godfather's explanation.

"Apparently, Bobby had gone into Mr Bland's room and discovered that like him, his mum must have had a bad dream, because she was asleep in John's bed..."

As my Godfather paused, I felt obliged to fill the momentary silence. "Oops..."

"So now you know why I suggested that you should stop digging Charlie, and although I'm sure that there must be a rational explanation, as to why having a bad dream should mean that you're wearing one of Mr Bland's denim shirts, might I suggest that you leave the study, without incriminating either of you any more than you already have..."

"Yes Commander..."

Despite my initial relief at being dismissed, I should have guessed that it might have been too good to be true.

"Oh, and one final thing Mrs Daltry..."

As if he was determined to leave us in no doubt as to the full extent of his displeasure, before proceeding, my Godfather waited, until I felt obliged to re-establish eye contact.

"In addition to being over the legal age of consent, Mr Bland is also a multi-disciplined Special Operative, whose extensive training at the taxpayer's expense should have rendered him more than capable of handling whatever occurred, without his protection assignment being discovered in his bed, wearing his shirt in the early hours of the morning, by her impressionable almost seven-year-old son..."

As if he were daring either of us to contradict him, Philip Maddox hesitated, before adding, "Now provided that I've made myself clear, if Mr Powell happens to be loitering on the other side of the study door, would you please ask him to join us immediately?"

"Of course Commander..."

In the hallway, Bill had been eavesdropping, but after I had been so contented in the early hours of the morning, I left the study disillusioned, downhearted and close to crying, so instead of doing as he had been ordered, he extended the immediately part of the command, by a few minutes, so that he could reassure me that despite having to follow routine procedure, the Commander's bark often proved to be far worse than his bite, and because John had been willing to update their Commanding Officer, before I had intervened everything would be fine. But in the meantime, while I was getting ready for breakfast, he suggested that it might be wise to update Lorna, preferably before our son could share the worst kept secret with her. Sound advice, but then after Bill went inside and he closed the door behind him, I heard my Godfather's demand for some kind of corroboration.

"And what the hell were you doing Mr Powell, when all this was taking place?"

"As far as I was aware Sir, Lorna and Bobby were asleep, and Mrs Daltry was in her own room, when I heard John explaining that he had finished his security sweep, but before he did the hand over, in light of the news about Bobby's biological father we had thought that she might like a nightcap, and the chance to take a sleeping tablet..."

"Is that correct Mr Bland?"

"Yes Sir, we were concerned that she might end up overthinking things, so I left the whisky and the tablet on the bedside cabinet and then, after I handed over to Bill I went to my own room to have a shower..."

"So there was nothing to suggests that any impropriety might occur?"

Irrespective of the outcome, John Bland knew that like Charlie Daltry had done during the Interview, it was imperative that to the best of his ability, he should tell the truth, the whole truth, and nothing but the truth, because any falsehood would be easily detected.

"No Sir, it wasn't until I left my en-suite that I realized she had entered my room and was locking the door..."

As Philip Maddox rose to his feet, and began to walk towards the window, his subordinate fell silent, which enabled his Commanding Officer to suggest. "You have my undivided attention Mr Bland, so please feel free to continue, safe in the knowledge that if at any time you haven't given me enough, I will ask for some additional clarification..."

Fleetingly, John and Bill exchanged a curious sideways glance and then, in the hope that honesty would still prove to be the best policy, Bland began his declaration.

"In no way can I blame Bill for not preventing what took place Sir, because after your Goddaughter exchanged her towelling robe for a full length chemise, she had crept along the landing in her bare feet, in order to proposition me, so that she could discover whether a man would be able to touch her, without her being reminded of what took place during those sixty minutes of her life." Pausing John waited, and when Philip Maddox remained silent, he found the courage to continue. "And despite knowing that what occurred would be categorized as gross misconduct, if you're expecting me to apologise for the decision I made as a Special Operative, then I am also unable to do so Sir…"

As Philip Maddox glanced over his shoulder yet again, John fell silent. "I'm intrigued Mr Bland would you please elaborate?"

"Of course," John replied, without any hesitation and then, he waited until the Commander turned away again, before commencing. "After undertaking extensive therapy with Dr James, your Goddaughter needed to be sure, and because it was as if she trusted me enough to know that despite whatever had passed between us to the contrary, I would never cause her any physical, mental or emotional harm, I was at least able to make certain that this matter was dealt with in the right way, including the establishment of a safe word, in case she needed to stop the proceedings at any time. In addition, through selecting some music and reassuring her that we would not be disturbed, I felt that I was creating the best possible environment in order to achieve a successful outcome…"

Silence, but then as expected the Commander asked, "Is there anything else you would like to add Mr Bland?"

"There is one other thing Sir. After creating what I believe to be the best possible environment, as I helped Charlie to rise to her feet, from the moment my lips brushed against hers I knew that I had been waiting, and dare I risk admitting actually hoping that the chance to be able to kiss her would arise…"

Unseen by his subordinates the Commander's features softened, and as a small smile crept onto his face he turned his attention to the other half of the dynamic duo.

"And what about you Mr Powell? Before I make a final decision, is there anything you would like to add, which might assist your partner's defence?"

Having pleaded guilty to gross misconduct, neither of the subordinates could understand why their Commanding Officer was prepared to listen to anything, which might lessen the offence, but after another curious glance passed between them, Bill also chose to tell the truth. "With regard to the incident Sir, there is something in connection with the long term physical, mental and emotional welfare of our primary protection assignment, which John has not mentioned, and because I believe it to be very relevant to the reason why he was prepared to jeopardise what has been an outstanding good conduct service record, I would like to bring it to your attention…"

"Very well, feel free to enlighten me…"

Even after the Commander finished giving his permission, Bill afforded him the opportunity to add anything else, and when he failed to do so, he began to explain. "Because John had attached a note to his locked bedroom door, which explained Charlie's whereabouts, by the time the next hand over was due, I had every reason to suspect what had taken place. However, in his defence, because I needed to be sure that our primary protection assignment was okay, after we walked back to his room, we discovered that probably for the first time in what might turn out to be the last three months, your Goddaughter must have got back into bed, and without the need for the introduction of any substance--such as alcohol or a sleeping tablet--she must have fallen into a deep sleep, which is probably the reason why she was still there with John lying awake beside her when Bobby found them…"

Yet more silence, before Philip Maddox glanced over his shoulder again. "In the early hours of the 30$^{th}$ June, can you remember what I told you Mr Bland with regard to my greatest concern?"

"Of course Sir," John replied, without any hesitation. "As a Commanding Officer instead of a Godfather you cautioned me that if for some reason, you failed to pull the necessary white rabbits out of their respect top hats at the negotiating table, then it would be most regrettable if I should be standing between Charlie Daltry and her destiny, because it would be such a waste of a good Operative…"

Appreciating his subordinate's accuracy, Philip Maddox reminded himself that when they were no longer operational, both Powell and Bland would make excellent negotiators.

"Evidently, the sleepless hours after the hand-over seem to have provided you with plenty of time to consider the implications of your actions…"

"Yes they did Sir…"

"And what about the consequences?"

"I've also given them a great deal of consideration, and I remain confident that if such a scenario were to arise, then I would have enough information at my disposal to know whether it was an unexpected threat to Mrs Daltry's life, or an unavoidable part of her destiny, but until I knew the guidelines and limitations within which we would be working, my primary objective would be to protect Charlie Daltry and Lorna and Bobby Clunnell…"

Half-turning, Philip Maddox announced. "You do realize that at this late stage, I should suspend you with immediate effect." Hesitating, he began to move back towards the desk. "And considering how hard Mr Powell has also worked towards achieving a satisfactory conclusion that would be most regrettable…"

Although both men heard the reference to a satisfactory conclusion, neither of them dared to do or say anything, which might mean prejudicing some kind of mitigating circumstances. "However, this was the first time a protection assignment has needed to be handled in this way, and after also taking into consideration that even though I knew the risks involved on the 30th June, I did not insist upon any special measures. Therefore, I am prepared to accept some of the responsibility for what has transpired…"

Since there had to be more, Bland and Powell continued to say and do nothing. "In addition, you will be relieved to learn that in this instance, I have every reason to believe that with Sarah-Roxanna's assistance, all of the necessary white rabbits were pulled out of their respective political top-hats at the negotiating table--in order to secure the complex deal--I set out to achieve before we began…"

By now, both men were too afraid of the consequences if they released the shared breath they seemed to be holding as the Commander approached his desk. "Therefore, having heard all the evidence, and taken into account that there are some mitigating circumstances, in this particular instance, I do not intend to suspend you Mr Bland. Nor do I expect both of you to withdraw from this assignment of your own volition…"

Finally, able to release that shared breath, the cavalry expressed their gratitude almost simultaneously. "Thank you Sir…"

Feeling a little weary, Philip Maddox sat down, before preparing to dismiss his subordinates. "In strictest confidence as part of that complex deal, as soon as I receive word from Henri Retand that everything is in place, I will expect you to be ready to leave for Paris, without anyone, except the three of us knowing…"

"Of course Sir…"

"In addition, after breakfast, I wish to see my Goddaughter together with the pair of you, so that I can explain what has been decided, at which time you will appreciate the need for discretion. Then, because it also has far-reaching implications for her, I would like you to warn Mrs Clunnell that we will need to have the pleasure of her company…"

"Although none of that should pose any problem Sir," Powell confirmed on their behalf. "With regard to Mrs Clunnell, if there are far-reaching implications are we to presume that initially, you will want to see her without Mrs Daltry present?"

"Oh I do apologise, I must be a little more weary than I imagined, but I should have made it clear that I want Mrs Clunnell to have the opportunity to make up her own mind about her future and therefore, not only do I want to see them individually, but with both of you present, I need them to be kept apart after each meeting, so that they can decide, when to discuss the proposal with each other, and as for Master Bobby Clunnell and his overactive imagination, as a result of him knowing about such things courtesy of Mrs Wesley, you can leave him to me…"

Pausing, he allowed the silence to linger, before adding. "So unless either of you can think of any additional clarification that might be beneficial that will be all for now?"

"Of course Sir…"

Relieved at having survived, reasonably unscathed, John Bland followed his partner to the door, but then like Charlie, he should have known that it was too good to be true, as the Commander remarked, "Oh and there is one more thing Mr Bland. Although I would not expect you to apologise for what happened, I was a little disconcerted by your admission that you had been surprised by your feelings with regard to having the opportunity to kiss my Goddaughter, so I do expect you to arrange to undertake some sessions with Dr James…"

"It was my intention to do that anyway Commander…"

"Good, because the damage is done, and while neither of you can promise for ever, and you both know the risks involved, especially for a man in your profession, I would have no objections if some kind of a personal relationship did develop…"

Then, with his subordinate rendered speechless, Philip Maddox was able to reverse the explanatory statement, he had used on $30^{th}$ June, so that there could be no misinterpretation. "I trust that you'll take on board what I'm telling you Mr Bland, not as your Commanding Officer, but as a Godfather whose Goddaughter has earned the right to some happiness, while she's still young enough to enjoy it, irrespective of its longitude…"

If you are wondering whether my actions would have been classed as further reckless behaviour, then strictly between you and me, I have to admit that after dealing with Lorna's initial amazement, when I told her about how I had virtually propositioned John Bland, in the early hours of the morning, after she expressed her genuine delight on my behalf, I was heading down to the dining room—most curious to learn why I could not hear my son's usual excited chattering--when I was ambushed, and forced to accompany John into the living room, where he reminded me--in a hushed voice--that prior to my bursting into the study he had everything under control, and because I could have jeopardized his plan, then the time had come to do something about my reckless behaviour.

My reward--sorry Freudian slip--my punishment was anticipatory, because as his lips were tormenting me by sensuously brushing against mine, John explained that since his Commanding Officer had refused to give him permission to beat me senseless, he had decided that he would be more than willing to play some of the erotic games to which, my husband had introduced me and then, intent on further torment as his hand began to work its way between my thighs, he added that he was most eager to teach me the error of my ways.

As for breakfast, because he had been unable to keep what must have become the worst ever kept secret, within the history of the secret making machinery, my son was more subdued than usual. However, as breakfast was coming to an end when my Godfather had asked me, if I would join him in his study, and my son seemed to be crest-fallen in case it meant that there would not be a football match, Bill had brought his misery to an end by ruffling his hair, as he reassured him that once our boring grown up business had been dealt with, then not only the cavalry, but also Lorna, and despite his weariness as a result of the last twenty-four hours, it was even his Uncle Philip's intention to join them outside.

Unbeknown to me, at my Godfather's request Bill had spoken to Lorna and as a result, she had agreed that as soon as I left the study, she would be waiting in the living room, ready to take my place, so that the Commander could talk to her in private.

As for me, despite the fact that John was standing a little to my right, and Bill was over by the cabinet, because the outcome of his negotiations with regard to my future, and whether there might be a chance of the three of us remaining together as a family meant so much to me, sitting in the chair opposite my Godfather, I was feeling a little apprehensive.

After opening the folder in front of him, the Commander began to explain. "During our 8:15 appointment, I spent the best part of forty-five minutes, justifying the actions I needed to undertake to ensure that my primary objective could be achieved by the end of the discussions, which were scheduled to take place immediately afterwards…"

As he paused, I suspected that my Godfather was allowing me the opportunity to respond, but while I longed to ask him whether he had been forced to change or even amend his primary objective, which he had outlined less than forty-eight hours ago, because I was afraid of receiving the wrong answer, I was condemned to suffer in silence.

"Therefore, by the designated time Sarah-Roxanna and I had returned to H.Q., where we had taken up residency in one of the Interview rooms, usually reserved for Persons of Interest, a room in which our Technical Support Team had used encrypted passwords to establish a secure satellite link with a prearranged location in Paris, so that the discussions could take place in complete privacy, because your husband's Sponsor and Handler had agreed that provided their identities were concealed, they were willing to seek an outcome, which would prove satisfactory to everyone concerned…"

This time when my Godfather paused, I heard this woman expressing her concern that such lengths had proved necessary. "Knowing you are a firm believer that there should be no grounds to justify you having to discuss--much less negotiate on a personal level with anyone known--or suspected--to be involved with any kind of subversive activity, I am truly sorry that you had no choice, except to enter into these discussions on my behalf Commander…"

In response, a small smile softened the corners of my Godfather's mouth. "Oh there's no need to feel remorseful Charlie, because it's my experience that in order to achieve the right result sometimes we don't have any choice, except to bend one's own rules. Besides, since Henri had succeeded in confirming the identities of the Sponsor and the Handler, I consoled myself with the fact that if I had chosen to do so, I could have had them both picked up and flown here, so that we could conduct the necessary Interview in person…"

In that same instant, I felt a sense of unease, because if the negotiations were being held under such intense security measures in order to satisfy Mark's Sponsor and Handler, why would Henri have wanted to confirm their identities? Maybe it was for future reference, but then perhaps fortunately, before a far more sinister reason could begin to develop, the Commander continued with his explanation.

"Although the discussions were delayed by their failure to arrive at the predesignated time, as one might have expected, we were immediately confronted by the fact that your husband had done his best to implicate you in his alternative lifestyle. However, even though they had never seen any of the content, and it might seem somewhat ironical, the fictitious piece of literature you created in order to protect yourself, provided you with a defence. But I will come back to your insurance policy in due course…"

How intriguing! Of course, although my husband did have those few pages in his possession, which I had given to him during the flight to Paris, when the gunmen took control of the Foray residence, Mark had taken them into the en-suite, so that he could use my cigarette lighter to burn them before rinsing the ashes down the sink.

"Firstly, we were able to substantiate that you were never a willing participant in your husband's extra curriculum activities and secondly, we were able to satisfy both parties that while he was amassing enough money to provide him with his early retirement pension, you never benefitted financially…"

Between you and me, if you remember rightly, at all times and in all places, Mark expected me to enact the role of the dutiful wife. So it only seemed natural that I should be curious to learn how my Godfather had managed to achieve such a result.

"In light of the public persona Mark expected me to portray at all times--such as the expensive designer clothes and shoes--might I ask how you managed to convince them?"

Silence, but then as my Godfather leant back in his Executive chair, his gaze drifted in John Bland's direction, which prompted his subordinate to attract my attention.

"Although it's a valid question Charlie, are you certain that you need to know?"

Momentarily confused, I shook my head. "Why is it some sort of state secret?"

Over by the cabinet, Bill unfolded his arms, before venturing to reply. "No it isn't a secret, but you might not like the answer…"

In response there was a sense of discomfort, but then instead of descending in a sedate manner, the silence more or less crashed around me, which was compounded by my attention being drawn to an unexpected movement on the other side of the desk--because after rising to his feet--my Godfather chose to detach himself from the scene, and as he began to walk towards the window like a thunder bolt realization dawned.

"Oh my God, you used extracts from the Interview…"

From his position over by the cabinet, Bill tried to justify their actions. "We had to make a choice and if we hadn't chosen the Interview, then we would have needed your permission to re-access not only your bank and savings accounts for the last three years, we would have also needed a more thorough inspection of your Trust Fund and then, if that didn't prove to be intrusive enough, we would have needed to repeat certain parts of the Interview, which we felt you might not find any less difficult to discuss, never mind describe the second time around…"

The moment I raised my hand, Bill fell silent in time to hear me gasp. "Please Bill, I need a few minutes…"

Respecting my request not only the cavalry, but also my Godfather remained still and silent, but then I heard the familiar sound of liquid being poured into what I assumed would turn out to be yet another crystal glass, and although John decided to crouch down beside the chair, so that his hand was resting on mine, he waited until his partner placed the aforementioned item on the desk in front of me, before he offered me some reassurance.

"There's no immediate rush Charlie. So as we've done in the past, you can take whatever time you need…"

Between you and me after we finished the Interview, I refused to allow myself to acknowledge that whilst listening to the playback Philip Maddox would hear me describing in such lurid detail, the reality of what my daily life with Mark Daltry was like--throughout the last three years. So when John picked up the crystal glass and he offered it to me, even though it struck me that the use of a pure malt whisky to restore my resolve had occurred so many times, especially in this room that it was in danger of turning into a nasty habit, I accepted it and after swallowing a mouthful in a most unladylike manner, I felt able to afford them an explanation.

"On June 29th after we had finished in the study, it was difficult enough coming to terms with the fact that my Godfather would hear me describing the less pleasant aspects of my marriage, but to have people like his Sponsor and Handler discover the truth about the way in which Mark Daltry treated me--behind closed doors--was almost too embarrassing for me to bear…"

Over by the window, my Godfather unclasped his hands from behind his back and half turned, but before he started to walk back to the desk, he offered me an unexpected apology. "Since our security screening failed to detect any subversive tendencies, either before or during the last three years, it's me who is embarrassed Charlie, because our duty of care proved to be sorely lacking. However, once both parties were satisfied we were able to determine the terms and conditions of a final settlement, and as part of the deal, we knew that they wanted us to give them the flash drive containing your fictitious piece of literature…"

Suddenly alarmed, I almost gasped. "But surely some of the people I named…"

Having reached the desk, as he sat back down in his Executive chair, my Godfather interrupted me. "Oh there's no need to be alarmed, because our Technical Support Team have managed to doctor your insurance policy, so that using the utmost skill to ensure that they could not be detected certain references have either been altered or eliminated…"

"And presumably, there was something you wanted in exchange…"

The Commander nodded. "Yes, and it proved to be another stumbling block for quite some time, but since the highest possible Authority had agreed, we made it clear that they would only acquire the flash drive, provided that they confirmed that Mark Daltry--albeit it under arrest for treason--would be allowed to return to the UK alive and unharmed…"

"When that happens, will I have to have any contact with him?"

On the other side of the desk, my Godfather shook his head. "There's no danger of that occurring, but the highest possible Authority agrees that his return will set an example to all Special Operations' personnel that such acts will never be allowed to go unpunished. So after they escort him home unharmed, your husband is destined to spend some considerable time, in a very dark hole hoping that I don't subsequently change my mind and give Mr Bland and Mr Powell permission to Interview him instead of our Security personnel, who intend to discover how he managed to evade detection for so long…"

Pausing, a smile crept onto my Godfather's face. "Then, once we're satisfied that there isn't anything else left to learn, Mark Daltry will be starting a life sentence for the betrayal of his country, which must have cost people--like Bobby's father--their lives. So in his case, life will mean life without there being any possibility of him applying for parole…"

Unable to stop myself, I remarked, "At least in prison, Mark will get a taste of his own medicine, when he gets the chance to learn--preferably on a nightly basis--what it must have been like to be one of the seventeen-year-old fair haired virgins, he used to abuse…"

Closing the folder, the Commander announced, "As soon as the discussions came to an end Sarah-Roxanna and I had a second meeting with the highest possible Authority, so that we could discuss not only your future, but also the future of the Clunnell family, and until I have spoken to Lorna in private, I do not intend to reveal the outcome to either of you. So if you don't mind waiting in the living room, I do believe that Mr Powell has arranged for Lorna to temporarily replace you…"

"Of course Commander…"

Naturally, I longed to ask him why he needed to see Lorna privately, but I erred on the side of caution, and because we had discussed what the options might be, and how she felt about the three of us being together permanently I decided to bide my time, and until my presence was once again required, I followed Bill out of the study.

"The Commander would like to see you now Lorna," Bill announced, as we entered the living room before he added, "And then Charlie will be re-joining us…"

Although no words needed to be spoken for the briefest of moment's our eyes met, and no doubt as a reaffirmation of the unanimity, we have shared over the last seven years, Lorna's fingertips brushed against mine, and I reminded myself that if my father had been unable to dissuade Lorna from becoming Bobby's surrogate mother, then I had nothing to fear from my Godfather and yet, it did not stop me from wishing that the walls had ears, but the only thing I overheard was when Bill must have opened the study door to usher Lorna inside.

"Ah Lorna, thank you so much for agreeing to wait in the living room, while I updated my Goddaughter." Philip Maddox announced and then, as he must have gestured towards the empty chair opposite him, I heard him suggest. "Please take a seat…"

"Since Margaret has managed to keep Bobby fully occupied in the kitchen, I enjoyed having a few moments to myself." Lorna replied, as she sat down. "But I must admit that I cannot begin to imagine why you should want to see me without Charlie being present?"

"It's merely a formality, because after yesterday's discussions came to an end, my last meeting was with the highest possible Authority, and it was suggested that I should make certain that you are aware of the personal implications, if the three of you were to be relocated together…"

"Now I'm doubly confused Philip, because from what Charlie explained, it was my understanding that you gone to Headquarters, so that you could manage to secure her continued safety and anonymity…"

Placing his elbows on the desk, the Commander smiled. "Yes I did, but while my discussions proved to be successful, we can never be one hundred per cent certain that any agreements reached will be wholly honoured…"

"If that's what concerns you Philip," Lorna interrupted him. "Then perhaps I should clarify my position…"

As the Commander extended one of his open hands across the desk, Lorna accepted his gesture as an indication of his willingness for her to proceed. "Although I'm aware that Charlie told you the reason why Colin agreed to have me Sectioned for my own safety and admitted, at his expense to the Psychiatric Wing of the Mayfield Clinic, I might as well have been dead, because I continued to be numb, incapable of feeling anything, until everything changed after Professor Morgan's arrival, and getting to know Charlie inspired me to work towards making the kind of recovery, which would enable me to be discharged..."

Hesitating, Lorna's gaze drifted from the Commander to his two subordinates who were listening in respectful silence. "As I'm confident that Mr Bland and Mr Powell would agree, when someone is responsible for the preservation of your life, then the bond between you is unbreakable. So without anyone knowing about our continued friendship--after our discharges--we kept in touch so that when she landed on my doorstep in Edinburgh, and she announced that because she was pregnant and Major Forsyth wanted her to have an abortion, she'd run away from home--without asking any awkward questions--I welcomed her into what had been the McCardle residence and then, when we hatched the plot for me to become Bobby's surrogate mother, I accepted that Charlie's life must have been littered with the kind of complications, which might one day make their presence felt…"

"Which I seem to recall you confirmed on the 23$^{rd}$ June," Philip Maddox added, as Lorna paused. "When my subordinates landed on your doorstep…"

Opposite him Lorna nodded. "That's correct, and believe me if we should get the chance to stay together as a family, we have discussed all of the possible short-term and long-term implications, and although I learnt about the open security file, which can never be closed in the delivery suite while Charlie was giving birth to Bobby, she has since told me about her marriage, and she has explained that if she hadn't managed to find a way to guarantee her continued existence, by the time she went to Paris in March, then she would not have survived. So I think you can appreciate that having examined all of our options, I can assure you that like John and Bill, we function as if we are moving parts in the same piece of machinery within which, I am more than willing to accept that there will always be a risk that something untoward might happen…"

Pausing again, Lorna continued to maintain eye contact with the Commander, before she added. "Besides, I don't doubt for a single moment that in order to cater for such eventualities you will have measures, which you intend to put in place…"

Impressed by her astuteness, the Commander's tone of voice was complimentary. "Yes I do, but I'll deal with them when Charlie re-joins us, because there is something else, something of a more personal nature, which I need you to consider…"

"Whatever it is Philip, surely it can't be that serious?"

Suddenly, the Commander's tone of voice was sombre, as he began to explain, "As you know until now, we have endeavoured to ensure that few people could make a connection between you and my Goddaughter, which is why we even referred to you as being Bobby's chaperone, when he attended Major Forsyth's funeral. Therefore, during any initial adjustment period, which could be for the first six months, I would prefer that the only contact you have with your brother is via hand delivered letters, or disposable mobile phones, which will be supplied by us, specifically for that purpose. However, Colin will be free to contact me at any time, and he will of course receive regular updates regarding the welfare of all three of you…"

On the other side of the desk, Lorna seemed pensive, before she replied, "Convincing Bobby that he cannot see his Uncle Colin might be a little tricky, but if there is no other way, then I'm sure the time spent in quarantine will soon come to pass…"

With a single glance in Bill Powell's direction, his subordinate left the study, while at the same time, John Bland collected the spare chair, which was next to the cabinet, and placed it beside Lorna.

Then, as I re-joined them, and I sat down in the empty chair, Lorna and I exchanged a knowledgeable glance and before the Commander could afford this young woman any kind of explanation, Lorna reassured me by answering the unasked question.

"There wasn't anything for either of us to worry about because Philip merely wanted to be sure that I understood that there will always be some kind of risk involved, and if the three of us are going to be relocated as a family unit--for several months--our contact with Colin will be restricted to letters and the occasional mobile phone call…"

Horrified at yet another big sacrifice on my behalf, which Lorna was going to have to make, my tone was apologetic. "But surely, there must be some way in which Colin…"

But my Godfather curtailed any speculation. "I'm afraid, it's non-negotiable…"

"It's not so bad," Lorna reassured me. "Because hopefully, we'll be so busy organizing our new home that everything will be back to normal in no time at all…"

Then, without any further delay, the Commander chose to enlighten both of us. "And since my subordinates will remain responsible for your overall protection, whenever they aren't on an assignment, they intend to make your relocation their home base, but I'm getting ahead of myself." Hesitating, he cast a glance towards the cabinet. "Mr Bland, do we still have the photographs, which were taken during the initial reconnaissance at Reybrook?"

"Yes Sir," John replied, as he slid open the top drawer of the cabinet so that he could retrieve an A4 envelope. "They were copied before the specifications for the refurbishment, and the internal and external security modifications were sent to Technical Support…"

Before removing the photographs, Philip Maddox explained, "Before I went to H.Q., I knew what I was aiming to achieve on your behalves, and although I had to use the Royal Seal of Approval as leverage, the highest possible Authority had no choice, except to agree that the unique qualities Charlie possesses could prove to be an invaluable resource. Therefore, provided I accept full responsibility for your continued safety and anonymity, there's no reason why you should not be able to continue living as a family unit in a place which will be known to no one, except yourselves, Mr Bland and Mr Powell, Patrick O'Keefe and Matthew Morton and myself…"

Pausing, the Commander's gaze drifted between his subordinates. "Gentlemen, do we have an update on how long Technical Support need to complete the necessary alterations?"

"O'Keefe spoke to the Team Leader two days ago Sir," Bill confirmed. "And since the security measures have so far been their number one priority, the workmen will need at least six to eight weeks to complete the internal refurbishment and restructuring…"

"In that case, since the summer holidays begin in two weeks, the three of you will remain at Manor Park, but as soon as I can arrange for a member of staff from our training programme to be available, I will expect you Charlie to update your firearms training to include assault rifles, while at the same time you can refresh your unarmed combat skills…"

"Of course Commander…"

Turning his attention to Lorna, he continued. "And bearing in mind that Mr Bland and Mr Powell will not be at the relocation site twenty-four hours a day, in order to cater for those moments when something untoward might happen, irrespective of how much you might abhor any kind of violence, I expect you to undertake the basic course in firearms training, so that you can point a gun at an intruder--or an assailant--in such a manner that they will be left in no doubt that you can--and if necessary will--shoot them…"

Lorna nodded her agreement. "Oh I'm sure that if either Charlie or Bobby were under threat from a third party, then I'd be more than capable of using a gun to defend them…"

Then, as the Commander's gaze drifted from Lorna to Charlie, he added, "In addition, you will both learn a Martial Art to a standard, which meets my subordinate's approval, with that same standard being sustained through regular practise…"

Between you and me, I did allow myself to consider that after I became a person, who was able to defend myself using a Martial Art, there would be a much fairer, and far healthier distribution of power, whenever John deemed me to have indulged in any additional reckless endangerment, but yet again, I managed to stop my gaze from drifting in his direction, because my Godfather was sliding the photographs out of the envelope.

"After Reybrook came into our possession two and a half years ago, apart from updating the security measures, so that it could safely remain empty for the first twelve months, although it has taken far longer than anticipated, the ground floor has now been redesigned and then, totally refurbished to the highest possible standard…"

After pausing long enough to slide the photographs across the desk, so that Lorna and I could see them, the Commander continued. "And since it had been turned into what proved to be an unprofitable guest house, all five bedrooms already had access to running water. So there are two on the ground floor, which now have en-suite facilities, and while we had started work on the upper level, the refurbishment has now become a number one priority, so that before you are relocated, the three upper bedrooms will have en-suite facilities. In addition, there is a separate annex which has a bedroom, living area, small kitchen and en suite facilities which will prove ideal whenever Colin comes to stay for the weekend…"

"And what about our possessions from Trafalgar Avenue Philip," Lorna asked. "Can they be transferred to Reybrook or will we have to leave them behind?"

"Oh, as soon as it became clear that neither of you would be able to resume living at your previous residences in Cheltenham Way, and Trafalgar Avenue at my request, and taking the utmost care, all of your personal possessions were packed up and placed into storage, so that once you have chosen what furniture you would like in your new home and who will be sleeping in which bedrooms on the upper level, all of the boxes will be relocated and unpacked, before your arrival…"

"And what about Bobby's education Philip?"

Undoubtedly, as a result of his negotiating skills, it was the first time I had felt comfortable addressing him in such an informal manner, and after casting an appreciative nod in my direction, he provided us with an answer.

"Firstly, I should explain that Reybrook was chosen as a safe house, because being built on higher ground, it is defendable, especially when you not only have an unrestricted view of the main road, but after turning off at the junction, you can also see any cars approaching the secure entrance, which leads to the Edwardian building…"

Pausing, my Godfather waited for us to locate the roads on the reconnaissance photographs, before he continued. "Secondly, when it came to Bobby's education, my initial consideration was his safety and anonymity and then, I took into account that he is far more advanced than other children of the same age, and if you follow the road through the valley, you pass Whitchurch Academy, which caters for boys and girls, who are deemed to be educationally advanced for their ages. On your behalves, I have taken the liberty of enrolling Bobby, in readiness for the Autumn term, but after you read the prospectus, and had a chance to discuss the options, if you would prefer him to be taught together with other seven-year-olds, then provided we can afford him the same unobtrusive protection, arrangements can be made for him to attend the Primary school in Whitchurch…"

With me acting as spokesperson, I offered my Godfather our gratitude. "Thank you Philip, there's obviously a great deal that we need to consider and discuss, but provided that it's what Bobby wants, and he does not come under any undue pressure to produce results, I think Lorna would agree that for security purposes, it might be best if he did attend the Academy as a day pupil…"

"Oh when it comes to him being allowed to develop at his own pace, I couldn't agree more Charlie, and because Margaret has reminded me that you are the closest thing I have to any kind of family, and my life won't be worth living if she believes I've been too tied up with official details to remember, we are both hoping that during the school holidays, you will all come and stay at Manor Park…"

At the thought of Bobby's indignation, I could not stop myself from laughing. "Since you have made such a big impression on him, and he has thoroughly enjoyed every minute of this adventure, somehow I think that our coming to stay during the holidays will be included in his personal terms and conditions before we can be relocated…"

Right on cue, the momentary silence in the study was disturbed, by the sound of voices in the hallway outside, as my son voiced his disillusionment. "Schucks Margaret, the study door is still closed. Surely, not even Uncle Philip could possibly have this much boring grown-up stuff to talk about?"

Taking pity on his housekeeper, my Godfather announced, "Although Margaret's done an excellent job keeping the youngster occupied, unless there is anything else anyone would like to add, perhaps we should adjourn, so that while we're entertaining Bobby on the makeshift football pitch, she can resume her normal routine.

Between you and me, later that same day with John and Bill in attendance, I had requested a further brief meeting with my Godfather, during which I explained that since I was deemed to be a valuable resource, if there were ever occasions, when my unique abilities might be of use to Special Operations, then I was only too willing to offer my assistance.

With regard to reckless endangerment, it was John's behaviour which turned out to be questionable, and despite having been reprimanded once, he seemed to disregard the danger that I might be discovered in the wrong bedroom, never mind the wrong bed, but then all that changed two days later with John and Bill's sudden disappearance.

## July 13th 18:10

While she was watching the evening news, Lorna drew my attention to a report about an incident on the left bank in Paris, during which an area had been sealed off, and as a precautionary measure nearby buildings had been evacuated, while an alleged attempt was made to retrieve a British trouble-shooting envoy who had been missing for several months, after he had attended a routine peace-keeping conference.

Although no organizations had claimed responsibility, it seemed to be too much of a coincidence and yet, if the incident was related to the exchange, which Commander Maddox had negotiated, then according to an eyewitness who claimed to have seen six bodies being removed from the scene, things cannot have gone according to plan, and if my suspicions were correct, then the media coverage would explain the inexplicable suddenness of John and Bill's disappearance. However, despite my mixed feelings about the incident, as I watched the Jaguar F series making its return journey up the driveway, taking into consideration the body count, it was a relief to know that they had both returned alive.

## July 13th 19:40

In need of an unhealthy measure of pure malt whisky, preferably savoured in the meditative silence of a relaxing bath, as John Bland pulled the keys from the ignition, he glanced at Bill Powell. Having failed to achieve the optimum outcome, it was regrettable that the Daltry file could not be closed, but in accordance with the orders they had been given, and with the assistance of Henri Retand, they had done whatever proved necessary to ensure that Charlie, Lorna and Bobby could move on with their life as a family unit.

In an ideal world, at the end of an assignment a pure malt whisky, savoured in a relaxing bath should have been the order of events, but as they were retrieving the overnight bags from the car, Charlie emerged from the Manor, and as she came rushing down the steps, in their direction, Bill remarked, "Charlie's expression seems to suggest that she's seen the evening news, and she isn't happy about the content of the unofficial report, which was leaked to the press..."

But John Bland was far too tired to reveal any undue concern. "She had to find out sooner or later, and in the end, it all comes down to what--or rather whose--version of events, she chooses to believe..."

As Charlie neared the two men, she slowed her pace until she achieved eye contact with John. "According to the news, there was an incident on the left bank in Paris..."

Hesitating, she tossed her head in Bill Powell's direction, and an accusing tone crept into her voice, as she demanded, "Is that where the pair of you have been?"

Under no obligation to either divulge his whereabouts or justify his actions Bill Powell chose to disregard the demand, and continued to walk towards the house, but Charlie would not be dismissed quite so easily, and when John also tried to move passed her, she caught hold of his arm. "Commander Maddox negotiated an agreement..."

In the hope that he could stop the accusation from being levelled, John turned to look at her, so that he could counter-challenge. "He negotiated an agreement over you Charlie..."

Failing to grasp the significance, Charlie interrupted him. "So presumably, the negotiated agreement whereby my husband was to be returned to Special Operations, in exchange for the flash drive never happened?"

"That's correct Charlie. Sometimes things don't go according to plan..."

"So do we even know whether he's alive or dead?"

After uttering a dissatisfied sigh, John felt obliged to explain. "Although we were supplied with the mandatory proof of life--twelve minutes later--when Henri's unarmed Operative approached the exchange point carrying not only a fake flash drive, but also the doctored article, your husband had yet again disappeared, which suggested that his Sponsor and Handler had never intended to honour their side of the agreement, and because there were other people who needed to be taken into consideration..."

As he continued, John noted that Charlie's grasp on his arm was beginning to loosen. "People like Lorna and her brother Colin McCardle, who have stood by you during the last seven years, and then there's the solicitor and the accountant, who have managed your Trust Fund ever since Bobby was born. Since none of them could be identified for fear of jeopardising their safety, before we left the Manor the orders we were given were quite clear, and if their willingness to do the exchange proved to be nothing more than another attempt to retrieve the flash drive, then we were to do whatever was necessary in order to ensure, the continued safety and anonymity of not only you, but also everybody else…"

Then, after shrugging his arm free, John began to follow his partner, until Charlie dared to level her accusation. "In that case, you must have been partly responsible for the dead bodies, which an eyewitness claimed they saw being removed from the scene…"

Although both men stopped in mid-stride, Powell glanced at his partner, and before he continued to walk towards the house, his expression left Bland in no doubt that the issue needed to be addressed, and when John recalled the contempt in Michelle Berloise's eyes, as she was levelling the gun for what would have been the last time and yet, with everybody who had posed a threat to the unarmed Operative having been eliminated, she had allowed herself to be taken alive. So when he turned to confront Charlie, and further inappropriate words threatened to emerge from between her lips, he kept her silent by suddenly reaching for her arm, and despite her gasped protest he yanked her towards him.

"Whether we were or not, it happens to be part of the job. In fact, it's an occupational hazard Charlie, and if we're ever going to have any peace at all, then I suggest you find a way to deal with it, because I don't need this kind of aggravation every time I come home at the end of an assignment…"

Initially, Charlie started shaking her head. "I don't understand…"

"Oh I think you do…"

"But I thought we'd agreed that it wasn't possible…"

John Bland smiled. "After reconsidering, I've decided to change my mind…"

"Oh I see…"

In that instant, the outrage reflected in Charlie's eyes was magnificent, and because Bland knew that once inside the house, she would continue to dispute his change of heart, and without considering the consequences, she would follow him upstairs and then, within the seclusion of his bedroom, he would enjoy turning that outrage to his own advantage by savouring every moment of her genuine reluctance as he began to undress her.

At the prospect of her forthcoming nakedness, John lowered his head, so that he could kiss her, and when Charlie tried to protest, because her Godfather and Lorna were watching from the study window, he placed a finger against her lips.

"There's no need to be concerned about the Commander, because on the day Bobby couldn't keep our secret, although he had no choice except to read both of us the riot act, as I was leaving the study, he suggested that since you deserved some happiness--speaking as a Godfather instead of my Commanding Officer--he would have no objections if a relationship were to develop, especially when we both know the risks involved, and neither of us can promise forever…"

Refusing to relinquish her outrage, Charlie demanded, "And what if I haven't changed my mind?"

Turning away, Bland laughed as he once again began walking towards the house. "Oh you will--not necessarily immediately--but nevertheless eventually…"

Upstairs in his bedroom, having not yet overcome every aspect of her negative self-image, she would not only be embarrassed, but also ashamed of her nakedness, and she would initially be too afraid to look at him in case she might discover the disdain and contempt, she had come to expect, instead of the delight she would bring to his weary features and yet, she would not run away from him.

From the top of the steps, the unmistakable sound of Bobby giggling, prompted him to look up, and when he discovered that sitting side by side on the top step, the youngster was no doubt the recipient of Bill's fatherly explanation on the scene in the driveway below and yet, for once John could not resent the knowledgeable smirk on his partner's face. But in the next instant, he sensed that Charlie Daltry was no longer following him.

As he looked back, she was standing six--or maybe even seven--paces away from him, and as if something had attracted her attention, she was staring out across the lake towards the distant trees and yet, almost immediately, she half-turned and smiled at him.

"You're right John, I would have changed my mind..."

In the early hours of the next morning, when he would be unable to avoid the inevitable rerunning of the incident, in the futile hope that he could change the sequence of events, John Bland would not be able to recall what had come first, his professional recognition of the threat to her continued existence, or Charlie's stating that she '*would have*' which suggested that she would never be able to do so, or perhaps the ear-piercing denial of a frightened seven-year old boy, as he had released his own warning about *the bad man, the bad man's back*. Nevertheless, from the other side of the lake as the barely audible crack from the recoil of a high-velocity firearm sent the protesting birds soaring into the sky, John dropped his overnight bag, but as he lurched forward in an attempt to snatch her from the path of the bullet, Charlie took a deliberate step away from him.

Of course based on the assumption that the flash drive would have been retrieved by Mark's Sponsor and Handler, someone must have decided that like Bobby's father, Charlie Daltry had outlived her usefulness. But while she was supposed to die instantaneously, and the deliberate step she had taken away from John Bland might have robbed the marks-person of the opportunity to readjust their aim, which meant that she was still alive, Charlie was unaware that John's hands were breaking her fall, and because in the immediate aftermath, she was partially paralysed, she could not feel him holding onto her, as he eased them both to the ground, so that he was shielding her from any further bullets.

Then, as the dull haze began to lift and some degree of sensitivity was restored, she could feel the warmth of his breath against her forehead and much to her relief, she could sense his hand cradling her head against his shoulder. But in the next heart-breaking moment, the terrified screams of a young child penetrated the temporary deafness, and despite the fact that the screaming confirmed that her son was alive, Charlie had no idea how many shots had been fired, and because he could have sustained a life-threatening injury, with the slightest of movements, she tried to draw John down towards her so that he could hear her.

"Bobby?"

Knowing that every second was crucial to Charlie's continued survival, in his mind John had been formulating a plan of action, and his initial priority was finding something to help him to lessen the blood loss, which was quite substantial, especially when he had checked her pulse and it was not only weak, but also erratic which in turn caused him to suspect that if anyone tried to move her without a hefty dose of morphine being administered, she might not be able to withstand the sudden onslaught of pain, and if she crashed, then they would need the portable defibrillator, which was kept inside the Manor in order to cater for such emergencies. So at least they would be able to resuscitate her and yet, in response to her request for an update regarding her son's welfare, not even John could be certain without glancing over his shoulder.

When it came to protecting a frightened seven-year old, clearly Bill had been successful, because he was easing himself away from the youngster, but once Bobby was upright, his partner was having to contend with his struggling as he tried to writhe himself free. But regardless of the noise--much to John's relief--through the microphone in his ear, he knew that the air ambulance, which would have been diverted from a less serious incident was due to reach them in five--or maybe six minutes.

"He's fine Charlie. You're the only casualty..."

Despite the seriousness of her situation, Bland did not want to consider that she might not survive, and because he was angry with her for having deprived him of the right to fulfil the terms and conditions of his Contract--even though it might have cost him his own life--as he managed to drag his overnight bag close enough to retrieve the hand towel from its contents, he demanded, "Damn it Charlie, what the fuck did you think you were doing?"

Of course, in the early hours of June 30th after John had opened the study door in readiness for his departure, because she had been eavesdropping she had overheard the Commander explaining not as a Godfather, but as his Commanding Officer why his subordinate should not find himself standing between Charlie Daltry and her destiny.

"It would have been a waste of a good operative," Charlie managed to gasp. "Especially when I need you alive…"

Having made the connection, John interrupted her. "So you must have been eavesdropping." Pausing, he shook his head. "And presumably, it never occurred to you that together with Bill, I might be good enough at my job to be able to protect all three of you?"

Then, he released a dissatisfied sigh, before he declared, "My God when it came to the beating the shit out of you option, I was too damn soft…"

When Charlie failed to respond, John noted that as if the air had suddenly begun to grow thin, she was having to fight for every breath, and from experience he knew that soon each of those breaths would need to be won with even more difficulty than the last. So there was a strong possibility that in the brain's determination to keep the heart beating speech was becoming a costly nonessential, but as if she knew the seriousness of her own situation, she dared to ask the question, he had been dreading.

"It's bad isn't it John?"

Initially, Bland considered deceiving her, but since he needed her cooperation, he explained, "Yes it is, but the good news is that I have seen worse, and in those instances the wounded parties survived. Plus, in approximately four minutes and thirty-two seconds after the air-ambulance lands not only will we have the benefit of a doctor and paramedic, O'Keefe and Morton are on their way up to the Manor. However, until all that happens you do realize that you're bleeding all over my favourite jacket…"

Although Charlie's barely audible laugh caused him to pause, his tone was more sombre, as he stated, "Seriously Charlie, you're losing far too much blood, so I don't have any choice, except to try and patch you up…"

Despite knowing what he needed to do in order to stop her from bleeding to death, Charlie mumbled her consent. "Do whatever you have to do…"

Hating what he was about to do, Bland hesitated, before he explained, "Although I'm going to use this towel to apply pressure to the bullet wound, the good news is that the next time you behave recklessly--and when it comes to somebody like you Charlie, there will be a next time--I might be prepared to take the pain I'm about to cause into consideration, before I beat you senseless?"

Yet again, Charlie uttered a barely audible laugh, but while it suggested that despite the gravity of her situation, she was prepared to fight for her continued survival, when he used the towel to apply pressure to the bullet wound, because she did not want to upset her son any more than was necessary, she tried to stifle her agonised gasping by burying her face in his jacket, and yet, as soon as the pain began to ease, as if she was aware of how close she had come to losing consciousness, in a barely audible voice, she levelled the kind of end of life special request, which caused John even more concern.

"I need to see my son…"

While the cavalry were continuously monitoring the constant relay of messages, which thanks to their discreet communication system was updating them, not only about the arrival of the air-ambulance, but also the progress of what had been confirmed as the manhunt for a marksman who was apparently working alone, despite Bobby's determination to be with his mother, Bill Powell had somehow managed to stop the distraught little boy from rushing down the steps,

Until there was firm evidence that he was not in any danger, Bill Powell would continue to afford the youngster his protection, but as soon as each new sighting began to confirm that the threat was moving away, although he picked Bobby up so that he could maintain some degree of control, he satisfied his need to be heading in the right direction, by starting to carry him down the steps towards his partner, and perhaps more importantly his biological mother.

Then, when he reached the bottom of the steps, there were two messages in quick succession, which confirmed definite sightings of the paid assassin, and because it was reasonably safe, Bill allowed the youngster to wriggle free, but as he slithered down his body until his feet touched the gravel, Powell paused and although it might be a futile request, he reinforced what would be their routine procedure in such matters.

"Alive--if possible take the marks-person alive…"

Beside them, Charlie heard the small running feet come to an abrupt halt, and as he fell to his knees beside his mother, Powell caught up with them in time to hear Bobby levelling his own accusation.

"After my last nightmare, I told John that the bad man was coming back with a big gun. So why didn't they stop him?"

"It's not their fault," Charlie managed to whisper. "One day you will understand…"

Momentarily, Bland and Powell were distracted by their need to ensure that the screech of tyres was nothing more suspicious than the result of O'Keefe bringing the classic British Racing Green Jaguar to an abrupt halt, before he and Morton raced up the steps to the Manor, but a few moments later, when Morton reappeared carrying the portable defibrillator, John overheard Charlie whispering to her son.

"Until the end of time I will always love you…"

"Charlie," John demanded, in an attempt to stop her eyelids from closing. "Come on Charlie, you have to try and stay with us…"

But it was too late. Charlie Daltry had lost far too much blood to sustain her consciousness and yet, as if they were acting on auto-pilot, in response to the cardiac arrest after Bill moved Bobby out of the way, he helped his partner to gently lower her to the ground and then, with an even more terrified little boy who seemed to be lost for words as he watched their every move, the cavalry began standard cardiopulmonary resuscitation. So once John made sure that her airway was clear, and his lips covered hers, he began to force second-hand oxygen into her lungs, and even though Bill must have broken at least one rib with his first forceful downward punch, he started the equally vital chest compressions, so that at the very least it would keep Charlie's vital organs alive long enough for Matthew Morton to charge the defibrillator, especially when they knew that the air-ambulance was about to land on the helipad.

Mercifully, as soon as the machine was ready, the doctor and paramedic reached them, but when the first shock was administered, it failed to produce the desired result. So after the paramedic prepared a syringe on his behalf--in an attempt to stimulate her heart--the doctor administered the injection, before he ordered the frequency to be increased, so that they could shock her again, and this time when he listened for any signs of life, he was able to announce--albeit with a degree of cautiousness.

"Although it's weak, we have a pulse. So before she can crash again, let's get her on board the air-ambulance as fast as possible…"

Knowing that there was only room for John to accompany her, it took nothing more than a single glance to pass between the two men for Bill to suddenly sweep Bobby up into his arms. Then, despite the youngster screaming at the top of his voice that he wanted to go with his mother--without so much as a backward glance--Bill began to carry him back towards the Manor, and even when Bobby started lashing out with his small fists, he did not relinquish his hold, and although there was a second helicopter about to land, until the youngster calmed down, there was no point in trying to reason with him.

After the initial shot had been fired, although Lorna Clunnell had reacted instinctively Philip Maddox had anticipated her movement, and as his arm prevented her from leaving his side, he explained that because Bland was taking care of his Goddaughter, and whilst monitoring not only the progress of the air-ambulance, but also the manhunt for the paid assassin, Powell had his hands full trying to protect Bobby. So the last thing his subordinates needed was the added responsibility if Lorna were to suddenly go rushing out of the Manor.

So despite finding it tortuous, as Lorna had bided her time, she held her breath, while they were trying to bring Charlie back from the dead, but when Powell swept the unsuspecting youngster up into his arms, hearing Bobby screaming at the top of his voice proved to be too much for her to bear. However, although the suddenness of her attempt to break free from the Commander was successful, because he knew that Patrick O'Keefe was standing in the doorway blocking her exit, Philip Maddox remained unperturbed and yet, finding herself overcome with a rare display of emotion, Lorna was unable to prevent the tears from rolling down her cheeks, as she beseeched O'Keefe.

"Please Patrick, I have to go to him…"

As Lorna found herself unable to continue, Patrick eased her towards him, and because his Commanding Officer had joined them, he continued to hold onto her, until her distress responded to his nearness, which enabled Philip Maddox to offer her an explanation.

"We know it's hard Lorna, but right now he's so angry he's lashing out at Powell, and if for some reason my Goddaughter doesn't survive, the last thing Bobby's going to need is to have to overcome the guilt of having lashed out and possibly hurt, the other mother he is going to need…"

Hesitating, he afforded her a few seconds to bring the emotion back under control, before he added. "There's another helicopter landing in precisely, three minutes and twenty-three seconds, and because they will be taking my Goddaughter straight into theatre, so that they can remove the bullet, after I find Bobby's jacket, I'll gather together not only his tablet and the book you are currently reading together, but also the computer games he likes to play, so that he will have plenty of things to occupy him while you're waiting…"

Although Lorna's face remained half-hidden in O'Keefe's shirt, she managed to express her gratitude. "Because I don't think I'm capable of doing it myself Philip, as well as arranging those things for us, if you can also find my bag that would be very kind…"

As Lorna felt the palm of his hand touching her back, his reply was almost apologetic. "Considering the circumstances Lorna, it's the least I can do…"

After moving slightly, so that Philip Maddox could leave the study, because Patrick O'Keefe was prepared to hold onto Lorna for as long as she needed, he took the opportunity to elaborate upon his Commanding Officer's explanation.

"Even if Bill had tried to explain that there was another helicopter on the way, so that it could take the three of you to the Mayfield Clinic, until Bobby calmed down he wouldn't have been able to grasp the significance…"

Then, a few minutes later, as the Commander re-joined them, Philip Maddox announced, "Although I've found everything Bobby might need and your bag was in the dining room, I couldn't find your jacket Lorna…"

"It's hanging on the stand by the front door," Lorna replied, but beyond the study silence suddenly descended, and after lifting her head until she could see the Commander's face, she asked, "Bobby's stopped screaming Philip. So can we please go now?"

"Of course you can, and as an added bonus Mr O'Keefe is going to escort you outside, so that after he helps Mr Powell to get you both on-board, he can accompany you during the flight to the Mayfield Clinic…"

Hesitating, he allowed a few tactful seconds to pass, before he added, "I will of course be receiving constant updates, and I do intend to join you all later, but until then, not only my thoughts and prayers, but also Margaret's will be with you and the rest of your family…"

"Thank you Philip, but if you have cause to doubt that Charlie can survive, I think we're going to need a miracle…"

Then, after stopping long enough for Lorna to slip her arms into her jacket, as promised O'Keefe escorted her outside, where Bobby was waiting to be transferred from Bill's arms into hers.

"Lorna," he sobbed, as his arms encircled her neck. "The bad man came back and shot mum and now they've taken her away…"

"I know Bobby I was watching from the study window. It must have been very frightening, especially when there wasn't room on the air-ambulance for any of us to go with her. However, Uncle Philip has arranged for another helicopter--which will be landing in a few minutes--to take us to the Mayfield Clinic and during the flight, I think you'll have to wear a proper headset to protect your ears…"

Instantly, Bobby's distress diminished. "Does that mean that I will be able to hear what the pilot and co-pilot are saying…"

Appreciating the speed with which Lorna's diversionary tactic had calmed him down, Bill was ready to reassure the youngster that they were still friends. "Yes you will Bobby…"

"I suppose that sounds pretty cool," Bobby conceded--albeit with a degree of reluctance--before he aimed his next question directly at Lorna. "Is mum going to be okay?"

Without even considering telling him a half-truth, Lorna treated the youngster's enquiry with the respect his request deserved.

"The truth is that I don't know Bobby. But Uncle Philip has arranged for one of the very best surgeons to operate on her as soon as the air-ambulance reaches the Mayfield Clinic, so we should know more after they remove the bullet and stop the bleeding…"

As she paused, Lorna afforded the young man the opportunity to question her further, but yet again, he seemed to be lost for words, which enabled her to explain.

"Right young man, now before I put you down, so that you can put your jacket on, I want you to listen very carefully. Since none of us knows what's going to happen next, I need you to start behaving like a very brave almost seven-year-old, who has been taught that if something occurs that you don't like, then hitting people--or even trying to lash out at them is totally unacceptable…"

Hesitating, Lorna allowed the youngster to grasp the implication, before she asked, "Do you understand what I'm telling you Bobby?"

"Yes Lorna…"

Having delivered his agreement with a degree of sheepishness, without being asked to do so. he looked over his shoulder at Powell. "I'm sorry Bill, I was only angry because I thought we were never going to see mum again…"

"And because it all happened so fast, I'm sorry that there wasn't time for me to explain about the other helicopter. However, although I doubt that Lorna and your mum will approve, in case you ever do need to defend yourself, I think we'll have to do some work in the gym on that upper right cut of yours, because I hardly felt a thing…"

Then, after taking the youngsters jacket from O'Keefe, he suggested. "Okay Mike Tyson Junior, it'll be a great deal breezier once we're air-borne, so as Lorna suggested you're going to need this on and then, provided you promise not to beat me up again, I'll carry you to the helipad…"

Unseen and unheard by Lorna or Bobby, at that precise moment a message from the air-ambulance confirmed that Charlie had crashed for a second time, and because they were having difficulty restarting her heart, the doctor had requested that the surgeon and theatre staff be ready to assume control as soon as they landed on the roof of the Mayfield Clinic, but since there was nothing to be gained from divulging that news to Lorna, although the two men exchanged a concerned glance, after Bill Powell yet again swept Bobby up into his arms, he and Patrick O'Keefe started to escort them to the helicopter, which despite having just touched down, still had its rotary blades turning in readiness for their immediate departure, once its passengers were on-board.

# EPILOGUE

"Good afternoon ladies and gentlemen. Please accept my apologies for keeping you waiting." Malcolm Banks announced, as soon as he stepped onto the mobile podium. "The P.M. has requested that the following short statement be released to the media. However, before disclosing the content, I would be grateful if you would note that since I am not in possession of all the details, I have not been given the necessary authorization in order to participate in the customary question and answer session…"

Then, after waiting for the murmuring to begin subsiding, he called the proceedings to order by clearing his throat, before he began to read the prepared statement.

**On behalf of Commander Philip Maddox, I would like to take this opportunity to confirm that on the 13$^{th}$ July at 19:48 the only child of Major William Charles and Joanna Mary Forsyth was targeted by someone who has since been identified as a paid assassin. If the person or persons responsible for issuing the Contract are watching or listening using our intelligence network, we will identify you, so that you can be held accountable and even if you continue to target those closest to us, our policy remains unchanged, we will neither yield to threats, nor negotiate with terrorists…"**

Then, when the return of the murmuring replaced the respectful silence, Malcolm Banks turned away from the microphone, and he had every intention of leaving the scene immediately until a knowledgeable journalist who was standing at the rear of the crowd dared to delay his departure, by posing the direct question to which every member of the group wanted an answer.

"Before you go back inside Mr Banks are you able to confirm whether Major Forsyth's daughter survived the assassination attempt?"

27732853R00167

Printed in Poland
by Amazon Fulfillment
Poland Sp. z o.o., Wrocław